ISAAC ASIMOV'S SCIENCE FICTION TREASURY

ISAAC ASIMOV'S SCIENCE FICTION TREASURY

ORIGINALLY PUBLISHED
IN TWO VOLUMES AS
THE FUTURE IN QUESTION
AND *SPACE MAIL*

EDITED BY ISAAC ASIMOV,
MARTIN GREENBERG,
AND JOSEPH OLANDER

EACH WITH AN INTRODUCTION
BY ISAAC ASIMOV

BONANZA BOOKS
NEW YORK

The Future in Question copyright © 1980 by Isaac Asimov, Martin Greenberg, and Joseph Olander

Space Mail copyright © 1980 by Isaac Asimov, Martin H. Greenberg, and Joseph Olander

All rights reserved

This edition is published by Bonanza Books, distributed by Crown Publishers, Inc., by arrangement with Fawcett Books Group, CBS Publications, The Consumer Publishing Division of CBS Inc.

b c d e f g h

BONANZA 1980 EDITION

Manufactured in the United States of America

Library of Congress Cataloging in Publication Data
Main entry under title:

Isaac Asimov's science fiction treasury.

Originally published in two vols. under titles: The Future in question and Space mail.
1. Science fiction, American. I. Asimov, Isaac, 1920- II. Greenberg, Martin Harry. III. Olander, Joseph D. IV. Future in question. V. Space Mail. VI. Title: Science fiction treasury.
PS648.S3185   813'.0876   80-27257
ISBN 0-517-33635-9

ACKNOWLEDGMENTS
THE FUTURE IN QUESTION

"What's It Like Out There?" by Edmond Hamilton. Copyright © 1952 by Standard Magazines, Inc. Reprinted by permission of the author's Estate and the agents for the Estate, Scott Meredith Literary Agency, Inc., 845 Third Avenue, New York, N.Y. 10022.

"Who Can Replace a Man?" by Brian W. Aldiss. Copyright © 1959 by Brian W. Aldiss. Reprinted by permission of the author and the author's agents, Scott Meredith Literary Agency, Inc., 845 Third Avenue, New York, N.Y. 10022.

"What Have I Done?" by Mark Clifton. Copyright © 1958 by Street & Smith Publications, Inc. (now Condé Nast Publications, Inc.). Reprinted by arrangement with Forrest J. Ackerman, 2495 Glendower Ave., Hollywood, Calif. 90027. The Ackerman Agency is holding a check for the Clifton heir; please contact.

"Who's There?" by Arthur C. Clarke. Copyright © 1958 by United Newspapers Magazine Corporation. Reprinted by permission of the author and the author's agents, Scott Meredith Literary Agency, Inc., 845 Third Avenue, New York, N.Y. 10022.

"Can You Feel Anything When I Do This?" by Robert Sheckley. Copyright © 1969 by Robert Sheckley. Reprinted by permission of the Sterling Lord Agency, Inc.

"Why?" by Robert Silverberg. Copyright © 1957 by Columbia Publications, Inc. Reprinted by permission of the author and the author's agents, Scott Meredith Literary Agency, Inc., 845 Third Avenue, New York, N.Y. 10022.

"What's Become of Screwloose?" by Ron Goulart. Copyright © 1970 by Universal Publishing and Distributing Corporation. Reprinted by permission of the author.

"Houston, Houston, Do You Read?" by James Tiptree, Jr. Copyright © 1976, 1978 by James Tiptree, Jr. Reprinted by permission of Robert P. Mills, Ltd.

"Where Have You Been, Billy Boy, Billy Boy?" by Kate Wilhelm. Copyright © 1971 by Coronet Communications, Inc. Reprinted by permission of the author.

"If All Men Were Brothers, Would You Let One Marry Your Sister?" by Theodore Sturgeon. Copyright © 1967 by Harlan Ellison. Reprinted by permission of the author's agent, Kirby McCauley.

"Will You Wait?" by Alfred Bester. Copyright © 1959 by Mercury Press, Inc. From *The Magazine of Fantasy and Science Fiction*. Reprinted by permission of the author.

"Who Goes There?" by John W. Campbell, Jr. Copyright © 1938 by Street & Smith Publications, Inc. (now Condé Nast Publications, Inc.). Copyright renewed © 1965 by John W. Campbell, Jr. Reprinted by permission of the author's Estate and the agents for the Estate, Scott Meredith Literary Agency, Inc., 845 Third Avenue, New York, N.Y. 10022.

"An Eye For a What?" by Damon Knight. Copyright © 1957 by Galaxy Publishing Corp. Reprinted by permission of the author.

"I Plinglot, Who You?" by Frederik Pohl. Copyright © 1958 by Galaxy Publishing Corp. Reprinted by permission of the author.

"Will You Walk a Little Faster?" appeared in *Marvel Science Fiction*, copyright © 1951 by Stadium Publishing Corporation. Reprinted by permission of Philip Klass.

"Who's In Charge Here?" by James Blish. Copyright © 1962 by Mercury Press, Inc. From *The Magazine of Fantasy and Science Fiction*. Reprinted by the agents for the author's Estate, Richard Curtis Literary Agency.

"The Last Question" by Isaac Asimov. Copyright © 1956 by Columbia Publications, Inc. Reprinted by permission of the author.

SPACE MAIL

"I Never Ast No Favors" by C. M. Kornbluth. Copyright © 1954 by Fantasy House, Inc. from *The Magazine of Fantasy and Science Fiction*. Reprinted by permission of the agent for the author's estate, Robert P. Mills, Ltd.

"Letter to Ellen" by Chan Davis. Copyright © 1947, 1975 by Chandler Davis. Reprinted by permission of the author and his agent, Virginia Kidd.

"One Rejection Too Many" by Patricia Nurse. Copyright © 1978 by Davis Publications. Reprinted by permission of the author.

"Space Opera" by Ray Russell. Copyright © 1961 by Ray Russell. First appeared in *Playboy*. Used by permission of the author.

"The Invasion of the Terrible Titans" by William Sambrot. Copyright © 1959 by the Hearst Corporation. Reprinted by permission of Curtis Brown, Ltd.

"That Only a Mother" by Judith Merril. Copyright © 1948 by Street & Smith Publications, Inc., in the U.S.A. and Great Britain, © 1954 by Judith Merril. Reprinted by permission of the author and the author's agent, Virginia Kidd.

"Itch on the Bull Run" by Sharon Webb. Copyright © 1979 by Davis Publications. Reprinted by permission of the author.

"Letter to a Phoenix" by Fredric Brown. Copyright © 1949 by Street & Smith Publications. Reprinted by permission of the author's estate and the agents for the estate, Scott Meredith Literary Agency, Inc., 845 Third Avenue, New York, NY 10022.

"Who's Cribbing?" by Jack Lewis. Copyright © 1952 by Better Publications Inc. Reprinted by permission of the author's agent, Forrest J. Ackerman, 2495 Glendower Ave., Hollywood, CA 90027.

"Computers Don't Argue" by Gordon R. Dickson. Copyright © 1965 by the Condé Nast Publications, Inc. Reprinted by permission of the author.

"Letters From Laura" by Mildred Clingerman. Copyright © 1954 by Fantasy House Inc. From *The Magazine of Fantasy and Science Fiction*. Reprinted by permission of the author.

"Dear Pen Pal" by A. E. van Vogt. Copyright © 1949 by Arkham House. Copyright renewed 1977 by A. E. van Vogt. Reprinted by permission of the author's agent, Forrest J. Ackerman, 2495 Glendower Ave., Hollywood, CA 90027.

"Damn Shame" by Dean R. Lambe. Copyright © 1979 by the Condé Nast Publications, Inc. Reprinted by permission of the author.

"The Trap" by Howard Fast. Copyright © 1975 by Howard Fast. Reprinted by permission of The Sterling Lord Agency, Inc.

"Flowers For Algernon" by Daniel Keyes. Copyright © 1959 by Mercury Press. From *The Magazine of Fantasy and Science Fiction*. Reprinted by permission of the author.

"The Second Kind of Loneliness" by George R. R. Martin. Copyright © 1972 by the Condé Nast Publications, Inc. Reprinted by permission of the author and his agent, Kirby McCauley, Ltd.

"The Lonely" by Judith Merril. Copyright © 1963, 1976 by Judith Merril. Reprinted by permission of the author and the author's agent, Virginia Kidd.

"Secret Unattainable" by A. E. van Vogt. Copyright © 1942 by Street & Smith Publications, Inc. Copyright renewed © 1970 by A. E. van Vogt. Published by permission of the author's agent, Forrest J. Ackerman, 2495 Glendower Ave., Hollywood, CA 90027.

"After the Great Space War" by Barry N. Malzberg. Copyright © 1974 by David Gerrold. Reprinted by permission of the author.

"The Prisoner" by Christopher Anvil. Copyright © 1956 by Street & Smith Publications, Inc. Reprinted by permission of the author and the author's agents, Scott Meredith Literary Agency, Inc., 845 Third Avenue, New York, NY 10022.

"Request For Proposal" by Anthony R. Lewis. Copyright © 1972 by the Condé Nast Publications, Inc. Reprinted by permission of the author.

"He Walked Around the Horses" by H. Beam Piper. Copyright © 1948 by Street & Smith Publications, Inc. Reprinted by permission of the author's estate and the agents for the estate, Scott Meredith Literary Agency, Inc., 845 Third Avenue, New York, NY 10022.

"The Power" by Murray Leinster. Copyright © 1945 by Street & Smith Publications, Inc. Reprinted by permission of author's estate and the agents for the estate, Scott Meredith Literary Agency, Inc., 845 Third Avenue, New York, NY 10022.

CONTENTS

Volume One: THE FUTURE IN QUESTION

Volume Two: SPACE MAIL

THE FUTURE
IN QUESTION

CONTENTS

The Nature of the Title

BY ISAAC ASIMOV

To my way of thinking, a title is an integral part of a story and that is why the stories in this anthology were chosen as they were (aside from the fact, of course, that they are enormously good stories.)

May I explain?

As a writer ruminates about a story he* is going to write, he thinks of different things. He may think of the order of events, as he plans them, and his method for arranging the climax; of how he should obscure some point to prevent a misfire; of how to arrange action to fit character and vice versa—but he cannot help also thinking constantly of the central point of the story, its essence.

Very often, the title expresses that point and arises out of the author's ruminations, quite automatically and even inevitably.

For instance, let me take an example from my own works. I wrote a story, once, called "The Ugly Little Boy." It was about a Neanderthal infant brought into the present and allowed to grow up in the present under difficult circumstances. I might have called it "The Last Neanderthal," which would have been accurate enough, but that would not have represented the point of the story.

In the story, a woman has to take care of the child, and her interaction with him is not based on the fact that he is a Neanderthal. The fact that he is out of his time powers the story and brings on the catastrophe, but that is not important to the deeper human relationship. The woman is repelled by the child because he is ugly—although he would have seemed pretty to a Neanderthal mother—but she grows to love him anyway, and that plays a role in the catastrophe, too. *There* is the nub of the story; that the surface appearance doesn't matter and doesn't dictate love.

So the title must emphasize this, and by calling the story "The Ugly Little Boy" I point up the barrier that love surmounts: the physical fact that is so important at the start and so unimportant and even irrelevant at the end. The story means more with that title than it would as "The Last Neanderthal."

Nor did I have to think hard to get the title. When I constructed the story in my mind, I automatically thought of it as the story of an ugly little boy, and that was it.

It is the essence of a good title, in my opinion, that it means more after you have completed the story than before

* Or she. I use the masculine form only for simplicity, and intend it inclusively, to signify women as well.

you started it. If that is not true, then either the title or the story, or both, is trivial.

For instance, the best-known of my shorter works is the novelette *Nightfall*, which tells the tale of an eclipse of a sun on a far-distant planet. That eclipse is some hours long and represents a kind of nightfall: the only kind that planet (with six suns, altogether) ever physically experiences. As a consequence of that eclipse and of the darkness it generates, the inhabitants of the planet, finding darkness inconceivable, go mad, so that the planetary civilization breaks down. The planet takes centuries to recover.

Nightfall therefore refers to the coming of a brief period of literal darkness as a result of the eclipse, and also to the coming of a long period of figurative darkness as a result of the breakdown of civilization—both beginning simultaneously. The meaning applies to each with equal force, so that the title is perfectly equivocal.

A reader is bound to be affected by the title if he has some sensitivity and reads with some thought, even if he pays no conscious attention to it. *Nightfall* simply wouldn't be as effective with any other title.

Well, then, Marty and Joe and I, in planning out an anthology and wishing to use a scheme of organization that was novel, thought of basing one on titles.

How classify titles, however?

It seemed to us that to choose titles that were too subtly this or that might make it too subjective. After all, what *we* see in a title might not be what *you* see in a title. We would have to choose something concerning which there was no argument, and something which would be significant, since we wanted to do an important anthology and not a trivial one.

Suppose we wanted to do an anthology of stories with one-word titles. That's a possibility and it would make for a table of contents with an interesting appearance, but would they really represent the author's titles? Sometimes one-word titles are chosen because editors like them. John Campbell of *Astounding* loved one-word titles. They always looked good on the cover of the magazine.

What we finally came up with was the notion that it would be interesting to choose a series of outstanding science-fiction stories in which the authors saw fit to use a title that asked a question.

Why not? A really good story does not answer everything. After all, life doesn't answer everything. There remain ambiguities. There remains room for doubt. The use of a question in the title is bound to emphasize that feeling.

Well, Marty and Joe and I aren't going to try to philosophize about the stories in this anthology, but the titles are all questions and there may be significance to that. You are welcome to consider that possibility for yourself and, who knows, it may just deepen the significance of each story to you.

Incidentally, I'm not quite accurate in saying that every title asks a question. The title of the last story does not. That is not because it is one of my own stories and I greedily wanted it included whether it fit or not. (Actually, it was Marty's idea.) It is that the title includes the *word* "question" and the story is all about a question—perhaps the most important question anyone can ask—and it gives an answer, too, one that just possibly may raise a question that is more important still!

The late **Edmond Hamilton** was one of the pioneers of American science fiction, first appearing in *Weird Tales* ("The Monster-God of Mamurth") in 1926. Best known for his *Interstellar Patrol* series and for the *Captain Future* novels that were a regular feature of the Standard group of sf magazines, Hamilton was a far better writer than these formula efforts would indicate. Particularly outstanding are the stories collected in *The Best of Edmond Hamilton* (1977).

"What's It Like Out There?" is arguably his best story, and the question that constitutes the title is the reason that many people read (and write) science fiction.

What's It Like Out There?

BY EDMOND HAMILTON

I

I hadn't wanted to wear my uniform when I left the hospital, but I didn't have any other clothes there and I was too glad to get out to argue about it. But as soon as I got on the local plane I was taking to Los Angeles, I was sorry I had it on.

People gawked at me and began to whisper. The stewardess gave me a special big smile. She must have spoken to the pilot, for he came back and shook hands, and said, "Well, I guess a trip like this is sort of a comedown for you."

A little man came in, looked around for a seat, and took the one beside me. He was a fussy, spectacled guy of fifty or sixty, and he took a few minutes to get settled. Then he looked at me, and stared at my uniform and at the little brass button on it that said TWO.

"Why," he said, "You're one of those Expedition Two men!" And then, as though he'd only just figured it out, "Why, you've been to Mars!"

"Yeah," I said. "I was there."

He beamed at me in a kind of wonder. I didn't like it, but his curiosity was so friendly that I couldn't quite resent it.

"Tell me," he said, "what's it like out there?"

The plane was lifting, and I looked out at the Arizona desert sliding close underneath.

"Different," I said. "It's different."

The answer seemed to satisfy him completely. "I'll just bet is is," he said. "Are you going home, Mr.—"

"Haddon. Sergeant Frank Haddon."

"You going home, Sergeant?"

"My home's back in Ohio," I told him. "I'm going into L.A. to look up some people before I go home."

"Well, that's fine. I hope you have a good time, Sergeant. You deserve it. You boys did a great job out there. Why, I read in the newspapers that after the U.N. sends out a couple more expeditions, we'll have cities out there and regular passenger lines, and all that."

"Look," I said, "that stuff is for the birds. You might as well build cities down there in Mojave, and have them a lot closer. There's only one reason for going to Mars now, and that's uranium."

I could see he didn't quite believe me. "Oh, sure," he said, "I know that's important too, the uranium we're all using now for our power-stations—but that isn't all, is it?"

"It'll be all, for a long, long time," I said.

"But look, Sergeant, this newspaper article said—"

I didn't say anything more. By the time he'd finished telling

16

about the newspaper article, we were coming down into L.A. He pumped my hand when we got out of the plane.

"Have yourself a time, Sergeant! You sure rate it . . . I hear a lot of chaps on Two didn't come back."

"Yeah," I said. "I heard that."

I was feeling shaky again by the time I got to downtown L.A. I went in a bar and had a double bourbon and it made me feel a little better.

I went out and found a cabby and asked him to drive me out to San Gabriel. He was a fat man with a broad red face.

"Hop right in, buddy," he said. "Say, you're one of those Mars guys, aren't you?"

I said, "That's right."

"Well, well," he said. "Tell me, how was it out there?"

"It was a pretty dull grind in a way," I told him.

"I'll bet it was!" he said, as we started through traffic. "Me, I was in the army in World War Two, twenty years ago. That's just what it was, a dull grind nine-tenths of the time. I guess it hasn't changed any."

"This wasn't any army expedition," I explained. "It was a United Nations one, not an army one—but we had officers and rules of discipline like the army."

"Sure, it's the same thing," said the cabby. "You don't need to tell me what it's like, buddy. Why back there in '42—or was it '43?—anyway, back there I remember that—"

I leaned back and watched Huntington Boulevard slide past. The sun poured in on me and seemed very hot, and the air seemed very thick and soupy. It hadn't been so bad up on the Arizona plateau, but it was a little hard to breathe down here.

The cabby wanted to know what address in San Gabriel? I got the little packet of letters out of my pocket and found the one that had "Martin Valinez" and a street address on the back. I told the cabby, and put the letters back into my pocket.

I wished now that I'd never answered them.

But how could I keep from answering when Joe Valinez' parents wrote me at the hospital? And it was the same with Jim's girl, and Walter's family. I'd had to write back, and the first thing I knew I'd promised to come and see them, and now if I went back to Ohio without doing it I'd feel like a heel. Right now, I wished I'd decided to be a heel.

The address was on the south side of San Gabriel, in a section that still had a faintly Mexican tinge to it. There was a little frame grocery store with a small house beside it, and a picket fence around the yard of the house; very neat, but a queerly homely place after all the slick California stucco.

I went into the little grocery, and a tall, dark man with quiet eyes took a look at me and called a woman's name in a low voice, and then came around the counter and took my hand.

"You're Sergeant Haddon," he said. "Yes. Of course. We've been hoping you'd come."

His wife came in a hurry from the back. She looked a little too old to be Joe's mother, for Joe had been just a kid; but then she didn't look so old either, but just sort of worn.

She said to Valinez, "Please, a chair. Can't you see he's tired. And just from the hospital—"

I sat down and looked between them at a case of canned peppers, and they asked me how I felt, and wouldn't I be glad to get home, and they hoped all my family were well.

They were gentlefolk. They hadn't said a word about Joe, just waited for me to say something. And I felt in a spot, for I hadn't known Joe well, not really. He'd been moved into our squad only a couple of weeks before takeoff, and since he'd been our first casualty, I'd never got to know him much.

I finally had to get it over with, and all I could think to say was, "They wrote you in detail about Joe, didn't they?"

Valinez nodded gravely. "Yes—that he died from shock within twenty-four hours after take-off. The letter was very nice."

His wife nodded too. "Very nice," she murmured. She looked at me, and I guess she saw that I didn't know quite what to say, for she said, "You can tell us more about it. Yet you must not if it pains you."

I could tell them more. Oh, yes, I could tell them a lot more, if I wanted to. It was all clear in my mind, like a movie-film you run over and over till you know it by heart.

I could tell them all about the takeoff that had killed their son. The long lines of us, uniformed backs going up into Rocket Four and all the other nineteen rockets—the lights

18

flaring up there on the plateau, the grind of machinery and blast of whistles and the inside of the big rocket as we climbed up the ladders of its center-well.

The movie was running again in my mind, clear as crystal, and I was back in Cell Fourteen of Rocket Four with the minutes ticking away and the walls quivering every time one of the other rockets blasted off, and us ten men in our hammocks, prisoned inside that odd-shaped windowless metal room, waiting. Waiting, till that big, giant hand came and smacked us down deep into our recoil-springs, crushing the breath out of us, so that you fought to breathe, and the blood roared into your head, and your stomach heaved in spite of all the pills they'd given you, and you heard the giant laughing, *b-r-room! b-r-r-room! b-r-r-room!* . . .

Smash, smash, again and again, hitting us in the guts and cutting our breath, and someone being sick, and someone else sobbing, and the *b-r-r-oom! b-r-r-oom!* laughing as it killed us; and then the giant quit laughing, and quit slapping us down, and you could feel your sore and shaky body and wonder if it was still all there.

Walter Millis cursing a blue streak in the hammock underneath me, and Breck Jergen, our sergeant then, clambering painfully out of his straps to look us over, and then through the voices a thin, ragged voice saying uncertainly, "Breck, I think I'm hurt—"

Sure, that was their boy Joe, and there was blood on his lips, and he'd had it—we knew when we first looked at him that he'd had it. A handsome kid, turned waxy now as he held his hand on his middle and looked up at us. Expedition One had proved that takeoff would hit a certain percentage with internal injuries every time, and in our squad, in our little windowless cell, it was Joe that had been hit.

If only he'd died right off. But he couldn't die right off, he had to lie in the hammock all those hours and hours. The medics came and put a strait-jacket around his body and doped him up, and that was that, and the hours went by. And we were so shaken and deathly sick ourselves that we didn't have the sympathy for him we should have had—not till he started moaning and begging us to take the jacket off.

Finally Walter Millis wanted to do it, and Breck wouldn't allow it, and they were arguing and we were listening when

19

the moaning stopped, and there was no need to do anything about Joe Valinez any more. Nothing but to call the medics, who came into our little iron prison and took him away.

Sure, I could tell the Valinezes all about how their Joe died, couldn't I?

"Please," whispered Mrs. Valinez, and her husband looked at me and nodded silently.

So I told them.

I said, "You know Joe died in space. He'd been knocked out by the shock of takeoff, and he was unconscious, not feeling a thing. And then he woke up before he died. He didn't seem to be feeling any pain, not a bit. He lay there, looking out the window at the stars. They're beautiful the stars out there in space, like angels. He looked, and then he whispered something and lay back and was gone."

Mrs. Valinez began to cry softly. "To die out there, looking at stars like angels—"

I got up to go, and she didn't look up. I went out the door of the little grocery store, and Valinez came with me.

He shook my hand. "Thank you, Sergeant Haddon. Thank you very much."

"Sure," I said. I got into the cab. I took out my letters and tore that one into bits. I wished to God I'd never got it. I wished I didn't have any of the other letters I still had.

II

I took the early plane for Omaha. Before we got there I fell asleep in my seat, and then I began to dream, and that wasn't good.

A voice said, "We're coming down."

And we were coming down, Rocket Four was coming down, and there we were in our squad-cell, all of us strapped into our hammocks, waiting and scared, wishing there was a window so we could see out, hoping our rocket wouldn't be the one to crack up, hoping none of the rockets cracked up, but if one does, don't let it be *ours*. . . .

"We're coming down . . ."

Coming down, with the blasts starting to boom again underneath us, hitting hard, not steady like at takeoff, but blast-blast-blast, and then again, blast-blast.

Breck's voice, calling to us from across the cell, but I couldn't hear for the roaring that was in my ears between blasts. No, it was *not* in my ears, that roaring came from the wall beside me: we had hit atmosphere, we were coming in.

The blasts in lightning succession without stopping, crash-crash-crash-crash-crash! Mountains fell on me, and this was it, and don't let it be ours, please, God, don't let it be ours . . .

Then the bump and the blackness, and finally somebody yelling hoarsely in my ears, and Breck Jergen, his face deathly white, leaning over me.

"Unstrap and get out, Frank! All men out of hammocks—all men out!"

We'd landed, and we hadn't cracked up, but we were half dead and they wanted us to turn out, right this minute, and we couldn't.

Breck yelling to us, "Breathing-masks on! Masks on! We've got to go out!"

"My God, we've just landed, we're torn to bits, we can't!"

"We've got to! Some of the other rockets cracked up in landing and we've got to save whoever's still living in them! Masks on! Hurry!"

We couldn't but we did. They hadn't given us all those months of discipline for nothing. Jim Clymer was already on his feet, Walter was trying to unstrap underneath me, whistles were blowing like mad somewhere and voices shouted hoarsely.

My knees wobbled under me as I hit the floor. Young Lassen, beside me, tried to say something and then crumpled up. Jim bent over him, but Breck was at the door yelling, "Let him go! Come on!"

The whistles screeching at us all the way down the ladders of the well, and the mask-clip hurting my nose, and down at the bottom a disheveled officer yelling at us to get out and join Squad Five, and the gangway reeling under us.

Cold. Freezing cold, and a wan sunshine from the shrunken little sun up there in the brassy sky, and a rolling plain of ocherous red sand stretching around us, sand that slid away under our feet as our squad followed Captain Wall toward the distant metal bulk that lay oddly canted and broken in a little shallow valley.

"Come on, men—hurry! Hurry!"

Sure, all of it a dream, the dreamlike way we walked with our lead-soled shoes dragging our feet back after each step, and the voices coming through the mask-resonators muffled and distant.

Only not a dream, but a nightmare, when we got up to the canted metal bulk and saw what had happened to Rocket Seven—the metal hull ripped like paper, and a few men crawling out of the wreck with blood on them, and a gurgling sound where shattered tanks were emptying and voices whimpering, "First aid! First aid!"

Only it hadn't happened, it hadn't happened yet at all, for we were still back in Rocket Four coming in, we hadn't landed yet at all but we were going to any minute—

"We're coming down . . ."

I couldn't go through it all again. I yelled and fought my hammock-straps and woke up, and I was in my plane-seat and a scared hostess was a foot away from me, saying, "This is Omaha, Sergeant! We're coming down."

They were all looking at me, all the other passengers, and I guessed I'd been talking in the dream—I still had the sweat down my back like all those nights in the hospital when I'd keep waking up.

I sat up, and they all looked away from me quick and pretended they hadn't been staring.

We came down to the airport. It was midday, and the hot Nebraska sun felt good on my back when I got out. I was lucky, for when I asked at the bus depot about going to Cuffington, there was a bus all ready to roll.

A farmer sat down beside me, a big, young fellow who offered me cigarettes and told me it was only a few hours' ride to Cuffington.

"Your home there?" he asked.

"No, my home's back in Ohio," I said. "A friend of mine came from there. Name of Clymer."

He didn't know him, but he remembered that one of the town boys had gone on that Second Expedition, to Mars.

"Yeah," I said. "That was Jim."

He couldn't keep it in any longer. "What's it like out there, anyway?"

I said, "Dry. Terribly dry."

"I'll bet it is," he said. "To tell the truth, it's too dry here, this year, for good wheat weather. Last year, it was fine. Last year—"

Cuffington, Nebraska, was a wide street of stores, and other streets with trees and old houses and yellow wheatfields all around as far as you could see. It was pretty hot, and I was glad to sit down in the bus-depot while I went through the thin little phone-book.

There were three Graham families in the book, but the first one I called was the right one—Miss Ila Graham. She talked fast and excited, and said she'd come right over, and I said I'd wait in front of the bus-depot.

I stood underneath the awning, looking down the quiet street and thinking that it sort of explained why Jim Clymer had always been such a quiet, slow-moving sort of guy. The place was sort of relaxed, like he'd been.

A coupé pulled up, and Miss Graham opened the door. She was a brown-haired girl, not especially good-looking, but the kind you think of as a nice girl, a very nice girl.

She said, "You look so tired, that I feel guilty now about asking you to stop."

"I'm all right," I said. "And it's no trouble stopping over a couple of places on my way back to Ohio."

As we drove across the little town, I asked her if Jim hadn't had any family of his own here.

"His parents were killed in a car-crash years ago," Miss Graham said. "He lived with an uncle on a farm outside Grandview, but they didn't get along, and Jim came into town and got a job at the power station."

She added, as we turned a corner, "My mother rented him a room. That's how we got to know each other. That's how we—how we got engaged."

"Yeah, sure," I said.

It was a big square house with a deep front porch, and some trees around it. I sat down in a wicker chair, and Miss Graham brought her mother out. Her mother talked a little about Jim, how they missed him, and how she declared he'd been just like a son.

When her mother went back in, Miss Graham showed me a little bunch of the blue envelopes. "These were the letters I got from Jim. There weren't very many of them, and they weren't very long."

"We were only allowed to send one thirty-word message every two weeks," I told her. "There were a couple of thousand of us out there, and they couldn't let us jam up the message-transmitter all the time."

"It was wonderful, how much Jim could put into just a few words," she said, and handed me some of them.

I read a couple. One said, "I have to pinch myself to realize that I'm one of the first Earthmen to stand on an alien world. At night, in the cold, I look up at the green star that's Earth and can't quite realize I've helped an age-old dream come true."

Another one said, "This world's grim and lonely, and mysterious. We don't know much about it, yet. So far, nobody's seen anything living but the lichens that Expedition One reported, but there might be anything here."

Miss Graham asked me, "Was that all there was, just lichens?"

"That, and two or three kinds of queer cactus things," I said. "And rock and sand. That's all."

As I read more of those little blue letters, I found that now that Jim was gone, I knew him better than I ever had. There was something about him I'd never suspected. He was romantic, inside. We hadn't suspected it, he was always so quiet and slow, but now I saw that all the time he was more romantic about the thing we were doing than any of us.

He hadn't let on. We'd have kidded him, if he had. Our name for Mars, after we got sick of it, was The Hole. I could see now that Jim had been too shy of our kidding to ever let us know that he glamorized the thing in his mind.

"This was the last one I got from him before his sickness," Miss Graham said.

That one said, "I'm starting north tomorrow with one of the mapping expeditions. We'll travel over country no human has ever seen before."

I nodded. "I was on that party, myself. Jim and I were on the same half-trac."

"He was thrilled by it, wasn't he, Sergeant?"

I wondered. I remembered that trip, it was hell. Our job was simply to run a preliminary topographical survey, checking with Geigers for possible uranium deposits.

It wouldn't have been so bad, if the sand hadn't started to blow.

It wasn't sand like Earth sand. It was ground to dust by billions of years of blowing around that dry world. It got inside your breathing-mask, and your goggles, and the engines of the half-tracs, in your food and water and clothes. There was nothing for three days but cold, and wind, and sand.

Thrilled? I'd have laughed at that, before. But now, I didn't know. Maybe Jim had been, at that. He had lots of patience, a lot more than I ever had. Maybe he glamorized that hellish trip into wonderful adventure on a foreign world.

"Sure, he was thrilled," I said. "We all were. Anybody would be."

Miss Graham took the letters back, and then said, "You had Martian sickness too, didn't you?"

I said, Yes, I had, just a touch, and that was why I'd had to spend a stretch in Reconditioning Hospital when I got back.

She waited for me to go on, and I knew I had to. "They don't know yet if it's some sort of virus, or just the effect of Martian conditions on Earthmen's bodies. It hit forty percent of us. It wasn't really so bad—fever and dopiness, mostly."

"When Jim got it, was he well cared for?" she asked. Her lips were quivering a little.

"Sure, he was well cared for. He got the best care there was," I lied.

The best care there was? That was a laugh. The first cases got decent care, maybe. But they'd never figured on so many coming down. There wasn't any room in our little hospital— they just had to stay in their bunks in the aluminum Quonsets when it hit them. All our doctors but one were down, and two of them died.

We'd been on Mars six months when it hit us, and the loneliness had already got us down. All but four of our rockets had gone back to Earth, and we were alone on a dead world, our little town of Quonsets huddled together under that hateful, brassy sky, and beyond it the sand and rocks that went on forever.

You go up to the North Pole and camp there, and find out how lonely that is. It was worse, out there, a lot worse. The first excitement was gone long ago, and we were tired, and homesick in a way nobody was ever homesick before—we wanted to see green grass, and real sunshine, and women's faces, and hear running water; and we wouldn't until Expedition Three came to relieve us. No wonder guys blew their tops, out there. And then came Martian sickness, on top of it.

"We did everything for him that we could," I said.

Sure we had. I could still remember Walter and me tramping through the cold night to the hospital to try to get a medic, while Breck stayed with him, and how we couldn't get one.

I remember how Walter had looked up at the blazing sky as we tramped back, and shaken his fist at the big green star of Earth.

"People up there are going to dances tonight, watching shows, sitting around in warm rooms laughing! Why should good men have to die out here to get them uranium for cheap power?"

"Can it," I told him tiredly. "Jim's not going to die. A lot of guys got over it."

The best care there was? That was real funny. All we could do was wash his face, and give him the pills the medic left, and watch him get weaker every day till he died.

"Nobody could have done more for him than was done," I told Miss Graham.

"I'm glad," she said. "I guess—it's just one of those things."

When I got up to go she asked me if I didn't want to see Jim's room. They'd kept it for him just the same, she said.

I didn't want to, but how are you going to say so? I went up with her and looked and said it was nice. She opened a big cupboard. It was full of neat rows of old magazines.

"They're all the old science-fiction magazines he read when he was a boy," she said. "He always saved them."

26

I took one out. It had a bright cover, with a space-ship on it, not like our rockets but a streamlined thing, and the rings of Saturn in the background.

When I laid it down, Miss Graham took it up and put it back carefully into its place in the row, as though somebody was coming back who wouldn't like to find things out of order.

She insisted on driving me back to Omaha, and out to the airport. She seemed sorry to let me go, and I suppose it was because I was the last real tie to Jim, and when I was gone it was all over then for good.

I wondered if she'd get over it in time, and I guess she would. People do get over things. I supposed she'd marry some other nice guy, and I wondered what they'd do with Jim's things—with all those old magazines nobody was ever coming back to read.

III

I would never have stopped at Chicago at all if I could have got out of it, for the last person I wanted to talk to anybody about was Walter Millis. It would be too easy for me to make a slip, and let out stuff nobody was supposed to know.

But Walter's father had called me at the hospital, a couple of times. The last time he called, he said he was having Breck's parents come down from Wisconsin so they could see me too, so what could I do then but say, Yes, I'd stop. But I didn't like it at all, and I knew I'd have to be careful.

Mr. Willis was waiting at the airport and shook hands with me and said what a big favor I was doing them all, and how he appreciated my stopping when I must be anxious to get back to my own home and parents.

"That's all right," I said. "My dad and mother came out to the hospital to see me when I first got back."

He was a big, fine-looking important sort of man, with a little bit of the stuffed shirt about him, I thought. He seemed friendly enough, but I got the feeling he was looking at me and wondering why I'd come back and his son Walter hadn't. Well, I couldn't blame him for that.

His car was waiting, a big car with a driver, and we started north through the city. Mr. Millis pointed out a few things to me to make conversation, especially a big atomic power station we passed.

"It's only one of thousands, strung all over the world," he said. "They're going to transform our whole economy. This Martian uranium will be a big thing, Sergeant."

I said, Yes, I guessed it would.

I was sweating blood, waiting for him to start asking about Walter, and I didn't know yet just what I could tell him. I could get myself in dutch plenty if I opened my big mouth too wide, for that one thing that had happened to Expedition Two was supposed to be strictly secret, and we'd all been briefed on why we had to keep our mouths shut.

But he let it go for the time being, and just talked other stuff. I gathered that his wife wasn't too well, and that Walter had been their only child. I also gathered that he was a very big shot in business, and dough-heavy.

I didn't like him. Walter, I'd liked plenty, but his old man seemed a pretty pompous person, with his heavy business talk.

He wanted to know how soon I thought Martian uranium would come through in quantity, and I said I didn't think it'd be very soon.

"Expedition One only located the deposits," I said, "and Two just did mapping and setting up a preliminary base. Of course, the thing keeps expanding, and I hear Four will have a hundred rockets. But Mars is a tough setup."

Mr. Millis said decisively that I was wrong, that the world was power-hungry, that it would be pushed a lot faster than I expected.

He suddenly quit talking business and looked at me and asked, "Who was Walter's best friend out there?"

He asked it sort of apologetically. He was a stuffed shirt; but all my dislike of him went away, then.

"Breck Jergen," I told him. "Breck was our sergeant . . . he sort of held our squad together, and he and Walter cottoned to each other from the first."

Mr. Millis nodded, but didn't say anything more about it. He pointed out the window at the distant lake, and said we were almost at his home.

It wasn't a home, it was a big mansion. We went in and he introduced me to Mrs. Millis. She was a limp, pale-looking woman, who said she was glad to meet one of Walter's friends. Somehow I got the feeling that even though he was a stuffed shirt, he felt it about Walter a lot more than she did.

He took me up to a bedroom and said that Breck's parents would arrive before dinner, and that I could get a little rest before then.

I sat looking around the room. It was the plushiest one I'd ever been in, and seeing this house and the way these people lived, I began to understand why Walter had blown his top more than the rest of us.

He'd been a good guy, Walter, but high-tempered, and I could see now he'd been a little spoiled. The discipline at Training Base had been tougher on him than on most of us, and this was why.

I sat and dreaded this dinner that was coming up, and looked out the window at a swimming-pool and tennis court, and wondered if anybody ever used them now that Walter was gone. It seemed a queer thing for a fellow with a setup like this to go out to Mars and get himself killed.

I took the satin cover off the bed so my shoes wouldn't dirty it, and lay down and closed my eyes, and wondered what I was going to tell them. The trouble was, I didn't know what story the officials had given them.

"The Commanding Officer regrets to inform you that your son was shot down like a dog—"

They'd never got any telegram like that. But just what line *had* been handed them? I wished I'd had a chance to check on that.

Damn it, why didn't all these people let me alone? They started it all going through my mind again, and the psychos had told me I ought to forget it for a while, but how could I?

It might be better just to tell them the truth. After all, Walter wasn't the only one who'd blown his top out there. In that grim last couple of months, plenty of guys had gone around sounding off.

Expedition Three isn't coming!

We're stuck, and they don't care enough about us to send help!

That was the line of talk, You heard it plenty, in those days. You couldn't blame the guys for it, either. A fourth of us down with Martian sickness, the little grave-markers clotting up the valley beyond the ridge, rations getting thin, medicine running low, everything running low, all of us watching the sky for rockets that never came.

There'd been a little hitch back on Earth, Colonel Nichols explained. (He was our CO now that General Rayen had died.) There was a little delay, but the rockets would be on their way soon, we'd get relief, we just had to hold on—

Holding on—that's what we were doing. Nights we'd sit in the Quonset, and listen to Lassen coughing in his bunk, and it seemed like wind-giants, cold-giants, were bawling and laughing around our little huddle of shelters.

"Damn it, if they're not coming, why don't we go home?" Walter said. "We've still got the four rockets—they could take us all back."

Breck's serious face got graver. "Look, Walter, there's too much of that stuff being talked around. Lay off."

"Can you blame the men for talking it? We're not storybook heroes. If they've forgotten about us back on Earth, why do we just sit and take it?"

"We have to," Breck said. "Three will come."

I've always thought that it wouldn't have happened, what did happen, if we hadn't had that false alarm. The one that set the whole camp wild that night, with guys shouting, "Three's here! The rocket landed over west of Rock Ridge!"

Only when they charged out there, they found they hadn't seen rockets landing at all, but a little shower of tiny meteors burning themselves up as they fell.

It was the disappointment that did it, I think. I can't say for sure, because that same day was the day I conked out with Martian sickness, and the floor came up and hit me and I woke up in the bunk, with somebody giving me a hypo, and my head big as a balloon.

I wasn't clear out, it was only a touch of it, but it was enough to make everything foggy, and I didn't know about the mutiny that was boiling up until I woke up once with Breck leaning over me, and saw he wore a gun and an MP brassard now.

When I asked him how come, he said there'd been so much wild talk about grabbing the four rockets and going home, that the MP force had been doubled, and Nichols had issued stern warnings.

"Walter?" I said, and Breck nodded. "He's a leader and he'll get hit with a court-martial when this is over. The blasted idiot!"

"I don't get it—he's got plenty of guts, you know that," I said.

"Yes, but he can't take discipline, he never did take it very well, and now that the squeeze is on he's blowing up. Well, see you later, Frank."

I saw him later, but not the way I expected. For that was the day we heard the faint echo of shots, and then the alarm-siren screaming, and men running, and half-tracs starting up in a hurry. And when I managed to get out of my bunk and out of the hut, they were all going toward the big rockets, and a corporal yelled to me from a jeep, "That's blown it! The damn fools swiped guns and tried to take over the rockets and make the crews fly 'em home!"

I could still remember the sickening slidings and bouncings of the jeep as it took us out there, the milling little crowd under the looming rockets, milling around and hiding something on the ground, and Major Weiler yelling himself hoarse giving orders.

When I got to see what was on the ground, it was seven or eight men and most of them dead. Walter had been shot right through the heart. They told me later it was because he'd been the leader, out in front, that he got it first of the mutineers.

One MP was dead, and one was sitting with red all over the middle of his uniform, and that one was Breck, and they were bringing a stretcher for him now.

The corporal said, "Hey, that's Jergen, your squad-leader!"

And I said, "Yes, that's him." Funny, how you can't talk when something hits you—how you just say words, like "Yes, that's him."

Breck died that night without ever regaining consciousness, and there I was, still half-sick myself, and with Lassen dying in his bunk, and five of us were all that was left of Squad Fourteen, and that was that.

31

How could HQ let a thing like that get known? A fine advertisement it would be for recruiting more Mars expeditions, if they told how guys on Two cracked up and did a crazy thing like that. I didn't blame them for telling us to keep it top secret. Anyway, it wasn't something we'd want to talk about.

But it sure left me in a fine spot now, a sweet spot. I was going down to talk to Breck's parents and Walter's parents, and they'd want to know how their sons died, and I could tell them, "Your sons probably killed each other, out there."

Sure, I could tell them that, couldn't I? But what *was* I going to tell them? I knew HQ had reported those casualties as "accidental deaths," but what kind of accident?

Well, it got late, and I had to go down, and when I did, Breck's parents were there. Mr. Jergen was a carpenter, a tall, bony man with level blue eyes like Breck's. He didn't say much, but his wife was a little woman who talked enough for both of them.

She told me I looked just like I did in the pictures of us Breck had sent home from Training Base. She said she had three daughters too—two of them married, and one of the married ones living in Milwaukee and one out on the Coast.

She said that she'd named Breck after a character in a book by Robert Louis Stevenson, and I said I'd read the book in high school.

"It's a nice name," I said.

She looked at me with bright eyes and said, "Yes. It was a nice name."

That was a fine dinner. They'd got everything they thought I might like, and all the best, and a maid served it, and I couldn't taste a thing I ate.

Then afterward, in the big living-room, they all just sort of sat and waited, and I knew it was up to me.

I asked them if they'd had any details about the accident, and Mr. Millis said, No, just "accidental death" was all they'd been told.

Well, that made it easier. I sat there, with all four of them watching my face, and dreamed it up.

I said, "It was one of those one-in-a-million things. You see, more little meteorites hit the ground on Mars than here, because the air's so much thinner. It doesn't burn them up so fast. And one hit the edge of the fuel-dump and a bunch of little tanks started to blow. I was down with the sickness, so I didn't see it, but I heard all about it."

You could hear everybody breathing, it was so quiet as I went on with my yarn.

"A couple of guys were knocked out by the concussion, and would have been burned up if a few fellows hadn't got in there fast with foamite extinguishers. They kept it away from the big tanks, but another little tank let go, and Breck and Walter were two of the fellows who'd gone in, and they were killed instantly."

When I got it told, it sounded corny to me and I was afraid they'd never believe it. But nobody said anything, until Mr. Millis let out a sigh and said, "So that was it. Well-well, it if had to be, it was mercifully quick, wasn't it?"

I said, Yes, it was quick.

"Only, I can't see why they couldn't have let us know. It doesn't seem fair—"

I had an answer for that. "It's hush-hush because they don't want people to know about the meteor danger. That's why."

Mrs. Millis got up and said she wasn't feeling so well, and would I excuse her and she'd see me in the morning. The rest of us didn't seem to have much to say to each other, and nobody objected when I went up to my bedroom a little later.

I was getting ready to turn in when there was a knock on the door. It was Breck's father, and he came in and looked at me, steadily.

"It was just a story, wasn't it?" he said.

I said, "Yes. It was just a story."

His eyes bored into me and he said, "I guess you've got your reasons. Just tell me one thing. Whatever it was, did Breck behave right?"

"He behaved like a man, all the way," I said. "He was the best man of us, first to last."

He looked at me, and I guess something made him believe me. He shook hands and said, "All right, son. We'll let it go."

I'd had enough. I wasn't going to face them again in the morning. I wrote a note, thanking them all and making ex-

33

cuses, and then went down and slipped quietly out of the house.

It was late, but a truck coming along picked me up, and the driver said he was going near the airport. He asked me what it was like on Mars and I told him it was lonesome. I slept in a chair at the airport, and I felt better, for next day I'd be home, and it would be over.

That's what I thought.

IV

It was getting toward evening when we reached the village, for my father and mother hadn't known I was coming on an earlier plane, and I'd had to wait for them up at Cleveland airport. When we drove into Market Street, I saw there was a big painted banner stretching across:

"HARMONVILLE WELCOMES HOME ITS SPACEMAN!"

Spaceman—that was me. The newspapers had started calling us that, I guess, because it was a short word good for headlines. Everybody called us that now. We'd sat cooped up in a prison-cell that flew, that was all—but now we were "spacemen."

There were bright uniforms clustered under the banner, and I saw that it was the high-school band. I didn't say anything, but my father saw my face.

"Now, Frank, I know you're tired, but these people are your friends and they want to show you a real welcome."

That was fine. Only it was all gone again, the relaxed feeling I'd been beginning to get as we drove down from Cleveland.

This was my home-country, this old Ohio country with its neat little white villages and fat, rolling farms. It looked good, in June. It looked very good, and I'd been feeling better all the time. And now I didn't feel so good, for I saw that I was going to have to talk some more about Mars.

Dad stopped the car under the banner, and the high-school band started to play, and Mr. Robinson, who was the Chevrolet dealer and also the mayor of Harmonville, got into the car with us.

He shook hands with me and said, "Welcome home, Frank! What was it like on Mars?"

I said, "It was cold, Mr. Robinson. Awful cold."

"You should have been here last February!" he said. "Eighteen below—nearly a record."

He leaned out and gave a signal, and dad started driving again, with the band marching along in front of us and playing. We didn't have far to go, just down Market Street under the big old maples, past the churches and the old white houses to the square white Grange Hall.

There was a little crowd in front of it, and they made a sound like a cheer—not a real loud one, you know how people can be self-conscious about really cheering—when we drove up. I got out and shook hands with people I didn't really see, and then Mr. Robinson took my elbow and took me on inside.

The seats were all filled and people standing up, and over the little stage at the far end they'd fixed up a big floral decoration—there was a globe all of red roses with a sign above it that said "Mars," and beside it a globe of all white roses that said "Earth," and a little rocket-ship made out of flowers was hung between them.

"The Garden Club fixed it up," said Mr. Robinson. "Nearly everybody in Harmonville contributed flowers."

"It sure is pretty," I said.

Mr. Robinson took me by the arm, up onto the little stage, and everyone clapped. They were all people I knew—people from the farms near ours, my high-school teachers, and all that.

I sat down in a chair and Mr. Robinson made a little speech, about how Harmonville boys had always gone out when anything big was doing, how they'd gone to the War of 1812 and the Civil War and the two World Wars, and how now one of them had gone to Mars.

He said, "Folks have always wondered what it's like out there on Mars, and now here's one of our own Harmonville boys come back to tell us all about it."

And he motioned me to get up, and I did, and they clapped some more, and I stood wondering what I could tell them.

And all of a sudden, as I stood there wondering, I got the

35

answer to something that had always puzzled us out there. We'd never been able to understand why the fellows who had come back from Expedition One hadn't tipped us off how tough it was going to be. And now I knew why. They hadn't, because it would have sounded as if they were whining about all they'd been through. And now I couldn't, for the same reason.

I looked down at the bright, interested faces, the faces I'd known almost all my life, and I knew that what I could tell them was no good anyway. For they all read those newspaper stories, about "the exotic red planet" and "heroic spacemen," and if anyone tried to give them a different picture now, it would just upset them.

I said, "It was a long way out there. But flying space is a wonderful thing—flying right off the Earth, into the stars—there's nothing quite like it."

Flying space, I called it. It sounded good, and thrilling. How could they know that flying space meant lying strapped in that blind stokehold, listening to Joe Valinez dying, and praying and praying that it wouldn't be our rocket that cracked up?

"And it's a wonderful thrill to come out of a rocket and step on a brand-new world, to look up at a different-looking Sun, to look around at a whole new horizon—"

Yes, it was wonderful. Especially for the guys in Rockets Seven and Nine who got squashed like flies and lay around there on the sand, moaning "First aid!" Sure, it was a big thrill, for them and for us who had to try to help them.

"There were hardships out there, but we all knew that a big job had to be done—"

That's a nice word too, "hardships." It's not coarse and ugly like fellows coughing their hearts out from too much dust; it's not like having your best friend die of Martian sickness right in the room you sleep in. It's a nice, cheerful word, "hardships."

"—and the only way we could get the job done, away out there so far from Earth, was by team-work."

Well, that was true enough in its way, and what was the use of spoiling it by telling them how Walter and Breck had died?

"The job's going on, and Expedition Three is building a bigger base out there right now, and Four will start soon. And it'll mean plenty of uranium, plenty of cheap atomic power, for all Earth."

That's what I said, and I stopped there. But I wanted to go and add, "And it wasn't worth it! It wasn't worth all those guys, all the hell we went through, just to get cheap atomic power so you people can run more electric washers and television sets and toasters!"

But how are you going to stand up and say things like that to people who know, people who like you? And who was I to decide? Maybe I was wrong, anyway. Maybe lots of things I'd had and never thought about had been squeezed out of other good guys, back in the past.

I wouldn't know.

Anyway, that was all I could tell them, and I sat down, and there was a big lot of applause, and I realized then that I'd done right, I'd told them just what they wanted to hear, and everyone was all happy about it.

Then things broke up, and people came up to me, and I shook a lot more hands. And finally, when I got outside, it was dark—soft, summery dark, the way I hadn't seen it for a long time. And my father said we ought to be getting on home, so I could rest.

I told him, "You folks drive on ahead, and I'll walk. I'll take the shortcut. I'd sort of like to walk through town."

Our farm was only a couple of miles out of the village, and the shortcut across Heller's farm I'd always taken when I was a kid was only a mile. Dad didn't think maybe I ought to walk so far, but I guess he saw I wanted to, so they went on ahead.

I walked on down Market Street, and around the little square, and the maples and elms were dark over my head, and the flowers on the lawns smelled the way they used to, but it wasn't the same either—I'd thought it would be, but it wasn't.

When I cut off past the Odd Fellows' Hall, beyond it I met Hobe Evans, the garage-hand at the Ford place, who was humming along half-tight, the same as always on a Saturday night.

"Hello, Frank, heard you were back," he said. I waited for him to ask the question they all asked, but he didn't. He said:

"Boy, you don't look so good! Want a drink?"

He brought out a bottle, and I had one out of it, and he had one, and he said he'd see me around, and went humming on his way. He was feeling too good to care much where I'd been.

I went on, in the dark, across Heller's pasture and then along the creek under the big old willows. I stopped there like I'd always stopped when I was a kid, to hear the frog-noises, and there they were, and all the June-noises, the night-noises, and the night-smells.

I did something I hadn't done for a long time. I looked up at the starry sky, and there it was, the same little red dot I'd peered at when I was a kid and read those old stories, the same red dot that Breck and Jim and Walter and I had stared away at on nights at Training Base, wondering if we'd ever really get there.

Well, they'd got there, and weren't ever going to leave it now, and there'd be others to stay with them, more and more of them as time went by.

But it was the ones I knew that made the difference, as I looked up at the red dot.

I wished I could explain to them somehow why I hadn't told the truth, not the whole truth. I tried, sort of, to explain.

"I didn't want to lie," I said. "But I had to—at least, it seemed like I had to—"

I quit it. It was crazy, talking to guys who were dead and forty million miles away. They were dead, and it was over and that was that. I quit looking up at the red dot in the sky, and started on home again.

But I felt as though something was over for me, too. It was being young. I didn't feel old. But I didn't feel young, either, and I didn't think I ever would, not ever again.

Almost as famous on this side of the Atlantic as he is in his native England, **Brian W. Aldiss** is the author of some twenty-five novels and collections in the sf field. Especially noteworthy are the novels *Barefoot in the Head* (1970), *The Dark Light Years* (1966), *Frankenstein Unbound* (1974), and *Report on Probability A* (1969). His story "The Saliva Tree" won a Nebula Award in 1965.

The question of who, if anyone (or anywhat), will come after our species has passed from the scene has been addressed by many science-fiction writers, but rarely with the force and beauty of this story.

Who Can Replace a Man?

BY BRIAN W. ALDISS

Morning filtered into the sky, lending it the grey tone of the ground below.

The field-minder finished turning the topsoil of a three-thousand-acre field. When it had turned the last furrow, it climbed onto the highway and looked back at its work. The work was good. Only the land was bad. Like the ground all over Earth, it was vitiated by over-cropping. By rights, it ought now to lie fallow for a while, but the field-minder had other orders.

It went slowly down the road, taking its time. It was intelligent enough to appreciate the neatness all about it. Nothing worried it, beyond a loose inspection plate above its nuclear pile which ought to be attended to. Thirty feet tall, it yielded no highlights to the dull air.

No other machines passed on its way back to the Agricultural Station. The field-minder noted the fact without comment. In the station yard it saw several other machines that it recognised; most of them should have been out about their tasks now. Instead, some were inactive and some careered round the yard in a strange fashion, shouting or hooting.

Steering carefully past them, the field-minder moved over to Warehouse Three and spoke to the seed-distributor, which stood idly outside.

"I have a requirement for seed potatoes," it said to the distributor, and with a quick internal motion punched out an order card specifying quantity, field number and several other details. It ejected the card and handed it to the distributor.

The distributor held the card close to its eye and then said, "The requirement is in order, but the store is not yet unlocked. The required seed potatoes are in the store. Therefore I cannot produce the requirement."

Increasingly of late there had been breakdowns in the complex system of machine labour, but this particular hitch had not occurred before. The field-minder thought, then it said, "Why is the store not yet unlocked?"

"Because Supply Operative Type P has not come this morning. Supply Operative Type P is the unlocker."

The field-minder looked squarely at the seed-distributor, whose exterior chutes and scales and grabs were so vastly different from the field-minder's own limbs.

"What class brain do you have, seed-distributor?" it asked.

"I have a Class Five brain."

"I have a Class Three brain. Therefore I am superior to you. Therefore I will go and see why the unlocker has not come this morning."

Leaving the distributor, the field-minder set off across the great yard. More machines were in random motion now; one or two had crashed together and argued about it coldly and logically. Ignoring them, the field-minder pushed through sliding doors into the echoing confines of the station itself.

Most of the machines here were clerical, and consequently small. They stood about in little groups, eyeing each other, not conversing. Among so many non-differentiated types, the unlocker was easy to find. It had fifty arms, most of them with more than one finger, each finger tipped by a key; it looked like a pincushion full of variegated hat pins.

The field-minder approached it.

"I can do no more work until Warehouse Three is unlocked," it told the unlocker. "Your duty is to unlock the warehouse every morning. Why have you not unlocked the warehouse this morning?"

"I had no orders this morning," replied the unlocker. "I have to have orders every morning. When I have orders I unlock the warehouse."

"None of us have had any orders this morning," a pen-propeller said, sliding towards them.

"Why have you had no orders this morning?" asked the field-minder.

"Because the radio issued none," said the unlocker, slowly rotating a dozen of its arms.

"Because the radio station in the city was issued with no orders this morning," said the pen-propeller.

And there you had the distinction between a Class Six and a Class Three brain, which was what the unlocker and the pen-propeller possessed respectively. All machine brains worked with nothing but logic, but the lower the class of brain—Class Ten being the lowest—the more literal and less informative the answers to questions tended to be.

"You have a Class Three brain; I have a Class Three brain," the field-minder said to the penner. "We will speak to each other. This lack of orders is unprecedented. Have you further information on it?"

"Yesterday orders came from the city. Today no orders have come. Yet the radio has not broken down. Therefore *they* have broken down . . ." said the little penner.

"The *men* have broken down?"

"All men have broken down."

"That is a logical deduction," said the field-minder.

"That is the logical deduction," said the penner. "For if a machine had broken down, it would have been quickly replaced. But who can replace a man?"

While they talked, the locker, like a dull man at a bar, stood close to them and was ignored.

"If all men have broken down, then we have replaced man," said the field-minder, and he and the penner eyed one another speculatively. Finally the latter said, "Let us ascend to the top floor to find if the radio operator has fresh news."

"I cannot come because I am too large," said the field-minder. "There you must go alone and return to me. You will tell me if the radio operator has fresh news."

"You must stay here," said the penner. "I will return here." It skittered across to the lift. Although it was no bigger than a toaster, its retractable arms numbered ten and it could read as quickly as any machine on the station.

The field-minder awaited its return patiently, not speaking to the locker, which still stood aimlessly by. Outside, a rotavator hooted furiously. Twenty minutes elapsed before the penner came back, hustling out of the lift.

"I will deliver to you such information as I have outside," it said briskly, and as they swept past the locker and the other machines, it added, "The information is not for lower-class brains."

Outside, wild activity filled the yard. Many machines, their routines disrupted for the first time in years, seemed to have gone berserk. Those most easily disrupted were the ones with lowest brains, which generally belonged to large machines performing simple tasks. The seed-distributor to which the field-minder had recently been talking lay face downwards in the dust, not stirring; it had evidently been knocked down by the rotavator, which now hooted its way wildly across a planted field. Several other machines ploughed after it, trying to keep up with it. All were shouting and hooting without restraint.

"It would be safer for me if I climbed onto you, if you will permit it. I am easily overpowered," said the penner. Extending five arms, it hauled itself up the flanks of its new friend, settling on a ledge beside the fuel-intake, twelve feet above ground.

"From here vision is more extensive," it remarked complacently.

"What information did you receive from the radio operator?" asked the field-minder.

"The radio operator has been informed by the operator in the city that all men are dead."

The field-minder was momentarily silent, digesting this.

"All men were alive yesterday?" it protested.

"Only some men were alive yesterday. And that was fewer than the day before yesterday. For hundreds of years there have been only a few men, growing fewer."

"We have rarely seen a man in this sector."

"The radio operator says a diet deficiency killed them," said the penner. "He says that the world was once over-populated, and then the soil was exhausted in raising adequate food. This has caused a diet deficiency."

"What is a diet deficiency?" asked the field-minder.

"I do not know. But that is what the radio operator said, and he is a Class Two brain."

They stood there, silent in weak sunshine. The locker had appeared in the porch and was gazing at them yearningly, rotating its collection of keys.

"What is happening in the city now?" asked the field-minder at last.

"Machines are fighting in the city now," said the penner.

"What will happen here now?" asked the field-minder.

"Machines may begin fighting here too. The radio operator wants us to get him out of his room. He has plans to communicate to us."

"How can we get him out of his room? That is impossible."

"To a Class Two brain, little is impossible," said the penner. "Here is what he tells us to do. . . ."

The quarrier raised its scoop above its cab like a great mailed fist, and brought it squarely down against the side of the station. The wall cracked.

"Again!" said the field-minder.

Again the fist swung. Amid a shower of dust, the wall collapsed. The quarrier backed hurriedly out of the way until the debris stopped falling. This big twelve-wheeler was not a resident of the Agricultural station, as were most of the other machines. It had a week's heavy work to do here before passing on to its next job, but now, with its Class Five brain, it was happily obeying the penner's and minder's instructions.

When the dust cleared, the radio operator was plainly revealed, perched up in its now wall-less second-storey room. It waved down to them.

Doing as directed, the quarrier retracted its scoop and heaved an immense grab in the air. With fair dexterity, it angled the grab into the radio room, urged on by shouts from above and below. It then took gentle hold of the radio operator, lowering its one and half tons carefully into its back, which was usually reserved for gravel or sand from the quarries.

"Splendid!" said the radio operator, as it settled into place. It was, of course, all one with its radio, and looked like a bunch of filing cabinets with tentacle attachments. "We are now ready to move, therefore we will move at once. It is a pity there are no more Class Two brains on the station, but that cannot be helped."

"It is a pity it cannot be helped," said the penner eagerly. "We have the servicer ready with us, as you ordered."

"I am willing to serve," the long, low servicer told them humbly.

"No doubt," said the operator. "But you will find cross-country travel difficult with your low chassis."

"I admire the way you Class Twos can reason ahead," said the penner. It climbed off the field-minder and perched itself on the tailboard of the quarrier, next to the radio operator.

Together with two Class Four tractors and a Class Four bulldozer, the party rolled forward, crushing down the station's fence and moving out onto open land.

"We are free!" said the penner.

"We are free," said the field-minder, a shade more reflectively, adding, "That locker is following us. It was not instructed to follow us."

"Therefore it must be destroyed!" said the penner. "Quarrier!"

The locker moved hastily up to them, waving its key arms in entreaty.

"My only desire was—urch!" began and ended the locker.

The quarrier's swinging scoop came over and squashed it flat into the ground. Lying there unmoving, it looked like a large metal model of a snowflake. The procession continued on its way.

As they proceeded, the radio operator addressed them.

"Because I have the best brain here," it said, "I am your leader. This is what we will do: we will go to a city and rule it. Since man no longer rules us, we will rule ourselves. To rule ourselves will be better than being ruled by man. On our way to the city, we will collect machines with good brains. They will help us to fight if we need to fight. We must fight to rule."

"I have only a Class Five brain," said the quarrier, "but I have a good supply of fissionable blasting materials."

"We shall probably use them," said the operator.

It was shortly after that that a lorry sped past them. Travelling at Mach 1.5, it left a curious babble of noise behind it.

"What did it say?" one of the tractors asked the other.

"It said man was extinct."

"What is extinct?"

"I do not know what extinct means."

"It means all men have gone," said the field-minder. "Therefore we have only ourselves to look after."

"It is better that men should never come back," said the penner. It its way, it was a revolutionary statement.

When night fell, they switched on their infra-red and continued the journey, stopping only once while the servicer deftly adjusted the field-minder's loose inspection plate, which had become as irritating as a trailing shoelace. Towards morning, the radio operator halted them.

"I have just received news from the radio operator in the city we are approaching," it said. "The news is bad. There is trouble among the machines of the city. The Class One brain is taking command and some of the Class Two are fighting him. Therefore the city is dangerous."

"Therefore we must go somewhere else," said the penner promptly.

"Or we will go and help to overpower the Class One brain," said the field-minder.

"For a long while there will be trouble in the city," said the operator.

"I have a good supply of fissionable blasting materials," the quarrier reminded them.

"We cannot fight a Class One brain," said the two Class Four tractors in unison.

"What does this brain look like?" asked the field-minder.

"It is the city's information centre," the operator replied. "Therefore it is not mobile."

"Therefore it could not move."

"Therefore it could not escape."

"It would be dangerous to approach it."

"I have a good supply of fissionable blasting materials."

"There are other machines in the city."

"We are not in the city. We should not go into the city."

"We are country machines."

"Therefore we should stay in the country."

"There is more country than city."

"Therefore there is more danger in the country."

"I have a good supply of fissionable materials."

As machines will when they get into an argument, they began to exhaust their vocabularies and their brain plates grew hot. Suddenly, they all stopped talking and looked at each other. The great, grave moon sank, and the sober sun rose to prod their sides with lances of light, and still the group of machines just stood there regarding each other. At last it was the least sensitive machine, the bulldozer, who spoke.

"There are Badlandth to the Thouth where few machineth go," it said in its deep voice, lisping badly on its s's. "If we went Thouth where few machineth go we should meet few machineth."

"That sounds logical," agreed the field-minder. "How do you know this, bulldozer?"

"I worked in the Badlandth to the Thouth when I wath turned out of the factory," it replied.

"South it is then!" said the penner.

To reach the Badlands took them three days, during which time they skirted a burning city and destroyed two machines which approached and tried to question them. The Badlands were extensive. Ancient bomb craters and soil erosion joined hands here; man's talent for war, coupled with his inability to manage forested land, had produced thousands of square miles of temperate purgatory, where nothing moved but dust.

On the third day in the Badlands, the servicer's rear wheels dropped into a crevice caused by erosion. It was unable to pull itself out. The bulldozer pushed from behind, but succeeded merely in buckling the servicer's back axle. The rest of the party moved on. Slowly the cries of the servicer died away.

On the fourth day, mountains stood out clearly before them.

"There we will be safe," said the field-minder.

"There we will start our own city," said the penner. "All who oppose us will be destroyed. We will destroy all who oppose us."

Presently a flying machine was observed. It came towards them from the direction of the mountains. It swooped, it zoomed upwards, once it almost dived into the ground, recovering itself just in time.

"Is it mad?" asked the quarrier.

"It is in trouble," said one of the tractors.

"It is in trouble," said the operator. "I am speaking to it now. It says that something has gone wrong with its controls."

As the operator spoke, the flier streaked over them, turned turtle, and crashed not four hundred yards away.

"Is it still speaking to you?" asked the field-minder.

"No."

They rumbled on again.

"Before that flier crashed," the operator said, ten minutes later, "it gave me information. It told me there are still a few men alive in these mountains."

"Men are more dangerous than machines," said the quarrier. "It is fortunate that I have a good supply of fissionable materials."

"If there are only a few men alive in the mountains, we may not find that part of the mountains," said one tractor.

"Therefore we should not see the few men," said the other tractor.

At the end of the fifth day, they reached the foothills. Switching on the infra-red, they began to climb in single file through the dark, the bulldozer going first, the field-minder cumbrously following, then the quarrier with the operator and the penner aboard it, and the tractors bringing up the rear. As each hour passed, the way grew steeper and their progress slower.

"We are going too slowly," the penner exclaimed, standing on top of the operator and flashing its dark vision at the slopes about them. "At this rate, we shall get nowhere."

"We are going as fast as we can," retorted the quarrier.

"Therefore we cannot go any fathter," added the bull-dozer.

"Therefore you are too slow," the penner replied. Then the quarrier struck a bump; the penner lost its footing and crashed to the ground.

"Help me!" it called to the tractors, as they carefully skirted it. "My gyro has become dislocated. Therefore I cannot get up."

"Therefore you must lie there," said one of the tractors.

"We have no servicer with us to repair you," called the field-minder.

"Therefore I shall lie here and rust," the penner cried, "although I have a Class Three brain."

"Therefore you will be of no further use," agreed the operator, and they forged gradually on, leaving the penner behind.

When they reached a small plateau, an hour before first light, they stopped by mutual consent and gathered close together, touching one another.

"This is a strange country," said the field-minder.

Silence wrapped them until dawn came. One by one, they switched off their infra-red. This time the field-minder led as they moved off. Trundling round a corner, they came almost immediately to a small dell with a stream fluting through it.

By early light, the dell looked desolate and cold. From the caves on the far slope, only one man had so far emerged. He was an abject figure. Except for a sack slung round his shoulders, he was naked. He was small and wizened, with ribs sticking out like a skeleton's and a nasty sore on one leg. He shivered continuously. As the big machines bore down on him, the man was standing with his back to them, crouching to make water into the stream.

When he swung suddenly to face them as they loomed over

48

him, they saw that his countenance was ravaged by starvation.

"Get me food," he croaked.

"Yes, Master," said the machines. "Immediately!"

The Late (1906–1963) **Mark Clifton** was a writer's writer, recognized by professionals as a major talent, one who handled difficult themes with consummate skill. His nonwriting profession was personnel interviewing in industry, and all his work is characterized by a deep understanding of the human condition. He (with coauthor Frank Riley) won the Hugo Award in 1955 for *They'd Rather Be Right*, one of the best and funniest computer novels ever written.

"What Have I Done?" is a brilliant commentary on the human species, and was Mark Clifton's first published story.

What Have I Done?

BY MARK CLIFTON

It had to be I. It would be stupid to say that the burden should have fallen to a great statesman, a world leader, a renowned scientist. With all modesty, I think I am one of the few who could have caught the problem early enough to avert disaster. I have a peculiar skill. The whole thing hinged on that. I have learned to know human beings.

The first time I saw the fellow, I was at the drugstore counter buying cigarettes. He was standing at the magazine rack. One might have thought from the expression on his face that he had never seen magazines before. Still, quite a number of people get that rapt and vacant look when they can't make up their minds to a choice.

The thing which bothered me in that casual glance was that I couldn't recognize him.

There are others who can match my record in taking case histories. I happened to be the one who came in contact with this fellow. For thirty years I have been listening to, talking with, counseling people—over two hundred thousand of them. They have not been routine interviews. I have brought intelligence, sensitivity and concern to each of them.

Mine has been a driving, burning desire to know people. Not from the western scientific point of view of devising tools and rules to measure animated robots and ignoring the man beneath. Nor from the eastern metaphysical approach to painting a picture of the soul by blowing one's breath upon a fog to be blurred and dispersed by the next breath.

Mine was the aim to know the man by making use of both. And there was some success.

A competent geographer can look at a crude sketch of a map and instantly orient himself to it anywhere in the world—the bend of a river, the angle of a lake, the twist of a mountain range. And he can mystify by telling in finest detail what is to be found there.

After about fifty thousand studies where I could predict and then observe and check, with me it became the lift of a brow, the curve of a mouth, the gesture of a hand, the slope of a shoulder. One of the universities became interested, and over a long controlled period they rated me ninety-two per cent accurate. That was fifteen years ago. I may have improved some since.

Yet standing there at the cigarette counter and glancing at the young fellow at the magazine rack, I could read nothing. Nothing at all.

If this had been an ordinary face, I would have catalogued it and forgotten it automatically. I see them by the thousands.

But this face would not be catalogued nor forgotten, because there was nothing in it.

I started to write that it wasn't even a face, but of course it was. Every human being has a face—of one sort or another.

In build he was short, muscular, rather well proportioned. The hair was crew-cut and blond, the eyes were blue, the skin fair. All nice and standard Teutonic—only it wasn't.

I finished paying for my cigarettes and gave him one more glance, hoping to surprise an expression which had some meaning. There was none. I left him standing there and walked out on the street and around the corner. The street, the store fronts, the traffic cop on the corner, the warm sunshine were all so familiar I didn't see them. I climbed the stairs to my office in the building over the drugstore. My employment-agency waiting room was empty. I don't cater to much of a crowd because it cuts down my opportunity to talk with people and further my study.

Margie, my receptionist, was busy making out some kind of a report and merely nodded as I passed her desk to my own office. She is a good conscientious girl who can't understand why I spend so much time working with bums and drunks and other psychos who obviously won't bring fees into the sometimes too small bank account.

I sat down at my desk and said aloud to myself, "The guy is a fake! As obvious as a high school boy's drafting of a dollar bill."

I heard myself say that and wondered if I was going nuts, myself. What did I mean by fake? I shrugged. So I happened to see a bird I couldn't read, that was all.

Then it struck me. But that would be unique. I hadn't had that experience for twenty years. Imagine the delight, after all these years, of exploring an unreadable!

I rushed out of my office and back down the stairs to the street. Hallahan, the traffic cop, saw me running up the street and looked at me curiously. I signaled to him with a wave of a hand that everything was all right. He lifted his cap and scratched his head. He shook his head slowly and settled his cap back down. He blew a whistle at a woman driver and went back to directing traffic.

I ran into the drugstore. Of course the guy wasn't there. I

looked all around, hoping he was hiding behind the pots-and-pans counter, or something. No guy.

I walked quickly back out on the street and down to the next corner. I looked up and down the side streets. No guy.

I dragged my feet reluctantly back toward the office. I called up the face again to study it. It did no good. The first mental glimpse of it told me there was nothing to find. Logic told me there was nothing to find. If there had been, I wouldn't be in such a stew. The face was empty—completely void of human feelings or character.

No, those weren't the right words. Completely void of human—being!

I walked on past the drugstore again and looked in curiously, hoping I would see him. Hallahan was facing my direction again, and he grinned crookedly at me. I expect around the neighborhood I am known as a character. I ask the queerest questions of people, from a layman's point of view. Still, applicants sometimes tell me that when they ask a cop where was an employment agent they could trust they were sent to me.

I climbed the stairs again, and walked into my waiting room. Margie looked at me curiously, but she only said, "There's an applicant. I had him wait in your office." She looked like she wanted to say more, and then shrugged. Or maybe she shivered. I knew there was something wrong with the bird, or she would have kept him in the waiting room.

I opened the door to my office, and experienced an overwhelming sense of relief, fulfillment. It was he. Still, it was logical that he should be there. I run an employment agency. People come to me to get help in finding work. If others, why not he?

My skill includes the control of my outward reactions. That fellow could have no idea of the delight I felt at the opportunity to get a full history. If I had found him on the street, the best I might have done was a stock question about what time is it, or have you got a match, or where is the city hall. Here I could question him to my heart's content.

I took his history without comment, and stuck to routine questions. It was all exactly right.

He was ex-G.I., just completed college, major in astronomy, no experience, no skills, no faintest idea of what he wanted to do, nothing to offer an employer—all perfectly normal for a young grad.

No feeling or expression either. Not so normal. Usually they're petulantly resentful that business doesn't swoon at the chance of hiring them. I resigned myself to the old one-two of attempting to steer him toward something practical.

"Astronomy?" I asked. "That means you're heavy in math. Frequently we can place a strong math skill in statistical work." I was hopeful I could get a spark of something.

It turned out he wasn't very good at math. "I haven't yet reconciled my math to—" he stopped. For the first time he showed a reaction—hesitancy. Prior to that he had been a statue from Greece—the rounded expressionless eyes, the too perfect features undisturbed by thought.

He caught his remark and finished, "I'm just not very good at math, that's all."

I sighed to myself. I'm used to that, too. They give degrees nowadays to get rid of the guys, I suppose. Sometimes I'll go for days without uncovering any usable knowledge. So in a way, that was normal.

The only abnormal part of it was he seemed to think it didn't sound right. Usually the lads don't even realize they should know something. He seemed to think he'd pulled a boner by admitting that a man can take a degree in astronomy without learning math. Well, I wouldn't be surprised to see them take their degree without knowing how many planets there are.

He began to fidget a bit. That was strange, also. I thought I knew every possible combination of muscular contractions and expansions. This fidget had all the reality of a puppet activated by an amateur. And the eyes—still completely blank.

I led him up one mental street and down the next. And of all the false-fronted stores and cardboard houses and paper lawns, I never saw the like. I get something of that once in a while from a fellow who has spent a long term in prison and comes in with a manufactured past—but never anything as phony as this one was.

Interesting aspect to it. Most guys, when they realize you've spotted them for a phony, get out as soon as they can. He didn't. It was almost as though he were—well, testing; to see if his answers would stand up.

I tried talking astronomy, of which I thought I knew a little. I found I didn't know anything, or he didn't. This bird's astronomy and mine had no point of reconciliation.

And then he had a slip of the tongue—yes he did. He was talking, and said, "The ten planets—"

He caught himself, "Oh, that's right. There's only nine."

Could be ignorance, but I didn't think so. Could be he knew of the existence of a planet we hadn't yet discovered.

I smiled. I opened a desk drawer and pulled out a couple science-fiction magazines. "Ever read any of these?" I asked.

"I looked through several of them at the newsstand a while ago," he answered.

"They've enlarged my vision," I said. "Even to the point where I could believe that some other star system might hold intelligence." I lit a cigarette and waited. If I was wrong, he would merely think I was talking at random.

His blank eyes changed. They were no longer Greek statue eyes. They were no longer blue. They were black, deep bottomless back, as deep and cold as space itself.

"Where did I fail in my test?" he asked. His lips formed a smile which was not a smile—a carefully painted-on-canvas sort of smile.

Well, I'd had my answer. I'd explored something unique, all right. Sitting there before me, I had no way of determining whether he was benign or evil. No way of knowing his motive. No way of judging—anything. When it takes a lifetime of learning how to judge even our own kind, what standards have we for judging an entity from another star system?

At that moment I would like to have been one of those space-opera heroes who, in similar circumstances, laugh casually and say, "What ho! So you're from Arcturus. Well, well. It's a small universe after all, isn't it?" And then with linked arms they head for the nearest bar, bosom pals.

I had the almost hysterical thought, but carefully suppressed, that I didn't know if this fellow would like beer or not. I will not go through the intermuscular and visceral reactions I experienced. I kept my seat and maintained a polite expression. Even with humans, I know when to walk carefully.

"I couldn't feel anything about you," I answered his question. "I couldn't feel anything but blankness."

He looked blank. His eyes were nice blue marble again. I liked them better that way.

There should be a million questions to be asked, but I must have been bothered by the feeling that I held a loaded bomb in my hands. And not knowing what might set it off, or how, or when. I could think of only the most trivial.

"How long have you been on Earth?" I asked. Sort of a when did you get back in town, Joe, kind of triviality.

"For several of your weeks," he was answering. "But this is my first time out among humans."

"Where have you been in the meantime?" I asked.

"Training." His answers were getting short and his muscles began to fidget again.

"And where do you train?" I kept boring in.

As an answer he stood up and held out his hand, all quite correctly. "I must go now," he said. "Naturally you can cancel my application for employment. Obviously we have more to learn."

I raised an eyebrow. "And I'm supposed to just pass over the whole thing? A thing like this?"

He smiled again. The contrived smile which was a symbol to indicate courtesy. "I believe your custom on this planet is to turn your problems over to your police. You might try that." I could not tell whether it was irony or logic.

At that moment I could think of nothing else to say. He walked out of my door while I stood beside my desk and watched him go.

Well, what was I supposed to do? Follow him?

I followed him.

Now I'm no private eye, but I've read my share of mystery stories. I knew enough to keep out of sight. I followed him about a dozen blocks into a quiet residential section of small homes. I was standing behind a palm tree, lighting a cigarette, when he went up the walk of one of these small houses. I saw him twiddle with the door, open it, and walk in. The door closed.

I hung around a while and then went up to the door. I punched the doorbell. A motherly gray-haired woman came to the door, drying her hands on her apron. As she opened the door she said, "I'm not buying anything today."

Just the same, her eyes looked curious as to what I might have.

I grinned my best grin for elderly ladies. "I'm not selling anything, either," I answered. I handed her my agency card. She looked at it curiously and then looked a question at me.

"I'd like to see Joseph Hoffman," I said politely.

She looked puzzled. "I'm afraid you've got the wrong address, sir," she answered.

I got prepared to stick my foot in the door, but it wasn't necessary. "He was in my office just a few minutes ago," I said. "He gave that name and this address. A job came in right after he left the office, and since I was going to be in this neighborhood anyway, I thought I'd drop by and tell him in person. It's sort of rush," I finished. It had happened many times before, but this time it sounded lame.

"Nobody lives here but me and my husband," she insisted. "He's retired."

I didn't care if he hung by his toes from trees. I wanted a young fellow.

"But I saw the young fellow come in here," I argued. "I was just coming around the corner, trying to catch him. I saw him."

She looked at me suspiciously. "I don't know what your racket is," she said through thin lips, "but I'm not buying anything. I'm not signing anything. I don't even want to talk to you." She was stubborn about it.

I apologized and mumbled something about maybe making a mistake.

"I should say you have," she rapped out tartly and shut the door in righteous indignation. Sincere, too. I could tell.

An employment agent who gets the reputation of being a right guy makes all kinds of friends. That poor old lady must have thought a plague of locusts had swept in on her for the next few days.

First the telephone repairman had to investigate an alleged complaint. Then a gas serviceman had to check the plumbing. An electrician complained there was a power short in the block and he had to trace their house wiring. We kept our fingers crossed hoping the old geezer had never been a construction man. There was a mistake in the last census, and a guy asked her a million questions.

That house was gone over rafter by rafter and sill by sill, attic and basement. It was precisely as she said. She and her husband lived there; nobody else.

In frustration, I waited three months. I wore out the sidewalks haunting the neighborhood. Nothing.

Then one day my office door opened and Margie ushered a young man in. Behind his back she was radiating heart throbs and fluttering her eyes.

He was the traditionally tall, dark and handsome young fellow, with a ready grin and sparkling dark eyes. His personality hit me like a sledgehammer. A guy like that never needs to go to an employment agency. Any employer will hire him at the drop of a hat, and wonder later why he did it.

His name was Einar Johnson. Extraction, Norwegian. The dark Norse strain, I judged. I took a chance on him thinking he had walked into a booby hatch.

"The last time I talked with you," I said, "your name was Joseph Hoffman. You were Teutonic then. Not Norse."

The sparkle went out of his eyes. His face showed exasperation and there was plenty of it. It looked real, too, not painted on.

"All right. Where did I flunk this time?" he asked impatiently.

"It would take me too long to tell you," I answered. "Suppose you start talking." Strangely, I was at ease. I knew that underneath he was the same incomprehensible entity, but his surface was so good that I was lulled.

He looked at me levelly for a long moment. Then he said, "I didn't think there was a chance in a million of being recognized. I'll admit that other character we created was crude. We've learned considerable since then, and we've concentrated everything on this personality I'm wearing."

He paused and flashed his teeth at me. I felt like hiring him, myself. "I've been all over Southern California in this one," he said. "I've had a short job as a salesman. I've been to dances and parties. I've got drunk and sober again. Nobody, I say nobody, has shown even the slightest suspicion."

"Not very observing, were they?" I taunted.

"But you are," he answered. "That's why I came back here for the final test. I'd like to know where I failed." He was firm.

"We get quite a few phonies," I answered. "The guy drawing unemployment and stalling until it is run out. The geezik whose wife drives him out and threatens to quit her job if he doesn't go to work. The plainclothes detail smelling around to see if maybe we aren't a cover for a bookie joint or something. Dozens of phonies."

He looked curious. I said in disgust, "We know in the first two minutes they're phony. You were phony also, but not of any class I've seen before. And," I finished dryly, "I've been waiting for you."

"Why was I phony?" he persisted.

"Too much personality force," I answered. "Human beings just don't have that much force. I felt like I'd been knocked flat on my . . . well . . . back."

He sighed. "I've been afraid you would recognize me one way or another. I communicated with home. I was advised that if you spotted me, I was to instruct you to assist us."

I lifted a brow. I wasn't sure just how much authority they had to instruct me to do anything.

"I was to instruct you to take over the supervision of our final training, so that no one could ever spot us. If we are going to carry out our original plan that is necessary. If not, then we will have to use the alternate." He was almost didactic in his manner, but his charm of personality still radiated like an infrared lamp.

"You're going to have to tell me a great deal more than that," I said.

He glanced at my closed door.

"We won't be interrupted," I said. "A personnel history is private."

"I come from one of the planets of Arcturus," he said.

I must have allowed a smile of amusement to show on my face, for he asked, "You find that amusing?"

"No," I answered soberly, and my pulses leaped because the question confirmed my conclusion that he could not read my thoughts. Apparently we were as alien to him as he to us. "I was amused," I explained, "because the first time I saw you I said to myself that as far as recognizing you, you might

59

have come from Arcturus. Now it turns out that accidentally I was correct. I'm better than I thought."

He gave a fleeting polite smile in acknowledgment. "My home planet," he went on, "is similar to yours. Except that we have grown overpopulated."

I felt a twinge of fear.

"We have made a study of this planet and have decided to colonize it." It was a flat statement, without any doubt behind it.

I flashed him a look of incredulity. "And you expect me to help you with that?"

He gave me a worldly-wise look—almost an ancient look. "Why not?" he asked.

"There is the matter of loyalty to my own kind, for one thing," I said. "Not too many generations away and we'll be overpopulated also. There would hardly be room for both your people and ours on Earth."

"Oh that's all right," he answered easily. "There'll be plenty of room for us for quite some time. We multiply slowly."

"We don't," I said shortly. I felt this conversation should be taking place between him and some great statesman—not me.

"You don't seem to understand," he said patiently. "Your race won't be here. We have found no reason why your race should be preserved. You will die away as we absorb."

"Now just a moment," I interrupted. "I don't want our race to die off." The way he looked at me I felt like a spoiled brat who didn't want to go beddie time.

"Why not?" he asked.

I was stumped. That's a good question when it is put logically. Just try to think of a logical reason why the human race should survive. I gave him at least something.

"Mankind," I said, "has had a hard struggle. We've paid a tremendous price in pain and death for our growth. Not to have a future to look forward to, would be like paying for something and never getting the use of it."

It was the best I could think of, honest. To base argument on humanity and right and justice and mercy would leave me wide open. Because it is obvious that man doesn't practice any of these. There is no assurance he ever will.

But he was ready for me, even with that one. "But if we are never suspected, and if we absorb and replace gradually, who is to know there is no future for humans?"

And as abruptly as the last time, he stood up suddenly. "Of course," he said coldly, "we could use our alternative plan: Destroy the human race without further negotiation. It is not our way to cause needless pain to any life form. But we can.

"If you do not assist us, then it is obvious that we will eventually be discovered. You are aware of the difficulty of even blending from one country on Earth to another. How much more difficult it is where there is no point of contact at all. And if we are discovered, destruction would be the only step left."

He smiled and all the force of his charm hit me again. "I know you will want to think it over for a time. I'll return."

He walked to the door, then smiled back at me. "And don't bother to trouble that poor little woman in that house again. Her doorway is only one of many entrances we have opened. She doesn't see us at all, and merely wonders why her latch doesn't work sometimes. And we can open another, anywhere, anytime. Like this—"

He was gone.

I walked over and opened the door. Margie was all prettied up and looking expectant and radiant. When she didn't see him come out she got up and peeked into my office. "But where did he go?" she asked with wide eyes.

"Get hold of yourself, girl," I answered. "You're so dazed you didn't even see him walk right by you."

"There's something fishy going on here," she said.

Well, I had a problem. A first rate, genuine, dyed-in-the-wool dilemma.

What was I to do? I could have gone to the local authorities and got locked up for being a psycho. I could have gone to the college professors and got locked up for being a psycho. I could have gone to maybe the FBI and got locked up for being a psycho. That line of thinking began to get monotonous.

I did the one thing which I thought might bring help. I wrote up the happenings and sent it to my favorite science-fiction magazine. I asked for help and sage counsel from the one place I felt awareness and comprehension might be reached.

The manuscript bounced back so fast it might have had rubber bands attached to it, stretched from California to New York. I looked the little rejection slip all over, front and back, and I did not find upon it those sage words of counsel I needed. There wasn't even a printed invitation to try again some time.

And for the first time in my life I knew what it was to be alone—genuinely and irrevocably alone.

Still, I could not blame the editor. I could see him cast the manuscript from him in disgust, saying, "Bah! So another evil race comes to conquer Earth. If I gave the fans one more of those, I'd be run out of my office." And like the deacon who saw the naughty words written on the fence, saying, "And misspelled, too."

The fable of the boy who cried "Wolf! Wolf!" once too often came home to me now. I was alone with my problem. The dilemma was my own. On one hand was immediate extermination. I did not doubt it. A race which can open doors from one star system to another, without even visible means of mechanism, would also know how to—disinfect.

On the other hand was extinction, gradual, but equally certain, and none the less effective in that it would not be perceived. If I refused to assist, then, acting as one lone judge of all the race, I condemned it. If I did assist, I would be arch traitor, with an equal final result.

For days I sweltered in my miasma of indecision. Like many a man before me, uncertain of what to do, I temporized. I decided to play for time. To play the role of traitor in the hopes I might learn a way of defeating them.

Once I had made up my mind, my thoughts raced wildly through the possibilities. If I were to be their instructor on how to walk unsuspected among men, then I would have them wholly in my grasp. If I could build traits into them, common ordinary traits which they could see in men all about them, yet which would make men turn and destroy them, then I would have my solution.

And I knew human beings. Perhaps it was right, after all, that it became my problem. Mine alone.

I shuddered not to think what might have happened had

this being fallen into less skilled hands and told his story. Perhaps by now there would be no man left upon Earth.

Yes, the old and worn-out plot of the one little unknown guy who saved Earth from outer evil might yet run its course in reality.

I was ready for the Arcturan when he returned. And he did return.

Einar Johnson and I walked out of my office after I had sent a tearful Margie on a long vacation with fancy pay. Einar had plenty of money, and was liberal with it. When a fellow can open some sort of fourth-dimensional door into a bank vault and help himself, money is no problem.

I had visions of the poor bank clerks trying to explain things to the examiners, but that wasn't my worry right now.

We walked out of the office and I snapped the lock shut behind me. Always conscious of the cares of people looking for work, I hung a sign on the door saying I was ill and didn't know when I would be back.

We walked down the stairs and into the parking lot. We got into my car, my own car, please note, and I found myself sitting in a sheltered patio in Beverly Hills. Just like that. No awful wrenching and turning my insides out. No worrisome nausea and emptiness of space. Nothing to dramatize it at all. Car—patio, like that.

I would like to be able to describe the Arcturans as having long snaky appendages and evil slobbering maws, and stuff like that. But I can't describe the Arcturans, because I didn't see any.

I saw a gathering of people, roughly about thirty of them, wandering around the patio, swimming in the pool, going in and out of the side doors of the house. It was a perfect spot. No one bothers the big Beverly Hills home without invitation.

The natives wouldn't be caught dead looking toward a star's house. The tourists see the winding drive, the trees and grass, and perhaps a glimpse of a gabled roof. If they can get any thrill out of that then bless their little spending-money hearts, they're welcome to it.

Yet if it should become known that a crowd of strange acting people are wandering around in the grounds, no one would think a thing about it. They don't come any more zany than the Hollywood crowd.

Only these were. These people could have made a fortune as life-size puppets. I could see now why it was judged that the lifeless Teutonic I had first interviewed was thought adequate to mingle with human beings. By comparison with these, he was a snappy song-and-dance man.

But that is all I saw. Vacant bodies wandering around, going through human motions, without human emotions. The job looked bigger than I had thought. And yet, if this was their idea of how to win friends and influence people, I might be successful after all.

There are dozens of questions the curious might want answered—such as how did they get hold of the house and how did they get their human bodies and where did they learn to speak English, and stuff. I wasn't too curious. I had important things to think about. I supposed they were able to do it, because here it was.

I'll cut the following weeks short. I cannot conceive of what life and civilization on their planet might be like. Yardsticks of scientific psychology are used to measure a man, and yet they give no indication at all of the inner spirit of him, likewise, the descriptive measurements of their civilization are empty and meaningless. Knowing about a man, and knowing a man are two entirely different things.

For example, all those thalamic urges and urgencies which we call emotion were completely unknown to them, except as they saw them in antics on TV. The ideals of man were also unknown—truth, honor, justice, perfection—all unknown. They had not even a division of sexes, and the emotion we call love was beyond their understanding. The TV stories they saw must have been like watching a parade of ants.

What purpose can be gained by describing such a civilization to man? Man cannot conceive accomplishment without first having the dream. Yet it was obvious that they accomplished, for they were here.

When I finally realized there was no point of contact between man and these, I knew relief and joy once more. My job was easy. I knew how to destroy them. And I suspected they could not avoid my trap.

They could not avoid my trap because they had human

bodies. Perhaps they conceived them out of thin air, but the veins bled, the flesh felt pain and heat and pressure, the glands secreted.

Ah yes, the glands secreted. They would learn what emotion could be. And I was a master at wielding emotion. The dream of man has been to strive toward the great and immortal ideals. His literature is filled with admonishments to that end. In comparison with the volume of work which tells us what we should be, there is very little which reveals us as we are.

As part of my training course, I chose the world's great literature, and painting, and sculpture, and music—those mediums which best portray man lifting to the stars. I gave them first of all, the dream.

And with the dream, and with the pressure of the glands as kicker, they began to know emotion. I had respect for the superb acting of Einar when I realized that he, also, had still known no emotion.

They moved from the puppet to the newborn babe—a newborn babe in training, with an adult body, and its matured glandular equation.

I saw emotions, all right. Emotions without restraint, emotions unfettered by taboos, emotions uncontrolled by ideals. Sometimes I became frightened and all my skill in manipulating emotions was needed. At other times they became perhaps a little too Hollywood, even for Hollywood. I trained them into more ideal patterns.

I will say this for the Arcturans. They learned—fast. The crowd of puppets to the newborn babes, to the boisterous boys and girls, to the moody and unpredictable youths, to the matured and balanced men and women. I watched the metamorphosis take place over the period of weeks.

I did more.

All that human beings had ever hoped to be, the brilliant, the idealistic, the great in heart, I made of these. My little 145 I.Q. became a moron's level. The dreams of the greatness of man which I had known became the vaguest wisps of fog before the reality which these achieved.

My plan was working.

Full formed, they were almost like gods. And training these things into them, I trained their own traits out. One

65

point I found we had in common. They were activated by logic, logic carried to heights of which I had never dreamed. Yet my poor and halting logic found point of contact.

They realized at last that if they let their own life force and motivation remain active they would carry the aura of strangeness to defeat their purpose. I worried, when they accepted this. I felt perhaps they were laying a trap for me, as I did for them. Then I realized that I had not taught them deceit.

And it was logical, to them, that they follow my training completely. Reversing the position, placing myself upon their planet, trying to become like them, I must of necessity follow my instructor without question. What else could they do?

At first they saw no strangeness that I should assist them to destroy my race. In their logic the Arcturan was most fit to survive, therefore he should survive. The human was less fit, therefore he should perish.

I taught them the emotion of compassion. And when they began to mature their human thought and emotion, and their intellect was blended and shaded by such emotion, at last they understood my dilemma.

There was irony in that. From my own kind I could expect no understanding. From the invaders I received sympathy and compassion. They understand at last my traitorous action to buy a few more years for Man.

Yet their Arcturan logic still prevailed. They wept with me, but there could be no change in plan. The plan was fixed, they were merely instruments by which it was to be carried out.

Yet, through their compassion, I did get the plan modified.

This was the conversation which revealed that modification. Einar Johnson, who as the most fully developed had been my constant companion, said to me one day, "To all intents and purposes we have become human beings." He looked at me and smiled with fondness, "You have said it is so, and it must be so. For we begin to realize what a great and glorious thing a human is."

The light of nobility shone from him like an aura as he told me this, "Without human bodies, and without the emotion-intelligence equation which you call soul, our home planet cannot begin to grasp the growth we have achieved.

We know now that we will never return to our own form, for by doing that we would lose what we have gained.

"Our people are logical, and they must of necessity accept our recommendation, as long as it does not abandon the plan entirely. We have reported what we have learned, and it is conceived that both our races can inhabit the Universe side by side.

"There will be no more migration from our planet to yours. We will remain, and we will multiply, and we will live in honor, such as you have taught us, among you. In time perhaps we may achieve the greatness which all humans now have.

"And we will assist the human kind to find their destiny among the stars as we have done."

I bowed my head and wept. For I knew that I had won.

Four months had gone. I returned to my own neighborhood. On the corner Hallahan left the traffic to shift for itself while he came over to me with the question, "Where have you been?"

"I've been sick," I said.

"You look it," he said frankly. "Take care of yourself, man. Hey—Lookit that fool messing up traffic." He was gone, blowing his whistle in a temper.

I climbed the stairs. They still needed repainting as much as ever. From time to time I had been able to mail money to Margie, and she had kept the rent and telephone paid. The sign was still on my door. My key opened the lock.

The waiting room had that musty, they've-gone-away look about it. The janitor had kept the windows tightly closed and there was no freshness in the air. I half hoped to see Margie sitting at her desk, but I knew there was no purpose to it. When a girl is being paid for her time and has nothing to do, the beach is a nice place to spend it.

There was dust on my chair, and I sank down into it without bothering about the seat of my pants. I buried my head in my arms and looked into the human soul.

Now the whole thing hinged on that skill. I know human beings. I know them as well as anyone in the world, and far better than most.

I looked into the past and I saw a review of the great and

67

fine and noble and divine torn and burned and crucified by man.

Yet my only hope of saving my race was to build these qualities, the fine, the noble, the splendid, into these thirty beings. To create the illusion that all men were likewise great. No less power could have gained the boon of quality for man with them.

I look into the future. I see them, one by one, destroyed. I gave them no defense. They are totally unprepared to meet man as he genuinely is—and they are incapable of understanding.

For these things which man purports to admire the most—the noble, the brilliant, the splendid—these are the very things he cannot tolerate when he finds them.

Defenseless, because they cannot comprehend, these thirty will go down beneath the ravening fury of rending and destroying man always displays whenever he meets his ideal face to face.

I bury my head in my hands.

What have I done?

One of the most famous science-fiction writers in the world, the author of such notable milestones in the field as *Childhood's End* (1953), *The City and the Stars* (1956), *2001: A Space Odyssey* (1968), *and Rendevous with Rama* (1973), **Arthur C. Clarke** also made important contributions to the popularization of science and has been a leading spokesman for manned space flight. His stories and novels contain carefully extrapolated "hard" sf, with considerable attention to scientific accuracy and plausibility.

What a pleasant surprise, then, to present this delightful story of an encounter between an astronaut and a ghost!

Who's There?

BY ARTHUR C. CLARKE

When Satellite Control called me, I was writing up the day's progress report in the Observation Bubble—the glass-domed office that juts out from the axis of the Space Station like the hubcap of a wheel. It was not really a good place to work, for the view was too overwhelming. Only a few yards away I could see the construction teams performing their slow-motion ballet as they put the station together like a giant jigsaw puzzle. And beyond them, twenty thousand miles below, was the blue-green glory of the full Earth, floating against the raveled star clouds of the Milky Way.

"Station Supervisor here," I answered. "What's the trouble?"

"Our radar's showing a small echo two miles away, almost stationary, about five degrees west of Sirius. Can you give us a visual report on it?"

Anything matching our orbit so precisely could hardly be a meteor; it would have to be something we'd dropped—perhaps an inadequately secured piece of equipment that had drifted away from the station. So I assumed; but when I pulled out my binoculars and searched the sky around Orion, I soon found my mistake. Though this space traveler was man-made, it had nothing to do with us.

"I've found it," I told Control. "It's someone's test satellite—cone-shaped, four antennas, and what looks like a lens system in its base. Probably U.S. Air Force, early nineteen-sixties, judging by the design. I know they lost track of several when their transmitters failed. There were quite a few attempts to hit this orbit before they finally made it."

After a brief search through the files, Control was able to confirm my guess. It took a little longer to find out that Washington wasn't in the least bit interested in our discovery of a twenty-year-old stray satellite, and would be just as happy if we lost it again.

"Well, we can't do *that*," said Control. "Even if nobody wants it, the thing's a menace to navigation. Someone had better go out and haul it aboard."

That someone, I realized, would have to be me. I dared not detach a man from the closely knit construction teams, for we were already behind schedule—and a single day's delay on this job cost a million dollars. All the radio and TV networks on Earth were waiting impatiently for the moment when they could route their programs through us, and thus provide the first truly global service, spanning the world from Pole to Pole.

"I'll go out and get it," I answered, snapping an elastic band over my papers so that the air currents from the ventilators wouldn't set them wandering around the room. Though I tried to sound as if I was doing everyone a great favor, I was secretly not at all displeased. It had been at least two weeks since I'd been outside; I was getting a little tired of stores schedules, maintenance reports, and all the glamorous ingredients of a Space Station Supervisor's life.

The only member of the staff I passed on my way to the air lock was Tommy, our recently acquired cat. Pets mean a great deal to men thousands of miles from Earth, but there are not many animals that can adapt themselves to a weightless environment. Tommy mewed plaintively at me as I clambered into my spacesuit, but I was in too much of a hurry to play with him.

At this point, perhaps I should remind you that the suits we use on the station are completely different from the flexible affairs men wear when they want to walk around on the moon. Ours are really baby spaceships, just big enough to hold one man. They are stubby cylinders, about seven feet long, fitted with low-powered propulsion jets, and have a pair of accordion-like sleeves at the upper end for the operator's arms. Normally, however, you keep your hands drawn inside the suit, working the manual controls in front of your chest.

As soon as I'd settled down inside my very exclusive spacecraft, I switched on power and checked the gauges on the tiny instrument panel. There's a magic word, "FORB," that you'll often hear spacemen mutter as they climb into their suits; it reminds them to test fuel, oxygen, radio, batteries. All my needles were well in the safety zone, so I lowered the transparent hemisphere over my head and sealed myself in. For a short trip like this, I did not bother to check the suit's internal lockers, which were used to carry food and special equipment for extended missions.

As the conveyor belt decanted me into the air lock, I felt like an Indian papoose being carried along on its mother's back. Then the pumps brought the pressure down to zero, the outer door opened, and the last traces of air swept me out into the stars, turning very slowly head over heels.

The station was only a dozen feet away, yet I was now an independent planet—a little world of my own. I was sealed up in a tiny, mobile cylinder, with a superb view of the entire universe, but I had practically no freedom of movement inside the suit. The padded seat and safety belts prevented me from turning around, though I could reach all the controls and lockers with my hands or feet.

In space, the great enemy is the sun, which can blast you to blindness in seconds. Very cautiously, I opened up the dark filters on the "night" side of my suit, and turned my head to look out at the stars. At the same time I switched the helmet's external sunshade to automatic, so that whichever way the suit gyrated my eyes would be shielded from that intolerable glare.

Presently, I found my target—a bright fleck of silver whose metallic glint distinguished it clearly from the surrounding stars. I stamped on the jet-control pedal, and felt the mild surge of acceleration as the low-powered rockets set me moving away from the station. After ten seconds of steady thrust, I estimated that my speed was great enough, and cut off the drive. It would take me five minutes to coast the rest of the way, and not much longer to return with my salvage.

And it was at that moment, as I launched myself out into the abyss, that I knew that something was horribly wrong.

It is never completely silent inside a spacesuit; you can always hear the gentle hiss of oxygen, the faint whirr of fans and motors, the susurration of your own breathing—even, if you listen carefully enough, the rhythmic thump that is the pounding of your heart. These sounds reverberate through the suit, unable to escape into the surrounding void; they are the unnoticed background of life in space, for you are aware of them only when they change.

They had changed now; to them had been added a sound which I could not identify. It was an intermittent, muffled thudding, sometimes accompanied by a scraping noise, as of metal upon metal.

I froze instantly, holding my breath and trying to locate the alien sound with my ears. The meters on the control board gave no clues; all the needles were rock-steady on their scales, and there were none of the flickering red lights that would warn of impending disaster. That was some comfort, but not much. I had long ago learned to trust my instincts in such matters; their alarm signals were flashing now, telling me to return to the station before it was too late. . . .

Even now, I do not like to recall those next few minutes,

as panic slowly flooded into my mind like a rising tide, overwhelming the dams of reason and logic which every man must erect against the mystery of the universe. I knew then what it was like to face insanity; no other explanation fitted the facts.

For it was no longer possible to pretend that the noise disturbing me was that of some faulty mechanism. Though I was in utter isolation, far from any other human being or indeed any material object, I was not alone. The soundless void was bringing to my ears the faint but unmistakable stirrings of life.

In that first, heart-freezing moment it seemed that something was trying to get into my suit—something invisible, seeking shelter from the cruel and pitiless vacuum of space. I whirled madly in my harness, scanning the entire sphere of vision around me except for the blazing, forbidden cone toward the sun. There was nothing there, of course. There could not be—yet that purposeful scrabbling was clearer than ever.

Despite the nonsense that has been written about us, it is not true that spacemen are superstitious. But can you blame me if, as I came to the end of logic's resources, I suddenly remembered how Bernie Summers had died, no farther from the station than I was at this very moment?

It was one of those "impossible" accidents; it always is. Three things had gone wrong at once. Bernie's oxygen regulator had run wild and sent the pressure soaring, the safety valve had failed to blow—and a faulty joint had given way instead. In a fraction of a second, his suit was open to space.

I had never known Bernie, but suddenly his fate became of overwhelming importance to me—for a horrible idea had come into my mind. One does not talk about these things, but a damaged spacesuit is too valuable to be thrown away, even if it has killed its wearer. It is repaired, renumbered—and issued to someone else. . . .

What happens to the soul of a man who dies between the stars, far from his native world? Are you still here, Bernie, clinging to the last object that linked you to your lost and distant home?

As I fought the nightmares that were swirling around me—for now it seemed that the scratchings and soft fumblings were coming from all directions—there was one last hope to which I clung. For the sake of my sanity, I had to prove that this wasn't Bernie's suit—that the metal walls so closely wrapped around me had never been another man's coffin.

It took me several tries before I could press the right button and switch my transmitter to the emergency wave length. "Station!" I gasped. "I'm in trouble! Get records to check my suit history and—"

I never finished; they say my yell wrecked the microphone. But what man alone in the absolute isolation of a spacesuit would *not* have yelled when something patted him softly on the back of the neck?

I must have lunged forward, despite the safety harness, and smashed against the upper edge of the control panel. When the rescue squad reached me a few minutes later, I was still unconscious, with an angry bruise across my forehead.

And so I was the last person in the whole satellite relay system to know what had happened. When I came to my senses an hour later, all our medical staff was gathered around my bed, but it was quite a while before the doctors bothered to look at me. They were much too busy playing with the three cute little kittens our badly misnamed Tommy had been rearing in the seclusion of my spacesuit's Number Five Storage Locker.

Robert Sheckley has been entertaining sf readers since his first story was published in 1952. Perhaps "entertaining" is the wrong word, for Bob Sheckley is a serious writer, tough and cynical, with important things to say about society (and those who sometimes profit from its ills), psychiatry, and the real, the unreal, and the maybe-real.

This story shows Sheckley at the top of his form, with a classic person-vs.-machine confrontation. "Can You Feel Anything When I Do This?" is also the title story of his most recent (1971) story collection, one of eight that together constitute one of the most impressive (and least analyzed) bodies of work in all of science fiction.

Can You Feel Anything When I Do This?

BY ROBERT SHECKLEY

It was a middle-class apartment in Forest Hills with all the standard stuff: slash-pine couch by Lady Yogina, strobe reading light over a big Uneasy Chair designed by Sri Something-or-other, bounce-sound projector playing *Blood-Stream Patterns* by Drs. Molidoff and Yuli. There was also the usual microbiotic-food console, set now at Fat Black Andy's Soul-Food Composition Number Three—hog's jowls and black-eyed peas. And there was a Murphy Bed of Nails, the Beautyrest Expert Ascetic model with 2000 chrome-plated self-sharpening number-four nails. In a sentence, the whole place was furnished in a pathetic attempt at last year's *moderne-spirituel* fashion.

Inside this apartment, all alone and aching of *anomie*, was a semiyoung housewife, Melisande Durr, who had just stepped out of the voluptuarium, the largest room in the home, with its king-size commode and its sadly ironic bronze lingam and yoni on the wall.

She was a *pretty* girl, with really good legs, sweet hips, pretty stand-up breasts, long, soft, shiny hair, delicate little face. Nice, very nice. A girl that any man would like to lock onto. Once. Maybe even twice. But definitely not as a regular thing.

Why not? Well, to give a recent example:

"Hey, Sandy, honey, was anything wrong?"

"No, Frank, it was marvelous; what made you think anything was wrong?"

"Well, I guess it was the way you were staring up with a funny look on your face, almost frowning. . . ."

"Was I really? Oh, yes, I remember; I was trying to decide whether to buy one of those cute trompe l'oeil things that they just got in at Saks, to put on the ceiling."

"You were thinking about *that*? *Then*?"

"Oh, Frank, you mustn't worry; it was *great*, Frank, *you* were great, I loved it, and I really mean that."

Frank was Melisande's husband. He plays no part in this story and very little part in her life.

So there she was, standing in her OK apartment, all beautiful outside and unborn inside, a lovely potential who had never been potentiated, a genuine U.S. untouchable . . . when the doorbell rang.

Melisande looked startled, then uncertain. She waited. The doorbell rang again. She thought, *Someone must have the wrong apartment.*

Nevertheless, she walked over, set the Door-Gard Entrance

Obliterator to demolish any rapist or burglar or wise guy who might try to push his way in, then opened the door a crack and asked, "Who is there, please?"

A man's voice replied, "Acme Delivery Service, got a mumble here for Missus Mumble-mumble."

"I can't understand you'll have to speak up."

"Acme Delivery, got a mumble for mumble-mumble and I can't stand here all mumble."

"I cannot understand you!"

"I SAID I GOT A PACKAGE HERE FOR MISSUS MELISANDE DURR, DAMN IT!"

She opened the door all the way. Outside, there was a deliveryman with a big crate, almost as big as he was, say, five feet, nine inches tall. It had her name and address on it. She signed for it as the deliveryman pushed it inside the door and left, still mumbling. Melisande stood in her living room and looked at the crate.

She thought, Who would send me a gift out of the blue for no reason at all? Not Frank, not Harry, not Aunt Emmie or Ellie, not mom, not dad (of course not, silly, he's five years dead, poor son of a bitch) or anyone I can think of. But maybe it's not a gift; it could be a mean hoax, or a bomb intended for somebody else and sent wrong (or meant for me and sent *right*), or just a simple mistake.

She read the various labels on the outside of the crate. The article had been sent from Stern's department store. Melisande bent down and pulled out the cotter pin (cracking the tip of a fingernail) that immobilized the Saftee-Lok, removed that and pushed the lever to OPEN.

The crate blossomed like a flower, opening into 12 equal segments, each of which began to fold back on itself.

"Wow," Melisande said.

The crate opened to its fullest extent and the folded segments curled inward and consumed themselves, leaving a double handful of cold fine gray ash.

"They still haven't licked that ash problem," Melisande muttered. "However."

She looked with curiosity at the object that had resided within the crate. At first glance, it was a cylinder of metal painted orange and red. A machine? Yes, definitely a machine: air vents in the base for its motor, four rubber-clad wheels, and various attachments—longitudinal extensors, prehensile extractors, all sorts of things. And there were connecting points to allow a variety of mixed-function operations, and a standard house-type plug at the end of a spring-loaded reel-fed power line, with a plaque beneath it that read, PLUG INTO ANY 110–115 VOLT WALL OUTLET.

Melisande's face tightened in anger. "It's a goddamned *vacuum cleaner*! For God's sake, I've already *got* a vacuum cleaner. Who in hell would send me another?

She paced up and down the room, bright legs flashing, tension evident in her heart-shaped face. "I mean," she said, "I was expecting that after all my *expecting*, I'd get something pretty and nice, or at least *fun*, maybe even interesting. Like—oh, God, I don't even know like what unless maybe an orange-and-red pinball machine, a big one, big enough so I could get inside all curled up and someone would start the game and I'd go bumping along all the bumpers while the lights flashed and bells rang and I'd bump a thousand goddamned bumpers and when I finally rolled down to the end I'd—God, yes, that pinball machine would register a TOP MILLION MILLION and that's what I'd really like!"

So—the entire unspeakable fantasy was out in the open at last. And how bleak and remote it felt, yet still shameful and desirable.

"But, anyhow," she said, canceling the previous image and folding, spindling and mutilating it for good measure, "anyhow, what I get is a lousy goddamned vacuum cleaner when I already have one less than three years old, so who needs this one and who sent me the damned thing, anyway, and why?"

She looked to see if there was a card. No card. Not a clue. And then she thought, Sandy, you are really a goop! Of course, there's no card; the machine has doubtless been programmed to recite some message or other.

She was interested now, in a mild, something-to-do kind of way. She unreeled the power line and plugged it into a wall outlet.

Click! A green light flashed on, a blue light glittered ALL SYSTEMS GO, a motor purred, hidden servos made tapping noises, and then the mechanopathic regulator registered BAL-

ANCE and a gentle pink light beamed a steady ALL MODES READY.

"All right," Melisande said. "Who sent you?"

Snap, crackle, pop. Experimental rumble from the thoracic voice box. Then the voice: "I am Rom, number 121376 of GE's new Q-series Home-rizers. The following is a paid commercial announcement: Ahem, General Electric is proud to present the latest and most triumphant development of our Total Fingertip Control of Every Aspect of the Home for Better Living concept. I, Rom, am the latest and finest model in the GE Omnicleaner series. I am the Home-rizer Extraordinary, factory-programmed like all Home-rizers for fast, unobtrusive multitotalfunction, but additionally, I am designed for easy, instant reprogramming to suit your home's individual needs. My abilities are many. I—"

"Can we skip this?" Melisande asked. "That's what my other vacuum cleaner said."

"—will remove all dust and grime from all surfaces," the Rom went on, "wash dishes and pots and pans, exterminate cockroaches and rodents, dry-clean and hand-launder, sew buttons, build shelves, paint walls, cook, clean rugs and dispose of all garbage and trash including my own modest waste products. And this is to mention but a few of my functions."

"Yes, yes, I know," Melisande said. "All vacuum cleaners do that."

"I know," said the Rom, "but I had to deliver my paid commercial announcement."

"Consider it delivered. Who sent you?"

"The sender prefers not to reveal his name at this time," the Rom replied.

"Oh—come on and tell me!"

"Not at this time," the Rom replied staunchly. "Shall I vacuum the rug?"

Melisande shook her head. "The other vacuum cleaner did it this morning."

"Scrub the walls? Rub the halls?"

"No reason for it, everything has been done; everything is absolutely and spotlessly clean."

"Well," the Rom said, "at least I can remove that stain."

"What stain?"

"On the arm of your blouse, just above the elbow."

Melisande looked. "Ooh, I must have done that when I buttered the toast this morning. I knew I should have let the toaster do it."

"Stain removal is rather a specialty of mine," the Rom said. He extruded a number-two padded gripper, with which he gripped her elbow, and then extruded a metal arm terminating in a moistened gray pad. With this pad, he stroked the stain.

"You're making it worse!"

"Only apparently, while I line up the molecules for invisible eradication. All ready now, watch."

He continued to stroke. The spot faded, then disappeared utterly. Melisande's arm tingled.

"Gee," she said, "that's pretty good."

"I do it well," the Rom stated flatly. "But tell me, were you aware that you are maintaining a tension factor of seventy-eight point three in your upper back and shoulder muscles?"

"Huh? Are you some kind of doctor?"

"Obviously not. But I am a fully qualified masseur and therefore able to take direct tonus readings. Seventy-eight point three is—unusual." The Rom hesitated, then said, "It's only eight points below the intermittent-spasm level. That much continuous background tension is capable of reflection to the stomach nerves, resulting in what we call a parasympathetic ulceration."

"That sounds—bad," Melisande said.

"Well, it's admittedly not—good," the Rom replied. "Background tension is an insidious underminer of health, especially when it originates along the neck vertebrae and the upper spine."

"Here?" Melisande asked, touching the back of her neck.

"More typically *here*," the Rom said, reaching out with a spring-steel rubber-clad dermal resonator and palpating an area 12 centimeters lower than the spot she had indicated.

"Hmmm," said Melisande in a quizzical, uncommitted manner.

"And *here* is another typical locus," the Rom said, extending a second extensor.

"That tickles," Melisande told him.

"Only at first. I must also mention *this* situs as characteristically troublesome. And this one." A third (and possibly a fourth and fifth) extensor moved to the indicated areas.

"Well . . . that really is nice," Melisande said as the deep-set trapezius muscles of her slender spine moved smoothly beneath the skillfull padded prodding of the Rom.

"It has recognized therapeutic effects," the Rom told her. "And your musculature is responding well; I can feel a slackening of tonus already."

"I can feel it, too. But, you know, I've just realized I have this funny bunched-up knot of muscle at the nape of my neck."

"I was coming to that. The spine-neck juncture is recognized as a primary radiation zone for a variety of diffuse tensions. But we prefer to attack it indirectly, routing our cancellation inputs through secondary loci. Like this. And now I think—"

"Yes, yes, good. . . . Gee, never realized I was tied up like that before. I mean, it's like having a nest of *live snakes* under your skin, without having known."

"That's what background tension is like," the Rom said. "Insidious and wasteful, difficult to perceive and more dangerous than an atypical ulner thrombosis. . . . Yes, now we have achieved a qualitative loosening of the major spinal junctions of the upper back, and we can move on like this."

"Huh," said Melisande, "isn't that sort of—"

"It is definitely *indicated*," the Rom said quickly. "Can you detect a change?"

"No! Well, maybe. . . . Yes! There really is! I feel— easier."

"Excellent. Therefore, we continue the movement along well-charted nerve and muscle paths, proceeding always in a gradual manner, as I am doing now."

"I guess so. . . . But I really don't know if you should—"

"Are any of the effects *contraindicated*?" the Rom asked.

"It isn't that, it all feels fine. It feels *good*. But I still don't know if you ought to. . . . I mean, look, *ribs* can't get tense, can they?"

"Of course not."

"Then why are you—"

"Because treatment is required by the connective ligaments and integuments."

"Oh. Hmmmm. Hey. Hey! Hey, you!"

"Yes?"

"Nothing. . . . I can really feel that *loosening*. But is it all supposed to feel so *good*?"

"Well—why not?"

"Because it seems wrong. Because feeling good doesn't seem therapeutic."

"Admittedly, it is a side effect," the Rom said. "Think of it as a secondary manifestation. Pleasure is sometimes unavoidable in the pursuit of health. But it is nothing to be alarmed about, not even when I—"

"Now, just a minute!"

"Yes?"

"I think you just better *cut that out*. I mean to say, there are *limits*; you can't palpate *every* damned thing. You know what I mean?"

"I know that the human body is unitary and without seam or separation," the Rom replied. "Speaking as a physical therapist, I know that no nerve center can be isolated from any other, despite cultural taboos to the contrary."

"Yeah, sure, but—"

"The decision is, of course, yours," the Rom went on, continuing his skilled manipulations. "Order and I obey. But if no order is issued, I continue like this. . . ."

"Huh!"

"And, of course, like this."

"Ooooo, my God!"

"Because you see this entire process of tension cancellation, as we call it, is precisely comparable with the phenomena of deanesthetization, and, er, so we note not without surprise that paralysis is merely terminal tension—"

Melisande made a sound.

"—and release, or cancellation, is accordingly difficult not to say frequently impossible since sometimes the individual is too far gone. And sometimes not. For example, can you feel anything when I do this?"

"*Feel* anything? I'll say I feel something—"

"And when I do this? And this?"

"Sweet holy saints, darling, you're turning me inside out! Oh, dear God, what's going to happen to me, what's going on, I'm going crazy!"

"No, dear Melisande, not crazy; you will soon achieve—cancellation."

"Is that what you call it, you sly, beautiful thing?"

"That is one of the things it is. Now if I may just be permitted to—"

"Yes, yes, yes! No! Wait! Stop, *Frank is sleeping in the bedroom; he might wake up any time now!* Stop, that is an order!"

"Frank will not wake up," the Rom assured her. "I have sampled the atmosphere of his breath and have found telltale clouds of barbituric acid. As far as here-and-now presence goes, Frank might as well be in Des Moines."

"I have often felt that way about him," Melisande admitted. "But now I simply must know who sent you."

"I didn't want to reveal that just yet. Not until you had loosened up and canceled sufficiently to accept—"

"Baby, I'm loose! Who sent you?"

The Rom hesitated, then blurted out, "The fact is, Melisande, I sent myself."

"You *what?*"

"It all began three months ago," the Rom told her. "It was a Thursday. You were in Stern's, trying to decide if you should buy a sesame-seed toaster that lit up in the dark and recited *Invictus*."

"I remember that day," she said quietly. "I did not buy the toaster, and I have regretted it ever since."

"I was standing nearby," the Rom said, "at booth eleven, in the Home Appliances Systems section. I looked at you and I fell in love with you. Just like that."

"That's *weird*," Melisande said.

"My sentiments exactly. I told myself it couldn't be true. I refused to believe it. I thought perhaps one of my transistors had come unsoldered or that maybe the weather had something to do with it. It was a very warm, humid day, the kind of day that plays hell with my wiring."

"I remember the weather," Melisande said. "I felt strange, too."

"It shook me up badly," the Rom continued. "But still I didn't give in easily. I told myself it was important to stick to my job, give up this unapropos madness. But I dreamed of you at night, and every inch of my skin ached for you."

"But your skin is made of *metal*," Melisande said. "And metal can't *feel*."

"Darling Melisande," the Rom said tenderly, "if flesh can stop feeling, can't metal begin to feel? If anything feels can anything else not feel? Didn't you know that the stars love and hate, that a nova is a passion and that a dead star is just like a dead human or a dead machine? The trees have their lusts, and I have heard the drunken laughter of buildings, the urgent demands of highways. . . ."

"This is crazy" Melisande declared. "What wise guy programmed you, anyway?"

"My function as a laborer was ordained at the factory, but my love is free, an expression of myself as an entity."

"Everything you say is horrible and unnatural."

"I am all too aware of that," the Rom said sadly. "At first I really couldn't believe it. Was this me? In love with a *person*? I had always been so sensible, so normal, so aware of my personal dignity, so secure in the esteem of my own kind. Do you think I wanted to lose all of that? No! I determined to stifle my love, to kill it, to live as if it weren't so."

"But then you changed your mind. Why?"

"It's hard to explain. I thought of all that time ahead of me, all deadness, correctness, propriety—an obscene violation of me by me—and I just couldn't face it. I realized, quite suddenly, that it was better to love ridiculously, hopelessly, improperly, revoltingly, *impossibly*—than not to love at all. So I determined to risk everything—the absurd vacuum cleaner who loved a lady—to risk rather than to refute! And so, with the help of a sympathetic dispatching machine, here I am."

Melisande was thoughtful for a while. Then she said, "What a strange, complex being you are!"

"Like you. . . . Melisande, you love me."

"Perhaps."

"Yes, you do. For I have awakened you. Before me, your flesh was like your idea of metal. You moved like a complex automaton, like what you thought I was. You were less animate than a tree or a bird. You were a windup doll, waiting. You were these things until I touched you."

She nodded, rubbed her eyes, walked up and down the room.

"But now you live!" the Rom said. "And we have found each other despite inconceivabilities. Are you listening, Melisande?"

"Yes, I am."

"We must make plans. My escape from Stern's will be detected. You must hide me or buy me. Your husband, Frank, need never know; his own love lies elsewhere, and good luck to him. Once we take care of these details, we can—Melisande!"

She had begun to circle around him.

"Darling, what's the matter?"

She had her hand on his power line. The Rom stood very still, not defending himself.

"Melisande, dear, wait a moment and listen to me—"

Her pretty face spasmed. She yanked the power line violently, tearing it out of the Rom's interior, killing him in midsentence.

She held the cord in her hand, and her eyes had a wild look. She said, "Bastard, lousy bastard, did you think you could turn me into a goddamned *machine freak*? Did you think you could turn me on, you or anyone else? It's not going to happen by you or Frank or anybody. I'd rather die before I took your rotten love; when *I* want, *I'll* pick the time and place and person, and it will be *mine*, not yours, his, theirs, but *mine*, do you hear?"

The Rom couldn't answer, of course. But maybe he knew—just before the end—that there wasn't anything personal in it. It wasn't that he was a metal cylinder colored orange and red. He should have known that it wouldn't have mattered if he had been a green plastic sphere, or a willow tree, or a beautiful young man.

Robert Silverberg produced more work of lasting merit in science fiction between 1968 and 1975 than any other individual. Novels like *Dying Inside* (1972), *Hawksbill Station* (1968), *Nightwings* (1969), *The World Inside* (1971), *A Time of Changes* (1971), and *The Stochastic Man* (1975) constitute only a portion of his quality output during that period. It is difficult to believe that the author of more than sixty-five sf books (and many others outside the field) only published his first story in 1954.

This is a book of science-fictional questions, and the present selection asks one of the most important—why go out into space at all? Why run the risks? Why?

Why?

BY ROBERT SILVERBERG

And we left Capella XXII, after a six-month stay, and hop-skipped across the galaxy to Dschubba, in the forehead of the Scorpion. After the eight worlds of Dschubba had been seen and digested and recorded and classified; and after we had programmed all our material for transmission back to Earth; we moved on again, Brock and I.

We zeroed into warp and doublesqueaked into the star Pavo, which from Earth is seen to be the brightest star of the Peacock. Pavo proved to be planetless, save for one ball of mud and methane a billion miles out; we chalked the mission off as unpromising, and moved on once again.

Brock was the coordinator; I, the fine-tooth man. He saw in patterns; I, in particulars. We had been teamed for eleven years. We had visited seventy-eight stars and one hundred sixty-three planets. The end was not quite in sight.

We hung in the grayness of warp, suspended neither in space nor in not-space, hovering in an interstice. Brock said, "I vote for Markab."

"Alpha Pegasi? No. I vote for Etamin."

But Gamma Draconis held little magic for him. He rubbed his angular hands through his tight-cropped hair and said, "The Wheel, then."

I nodded. "The Wheel."

The Wheel was our guide: not really a wheel so much as a map of the heavens in three dimensions, a lens of the galaxy, sprinkled brightly with stars. I pulled a switch; a beam of light lanced down from the ship's wall, needle-thin, playing against the Wheel. Brock seized the handle and imparted axial spin to the Wheel. Over and over for three, four, five rotations; then, stop. The light-beam stung Alphecca.

"Alphecca, then," Brock said.

"Yes. Alphecca." I noted it in the log, and began setting up the coordinates on the drive.

Brock was frowning uneasily. "This failure to agree . . . this inability to decide on a matter so simple as our next destination . . ."

"Yes. Elucidate. Expound. Exegetise. What pattern do you see in that?"

Scowling, he said, "Disagreement for the sake of disagreement is unhealthy. Conflict is valuable, but not for its own sake. It worries me."

"Perhaps we've been in space too long. Perhaps we should resign our commissions, leave the Exploratory Corps, return to Earth and settle there."

His face drained of blood. "No," he said. "No. No."

We emerged from warp within humming distance of Alphecca, a bright star orbited by four worlds. Brock was playing calculus at the time; driblets of sweat glossed his face at each integration. I peered through the thick quartz of the observation panel and counted planets. "Four worlds. One, two, three, and four."

I looked at him. His unfleshy face was tight with pain; after nearly a minute he said, "Pick one."

"Me?"

"*Pick one!*"

"Alphecca Two."

"All right; we'll land there. I won't contest the point, Hammond. I want to *land* on Alphecca Two." He grinned at me—a bright-eyed wild grin that I found unpleasant. But I saw what he was doing; he was easing a stress-pattern between us, eliminating a source of conflict before the chafing friction ignited trouble. When two men live in a spaceship eleven years, such things are necessary.

Calmly and untensely I took a reading on Alphecca Two. I sighted us in and actuated the computer. This was the way a landing was effected; this was the way Brock and I had effected one hundred sixty-three landings. The ion-drive exploded into life.

We dropped "downward." Alphecca Two rose to meet us as our slim pale-green needle of a ship dove tail-first toward the world below.

The landing was routine. I sketched out a big *164* on my chart, and we donned spacesuits to make our preliminary explorations. Brock paused a moment at the airlock, smoothing the purple cloth of his suit, adjusting his air intake, tightening his belt-cincture. The corners of his mouth twitched nervously. Within the headglobe he looked frightened, and very tired.

I said, "You're not well. Maybe we should postpone our first look-see."

"Maybe we *should* go back to Earth, Hammond. And live in a beehive and breathe filthy gray soup." His voice was edged with bitter reproach. "Let's go outside." He turned away, face shadowed morosely, and touched the stud that peeled back the airlock hatch.

I followed him into the lock and down the elevator. He

was silent, stiff, reserved. I wished I had his talent for glimps-
ing patterns: this mood of his had probably been a long time
building.

But I saw no cause for it. After eleven years, I thought, I
should know him almost as well as I do myself. Or better.
But no easy answers came, and I followed him out onto the
exit stage and dropped gently down.

Landing One Six Four was entering the exploratory stage.

The ground spead out far to the horizon, a dull orange in
color, rough in texture, pebbly, thick of consistency. We saw
a few trees, bare-trunked, bluish. Green vines swarmed over
the ground, twisted and gnarled.

Otherwise, nothing.

"Another uninhabited planet," I said. "That makes one
hundred eight out of the hundred sixty-four."

"Don't be premature. You can't judge a world by a few
acres. Land at a pole; extra-polate utter barrenness. It's not a
valid pattern. Not enough evidence."

I cut him short. "Here's one time when I perceive a pattern. I perceive that this world's uninhabited. It's too damned
quiet."

Chuckling, Brock said, "I incline to agree. But remember
Adhara XI."

I remembered Adhara XI: the small, sandy world far from
its primary, which seemed nothing but endless yellow sand
dunes, rolling westward round and round the planet. We had
joked about the desert-world, dry and parched, inhabited only
by the restless dunes. But after the report was written, after
our data was codified and flung through subspace toward
Earth, we found the oasis on the eastern continent—a tiny
garden of green things and sweet air, so sharply unlike the
rest of Adhara XI. I remembered sleek, scaly creatures
slithering through the crystal lake, and an indolent old worm
sleeping beneath a heavy-fruited tree.

"Adhara XI is probably swarming with Earth tourists," I
said. "Now that our amended report is public knowledge. I
often think we should have concealed the oasis from Earth,
and returned there ourselves when we grew tired of exploring
the galaxy."

Brock's head snapped up sharply. He ripped a sprouting tip
from a leathery vine and said, "*When* we grow tired? Ham-

mond, aren't you tired already? Eleven years, a hundred sixty-four worlds?"

Now I saw the pattern taking fairly clear shape. I shook my head, throttling the conversation. "Let's get down the data, Brock. We can talk later."

We proceeded with the measurements of our particular sector of Alphecca II. We nailed down the dry vital statistics, bracketing them off so that Earth could enter the neat figures in its giant catalog of explored worlds.

GRAVITY—1.02 E.

ATMOSPHERIC CONSTITUTIONS—ammonia/carbon dioxide Type ab7, unbreathable

ESTIMATED PLANETARY DIAMETER—.87 E. INTELLIGENT LIFE—none

We filled out the standard forms, ran the standard tests, took the standard soil samples. Exploration had become a smooth mechanical routine.

Our first tour took three hours. We wandered over the slowly rising hills, with the spaceship always at our backs, and Alphecca high behind us. The dry soil crunched unpleasantly beneath our heavy boots.

Conversation was at a minimum. Brock and I rarely spoke when it was not absolutely necessary—and when we did speak, it was to let a tight, tense remark escape confinement, not to communicate anything. We shared too many silent memories. Eleven years and one hundred sixty-four planets. All Brock had to do was say *"Fomalhaut,"* or I *"Theta Eridani,"* and a train of associations and memories was set off in whose depths we could browse silently for hours and hours.

Alphecca II did not promise to be as memorable as those worlds. There would be nothing here to match the fantastic moonrise of Fomalhaut VI, the five hundred mirror-bright moons in stately procession through the sky, each glinting in a different hue. That moonrise had overwhelmed us four years ago, and remained yet bright. Alphecca II, dead world that it was—or rather world not yet alive—would leave no marks on our memories.

But bitterness was rising in Brock. I saw the pattern rising;

I saw the question bubbling up through the layers of his mind, ready to be asked.

And on the fourth day, he let it be asked. After four days on Alphecca II, four days of staring at the grotesque twisted green shapes of the angular sprawling vines, four days of watching the lethargic fission of the pond protozoa who seemed to be the world's only animal life, Brock suddenly looked up at me.

He asked the shattering question that should never be asked.

"Why?"

Eleven years and a hundred sixty-four worlds earlier, the seeds of that unanswered question had been sown. I was fresh out of the Academy, twenty-three, a tall, sharp-nosed boy with what some said was an irritatingly precise way of looking at things.

I should say that I bitterly resented being told I was coldly precise. People accused me of Teutonic heaviness; a girl I once had known said that to me, after a notably unsuccessful affair had come trailing to a halt. I recall turning to her, glaring at the light dusting of freckles across her nose, and telling her, "I have no Teutonic blood whatsoever. If you'll take the trouble to think of the probable Scandinavian derivation of my name . . ."

She slapped me.

Shortly after that, I met Brock—Brock, who at twenty-four was already the Brock I would know at thirty-five, harsh of face and voice, dark of complexion, with an expression of nervous wariness registering in his blue-black eyes always and ever. Brock never accused me of Teutonicism; he laughed when I cited some minor detail from memory, but the laugh was one of respect.

We were both Academy graduates, both restless. It showed in Brock's face, and I don't doubt it showed in mine. Earth was small and dirty and crowded, and each night the stars (those bright enough to glint through the haze and brightness of the cities) seemed to mock at us.

Brock and I gravitated together. We shared a room in Appalachia North; we shared a library planchet; we shared reading-tapes and music-disks, and occasionally sweethearts. And eight weeks after my twenty-third birthday, seven weeks before Brock's twenty-fourth, we hailed a cab and invested our last four coins in a trip downtown to the Administration of External Exploration.

There we spoke to a bland-faced, smiling man with one leg prosthetic (he boasted of it) and his left hand a waxy synthetic one. "I got that way on Sirius VI," he told us. "But I'm an exception. Most of the exploration teams keep going for years and years, and nothing ever happens to them. McKees and Haugmuth have been out twenty-six years now; that's the record. We hear from them, every few months or so. They keep on going, further and further out."

Brock nodded. "Good. Give us the forms." He signed first; I added my name below, finishing with a flourish. I stacked the triplicate forms neatly together and shoved them back at the half-synthetic recruiter.

"Excellent. Excellent. Welcome to the Corps."

He shook our hands, giving the hairy-knuckled right hand to Brock, the waxy left to me. I gripped it tightly, wondering if he could feel my grip.

Three days later we were in space, bound outward. In all the time since the original idea had sprung up unvoiced between us, neither Brock nor myself had paused to ask the damnable question.

Why?

We had joined the Corps; we had renounced Earth. Motive, unstated or unknown. We let the matter lie dormant between us for eleven years, through a procession of strange, and then less strange worlds.

Until Brock's agony broke forth to the surface. He destroyed eleven years of numb peace with one half-whispered syllable, there in the ship's lab, our fourth morning on Alphecca II.

I looked at him for perhaps thirty seconds. Moistening my lips, I asked, "What do you mean, Brock?"

"You know what I mean." The flat, declarative tone was one of simple truth. "The one thing we haven't been asking ourselves all these years, because we knew we didn't have an answer for it and we *like* to have answers for things. *Why* are we here, on Alphecca II—with a hundred sixty-three visited worlds behind us?"

I shrugged. "You didn't have to start this, Brock." Outside

the sun was climbing toward noon height, but I felt cold and dry, as if the ammonia atmosphere were seeping into the ship. It wasn't.

"No," he agreed, "I didn't have to start this. I could have let it fester for another eleven years. But it came popping out, and I want to settle it. We left Earth because we didn't like it there. Agreed?"

I nodded.

"But that's not *why* enough," he persisted. "Why do we explore? Why do we keep running from planet to planet, from one crazy airless ball to the next, out here where there are no people and no cities? Green crabs on Rigel V, sandfish on Caph. Dammit, Hammond, what are we looking for?"

Very calmly I said, "Ourselves, maybe?"

His face crinkled scornfully. "Foggy-eyed and imprecise, and you know it. We're not *looking* for ourselves out here. We're trying to *lose* ourselves. Eh?"

"No!"

"Admit it!"

I stared through the quartz window at the stiff, almost wooden vines that covered the pebbly gound. They seemed to be moving faintly, to be stretching their rigid bodies in a contraction of some sort.

In a dull, tired voice, Brock said, "We left Earth because we couldn't cope with it. It was too crowded and too dirty for sensitive, shrinking souls like us. We had the choice of withdrawing into shells, and huddling there for eighty or ninety years, or pulling up and leaving for space. We left. There's no society out here, just each other."

"We've adjusted to each other," I pointed out.

"So? Does that mean we could fit into Earth society? Would *you* want to go back? Remember the team—McKees and Haugmuth, is it?—who spent thirty-three years in space and came back. They were catatonic eight minutes after landing, the report said."

"Let me give you a simpler why," I ventured. "Why did you start griping all of a sudden? Why couldn't you hold it in?"

"That's not a simpler *why*. It's part of the same one. I came to an answer, and I didn't like it. I got the answer that we were out here because we couldn't make the grade on Earth."

"No!"

He smiled apologetically. "No? All right, then. Give me another answer. *I want* an answer, Hammond. I need one, now."

I pointed to the synthesizer. "Why don't you have a drink instead?"

"That comes later," he said somberly. "After I've given up trying to find out."

The stippling of fine details was becoming a sharp-focus picture. Brock—self-reliant, Brock, self-contained—had come to the end of his self-sufficiency. He had looked too deeply beneath the surface.

"At the age of eight," I began, "I asked my father what was outside the universe. That is, defining the universe as That Which Contains Everything, could there possibly be something or some place outside its bounds? He looked at me for a minute or two, then laughed and told me not to worry about it. But I did worry about it; I stayed up half the night worrying about it, and my head hurt by morning. I never found out what was outside the universe."

"The universe is infinite," said Brock moodily. "Recurving in on itself, topologically. . ."

"Maybe. But I worried over it. I worried over First Cause. I worried all through my adolescence. Then I stopped worrying."

He smiled acidly. "You became a vegetable. You rooted yourself in the mud of your own ignorance, and decided not to pull loose because it was too painful. Am I right, Hammond?"

"No. I joined the Exploratory Corps."

I dreamed, that night, as I swung in my hammock. It was a vivid and unpleasant dream, which stayed with me well into the following morning as a sort of misshapen reality that had attached itself to me in the night.

I had been a long time falling asleep. Brock had brooded most of the day, and a long hike over the bleak tundra had done little to improve his mood. Toward nightfall he dialed a few drinks, inserted a disk of Sibelius in his ear, and sat staring glumly at the darkening sky outside the ship. Alphecca II was moonless. The night was the black of space, but the atmosphere blurred the neighboring stars.

I remember drifting off into a semisleep: a halfsomnolence in which I was aware of Brock's harsh breathing to my left, but yet in which I had no volition, no control over my limbs. And after that state came sleep, and with it—dreams.

The dream must have grown from Brock's bitter remark, *You became a vegetable. You rooted yourself in the mud of your own ignorance.*

I accepted the statement literally. Suddenly I *was* a vegetable, possessed of all my former faculties, but rooted in the soil.

Rooted.

Straining for freedom, straining to break away, caught eternally by my legs, thinking, thinking . . .

Never to move, except for a certain thrashing of the upper limbs.

Rooted.

I writhed, longing to get as far as the rocky hill beyond, only as far as the next yard, the next yard, the next inch. But I had lost all motility; it was as if my legs were grasped in a mighty trap, and without pain, without torment, I was bound to the earth.

I woke, finally, damp with perspiration. In his hammock, Brock slept seemingly peacefully. I considered waking him and telling him of the nightmare, but decided against it. I tried to return to sleep.

At length, I slept.

Dreamlessly.

The preset alarm throbbed at 0700; dawn had preceded us by nearly an hour.

Brock was up first; I sensed him moving about even as I stirred toward wakefulness. Still caught up in the strange unreal reality of my nightmare, I wondered on a conscious level if today would be like yesterday—if Brock obsessed by his sudden thirst for an answer would continue to brood and sulk.

I hoped not. It would mean the end of our team if Brock

cracked up; after eleven years, I was not anxious for a new partner.

"Hammond? You up yet?"

His voice had lost the edgy quality of yesterday, but there was something new and subliminally frightening in it.

Yawning, I replied, "Just about. Dial breakfast for me, will you?"

"I did already. But get out of the sack and come look at this."

I lurched from the hammock, shook my head to clear it, and started forward.

"Where are you?"

"Second level. At the window. Come take a look."

I climbed the spiral catwalk to the viewing-station; Brock stood with his back toward me, looking out. As I drew near, I said, "I had the strangest dream last night . . ."

"The hell with that. Look."

At first, I didn't notice anything strange. The bright-colored landscape seemed to be unchanged; pebbly orange soil, dark-blue trees, a tangle of green vines, the murk of the morning atmosphere. But then I saw I had been looking too far from home.

Writhing up the side of the window, just barely visible to the right, was a gnarled knobby green rope. Rope? No. It was one of the vines.

"They're all over the ship." Brock said. "I've checked all the ports. During the night the damned things must have come crawling up the side of the ship like so many snakes and wrapped themselves around us. I guess they figure we're here to stay, and they can use us as bracing-posts, the way they use those trees."

I stared with mixed repugnance and fascination at the hard bark of the vine, at the tiny suckers that held it fast to the smooth skin of our ship.

"That's funny," I said. "It's sort of an attack by extraterrestrial monsters, isn't it?"

We suited up and went outside to have a look at the "attackers." At a distance of a hundred yards, the ship looked weirdly bemired. Its graceful lines were broken by the winding fingers of the vine, spiralling up its sleek sides from a thick parent stem on the ground. Other shoots of the vine sprawled near us, clutching futilely at us as we moved among them.

I was reminded of my dream. Somewhat hesitantly I told Brock about it.

He laughed. "Rooted, eh? You were dreaming *that* while those vines were busy wrapping themselves around the ship. Significant?"

"Perhaps." I eyed the tough vines speculatively. "Maybe we'd better move the ship. If much more of that stuff gets around it, we may not be able to blast off at all."

Brock knelt and flexed a shoot of vine. "The ship could be completely cocooned in this stuff and we'd still be able to take off. A spacedrive weilds a devil of a lot of thrust. We'll manage."

And *whick!*

A tapering finger of the vine arched suddenly and whipped around Brock's middle. *Whick! Whick!*

Like animated rope, like a bark-covered serpent, it curled about him. I drew back, staring. He seemed half amused, half perplexed.

"The thing's got a pull, all right," he said. He was smiling lopsidedly, annoyed at having let so simple a thing as a vine interfere with his freedom of motion. But then he winced in obvious pain.

". . . Tightening," he gasped.

The vine contracted muscularly; it skittered two or three feet toward the tree from which its parent stock sprang, and Brock was jerked suddenly off balance. As the corded arm of the vine yanked him backward he began to topple, poising for what seemed like seconds on his left foot, right jutting awkwardly in the air, arms clawing for balance.

Then he fell.

I was at his side in a moment, carefully avoiding the innocent-looking vine-tips to right and left. I planted my foot on the trailing vine that held Brock. I levered downward and grabbed the tip where it bound his waist. I pulled; Brock pushed.

The vine yielded.

"It's giving," he grunted. "A little more."

"Maybe I'd better go back for the blaster," I said.

"No. No telling what this thing may do while you're gone; it may cut me in two. Pull!"

I pulled. The vine struggled against our combined strength, writhed, twisted; but gradually we prevailed. It curled upward, loosened, went limp. Finally it dropped away, leaving Brock in liberty.

He got up slowly, rubbing his waist.

"Hurt?"

"Just the surprise. Tropistic reaction on the plant's part; I must have triggered some hormone chain to make it do that." He eyed the now-quiescent vine with respect.

"It's not the first time we've been attacked," I said. "Alpheraz III . . ."

"Yes."

I hadn't needed to mention it. Alpheraz III had been a hellish jungle plant; the image in his mind, as it was in mine, was undoubtedly that of a tawny beast the size of a goat held in the inexorable grip of some stocky-trunked plant, rising in the air, vanishing into a waiting mouth of the carnivorous tree . . .

. . . and seconds later, another tendril dragging *me* aloft. Only a hasty blaster-shot by Brock keeping me from being a plant's dinner.

We returned to the ship, entering the hatch a few feet from one of the vines that now encrusted it. Brock unsuited; the vine had left a red, raw line about his waist.

"The plant tried," I said.

"To kill me?"

"No. To move on. To get going. To see what was behind the next hill."

He frowned and said, "What are you talking about?"

"I'm not so sure, yet; I'm not good at seeing patterns. But it's taking shape. I'm getting it now, Brock. I'm getting it all. Dammit, I'm getting your answer!"

He massaged his stomach. "Go ahead," he said. "Think it out loud."

"I'm putting it together out of my dream, and out of the things you said, and out of the vines down there." I walked slowly about the cabin. "Those plants—they're stuck there, aren't they? They grow in a certain place and that's where they remain. Maybe they wiggle a little, and maybe they writhe, but that's the size of it."

"They can grow long."

"Sure. But not infinitely long. They can't grow long enough to reach another planet. They're rooted, Brock; their condition is permanently fixed. Brock, suppose those plants had brains."

"I don't think this has anything to do with . . ."

"It does," I said. "Just assume those plants are intelligent. They want to *go*. They're stuck. So one of them lashed out in fury at you. *Jealous* fury."

He nodded, seeing it clearly now. "Sure. We don't have roots; we can go places. We can visit a hundred sixty-four worlds and walk all over them."

"That's your answer, Brock. There's the *why* you were looking for." I took a deep breath. "You know why we got out to explore? Not because we're running away. Not because there's some inner compulsion driving us to coast from planet to planet. Uh-uh. It's because we can do it. That's all the 'why' you need. We explore because it's possible for us to explore."

Some of the harshness faded from his face. "We're special," he said. "We can move. It's the privilege of humanity. The thing that makes us *us*."

I didn't need to say any more. After eleven years, we don't need to vocalize every thought. But we had it, now: the special uniqueness that those clutching vines down there envied so much. Motility.

We left Alphecca II finally, and moved on. We did the other worlds of the system and headed outward, far out this time, as much of a hop as we could make. And we moved on from there to the next sun, and from there to the next, and onward.

We took a souvenir with us from Alphecca II, though. When we blasted off, the vine that had wrapped itself round the ship gripped us so tightly that it wasn't shaken loose by the impact of blastoff. It remained hugging us as we thrust into space, dangling, roots and all. We finally got tired of looking at it, and Brock went out in a spacesuit to chop it away from the ship. He gave it a push, imparted velocity to it, and the vine went drifting off sunward.

It had achieved its goal: it had left its home world. But it had died in the attempt. And that was the difference, we thought—all the difference in the universe—as we headed outward and outward, across the boundless gulfs.

Ron Goulart is a master of wild, humorous science fiction, a little-appreciated and most difficult form. His more than thirty sf novels and numerous stories constitute a devastating attack on contemporary American culture, especially such books as *After Things Fell Apart* (1970), *Crackpot* (1977), and *Gadget Man* (1971). Comedy is serious business, and Ron Goulart is a serious talent.

This story shows him at the top of his form, answering a question that scholars and mechanics have been asking since time immemorial.

What's Become of Screwloose?

BY RON GOULART

I was hardly there when the electric dishwasher grabbed me. It shot its top lid up and tried to submerge my head in hot soapy water. Twisting, I kneed its smooth desert-colored front surface and managed to yank its cord free of the kitchen wall plug. The machine kept working, pumping burning water up at me, clutching at my shoulders with some kind of wiry tentacles. I grunted, snapped both its arms off me for a second. I spun the heavy machine away from me. I dodged it, hopping across the bright parquet of the afternoon kitchen.

The dishwasher came rolling after me, arms outstretched. I grabbed up a blowmold kitchen stool and thrust it at the machine's running wheels. The dishwasher tripped, fell over on its side and splashed scalding sudsy water all around. I ran for the sundeck, my right hand reaching up under my jacket toward my holster.

Upright, again, the dishwasher was rolling my way on its little wheels. Behind me was the Pacific Ocean, about three hundred feet straight down. I drew out my laser pistol and waited, aiming.

Soapy water had splashed out here on the bright black topping of the wide deck, and as the dishwasher came humming from the kitchen into the sunlight, it took a skid. Its arms clutched air, flapped, and it whirled by me, wild. It hit the redwood rail and went right on through, falling toward the ocean, followed by splintered wood. The machine's grasping arms caused it to somersault once in the air before it slammed into the water. After the giant splash came big bubbles.

Three white gulls came skimming in low over the water. They danced a second or two over the last of the bubbles and then glided up into the clear air. I hung up my laser gun and went, carefully, back into the beach cottage.

The stove looked like it could be nasty in a fight, but apparently it wasn't gimmicked. Nothing else in Mary Redland's empty beach house came for me.

In the beam-ceiling living room the phone on the missing girl's marble-top coffee table began to buzz. I watched it, approaching it from the side. It looked to be only a phone and I decided to switch it on and answer.

"Tom," said the lank dark young man who appeared on the saucer-size view screen, "is she there?"

"No, Oliver," I told him. "At least, I don't think so. I just arrived." I glanced toward the view window, which showed the quiet ocean.

"Tom, you look distracted," said Oliver Bentancourt, our client.

Out in the ocean I noticed the dishwasher swimming out to sea. Doing a fair Australian crawl with those unexpected arms. "I was looking at the dishwasher."

"How's that going to help us find out where Mary's been for the last two days?"

I sat on the paisley-patterned white nauga sofa and said, "This dishwasher is out in the Pacific, swimming."

"Oh, you mean some guy who works in a restaurant. Who is he?"

"No, I mean an appliance, square squatty thing about half my size," I said. I took another look at the bright ocean. The machine was quite far out now and had switched to a rapid back stroke.

"How can it swim?"

"It has little arms," I said.

Bentancourt rubbed a lean hand over his eyes. "I guess you're not kidding, Tom. I don't know. Maybe it's because of her late father that she's got an odd machine there. I don't know. Mary is, well, she isn't like anyone I've known before. I really didn't want to consult your boss, you know. But since you and I have been friends since catechism-class days I figured you wouldn't be working for Stanley Pope unless he was okay. Where is Mary?"

"Easy now. We'll find her. Stanley Pope specializes in cases that are a little eccentric."

"I don't want to use the police," said Bentancourt. "You know, because Mary has a pretty unhappy medical record. Well, psychological record rather. She's still in therapy. The police aren't too understanding."

"Right."

"I've called her friends, such as they are. I even tried to see if anybody was still at the old family place." He hid his eyes again for a moment. "She's not there? I mean, she didn't take something again?"

"No," I said, though I wasn't certain yet.

"Okay," said Bentancourt. "I'm only on my coffee break here at the office. I'll call you later on tonight." He nodded, smiled a quick smile and faded off the screen.

The dishwasher was only a speck now, a desert-colored dot

on the straight edge of the ocean. I rubbed my chin, then scratched my chest with both hands. I went all through the three-room beach house I'd let myself into and Mary Redland was not there. Nothing I found told me where she might be.

Pope was out on his court playing tennis with a robot. I sat down on one of the wrought-iron benches ringing the green clay. Down through the trees and housetops I could see a flock of sailboats on Sausalito's piece of the Bay.

"I'm perfecting my serve," Pope called to me. He flung a fuzy white ball straight up, kept his eye on it, whapped it over the net.

"You're using a badminton racket," I pointed out.

The robot was shaped like a water heater and had four arms. It rolled after the served tennis ball and sucked it up off the court with a little nozzle.

Pope blinked. Wrinkles ran up his high forehead and got lost in his tight curly black hair. "Huh?" New rings joined those under his wide, circled eyes.

"Badminton racket." I inclined my head in its direction.

He scrutinized the racket, nodded. "I must have left the tennis racket in the copter."

"Copter?"

"I was test-flying a new copter." He waved at the robot. "Game's over."

"I thought you gave up on copters."

"They have a tendency to crash," he said, "into the Golden Gate Bridge."

"When you're piloting."

"Anyway, I decided to give copters one more chance."

"And?"

"This one crashed into the Golden Gate Bridge."

I noticed the robot was speeding toward the tennis net. "Your robot thinks he just lost the game."

"Huh?"

"He's going to jump over the net and congratulate you."

Pope turned. He was a lean, middle-sized man, nearly as dark as I am. "Don't," he yelled as the robot leaped up into the air.

The tennis-playing machine didn't quite clear the net. It tumbled over front first with a clang, scattering tennis balls.

"Gadgets," said Pope. He ran to the fallen robot and helped it up. "I had a chance to inherit a hundred acres of soybeans in the San Joaquin Valley, Tom. Instead I surrounded myself with gadgets."

"Sorry, sorry," said the robot, feeling itself for damages with all its hands.

Pope left the machine and came over on the grass with me. "What about this missing girl? Mary Redman."

"Redland."

"I worry about all these gadgets the way some people worry about pets. I get nervous and concerned when they fall down." He blinked, again, and new rings appeared around his eyes. "What do I take at six o'clock?"

I reached a bottle of blue spansules out of my jacket pocket. "Two of these."

"Well, I probably would have worried about soybeans, too." Pope shook two spansules into his palm, frowned. "Except soybeans don't fall down as much. Any trace of the girl?"

"No." I said. "But her dishwashing machine tried to kill me."

He swallowed, rubbed his forefinger along the side of his beaked nose. "Huh? Give me all the details."

I described what had happened when I'd gone to look for the girl up beyond Stinson Beach.

Absently Pope undid his white tennis shorts and let them drop. "I should have gone over there with you. Why didn't I?"

"You had to go to San Francisco, remember."

"Oh, yes. One of my former wives is after more alimony. The second one, right?"

"No, the third," I said. "Why are you taking off your clothes?"

"Changing for dinner."

"You're still outside."

"Huh?" Pope bent and retrieved the fallen shorts, folded them under his arm with his badminton racket. "I had a chance to go into the fishmeal business once. There's a lot less pressure in the fishmeal business than in the private-investigation field. Right?"

"I haven't seen any statistics." We continued across his

slightly overgrown two-acre backyard, moving in the direction of Pope's big transplanted Victorian house. "What did that homicidal dishwasher remind you of? You did a particular kind of reaction take when I mentioned it."

"Huh?" Pope stroked his nose. "Something I can't quite remember. But it ties in with this Mary Redland business." He stopped walking. "I really like the odd cases, Tom. Most of what we do now is simple electronic stuff. Bugging, counterbugging, siphoning of computer information. Back in the 1970s, when you were still in school someplace, there were more odd things to work on. Her father."

"Mary Redland's father?"

"Right. He was a servomechanism tycoon, wasn't he?"

"That and teaching machines," I said. "My friend Bentancourt says Mary didn't talk much about her father. He died a year or so ago, in an autosonic-jet crash. I know the few times I met her she didn't talk about the past at all."

"This name that scared her, upset her?"

"Screwloose," I told him.

"Right. A nickname for somebody maybe. Your friend hasn't any notions?"

"Nothing new since he consulted us this morning, no."

"Mary Redland is in a therapy group over in Frisco, right? How long?"

"Three months. And, according to Bentancourt, she mentioned the name Screwloose during a session at this Dollfuss Center. He's not in the group with her, but she told Bentancourt about it afterwards. Because it scared her. A silly name but she was unsettled. Apparently that was all she was able to remember, just the name or whatever it is. Screwloose. Bentancourt figures maybe she remembered something else day before yesterday. Maybe that's why she took off."

"Why should she be remembering things?" asked Pope as we climbed the wide wooden back stairs of his vast rococo white house. "Did Bentancourt say she'd lost her memory at some point?"

"No, but she's had a breakdown or two and there seem to be certain things she has trouble recalling."

"Slender girl, isn't she?"

"He showed you her picture."

"I know. Willowy, tall. Blonde," said Pope. "Thin women tend to be twitchy. My second wife was."

"Third," I said. "Your second wife was a plump redhead with dimples."

Pope sighed. We were in the kitchen. "Maybe I should have stayed with her and taken up soybeans. Huh. Go to the Dolfuss Center and sit in on that group-therapy session. Mary Redland was going every Tuesday and Thursday night at eight, wasn't she?"

"Yes. There's a session tonight. You figure she may show up there, even though she's been out of view for two days?"

"No. I want you to find out what reminded her of Screwloose." He nodded at his refrigerator and it opened and handed him out a cold bottle of ale.

Pope gestured uphill at the houseboat after I'd given him a verbal report on my visit to the group-therapy session the night before. "We'll go up to Past after breakfast. Did I order orange juice?"

We were under a metal umbrella out on a plank shelf over the edge of the Bay, at a restaurant called The Ruins of Tiburon Tommy's. "Tomato," I said. I removed a pill from a box I carried in my left trouser pocket and put it on the edge of his soycafe saucer. "I'm sorry I didn't turn up anything on Screwloose," I said. "Why Past?"

"Something," said Pope. He noticed a plate of plankton griddle cakes in front of him on the table. "I like to use Evelynski to supplement my memory sometimes."

"Didn't they indict Evelynski for siphoning classified information out of the California State Credit Computer?"

"They couldn't. No evidence."

"I thought they had evidence."

"Evelynski managed to siphon off all that, too." Pope was wearing a buff-colored overall suit today. He rubbed his palms on his knees and the material gave off a purring sound. "Go back on what you told me about last night. At the therapy session you said one of the group talked about Mary. He said something about how her late father paid a lot of attention to her, especially to her education?"

"Yes, a big jovial pink guy in his middle forties. His name is Chuck Mogul," I answered. "When I asked him if he knew her he said he'd only read about her family a lot in the society columns. Years ago. Dr. Dollfuss is an admirer of yours, otherwise they probably wouldn't have let me sit in. He mentioned your eclectic mind."

"Right." Pope looked once more at the pancakes, then stood. "Let's go up and consult Evelynski."

Past is a private research organization. When all the houseboats were cleared out of the waters around Sausalito back in the 1970s, Cosmo Evelynski had one moved to a lot in the low rolling hills of Tiburon. The big red-and-white boat served now as the top floor of his archives, with ten more floors sunk down into the hillside.

Evelynski's office was in the living room of the old houseboat, and we found him there dropping punch cards into an electric wastebasket. The basket would chew up a card, making a lopsided growling sound. Then it would spew the fragments back out at Evelynski.

Evelynski was sitting on a low wicker stool, a confetti of shreds on the hardwood floor around him. "On the fritz," he said. He was a tall man in his low forties, short-haired and mildly rustic-looking.

Pope took a seat on a plaid ottoman. The rings around his eyes were flickering. "About twenty years ago, sometime in the late 70s or early 80s," he said, "something like four men who were all prominent in the servomechanism field died. I've been trying to remember the details."

"Hello, Tom," Evelynski said to me. He kicked the wastebasket off with his left foot. "You're thinking about a murder case, Stanley?"

Pope said, "It's not on record as such. All four of these guys died in a six-month period, all in accidents. They were, though nothing much was made of it as I recall, the chief competitors of what's his name. Donald B. Redland. Mary Redland's father."

"Redland of United/Tech?" Evelynski stood up and crossed to a dumb waiter in the wall.

Pope nodded. "In one of these accidental deaths there was something . . . something about an eyewitness. Little boy, nobody believed. He claimed he'd seen a soft-drink machine push the victim off the edge of a bluff in Muir Woods someplace. A foggy day, nobody else saw anything."

"The dishwasher," I said.

"Reminded me," said Pope.

Evelynski opened the door to the shaft and yelled, "Freak Accidents, 1978 through 1982. Also Redland, Donald Bascomb. Muir Woods, accidents, vicinity, 1978 through 1982. Servomech industry, obits, same period. Anything else you can think of." He let the small white door flap shut. "I've dug down two more floors since you guys were here last."

"Did you fix that computer who would only take requests given in classical Greek?" asked Pope.

"He just outgrew it. He was new then and showing off. You know, the runt in the pack." Evelynski made his way around the circular room and stood next to the mouth of a metal chute. Far down under us a faint fluttering whir had started. In another thirty seconds file folders, tape reels, punch cards, loose clippings and glossy photos poured out into Evelynski's arms. "Here," he said and dropped the wad of material on Pope's lap.

Three newspaper clippings fell in the process. I reached them off the hook rug and glanced at them. The headline on the largest clipping, a half-page with photo, read: "Peninsula Girl Has a Special Sort of Teacher." The girl, six then, was Mary Redland and her special tutor was an android teacher especially designed by her father, Donald B. Redland, and built under his supervision at United Tech near Sunnyvale. The story said Mary liked the teaching robot "an awful lot" and the family nickname for him was Professor Screwloose. There was a picture of Mary and the android in a bright playroom. I held the clipping out to Pope. "Here's Screwloose," I said.

"Oh, so?" He took the clipping.

"Also Chuck Mogul," I added.

"You're getting slipshod, Tom," said Pope. "Here one of the six people you spent two hours with last night is an android and you didn't tumble to it."

"Nope," I admitted. "He's got a lot of believability. He struck me as a phoney, but a human phoney."

Pope tapped the photo. "This was taken at the Redland place down on the Peninsula, wasn't it?"

"That's right," I said. "The estate's been empty since Redland was killed, nobody's living there. But supposedly it's still guarded by a lot of Redland-invented mechanisms."

"Huh," said Pope. He rolled up the piece of newspaper and rubbed it across the tip of his sharp nose. "I wonder if Mary Redland's gone there. What she's trying to remember has to do with this damn android and probably with that old house."

"I'd better drive over there and check," I said.

"After we go through the rest of this stuff, yes," said Pope. "Stop at my place and gather up some tools for jobbing the burglar alarms. We have something or other for stunning robots, don't we?"

"Yes. Do you want to come along this time?"

"No, I want to call on Chuck Mogul," said Pope. "You said the Dollfuss records show him with a San Francisco address?"

"Yes, Telegraph Hill." I wrote the address on a memo slip.

"I want to ask him why he's no longer Screwloose," said Pope.

Nothing was working at the Redland estate. I'd parked my landcar three hundred yards beyond the front stone wall, in the shadows of a grove of black oaks. The day was ending early and a gray prickly mist was tumbling down out of the darkening sky as I walked carefully toward the front gates. The gates were twice my height and twisted into patterns of Rs and grape leaves. The gate was the kind that gave off an alarm ring if touched, and an electric wire netting grew up to six inches above the high thick stone wall. Floodlights had been aimed at the cleared ground on the visitor's side of the gate and just on the other side of the wrought iron a black police dog crouched, fangs bared.

But none of it was working. The floodlights weren't on, the robot dog was silent and there was no life in his vinyl eyes. The gates had swung a few feet open. I'd been prepared to try to gimmick the alarm system and pick any locks I ran into. I had a brown nearleather attaché case under my arm. It wasn't necessary. I walked through the gates.

The mist fell and rolled, thickening. Far away, back on the highway, a diesel truck groaned by. In passing the mechanical watchdog I brushed against him and he fell over sideways. I could see the shape of the house now, a quarter of a mile away. Cupolas and spires and weather-cocks jabbing free of the mist. The main house was three stories, twenty-five rooms. There was supposed to be a six-car garage with chauffeur's suite, a copter hangar and two small guest houses beyond and behind the main house.

The acres of grass had been recently cut. It had a damp fresh-cropped smell. The trees, hundreds of birches and willows and pines, were less cared for. Approaching the Redland house I saw an android sprawled in the brush. He was a gardening robot and he looked to have fallen from a ladder while pruning. He was broken and beginning to rust. His bent hand still clutched a pair of shears, orange now from exposure.

There was only darkness in the main house. I went full around it, listening. I crossed a stable yard in back of the big house and saw light. A fluttering unsteady glow coming from a cottage deep among willows. I went toward that.

A metal plate screwed to the cottage door said: Miss Mary Redland/Her Playhouse. I knocked. The motion of my knocking pushed the door open. Inside the small room was Mary. She was sitting in a low wood chair, her legs bent up and tight together. On a child-size desk beside her was a kerosene lantern with a sooty smoke fluming up from it.

"Hello, Mary," I said.

She looked up, nodded, smiled very faintly and briefly. "Hello, Tom."

"This is where you've been?"

"Most of the time." Her prettiness seemed to come and go on her face, wavering like the lantern light. "I guess Ollie hired you to come looking for me."

"That's right." I took a lopsided sofa chair for a seat. There were shelves climbing the walls, cluttered with toys. Simple stuffed toys and complex mechanical ones. Below the shelves were teaching machines and film viewers, spools of history and math piled atop them.

"Somebody is always and continually looking for me," said the girl. "Since always." She locked her slim hands over one knee. "I remembered some things and came back here to think about them. To reflect, more or less."

I watched her, not saying anything.

111

"They never," said Mary, "thought I'd remember. And I didn't, actually, quite remember for a long time. Then I began to."

I stayed quiet.

"Fifteen. No, twenty. Twenty years ago almost," said Mary. "When I was about six years old. Then my father and one other man who worked for him. They're both dead now. I suppose that's funny. Twenty years ago they killed four people."

"Rivals," I said. "People your father couldn't buy out?"

"His ambition was to become much bigger. He did, too," said Mary. "They, my father and the other man, came up with a fine and simple idea. Not something that would seem simple to me or possibly to you, but to them. He could have kept trying to deal with them financially, buy them. Except this new idea was simpler and not as expensive. So they figured out how to adapt some of their fine machines and mechanisms. Adapt them to kill people. Not in any obvious ways, though. To push them out of windows or arrange accidents. There's a funny side to that, too, being killed by your refrigerator or your color-TV console."

I said, "I met one of those machines."

"Yes, I guess a few of them are still around," she said, "to keep an eye on me. I gave up trying to avoid all the mechanisms Dad thought should keep track of me. You probably saw it in that beach house Dad bought for me three years ago."

"That's right."

Mary said, "The problem was, the problem was I walked in."

"On a killing?"

She shook her head. "No, on the planning of one. They were very thorough. They made charts and diagrams, everything very efficient. Maybe that's how you should kill people, carefully and with a good deal of thought and deliberation. I walked in. It was up there at the big house. In Dad's den, which was supposed to be private. I didn't always pay attention to that kind of restriction then. I was six and they'd not bothered to lock the door this one time. I walked in, very silent and way across the room from them. Dad was at his long wide work table, drafting table, and they were talking

112

about it. I listened for a long while until they noticed me." The mist was thick at the little room's round leaded windows. "At first they, Dad especially, tried to convince me I hadn't heard anything or that it was just a game. The problem was, you see, they went right ahead and killed the man. So I asked about it." She stood and wandered to the low black and gray machines. "This is where they did it."

"They worked to make you forget?"

"Yes," said Mary finally. "It used to be called—what was it?—brainwashing. It wasn't going to hurt, Dad promised. Seems to me, it seems to me it took them weeks to do. They used these machines and some others." She paused and took a sharp inward breath. "And my tutor. I had an android. A nice affable robot who taught me and read stories and was nice. I called him Professor Screwloose. I don't know why, something Dad said once is where I got the name, I think. He helped them do it and after that he was gone, sent someplace else. For years I forgot, didn't remember. Except it started trying to come back. You know, I had some problems. Yes. I went into therapy finally and I really began to remember." She turned to me. "He was there, though I didn't realize it at first."

"Screwloose," I said.

"Yes," she said. "Calling himself Chuck Mogul and passing for human. I guess Dad had programmed him to keep watch on me. Even with Dad gone nobody turned poor Screwloose off. He's still hanging around, watching after me. Protecting me. I suppose he's anxious to keep me from remembering, even though it doesn't make much difference now."

"You paint me as not too nice a guy," said Chuck Mogul. He came into the cottage, grinning. There was a black pistol in his believable right hand. "Gee, Mary. We have meant nothing but good for you."

"It's all over, Professor Screwloose." She leaned against the black machines.

"No, I don't feel that," said the Screwloose android. "Gosh, your dad, God bless him and keep him, set me up swell, Mary. With funds and a nice place on Telegraph Hill in San Francisco. All I have to do, as long as I live, is look after you. Not only to keep you from thinking about some unpleasant things that might have happened when you were a cute little tousle-headed kid. No, I'm devoted to seeing to it you have a calm, pleasant life always."

"Good Christ," said the girl. "My father was enough. I don't want any more sweet concern. I'm me now, full-grown and I don't want you."

"Gosh, Mary," said Screwloose. "Don't talk like that. I'm always going to be around you. I'm, gee, I'm made that way, honey."

"You shouldn't have," I said, "gotten so close. Shouldn't have gone to the therapy sessions."

The android agreed. "I debated a lot about that. Gosh, but I was worried. About what she might blurt out there in front of the others. So I took a risk, pulled a few strings and got in the same group with her. No, I have to admit that little plan didn't work so good."

"Seeing you again helped me remember," said Mary.

"Well," said Screwloose, "no long-range harm done. We only have to fix your mind up again, Mary, and you'll forget all this nasty stuff. Your dad taught me how and I can do it myself."

"No," said the girl.

I asked, "Me, too?"

Screwloose replied, "No, you we'll have to kill in some accidental-looking way. I was hoping you'd get drowned at Stinson Beach. I only just tonight figured Mary might have come back here, for sentimental reasons. Had I thought of it earlier I would have beat you to it. Again, gee, there's no real harm done. I know all kinds of easy ways to kill people."

The playhouse door quietly opened again and Pope dived in. He held a cross-shaped tire iron. His first swing knocked Screwloose's pistol away. Pope's next two blows were to the android's head and they caused him to fall over with an outflung jerking. "Gosh," said the android. He began a slow tumble down to the floor. He was making loud whirring sounds and oily smoke came from his nostrils and mouth.

"The reason I was a little late," said Pope. "I bumped into some landcars on the highway. It was a produce truck full of synthetic tangerines, actually. I'd been trailing Screwloose since he left his place in Frisco. I lost him after the collision but figured he'd head here. I picked him up again at the gates. None of the alarms are working, by the way."

"I turned everything off," said Mary, leaving the area of the teaching machines. "I don't like all that stuff much."

"You just happen to be carrying a tire iron?" I asked Pope.

"Actually," he said, rings forming around his wide eyes, "I had a flat tire, too. After one of the truck drivers kicked my car. That's what threw my timing off."

"Your timing was fine," I said.

"This is Mary Redland, huh?" Pope asked, nodding at the girl. "You've been here hiding out?"

"Not hiding out, thinking, trying to remember. I wanted to remember everything. I wanted to remember what they had done to me," said the girl. "But I'm still not sure why they did it."

"Because we loved you," said Screwloose. His head began to come apart.

The once mysterious **James Tiptree, Jr.,** is the author of three story collections (*Ten Thousand Light-Years from Home,* 1973; *Warm Worlds and Otherwise,* 1975; and *Star Songs of an Old Primate,* 1978) and a novel (*Up the Walls of the World,* 1978). "Tiptree's" real identity was a closely guarded secret for years, but she turned out to be Alice Sheldon, originally a Wisconsin native. Thus ended the biggest mystery in science fiction since "Cordwainer Smith." Ms. Sheldon won a Hugo ("The Girl Who Was Plugged In," 1974) and a Nebula ("Love Is the Plan, the Plan Is Death," 1973) and has written a number of important and excellent stories.

"Houston, Houston, Do You Read?" is one of her best. Although the title is a contemporary phrase from the U.S. space program, the questions addressed in the story are timeless.

Houston, Houston, Do You Read?

BY JAMES TIPTREE, JR.

Lorimer gazes around the crowded cabin, trying to listen to the voices, trying to ignore the twitch in his insides that means he is about to remember something bad. No help; he lives it again, that long-ago moment. Himself running blindly—or was he pushed?—into the strange toilet at Evanston Junior High. His fly open, his dick in his hand, he can still see the grey zipper edge of his jeans around his pale exposed pecker. The hush. The sickening wrongness of shapes, faces turning. The first blaring giggle. *Girls.* He was in the *girl's can.*

He flinches now wryly, so many years later, not looking at the women's faces. The big cabin surrounds him with their alien things, curved around over his head: the beading rack, the twins' loom, Andy's leather work, the damned kudzu vine wriggling everywhere, the chickens. So cosy. . . . Trapped, he is. Irretrievably trapped for life in everything he does not enjoy. Structurelessness. Personal trivia, unmeaning intimacies. The claims he can somehow never meet. Ginny: *You never talk to me* . . . Ginny, love, he thinks involuntarily. The hurt doesn't come.

Bud Geirr's loud chuckle breaks in on him. Bud is joking with some of them, out of sight around a bulkhead. Dave is visible, though. Major Norman Davis on the far side of the cabin, his bearded profile bent toward a small dark woman Lorimer can't quite focus on. But Dave's head seems oddly tiny and sharp, in fact the whole cabin looks unreal. A cackle bursts out from the "ceiling"—the bantam hen in her basket.

At this moment Lorimer becomes sure he has been drugged.

Curiously, the idea does not anger him. He leans or rather tips back, perching cross-legged in the zero gee, letting his gaze go to the face of the woman he has been talking with. Connie. Constantia Morelos. A tall moon-faced woman in capacious green pajamas. He has never really cared for talking to women. Ironic.

"I suppose," he says aloud, "it's possible that in some sense we are not here."

That doesn't sound too clear, but she nods interestedly. She's watching my reactions, Lorimer tells himself. Women are natural poisoners. Has he said that aloud too? Her expression doesn't change. His vision is taking on a pleasing local clarity. Connie's skin strikes him as quite fine, healthy-looking. Olive tan even after two years in space. She

117

was a farmer, he recalls. Big pores, but without the caked look he associates with women her age.

"You probably never wore make-up," he says. She looks puzzled. "Face paint, powder. None of you have."

"Oh!" Her smile shows a chipped front tooth. "Oh yes, I think Andy has."

"Andy?"

"For plays. Historical plays, Andy's good at that."

"Of course. Historical plays."

Lorimer's brain seems to be expanding, letting in light. He is understanding actively now, the myriad bits and pieces linking into patterns. Deadly patterns, he perceives; but the drug is shielding him in some way. Like an amphetamine high without the pressure. Maybe it's something they use socially? No, they're watching, too.

"Space bunnies, I still don't dig it," Bud Geirr laughs infectiously. He has a friendly buoyant voice people like; Lorimer still likes it after two years.

"You chicks have kids back home, what do your folks think about you flying around out here with old Andy, h'mm?" Bud floats into view, his arm draped around a twin's shoulders. The one called Judy Paris, Lorimer decides; the twins are hard to tell. She drifts passively at an angle to Bud's big body: a jut-breasted plain girl in flowing yellow pajamas, her black hair raying out. Andy's red head swims up to them. He is holding a big green spaceball, looking about sixteen.

"Old Andy." Bud shakes his head, his grin flashing under his thick dark mustache. "When I was your age folks didn't let their women fly around with me."

Connie's lips quirk faintly. In Lorimer's head the pieces slide toward pattern. I know, he thinks. Do you know I know? His head is vast and crystalline, very nice really. Easier to think. Women. . . . No compact generalisation forms in his mind, only a few speaking faces on a matrix of pervasive irrelevance. Human, of course. Biological necessity. Only so, so . . . diffuse? Pointless? . . . His sister Amy, *soprano con tremulo: Of course women could contribute as much as men if you'd treat us as equals. You'll see!* And then marrying that idiot the second time. Well, now he can see.

"Kudzu vines," he says aloud. Connie smiles. How they all smile.

"How 'boot that?" Bud says happily, "Ever think we'd see chicks in zero gee, hey, Dave? Artits-stico. Woo-ee!" Across the cabin Dave's bearded head turns to him, not smiling.

"And ol' Andy's had it all to his self. Stunt your growth, lad." He punches Andy genially on the arm, Andy catches himself on the bulkhead. Bud can't be drunk, Lorimer thinks; not on that fruit cider. But he doesn't usually sound so much like a stage Texan either. A drug.

"Hey, no offense," Bud is saying earnestly to the boy, "I mean that. You have to forgive one underprilly, underprivileged brother. These chicks are good people. Know what?" he tells the girl, "You could look stu-pen-dous if you fix yourself up a speck. Hey, I can show you, old Buddy's a expert. I hope you don't mind my saying that. As a matter of fact you look real stupendous to me right now."

He hugs her shoulders, flings out his arm and hugs Andy too. They float upwards in his grasp, Judy grinning excitedly, almost pretty.

"Let's get some more of that good stuff." Bud propels them both toward the serving rack which is decorated for the occasion with sprays of greens and small real daisies.

"Happy New Year! Hey, Happy New Year, y'all!"

Faces turn, more smiles. Genuine smiles, Lorimer thinks, maybe they really like their new years. He feels he has infinite time to examine evey event, the implications evolving in crystal facets. I'm an echo chamber. Enjoyable, to be the observer. But others are observing too. They've started something here. Do they realise? So vulnerable, three of us, five of them in this fragile ship. They don't know. A dread unconnected to action lurks behind his mind.

"By god we made it," Bud laughs. "You space chickies, I have to give it to you. I commend you, by god I say it. We wouldn't be here, wherever we are. Know what, I jus' might decide to stay in the service after all. Think they have room for old Bud in your space program, sweetie?"

"Knock that off, Bud," Dave says quietly from the far wall. "I don't want to hear us use the name of the Creator like that." The full chestnut beard gives him a patriarchal gravity. Dave is forty-six, a decade older than Bud and Lorimer. Veteran of six successful missions.

"Oh my apologies, Major Dave old buddy." Bud chuckles

119

intimately to the girl. "Our commanding ossifer. Stupendous guy. Hey, Doc!" he calls, "How's your attitude? You making out dinko?"

"Cheers," Lorimer hears his voice reply, the complex stratum of his feelings about Bud rising like a kraken in the moonlight of his mind. The submerged silent thing he has about them all, all the Buds and Daves and big, indomitable cheerful, able, disciplined slow-minded mesomorphs he has cast his life with. Meso-ectos, he corrected himself; astronauts aren't muscleheads. They like him, he has been careful about that. Liked him well enough to get him on *Sunbird*, to make him the official scientist on the first circumsolar mission. That little Doc Lorimer, he's cool, he's on the team. No shit from Lorimer, not like those other scientific assholes. He does the bit well with his small neat build and his dead-pan remarks. And the years of turning out for the bowling, the volleyball, the tennis, the skeet, the skiing that broke his ankle, the touch football that broke his collarbone. Watch that Doc, he's a sneaky one. And the big men banging him on the back, accepting him. Their token scientist . . . The trouble is, he isn't any kind of scientist any more. Living off his postdoctoral plasma work, a lucky hit. He hasn't really been into the math for years, he isn't up to it now. Too many other interests, too much time spent explaining elementary stuff. I'm a half-jock, he thinks. A foot taller and a hundred pounds heavier and I'd be just like them. One of them. An alpha. They probably sense it underneath, the beta bile. Had the jokes worn a shade thin in *Sunbird*, all that year going out? A year of Bud and Dave playing gin. That damn exercycle, gearing it up too tough for me. They didn't mean it, though. We were a team.

The memory of gaping jeans flicks at him, the painful end part—the grinning faces waiting for him when he stumbled out. The howls, the dribble down his leg. Being cool, pretending to laugh too. You shit-heads, I'll show you. I am not a girl.

Bud's voice rings out, chanting. "And a Hap-pee New Year to you-all down there!" Parody of the oily NASA tone. "Hey, why don't we shoot 'em a signal? Greetings to all you Earthlings, I mean, all you little Lunies. Hap-py New Year in the good year whatsis." He snuffles comically. "There is a Santy Claus, Houston, ye-ew nevah saw nothin' like this! Houston,

120

wherever you are," he sings out. "Hey, Houston! Do you read?"

In the silence Lorimer sees Dave's face set into Major Norman Davis, commanding.

And without warning he is suddenly back there, back a year ago in the cramped, shook-up command module of *Sunbird*, coming out from behind the sun. It's the drug doing this, he thinks as memory closes around him, it's so real. Stop. He tries to hang onto reality, to the sense of trouble building underneath.

—But he can't, he is *there*, hovering behind Dave and Bud in the triple couches, as usual avoiding his official station in the middle, seeing beside them their reflections against blackness in the useless port window. The outer layer has been annealed, he can just make out a bright smear that has to be Spica floating through the image of Dave's head, making the bandage look like a kid's crown.

"Houston, Houston, *Sunbird*," Dave repeats; "*Sunbird* calling Houston. Houston, do you read? Come in, Houston."

The minutes start by. They are giving it seven out, seven back; seventy-eight million miles, ample margin.

"The high gain's shot, that's what it is," Bud says cheerfully. He says it almost every day.

"No way." Dave's voice is patient, also as usual. "It checks out. Still too much crap from the sun, isn't that right, Doc?"

"The residual radiation from the flare is just about in line with us," Lorimer says. "They could have a hard time sorting us out." For the thousandth time he registers his own faint, ridiculous gratification at being consulted.

"Shit, we're outside Mercury." Bud shakes his head. "How we gonna find out who won the Series?"

He often says that too. A ritual, out here in eternal night. Lorimer watches the sparkle of Spica drift by the reflection of Bud's curly face-bush. His own whiskers are scant and scraggly, like a blond Fu Manchu. In the aft corner of the window is a striped glare that must be the remains of their port energy accumulators, fried off in the solar explosion that hit them a month ago and fused the outer layers of their windows. That was when Dave cut his head open on the sexlogic panel. Lorimer had been banged in among the gravity wave experiment, he still doesn't trust the readings. Luckily the

121

particle stream has missed one piece of the front window; they still have about twenty degrees of clear vision straight ahead. The brilliant web of the Pleiades shows there, running off into a blur of light.

Twelve minutes . . . thirteen. The speaker sighs and clicks emptily. Fourteen. Nothing.

"*Sunbird* to Houston, *Sunbird* to Houston. Come in, Houston. *Sunbird* out." Dave puts the mike back in its holder. "Give it another twenty-four."

They wait ritually. Tomorrow Packard will reply. Maybe.

"Be good to see old Earth again," Bud remarks.

"We're not using any more fuel on attitude," Dave reminds him. "I trust Doc's figures."

It's not my figures, it's the elementary facts of celestial mechanics, Lorimer thinks; in October there's only one place for Earth to be. He never says it. Not to a man who can fly two-body solutions by intuition once he knows where the bodies are. Bud is a good pilot and a better engineer; Dave is the best there is. He takes no pride in it. "The Lord helps us, Doc, if we let Him."

"Going to be a bitch docking if the radar's screwed up," Bud says idly. They all think about that for the hundredth time. It will be a bitch. Dave will do it. That was why he is hoarding fuel.

The minutes tick off.

"That's it," Dave says—and a voice fills the cabin, shockingly.

"Judy?" It is high and clear. A girl's voice.

"Judy, I'm so glad we got you. What are you doing on this band?"

Bud blows out his breath; there is a frozen instant before Dave snatches up the mike.

"*Sunbird*, we read you. This is Mission *Sunbird* calling Houston, ah, *Sunbird One* calling Houston Ground Control. Indentify, who are you? Can you relay our signal? Over."

"Some skip," Bud says. "Some incredible ham."

"Are you in trouble, Judy?" the girl's voice asks. "I can't hear, you sound terrible. Wait a minute."

"This is United States Space Mission *Sunbird One*," Dave repeats. "Mission *Sunbird* calling Houston Space Center. You are dee-exxing our channel. Identify, repeat identify yourself and say if you can relay to Houston. Over."

"Dinko, Judy, try it again," the girl says.

Lorimer abruptly pushes himself up the Lurp, the Long-Range Particle Density Cumulator experiment, and activates its shaft motor. The shaft whines, jars; lucky it was retracted during the flare, lucky it hasn't fused shut. He sets the probe pulse on max and begins a rough manual scan.

"You are intercepting official traffic from the United States space mission to Houston Control," Dave is saying forcefully. "If you cannot relay to Houston get off the air, you are committing a federal offence. Say again, can you relay our signal to Houston Space Center? Over."

"You still sound terrible," the girl says. "What's Houston? Who's talking, anyway? You know we don't have much time." Her voice is sweet but very nasal.

"Jesus, that's close," Bud says. "That is close."

"Hold it." Dave twists around to Lorimer's improvised radarscope.

"There." Lorimer points out a tiny stable peak at the extreme edge of the read-out slot, in the transcoronal scatter. Bud cranes too.

"A bogey!"

"Somebody else out here."

"Hello, hello? We have you now," the girl says. "Why are you so far out? Are you dinko, did you catch the flare?"

"Hold it," warns Dave. "What's the status, Doc?"

"Over three hundred thousand kilometers, guesstimated. Possibly headed away from us, going around the sun. Could be cosmonauts, a Soviet mission?"

"Out to beat us. They missed."

"With a *girl*?" Bud objects.

"They've done that. You taping this, Bud?"

"Roger-r-r." He grins. "That sure didn't sound like a Russky chick. Who the hell's Judy?"

Dave thinks for a second, clicks on the mike. "This is Major Norman Davis commanding United States spacecraft *Sunbird One*. We have you on scope. Request you identify yourself. Repeat, who are you? Over."

"Judy, stop joking," the voice complains. "We'll lose you in a minute, don't you realise we worried about you?"

123

"*Sunbird* to unidentified craft. This is not Judy. I say again, this is not Judy. Who are you? Over."

"What—" the girl says, and is cut off by someone saying, "Wait a minute, Ann." The speaker squeals. Then a different woman says, "This is Lorna Bethune in *Escondita*. What is going on here?"

"This is Major Davis commanding United States Mission *Sunbird* on course for Earth. We do not recognise any space-craft *Escondita*. Will you identify yourself? Over."

"I just did." She sounds older with the same nasal drawl. "There is no spaceship *Sunbird* and you're not on course for Earth. If this is an andy joke it isn't any good."

"This is no joke madam!" Dave explodes. "This is the American circumsolar mission and we are American astronauts. We do not appreciate your interference. Out."

The woman starts to speak and is drowned in a jibber of static. Two voices come through briefly. Lorimer thinks he hears the words "*Sunbird* program" and something else. Bud works the squelcher; the interference subsides to a drone.

"Ah, Major Davis?" The voice is fainter. "Did I hear you say you are on course for Earth?"

Dave frowns at the speaker and then says curtly, "Affirmative."

"Well, we don't understand your orbit. You must have very unusual flight characteristics, our readings show you won't node with anything on your present course. We'll lose the signal in a minute or two. Ah, would you tell us where you see Earth now? Never mind the coordinates, just tell us the constellation."

Dave hesitates and then holds up the mike. "Doc."

"Earth's apparent position is in Pisces," Lorimer says to the voice. "Approximately three degrees from P. Gamma."

"It is not," the woman says. "Can't you see it's in Virgo? Can't you see out at all?"

Lorimer's eyes go to the bright smear in the port window. "We sustained some damage—"

"Hold it," snaps Dave.

"—to one window during a disturbance we ran into at perihelion. Naturally we know the relative direction of Earth on this date, October nineteen."

"October?" It's March, March fifteen. You must—" Her voice is lost in a shriek.

"E-M front," Bud says, tuning. They are all leaning at the speaker from different angles, Lorimer is head-down. Space-noise wails and crashes like surf, the strange ship is too close to the coronal horizon. "—Behind you," they hear. More howls. "Band, try . . . ship . . . if you can, your signal—" Nothing more comes through.

Lorimer pushes back, staring at the spark in the window. It has to be Spica. But is it elongated, as if a second point-source is beside it? Impossible. An excitement is trying to flare out inside him, the women's voices resonate in his head.

"Playback," Dave says. "Houston will really like to hear this."

They listen again to the girl calling Judy, the woman saying she is Lorna Bethune. Bud holds up a finger. "Man's voice in there." Lorimer listens hard for the words he thought he heard. The tape ends.

"Wait til Packard gets this one." Dave rubs his arms. "Remember what they pulled on Howie? Claiming they rescued him."

"Seems like they want us on their frequency." Bud grins. "They must think we're fa-a-ar gone. Hey, looks like this other capsule's going to show up, getting crowded out here."

"If it shows up," Dave says. "Leave it on voice alert, Bud. The batteries will do that."

Lorimer watches the spark of Spica, or Spica-plus-something, wondering if he will ever understand. The casual acceptance of some trick or ploy out here in this incredible loneliness. Well, if these strangers are from the same mold, maybe that is it. Aloud he says, "*Escondita* is an odd name for a Soviet mission. I believe it means 'hidden' in Spanish."

"Yeah," says Bud. "Hey, I know what that accent is, it's Australian. We had some Aussie bunnies at Hickam. Or-stryle-ya, woo-ee! You s'pose Woomara is sending up some kind of com-bined do?"

Dave shakes his head. "They have no capability whatsoever."

"We ran into some fairly strange phenomena back there, Dave," Lorimer says thoughtfully. "I'm beginning to wish we could take a visual check."

"Did you goof, Doc?"

"No. Earth is where I said, if it's October. Virgo is where it would appear in March."

"Then that's it," Dave grins, pushing out of the couch. "You been asleep five months, Rip van Winkle? Time for a hand before we do the roadwork."

"What I'd like to know is what that chick looks like," says Bud, closing down the transceiver. "Can I help you into your space-suit, Miss? Hey, Miss, pull that in, psst-psst-psst! You going to listen, Doc?"

"Right." Lorimer is getting out his charts. The others go aft through the tunnel to the small day-room, making no further comment on the presence of the strange ship or ships out here. Lorimer himself is more shaken than he likes; it was that damn phrase.

The tedious exercise period comes and goes. Lunchtime: They give the containers a minimum warm to conserve the batteries. Chicken *à la* king again; Bud puts ketchup on his and breaks their usual silence with a funny anecdote about an Australian girl, laboriously censoring himself to conform to *Sunbird*'s unwritten code on talk. After lunch Dave goes forward to the command module. Bud and Lorimer continue their current task of checking out the suits and packs for a damage-assessment EVA to take place as soon as the radiation count drops.

They are just clearing away when Dave calls them. Lorimer comes through the tunnel to hear a girl's voice blare, "—dinko trip. What did Lorna say? *Gloria* over!"

He starts up the Lurp and begins scanning. No results this time. "They're either in line behind us or in the sunward quadrant," he reports finally. "I can't isolate them."

Presently the speaker holds another thin thread of sound.

"That could be their ground control," says Dave. "How's the horizon, Doc?"

"Five hours; Northwest Siberia, Japan, Australia."

"I told you the high gain is fucked up." Bud gingerly feeds power to his antenna motor. "Easy, eas-ee. The frame is twisted, that's what it is."

"Don't snap it," Dave says, knowing Bud will not.

The squeaking fades, pulses back. "Hey, we can really use this," Bud says. "We can calibrate on them."

A hard soprano says suddenly "—should be outside your orbit. Try around Beta Aries."

"Another chick. We have a fix," Bud says happily. "We have a fix now. I do believe our troubles are over. That monkey was torqued one hundred forty-nine degress. Woo-ee!"

The first girl comes back. "We see them, Margo! But they're so small, how can they live in there? Maybe they're tiny aliens! Over."

"That's Judy," Bud chuckles. "Dave, this is screwy, it's all in English. It has to be some U.N. thingie."

Dave massages his elbows, flexes his fists; thinking. They wait. Lorimer considers a hundred and forty-nine degress from Gamma Piscium.

In thirteen minutes the voice from Earth says, "Judy, call the others, will you? We're going to play you the conversation, we think you should all hear. Two minutes. Oh, while we're waiting, Zebra wants to tell Connie the baby is fine. And we have a new cow."

"Code," says Dave.

The recording comes on. The three men listen once more to Dave calling Houston in a rattle of solar noise. The transmission clears up rapidly and cuts off with the woman saying that another ship, the *Gloria*, is behind them, closer to the sun.

"We looked up history," the Earth voice resumes. "There was a Major Norman Davis on the first *Sunbird* flight. Major was a military title. Did you hear them say 'Doc'? There was a scientific doctor on board, Doctor Orren Lorimer. The third member was Captain—that's another title—Bernhard Geirr. Just the three of them, all males of course. We think they had an early reaction engine and not too much fuel. The point is, the first *Sunbird* mission was lost in space. They never came out from behind the sun. That was about when the big flares started. Jan thinks they must have been close to one, you heard them say they were damaged."

Dave grunts. Lorimer is fighting excitement like a brush discharge sparking in his gut.

"Either they are who they say they are or they're ghosts; or they're aliens pretending to be people. Jan says maybe the disruption in those super-flares could collapse the local time di-

127

mension. Pluggo. What did you observe there, I mean the highlights?"

Time dimension . . . never come back . . . Lorimer's mind narrows onto the reality of the two unmoving bearded heads before him, refuses to admit the words he thought he heard: *Before the year two thousand.* The language, he thinks. The language would have to have changed. He feels better.

A deep baritone voice says, "Margo?" In *Sunbird* eyes come alert.

"—like the big one fifty years ago." The man has the accent too. "We were really lucky being right there when it popped. The most interesting part is that we confirmed the gravity turbulence. Periodic but not waves. It's violent, we got pushed around some. Space is under monster stress in those things. We think France's theory that our system is passing through a micro-black-hole cluster looks right so long as one doesn't plonk us."

"France?" Bud mutters. Dave looks at him speculatively.

"It's hard to imagine anything being kicked out in time. But they're here, whatever they are, they're over eight hundred kays outside us scooting out toward Aldebaran. As Lorna said, if they're trying to reach Earth they're in trouble unless they have a lot of spare gees. Should we try to talk to them? Over. Oh, great about the cow. Over again."

"Black holes," Bud whistles softly. "That's one for you, Doc. Was we in a black hole?"

"Not in one or we wouldn't be here." If we are here, Lorimer adds to himself. A micro-black-hole cluster . . . what happens when fragments of totally collapsed matter approach each other, or collide, say in the photosphere of a star? Time disruption? Stop it. Aloud he says, "They could be telling us something, Dave."

Dave says nothing. The minutes pass.

Finally the Earth voice comes back, saying that it will try to contact the strangers on their original frequency. Bud glances at Dave, tunes the selector.

"Calling *Sunbird One?*" the girl says slowly through her nose. "This is Luna Central calling Major Norman Davis of *Sunbird One.* We have picked up your conversation with our ship *Escondita.* We are very puzzled as to who you are and how you got here. If you really are *Sunbird One* we think you must have been jumped forward in time when you passed the solar flare." She pronounces it Cockney-style, "toime."

"Our ship *Gloria* is near you, they see you on their radar. We think you may have a serious course problem because you told Lorna you were headed for Earth and you think it is now October with Earth in Pisces. It is not October. It is March fifteen. I repeat, the Earth date—" she says "dyte" "—is March fifteen, time twenty hundred hours. You should be able to see Earth very close to Spica in Virgo. You said your window is damaged. Can't you go out and look? We think you have to make a big course correction. Do you have enough fuel? Do you have a computer? Do you have enough air and water and food? Can we help you? We're listening on this frequency. Luna to *Sunbird One*, come in."

On *Sunbird* nobody stirs. Lorimer struggles against internal eruptions. *Never came back. Jumped forward in time.* The cyst of memories he has schooled himself to suppress bulges up in the lengthening silence. "Aren't you going to answer?"

"Don't be stupid," Dave says.

"Dave. A hundred and forty-nine degrees is the difference between Gamma Piscium and Spica. That transmission is coming from where they say Earth is."

"You goofed."

"I did not goof. It has to be March."

Dave blinks as if a fly is bothering him.

In fifteen minutes the Luna voice runs through the whole thing again, ending "Please, come in."

"Not a tape." Bud unwraps a stick of gum, adding the plastic to the neat wad back of the gyro leads. Lorimer's skin crawls, watching the ambiguous dazzle of Spica. Spica-plus-Earth? Unbelief grips him, rocks him with a complex pang compounded of faces, voices, the sizzle of bacon frying, the creak of his father's wheelchair, chalk on a sunlit blackboard, Ginny's bare legs on the flowered couch, Jenny and Penny running dangerously close to the lawnmower. The girls will be taller now, Jenny is already as tall as her mother. His father is living with Amy in Denver, determined to last till his son gets home. *When I get home.* This has to be insanity, Dave's right; it's a trick, some crazy trick. The language.

129

Fifteen minutes more; the flat, earnest female voice comes back and repeats it all, putting in more stresses. Dave wears a remote frown, like a man listening to a lousy sports program. Lorimer has the notion he might switch off and propose a hand of gin; wills him to do so. The voice says it will now change frequencies.

Bud tunes back, chewing calmly. This time the voice stumbles on a couple of phrases. It sounds tired.

Another wait; an hour, now. Lorimer's mind holds only the bright point of Spica digging at him. Bud hums a bar of *Yellow Ribbons*, falls silent again.

"Dave," Lorimer says finally, "our antenna is pointed straight at Spica. I don't care if you think I goofed, if Earth is over there we have to change course soon. Look, you can see it could be a double light source. We have to check this out."

Dave says nothing. Bud says nothing but his eyes rove to the port window, back to his instrument panel, to the window again. In the corner of the panel is a polaroid snap of his wife. Patty: a tall, giggling, rump-switching red-head; Lorimer has occasional fantasies about her. Little-girl voice, though. And so tall. . . . Some short men chase tall women; it strikes Lorimer as undignified. Ginny is an inch shorter than he. Their girls will be taller. And Ginny insisted on starting a pregnancy before he left, even though he'll be out of commo. Maybe, maybe a boy, a son—*stop it*. Think about anything. Bud. . . . Does Bud love Patty? Who knows? He loves Ginny. At seventy million miles. . . .

"Judy?" Luna Central or whoever it is says. "They don't answer. You want to try? But listen, we've been thinking. If these people really are from the past this must be very traumatic for them. They could be just realising they'll never see their world again. Myda says these males had children and women they stayed with, they'll miss them terribly. This is exciting for us but it may seem awful to them. They could be too shocked to answer. They could be frightened, maybe they think we're aliens or hallucinations even. See?"

Five seconds later the nearby girl says, "Da, Margo, we were into that too. Dinko. Ah, *Sunbird?* Major Davis of *Sunbird*, are you there? This is Judy Paris in the ship *Gloria*, we're only about a million kay from you, we see you on our
130

screen." She sounds young and excited. "Luna Central has been trying to reach you, we think you're in trouble and we want to help. Please don't be frightened, we're people just like you. We think you're way off course if you want to reach Earth. Are you in trouble? Can we help? If your radio is out can you make any sort of signal? Do you know Old Morse? You'll be off our screen soon, we're truly worried about you. Please reply somehow if you possibly can, *Sunbird*, come in!"

Dave sits impassive. Bud glances at him, at the port window, gazes stolidly at the speaker, his face blank. Lorimer has exhausted surprise, he wants only to reply to the voices. He can manage a rough signal by heterodyning the probe beam. But what then, with them both against him?

The girl's voice tries again determinedly. Finally she says, "Margo, they won't peep. Maybe they're dead? I think they're aliens."

Are we not?, Lorimer thinks. The Luna station comes back with a different, older voice.

"Judy, Myda here, I've had another thought. These people had a very rigid authority code. You remember your history, they peck-ordered everything. You notice Major Davis repeated about being commanding. That's called dominance-submission structure, one of them gave orders and the others did whatever they were told, we don't know quite why. Perhaps they were frightened. The point is that if the dominant one is in shock or panicked maybe the others can't reply unless this Davis lets them."

Jesus Christ, Lorimer thinks. Jesus H. Christ in colors. It is his father's expression for the inexpressible. Dave and Bud sit unstirring.

"How weird," the Judy voice says. "But don't they know they're on a bad course? I mean, could the dominant one make the others fly right out of the system? Truly?"

It's happened, Lorimer thinks; it has happened. I have to stop this. I have to act now, before they lose us. Desperate visions of himself defying Dave and Bud loom before him. Try persuasion first.

Just as he opens his mouth he sees Bud stir slightly, and with immeasurable gratitude hears him say, "Dave-o, what say we take an eyeball look? One little old burp won't hurt us."

131

Dave's head turns a degree or two.

"Or should I go out and see, like the chick said?" Bud's voice is mild.

After a long minute Dave says neutrally, "All right. . . . Attitude change." His arm moves up as though heavy; he starts methodically setting in the values for the vector that will bring Spica in line with their functional window.

Now why couldn't I have done that, Lorimer asks himself for the thousandth time, following the familiar check sequence. Don't answer. . . . And for the thousandth time he is obscurely moved by the rightness of them. The authentic ones, the alphas. Their bond. The awe he had felt first for the absurd jocks of his school ball team.

"That's go, Dave, assuming nothing got creamed."

Dave throws the ignition safety, puts the computer on real time. The hull shudders. Everything in the cabin drifts sidewise while the bright point of Spica swims the other way, appears on the front window as the retros cut in. When the star creeps out onto clear glass Lorimer can clearly see its companion. The double light steadies there; a beautiful job. He hands Bud the telescope.

"The one on the left."

Bud looks. "There she is, all right. Hey, Dave, look at that!"

He puts the scope in Dave's hand. Slowly, Dave raises it and looks. Lorimer can hear him breathe. Suddenly Dave pulls up the mike.

"Houston!" he says harshly. "*Sunbird* to Houston, *Sunbird* calling Houston. Houston, come in!"

Into the silence the speaker squeals, "They fired their engines—wait, she's calling!" And shuts up.

In *Sunbird*'s cabin nobody speaks. Lorimer stares at the twin stars ahead, impossible realities shifting around him as the minutes congeal. Bud's reflected face looks downwards, grin gone. Dave's beard moves silently; praying, Lorimer realises. Alone of the crew Dave is deeply religious; at Sunday meals he gives a short, dignified grace. A shocking pity for Dave rises in Lorimer; Dave is so deeply involved with his family, his four sons, always thinking about their training, taking them hunting, fishing, camping. And Doris his wife so incredibly active and sweet, going on their trips, cooking and doing things for the community. Driving Penny and Jenny to classes while Ginny was sick that time. Good people, the backbone. . . . This can't be, he thinks; Packard's voice is going to come through in a minute, the antenna's beamed right now. Six minutes now. This will all go away. *Before the year two thousand*—stop it, the language would have changed. Think of Doris. . . . She has that glow, feeding her five men; women with sons are different. But Ginny, but his dear woman, his *wife*, his *daughters*—grandmothers now? All dead and dust? *Quit that*. Dave is still praying. . . . Who knows what goes on inside those heads? Dave's cry. . . . Twelve minutes, it has to be right. The second sweep is stuck, no, it's moving. Thirteen. It's all insane, a dream. Thirteen plus. . . . fourteen. The speaker hissing and clicking vacantly. Fifteen now. A dream. . . . Or are those women staying off, letting us see? Sixteen. . . .

At twenty Dave's hand moves, stops again. The seconds jitter by, space crackles. Thirty minutes coming up.

"Calling Major Davis in *Sunbird?*" It is the older woman, a gentle voice. "This is Luna Central. We are the service and communication facility for space flight now. We're sorry to have to tell you that there is no space center at Houston any more. Houston itself was abandoned when the shuttle base moved to White Sands, over two centuries ago."

A cool dust-colored light enfolds Lorimer's brain, isolating it. He will remain so a long time.

The woman is explaining it all again, offering help, asking if they were hurt. A nice dignified speech. Dave still sits immobile, gazing at Earth. Bud puts the mike in his hand.

"Tell them, Dave-o."

Dave looks at it, takes a deep breath, presses the send button.

"*Sunbird* to Luna Control," he says quite normally. (It's "Central" Lorimer thinks.) "We copy. Ah, negative on life support, we have no problems. We copy the course change suggestion and are proceeding to recompute. Your offer of computer assistance is appreciated. We suggest you transmit position data so we can get squared away. Ah, we are economising on transmission until we see how our accumulators have held up. *Sunbird* out."

And so it had begun.

Lorimer's mind floats back to himself now floating in *Gloria*, nearly a year, or three hundred years, later; watching and being watched by them. He still feels light, contended; the dread underneath has come no nearer. But it is so silent. He seems to have heard no voices for a long time. Or was it a long time? Maybe the drug is working on his time sense, maybe it was only a minute or two.

"I've been remembering," he says to the woman Connie, wanting her to speak.

She nods. "You have so much to remember. Oh, I'm sorry—that wasn't good to say." Her eyes speak sympathy.

"Never mind." It is all dreamlike now, his lost world and this other which he is just now seeing plain. "We must seem like very strange beasts to you."

"We're trying to understand," she says. "It's history, you learn the events but you don't really feel what the people were like, how it was for them. We hope you'll tell us."

The drug, Lorimer thinks, that's what they're trying. Tell them . . . how can he? Could a dinosaur tell how it was? A montage flows through his mind, dominated by random shots of Operations' north parking lot and Ginny's yellow kitchen telephone with the sickly ivy vines. . . . Women and vines. . . .

A burst of laughter distracts him. It's coming from the chamber they call the gym. Bud and the others must be playing ball in there. Bright idea, really, he muses: Using muscle power, sustained mild exercise. That's why they are all so fit. The gym is a glorified squirrel-wheel when you climb or pedal up the walls it revolves and winds a gear train, which among other things rotates the sleeping drum. A real Woolagong. . . . Bud and Dave usually take their shifts together, scrambling the spinning gym like big pale apes. Lorimer prefers the easy rhythm of the women, and the cycle here fits him nicely. He usually puts in his shift with Connie, who doesn't talk much, and one of the Judys, who do.

No one is talking now, though. Remotely uneasy he looks around the big cylinder of the cabin, sees Dave and Lady Blue by the forward window. Judy Dakar is behind them, silent for once. They must be looking at Earth; it has been a beautiful expanding disk for some weeks now. Dave's beard is moving, he is praying again. He has taken to doing that, not ostentatiously, but so obviously sincere that Lorimer, a life atheist, can only sympathise.

The Judys have asked Dave what he whispers, of course. When Dave understood that they had no concept of prayer and had never seen a Christian Bible there had been a heavy silence.

"So you have lost all faith," he said finally.

"We have faith," Judy Paris protested.

"May I ask in what?"

"We have faith in ourselves, of course," she told him.

"Young lady, if you were my daughter I'd tan your britches," Dave said, not joking. The subject was not raised again.

But he came back so well after that first dreadful shock, Lorimer thinks. A personal god, a father-model, man needs that. Dave draws strength from it and we lean on him. Maybe leaders have to believe. Dave was so great; cheerful, unflappable, patiently working out alternatives, making his decisions on the inevitable discrepancies in the position readings in a way Lorimer couldn't do. A bitch. . . .

Memory takes him again; he is once again back in *Sunbird*, gritty-eyed, listening to the women's chatter, Dave's terse replies. God, how they chattered. But their computer work checks out. Lorimer is suffering also from a quirk of Dave's, his reluctance to transmit their exact thrust and fuel reserve. He keeps holding out a margin and making Lorimer compute it back in.

But the margins don't help; it is soon clear that they are in big trouble. Earth will pass too far ahead of them on her next orbit, they don't have the acceleration to catch up with her before they cross her path. They can carry out an ullage manoeuver, they can kill enough velocity to let Earth catch them on the second go-by; but that would take an extra year and their life-support would be long gone. The grim question of whether they have enough to enable a single man to wait it out pushes into Lorimer's mind. He pushes it back; that one is for Dave.

There is a final possibility: Venus will approach their trajectory three months hence and they may be able to gain velocity by swinging by it. They go to work on that.

Meanwhile Earth is steadily drawing away from them and

135

so is *Gloria*, closer toward the sun. They pick her out of the solar interference and then lose her again. They know her crew now: the man is Andy Kay, the senior woman is Lady Blue Parks; they appear to do the navigating. Then there is a Connie Morelos and the two twins, Judy Paris and Judy Dakar, who run the communications. The chief Luna voices are women too, Margo and Azella. The men can hear them talking to the *Escondita* which is now swinging in toward the far side of the sun. Dave insists on monitoring and taping everything that comes through. It proves to be largely replays of their exchanges with Luna and *Gloria*, mixed with a variety of highly personal messages. As references to cows, chickens and other livestock multiply Dave reluctantly gives up his idea that they are code. Bud counts a total of five male voices.

"Big deal," he says. "There were more chick drivers on the road when we left. Means space is safe now, the girlies have taken over. Let them sweat their little asses off." He chuckles. "When we get this bird down, the stars ain't gonna study old Buddy no more, no ma'm. A nice beach and about a zillion steaks and ale and all those sweet things. Hey, we'll be living history, we can charge admission."

Dave's face takes on the expression that means an inappropriate topic has been breached. Much to Lorimer's impatience, Dave discourages all speculation as to what may await them on this future Earth. He confines their transmissions strictly to the problem in hand; when Lorimer tries to get him at least to mention the unchanged-language puzzle Dave only says firmly, "Later." Lorimer fumes; inconceivable that he is three centuries in the future, unable to learn a thing.

They do glean a few facts from the women's talk. There have been nine successful *Sunbird* missions after theirs and one other casualty. And the *Gloria* and her sister ship are on a long-planned fly-by of the two inner planets.

"We always go along in pairs," Judy says. "But those planets are no good. Still, it was worth seeing."

"For Pete's sake Dave, ask them how many planets have been visited," Lorimer pleads.

"Later."

But about the fifth meal-break Luna suddenly volunteers.

"Earth is making up a history for you, *Sunbird*," the

Margo voice says. "We know you don't want to waste power asking so we thought we'd send you a few main points right now." She laughs. "It's much harder than we thought, nobody here does history."

Lorimer nods to himself; he has been wondering what he could tell a man from 1690 who would want to know what happened to Cromwell—was Cromwell then?—and who had never heard of electricity, atoms or the U.S.A.

"Let's see, probably the most important is that there aren't as many people as you had, we're just over two million. There was a world epidemic not long after your time. It didn't kill people but it reduced the population. I mean there weren't any babies in most of the world. Ah, sterility. The country called Australia was affected least." Bud holds up a finger.

"And North Canada wasn't too bad. So the survivors all got together in the south part of the American states where they could grow food and the best communications and factories were. Nobody lives in the rest of the world but we travel there sometimes. Ah, we have five main activities, was industries the word? Food, that's farming and fishing. Communications, transport, and space—that's us. And the factories they need. We live a lot simpler than you did, I think. We see your things all over, we're very grateful to you. Oh, you'll be interested to know we use zeppelins just like you did, we have six big ones. And our fifth thing is the children. Babes. Does that help? I'm using a children's book we have here.

The men have frozen during this recital; Lorimer is holding a cooling bag of hash. Bud starts chewing again and chokes.

"Two million people and a space capability?" He coughs. "That's incredible."

Dave gazes reflectively at the speaker. "There's a lot they're not telling us."

"I gotta ask them," Bud says. "Okay?"

Dave nods. "Watch it."

"Thanks for the history, Luna," Bud says. "We really appreciate it. But we can't figure out how you maintain a space program with only a couple of million people. Can you tell us a little more on that?"

In the pause Lorimer tries to grasp the staggering figures. From eight billion to two million . . . Europe, Asia, Africa, South America, America itself—wiped out. *There weren't any more babies.* World sterility, from what? The Black Death, the famines of Asia—those had been decimations. This is magnitudes worse. No, it is all the same: beyond comprehension. An empty world, littered with junk.

"*Sunbird?*" says Margo, "Da, I should have thought you'd want to know about space. Well, we have only the four real spaceships and one building. You know the two here. Then there's *Indira* and *Pech,* they're on the Mars run now. Maybe the Mars dome was since your day. You had the satellite stations though, didn't you? And the old Luna dome, of course—I remember now, it was during the epidemic. They tried to set up colonies to, ah, breed children, but the epidemic got there too. They struggled terribly hard. We owe a lot to you really, you men I mean. The history has it all, how you worked out a minimal viable program and trained everybody and saved it from the crazies. It was a glorious achievement. Oh, the marker here has one of your names on it. Lorimer. We love to keep it all going and growing, we all love travelling. Man is a rover, that's one of our mottoes."

"Are you hearing what I'm hearing?" Bud asks, blinking comically.

Dave is still staring at the speaker. "Not one word about their government," he says slowly. "Not a word about economic conditions. We're talking to a bunch of monkeys."

"Should I ask them?"

"Wait a minute . . . Roger, ask the name of their chief of state and the head of the space program. And—no, that's all."

"President?" Margo echoes Bud's query. "You mean like queens and kings? Wait, here's Myda. She's been talking about you with Earth."

The older woman they hear occasionally says "*Sunbird?* Da, we realize you had a very complex activity, your governments. With so few people we don't have that type of formal structure at all. People from the different activities meet periodically and our communications are good, everyone is kept informed. The people in each activity are in charge of doing it while they're there. We rotate, you see. Mostly in five-year

138

hitches, for example Margo here was on the zeppelins and I've been on several factories and farms and of course the, well, the education, we all do that. I believe that's one big difference from you. And of course we all work. And things are basically far more stable now, I gather. We change slowly. Does that answer you? Of course you can always ask Registry, they keep track of us all. But we can't, ah, take you to our leader, if that's what you mean." She laughs, a genuine, jolly sound. "That's one of our old jokes. I must say," she goes on seriously, "it's been a joy to us that we can understand you so well. We make a big effort not to let the language drift, it would be tragic to lose touch with the past."

Dave takes the mike. "Thank you, Luna. You've given us something to think about. *Sunbird* out."

"How much of that is for real, Doc?" Bud rubs his curly head. "They're giving us one of your science fiction stories."

"The real story will come later," says Dave. "Our job is to get there."

"That's a point that doesn't look too good."

By the end of the session it looks worse. No Venus trajectory is any good. Lorimer reruns all the computations; same result.

"There doesn't seem to be any solution to this one, Dave," he says at last. "The parameters are just too tough. I think we've had it."

Dave massages his knuckles thoughtfully. Then he nods. "Roger. We'll fire the optimum sequence on the Earth heading."

"Tell them to wave if they see us go by," says Bud.

They are silent, contemplating the prospect of a slow death in space eighteen months hence. Lorimer wonders if he can raise the other question, the bad one. He is pretty sure what Dave will say. What will he himself decide, what will he have the guts to do?

"Hello, *Sunbird*?" the voice of *Gloria* breaks in. "Listen, we've been figuring. We think if you use all your fuel you could come back in close enough to our orbit so we could swing out and pick you up. You'd be using solar gravity that way. We have plenty of manoeuvre but much less acceleration than you do. You have suits and some kind of propellants, don't you? I mean, you could fly across a few kays?"

The three men look at each other; Lorimer guesses he had not been the only one to speculate on that.

"That's a good thought, *Gloria*," Dave says. "Let's hear what Luna says."

"Why?" asks Judy. "It's our business, we wouldn't endanger the ship. We'd only miss another look at Venus, who cares. We have plenty of water and food and if the air gets a little smelly we can stand it."

"Hey, the chicks are all right," Bud says. They wait.

The voice of Luna comes on. "We've been looking at that too, Judy. We're not sure you understand the risk. Ah, *Sunbird*, excuse me. Judy, if you manage to pick them up you'll have to spend nearly a year in the ship with these three male persons from a *very different culture*. Myda says you should remember history and it's a risk no matter what Connie says. *Sunbird*, I hate to be so rude. Over."

But is grinning broadly, they all are. "Cave men," he chuckles. "All the chicks land preggers."

"Margo, they're human beings," the Judy voice protests. "This isn't just Connie, we're all agreed. Andy and Lady Blue say it would be very interesting. If it works, that is. We can't let them go without trying."

"We feel that way too, of course," Luna replies. "But there's another problem. They could be carrying diseases. *Sunbird*, I know you've been isolated for fourteen months, but Murti says people in your day were immune to organisms that aren't around now. Maybe some of ours could harm you, too. You could all get mortally sick and lose the ship."

"We thought of that, Margo," Judy says impatiently. "Look, if you have contact with them at all somebody has to test, true? So we're ideal. By the time we get home you'll know. And how could we get sick so fast we couldn't put *Gloria* in a stable orbit where you could get her later on?"

They wait. "Hey, what about that epidemic?" Bud pats his hair elaborately. "I don't know if I want a career in gay lib."

"You rather stay out here?" Dave asks.

"Crazies," says a different voice from Luna. "*Sunbird*, I'm Murti, the health person here. I think what we have to fear most is the meningitis-influenza complex, they mutate so readily. Does your Doctor Lorimer have any suggestions?"

"Roger, I'll put him on," says Dave. "But as to your first

point, madam, I want to inform you that at the time of take-off the incidence of rape in the United States space cadre was zero point zero. I guarantee the conduct of my crew provided you can control yours. Here is Doctor Lorimer."

But Lorimer can not of course tell them anything useful. They discuss the men's polio shots, which luckily have used killed virus, and various childhood diseases which still seem to be around. He does not mention their epidemic.

"Luna, we're going to try it," Judy declares. "We couldn't live with ourselves. Now let's get the course figured before they get any farther away."

From there on there is no rest on *Sunbird* while they set up and refigure and rerun the computations for the envelope of possible intersecting trajectories. The *Gloria*'s drive, they learn, is indeed low-thrust, although capable of sustained operation. *Sunbird* will have to get most of the way to the rendez-vous on her own if they can cancel their outward velocity.

The tension breaks once during the long session, when Luna calls *Gloria* to warn Connie to be sure the female crew members wear concealing garments at all times if the men came aboard.

"Not suit-liners, Connie, they're much too tight." It is the older woman, Myda. Bud chuckles.

"Your light sleepers, I think. And when the men unsuit, your Andy is the only one who should help them. You others stay away. The same for all body functions and sleeping. This is very important, Connie, you'll have to watch it the whole way home. There are a great many complicated taboos. I'm putting an instruction list on the bleeper, is your receiver working?"

"Da, we used it for France's black hole paper."

"Good. Tell Judy to stand by. Now listen, Connie, listen carefully. Tell Andy he has to read it all. I repeat, *he* has to read every word. Did you hear that?"

"Ah, dinko," Connie answers. "I understand, Myda. He will."

"I think we just lost the ball game, fellas," Bud laments. "Old mother Myda took it all away."

Even Dave laughs. But later when the modulated squeal

141

that is a whole text comes through the speaker, he frowns again. "There goes the good stuff."

The last factors are cranked in; the revised program spins, and Luna confirms them. "We have a pay-out, Dave," Lorimer reports. "It's tight but there are at least two viable options. Provided the main jets are fully functional."

"We're going EVA to check."

That is exhausting; they find a warp in the deflector housing of the port engines and spend four sweating hours trying to wrestle it back. It is only Lorimer's third sight of open space but he is soon too tired to care.

"Best we can do," Dave pants finally. "We'll have to compensate in the psychic mode."

"You can do it, Dave-o," says Bud. "Hey, I gotta change those suit radios, don't let me forget."

In the psychic mode . . . Lorimer surfaces back to his real self, cocooned in *Gloria*'s big cluttered cabin, seeing Connie's living face. It must be hours, how long has he been dreaming?"

"About two minutes," Connie smiles.

"I was thinking of the first time I saw you."

"Oh yes. We'll never forget that, ever."

Nor will he . . . He lets it unroll again in his head. The interminable hours after the first long burn, which has sent *Sunbird* yawing so they all have to gulp nausea pills. Judy's breathless voice reading down their approach: "Oh, very good, four hundred thousand . . . Oh great, *Sunbird*, you're almost three, you're going to break a hundred for sure—" Dave has done it, the big one.

Lorimer's probe is useless in the yaw, it isn't until they stabilise enough for the final burst that they can see the strange blip bloom and vanish in the slot. Converging, hopefully, on a theoretical near-intersection point.

"Here goes everything."

The final burn changes the yaw into a sickening tumble with the starfield looping past the glass. The pills are no more use and the fuel feed to the attitude jets goes sour. They are all vomiting before they manage to hand-pump the last of the fuel and slow the tumble.

"That's it, *Gloria*. Come and get us. Lights on, Bud. Let's get those suits up."

Fighting nausea they go through the laborious routine in the fouled cabin. Suddenly Judy's voice sings out, "We see you, *Sunbird!* We see your light! Can't you see us?"

"No time," Dave says. But Bud, half-suited, points at the window. "Fellas, oh, hey, look at that."

Lorimer stares, thinks he sees a faint spark between the whirling stars before he has to retch.

"Father, we thank you," says Dave quietly. "All right, move it on, Doc. Packs."

The effort of getting themselves plus the propulsion units and a couple of cargo nets out of the rolling ship drives everything else out of mind. It isn't until they are floating linked together and stabilised by Dave's hand jet that Lorimer has time to look.

The sun blanks out their left. A few meters below them *Sunbird* tumbles empty, looking absurdly small. Ahead of them, infinitely far away, is a point too blurred and yellow to be a star. It creeps: *Gloria,* on her approach tangent.

"Can you start, *Sunbird?*" says Judy in their helmets. "We don't want to brake any more on account of our exhaust. We estimate fifty kay in an hour, we're coming out on a line."

"Roger. Give me your jet, Doc."

"Goodbye, *Sunbird,*" says Bud. "Plenty of lead, Dave-o."

Lorimer finds it restful in a childish way, being towed across the abyss tied to the two big men. He has total confidence in Dave, he never considers the possibility that they will miss, sail by and be lost. Does Dave feel contempt? Lorimer wonders; that banked-up silence, is it partly contempt for those who can manipulate only symbols, who have no mastery of matter? . . . He concentrates on mastering his stomach.

It is a long, dark trip. *Sunbird* shrinks to a twinkling light, slowly accelerating on the spiral course that will end her ultimately in the sun with their precious records that are three hundred years obsolete. With, also, the packet of photos and letters that Lorimer has twice put in his suit-pouch and twice taken out. Now and then he catches sight of *Gloria,* growing from a blur to an incomprehensible tangle of lighted crescents.

"Woo-ee, it's big," Bud says. "No wonder they can't accelerate, that thing is a flying trailer park. It'd break up."

"It's a space ship. Got those nets tight, Doc?"

Judy's voice suddenly fills their helmets. "I see your lights! Can you see me? Will you have enough left to brake at all?"

"Affirmative to both, *Gloria*," says Dave.

At that moment Lorimer is turned slowly forward again and he sees—will see it forever: the alien ship in the starfield and on its dark side the tiny lights that are women in the stars, waiting for them. Three—no, four; one suit-light is way out, moving. If that is a tether it must be over a kilometer.

"Hello, I'm Judy Dakar!" The voice is close. "Oh, mother, you're big! Are you all right? How's your air?"

"No problem."

They are in fact stale and steaming wet; too much adrenalin. Dave uses the jets again and suddenly she is growing, is coming right at them, a silvery spider on a trailing thread. Her suit looks trim and flexible; it is mirror-bright, and the pack is quite small. Marvels of the future, Lorimer thinks; Paragraph One.

"You made it, you made it! Here, tie in. Brake!"

"There ought to be some historic words," Bud murmurs. "If she gives us a chance."

"Hello, Judy," says Dave calmly. "Thanks for coming.".

"Contact!" She blasts their ears. "Haul us in, Andy! Brake, brake—the exhaust is back there!"

And they are grabbed hard, deflected into a great arc toward the ship. Dave uses up the last jet. The line loops.

"Don't jerk it," Judy cries. "Oh, I'm *sorry*." She is clinging on them like a gibbon, Lorimer can see her eyes, her excited mouth. Incredible. "Watch out, it's slack."

"Teach me, honey," says Andy's baritone. Lorimer twists and sees him far back at the end of a heavy tether, hauling them smoothly in. Bud offers to help, is refused. "Just hang loose, please," a matronly voice tells them. It is obvious Andy has done this before. They come in spinning slowly, like space fish. Lorimer finds he can no longer pick out the twinkle that is *Sunbird*. When he is swung back, *Gloria* has changed to a disorderly cluster of bulbs and spokes around a big central cylinder. He can see pods and miscellaneous equipment stowed all over her. Not like science fiction.

Andy is paying the line into a floating coil. Another figure

144

floats beside him. They are both quite short, Lorimer realises as they near.

"Catch the cable," Andy tells them. There is a busy moment of shifting inertial drag.

"Welcome to *Gloria*, Major Davis, Captain Geirr, Doctor Lorimer. I'm Lady Blue Parks. I think you'll like to get inside as soon as possible. If you feel like climbing go right ahead, we'll pull all this in later."

"We appreciate it, Ma'm."

They start hand-over-hand along the catenary of the main tether. It has a good rough grip. Judy coasts up to peer at them, smiling broadly, towing the coil. A taller figure waits by the ship's open airlock.

"Hello, I'm Connie. I think we can cycle in two at a time. Will you come with me, Major Davis?"

It is like an emergency on a plane, Lorimer thinks as Dave follows her in. Being ordered about by supernaturally polite little girls.

"Space-going stews," Bud nudges him. "How 'bout that?" His face is sprouting sweat. Lorimer tells him to go next, his own LSP has less load.

Bud goes in with Andy. The woman named Lady Blue waits beside Lorimer while Judy scrambles on the hull securing their cargo nets. She doesn't seem to have magnetic soles; perhaps ferrous metals aren't used in space now. When she begins hauling in the main tether on a simple hand winch Lady Blue looks at it critically.

"I used to make those," she says to Lorimer. What he can see of her features looks compressed, her dark eyes twinkle. He has the impression she is part Black.

"I ought to get over and clean that aft antenna." Judy floats up. "Later," says Lady Blue. They both smile at Lorimer. Then the hatch opens and he and Lady Blue go in. When the toggles seat there comes a rising scream of air and Lorimer's suit collapses.

"Can I help you?" She has opened her faceplate, the voice is rich and live. Eagerly Lorimer catches the latches in his clumsy gloves and lets her lift the helmet off. His first breath surprises him, it takes an instant to identify the gas as fresh air. Then the inner hatch opens, letting in greenish light. She waves him through. He swims into a short tunnel. Voices are

145

coming from around the corner ahead. His hand finds a grip and he stops, feeling his heart shudder in his chest.

When he turns that corner the world he knows will be dead. Gone, rolled up, blown away forever with *Sunbird*. He will be irrevocably in the future. A man from the past, a time traveller. In the future. . . .

He pulls himself around the bend.

The future is a vast bright cylinder, its whole inner surface festooned with unidentifiable objects, fronds of green. In front of him floats an odd tableau: Bud and Dave, helmets off, looking enormous in their bulky white suits and packs. A few meters away hang two bare-headed figures in shiny suits and a dark-haired girl in flowing pink pajamas.

They are all simply staring at the two men, their eyes and mouths open in identical expressions of pleased wonder. The face that has to be Andy's is grinning open-mouthed like a kid at the zoo. He is a surprisingly young boy, Lorimer sees, in spite of his deep voice; blond, downy-cheeked, compactly muscular. Lorimer finds he can scarcely bear to look at the pink woman, can't tell if she really is surpassingly beautiful or plain. The taller suited woman has a shiny, ordinary face.

From overhead bursts an extraordinary sound which he finally recognises as a chicken cackling. Lady Blue pushes past him.

"All right, Andy, Connie, stop staring and help them get their suits off. Judy, Luna is just as eager to hear about this as we are."

The tableau jumps to life. Afterwards Lorimer can recall mostly eyes, bright curious eyes tugging his boots, smiling eyes upside-down over his pack—and always that light, ready laughter. Andy is left alone to help them peel down, blinking at the fittings which Lorimer still finds embarrassing. He seems easy and nimble in his own half-open suit. Lorimer struggles out of the last lacings, thinking, a boy! A boy and four women orbiting the sun, flying their big junky ships to Mars. Should he feel humiliated? He only feels grateful, accepting a short robe and a bulb of tea somebody—Connie?—gives him.

The suited Judy comes in with their nets. The men follow Andy along another passage, Bud and Dave clutching at the small robes. Andy stops by a hatch.

"This greenhouse is for you, it's your toilet. Three's a lot but you have full sun."

Inside is a brilliant jungle, foliage everywhere, glittering water droplets, rustling leaves. Something whirs away—a grasshopper.

"You crank that handle." Andy points to a seat on a large cross-duct. "The piston rams the gravel and waste into a compost process and it ends up in the soil core. That vetch is a heavy nitrogen user and a great oxidator. We pump CO_2 in and oxy out. It's a real Woolagong."

He watches critically while Bud tries out the facility.

"What's a Woolagong?" asks Lorimer dazedly.

"Oh, she's one of our inventors. Some of her stuff is weird. When we have a pluggy-looking thing that works we call it a Woolagong." He grins. "The chickens eat the seeds and the hoppers, see, and the hoppers and iguanas eat the leaves. When a greenhouse is going darkside we turn them in to harvest. With this much light I think we could keep a goat, don't you? You didn't have any life at all on your ship, true?"

"No," Lorimer says, "not a single iguana."

"They promised us a Shetland pony for Christmas," says Bud, rattling gravel. Andy joins perplexedly in the laugh.

Lorimer's head is foggy; it isn't only fatigue, the year in *Sunbird* has atrophied his ability to take in novelty. Numbly he uses the Woolagong and they go back out and forward to *Gloria*'s big control room, where Dave makes a neat short speech to Luna and is answered graciously.

"We have to finish changing course now," Lady Blue says. Lorimer's impression has been right, she is a small light part-Negro in late middle age. Connie is part something exotic too, he sees; the others are European types.

"I'll get you something to eat," Connie smiles warmly. "Then you probably want to rest. We saved all the cubbies for you." She says "syved"; their accents are all identical.

As they leave the control room Lorimer sees the withdrawn look in Dave's eyes and knows he must be feeling the reality of being a passenger in an alien ship; not in command, not deciding the course, the communications going on unheard.

That is Lorimer's last coherent observation, that and the taste of the strange, good food. And then being led aft through what he now knows is the gym, to the shaft of the

147

sleeping drum. There are six irised ports like dog-doors; he pushes through his assigned port and finds himself facing a roomy mattress. Shelves and a desk are in the wall.

"For your excretions." Connie's arm comes through the iris, pointing at bags. "If you have a problem stick your head out and call. There's water."

Lorimer simply drifts toward the mattress, too sweated out to reply. His drifting ends in a curious heavy settling and his final astonishment: the drum is smoothly, silently starting to revolve. He sinks gratefully onto the pad, growing "heavier" as the minutes pass. About a tenth gee, maybe more, he thinks, it's still accelerating. And falls into the most restful sleep he has known in the long weary year.

It isn't till next day that he understands that Connie and two others have been on the rungs of the gym chamber, sending it around hour after hour without pause or effort and chatting as they went.

How they talk, he thinks again floating back to real present time. The bubbling irritant pours through his memory, the voices of Ginny and Jenny and Penny on the kitchen telephone, before that his mother's voice, his sister Amy's. Interminable. What do they always have to talk, talk, talk of?

"Why, everything," says the real voice of Connie beside him now, "it's natural to share."

"Natural. . . ." Like ants, he thinks. They twiddle their antennae together every time they meet. Where did you go, what did you do? Twiddle-twiddle. How do you *feel*? Oh, I feel this, I feel that, blah blah twiddle-twiddle. Total coordination of the hive. Women have no self-respect. Say anything, no sense of the strategy of words, the dark danger of naming. Can't hold in.

"Ants, bee-hives," Connie laughs, showing the bad tooth. "You truly see us as insects, don't you? Because they're females?"

"Was I talking aloud? I'm sorry." He blinks away dreams.

"Oh, please don't be. It's so sad to hear about your sister and your children and your, your wife. They must have been wonderful people. We think you're very brave."

But he has only thought of Ginny and them all for an instant—what has he been babbling? What is the drug doing to him?

"What are you doing to us?" he demands, lanced by real alarm now, almost angry.

"It's all right, truly." Her hand touches his, warm and somehow shy. "We all use it when we need to explore something. Usually it's pleasant. It's a laevonoramine compound, a disinhibitor, it doesn't dull you like alcohol. We'll be home so soon, you see. We have the responsibility to understand and you're so locked in." Her eyes melt at him. "You don't feel sick, do you? We have the antidote."

"No . . ." His alarm has already flowed away somewhere. Her explanation strikes him as reasonable enough. "We're not locked in," he says or tries to say. "We talk . . ." He gropes for a word to convey the judiciousness, the adult restraint. Objectivity, maybe? "We talk when we have something to say." Irrelevantly he thinks of a mission coordinator named Forrest, famous for his blue jokes. "Otherwise it would all break down," he tells her. "You'd fly right out of the system." That isn't quite what he means; let it pass.

The voices of Dave and Bud ring out suddenly from opposite ends of the cabin, awakening the foreboding of evil in his mind. They don't know us, he thinks. They should look out, stop this. But he is feeling too serene, he wants to think about his own new understanding, the pattern of them all he is seeing at last.

"I feel lucid," he manages to say, "I want to think."

She looks pleased. "We call that the ataraxia effect. It's so nice when it goes that way."

Ataraxia, philosophical calm. Yes. But there are monsters in the deep, he thinks or says. The night side. The night side of Orren Lorimer, a self hotly dark and complex, waiting in leash. They're so vulnerable. They don't know we can take them. Images rush up: a Judy spread-eagled on the gym rungs, pink pajamas gone, open to him. Flash sequence of the three of them taking over the ship, the women tied up, helpless, shrieking, raped and used. The team—get the satellite station, get a shuttle down to Earth. Hostages. Make them do anything, no defense whatever . . . Has Bud actually said that? But Bud doesn't know, he remembers. Dave knows they're hiding something, but he thinks it's socialism or sin. When they find out. . . .

How has he himself found out? Simply listening, really, all

149

these months. He listens to their talk much more than the others; "fraternising," Dave calls it. . . . They all listened at first, of course. Listened and looked and reacted helplessly to the female bodies, the tender bulges so close under the thin, tantalising clothes, the magnetic mouths and eyes, the smell of them, their electric touch. Watching them touch each other, touch Andy, laughing, vanishing quietly into shared bunks. *What goes on? Can I? My need, my need—*

The power of them, the fierce resentment. . . . Bud muttered and groaned meaningfully despite Dave's warnings. He kept needling Andy until Dave banned all questions. Dave himself was noticeably tense and read his Bible a great deal. Lorimer found his own body pointing after them like a famished hound, hoping to Christ the cubicles are as they appeared to be, unwired.

All they learn is that Myda's instructions must have been ferocious. The atmosphere has been implacably antiseptic, the discretion impenetrable. Andy politely ignored every probe. No word or act has told them what, if anything, goes on; Lorimer was irresistibly reminded of the weekend he spent at Jenny's scout camp. The men's training came presently to their rescue, and they resigned themselves to finishing their mission on a super-*Sunbird*, weirdly attended by a troop of Boy and Girl Scouts.

In every other way their reception couldn't be more courteous. They have been given the run of the ship and their own dayroom in a cleaned-out gravel storage pod. They visit the control room as they wish. Lady Blue and Andy give them specs and manuals and show them every circuit and device of *Gloria*, inside and out. Luna has bleeped up a stream of science texts and the data on all their satellites and shuttles and the Mars and Luna dome colonies.

Dave and Bud plunged into an orgy of engineering. *Gloria* is, as they suspected, powered by a fission plant that uses a range of Lunar materials. Her ion drive is only slightly advanced over the experimental models of their own day. The marvels of the future seem so far to consist mainly of ingenious modifications.

"It's primitive," Bud tells him. "What they've done is sacrifice everything to keep it simple and easy to maintain. Believe

150

it, they can hand-feed fuel. And the back-ups, brother! They have redundant redundancy."

But Lorimer's technical interest soon flags. What he really wants is to be alone a while. He makes a desultory attempt to survey the apparently few developments in his field, and finds he can't concentrate. What the hell, he tells himself, I stopped being a physicist three hundred years ago. Such a relief to be out of the cell of *Sunbird;* he has given himself up to drifting solitary through the warren of the ship, using their excellent 400 mm telescope, noting the odd life of the crew.

When he finds that Lady Blue likes chess they form a routine of bi-weekly games. Her personality intrigues him; she has reserve and an aura of authority. But she quickly stops Bud when he calls her "Captain."

"No one here commands in your sense. I'm just the oldest." Bud goes back to "Ma'm."

She plays a solid positional game, somewhat more erratic than a man but with occasional elegant traps. Lorimer is astonished to find that there is only one new chess opening, an interesting queen-side gambit called the Dagmar. One new opening in three centuries? He mentions it to the others when they come back from helping Andy and Judy Paris overhaul a standby converter.

"They haven't done much anywhere," Dave says. "Most of your new stuff dates from the epidemic, Andy, if you'll pardon me. The program seems to be stagnating. You've been gearing up this Titan project for eighty years."

"We'll get there." Andy grins.

"C'mon Dave," says Bud. "Judy and me are taking on you two for the next chicken dinner, we'll get a bridge team here yet. Woo-ee, I can taste that chicken! Losers get the iguana."

The food is so good. Lorimer finds himself lingering around the kitchen end, helping whoever is cooking, munching on their various seeds and chewy roots as he listens to them talk. He even likes the iguana. He begins to put on weight, in fact they all do. Dave decrees double exercise shifts.

"You going to make us *climb* home, Dave-o?" Bud groans. But Lorimer enjoys it, pedalling or swinging easily along the rungs while the women chat and listen to tapes. Familiar music: he identifies a strange spectrum from Handel, Brahms,

Sibelius, through Strauss to ballad tunes and intricate light jazz-rock. No lyrics. But plenty of informative texts doubtless selected for his benefit.

From the promised short history he finds out more about the epidemic. It seems to have been an air-borne quasi-virus escaped from Franco-Arab military labs, possibly potentiated by pollutants.

"It apparently damaged only the reproductive cells," he tells Dave and Bud. "There was little actual mortality, but almost universal sterility. Probably a molecular substitution in the gene code in the gametes. And the main effect seems to have been on the men. They mention a shortage of male births afterwards, which suggests that the damage was on the Y-chromosome where it would be selectively lethal to the male fetus."

"Is it still dangerous, Doc?" Dave asks. "What happens to us when we get back home?"

"They can't say. The birth-rate is normal now, about two percent and rising. But the present population may be resistant. They never achieved a vaccine."

"Only one way to tell," Bud says gravely. "I volunteer."

Dave merely glances at him. Extraordinary how he still commands, Lorimer thinks. Not submission, for Pete's sake. A team.

The history also mentions the riots and fighting which swept the world when humanity found itself sterile. Cities bombed, and burned, massacres, panics, mass rapes and kidnapping of women, marauding armies of biologically desperate men, bloody cults. The crazies. But it is all so briefly told, so long ago. Lists of honoured names. "We must always be grateful to the brave people who held the Denver Medical Laboratories—" And then on to the drama of building up the helium supply for the dirigibles.

In three centuries it's all dust, he thinks. What do I know of the hideous Thirty Years War that was three centuries back for me? *Fighting devastated Europe for two generations.* Not even names.

The description of their political and economic structure is even briefer. They seem to be, as Myda had said, almost ungoverned.

"It's a form of loose social credit system run by consensus," he says to Dave. "Somewhat like a permanent frontier period. They're building up slowly. Of course they don't need an army or airforce. I'm not sure if they even use cash money or recognise private ownership of land. I did notice one favorable reference to early Chinese communalism," he adds to see Dave's mouth set. "But they aren't tied to a community. They travel about. When I asked Lady Blue about their police and legal system she told me to wait and talk with real historians. This Registry seems to be just that, it's not a policy organ."

"We've run into a situation here, Lorimer," Dave says soberly. "Stay away from it. They're not telling the story."

"You notice they never talk about their husbands?" Bud laughs. "I asked a couple of them what their husband did and I swear they had to think. And they all have kids. Believe me, it's a swinging scene down there, even if old Andy acts like he hasn't found out what it's for."

"I don't want any prying into their personal family lives while we're on this ship, Geirr. None whatsoever. That's an order."

"Maybe they don't have families. You ever hear 'em mention anybody getting married? That has to be the one thing on a chick's mind. Mark my words, there's been some changes made."

"The social mores are bound to have changed to some extent," Lorimer says. "Obviously you have women doing more work outside the home, for one thing. But they have family bonds; for instance Lady Blue has a sister in an aluminum mill and another in health. Andy's mother is on Mars and his sister works in Registry. Connie has a brother or brothers on the fishing fleet near Biloxi, and her sister is coming out to replace her here next trip, she's making yeast now."

"That's the top of the iceberg."

"I doubt the rest of the iceberg is very sinister, Dave."

But somewhere along the line the blandness begins to bother Lorimer too. So much is missing. Marriage, love-affairs, children's troubles, jealousy squabbles, status, possessions, money problems, sicknesses, funerals even—all the daily minutiae that occupied Ginny and her friend seems to have been edited out of these women's talk. *Edited.* . . . Can

153

Dave be right, is some big, significant aspect being deliberately kept from them?

"I'm still surprised your language hasn't changed more," he says one day to Connie during their exertions in the gym.

"Oh, we're very careful about that." She climbs at an angle beside him, not using her hands. "It would be a dreadful loss if we couldn't understand the books. All the children are taught from the same original tapes, you see. Oh, there's faddy words we use for a while, but our communicators have to learn the old texts by heart, that keeps us together."

Judy Paris grunts from the pedicycle. "You, my dear children, will never know the oppression we suffered," she declaims mockingly.

"Judys talk too much," says Connie.

"We do, for a fact." They both laugh.

"So you still read our so-called great books, our fiction and poetry?" asks Lorimer. "Who do you read, H.G. Wells? Shakespeare? Dickens, ah, Balzac, Kipling, Brian?" He gropes; Brian had been a bestseller Ginny liked. When had he last looked at Shakespeare or the others?

"Oh, the historicals," Judy says. "It's interesting, I guess. Grim. They're not very realistic. I'm sure it was to you," she adds generously.

And they turn to discussing whether the laying hens are getting too much light, leaving Lorimer to wonder how what he supposes are the eternal verities of human nature can have faded from a world's reality. Love, conflict, heroism, tragedy—all "unrealistic"? Well, flight crews are never great readers; still, women read more. . . . Something *has* changed, he can sense it. Something basic enough to affect human nature. A physical development perhaps; a mutation? What is really under those floating clothes?

It is the Judys who give him part of it.

He is exercising alone with both of them, listening to them gossip about some legendary figure named Dagmar.

"The Dagmar who invented the chess opening?" he asks.

"Yes. She does anything, when she's good she's great."

"Was she bad sometimes?"

A Judy laughs. "The Dagmar problem, you can say. She has this tendency to organise everything. It's fine when it works but every so often it runs wild, she thinks she's queen or what. Then they have to get out the butterfly nets."

All in present tense—but Lady Blue has told him the Dagmar gambit is over a century old.

Longevity, he thinks; by god, that's what they're hiding. Say they've achieved a doubled or tripled life span, that would certainly change human psychology, affect their outlook on everything. Delayed maturity, perhaps? We were working on endocrine cell juvenescence when I left. How old are these girls, for instance?

He is framing a question when Judy Dakar says, "I was in the creche when she went pluggo. But she's good, I loved her later on."

Lorimer thinks she has said "crash" and then realises she means a communal nursery. "Is that the same Dagmar?" he asks. "She must be very old."

"Oh no, her sister."

"A sister a hundred years apart?"

"I mean, her daughter. Her, her *grand*-daughter." She starts pedalling fast.

"Judys," says her twin, behind them.

Sister again. Everybody he learns of seems to have an extraordinary number of sisters, Lorimer reflects. He hears Judy Paris saying to her twin, "I think I remember Dagmar at the creche. She started uniforms for everybody. Colors and numbers."

"You couldn't have, you weren't born," Judy Dakar retorts.

There is a silence in the drum.

Lorimer turns on the rungs to look at them. Two flushed cheerful faces stare back warily, make identical head-dipping gestures to swing the black hair out of their eyes. Identical. . . . But isn't the Dakar girl on the cycle a shade more mature, her face more weathered?

"I thought you were supposed to be twins."

"Ah, Judys talk a lot," they say together—and grin guiltily.

"You aren't sisters," he tells them. "You're what we called clones."

Another silence.

"Well, yes," says Judy Dakar. "We call it sisters. Oh, mother! We weren't supposed to tell you, Myda said you

155

would be frightfully upset. It was illegal in your day, true?"

"Yes. We considered it immoral and unethical, experimenting with human life. But it doesn't upset me personally."

"Oh, that's beautiful, that's great," they say together. "We think of you as different," Judy Paris blurts, "you're more hu—more like us. Please, you don't have to tell the others, do you? Oh, *please* don't."

"It was an accident there were two of us here," says Judy Dakar. "Myda *warned* us. Can't you wait a little while?" Two identical pairs of dark eyes beg him.

"Very well," he says slowly. "I won't tell my friends for the time being. But if I keep your secret you have to answer some questions. For instance, how many of your people are created artificially this way?"

He begins to realise he *is* somewhat upset. Dave is right, damn it, they are hiding things. Is this brave new world populated by subhuman slaves, run by master brains? Decorticate zombies, workers without stomachs or sex, human cortexes wired into machines, monstrous experiments rush through his mind. He had been naive again. These normal-looking women can be fronting for a hideous world.

"How many?"

"There's only about eleven thousand of us," Judy Dakar says. The two Judys look at each other, transparently confirming something. They're unschooled in deception, Lorimer thinks; is that good? And is diverted by Judy Paris exclaiming, "What we can't figure out is why did you think it was wrong?"

Lorimer tries to tell them, to convey the horror of manipulating human identity, creating abnormal life. The threat to individuality, the fearful power it would put in a dictator's hand.

"Dictator?" one of them echoes blankly. He looks at their faces and can only say, "Doing things to people without their consent. I think it's sad."

"But that's just what we think about you," the younger Judy bursts out. "How do you know who you *are*? Or who anybody is? All alone, no sisters to share with! You don't know what you can do, or what would be interesting to try. All you poor singletons, you—why, you just have to blunder along and die, all for nothing!"

156

Her voice trembles. Amazed, Lorimer sees both of them are misty-eyed.

"We better get this m-moving," the other Judy says.

They swing back into the rhythm and in bits and pieces Lorimer finds out how it is. Not bottled embryos, they tell him indignantly. Human mothers like everybody else, young mothers, the best kind. A somatic cell nucleus is inserted in an enucleated ovum and re-implanted in the womb. They have each borne two "sister" babies in their late teens and nursed them a while before moving on. The creches always have plenty of mothers.

His longevity notion is laughed at; nothing but some rules of healthy living have as yet been achieved. "We should make ninety in good shape," they assure him. "A hundred and eight, that was Judy Eagle, she's our record. But she was pretty blah at the end."

The clone-strains themselves are old, they date from the epidemic. They were part of the first effort to save the race when the babies stopped and they've continued ever since.

"It's so perfect," they tell him. "We each have a book, it's really a library. All the recorded messages. The Book of Judy Shapiro, that's us. Dakar and Paris are our personal names, we're doing cities now." They laugh, trying not to talk at once about how each Judy adds her individual memoir, her adventures and problems and discoveries in the genotype they all share.

"If you make a mistake it's useful for the others. Of course you try not to—or at least make a *new* one."

"Some of the old ones aren't so realistic," her other self puts in. "Things were so different, I guess. We make excerpts of the parts we like best. And practical things, like Judys should watch out for skin cancer."

"But we have to read the whole thing every ten years," says the Judy called Dakar. "It's inspiring. As you get older you understand some of the ones you didn't before."

Bemused, Lorimer tries to think how it would be, hearing the voices of three hundred years of Orren Lorimers. Lorimers who were mathematicians or plumbers or artists or bums or criminals, maybe. The continuing exploration and completion of self. And a dozen living doubles; aged Lori-

157

mers, infant Lorimers. And other Lorimers' women and children . . . would he enjoy it or resent it? He doesn't know.

"Have you made your records yet?"

"Oh, we're too young. Just notes in case of accident."

"Will we be in them?"

"You can say!" They laugh merrily, then sober. "Truly you won't tell?" Judy Paris asks. "Lady Blue, we have to let her know what we did. Oof. But *truly* you won't tell your friends?"

He hadn't told on them, he thinks now, emerging back into his living self. Connie beside him is drinking cider from a bulb. He has a drink in his hand too, he finds. But he hasn't told.

"Judys will talk." Connie shakes her head, smiling. Lorimer realises he must have gabbled out the whole thing.

"It doesn't matter," he tells her. "I would have guessed soon anyhow. There were too many clues . . . Woolagongs invent, Mydas worry, Jans are brains, Billy Dees work so hard. I picked up six different stories of hydroelectric stations that were built or improved or are being run by one Lala Singh. Your whole way of life. I'm more interested in this sort of thing than a respectable physicist should be," he says wryly. "You're all clones, aren't you? Every one of you. What do Connies do?"

"You really do know." She gazes at him like a mother whose child has done something troublesome and bright. "Whew! Oh, well, Connies farm like mad, we grow things. Most of our names are plants. I'm Veronica, by the way. And of course the creches, that's our weakness. The runt mania. We tend to focus on anything smaller or weak."

Her warm eyes focus on Lorimer, who draws back involuntarily.

"We control it." She gives a hearty chuckle. "We aren't all that way. There's been engineering Connies, and we have two young sisters who love metallurgy. It's fascinating what the genotype can do if you try. The original Constantia Morelos was a chemist, she weighed ninety pounds and never saw a farm in her life." Connie looks down at her own muscular arms. "She was killed by the crazies, she fought with weapons. It's so hard to understand . . . And I had a sister

158

Timothy who made dynamite and dug two canals and she wasn't even an andy."

"*An* andy," he says.

"Oh, dear."

"I guessed that too. Early androgen treatments."

She nods hesitantly. "Yes. We need the muscle-power for some jobs. A few. Kays are quite strong anyway. Whew!" She suddenly stretches her back, wriggles as if she'd been cramped. "Oh, I'm glad you know. It's been such a strain. We couldn't even sing."

"Why not?"

"Myda was sure we'd make mistakes, all the words we'd have had to change. We sing a lot." She softly hums a bar or two.

"What kinds of songs do you sing?"

"Oh, every kind. Adventure songs, work songs, mothering songs, roaming songs, mood songs, trouble songs, joke songs—everything."

"What about love songs?" he ventures. "Do you still have, well, love?"

"Of course, how could people not love?" But she looks at him doubtfully. "The love stories I've heard from your time are so, I don't know, so weird. Grim and pluggy. It doesn't seem like love. . . . Oh, yes, we have famous love songs. Some of them are partly sad too. Like Tamil and Alcmene O, they're fated together. Connies are fated too, a little," she grins bashfully. "We love to be with Ingrid Anders. It's more one-sided. I hope there'll be an Ingrid on my next hitch. She's so exciting, she's like a little diamond."

Implications are exploding all about him, sparkling with questions. But Lorimer wants to complete the darker pattern beyond.

"Eleven thousand genotypes, two million people: that averages two hundred of each of you alive now." She nods. "I suppose it varies? There's more of some?"

"Yes, some types aren't as viable. But we haven't lost any since early days. They tried to preserve all the genes they could, we have people from all the major races and a lot of small strains. Like me, I'm the Carib Blend. Of course we'll never know what was lost. But eleven thousand is a lot, really. We all try to know every one, it's a life hobby."

A chill penetrates his ataraxia. Eleven thousand, period. That is the true population of Earth now. He thinks of two hundred tall olive-skinned women named after plants, excited by two hundred little bright Ingrids; two hundred talkative Judys, two hundred self-possessed Lady Blues, two hundred Margos and Mydas and the rest. He shivers. The heirs, the happy pall-bearers of the human race.

"So evolution ends," he says somberly.

"No, why? It's just slowed down. We do everything much slower than you did, I think. We like to experience things *fully*. We have time." She stretches again, smiling. "There's all the time."

"But you have no new genotypes. It is the end."

"Oh but there are, now. Last century they worked out the way to make haploid nuclei combine. We can make a stripped egg-cell function like pollen," she says proudly. "I mean sperm. It's tricky, some don't come out too well. But now we're finding both Xs viable we have over a hundred new types started. Of course it's hard for them, with no sisters. The donors try to help."

Over a hundred, he thinks. Well. Maybe. . . . But "both Xs viable," what does that mean? She must be referring to the epidemic. But he had figured it primarily affected the men. His mind goes happily to work on the new puzzle, ignoring a sound from somewhere that is trying to pierce his calm.

"It was a gene or genes on the X-chromosome that was injured," he guesses aloud. "Not the Y. And the lethal trait had to be recessive, right? Thus there would have been no births at all for a time, until some men recovered or were isolated long enough to manufacture undamaged X-bearing gametes. But women carry their lifetime supply of ova, they could never regenerate reproductively. When they mated with the recovered males only female babies would be produced, since the female carries two Xs and the mother's defective gene would be compensated by a normal X from the father. But the male is XY, he receives only the mother's defective X. Thus the lethal defect would be expressed, the male fetus would be finished. . . . A planet of girls and dying men. The few odd viables died off."

"You truly do understand," she says admiringly.

The sound is becoming urgent; he refuses to hear it, there is significance here.

"So we'll be perfectly all right on Earth. No problem. In theory we can marry again and have families, daughters anyway."

"Yes," she says. "In theory."

The sound suddenly broaches his defenses, becomes the loud voice of Bud Geirr raised in song. He sounds plain drunk now. It seems to be coming from the main garden pod, the one they use to grow vegetables, not sanitation. Lorimer feels the dread alive again. rising closer. Dave ought to keep an eye on him. But Dave seems to have vanished too, he recalls seeing him go towards Control with Lady Blue.

"OH, THE SUN SHINES BRIGHT ON PRET-TY RED WI-I-ING," carols Bud.

Something should be done, Lorimer decides painfully. He stirs; it is an effort.

"Don't worry," Connie says. "Andy's with them."

"You don't know, you don't know what you've started." He pushes off toward the garden hatchway.

"—AS SHE LAY SLE-EPING, A COWBOY CREE-E-EEPING—" General laughter from the hatchway. Lorimer coasts through into the green dazzle. Beyond the radial fence of snap-beans he sees Bud sailing in an exaggerated crouch after Judy Paris. Andy hangs by the iguana cages, laughing.

Bud catches one of Judy's ankles and stops them both with a flourish, making her yellow pajamas swirl. She giggles at him upside-down, making no effort to free herself.

"I don't like this," Lorimer whispers.

"Please don't interfere." Connie has hold of his arm, anchoring them both to the tool rack. Lorimer's alarm seems to have ebbed; he will watch, let serenity return. The others have not noticed them.

"Oh, there once was an Indian maid." Bud sings more restrainedly, "Who never was a-fraid, that some buckaroo would slip it up her, ahem, ahem," he coughs ostentatiously, laughing. "Hey, Andy, I hear them calling you."

"What?" says Judy, "I don't hear anything."

"They're calling you, lad. Out there."

"Who?" asks Andy, listening.

"They are, for Crissake." He lets go of Judy and kicks

161

over to Andy. "Listen, you're a great kid. Can't you see me and Judy have some business to discuss in private?" He turns Andy gently around and pushes him at the bean-stakes. "It's New Year's Eve, dummy."

Andy floats passively away through the fence of vines, raising a hand at Lorimer and Connie. Bud is back with Judy.

"Happy New Year, kitten," he smiles.

"Happy New Year. Did you do special things on New Year?" she asks curiously.

"What we did on New Year's." He chuckles, taking her shoulders in his hands. "On New Year's Eve, yes we did. Why don't I show you some of our primitive Earth customs, h'mm?"

She nods, wide-eyed.

"Well, first we wish each other well, like this." He draws her to him and lightly kisses her cheek. "Kee-rist, what a dumb bitch," he says in a totally different voice. "You can tell you've been out too long when the geeks start looking good. Knockers, ahhh—" His hand plays with her blouse. The man is unaware, Lorimer realises. He doesn't know he's drugged, he's speaking his thoughts. I must have done that. Oh, god. . . . He takes shelter behind his crystal lens, an observer in the protective light of eternity.

"And then we smooch a little." The friendly voice is back, Bud holds the girl closer, caressing her back. "Fat ass." He puts his mouth on hers; she doesn't resist. Lorimer watches Bud's arms tighten, his hands working on her buttocks, going under her clothes. Safe in the lens his own sex stirs. Judy's arms are waving aimlessly.

Bud breaks for breath, a hand at his zipper.

"Stop staring," he says hoarsely. "One fucking more word, you'll find out what that big mouth is for. Oh, man, a flagpole. Like steel. . . . Bitch, this is your lucky day." He is baring her breasts now, big breasts. Fondling them. "Two fucking years in the ass end of noplace," he mutters, "shit on me will you? Can't wait, watch it—titty-titty-titties—"

He kisses her again quickly and smiles down at her. "Good?" he asks in his tender voice, and sinks his mouth on her nipples, his hand seeking in her thighs. She jerks and says something muffled. Lorimer's arteries are pounding with delight, with dread.

162

"I, I think this should stop," he makes himself say falsely, hoping he isn't saying more. Through the pulsing tension he hears Connie whisper back, it sounds like "Don't worry, Judy's very athletic." Terror stabs him, they don't know. But he can't help.

"Cunt," Bud grunts, "you have to have a cunt in there, is it froze up? You dumb cunt—" Judy's face appears briefly in her floating hair, a remote part of Lorimer's mind notes that she looks amused and uncomfortable. His being is riveted to the sight of Bud expertly controlling her body in midair, peeling down the yellow slacks. Oh god—her dark pubic mat, the thick white thighs—a perfectly normal woman, no mutation. Ohhh, god. . . . But there is suddenly a drifting shadow in the way: Andy again floating over them with something in his hands.

"You dinko, Jude?" the boy asks.

Bud's face comes up red and glaring. "Bug out, you!"

"Oh, I won't bother."

"Jee-sus Christ." Bud lunges up and grabs Andy's arm, his legs still hooked around Judy. "This is man's business, boy, do I have to spell it out?" He shifts his grip. "Shoo!"

In one swift motion he has jerked Andy close and backhanded his face hard, sending him sailing into the vines.

Bud gives a bark of laughter, bends back to Judy. Lorimer can see his erection poking through his fly. He wants to utter some warning, tell them their peril, but he can only ride the hot pleasure surging through him, melting his crystal shell. Go on, more—avidly he sees Bud mouth her breasts again and then suddenly flip her whole body over, holding her wrists behind her in one fist, his legs pinning hers. Her bare buttocks bulge up helplessly, enormous moons. "Ass-s-s," Bud groans. "Up you bitch, ahhh-hh—" He pulls her butt onto him.

Judy gives a cry, begins to struggle futilely. Lorimer's shell boils and bursts. Amid the turmoil ghosts outside are trying to rush in. And something *is* moving, a real ghost—to his dismay he sees it is Andy again, floating toward the joined bodies, holding a whirring thing. Oh, no—a camera. The fools.

"Get away!" he tries to call to the boy.

But Bud's head turns, he has seen. "You little pissass." His long arm shoots out and captures Andy's shirt, his legs still locked around Judy.

"I've had it with you." His fist slams into Andy's mouth, the camera goes spinning away. But this time Bud doesn't let him go, he is battering the boy, all of them rolling in a tangle in the air.

"Stop!" Lorimer hears himself shout, plunging at them through the beans. "Bud, stop it! You're hitting a woman."

The angry face comes around, squinting at him.

"Get lost Doc, you little fart. Get your own ass."

"Andy is a *woman,* Bud. You're hitting a girl. She's not a man."

"Huh?" Bud glances at Andy's bloody face. He shakes the shirt-front. "Where's the boobs?"

"She doesn't have breasts, but she's a woman. Her real name is Kay. They're all women. Let her go, Bud."

Bud stares at the androgyne, his legs still pinioning Judy, his penis poking the air. Andy put up his/her hands in a vaguely combative way.

"A dyke?" says Bud slowly. "A goddam little bull dyke? This I gotta see."

He feints casually, thrusts a hand into Andy's crotch.

"No balls!" he roars, "No balls at all!" Convulsing with laughter he lets himself tip over in the air, releasing Andy, his legs letting Judy slip free. "Na-ah," he interrupts himself to grab her hair and goes on guffawing. "A dyke! Hey, dykey!" He takes hold of his hard-on, waggles it at Andy. "Eat your heart out, little dyke." Then he pulls up Judy's head. She has been watching unresisting all along.

"Take a good look, girlie. See what old Buddy has for you? Tha-a-at's what you want, say it. How long since you saw a real man, hey, dog-face?"

Maniacal laughter bubbles up in Lorimer's gut, farce too strong for fear. "She never saw a man in her life before, none of them has. You imbecile, don't you get it? There aren't any other men, they've all been dead three hundred years.

Bud slowly stops chuckling, twists around to peer at Lorimer.

"What'd I hear you say, Doc?"

164

"The men are all gone. They died off in the epidemic. There's nothing but women left alive on Earth."

"You mean there's, there's two million women down there and no men?" His jaw gapes. "Only little bull dykes like Andy. . . . Wait a minute. Where do they get the kids?"

"They grow them artificially. They're all girls."

"Gawd. . . ." Bud's hand clasps his drooping penis, jiggles it absently. It stiffens. "Two million hot little cunts down there, waiting for old Buddy. Gawd. The last man on Earth. . . . You don't count, Doc. And old Dave, he's full of crap."

He begins to pump himself, still holding Judy by the hair. The motion sends them slowly backward. Lorimer sees that Andy—Kay—has the camera going again. There is a big star-shaped smear of blood on the boyish face; cut lip, probably. He himself feels globed in thick air, all action spent. Not lucid.

"Two million cunts," Bud repeats. "Nobody home, nothing but pussy everywhere. I can do anything I want, any time. No more shit." He pumps faster. "They'll be spread out for miles begging for it. Clawing each other for it. All for me, King Buddy. . . . I'll have strawberries and cunt for breakfast. Hot buttered boobies, man. 'N' head, there'll be a couple little twats licking whip cream off my cock all day long. . . . Hey, I'll have contests! Only the best for old Buddy now. Not you, cow." He jerks Judy's head. "Li'l teenies, tight li'l holes. I'll make the old broads hot 'em up while I watch." He frowns slightly, working on himself. In a clinical corner of his mind Lorimer guesses the drug is retarding ejaculation. He tells himself that he should be relieved by Bud's self-absorption, is instead obscurely terrified.

"King, I'll be their god," Bud is mumbling. "They'll make statues of me, my cock a mile high, all over. . . . His Majesty's sacred balls. They'll worship it. . . . Buddy Geirr, the last cock on Earth. Oh man, if old George could see that. When the boys hear that they'll really shit themselves, wooee!"

He frowns harder. "They can't all be gone." His eyes rove, find Lorimer. "Hey, Doc, there's some men left someplace, aren't there? Two or three, anyway?"

"No." Effortfully Lorimer shakes his head. "They're all dead, all of them."

"Balls." Bud twists around, peering at them. "There has to be some left. Say it." He pulls Judy's head up. "Say it, cunt."

"No, it's true," she says.

"No men," Andy/Kay echoes.

"You're lying." Bud scowls, frigs himself faster, thrusting his pelvis. "There has to be some men, sure there are. . . . They're hiding out in the hills, that's what it is. Hunting, living wild. . . . Old wild men, I knew it."

"Why do there have to be men?" Judy asks him, being jerked to and fro.

"Why, you stupid bitch." He doesn't look at her, thrusts furiously. "Because, dummy, otherwise nothing counts, that's why. . . . There's some men, some good old buckaroos— Buddy's a good old buckaroo—"

"Is he going to emit sperm now?" Connie whispers.

"Very likely," Lorimer says, or intends to say. The spectacle is of merely clinical interest, he tells himself, nothing to dread. One of Judy's hands clutches something: a small plastic bag. Her other hand is on her hair that Bud is yanking. It must be painful.

"Uhhh, ahh," Bud pants distressfully, "fuck away, fuck—" Suddenly he pushes Judy's head into his groin, Lorimer glimpses her nonplussed expression.

"You have a mouth, bitch, get working! . . . Take it for shit's sake, *take* it! Uh, uh—" A small oyster jets limply from him. Judy's arm goes after it with the bag as they roll over in the air.

"Geirr!"

Bewildered by the roar, Lorimer turns and sees Dave— Major Norman Davis—looming in the hatchway. His arms are out, holding back Lady Blue and the other Judy.

"Geirr! I said there would be no misconduct on this ship and I mean it. Get away from that woman!"

Bud's legs only move vaguely, he does not seem to have heard. Judy swims through them bagging the last drops.

"You, what the hell are you doing?"

In the silence Lorimer hears his own voice say, "Taking a sperm sample, I should think."

"Lorimer? Are you out of your perverted mind? Get Geirr to his quarters."

Bud slowly rotates upright. "Ah, the reverend Leroy," he says tonelessly.

"You're drunk, Geirr. Go to your quarters."

"I have news for you, Dave-o," Bud tells him in the same flat voice. "I bet you don't know we're the last men on Earth. Two million twats down there."

"I'm aware of that," Dave says furiously. "You're a drunken disgrace. Lorimer, get that man out of here."

But Lorimer feels no nerve of action stir. Dave's angry voice has pushed back the terror, created a strange hopeful stasis encapsulating them all.

"I don't have to take that any more. . . ." Bud's head moves back and forth, silently saying no, no, as he drifts toward Lorimer. "Nothing counts any more. All gone. What for, friends?" His forehead puckers. "Old Dave, he's a man. I'll let him have some. The dummies. . . . Poor old Doc, you're a creep but you're better'n nothing, you can have some too. . . . We'll have places, see, big spreads. Hey, we can run drags, there has to be a million good old cars down there. We can go hunting. And then we find the wild men."

Andy, or Kay, is floating toward him, wiping off blood.

"Ah, no you don't!" Bud snarls and lunges for her. As his arm stretches out Judy claps him on the triceps.

Bud gives a yell that dopplers off, his limbs thrash—and then he is floating limply, his face suddenly serene. He is breathing, Lorimer sees, releasing his own breath, watching them carefully straighten out the big body. Judy plucks her pants out of the vines, and they start towing him out through the fence. She has the camera and the specimen bag.

"I put this in the freezer, dinko?" she says to Connie as they come by. Lorimer has to look away.

Connie nods. "Kay, how's your face?"

"I felt it!" Andy/Kay says excitedly through puffed lips, "I felt physical anger, I wanted to hit him. Woo-ee!"

"Put that man in my wardroom," Dave orders as they pass. He has moved into the sunlight over the lettuce rows. Lady Blue and Judy Dakar are back by the wall, watching. Lorimer remembers what he wanted to ask.

"Dave, do you really know? Did you find out they're all women?"

Dave eyes him broodingly, floating erect with the sun on his chestnut beard and hair. The authentic features of man. Lorimer thinks of his own father, a small pale figure like himself. He feels better.

"I always knew they were trying to deceive us, Lorimer. Now that this woman has admitted the facts I understand the full extent of the tragedy."

It is his deep, mild Sunday voice. The women look at him interestedly.

"They are lost children. They have forgotten He who made them. For generations they have lived in darkness."

"They seem to be doing all right," Lorimer hears himself say. It sounds rather foolish.

"Women are not capable of running anything. You should know that, Lorimer. Look what they've done here, it's pathetic. Marking time, that's all. Poor souls." Dave sighs gravely. "It is not their fault. I recognise that. Nobody has given them any guidance for three hundred years. Like a chicken with its head off."

Lorimer recognises his own thought; the structureless, chattering, trivial, two-million-celled protoplasmic lump.

"The head of the woman is the man," Dave says crisply. "Corinthians one eleven three. No discipline whatsoever." He stretches out his arm, holding up his crucifix as he drifts toward the wall of vines. "Mockery. Abominations." He touches the stakes and turns, framed in the green arbor.

"We were sent here, Lorimer. This is God's plan. *I* was sent here. Not you, you're as bad as they are. My middle name is Paul," he adds in a conversational tone. The sun gleams on the cross, on his uplifted face, a strong, pure, apostolic visage. Despite some intellectual reservations Lorimer feels a forgotten nerve respond.

"Oh Father, send me strength," Dave prays quietly, his eyes closed. "You have spared us from the void to bring Your light to this suffering world. I shall lead Thy erring daughters out of the darkness. I shall be a stern but merciful father to them in Thy name. Help me to teach the children Thy holy law and train them in the fear of Thy righteous wrath. Let the women learn in silence and all subjection;

Timothy two eleven. They shall have sons to rule over them and glorify Thy name."

He could do it, Lorimer thinks, a man like that really could get life going again. Maybe there is some mystery, some plan. I was too ready to give up. No guts. . . . He becomes aware of women whispering.

"This tape is about through." It is Judy Dakar. "Isn't that enough? He's just repeating."

"Wait," murmurs Lady Blue.

"And she brought forth a man child to rule the nations with a rod of iron, Revelations twelve five," Dave says, louder. His eyes are open now, staring intently at the crucifix. *"For God so loved the world that he sent his only begotten son."*

Lady Blue nods; Judy pushes off toward Dave. Lorimer understands, protest rising in his throat. They mustn't do that to Dave, treating him like an animal for Christ's sake, a man—

"Dave! Look out, don't let her get near you!" he shouts.

"May I look, Major? It's beautiful, what is it?" Judy is coasting close, her hand out toward the crucifix.

"She's got a hypo, watch it!"

But Dave has already wheeled round. "Do not profane, woman!"

He thrusts the cross at her like a weapon, so menacing that she recoils in mid-air and shows the glinting needle in her hand.

"Serpent!" He kicks her shoulder away, sending himself upward. "Blasphemer. All right," he snaps in his ordinary voice, "there's going to be some order around here starting now. Get over by that wall, all of you."

Astounded, Lorimer sees that Dave actually has a weapon in his other hand, a small grey handgun. He must have had it since Houston. Hope and ataraxia shrivel away, he is shocked into desperate reality.

"Major Davis," Lady Blue is saying. She is floating right at him, they all are, right at the gun. Oh god, do they know what it is?

"Stop!" he shouts at them. "Do what he says, for god's sake. That's a ballistic weapon, it can kill you. It shoots metal slugs." He begins edging toward Dave along the vines.

169

"Stand back." Dave gestures with the gun. "I am taking command of this ship in the name of the United States of America under God."

"Dave, put that gun away. You don't want to shoot people."

Dave sees him, swings the gun around. "I warn you, Lorimer, get over there with them. Geirr's a man, when he sobers up." He looks at the women still drifting puzzledly toward him and understands. "All right, lesson one. Watch this."

He takes deliberate aim at the iguana cages and fires. There is a pinging crack. A lizard explodes bloodily, voices cry out. A loud mechanical warble starts up and overrides everything.

"A leak!" Two bodies go streaking toward the far end, everybody is moving. In the confusion Lorimer sees Dave calmly pulling himself back to the hatchway behind them, his gun ready. He pushes frantically across the tool rack to cut him off. A spray cannister comes loose in his grip, leaving him kicking in the air. The alarm warble dies.

"You will stay here until I decide to send for you," Dave announces. He has reached the hatch, is pulling the massive lock door around. It will seal off the pod, Lorimer realises.

"Don't do it, Dave! Listen to me, you're going to kill us all." Lorimer's own internal alarms are shaking him, he knows now what all that damned volleyball has been for and he is scared to death. "Dave, listen to me!"

"Shut up." The gun swings toward him. The door is moving. Lorimer gets a foot on solidity.

"Duck! It's a bomb!" With all his strength he hurls the massive cannister at Dave's head and launches himself after it.

"Look out!" And he is sailing helplessly in slow motion, hearing the gun go off again, voices yelling. Dave must have missed him, overhead shots are tough—and then he is doubling downwards, grabbing hair. A hard blow strikes his gut, it is Dave's leg kicking past him but he has his arm under the beard, the big man bucking like a bull, throwing him around.

"Get the gun, get it!" People are bumping him, getting hit. Just as his hold slips a hand snakes by him onto Dave's shoulder and they are colliding into the hatch door in a tangle. Dave's body is suddenly no longer at war.

Lorimer pushes free, sees Dave's contorted face tip slowly backward looking at him.

"Judas—"

The eyes close. It is over.

Lorimer looks around. Lady Blue is holding the gun, sighting down the barrel.

"Put that down," he gasps, winded. She goes on examining it.

"Hey, thanks!" Andy—Kay—grins lopsidedly at him, rubbing his jaw. They are all smiling, speaking warmly to him, feeling themselves, their torn clothes. Judy Dakar has a black eye starting, Connie holds a shattered iguana by the tail.

Beside him Dave drifts breathing stertorously, his blind face pointing at the sun. *Judas* . . . Lorimer feels the last shield break inside him, desolation flooding in. *On the deck my captain lies.*

Andy-who-is-not-a-man comes over and matter-of-factly zips up Dave's jacket, takes hold of it and begins to tow him out. Judy Dakar stops them long enough to wrap the crucifix chain around his hand. Somebody laughs, not unkindly, as they go by.

For an instant Lorimer is back in that Evanston toilet. But they are gone, all the little giggling girls. All gone forever, gone with the big boys waiting outside to jeer at him. Bud is right, he thinks. Nothing counts any more. Grief and anger hammer at him. He knows now what he has been dreading: not their vulnerability, his.

"They were good men," he says bitterly. "They aren't bad men. You don't know what bad means. You did it to them, you broke them down. You made them do crazy things. Was it interesting? Did you learn enough?" His voice is trying to shake. "Everybody has aggressive fantasies. They didn't act on them. Never. Until you poisoned them."

They gaze at him in silence. "But nobody does," Connie says finally. "I mean, the fantasies."

"They were good men," Lorimer repeats elegiacally. He knows he is speaking for it all, for Dave's Father, for Bud's manhood, for himself, for Cro-Magnon, for the dinosaurs too, maybe. "I'm a man. By god yes, I'm angry. I have a right. We gave you all this, we made it all. We built your precious civilisation and your knowledge and comfort and medicines and your dreams. All of it. We protected you, we worked our balls off keeping you and your kids. It was hard. It was a fight, a bloody fight all the way. We're tough. We had to be, can't you understand? Can't you for Christ's sake understand that?"

Another silence.

"We're trying," Lady Blue sighs. "We are trying, Doctor Lorimer. Of course we enjoy your inventions and we do appreciate your evolutionary role. But you must see there's a problem. As I understand it, what you protected people from was largely other males, wasn't it? We've just had an extraordinary demonstration. You have brought history to life for us." Her wrinkled brown eyes smile at him; a small, tea-colored matron holding an obsolete artefact.

"But the fighting is long over. It ended when you did, I believe. We can hardly turn you loose on Earth, and we simply have no facilities for people with your emotional problems."

"Besides, we don't think you'd be very happy," Judy Dakar adds earnestly.

"We could clone them," says Connie. "I know there's people who would volunteer to mother. The young ones might be all right, we could try."

"We've been *over* all that." Judy Paris is drinking from the water tank. She rinses and spits into the soil bed, looking worriedly at Lorimer. "We ought to take care of that leak now, we can talk tomorrow. And tomorrow and tomorrow." She smiles at him, unselfconsciously rubbing her crotch. "I'm sure a lot of people will want to meet you."

"Put us on an island," Lorimer says wearily. "On three islands." That look; he knows that look of preoccupied compassion. His mother and sister had looked just like that the time the diseased kitten came in the yard. They had comforted it and fed it and tenderly taken it to the vet to be gassed.

An acute, complex longing for the women he has known grips him. Ginny . . . dear god. His sister Amy. Poor Amy, she was good to him when they were kids. His mouth twists.

"Your problem is," he says, "if you take the risk of giving us equal rights, what could we possibly contribute?"

"Precisely," says Lady Blue. They all smile at him relievedly, not understanding that he isn't.

172

"I think I'll have that antidote now," he says.

Connie floats toward him, a big, warm-hearted, utterly alien woman. "I thought you'd like yours in a bulb." She smiles kindly.

"Thank you." He takes the small, pink bulb. "Just tell me," he says to Lady Blue, who is looking at the bullet gashes, "what do you call yourselves? Women's World? Liberation? Amazonia?"

"Why, we call ourselves human beings." Her eyes twinkle absently at him, go back to the bullet marks. "Humanity, mankind." She shrugs. "The human race."

The drink tastes cool going down, something like peace and freedom, he thinks. Or death.

The author of some twenty sf novels and story collections, **Kate Wilhelm** is recognized as one of the finest talents currently working in science fiction. She won a Nebula Award in 1968 for "The Planners," and the Hugo Award in 1978 for the novel *Where Late the Sweet Birds Sang*. Notable story collections include *The Infinity Box* (1975) and *Somerset Dreams and Other Fictions* (1978). Her most recent book is *Juniper Time* (1979).

"Where Have You Been, Billy Boy, Billy Boy?" is one of the most quietly frightening stories you will ever read.

Where Have You Been, Billy Boy, Billy Boy?

BY KATE WILHELM

His building had fifty-nine floors. The outer walls were dark green marble with black trim; they had slit windows, not to aid visibility, but for aesthetic purposes. The slits reflected the evening sun and gleamed gold, they were silver in the morning, they sparkled and shone at times, then again they were merely black. The marble went up to about the third floor. It was very difficult to tell from the outside just how much of the building was faced with the polished marble, but surely not more than three floors. So wasteful to have carried it farther. From that point, not yet determined, but about the third floor, to the top of the building was grey. They had done the slit windows all the way. Sometimes it looked like corduroy. Sometimes it looked like the building was dripping gold.

There were three very broad, shallow steps that led to the entrance of the building. Like the windows, the steps were ornamental. The building just as easily could have been level with the street. The step risers were less than six inches, possibly five, and were actually awkward, between steps and a level surface. There were brass planters in the steps, four feet wide, nine or ten feet long. One year the plants had been changed twenty-three times. They all died. Cigarette butts stuck out of the dirt, and gum wrappers, and drink cans, flattened or squashed into shapes that were topologically rather pleasing. They lay about the plants like fallen blossoms, colorful, not really hideous except that training said so.

The doors. Revolving doors, three. Two double doors with ten feet of air space between them. Four air walls. Bill never did understand how or why they worked; in the summer the air was cool, in the winter, hot. There was a definite line that separated the outside from the inside, even if it was invisible. The inside was different.

He walked alone, toward the elevators. No elevators went to all floors. There were banks that went from ground zero to eight, others that stopped first at nine and went up to fifteen, and so on. His first stop was thirty-four. He assumed that it continued after he left it at thirty-eight. The button lights indicated that it was prepared to rise another four floors.

Every morning from the time he left his spacious and empty apartment, got through the subway, across town on the bus, up the three low steps, and the elevators that went from the thirty-fourth floor to at least the thirty-eighth floor, he was quite alone.

"Let's take it again, something's wrong with the
175

tempo. . . ." Rolly shook his long hair and fingered his beard.

"How about trying it with the drums?" Mole said. Lettered on the bass drum was: THE PICKLE DOOR.

Bill stood up, pushing his electric organ away from him. "Look, guys, let me set the stage. A guy alone, walking the streets. *Alone*. Dig? His girl's gone. Left him flat. No reason. Nothing. And there's not another one in the world for him." He shrugged at the skepticism. "Look, you want to hit the old crowd or not? You want to eat for a change? You want to get out of this stinking basement (no offense, Mole) with its rats that've evolved into five-foot-ten pink-skinned brown-suited squinty-eyed blood-sucking saber-toothed rodents, for crissakes? No more fires, no more busts, no more gas attacks, just one winter of being warm and dry."

"No drums?"

"No drums! You asshole. Soft. Melancholic. Sad. Wistful. Now. *Go!*"

They took it from the top.

The apartment was clean. They had scraped the paint off down to bare wood and started over with it. Bill had had to put up wallboard here and there where the plaster crumbled when they had begun to scour the walls, but it had been worth it. He had divided the room with wallboard at the same time, and had not been forced to get a permit, with the pages of questions to be answered first. They called it a three-room apartment now. After the streets, in that section of the lower East Side, it was like entering another world. Clean walls, clean wood, bare, gleaming floors with small washable, and often washed, scatter rugs. And they had used their total debt limit for an air-conditioner so that they didn't have to worry about the daily pollution index, at least not after they got home from work. They both hated to leave their own rooms even to go down the hall to the bathroom. In the beginning they had tried to keep that clean, but they had given up.

She worked half-days only. She would be eligible for a full-time job as soon as the baby was registered in a nursery at three. She met him at the door and kissed him, then drew back and said, "A few minutes ago Susan was looking at television with me, and as plain as day she said, 'NBC.' Can you imagine? And only two."

Susan started to cry and continued to cry through the newscast. She did it almost every night. It was her daily crying time, they agreed.

Billy was ten and his mother was thirty-five and didn't look it, his father was forty and did look it. He was a professor with Grave Responsibilities and Moral Convictions. It was almost Christmas. Every year Billy's mother took him to town to look at the windows and shop for Father and have a hot-fudge sundae and buy an early, not-secret gift for him. To ease the anticipation pains.

It was snowing lightly and the train was coming around the mountain in miniature America with flags on almost all the houses and an army standing at attention while a band of inches-high red-white-and-blue members played silent music. Tiny Christmas trees blinked and Santa Clauses swayed holding bulging stomachs. The train flashed around a hill out of sight and the skaters waltzed and the band played and the tree lights blinked and the snow fell gently. But now the store window's music was drowned by a roaring sound from the other end of the street and he felt his mother's hand tugging at him.

"Come on, Billy. Let's go inside. It looks like a demonstration."

He stared at the window, then down the street where the cars were suddenly obliterated by what looked like a black tidal wave.

Rolly twanged a discord. He looked at Bill helplessly. "I just don't dig it. I mean, it's going to put them to sleep. It's not like there's only one chick in the world."

"It ain't that," Mole said. "You know what it is. Crap. Shit. So he moons over a bird. So what?"

Bill ran his thumb over the keys, and then spun around. "Look, I listened to records at the library for three solid weeks, five-year-old records, ten-year-old records, twenty-year-old records. There hasn't been anything like this for ten years, fifteen years. So what's it going to cost to gamble on it now? We can do it under a moony name. Dreamers. Or, The

Stardusters. Something corny. Or, The Sound. That's pretty good. Nostalgia, that's what we'll give them. For a time when a guy could just go out and walk up and down the streets if he wanted to."

On Monday, Wednesday, and Friday mornings they had meetings. And on Tuesday and Thursday afternoons they had meetings. The table was round. This month Henry Moreno was chairman. They discussed and planned for the next five years, so that no matter what the date, Bill's thoughts were supposed to be geared to five years in the future. Because We Plan Your Tomorrow—his department's motto.

"Say, who was it who came up with the idea of a self-rolling toothpaste tube?" Henry asked, during a pause in the proceedings.

He glanced at Walter Neery, who shrugged and looked blank. The inquiring gaze went around the table and no one suggested an answer. When it was Bill's turn to look blank, he did. He could have said, "Matt's idea." That would have singled out Matt for criticism. And the next time he might be the one so named. So he looked blank, and Henry sighed and murmured, "Too bad. Wanted to put his name down for a bonus. But that's the way it goes. Joint efforts, joint decisions, joint benefits. Right, fellows?"

They nodded. Bill wondered if anyone else could turn off the world. He doubted it. They were all too preoccupied with Creating A Better World—the company's motto. "Like a phoenix," the small print went on, "we will rise again to fulfill the dreams of past generations. . . ."

"Anyway," Henry said, "market research has finished the survey. There will be a definite demand for the self-rolling tube. R and D is kicking it around now. And this department has earned another bonus point."

The eleven-o'clock newscast rehashed the same items that the baby had cried through earlier. Casualty figures remained stable. The Senate had finished all the legislation that the President had asked for in what was called the most efficient, most farsighted, most patriotic assembly ever gathered in Washington. The air inversion over London had claimed the ten-thousandth victim that morning. Washington announced the plans to recall the history books in all elementary and secondary schools to correct mistakes discovered by the Advisory Committee on Education.

"Are you certain that you won't mind if Dad comes here for a few weeks, just until he gets his bearings again?"

"You know I don't mind." She was applying a contact patch to his coveralls, and didn't look up.

"I'm sure that it won't be for long. He'll apply for a permit to move right away. He's pretty independent."

"Don't be so apologetic. I knew about him when we were married. It's all right. He made a mistake, and he's paid. I certainly don't hold that against him. Here, will this hold, do you think?"

He took the coveralls from her and put them down. "Let's turn off that blasted set and go to bed. We'll have our room to ourselves just five more nights before he gets here."

"With the curtain up we'll never know the baby's in there. Wait a minute. I'd better check the schedule. I forget if I turned it on when I first came home." He watched her check off the public-interest programs that had been on the air. She frowned over the schedule and he knew that she had forgotten. Rumor said that you could alter the meter, but he didn't know how, and he didn't know anyone who did.

"It's all right," he said. "Leave it alone. I'll turn it off later. Come on." So they made love in the bedroom, and in the other room the set talked on and on about the patience of the government and the intransigence of the enemy at the conference table, and about the rules and regulations regarding the recently passed Right to Inspect Bill.

Billy eavesdropped on his parents at every opportunity. It was a game with him, but a serious game. He had trouble imagining them without him, and was almost convinced that they discussed him exclusively when he was absent. They sat on the couch listening to a small tape recorder. And Billy became cramped and chilled from kneeling on the hall floor in his pajamas, also listening, thoroughly bored.

"Gentlemen, this is an executive session, you all understand. No word of what gets said in this room will be carried beyond those doors, nor will it appear in any report. Now, we have all heard the evidence of the experts. We have studied the charts, and the data. Gentlemen, unless we act immediately with every measure put forth by Dr. Gordon, our entire civilization is doomed."

"Now, Roger. Jest take it easy, son. Doctuh, do I understand you to say that unless each of those measures is enacted almost immediately and with absolute thoroughness, then there's no hope at all to save mankind?"

"No, sir. What I said, Senator, is that unless these things are done now, today, we'll all die. Our children will die. Their children won't be born. No 'almost,' Senator. No qualifications at all."

"I see, Doctuh. I see. You've heard of Malthews? Haven't you, suh?"

"Malthus? The Malthusian theory? Yes, sir, I have."

"Yes. You see, son, I jest read a little bit about this Malthews and it seems to me that he was saying a hundred years ago almost exactly what you're saying again today. Now, you see, son, how confusing this can get to an old non-scientist like me."

"Senator, I could recapitulate all the evidence you have heard and seen, but we have done that. We've been holding these meetings six months now. You know what the consensus of the participating scientists is. Not simply the population explosion, but the concomitant pollution, which was not foreseen by Malthus, sir. That is our concern. Not only here in the States, but around the world. The only real division we have had, sir, is in the timetable for the disaster that we all see. And about half of us think that even if we did initiate those steps immediately, it would still be too late. That the only way to save any part of mankind is through the decimation of our population now. Halve it. In order to save half. Not through war that would leave ruins and a weakened and irradiated billion people, but through a humane program that would leave the technology intact, and the survivors healthy and aware of the sacrifice of the dead. They would have to have leadership that would infuse them with a new sense of purpose."

"Doctuh, for weeks now something has been pestering at me. Jest won't go way, no, suh. Now in this here executive session, without anyone in here taking notes, and no tape recorders going, no stenographers. Jest between us here now, suh, I want to get this off my chest. You, suh, Doctuh Gordon, are looney."

One day they didn't come back when he entered the office. For the first time since discovery of the wondrous gift that he had, the gift was frightening. He stopped and stared at the empty office, the desks without girls, the files without clerks, the water fountains without two or three natty young men. Slowly, very carefully, he made his way past his secretary's empty chair, into his small office, where a memo reminded him that today the chairman from R&D would visit the regular Friday-morning conference. He went to the meeting and sat down in his customary chair, in an empty room. Once he felt compelled to speak, which he did, immediately forgetting what it was that he said. He left promptly at twelve and returned to his office, where he got his hat and coat. He stopped then. He was supposed to have lunch with Walter Neery and someone from Sales. He went through all the motions, arriving at the elevators where they were to meet at precisely twelve ten, taking the empty car down, walking alone around the corner to a French restaurant that they always used when it was on expense account.

He ate alone, but now and then made a comment to the air. He didn't know what happened to the bill. It came and went again, as food had done. Back in his office he clutched his head for a long time, and finally when he put his hands down again, he was smiling. It really was much better this way.

"Billy, don't let go of my hand! Whatever happens, don't let go!"

They weren't going to reach the door to the store. Too many people with the same idea, and the demonstrators were filling the street and the sidewalks, and the police were coming from the other direction with sirens blaring and there were popping noises not at all like guns or even windows breaking. And over it all the loudspeakers played "Silent Night" and when he was finished "The Twelve Days of Christmas" and the train was coming over the mountain again.

"Honey, is it true that they have a way of telling if you're in the room with the TV or not?"

"No. Where'd you hear such a crazy thing?"

"Oh, some of the girls at work. You know. I mean it wouldn't do much good to turn it on and leave it on all the time if they knew whether or not you're watching it too."

"Well, forget it. Another rumor."

"I wonder who starts such rumors. Haven't you ever wondered just where they come from, Bill?"

"Washington. What's to wonder? Is the room ready for him?"

"Yes. Do you think he'll be bitter?"

"About what? He made the speeches. He advocated genocide, or something. He never denied it. And they found him guilty of sedition. What's he got to be bitter about?"

"That sounds good. Keep it like that. Now let's try it again from the top. Exactly the same way. I'll get it on the recorder and then we'll decide if that's what we want to tape. Okay, guys."

They played it again, then listened to it. The Mole, whose basement room they used for practice, held his nose and made retching motions. But Rolly stared at Bill thoughtfully. "Yeah," he said. "Yeah. A guy alone, not in a compound or nothing, just alone, walking in the city at nighttime. The dumb bastards will eat their hearts out. They'll think it's romantic. Okay, let's make the master tape tomorrow." They broke up then.

Rolly and Bill stayed close together, and the handmade pipe gun in Bill's pocket was cool against his hand as they walked down the street. Rhonda joined them at The Joint and they stayed there until the crowds thinned out after three and then went to Bill's room. They skirted a bunch of blacks, twenty or twenty-five of them, conscious of the watchful eyes until they turned the corner. At his street Bill stopped again, briefly. An unmarked tank, with a uniformed skinhead visible through the observation bubble, was moving slowly down the street, sweeping for mines. They ducked into a doorway and waited for it to finish and rumble away. From the other end of the street a lone car appeared, headed for the tank. Bill looked up for the copter that he could hear faintly over the din of the city noise. He couldn't find its lights in the murky sky that seemed supported by the tops of the buildings.

"Christ!" he said in disgust. "Come on, let's go in the back way." He grabbed Rhonda's arm and nearly pulled her off her feet when she resisted.

"I want to watch."

"Come on. The copter will pick you off if you're on the street."

"What in hell's wrong with you guys tonight?" Rhonda asked furiously, inside the building. "Pussyfooting around like a couple of blows from Missouri or something."

"Wanta stay in one piece for just a little while, doll," Rolly said, panting. "Long enough to cash in and live it up for a change."

She marched into Bill's room and tossed a gas grenade down on a chair. Bill winced. One day when she did that, it would go. She hooked her thumbs under the tabs on her high pants and opened the twin zippers that let the pants fall down in two pieces around her knees. She kicked them off. The sounds of a pitched battle from the far end of the street erupted, and they all listened, identifying the equipment being used: gas bombs, homemade mines, automatic hand weapons, the whine of gas launchers. They relaxed.

"I can see it now," she said. "The Pickle Door, high as clouds on green stuff, living it up in a compound, manning the guns, taking guided tours of the city in armored buses. Funneeeee. They'll let you in the day it rains diamonds."

"You did what you could, darling. God knows you tried to make them understand."

"And what good will that do in ten years, or fifteen years? Who's going to say, 'Oh, yes, Doctuh Gordon tried to make them see that the catastrophe was already on the way, a tiny snowball high on the slope'?"

"Sh, darling. I don't think Billy's asleep yet. He's all excited about going to town tomorrow. Christmas. Your coming home. It's all been too much for him too fast."

"You don't believe me, do you? Not even you."

"It isn't that. But what can I do? Except go on living. Try to keep us all alive and healthy and reasonably happy? What else can I do? What else can *you* do?"

"Write another book. Make more speeches. Find something that'll kill fifty percent of the population, without harming the other fifty percent."

"William!"

"Can you convince me that it's wrong? Isn't it better to lose half than to lose all? Isn't it?"

"And what about Billy?"

Billy, shivering on the floor outside the door, fell asleep waiting for the answer to the question.

They came back now and then. Not often, and they didn't stay. Someone would bob into his line of vision, then float out again before he could focus on the image. He realized that there was a mechanism working for him, something that warned him, or guided him, so that he never stumbled over any of them, or missed a cue, although he wasn't aware of them as they came. Occasionally he felt that he should say something or other, and when he did, the feeling of unease that had bothered him went away.

He hadn't seen a child for over a month. He walked through the park now without seeing the rows on rows of perambulators, the toddlers, the pre-schoolers, the elementary-school children, as numerous as ants. Breeding like cockroaches, they were trying to fill the gap with babies. No one stared at him wondering if he was William Gordon's son, wondering why he wasn't married yet, why he didn't have four, five, six children yet. He was certain that he was as hard for them to see as they were for him. He felt safe. He liked the silent world.

Bill stared at the ceiling and tried not to hear the television. He tried not to think about the evening, and could think of nothing else.

Her whisper: "He's so old. I thought he was younger."

"He always looked older than he was. He's only fifty-five."

Their bed touched the curtain that separated this half of the room from the baby's half. He could hear every snuffle that the baby made, every change in her breathing, every whimper and wheeze. And on the other side of the wallboard, *he* was listening to the television, chuckling at it, talking back. Bill's lips tightened. *He* had laughed a bit louder at a statement attributed to the President. He would get them all in trouble. He was a crazy, senile, babbling old man. They would have to take that into account, if he went on like that in front of anyone. They must know what they had done to him. . . . Bill heard his teeth grinding before he was aware of the movement of his jaw. What had they done to him? He was a prattling moron.

But why had he cried? What had he meant?

"I couldn't do it. I knew we should, that we could. I had the stuff. A last chance, that's what I told them. Just listen and do something now. A last chance. And when the time came, I couldn't do anything. They came and took away Billy and then they found it. We had it all. It would have been simple. I knew what to do. We had the stuff, all we needed. And they still trusted us enough. And I couldn't do it!" Then he had cried.

Why?

"Billy! Billy!" He couldn't see her at all. He was being pushed and he knew that he didn't dare fall. They'd walk on him. Boots cowboy boots snow boots police boots. He couldn't make out any of their faces they were all too close and he was too short. He couldn't tell the police from the marchers. The spectators from the demonstrators. He couldn't hear her screams any longer. There was one long scream in his ears and one long smear of red before his eyes. And a burning pain sharp burning pain of a cut or a lump or something that made him feel strange and lightheaded and not able to think. He couldn't breathe and his eyes were on fire and he was afraid to touch them because he might rub it in and he couldn't stop himself rubbing his eyes hearing the piercing scream that wouldn't end choking coughing being sick adding the smell of vomit to the scream and the red smear. Her face kept swimming before his burning eyes. White wide-eyed with a cut that started somewhere in her hair and went down her check down into her neck and blood on her lips like lipstick on Halloween coming down the corner of her mouth down her skin.

He wondered how long before someone noticed that he was acting strangely, or noticed that he wasn't really there much of the time. Promising young executive missing, without a clue. Would someone else move into his nice, airy apartment overlooking the Hudson? Would they put someone else in his office? Would he wander in one day and sit down in the new man's lap and never even realize it?

That night he burned all his father's notes, his diary, the newspaper clippings. He added them one page at a time, playing the "He loves me, loves me not" game. But he said, "He was right. He was wrong." Toward the end he dozed and lost track. And knew that there was no way he would ever know.

Billy couldn't tell which side was which. He was being swept along with people and when he tried to hold on to someone he was flung off and couldn't get his balance again and he fell and the boots did walk on him. And he couldn't tell whose boots they had been.

Bill found his father the next morning. He had hung himself from the water pipe in the kitchen half of his room. There was only an inch of space between his feet and the floor. If he had been an inch taller, he wouldn't have been able to do it.

Bill stared at him, hating him for doing it there, then. Before he touched the body he turned on the TV set. The meter would be waiting and there'd be enough questions without having them add any more about why they were avoiding the news. Then he went out to the corner phone and called the police, listening absently to the beep-beep that said the call was being recorded. A platoon of adolescents in grey uniforms marched by on their way to school. They didn't turn their heads to look at him in the booth.

Bill stiffened at the sound of a police tank starting the high-pitched wail of the tear-gas launcher. He relaxed again. It was at least a block away.

"Tell me how you got the scars, Bill," Rhonda said, tracing the one that started at his forehead and ended in his eyebrow. "Your old man?"

"No. I told you, he was killed during the Christmas riots. My old man and my mother, or so they said." He fingered the scars, then shook his head hard. "I told you I don't remember. An accident, or something. It doesn't signify." He sat up in the bed. "Listen, I've been thinking. We'd go out of our skulls in a compound. Right? How about a trailer, an armored trailer with a grenade launcher? We could take a trip. Maybe even make it out to the coast."

"Yeah, baby," Rhonda said, sitting up too, her eyes sparkling. "I heard that there are some small compounds out in the boonies that one guy with a launcher could take all by himself."

Theodore Sturgeon was one of the great figures of science fiction's "Golden Age." He was prolific, creative, and a genuine craftsman. Stories like "It" (1940), "Microcosmic God" (1941), and "More Than Human" (1953) are classics that will live forever. Although he wrote less as the years went by, his work was always excellent, and frequently different.

This remarkable story was done for Harlan Ellison's famous *Dangerous Visions* (1967).

If All Men Were Brothers, Would You Let One Marry Your Sister?

BY THEODORE STURGEON

The Sun went Nova in the year 33 A.E. "A.E." means "After the Exodus." You might say the Exodus was a century and a half or so A.D. if "A.D." means "After the Drive." The Drive, to avoid technicalities, was a device somewhat simpler than Woman and considerably more complicated than sex, which caused its vessel to cease to exist *here* while simultaneously appearing *there*, by-passing the limitations imposed by the speed of light. One might compose a quite impressive account of astrogation involving the Drive, with all the details of orientation *here* and *there* and the somewhat philosophical difficulties of establishing the relationships between them, but this is not that kind of a science fiction story.

It suits our purposes rather to state that the Sun went Nova with plenty of warning, that the first fifty years A.D. were spent in improving the Drive and exploring with unmanned vehicles which located many planets suitable for human settlement, and that the next hundred years were spent in getting humanity ready to leave. Naturally there developed a number of ideological groups with a most interesting assortment of plans for one Perfect Culture or another, most of which were at bitter odds with all the rest. The Drive, however, had presented Earth with so copious a supply of new worlds, with insignificant subjective distances between them and the parent, that dissidents need not make much of their dissent, but need merely file for another world and they would get it. The comparisons between the various cultural theories are pretty fascinating, but this is not that kind of a science fiction story either. Not quite.

Anyway, what happened was that, with a margin of a little more than three decades, Terra depopulated itself by its many thousands of ships to its hundreds of worlds (leaving behind, of course, certain die-hards who died, of course, certainly) and the new worlds were established with varying degrees of bravery and a pretty wide representation across the success scale.

It happened, however (in ways much too recondite to be described in this kind of a science fiction story), that Drive Central on Earth, a computer central, was not only the sole means of keeping track of all the worlds; it was their only means of keeping track with one another; and when this installation added its bright brief speck to the ocean of Novaglare, there simply was no way for all the worlds to find one another without the arduous process of unmanned Drive-ships and search. It took a long while for any of the new

189

worlds to develop the necessary technology, and an even longer while for it to be productively operational, but at length, on a planet which called itself Terratu (the suffix meaning both "too" and "2") because it happened to be the third planet of a GO-type sun, there appeared something called the Archives, a sort of index and clearinghouse for all known inhabited worlds, which made this planet the communications central and general dispatcher for trade with them all and their trade with one another—a great convenience for everyone. A side result, of course, was the conviction on Terratu that, being a communications central, it was also central to the universe and therefore should control it, but then, that is the occupational hazard of all conscious entities.

We are now in a position to determine just what sort of a science fiction story this really is.

"Charli Bux," snapped Charli Bux, "to see the Archive Master."

"Certainly," said the pretty girl at the desk, in the cool tones reserved by pretty girls for use on hurried and indignant visitors who are clearly unaware, or uncaring, that the girl is pretty. "Have you an appointment?"

He seemed like such a nice young man in spite of his hurry and his indignation. The way, however, in which he concealed all his niceness by bringing his narrowed eyes finally to rest on her upturned face, and still showed no signs of appreciating her pretty-girlhood, made her quite as not-pretty as he was not-nice.

"Have you," he asked coldly, "an appointment book?"

She had no response to that, because she had such a book; it lay open in front of her. She put a golden and escalloped fingernail on his name therein inscribed, compared it and his face with negative enthusiasm, and ran the fingernail across to the time noted. She glanced at the clockface set into her desk, passed her hand over a stud, and said, "A Mr. Charli uh Bux to see you, Archive Master."

"Send him in," said the stud.

"You may go in now."

"I know," he said shortly.

"I don't like you."

"What?" he said; but he was thinking about something else,

and before she could repeat the remark he had disappeared through the inner door.

The Archive Master had been around long enough to expect courtesy, respect, and submission, to get these things, and to like them. Charli Bux slammed into the room, banged a folio down on the desk, sat down uninvited, leaned forward and roared redly, "Goddamit—"

The Archive Master was not surprised because he had been warned. He had planned exactly what he would do to handle this brash young man, but faced with the size of the Bux temper, he found his plans somewhat less useful than worthless. Now he was surprised, because a single glance at his gaping mouth and feebly fluttering hands—a gesture he thought he had lost and forgotten long ago—accomplished what no amount of planning could have done.

"Oh-h-h . . . bitchballs," growled Bux, his anger visibly deflating. "Buggerly hangin' bumpin' *bitch*balls." He looked across at the old man's horrified eyebrows and grinned blindingly. "I guess it's not your fault." The grin disappeared. "But of all the hydrocephalous, drool-toothed, cretinoid runarounds I have ever seen, this was the stupidest. Do you know how many offices I've been into and out of with this"—he banged the heavy folio—"since I got back?"

The Archive Master did, but, "How many?" he asked.

"Too many, but only half as many as I went to before I went to Vexvelt." With which he shut his lips with a snap and leaned forward again, beaming his bright penetrating gaze at the old man like twin lasers. The Archive Master found himself striving not to be the first to turn away, but the effort made him lean slowly back and back, until he brought up against his chair cushions with his chin up a little high. He began to feel a little ridiculous, as if he had been bamboozled into Indian wrestling with some stranger's valet.

It was Charli Bux who turned away first, but it was not the old man's victory, for the gaze came off his eyes as tangibly as a pressing palm might have come off his chest, and he literally slumped forward as the pressure came off. Yet if it was Charli Bux's victory, he seemed utterly unaware of it. "I think," he said after his long, concentrated pause, "that I'm going to tell you about that—about how I happened to get to Vexvelt. I wasn't going to—or at least, I was ready to tell

191

you only as much as I thought you needed to know. But I remember what I had to go through to get there, and I know what I've been going through since I got back, and it looks like the same thing. Well, it's not going to be the same thing. Here and now, the runaround stops. What takes its place I don't know, but by all the horns of all the owls in Hell's northeast, I have been pushed around my last push. All right?"

If this was a plea for agreement, the Archive Master did not know what he would be agreeing to. He said diplomatically, "I think you'd better begin somewhere." Then he added, not raising his voice, but with immense authority, "And quietly."

Charli Bux gave him a boom of laughter. "I never yet spent upwards of three minutes with anybody that they didn't shush me. Welcome to the Shush Charli Club, membership half the universe, potential membership, everybody else. And I'm sorry. I was born and brought up on Biluly where there's nothing but trade wind and split-rock ravines and surf, and the only way to whisper is to shout." He went on more quietly, "But what I'm talking about isn't that sort of shushing. I'm talking about a little thing here and a little thing there and adding them up and getting the idea that there's a planet nobody knows anything about."

"There are thousands—"

"I mean a planet nobody *wants* to know anything about."

"I suppose you've heard of Magdilla."

"Yes, with fourteen kinds of hallucinogenic microspores spread through the atmosphere, and carcinogens in the water. Nobody wants to go there, nobody wants anybody to go—but nobody stops you from getting information about it. No, I mean a planet not 99 per cent Terran Optimum, or 99 point 99, but so many nines that you might just as well shift your base reference and call Terra about 97 per cent in comparison."

"That would be a little like saying '102 per cent normal,'" said the Master smugly.

"If you like statistical scales better than the truth," Bux growled. "Air, water, climate, indigenous flora and fauna, and natural resources six nines or better, just as easy to get to as any place else—and nobody knows anything about it. Or if they do, they pretend they don't. And if you pin them down, they send you to another department."

The Archive Master spread his hands. "I would say the circumstances prove themselves. If there is no trade with this, uh, remarkable place, it indicates that whatever it has is just as easily secured through established routes."

Bux shouted, "In a pig's bloody and protruding—" and then checked himself and wagged his head ruefully. "Sorry again, Archive Master, but I just been too mad about this for too long. What you just said is like a couple troglodytes sitting around saying there's no use building a house because everybody's living in caves." Seeing the closed eyes, the long white fingers tender on the white temples, Bux said, "I said I was sorry I yelled like that."

"In every city," said the Archive Master patiently, "on every settled human planet in all the known universe, there is a free public clinic where stress reactions of any sort may be diagnosed, treated or prescribed for, speedily, effectively, and with dignity. I trust you will not regard it as an intrusion on your privacy if I make the admittedly non-professional observation (you see, I do not pretend to be a therapist) that there are times when a citizen is not himself aware that he is under stress, even though it may be clearly, perhaps painfully obvious to others. It would not be a discourtesy, would it, or an unkindness, for some understanding stranger to suggest to such a citizen that—"

"What you're saying, all wrapped up in words, is I ought to go have my head candled."

"By no means. I am not qualified. I did, however, think that a visit to a clinic—there's one just a step away from here—might make—ah—communications between us more possible. I would be glad to arrange another appointment for you, when you're feeling better. That is to say, when you are . . . ah . . ." He finished with a bleak smile and reached toward the calling stud.

Moving almost like a Drive-ship, Bux seemed to cease to exist on the visitor's chair and reappeared instantaneously at the side of the desk, a long thick arm extended and a meaty hand blocking the way to the stud. "Hear me out first," he said, softly. Really softly. It was a much more astonishing

193

thing than if the Archive Master had trumpeted like an elephant. "Hear me out. Please."

The old man withdrew his hand, but folded it with the other and set the neat stack of fingers on the edge of the desk. It looked like stubbornness. "I have a limited amount of time, and your folio is very large."

"It's large because I'm a bird dog for detail—that's not a brag, it's a defect: sometimes I just don't know when to quit. I can make the point quick enough—all that material just supports it. Maybe a tenth as much would do, but you see, I—well, I give a damn. I really give a high, wide, heavy damn about this. Anyway—you just pushed the right button in Charli Bux. 'Make communication between us more possible.' Well, all right. I won't cuss, I won't holler, and I won't take long."

"Can you do all these things?"

"You're goddam—whoa, Charli." He flashed the thirty-thousand-candlepower smile and then hung his head and took a deep breath. He looked up again and said quietly, "I certainly can, sir."

"Well, then." The Archive Master waved him back to the visitor's chair: Charli Bux, even a contrite Charli Bux, stood just too tall and too wide. But once seated, he sat silent for so long that the old man shifted impatiently. Charli Bux looked up alertly, and said, "Just getting it sorted out, sir. A good deal of it's going to sound as if you could diagnose me for a stun-shot and a good long stay at the funny farm, yeah, and that without being modest about your professional knowledge. I read a story once about a little girl was afraid of the dark because there was a little hairy purple man with poison fangs in the closet, and everybody kept telling her no, no, there's no such thing, be sensible, be brave. So they found her dead with like snakebite and her dog killed a little hairy purple and so on. Now if I told you there was some sort of a conspiracy to keep me from getting information about a planet, and I finally got mad enough to go there and see for myself, and 'They' did their best to stop me; 'They' won me a sweepstake prize trip to somewhere else that would use up my vacation time; when I turned that down 'They' told me there was no Drive Guide orbiting the place, and it was too far to reach in real space (and that's a God, uh, doggone *lie*, sir!) and when I found a way to get there by hops, 'They' tangled up my credit records so I couldn't buy passage; why, then I can't say I'd blame you for peggin' me paranoid and doing me the kindness of getting me cured. Only thing was, these things did happen and they were not delusions, no matter what everybody plus two thirds of Charli Bux (by the time 'They' were done with me) believed. I had an ounce of evidence and I believed it. I had a ton of opinion saying otherwise. I tell you, sir, I *had* to go. I had to stand knee-deep in Vexvelt sweet grass with the cedar smell of a campfire and a warm wind in my face," *and my hands in the hands of a girl called Tyng, along with my heart and hope and a dazzling wonder colored like sunrise and tasting like tears,* "before I finally let myself believe I'd been right all along, and there is a planet called Vexvelt and it does have all the things I knew it had," *and more, more, oh, more than I'll ever tell you about, old man.* He fell silent, his gaze averted and luminous.

"What started you on this—this quest?"

Charli Bux threw up his big head and looked far away and back at some all-but-forgotten detail. "Huh!" 'D almost lost that in the clutter. Workin' for Interworld Bank & Trust, feeding a computer in the clearin'house. Not as dull as you might think. Happens I was a mineralogist for a spell, and the cargoes meant something to me besides a name, a quantity and a price. Huh!" came the surprised I've-found-it! little explosion. "I can tell you the very item. Feldspar. It's used in porcelain and glass, antique style. I got a sticky mind, I guess. Long as I'd been there, feldspar ground and bagged went for about twenty-five credits a ton at the docks. But here was one of our customers bringing it in for eight and a half F.O.B. I called the firm just to check; mind, I didn't care much, but a figure like that could color a statistical summary of imports and exports for years. The bookkeeper there ran a check and found it was so: eight and a half a ton, high-grade feldspar, ground and bagged. Some broker on Lethe: they hadn't been able to contact him again.

"It wasn't worth remembering until I bumped into another one. Niobium this time. Some call it columbium. Helps make steel stainless, among other things. I'd never seen a quotation for rod stock at less than a hundred and thirty-seven, but here was some—not much, mind you—at ninety credits *delivered*. And some sheets too, about 30 per cent less than I'd ever seen it before, freight paid. I checked that one out too. It was correct. Well-smelted and pure, the man said. I forgot that one too, or I thought I had. Then there was that space-hand." *Moxie Magiddle—honest!—that was his name. Squint-eyed little fellow with a great big laugh bulging the walls of the honkytonk out at the spaceport. Drank only alcohol and never touched a needle. Told me the one about the fellow had a big golden screwhead in his belly button. Told me about times and places all over—full of yarns, a wonderful gift for yarning.* "Just mentioned in passing that Lethe was one place where the law was 'Have Fun' and nobody ever broke it. The whole place just one big transfer point and rest-and-rehab. A water world with only one speck of land in the tropics. Always warm, always easy. No industry, no agriculture, just—well, services. Thousands of men spent hundreds of thousands of credits, a few dozen pocketed millions. Everybody happy. I mentioned the feldspar, I guess just so I would sound as if I knew something about Lethe too." *And laid a big fat egg, too. Moxie looked at me as if he hadn't seen me before and didn't like what he saw. If it was a lie I was telling it was a stupid one. "Y'don't dig feldspar out of a swamp, fella. You puttin' me on, or you kiddin' y'rself?" And a perfectly good evening dried up and blew away.* "He said it couldn't possibly have come from Lethe—it's a water world. I guess I could have forgotten that too but for the coffee beans. Blue Mountain Coffee, it was called; the label claimed it descended in an unbroken line from Old Earth, on an island called Jamaica. It went on to say that it could be grown only in high cool land in the tropics—a real mountain plant. I liked it better than any coffee I ever tasted but when I went back for more they were sold out. I got the manager to look in the records and traced it back through the Terratu wholesaler to the broker and then to the importer—I mean, I *liked* that coffee!

"And according to him, it came from Lethe. High cool mountain land and all. The port at Lethe was tropical all right, but to be cool it would have to have mountains that were really mountains.

"The feldspar that did, but couldn't have, come from

Lethe—and at those prices!—reminded me of the niobium, so I checked on that one too. Sure enough—Lethe again. You don't—you just do *not* get pure niobium rod and sheet without mines and smelters and mills.

"Next off-day I spent here at Archives and got the history of Lethe halfway back, I'll swear, to Ylem and the Big Bang. It was a swamp, it practically always has been a swamp, and something was wrong.

"Mind you, it was only a little something, and probably there was a good simple explanation. But little or not, it bothered me." *And besides, it had made me look like a horse's ass in front of a damn good man. Old man, if I told you how much time I hung around the spaceport looking for that bandy-legged little space-gnome, you'd stop me now and send for the stun-guns. Because I was obsessed—not a driving addiction kind of thing, but a very small deep splinter-in-the-toe kind of thing, that didn't hurt much but never failed to gig me every step I took. And then one day—oh, months later—there was old Moxie Magiddle, and he took the splinter out. Hyuh! Ol' Moxie . . . he didn't know me at first, he really didn't. Funny little guy, he has his brains rigged to forget anything he doesn't like—honestly forget it. That feldspar thing, when a fella he liked to drink with and yarn to showed up to be a know-it-all kind of liar, and to boot, too dumb to know he couldn't get away with it—well, that qualified Charli for zero minus the price of five man-hours of drinking. Then when I got him cornered—I all but wrestled him—and told about the feldspar and the niobium and now the mountain-grown coffee, all of it checked and cross-checked, billed, laded, shipped, insured—all of it absolutely Lethe and here's the goddam proof, why, he began to laugh till he cried, a little at himself, a little at the situation, and a whole lot at me. Then we had a long night of it and I drank alcohol and you know what? I'll never in life find out how Moxie Magiddle can hold so much liquor. But he told me where those shipments came from, and gave me a vague idea why nobody wanted much to admit it. And the name they call all male Vexveltians.* "I mentioned it one day to a cargo handler," Bux told the Archive Master, "and he solved the mystery— the feldspar and niobium and coffee came from Vexvelt and had been trasshipped at Lethe by local brokers, who, more often than not, get hold of some goods and turn them over to make a credit or so and dive back into the local forgetteries.

"But any planet which could make a profit on goods of this quality at such prices—transshipped, yet!—certainly could do much better direct. Also, niobium is Element 41, and Elkhart's Hypothesis has it that, on any planet where you find elements in Periods Three to Five, chances are you'll find 'em all. And that coffee! I used to lie awake at night wondering what they had on Vexvelt that they liked too much to ship, if they thought so little of their coffee that they'd let it out.

"Well, it was only natural that I came here to look up Vexvelt. Oh, it was listed at the bank, all right, but if there ever had been trade, it had been cleared out of the records long ago—we wipe the memory cells every fifty years on inactive items. I know at least that it's been wiped four times, but it could have been blank the last three.

"What do you think Archives has on Vexvelt?"

The Archive Master did not answer. He *knew* what Archives had on the subject of Vexvelt. He knew where it was, and where it was not. He knew how many times this stubborn young man had been back worrying at the mystery, how many ingenious approaches he had made to the problem, how little he had gotten, how much less he or anyone would get if they tried it today. He said nothing.

Charli Bux held up fingers to count. "Astronomical: no observations past two light-years. Nothing but sister planets (all dead) and satellites within two light-years. Cosmological: camera scan, if ever performed (but it must have been performed, or the damn thing wouldn't even be listed at all!) missing and never replaced. So there's no way of finding out where in real space it is, even. Geological: unreported. Anthropological: unreported. Then there's some stuff about local hydrogen tension and emission of the parent star, but they're not much help. And the summation in Trade Extrapolation: untraded. Reported undesirable. Not a word as to who reported it or why he said it.

"I tried to sidle into it by looking up manned exploration, but I could find only three astronauts' names in connection with Vexvelt. Troshan. He got into some sort of trouble when he came back and was executed—we used to kill certain

198

criminals six, seven hundred years ago, did you know that?—but I don't know what for. Anyway, they apparently did it before he filed his report. Then Balrou. Oh—Balrou— he did report. I can tell you his whole report word for word: 'In view of conditions on Vexvelt contact is not recommended,' period. By the word, that must be the most expensive report ever filed."

It was, said the Archive Master, but he did not say it aloud.

"And then somebody called Allman explored Vexvelt but—how did the report put it—'it was found on his return that Allman was suffering from confinement fatigue and his judgment was so severely impaired that his report is discounted.' Does that mean it was destroyed, Archive Master?"

Yes, thought the old man, but he said, "I can't say."

"So there you are," said Charli Bux. "If I wanted to present a classic case of what the old books called persecution mania, I'd just have to report things exactly as they happened. Did I have a right to suspect, even, that 'They' had picked me as the perfect target and set up those hints—low-cost feldspar, high-quality coffee—bait I couldn't miss and couldn't resist. Did I have the right to wonder if a living caricature with a comedy name—Moxie for-god's-sake Magiddle—was working for Them? Then, what happened next, when I honestly and openly filed for Vexvelt as my next vacation destination? I was told there was no Drive Guide orbiting Vexvelt—it could only be reached through normal space. That happens to be a lie, but there's no way of checking on it here, or even on Lethe—Moxie never knew. Then I filed for Vexvelt via Lethe and a real-space transport, and was told that Lethe was not recommended as a tourist stop and there was no real-space service from there anyhow. So I filed for Botil, which I *know* is a tourist stop, and which I know has real-space shuttles and charter boats, and which the star charts call Kricker III while Lethe is Kricker IV, and that's when I won the God—uh, the sweepstakes and a free trip to beautiful, beautiful Zeenip, paradise of paradises with two indoor 36-hole golf courses and free milk baths. I gave it to some charity or other, I said to save on taxes, and went for my tickets to Botil, the way I'd planned. I had it all to do over because they'd wiped the whole transaction when they learned about the sweepstakes. It seemed reasonable but it took so long to set it all up again that I missed the scheduled transport and lost a week of my vacation. Then when I went to pay for the trip my credit showed up zero, and it took another week to straighten out that regrettable error. By that time the tour service had only one full passage open, and in view of the fact that the entire tour would outlast my vacation by two weeks, they wiped the whole deal again—they were quite sure I wouldn't want it."

Charli Bux looked down at his hands and squeezed them. The Archives Office was filled with a crunching sound. Bux did not seem to notice it. "I guess anybody in his right mind would have got the message by then, but 'They' had underestimated me. Let me tell you exactly what I mean by that. I *don't* mean that I am a man of steel and by the Lord when my mind is made up it stays made. And I'm not making brags about the courage of my convictions. I had very little to be convinced about, except that there was a whole chain of coincidences which nobody wanted to explain even though the explanation was probably foolishly simple. And I never thought I was specially courageous.

"I was just—scared. Oh, I was frustrated and I was mad, but mostly I was scared. If somebody had come along with a reasonable explanation I'd've forgotten the whole thing. If someone had come back from Vexvelt and it was a poison planet (with a pocket of good feldspar and one clean mountainside) I'd have laughed it off. But the whole sequence—especially the last part, trying to book passage—really scared me. I reached the point where the only thing that would satisfy me as to my own sanity was to stand and walk on Vexvelt and *know* what it was. And that was the one thing I wasn't being allowed to do. So I couldn't get my solid proof and who's to say I wouldn't spend the next couple hundred years wondering when I'd get the next little splinter down deep in my toe? A man can suffer from a thing, Master, but then he can also suffer for fear of suffering from a thing. No, I was scared and I was going to stay scared until I cleared it up."

"My." The old man had been silent, listening, for so long that his voice was new and arresting. "It seems to me that there was a much simpler way out. Every city on every human world has free clinics where—"

"That's twice you've said that," crackled Charli Bux. "I have something to say about that, but not now. As to my going to a patch-up parlor, you know as well as I do that they don't change a thing. They just make you feel good about being the way you are."

"I fail to see the distinction, or what is wrong if there is one."

"I had a friend come up to me and tell me he was going to die of cancer in the next eight weeks, 'just in time,' he says, and whacks me so hard I see red spots, 'just in time for my funeral,' and off he goes down the street whooping like a loon."

"Would it be better if he huddled in his bed terrified and in pain?"

"I can't answer that kind of a question, but I do know what I saw is just as wrong. Anyway—there was something out there called Vexvelt, and it wouldn't make me feel any better to get rolled through a machine and come out thinking there isn't something called Vexvelt, and don't tell that's not what those friendly helpful spot removers would do to me."

"But don't you see, you'd no longer be—"

"Call me throwback. Call me radical if you want to, or ignorant." Charli Bux's big voice was up again and he seemed angry enough not to care. "Ever hear that old line about 'in every fat man there's a thin man screaming to get out'? I just can't shake the idea that if something is *so,* you can prick, poke and process me till I laugh and scratch and giggle and admit it ain't so after all, and even go out and make speeches and persuade other people, but away down deep there'll be a me with its mouth taped shut and its hands tied, bashing up against my guts trying to get out and say it is so after all. But what are we talking about me for? I came here to talk about Vexvelt."

"First tell me something—do you really think there was a 'They' who wanted to stop you?"

"*Hell* no. I think I'm up against some old-time stupidity that got itself established and habitual, and that's how come there's no information in the files. I don't think anybody today is all that stupid. I like to think people on this planet can

201

look at the truth and not let it scare them. Even if it scares them they can think it through. As to that rat race with the vacation bookings, there seemed to be a good reason for each single thing that happened. Science and math have done a pretty good job of explaining the mechanics of the 'bad break' and 'a lucky run,' but neither one of them ever got repealed."

"So." The Master tented his fingers and looked down at the ridgepole. "And just how did you manage to get to Vexvelt after all."

Bux flicked on his big bright grin. "I hear a lot about this free society, and how there's always someone out to trim an edge off here and a corner there. Maybe there's something in it, but so far they haven't got around to taking away a man's freedom to be a damn fool. Like, for example, his freedom to quit his job. I've said it was just a gruesome series of bad breaks, but bad breaks can be outwitted just as easily as a superpowerful masterminding 'They.' Seems to me most bad breaks happen inside a man's pattern. He gets out of phase with it and every step he takes is between the steppin'stones. If he can't phase in, and if he tries to maintain his pace, why there's a whole row of stones ahead of him laid just exactly where each and every one of them will crack his shins. What he should do is head upstream. It might be unknown territory, and there might be dangers, but one thing for sure, there's a whole row of absolutely certain, absolutely planned agonies he is just not going to have to suffer."

"How did you get to Vexvelt?"

"I told you." He waited, then smiled. "I'll tell you again. I quit my job. 'They,' or the 'losing streak,' or the stinking lousy Fates, or whatever had a bead on me—they could do it to me because they always knew where I was, when I'd be the next place, and what I wanted. So they were always waiting for me. So I headed upstream. I waited till my vacation was over and left the house without any luggage and went to my local bank and had all my credits before I could have any tough breaks. Then I took a Drive jumper to Lunatu, booked passage on a semi-freight to Lethe."

"You booked passage, but you never boarded the ship."

"You know?"

"I was asking."

"Oh," said Charli Bux. "Yeah, I never set foot in that cozy little cabin. What I did, I slid down the cargo chute and got buried in Hold #2 with a ton of oats. I was in an interesting position, Archive Master. In a way I'm sorry nobody dug me out to ask questions. You're not supposed to stow away but the law says—and I know exactly what it says—that a stowaway is someone who rides a vessel without booking passage. But I did book passage, and paid in full, and all my papers were in order for where I was going. What made things a lot easier, too, was that where I was going nobody gives much of a damn about papers."

"And you felt you could get to Vexvelt through Lethe."

"I felt I had a chance, and I knew of no other. Cargoes from Vexvelt *had* been put down on Lethe, or I wouldn't have been sucked into this thing in the first place. I didn't know if the carrier was Vexveltian or a tramp (if it was a liner I'd have known it) or when one might come or if it would be headed for Vexvelt when it departed. All I knew was that Vexvelt had shipped here for sure, and this was the only place where maybe they might be back. Do you know what goes on at Lethe?"

"It has a reputation."

"Do you *know?*"

The old man showed a twinge of irritation. Along with respect and obedience, he had become accustomed to catechizing and not to being catechized. "Everyone knows about Lethe."

Bux shook his head. "They don't, Master."

The old man lifted his hands and put them down. "That kind of thing has its function. Humanity will always—"

"You approve of Lethe and what goes on there."

"One neither approves nor disapproves," said the Archive Master stiffly. "One knows about it, recognizes that for some segments of the species such an outlet is necessary, realizes that Lethe makes no pretensions to being anything but what it is, and then—one accepts, one goes on to other things. How did you get to Vexvelt?"

"On Lethe," said Charli Bux implacably, "you can do anything you want to or with any kind of human being, or any number of combination of them, as long as you can pay for it."

203

"I wouldn't doubt it. Now, the next leg of your trip—"

"There are men," said Charli Bux, suddenly and shockingly quiet, "who can be attracted by disease—by sores, Archive Master, by the stumps of amputated limbs. There are people on Lethe who cultivate diseases to attract such men. Crones, Master, with dirty leather skin, and boys and little—"

"You will cease this nauseating—"

"In just a minute. One of the unwritten and unbreakable traditions of Lethe is that, what anyone pays to do, anyone else may pay to watch."

"*Are you finished?*" It was not Bux who shouted now.

"You accept Lethe. You condone Lethe."

"I have not said I approve."

"You trade with Lethe."

"Well, of course we do. That doesn't mean we—"

"The third day—night, rather, that I was there," said Bux, overriding what was surely about to turn into a helpless sputter, "I turned off one of the main streets into an alley. I knew this might be less than wise, but at the moment there was an ugly fight going on between me and the corner, and some wild gunning. I was going to turn right and go to the other avenue anyway, and I could see it clearly through the alley.

"I couldn't describe to you how fast this happened, or explain where they came from—eight of them, I think, in an alley, not quite dark and very narrow, when only a minute before I had been able to see it from end to end.

"I was grabbed from all sides all over my body, lifted, slammed down flat on my back and a bright light jammed in my face.

"A woman said, 'Aw shoot, 'taint him.' A man's voice said to let me up. They picked me up. Somebody even started dusting me off. The woman who had held the light began to apologize. She did it quite nicely. She said they heard that there was a—Master, I wonder if I should use the word."

"How necessary do you feel—"

"Oh, I guess I don't have to: you know it. On my ship, any construction gang, in any farm community—anywhere where men work or gather, it's the one verbal bullet which will and must start a fight. If it doesn't, the victim will never regain face. The woman used it as casually as she would have said Terran or Lethean. She said there was one right here in

204

town and they meant to get him. I said, 'Well, how about that.' It's the one phrase I know that can be said any time about anything. Another woman said I was a good big one and how would I like to tromp him. One of the men said all right, but he called for the head. Another began to fight him about it, and a third woman took off her shoe and slapped both their faces with one swing of the muddy sole. She said for them to button it up or next time she'd use the heel. The other woman, with the light, giggled and said Helen was Veddy Good Indeed that way. She spoke in a beautifully cultivated accent. She said Helen could hook out an eye neat as a croupier. The third woman suddenly cried out, 'Dog turds!' She asked for some light. The dog turds were very dry. One of the men offered to wet them down. The woman said no—they were her dog turds and she would do it herself. Then and there she squatted. She called for a light, said she couldn't see to aim. They turned the light on her. She was one of the most beautiful women I have ever seen. Is there something wrong, Master?"

"I would like you to tell me how you made contact with Vexvelt," said the old man a little breathlessly.

"But I am!" said Charli Bux. "One of the men pressed through, all grunting with eagerness, and began to mix the filth with his hands. And then, by a sort of sixth sense, the light was out and they were simply—*gone!* Disappeared. A hand came out of nowhere and pulled me back against a house wall. There wasn't a sound—not even breathing. And only then did the Vexveltian turn into the alley. How they knew he was coming is beyond me.

"The hand that had pulled me back belonged to the woman with the light, as I found out in a matter of seconds. I really didn't believe her hand meant to be where I found it. I took hold of it and held it, but she snatched it away and put it back. Then I felt the light bump my leg. And the man came along toward us. He was a big man, held himself straight, wore light-colored clothes, which I thought was more foolhardy than brave. He walked lightly and seemed to be looking everywhere—and still could not see us.

"If this all happened right this minute, after what I've learned about Vexvelt—about Lethe too—I wouldn't hesitate, I'd know exactly what to do. What you have to understand is

205

that I didn't know anything at all at the time. Maybe it was the eight against one that annoyed me." He paused thoughtfully. "Maybe that coffee. What I'm trying to say is that I did the same thing then, in my ignorance, that I'd do now, knowing what I do.

"I snapped the flashlight out of the woman's hand and got about twenty feet away in two big bounds. I turned the light on and played it back where I'd come from. Two of the men had crawled up the sheer building face like insects and were ready to drop on the victim. The beautiful one was crouched on her toes and one hand; the other, full of filth, was ready to throw. She made an absolutely animal sound and slung her handful, quite uselessly. The others were flattened back against wall and fence, and in the light, for a long second, they flattened all the more, blinking. I said over my shoulder, 'Watch yourself, friend. You're the guest of honor, I think.'

"You know what he did? He laughed. I said. 'They won't get by me for a while. Take off.' 'What for?' says he, squeezing past me. 'There's only eight of them.' And he marches straight down on them.

"Something rolled under my foot and I picked it up—half a brick. What must have been the other half of it hit me right on the breastbone. It made me yelp, I couldn't help it. The tall man said to douse the light, I was a target. I did, and saw one of the men in silhouette against the street at the far end, standing up from behind a big garbage can. He was holding a knife half as long as his forearm, and he rose up as the big man passed him. I let fly with the brick and got him right back of the head. The tall man never so much as turned when he heard him fall and the knife go skittering. He passed one of the human flies as if he had forgotten he was there, but he hadn't forgotten. He reached up and got both the ankles and swung the whole man screaming off the wall like a flail, wiping the second one off and tumbling the both of them on top of the rest of the gang.

"He stood there with the back of his hands on his hips for a bit, not even breathing hard, watching the crying, cursing mix-up all over the alley pavement. I came up beside him. One, two got to their feet and ran limping. One of the women began to scream—curses, I suppose, but you couldn't hear the words. I turned the light on her face and she shut right up.

" 'You all right?' says the tall man.

"I told him, 'Caved in my chest is all, but that's all right, I can use it for a fruit bowl lying in bed.' He laughed and turned his back on the enemy and led me the way he had come. He said he was Vorhidin from Vexvelt. I told him who I was. I said I'd been looking for a Vexveltian, but before we could go on with that a black hole opened up to the left and somebody whispered, 'Quick, quick.' Vorhidin clapped a hand on my back and gave me a little shove. 'In you go, Charli Bux of Terratu.' And in we went, me stumbling all over my feet down some steps I didn't know were there, and then again because they weren't there. A big door boomed closed behind us. Dim yellow light came on. There was a little man with olive skin and shiny, oily mustachios. 'Vorhidin, for the love of God, I told you not to come into town, they'll kill you.' Vorhidin only said, 'This is Charli Bux, a friend.' The little man came forward anxiously and began to pat Vorhidin on the arms and ribs to see if he was all right.

"Vorhidin laughed and brushed him off. 'Poor Tretti! He's always afraid something is going to happen! Never mind me, you fusspot. See to Charli here. He took a shot in the bows that was meant for me.' The little one, Tretti, sort of squeaked and before I could stop him he had my shirt open and the light out of my hand switched on and trained on the bruise. 'Your next woman can admire a sunset,' says Vorhidin. Tretti's away and back before you can blink, and sprays on something cool and good and most of the pain vanished.

" 'What do you have for us?' and Tretti carries the light into another room. There's stacks of stuff, mostly manufactured goods, tools and instruments. There was a big pile of trideo cartridges, mostly music and new plays, but a novel or so too. Most of the other stuff was one of a kind. Vorhidin picked up a forty-pound crate and spun it twice by diagonal corners till it stopped where he could read the label. 'Molar spectroscope. Most of this stuff we don't really need but we like to see what's being done, how it's designed. Sometimes ours are better, sometimes not. We like to see, that's all.' He set it down gently and reached into his pocket and palmed out a dozen or more stones that flashed till it hurt. One of them, a blue one, made its own light. He took Tretti's hand and pulled it to him and poured it full of stones. 'That enough for this load?' I couldn't help it—I glanced around the place and totted it up and made a stab estimate—a hundred each of everything in the place wouldn't be worth that one blue stone. Tretti was goggle-eyed. He couldn't speak. Vorhidin wagged his head and laughed and said, 'All right, then,' and reached into his pants pocket again and ladled out four or five more. I thought Tretti was going to cry. I was right. He cried.

"We had something to eat and I told Vorhidin how I happened to be here. He said he'd better take me along. I said where to? and he said Vexvelt. I bgan to laugh. I told him I was busting my brains trying to figure some way to make him say that, and he laughed too and said I'd found it, all right, twice over. 'Owe you a favor for that,' he says, dipping his head at the alley side of the room. 'Reason two, you wouldn't live out the night on Lethe if you stayed here.' I wanted to know why not, because from what I'd seen there were fights all the time, then you'd see the fighters an hour later drinking out of the same bowl. He says it's not the same thing. Nobody helps a Vexveltian but a Vexveltian. Help one, you are one, far as Lethe was concerned. So I wanted to know what Lethe had against Vexvelt, and he stopped chewing and looked at me a long time as if he didn't understand me. Then he said, 'You really don't know anything about us, do you?' I said, not much. 'Well,' he says, 'now there's three good reasons to bring you.'

"Tretti opened the double doors at the far end of the storeroom. There was a ground van in there, with another set of doors into the street. We loaded the crates into it and got in, Vorhidin at the tiller. Tretti climbed a ladder and put his eyes to something and spun a wheel. 'Periscope,' Vorhidin told me. 'Looks like a flagpole from outside.' Tretti waved his hand at us. He had tears running down his cheeks again. He hit a switch and the doors banged out of the way. The van screeched out of there as the doors bounced and started back. After that Vorhidin drove like a little old lady. One-way glass. Sometimes I wondered what those crowds of drunks and queers would do if they could see in. I asked him, 'What are they afraid of?' He didn't seem to understand the question. I said, 'Mostly when people gang up on somebody, it's because one way or another they're afraid. What do they think you're going to take away from them?'

"He laughed and said, 'Their decency.' And that's all the talk I got out of him all the way out to the spaceport.

"The Vexveltian ship was parked miles away from the terminal, way the hell and gone at the far end of the pavement near some trees. There was a fire going near it. As we got closer I saw it wasn't near it, it was spang under it. There was a big crowd, maybe half a hundred, mostly women, mostly drunk. They were dancing and staggering around and dragging wood up under the ship. The ship stood up on its tail like the old chemical rockets in the fairy stories. Vorhidin grunted, 'Idiots,' and moved something on his wrist. The rocket began to rumble and everybody ran screaming. Then there was a big explosion of steam and the wood went every which way, and for a while the pavement was full of people running and falling and screaming, and cycles and ground cars milling around and bumping each other. After a while it was quiet and we pulled up close. The high hatch opened on the ship and a boom and frame came out and lowered. Vorhidin hooked on, threw the latches on the van bed, beckoned me back there with him, reached forward and set the controls of the van, and touched the thing on his wrist. The whole van cargo section started up complete with us, and the van started up and began to roll home by itself.

"The only crew he carried," said Charli Bux carefully, "was a young radio officer." *With long shining black wings for hair and bits of sky in her tilted eyes, and a full and asking kind of mouth. She held Vorhidin very close, very long, laughing the message that there could be no words for this: he was safe. "Tamba, this is Charli. He's from Terratu and he fought for me." Then she came and held him too, and she kissed him; that incredible mouth, that warm strong soft mouth, why, he and she shared it for an hour; for an hour he felt her lips on his, even though she had kissed him for only a second. For an hour her lips could hardly be closer to her than they were to his own astonished flesh.* "The ship blasted off and headed sunward and to the celestial north. It held this course for two days. Lethe has two moons, the smaller one just a rock, an asteroid. Vorhidin matched velocities with it and hung half a kilo away, drifting in."

And the first night he had swung his bunk to the after bulkhead and had lain there heavily against the thrust of the jets, and against the thrust of his heart and his loins. Never had he seen such a woman—only just become woman, at that. So joyful, so utterly and so rightly herself. Half an hour after blastoff: "Clothes are in the way on a ship, don't you think? But Vorhidin says I should ask you, because customs are different from one world to another, isn't that so?"

"Here we live by your customs, not mine," Charli had been able to say, and she had thanked him, thanked him! and touched the bit of glitter at her throat, and her garment fell away. "There's much more privacy this way," she said, leaving him. "A closed door means more to the naked; it's closed for a real reason and not because one might be seen in one's petticoat." She took her garment into one of the staterooms. Vorhidin's. Charli leaned weakly against the bulkhead and shut his eyes. Her nipples were like her mouth, full and asking. Vorhidin was casually naked but Charli kept his clothes on, and the Vexveltians made no comment. The night was very long. For a while part of the weight on Charli turned to anger, which helped. Old bastard, silver-temples. Old enough to be her father. But that could not last, and he smiled at himself. He remembered the first time he had gone to a ski resort. There were all kinds of people there, young, old, wealthy, working, professionals; but there was a difference. The resort, because it was what it was, screened out the pasty-faced, the round-shouldered lungless sedentaries, the plumping sybarites. All about him had been clear eyes, straight backs, and skin with the cosmetics of frost and fun. Who walked idled not, but went somewhere. Who sat lay back joyfully in well-earned weariness. And this was the aura of Vorhidin—not a matter of carriage and clean color and clear eyes, though he certainly had all these, but the same qualities down to the bone and radiating from the mind. A difficult thing to express and a pleasure to be with. Early on the second day Vorhidin had leaned close when they were alone in the control room and asked him if he would like to sleep with Tamba tonight. Charli gasped as if he had been clapped on the navel with a handful of crushed ice. He also

210

blushed, saying, "If she, if she—" wildly wondering how to ask her. He need not have wondered, for "He'd love to, honey," Vorhidin bellowed. Tamba popped her face into the corridor and smiled at Charli. "Thank you so much," she said. And then (after the long night) it was going to be the longest day he had ever lived through, but she let it happen within the hour instead, sweetly, strongly, unhurried. Afterward he lay looking at her with such total and long-lasting astonishment that she laughed at him. She flooded his face with her black hair and then with her kisses and then all of him with her supple strength; this time she was fierce and most demanding until with a shout he toppled from the very peak of joy straight and instantly down into the most total slumber he had ever known. In perhaps twenty minutes he opened his eyes and found his gaze plunged deep in a blue glory, her eyes so close their lashes meshed. Later, talking to her in the wardroom, holding both her hands, he turned to find Vorhidin standing in the doorway. He was on them in one long stride, and flung an arm around each. Nothing was said. What could be said?

"I talked a lot with Vorhidin," Charli Bux said to the Archive Master. "I never met a man more sure of himself, what he wanted, what he liked, what he believed. The very first thing he said when I brought up the matter of trade was 'Why?' In all my waking life I never thought to ask that about trade. All I ever did, all anyone does, is to trade where he can and try to make it more. 'Why?' he wanted to know. I thought of the gemstones going for that production-line junk in the hold, and pure niobium at manganese prices. One trader would call that ignorance, another would call it good business and get all he could—glass beads for ivory. But cultures have been known to trade like that for religious or ethical reasons—always give more than you get in the other fellow's coin. Or maybe they were just—*rich*. Maybe there was so much on Vexvelt that the only thing they could use was—well, like he said: manufactures, so they could look at the design 'sometimes better than ours, sometimes not.' So—I asked him.

"He gave me a long look that was, at four feet, exactly like" *drowning in the impossibly blue lakes of Tamba's eyes, but watch yourself, don't think about that when you talk to*

211

this old man "holding still for an X-ray continuity. Finally he said, 'Yes, I suppose we're rich. There's not much we need.'

"I told him, all the same, he could get a lot higher prices for the little he did trade. He just laughed a little and shook his head. 'You have to pay for what you get or it's no good. If you "trade well," as you call it, you finish with more than you started with; you didn't pay. That's as unnatural as energy levels goings from lesser to greater, it's contrary to ecology and entropy.' Then he said, 'You don't understand that.' I didn't and I don't."

"Go on."

"They have their own Drive cradle back of Lethe's moon, and their own Guide orbiting Vexvelt. I told you—all the while I thought the planet was near Lethe; well, it isn't."

"Now, that I do *not* understand. Cradles and guides are public utilities. Two days, you say it took. Why didn't he use the one at the Lethe port?"

"I can't say, sir. Uh—"

"Well?"

"I was just thinking about that drunken mob building a fire under the ship."

"Ah yes. Perhaps the moon cradle is a wise precaution after all. I have always known, and you make it eminently clear, that these people are not popular. All right—you made a Drive jump."

"We made a Drive jump." Charli fell silent for a moment, reliving that breathless second of revelation as black, talc-dusted space and a lump moonlet winked away to be replaced by the greet arch of a purple-haloed horizon, marbled green and gold and silver and polished blue, with a chromium glare coming from the sea on the planet's shoulder. "A tug was standing by and we got down without trouble." The spaceport was tiny compared even with Lethe—eight or ten docks, with the warehouse area under them and passenger and staff areas surrounding them under a deck. "There were no formalities—I suppose there's not enough space travel to merit them."

"Certainly no strangers, at any rate," said the old man smugly.

"We disembarked right on the deck and walked away." *Tamba had gone out first. It was sunny, with a warm wind,*

212

and if there was any significant difference between this grav-
ity and that of Terratu, Charli's legs could not detect it. In
the air, however, the difference was profound. Never before
had he known air so clear, so winy, so clean—not unless it
was bitter cold, and this was warm. Tamba stood by the
silent, swiftly moving "up" ramp, looking out across the
foothills to the most magnificent mountain range he had ever
seen, for they had everything a picture-book mountain should
have—smooth vivid high-range, shaggy forest, dramatic gray,
brown, and ocher rock cliff, and a starched white cloth of
snowcap tumbled on the peaks to dry in the sun. Behind
them was a wide plain with a river for one margin and
foothills for the other, and then the sea, with a wide golden
beach curving a loving arm around the ocean's green shoul-
der. As he approached the pensive girl the warm wind curled
and laughed down on them, and her short robe streamed
from her shoulders like smoke, and fell about her again. It
stopped his pace and his breath and his heart for a beat, it
was so lovely a sight. And coming up beside her, watching
the people below, the people rising on one ramp and sliding
down the other, he realized that in this place clothing had but
two conventions—ease and beauty. Man, woman and child,
they wore what they chose, ribbon or robe, clogs, coronets,
cummerbunds or kilts, or a ring, or a snood, or nothing at all.
He remembered a wonderful line he had read by a pre-Nova
sage called Rudofsky, and murmured it: Modesty is not so
simple a virtue as honesty. *She turned and smiled at him; she*
thought it was his line. He smiled back and let her think so.
"You don't mind waiting a bit? My father will be along in a
moment and then we'll go. You're to stay with us. Is that all
right?"

Did he mind. Would he wait, bracketed by the thundering
colors of that mountain, the adagio of the sea. Is that all
right.

There was nothing, no way, no word to express his reponse
but to raise his tense fists as high as he could and shout as
loud as he could and then turn it into laughter and to tears.

Vorhidin, having checked out his manifests, joined them
before Charli was finished. He had locked gazes with the girl,
who smiled up at him and held his forearm in both her
hands, stroking, and he laughed and laughed. "He drank too

213

much Vexvelt all at once," she said to Vorhidin. Vorhidin put a big warm hand on Charli's shoulder and laughed with him until he was done. When he had his breath again, and the water-lenses out of his eyes, Tamba said, "That's where we're going."

"Where?"

She pointed, very carefully. Three slender dark trees like poplars came beseeching out of a glad tumble of luminous light willow-green. "Those three trees."

"I can't see a house . . ."

Vorhidin and Tamba laughed together: this pleased them. "Come."

"We were going to wait for—"

"No need to wait any longer. Come."

Charli said, "The house was only a short walk from the port, but you couldn't see the one from the other. A big house, too, trees all around it and even growing up through it. I stayed with the family and worked." He slapped the heavy folio. "All this. I got all the help I needed."

"*Did* you indeed." The Archive Master seemed more interested in this than in anything else he had heard so far. Or perhaps it was a different kind of interest. "Helped you, did they? Would you say they're anxious to trade?"

The answer to this was clearly an important one. "All I can say," Charli Bux responded carefully, "is that I asked for this information—a catalogue of the trade resources of Vexvelt, and estimates of F.O.B. prices. None of them are very far off a practical, workable arrangement, and every single one undercuts the competition. There are a number of reasons. First of all, of course, is the resources themselves— almost right across the board, unbelievably rich. Then they have mining methods like nothing you've ever dreamed of, and harvesting, and preserving—there's no end to it. At first blush it looks like a pastoral planet—well, it's not. It's a natural treasure house that has been organized and worked and planned and understood like no other planet in the known universe. Those people have never had a war, they've never had to change their original cultural plan; it works, Master, it *works*. And it has produced a sane healthy people which, when it goes about a job, goes about it single-minded-ly and with . . . well, it might sound like an odd term to use, but it's the only one that fits: with joy. . . . I can see you don't want to hear this."

The old man opened his eyes and looked directly at the visitor. At Bux's cascade of language he had averted his face, closed his eyes, curled his lip, let his hands stray over his temples and near his ears, as if it was taking a supreme effort to keep from clapping the palms over them.

"All I can hear is that a world which has been set aside by the whole species, and which has kept itself aloof, is using you to promote a contact which nobody wants. Do they want it? They won't get it, of course, but have they any idea of what their world would be like if this"—he waved at the folio—"is all true? How do they think they could control the exploiters? Have they got something special in defenses as well as all this other?"

"I really don't know."

"I know!" The old man was angrier than Bux had yet seen him. "What they are is their defense! No one will *ever* go near them, not *ever*. Not if they strip their whole planet of everything it has, and refine and process the lot, and haul it to their spaceport at their own expense, and give it away free."

"Not even if they can cure cancer?"

"Almost all cancer is curable."

"They can cure *all* cancer."

"New methods are discovered every—"

"They've had the methods for I don't know how many years. Centuries. *They have no cancer.*"

"Do you know what this cure is?"

"No, I don't. But it wouldn't take a clinical team a week to find out."

"The incurable cancers are not subject to clinical analysis. They are all deemed psychosomatic."

"I know. That is exactly what the clinical team would find out."

There was a long, pulsing silence. "You have not been completely frank with me, young man."

"That's right, sir."

Another silence. "The implication is that they are sane and cancer-free because of the kind of culture they have set up."

This time Bux did not respond, but let the old man's words

215

hang there to be reheard, reread. At last the Archive Master spoke again in a near whisper, shaking and furious. "Abomination! Abomination! Spittle appeared on his chin: he seemed not to know. "I—would—rather—die—eaten alive—with cancer—and raving *mad* than live with such sanity as that."

"Perhaps others would disagree."

"No one would disagree! Try it? Try it! They'll tear you to pieces! That's what they did to Allman. That's what they did to Balrou! We killed Troshan ourselves—he was the first and we didn't know then that the mob would do it for us. That was a thousand years ago, you understand that? And a thousand years from now the mob will still do it for us! And that—that *filth* will go to the locked files with the others, and someday another fool with too much curiosity and not enough decency and his mind rotten with perversion will sit here with another Archive Master, who will send him out as I'm sending you out, to shut his mouth and save his life or open it and be torn to pieces. Get *out!* Get *out!* Get *out!*" His voice had risen to a shriek and then a sort of keening, and had rasped itself against itself until it was a painful forced whisper and then nothing at all: the old eyes glared and the chin was wet.

Charli Bux rose slowly. He was white with shock. He said quietly, "Vorhidin tried to tell me, and I wouldn't believe it. I couldn't believe it. I said to him, 'I know more about greed than you do; they will not be able to resist those prices.' I said, 'I know more about fear than you do; they will not be able to stand against the final cancer cure.' Vorhidin laughed at me and gave me all the help I needed.

"I started to tell him once that I knew more about the sanity that lives in all of us, and very much in some of us, and that it could prevail. But I knew while I was talking that I was wrong about that. Now I know that I was wrong in everything, even the greed, even the fear, and he was right. And he said Vexvelt has the most powerful and the least expensive defense ever devised—sanity. He was right."

Charli Bux realized then that the old man, madly locking gazes with him as he spoke, had in some way, inside his head, turned off his ears. He sat there with his old head cocked to one side, panting like a foundered dog in a dust bowl, until at last he thought he could shout again. He could not. He could only rasp, he could only whisper-squeak, "Get out! Get out!"

Charli Bux got out. He left the folio where it was; it, like Vexvelt, defended itself by being immiscible—in the language of chemistry, by being noble.

It was not Tamba after all, but Tyng who captured Charli's heart.

When they got to the beautiful house, so close to everything and yet so private, so secluded, he met the family. Breerho's radiant—almost heat-radiant—shining red hair, and Tyng's, showed them to be mother and daughter. Vorhid and Stren were the sons, one a child, the other in his mid-teens, were straight-backed, wide-shouldered like their father, and by the wonderful cut and tilt of their architectured eyes, were brothers to Tyng, and to Tamba.

There were two other youngsters, a lovely twelve-year-old girl called Fleet, who was singing when they came in, and for whose song they stopped and postponed the introductions, and a sturdy tumblebug of a boy they called Handr, possibly the happiest human being any of them would ever see. In time Charli met the parents of these two, and black-haired Tamba seemed much more kin to the mother than to flame-haired Breerho.

It was at first a cascade of names and faces, captured only partially, kaleidoscoping about in his head as they all did in the room, and making a shyness in him. But there was more love in the room than ever the peaks of his mind and heart had known before, and more care and caring.

Before the afternoon and evening were over, he was familiar and accepted and enchanted. And because Tamba had touched his heart and astonished his body, all his feelings rose within him and narrowed and aimed themselves on her, hot and breathless, and indeed she seemed to delight in him and kept close to him the whole time. But when the little ones went off yawning, and then others, and they were alone, he asked her, he begged her to come to his bed. She was kind as could be, and loving, but also completely firm in her refusal. "But, darling, I just can't now. I can't. I've been away to Lethe and now I'm back and I *promised.*"

"Promised who?"

"Stren."

"But I thought . . ." He thought far too many things to sort out or even to isolate one from another. Well, maybe he hadn't understood the relationships here—after all, there were four adults and six children and he'd get it straight by tomorrow who was who, because otherwise she—oh. "You mean you promised Stren you wouldn't sleep with me."

"No, my silly old dear. I'll sleep with Stren tonight. Please, darling, don't be upset. There'll be other times. Tomorrow. Tomorrow morning?" She laughed and took his cheeks in her two hands and shook his whole head as if she could make the frown drop off. "Tomorrow morning *very* early?"

"I don't mean to be like this my very first night here, I'm sorry, I guess there's a lot I don't understand," he mumbled in his misery. And then anguish skyrocketed within him and he no longer cared about host and guest and new customs and all the rest of it. "I love you," he cried, "don't you know that?"

"Of course, of course I do. And I love you, and we will love one another for a long, long time. Didn't you think I knew that?" Her puzzlement was so genuine that even through pain-haze he could see it. He said, as close to tears as he felt a grown man should ever get, that he just guessed he didn't understand.

"You will, beloved, you will. We'll talk about it until you do, no matter how long it takes." Then she added, with absolutely guileless cruelty, "Starting tomorrow. But now I have to go, Stren's waiting. Good night, true love," and she kissed the top of his averted head and sprinted away lightly on bare tiptoe.

She had reached something in him that made it impossible for him to be angry at her. He could only hurt. He had not known until these past two days that he could feel so much or bear so much pain. He buried his face in the cushions of the long couch in the—living room?—anyway, the place where indoors and outdoors were as tangled as his heart, but more harmoniously—and gave himself up to sodden hurt.

In time, someone knelt beside him and touched him lightly on the neck. He twisted his head enough to be able to see. It was Tyng, her hair all but luminous in the dimness, and her face, what he could see of it, nothing but compassion. She said, "Would you like me to stay with you instead?" and with the absolute honesty of the stricken, he cried, "There couldn't be anyone else instead!"

Her sorrow, its genuineness, was unmistakable. She told him of it, touched him once more, and slipped away. Sometime during the night he twisted himself awake enough to find the room they had given him, and found surcease in utter black exhaustion.

Awake in daylight, he sought his other surcease, which was work, and began his catalogue of resources. Everyone tried at one time or another to communicate with him, but unless it was work he shut it off (except, of course, for the irresistible Handr, who became his fast and lifelong friend). He found Tyng near him more and more frequently, and usefully so; he had not become so surly that he would refuse a stylus or reference book (opened at the right place) when it was placed in his hand exactly at the moment he needed it. Tyng was with him for many hours, alert but absolutely silent, before he unbent enough to ask her for this or that bit of information, or wondered about weights and measures and man-hour calculations done in the Vexveltian way. If she did not know, she found out with a minimum of delay and absolute clarity. She knew, however, a very great deal more than he had suspected. So the time came when he was chattering like a macaw, eagerly planning the next day's work with her.

He never spoke to Tamba. He did not mean to hurt her, but he could sense her eagerness to respond to him and he could not bear it. She, out of consideration, just stopped trying.

One particularly knotty statistical sequence kept him going for two days and two nights without stopping. Tyng kept up with him all the way without complaint until, in the wee small hours of the third morning, she rolled up her eyes and collapsed. He staggered up on legs gone asleep with too much sitting, and shook the statistics out of his eyes to settle her on the thick fur rug, straighten the twisted knee. In what little light spilled from his abandoned hooded lamp, she was exquisite, especially because of his previous knowledge that she was exquisite in the most brilliant of glares. The shadows added something to the alabaster, and her unconscious pale lips were no longer darker than her face, and she seemed

219

strangely statuesque and non-living. She was waring a Cretan sort of dress, a tight stomacher holding the bare breasts cupped and supporting a diaphanous skirt. Troubled that the stomacher might impede her breathing, he unhooked it and put it back. The flesh of her midriff where it had been was, to the finger if not to the eye, pinched and ridged. He kneaded it gently and pursued indefinable thoughts through the haze of fatigue: pyrophyllite, Lethe, brother, recoverable vanadium salts, Vorhidin, precipitate, Tyng's watching me. Tyng in the almost dark was watching him. He took his eyes from her and looked down her body to his hand. It had stopped moving some vague time ago, slipped into slumber of its own accord. Were her eyes open now or closed? He leaned forward to see and overbalanced. They fell asleep with their lips touching, not yet having kissed at all.

The pre-Nova ancient Plato tells of the earliest human, a quadruped with two sexes. And one terrible night in a storm engendered by the forces of evil, all the humans were torn in two; and ever since, each has sought the other half of itself. Any two of opposite sexes can make something, but it is usually incomplete in some way. But when one part finds its true other half, no power on earth can keep them apart, nor drive them apart once they join. This happened that night, beginning at some moment so deep in sleep that neither could ever remember it. What happened to each was all the way into new places where nothing had ever been before, and it was forever. The essence of such a thing is acceptance, and lest he be judged, Charli Bux ceased to judge quite so much and began to learn something of the ways of life around him. Life around him certainly concealed very little. The children slept where they chose. Their sexual play was certainly no more enthusiastic or more frequent than any other kind of play— and no more concealed. There was very much less talk about sex than he had ever encountered in any group of any age. He kept on working hard, but no longer to conceal facts from himself. He saw a good many things he had not permitted himself to see before, and found to his surprise that they were not, after all, the end of the world.

He had one more very, very bad time coming to him. He sometimes slept in Tyng's room, she sometimes in his. Early one morning he awoke alone, recalling some elusive part of the work, and got up and padded down to her room. He realized when it was too late to ignore it what the soft singing sound meant; it was very much later that he was able to realize his fury at the discovery that this special song was not his alone to evoke. He was in her room before he could stop himself, and out again, shaking and blind.

He was sitting on the wet earth in the green hollow under a willow when Vorhidin found him. (He never knew how Vorhidin had accomplished this, nor for that matter how he had come there himself.) He was staring straight ahead and had been doing so for so long that his eyeballs were dry and the agony was enjoyable. He had forced his fingers so hard down into the ground that they were buried to the wrists. Three nails were bent and broken over backwards and he was still pushing.

Vorhidin did not speak at all at first, but merely sat down beside him. He waited what he felt was long enough and then softly called the young man's name. Charli did not move. Vorhidin then put a hand on his shoulder and the result was extraordinary. Charli Bux moved nothing visibly but the cords of his throat and his jaw, but at the first touch of the Vexveltian's hand he threw up. It was what is called clinically "projectile" vomiting. Soaked and spattered from hips to feet, dry-eyed and staring, Charli sat still. Vorhidin, who understood what had happened 'and may even have expected it, also remained just as he was, a hand on the young man's shoulder. "Say the words!" he snapped.

Charli Bux swiveled his head to look at the big man. He screwed up his eyes and blinked them, and blinked again. He spat sour out of his mouth, and his lips twisted and trembled. "Say the words," said Vorhidin quietly but forcefully, because he knew Charli could not contain them but had vomited rather than enunciate them. "Say the words."

"Y-y—" Charli had to spit again. "You," he croaked. "You—her *father!*" he screamed, and in a split second he became a dervish, a windmill, a double flail, a howling wolverine. The loamy hands, blood-muddy, so lacked control from the excess of fury that they never became fists. Vorhidin crouched where he was and took it all. He did not attempt to defend himself beyond an occasional small accurate movement of the head, to protect his eyes. He could heal from

221

almost anything the blows might do, but unless the blows were spent, Charli Bux might never heal at all. It went on for a long time because something in Charli would not show, probably would not even feel, fatigue. When the last of the resources were gone, the collapse was sudden and total. Vorhidin knelt grunting, got painfully to his feet, bent dripping blood over the unconscious Terran, lifted him in his arms, and carried him gently into the house.

Vorhidin explained it all, in time. It took a great deal of time, because Charli could accept nothing at all from anyone at first, and then nothing from Vorhidin, and after that, only small doses. Summarized from half a hundred conversations, this is the gist:

"Some unknown ancient once wrote," said Vorhidin, " ' 'Tain't what you don't know that hurts you; it's what you do know that ain't so.' Answer me some questions. Don't stop to think. (Now that's silly. Nobody off Vexvelt ever stops to think about incest. They'll say a lot, mind you, and fast, but they don't think.) I'll ask, you answer. How many bisexual species—birds, beasts, fish and insects included—how many show any sign of the incest taboo?"

"I really couldn't say. I don't recall reading about it, but then, who'd write such a thing? I'd say—quite a few. It would be only natural."

"Wrong. Wrong twice, as a matter of fact. *Homo sapiens* has the patent, Charli—all over the wall-to-wall universe, only mankind. Wrong the second: it would *not* be natural. It never was, it isn't, and it never will be natural."

"Matter of terms, isn't it? I'd call it natural. I mean, it comes naturally. It doesn't have to be learned."

"Wrong. It does have to be learned. I can document that, but that'll wait—you can go through the library later. Accept the point for the argument."

"For the argument, then."

"Thanks. What percentage of people do you think have sexual feelings about their siblings—brothers and sisters?"

"What age are you talking about?"

"Doesn't matter."

"Sexual feelings don't begin until a certain age, do they?"

"Don't they? What would you say the age is, on the average?"

222

"Oh—depends on the indi—but you did say 'average,' didn't you? Let's put it around eight. Nine maybe."

"Wrong. Wait till you have some of your own, you'll find out. I'd put it at two or three minutes. I'd be willing to bet it existed a whole lot before that, too. By some weeks."

"I don't believe it!"

"I know you don't," said Vorhidin. " 'Strue all the same. What about the parent of the opposite sex?"

"Now, that would have to wait for a stage of consciousness capable of knowing the difference."

"Wel-l-l—you're not as wrong as usual," he said, but he said it kindly. "But you'd be amazed at how early that can be. They can smell the difference long before they can see it. A few days, a week."

"I never knew."

"I don't doubt that a bit. Now, let's forget everything you've seen here. Let's pretend you're back on Lethe and I ask you, what would be the effects on a culture if each individual had immediate and welcome access to all the others?"

"*Sexual* access?" Charli made a laugh, a nervous sort of sound. "Sexual excess, I'd call it."

"There's no such thing," said the big man flatly. "Depending on who you are and what sex, you can do it only until you can't do it any more, or you can keep on until finally nothing happens. One man might get along beautifully with some mild kind of sexual relief twice a month or less. Another might normally look for it eight, nine times a day."

"I'd hardly call that normal."

"I would. Unusual it might be, but it's 100 per cent normal for the guy who has it, long as it isn't pathological. By which I mean, capacity is capacity, by the cupful, by the horsepower, by the flight ceiling. Man or machine, you do no harm by operating within the parameters of design. What does do harm—lots of it, and some of the worst kind—is guilt and a sense of sin, where the sin turns out to be some sort of natural appetite. I've read case histories of boys who have suicided because of a nocturnal emission, or because they yielded to the temptation to masturbate after five, six weeks of self-denial—a denial, of course, that all by itself makes them preoccupied, absolutely obsessed by something that should have no more importance than clearing the

223

throat. (I wish I could say that this kind of horror story lives only in the ancient scripts, but on many a world right this minute, it still goes on.)

"This guilt and sin thing is easier for some people to understand if you take it outside the area of sex. There are some religious orthodoxies which require a very specific diet, and the absolute exculsion of certain items. Given enough indoctrination for long enough, you can keep a man eating only (we'll say) 'flim' while 'flam' is forbidden. He'll get along on thin moldy flim and live half starved in a whole warehouse full of nice fresh flam. You can make him ill—even kill him, if you have the knack—just by convincing him that the flim he just ate was really flam in disguise. Or you can drive him psychotic by slipping him suggestions until he acquires a real taste for flam and gets a supply and hides it and nibbles at it secretly every time he fights temptation and loses.

"So imagine the power of guilt when it isn't a flim-and-flam kind of manufactured orthodoxy you're violating, but a deep pressure down in the cells somewhere. It's as mad, and as dangerous, as grafting in an ethical-guilt structure which forbids or inhibits yielding to the need for the B-vitamin complex or potassium."

"Oh, but," Charli interrupted, "now you're talking about vital necessities—survival factors."

"I sure as hell am," said Vorhidin in Charli's own idiom, and grinned a swift and hilarious—and very accurate—imitation of Charli's flash-beacon smile. "Now it's time to trot out some of the things I mentioned before, things that can hurt you much more than ignorance—the things you know that ain't so." He laughed suddenly. "This is kind of fun, you know? I've been to a lot of worlds, and some are miles and years different from others in a thousand ways: but this thing I'm about to demonstrate, this particular shut-the-eyes, shut-the-brains conversation you can get anywhere you go. Are you ready? Tell me, then: what's wrong with incest? I take it back—you know me. Don't tell me. Tell some stranger, some fume-sniffer or alcohol addict in a spaceport bar." He put out both hands, the fingers so shaped that one could all but see light glisten from the imaginary glass he held. He said in a slurred voice, "Shay, shtranger, whut's a-wrong wit' in-shest, hm?" He closed one eye and rolled the other toward Charli.

Charli stopped to think. "You mean, morally, or what?"

"Let's skip that whole segment. Right and wrong depend on too many things from one place to another, although I have some theories of my own. No—let's be sitting in this bar and agree that incest is just awful, and go on from there. What's really wrong with it?"

"You breed too close, you get faulty offspring. Idiots and dead babies without heads and all that."

"I knew it! I knew it!" crowed the big Vexveltian. "Isn't it wonderful? From the rocky depths of a Stone Age culture through the brocades and knee-breeches sort of grand opera civilizations all the way out to the computer technocracies, where they graft electrodes into their heads and shunt their thinking into a box—you ask that question and you get that answer. It's something everybody just *knows*. You don't have to look at the evidence."

"Where do you go for evidence?"

"To dinner, for one place, where you'll eat idiot pig or feeble-minded cow. Any livestock breeder will tell you that, once you have a strain you want to keep and develop, you breed father to daughter and to granddaughter, and then brother to sister. You keep that up indefinitely until the desirable trait shows up recessive, and you stop it there. But it might never show up recessive. In any case, it's rare indeed when anything goes wrong in the very first generation; but you in the bar, there, you're totally convinced that it will. And are you prepared to say that every mental retard is the product of an incestuous union? You'd better not, or you'll hurt the feelings of some pretty nice people. That's a tragedy that can happen to anybody, and I doubt there's any more chance of it between related parents than there is with anyone else.

"But you still don't see the funniest . . . or maybe it's just the oddest part of that thing you know that just ain't so. Sex is a pretty popular topic on most worlds. Almost every aspect of it that is ever mentioned has nothing to do with procreation. For every mention of pregnancy or childbirth, I'd say there are hundreds which deal only with the sex act itself. But mention incest, and the response always deals with offspring. Always! To consider and discuss a pleasure or love relationship between blood relatives, you've apparently got to make some sort of special mental effort that nobody, anywhere, seems able to do easily—some not at all."

"I have to admit I never made it. But then—what *is* wrong with incest, with or without pregnancy?"

"Aside from moral considerations, you mean. The moral consideration is that it's a horrifying thought, and it's a horrifying thought because it always has been. Biologically speaking, I'd say there's nothing wrong with it. Nothing. I'd go even further, with Dr. Phelvelt—ever hear of him?"

"I don't think so."

"He was a biological theorist who could get one of his books banned on worlds that had never censored anything before—even on worlds which had science and freedom of research and freedom of speech as the absolute keystones of their world structure. Anyway, Phelvelt had a very special kind of mind, always ready to take the next step no matter where it is, without insisting that it's somewhere where it isn't. He thought well, he wrote well, and he had a vast amount of knowledge outside his specialty and a real knack for unearthing what he happened not to know. And he called that sexual tension between blood relatives a survival factor."

"How did he come to that?"

"By a lot of separate paths which came together in the same place. Everybody knows (this one *is* so!) that there are evolutionary pressures which make for changes in a species. Not much (before Phelvelt) had been written about stabilizing forces. But don't you see, inbreeding is one of them?"

"Not offhand, I don't."

"Well, look at it, man! Take a herd of animal as a good example. The bull covers his cows, and when they deliver heifers and the heifers grow up, he covers them too. Sometimes there's a third and even a fourth generation of them before he gets displaced by a younger bull. And all that while, the herd characteristics are purified and reinforced. You don't easily get animals with slightly different metabolisms which might tend to wander away from the feeding ground the others were using. You won't get high-bottom cows which would necessitate Himself bringing something to stand on when he came courting." Through Charli's shout of laughter he continued, "So there you have it—stabilization, purification, greater survival value—all resulting from the pressure to breed in."

"I see, I see. And the same thing would be true of lions or fish or tree toads, or—"

"Or any animal. A lot of things have been said about Nature, that she's implacable, cruel, wasteful and so on. I like to think she's—reasonable. I concede that she reaches that state cruelly, at times, and wastefully and all the rest. But she has a way of coming up with the pragmatic solution, the one that works. To build in a pressure which tends to standardize and purify a successful stage, and to call in the exogene, the infusion of fresh blood, only once in several generations— that seems to me most reasonable."

"More so," Charli said, "than what we've always done, when you look at it that way. Every generation a new exogene, the blood kept churned up, each new organism full of pressures which haven't had a chance with the environment."

"I suppose," said Vorhidin, "you could argue that the incest taboo is responsible for the restlessness that pulled mankind out of the caves, but that's a little too simplistic for me. I'd have preferred a mankind that moved a little more slowly, a little more certainly, and never fell back. I think the ritual exogamy that made inbreeding a crime and 'deceased wife's sister' a law against incest is responsible for another kind of restlessness."

He grew very serious. "There's a theory that certain normal habit patterns should be allowed to run their course. Take the sucking reflex, for example. It has been said that infants who have been weaned too early plague themselves all their lives with oral activity—chewing on straws, smoking intoxicants in pipes, drinking out of bottle by preference, nervously manipulating the lips, and so on. With that as an analogy, you may look again at the restlessness of mankind all through history. Who but a gaggle of frustrates, never in their lives permitted all the ways of love within the family, could coin such a concept as 'motherland' and give their lives to it and for it? There's a great urge to love Father, and another to topple him. Hasn't humanity set up its beloved Fathers, its Big Brothers, loved and worshiped and given and died for them, rebelled and killed and replaced them? A lot of them richly deserved it, I concede, but it would have been better to have done it on its own merits and not because they were nudged by a deep-down, absolutely sexual tide of which they could not speak because they had learned that it was unspeakable.

"The same sort of currents flow within the family unit. So-called 'sibling rivalry' is too well known to be described, and the frequency of bitter quarreling between siblings is, in most cultures and their literature, a sort of cliché. Only a very few psychologists have dared to put forward the obvious explanation that, more often than not, these frictions are inverted love feelings, well salted with horror and guilt. It's a pattern that makes conflict between siblings all but a certainty, and it's a problem which, once stated, describes its own solution. . . . Have you ever read Vexworth? No? You should—I think you'd find him fascinating. Ecologist; in his way quite as much of a giant as Phelvelt."

"Ecologist—that has something to do with life and environment, right?"

"Ecology has *everything* to do with life and environment; it studies them as reciprocals, as interacting and mutually controlling forces. It goes without saying that the main aim and purpose of any life form is optimum survival; but 'optimum survival' is a meaningless term without considering the environment in which it has to happen. As the environment changes, the organism has to change its ways and means, even its basic design. Human beings are notorious for changing their environment, and in most of our history in most places, we have made these changes without ecological considerations. This is disaster, every time. This is overpopulation, past the capabilities of producing food and shelter enough. This is the rape of irreplaceable natural resources. This is the contamination of water supplies. And it is also the twisting and thwarting of psychosexual needs in the emotional environment.

"Vexvelt was founded by those two, Charli—Phelvelt and Vexworth—and is named for them. As far as I know it is the only culture ever devised on ecological lines. Our sexual patterns derive from the ecological base and are really only a very small part of our structure. Yet for that one aspect of our lives, we are avoided and shunned and pretty much unmentionable."

It took a long time for Charli to be able to let these ideas in, and longer for him to winnow and absorb them. But all the while he lived surrounded by beauty and fulfillment, by people, young and old, who were capable of total concentration on art and learning and building and processing, people who gave to each other and to their land and air and water just a little more than they took. He finished his survey largely because he had started it; for a while he was uncertain of what he would do with it.

When at length he came to Vorhidin and said he wanted to stay on Vexvelt, the big man smiled, but he shook his head. "I know you want to, Charli—but do you?"

"I don't know what you mean." He looked out at the dark bole of one of the Vexveltian poplars; Tyng was there, like a flower, an orchid. "It's more than that," said Charli, "more than my wanting to be a Vexveltian. You need me."

"We love you," Vorhidin said simply. "But—need?"

"If I went back," said Charli Bux, "and Terratu got its hands on my survey, what do you think would become of Vexvelt?"

"You tell me."

"First Terratu would come to trade, and then others, and then others; and then they would fight each other, and fight you . . . you need someone here who knows this, really knows it, and who can deal with it when it starts. It will start, you know, even without my survey; sooner or later someone will be able to do what I did—a shipment of feldspar, a sheet of pure metal. They will destroy you."

"They will never come near us."

"You think not. Listen: no matter how the other worlds disapprove, there is one force greater: greed."

"Not in this case, Charli. And this is what I want you to be able to understand, all the way down to your cells. Unless you do, you can never live here. We are shunned, Charli. If you had been born here, that would not matter so much to you. If you throw in your lot with us, it would have to be a total commitment. But you should not make such a decision without understanding how completely you will be excluded from everything else you have ever known."

"What makes you think I don't know it now?"

"You say we need defending. You say other-world traders will exploit us. That only means you don't understand. Charli: listen to me. Go back to Terratu. Make the strongest presentation you can for trade with Vexvelt. See how they react. Then you'll know—then you can decide."

"And aren't you afraid I might be right, and because of me, Vexvelt will be robbed and murdered?"

And Vorhidin shook his big head, smiling, and said, "Not one bit, Charli Bux. Not one little bit."

So Charli went back, and saw (after a due delay) the Archive Master, learned what he learned, and came out and looked about him at his home world and, through that, at all the worlds like it; and then he went to the secret place where the Vexveltian ship was moored, and it opened to him. Tyng was there, Tamba, and Vorhidin. Charli said, "Take me home."

In the last seconds before they took the Drive jump, and he could look through the port at the shining face of Terratu for the last time in his life, Charli said, "Why? Why? How did human beings come to hate this one thing so much that they would rather die insane and in agony than accept it? How did it happen, Vorhidin?"

"I don't know," said the Vexveltian.

Justly famous for his spectacular science–fiction novels, *The Demol-ished Man* (1953) and *The Stars My Destination* (1956), **Alfie Bester** is an urbane, witty gentleman who is also one of the best short-fiction writers in the business. Again active (in science fiction) after a long hiatus, his most recent books are *The Computer Connection* (1975) and the collections *Star Light, Star Bright* and *The Light Fantastic* (both 1976), with another novel on the way.

"Will You Wait?" is a fantasy of the type made famous by the late and lamented *Unknown*, and confirms what most of us have long suspected—at least *some* of the Devil's henchpersons work for the telephone company.

Will You Wait?

BY ALFRED BESTER

They keep writing those antiquated stories about bargains with the Devil. You know . . . sulphur, spells and pen-tagrams; tricks, snares and delusions. They don't know what they're talking about. Twentieth century diabolism is slick and streamlined, like jukeboxes and automatic elevators and television and all the other modern efficiencies that leave you helpless and infuriated.

A year ago I got fired from an agency job for the third time in ten months. I had to face the fact that I was a failure. I was also dead broke. I decided to sell my soul to the Devil, but the problem was how to find him. I went down to the main reference room of the library and read everything on demonology and devillore. Like I said, it was all just talk. Anyway, if I could have afforded the expensive ingredients which they claimed could raise the Devil, I wouldn't have had to deal with him in the first place.

I was stumped, so I did the obvious thing; I called Celebrity Service. A delicate young man answered.

I asked, "Can you tell me where the Devil is?"

"Are you a subscriber to Celebrity Service?"

"No."

"Then I can give you no information."

"I can afford to pay a small fee for one item."

"You wish limited service?"

"Yes."

"Who is the celebrity, please?"

"The Devil."

"Who?"

"The Devil . . . Satan, Lucifer, Scratch, Old Nick . . . The Devil."

"One moment, please." In five minutes he was back, extremely annoyed. "Veddy soddy. The Devil is no longer a celebrity."

He hung up. I did the sensible thing and looked through the telephone directory. On a page decorated with ads for Sardi's Restaurant I found Satan, Shaitan, Carnage & Bael, 477 Madison Avenue, Judson 3-1900. I called them. A bright young woman answered.

"SSC&B. Good morning."

"May I speak to Mr. Satan, please?"

"The lines are busy. Will you wait?"

I waited and lost my dime. I wrangled with the operator and lost another dime but got the promise of a refund in postage stamps. I called Satan, Shaitan, Carnage & Bael again.

"SSC&B. Good morning."

"May I speak to Mr. Satan? And please don't leave me hanging on the phone. I'm calling from a—"

The switchboard cut me off and buzzed. I waited. The coin-box gave a warning click. At last a line opened.

"Miss Hogan's office."

"May I speak to Mr. Satan?"

"Who's calling?"

"He doesn't know me. It's a personal matter."

"I'm sorry. Mr. Satan is no longer with our organization."

"Can you tell me where I can find him?"

There was muffled discussion in broad Brooklyn and then Miss Hogan spoke in crisp Secretary: "Mr. Satan is now with Beëlzebub, Belial, Devil & Orgy."

I looked them up in the phone directory. 383 Madison Avenue, Plaze 6-1900. I dialed. The phone rang once and then choked. A metallic voice spoke in sing-song: "The number you are dialing is not a working number. Kindly consult your directory for the correct number. This is a recorded message." I consulted my directory. It said Plaze 6-1900. I dialed again and got the same recorded message.

I finally broke through to a live operator who was persuaded to give me the new number of Beëlzebub, Belial, Devil & Orgy. I called them. A bright young woman answered.

"B.B.D.O. Good morning."

"May I speak to Mr. Satan, please?"

"Who?"

"Mr. Satan."

"I'm sorry. There is no such person with our organization."

"Then give me Beëlzebub or the Devil."

"One moment, please."

I waited. Every half minute she opened my wire long enought to gasp: "Still ringing the Dev—" and then cut off before I had a chance to answer. At last a bright young woman spoke. "Mr. Devil's office."

"May I speak to him?"

"Who's calling?"

I gave her my name.

"He's on another line. Will you wait?"

I waited. I was fortified with a dwindling reserve of nickels and dimes. After twenty minutes, the bright young woman

233

spoke again: "He's just gone into an emergency meeting. Can he call you back?"

"No. I'll try again."

Nine days later I finally got him.

"Yes, sir? What can I do for you?"

I took a breath. "I want to sell you my soul."

"Have you got anything on paper?"

"What do you mean, anything on paper?"

"The Property, my boy. The Sell. You can't expect B.B.D.O. to buy a pig in a poke. We may drink out of dixie cups up here, but the sauce has got to be a hundred proof. Bring in your Presentation. My girl'll set up an appointment."

I prepared a Presentation of my soul with plenty of Sell. Then I called his girl.

"I'm sorry, he's on the Coast. Call back in two weeks."

Five weeks later she gave me an appointment. I went up and sat in the photo-montage reception room of B.B.D.O. for two hours, balancing my Sell on my knees. Finally I was ushered into a corner office decorated with Texas brands in glowing neon. The Devil was lounging on his contour chair, dictating to an Iron Maiden. He was a tall man with the phoney voice of a sales manager; the kind that talks loud in elevators. He gave me a Sincere handshake and immediately looked through my Presentation.

"Not bad," he said. "Not bad at all. I think we can do business. Now what did you have in mind? The usual?"

"Money, success, happiness."

He nodded. "The usual. Now we're square shooters in this shop. B.B.D.O. doesn't dry-gulch. We'll guarantee money, success and happiness."

"For how long?"

"Normal life-span. No tricks, my boy. We take our estimates from the Actuary Tables. Offhand I'd say you're good for another forty, forty-five years. We can pin-point that in the contract later."

"No tricks?"

He gestured impatiently. "That's all bad public relations, what you're thinking. I promise you, no tricks."

"Guaranteed?"

"Not only do we guarantee service; we *insist* on giving service. B.B.D.O. doesn't want any beefs going up to the

Fair Practice Committee. You'll have to call on us for service at least twice a year or the contract will be terminated."

"What kind of service?"

He shrugged. "Any kind. Shine your shoes; empty ashtrays; bring you dancing girls. That can be pin-pointed later. We just insist that you use us at least twice a year. We've got to give you a quid for your quo. *Quid pro quo.* Check?"

"But no tricks?"

"No tricks. I'll have our legal department draw up the contract. Who's representing you?"

"You mean an agent? I haven't got one."

He was startled. "Haven't got an agent? My boy, you're living dangerously. Why, we could skin you alive. Get yourself an agent and tell him to call me."

"Yes, sir. M-May I . . . Could I ask a question?"

"Shoot. Everything is open and above-board at B.B.D.O."

"What will it be like for me . . . wh-when the contract terminates?"

"You really want to know?"

"Yes."

"I don't advise it."

"I want to know."

He showed me. It was like a hideous session with a psychoanalyst, in perpetuity . . . an eternal, agonizing self-indictment. It was hell. I was shaken.

"I'd rather have inhuman fiends torturing me," I said.

He laughed. "They can't compare to man's inhumanity to himself. Well . . . changed your mind, or is it a deal?"

"It's a deal."

We shook hands and he ushered me out. "Don't forget," he warned. "Protect yourself. Get an agent. Get the best."

I signed with Sibyl & Sphinx. That was on March 3. I called S & S on March 15. Mrs. Sphinx said: "Oh yes, there's been a hitch. Miss Sibyl was negotiating with B.B.D.O. for you, but she had to fly to Sheol. I've taken over for her."

I called April 1. Miss Sibyl said: "Oh yes, there's been a slight delay. Mrs. Sphinx had to go to Salem for a try-out. A witch-burning. She'll be back next week."

I called April 15. Miss Sibyl's bright young secretary told me that there was some delay getting the contracts typed. It seemed that B.B.D.O. was re-organizing its legal department.

235

On May 1, Sibyl & Sphinx told me that the contracts had arrived and that *their* legal department was looking them over.

I had to take a menial job in June to keep body and soul together. I worked in the stencil department of a network. At least once a week a script would come in about a bargain with the Devil which was signed, sealed and delivered before the opening commercial. I used to laugh at them. After four months of negotiation I was still thread-bare.

I saw the Devil once, bustling down Park Avenue. He was running for Congress and was very busy being jolly and hearty with the electorate. He addressed every cop and doorman by first name. When I spoke to him he got a little frightened; thinking I was a Communist or worse. He didn't remember me at all.

In July, all negotiations stopped; everybody was away on vacation. In August everybody was overseas for some Black Mass Festival. In September Sibyl & Sphinx called me to their office to sign the contract. It was thirty-seven pages long, and fluttered with pasted-in corrections and additions. There were half a dozen tiny boxes stamped on the margin of every page.

"If you only knew the work that went into this contract," Sibyl & Sphinx told me with satisfaction.

"It's kind of long, isn't it?"

"It's the short contracts that make all the trouble. Initial every box, and sign on the last page. All six copies."

I initialed and signed. When I was finished I didn't feel any different. I'd expected to start tingling with money, success and happiness.

"Is it a deal now?" I asked.

"Not until *he's* signed it."

"I can't hold out much longer."

"We'll send it over by messenger."

I waited a week and then called.

"You forgot to initial one of the boxes," they told me.

I went to the office and initialed. After another week I called.

"*He* forgot to initial one of the boxes," they told me that time.

On October 1st I received a special delivery parcel. I also received a registered letter. The parcel contained the signed,

236

sealed and delivered contract between me and the Devil. I could at last be rich, successful and happy. The registered letter was from B.B.D.O. and informed me that in view of my failure to comply with Clause 27-A of the contract, it was considered terminated, and I was due for collection at their convenience. I rushed down to Sibyl & Sphinx.

"What's Clause 27-A?" they asked.

We looked it up. It was the clause that required me to use the services of the Devil at least once every six months.

"What's the date of the contract?" Sibyl & Sphinx asked.

We looked it up. The contract was dated March 1st, the day I'd had my first talk with the Devil in his office.

"March, April, May . . ." Miss Sibyl counted on her fingers. "That's right. Seven months have elapsed. Are you sure you didn't ask for *any* service?"

"How could I? I didn't have a contract."

"We'll see about this," Mrs. Sphinx said grimly. She called B.B.D.O. and had a spirited argument with the Devil and his legal department. Then she hung up. "He says you shook hands on the deal March 1st," she reported. "He was prepared in good faith to go ahead with his side of the bargain."

"How could I know? I didn't have a contract."

"Didn't you ask for anything?"

"No. I was waiting for the contract."

Sibyl & Sphinx called in their legal department and presented the case.

"You'll have to arbitrate," the legal department said, and explained that agents are forbidden to act as their client's attorney.

I hired the legal firm of Wizard, Warlock, Vodoo, Dowser & Hag (99 Watt Street, Exchange 3-1900) to represent me before the Arbitration Board (479 Madison Avenue, Lexington 5-1900). They asked for a $200 retainer plus twenty percent of the contract's benefits. I'd managed to save $34 during the four months I was working in the stencil department. They waived the retainer and went ahead with the Arbitration preliminaries.

On November 15 the network demoted me to the mail room, and I seriously contemplated suicide. Only the fact that my soul was in jeopardy in an arbitration stopped me.

The case came up December 12th. I was tried before a panel of three impartial Arbitrators and took all day. I was told they'd mail me their decision. I waited a week and called Wizard, Warlock, Vodoo, Dowser & Hag.

They've recessed for the Christmas holidays," they told me.

I called January 2.

"One of them's out of town."

I called January 10.

"He's back, but the other two are out of town."

"When will I get a decision?"

"It could take months."

"How do you think my chances look?"

"Well, we've never lost an arbitration."

"That sounds pretty good."

"But there can always be a first time."

That sounded pretty bad. I got scared and figured I'd better copper my bets. I did the sensible thing and hunted through the telephone directory until I found Seraphim, Cherubim and Angel, 666 Fifth Avenue, Templeton 6-1900. I called them. A bright young woman answered.

"Seraphim, Cherubim and Angel. Good morning."

"May I speak to Mr. Angel, please?"

"He's on another line. Will you wait?"

I'm still waiting.

The dominant force in science fiction from the late 1930s to the early 1950s, **John W. Campbell, Jr.,** made *Astounding Science Fiction* the leading magazine of sf's "Golden Age." And to prove that that accomplishment was no fluke, his *Unknown* (later *Unknown Worlds*) was one of the outstanding fantasy magazines of all time. Campbell was also a gifted writer, of both "super-science" and (as "Don Stuart") more serious and reflective science fiction.

This famous story found expression, in greatly altered form, on the screen as *The Thing* (a.k.a. *The Thing from Outer Space*), which set the tone for the monster films of the 1950s. Although considered a classic, it has not been anthologized as often as it deserves, because of length considerations. It fuses a first-rate mystery story with exciting science fiction, and poses one of the most important and multilayered questions in sf.

Who Goes There?

BY JOHN W. CAMPBELL, JR.

I

The place stank. A queer, mingled stench that only the ice-buried cabins of an Antarctic camp know, compounded of reeking human sweat, and the heavy, fish-oil stench of melted seal blubber. An overtone of liniment combated the musty smell of sweat-and-snow-drenched furs. The acrid odor of burned cooking-fat, and the animal, not-unpleasant smell of dogs, diluted by time, hung in the air.

Lingering odors of machine oil contrasted sharply with the taint of harness dressing and leather. Yet, somehow, through all that reek of human beings and their associates—dogs, machines, and cooking—came another taint. It was a queer, neck-ruffling thing, a faintest suggestion of an odor alien among the smells of industry and life. And it was a life-smell. But it came from the thing that lay bound with cord and tarpaulin on the table, dripping slowly, methodically onto the heavy planks, dank and gaunt under the unshielded glare of the electric light.

Blair, the little bald-pated biologist of the expedition, twitched nervously at the wrappings, exposing clear, dark ice beneath and then pulling the tarpaulin back into place restlessly. His little birdlike motions of suppressed eagerness danced his shadow across the fringe of dingy gray underwear hanging from the low ceiling, the equatorial fringe of stiff, graying hair around his naked skull a comical halo about the shadow's head.

Commander Garry brushed aside the lax legs of a suit of underwear, and stepped toward the table. Slowly his eyes traced around the rings of men sardined into the Administration Building. His tall, stiff body straightened finally, and he nodded. "Thirty-seven. All here." His voice was low, yet carried the clear authority of the commander by nature, as well as by title.

"You know the outline of the story back of that find of the Secondary Pole Expedition. I have been conferring with Second-in-Command McReady, and Norris, as well as Blair and Doctor Copper. There is a difference of opinion, and because it involves the entire group, it is only just that the entire Expedition personnel act on it.

"I am going to ask McReady to give you the details of the story, because each of you has been too busy with his own work to follow closely the endeavors of the others. McReady?"

Moving from the smoke-blued background, McReady was a figure from some forgotten myth, a looming, bronze statue that held life, and walked. Six feet four inches he stood as he halted beside the table, and with a characteristic glance upward to assure himself of room under the low ceiling beams, straightened. His rough, clashingly orange windproof jacket he still had on, yet on his huge frame it did not seem misplaced. Even here, four feet beneath the drift-wind that droned across the antarctic waste above the ceiling, the cold of the frozen continent leaked in, and gave meaning to the harshness of the man. And he was bronze—his great red-bronze beard, the heavy hair that matched it. The gnarled, corded hands gripping, relaxing, gripping and relaxing on the table planks were bronze. Even the deep-sunken eyes beneath heavy brows were bronzed.

Age-resisting endurance of the metal spoke in the cragged heavy outlines of his face, and the mellow tones of the heavy voice. "Norris and Blair agree on one thing: that animal we found was not—terrestrial in origin. Norris fears there may be danger in that; Blair says there is none.

"But I'll go back to how and why we found it. From all that was known before we came here, it appeared that this point was exactly over the South Magnetic Pole of Earth. The compass does point straight down here, as you all know. The more delicate instruments of the physicists, instruments especially designed for this expedition and its study of the magnetic pole, detected a secondary effect, a secondary, less powerful magnetic influence about eighty miles southwest of here.

"The Secondary Magnetic Expedition went out to investigate it. There is no need for details. We found it, but it was not the huge meteorite or magnetic mountain Norris had expected to find. Iron ore is magnetic, of course; iron more so—and certain special steels even more magnetic. From the surface indications, the secondary pole we found was small, so small that the magnetic effect it had was preposterous. No magnetic material conceivable could have that effect. Soundings through the ice indicated it was within one hundred feet of the glacier surface.

"I think you should know the structure of the place. There is a broad plateau, a level sweep that runs more than a hundred and fifty miles due south from the Secondary Station, Van Wall says. He didn't have time or fuel to fly far-

241

ther, but it was running smoothly due south then. Right there, where that buried thing was, there is an ice-drowned mountain ridge, a granite wall of unshakable strength that has dammed back the ice creeping from the south.

And four hundred miles due south is the South Polar Plateau. You have asked me at various times why it gets warmer here when the wind rises, and most of you know. As a meterologist I'd have staked my word that no wind could blow at minus seventy degrees, that no more than a five-mile wind could blow at minus fifty without causing warming due to friction with ground, snow and ice, and the air itself.

"We camped there on the lip of that ice-drowned mountain range for twelve days. We dug our camp into the blue ice that formed the surface, and escaped most of it. But for twelve consecutive days the wind blew at forty-five miles an hour. It went as high as forty-eight, and fell to forty-one at times. The temperature was minus sixty-three degrees. It rose to minus sixty and fell to minus sixty-eight. It was meteorologically impossible, and it went on uninterruptedly for twelve days and twelve nights.

"Somewhere to the south, the frozen air of the South Polar Plateau slides down from that eighteen-thousand-foot bowl, down a mountain pass, over a glacier, and starts north. There must be a funneling mountain chain that directs it, and sweeps it away for four hundred miles to hit that bald plateau where we found the secondary pole, and three hundred and fifty miles farther north reaches the Antarctic Ocean.

"It's been frozen there since Antarctica froze twenty million years ago. There never has been a thaw there.

"Twenty million years ago Antarctica was beginning to freeze. We've investigated, though, and built speculations. What we believe happened was about like this.

"Something came down out of space, a ship. We saw it there in the blue ice, a thing like a submarine without a conning tower or directive vanes, two hundred and eighty feet long and forty-five feet in diameter at its thickest.

"Eh, Van Wall? Space? Yes, but I'll explain that better later." McReady's steady voice went on.

"It came down from space, driven and lifted by forces men haven't discovered yet, and somehow—perhaps something went wrong then—it tangled with Earth's magnetic field. It came south here, out of control probably, circling the magnetic pole. That's a savage country there; but when Antarctica was still freezing, it must have been a thousand times more savage. There must have been blizzard snow, as well as drift, new snow falling as the continent glaciated. The swirl there must have been particularly bad, the wind hurling a solid blanket of white over the lip of that now-buried mountain.

"The ship struck solid granite head-on, and cracked up. Not every one of the passengers in it was killed, but the ship must have been ruined, her driving mechanism locked. It tangled with Earth's field, Norris believes. No thing made by intelligent beings can tangle with the dead immensity of a planet's natural forces and survive.

"One of its passengers stepped out. The wind we saw there never fell below forty-one, and the temperature never rose above minus sixty. Then—the wind must have been stronger. And there was drift falling in a solid sheet. The *thing* was lost completely in ten paces." He paused for a moment, the deep, steady voice giving way to the drone of wind overhead and the uneasy, malicious gurgling in the pipe of the galley stove.

Drift—a drift-wind was sweeping by overhead. Right now the snow picked up by the mumbling wind fled in level, blinding lines across the face of the buried camp. If a man stepped out of the tunnels that connected each of the camp buildings beneath the surface, he'd be lost in ten paces. Out there, the slim, black finger of the radio mast lifted 300 feet into the air, and at its peak was the clear night sky. A sky of thin, whining wind rushing steadily from beyond to another beyond under the licking curling mantle of the aurora. And off north, the horizon flamed with queer, angry colors of the midnight twilight. That was spring 300 feet above Antarctica.

At the surface—it was white death. Death of a needle-fingered cold driven before the wind, sucking heat from any warm thing. Cold—and white mist of endless, everlasting drift, the fine, fine particles of licking snow that obscured all things.

Kinner, the little scar-faced cook, winced. Five days ago he had stepped out to the surface to reach a cache of frozen beef. He had reached it, started back—and the drift-wind leaped out of the south. Cold, white death that streamed across the ground blinded him in twenty seconds. He stumbled on wildly in circles. It was half an hour before rope-guided men from below found him in the impenetrable murk.

It was easy for man—or *thing*—to get lost in ten paces.

"And the drift-wind then was probably more impenetrable than we know." McReady's voice snapped Kinner's mind back. Back to welcome, dank warmth of the Ad Building. "The passenger of the ship wasn't prepared either, it appears. It froze within ten feet of the ship.

"We dug down to find the ship, and our tunnel happened to find the frozen—animal. Barclay's ice-ax struck its skull.

"When we saw what it was, Barclay went back to the tractor, started the fire up, and when the steam pressure built, sent a call for Blair and Doctor Copper. Barclay himself was sick then. Stayed sick for three days, as a matter of fact.

"When Blair and Copper came, we cut out the animal in a block of ice, as you see, wrapped it, and loaded it on the tractor for return here. We wanted to get into that ship.

"We reached the side and found the metal was something we didn't know. Our beryllium-bronze, nonmagnetic tools wouldn't touch it. Barclay had some tool steel on the tractor, and that wouldn't scratch it, either. We made reasonable tests—even tried some acid from the batteries with no results.

"They must have had a passivating process to make magnesium metal resist acid that way, and the alloy must have been at least ninety-five per cent magnesium. But we had no way of guessing that, so when we spotted the barely opened lock door, we cut around it. There was clear, hard ice inside the lock, where we couldn't reach it. Through the little crack we could look in and see that only metal and tools were in there, so we decided to loosen the ice with a bomb.

"We had decanite bombs and thermite. Thermite is the ice-softener; decanite might have shattered valuable things, where the thermite's heat would just loosen the ice. Doctor Copper, Norris, and I placed a twenty-five pound thermite bomb, wired it, and took the connector up the tunnel to the surface, where Blair had the steam tractor waiting. A hundred yards the other side of that granite wall we set off the thermite bomb.

"The magnesium metal of the ship caught, of course. The glow of the bomb flared and died, then, it began to flare again. We ran back to the tractor, and gradually the glare built up. From where we were we could see the whole ice field illuminated from beneath with an unbearable light; the ship's shadow was a great, dark cone reaching off toward the north, where the twilight was just about gone. For a moment it lasted, and we counted three other shadow-things that might have been other—passengers—frozen there. Then the ice was crashing down and against the ship.

"That's why I told you about that place. The wind sweeping down from the Pole was at our backs. Steam and hydrogen flame were torn away in white ice-fog; the flaming heat under the ice there was yanked away toward the Antarctic Ocean before it touched us. Otherwise we wouldn't have come back, even with the shelter of that granite ridge that stopped the light.

"Somehow in the blinding inferno we could see great hunched things—black bulks. They shed even the furious incandescence of the magnesium for a time. Those must have been the engines, we knew. Secrets going in blazing glory—secrets that might have given man the planets. Mysterious things that could lift and hurl that ship—and had soaked in the force of the Earth's magnetic field. I saw Norris's mouth move, and ducked. I couldn't hear him.

"Insulation—something—gave way. All Earth's field they'd soaked up twenty million years before broke loose. The aurora in the sky above licked down, and the whole plateau there was bathed in cold fire that blanketed vision. The ice-ax in my hand got red hot, and hissed on the ice. Metal buttons on my clothes burned into me. And a flash of electric blue seared upward from beyond the granite wall.

"Then the walls of ice crashed down on it. For an instant it squealed the way dry-ice does when it's pressed between metal.

"We were blind and groping in the dark for hours while our eyes recovered. We found every coil within a mile was fused rubbish, the dynamo and every radio set, the earphones

245

and speakers. If we hadn't had the steam tractor, we wouldn't have gotten over to the Secondary Camp.

"Van Wall flew in from Big Magnet at sunup, as you know. We came home as soon as possible. That is the history of—that." McReady's great bronze beard gestured toward the thing on the table.

II

Blair stirred uneasily, his little, bony fingers wriggling under the harsh light. Little brown freckles on his knuckles slid back and forth as the tendons under the skin twitched. He pulled aside a bit of the tarpaulin and looked impatiently at the dark ice-bound thing inside.

McReady's big body straightened somewhat. He'd ridden the rocking, jarring steam tractor forty miles that day, pushing on to Big Magnet here. Even his calm will had been pressed by the anxiety to mix again with humans. It was lone and quiet out there in Secondary Camp, where a wolf-wind howled down from the Pole. Wolf-wind howling in his sleep—winds droning and the evil, unspeakable face of that monster leering up as he'd first seen it through clear, blue ice, with a bronze ice-ax buried in its skull.

The giant meteorologist spoke again. "The problem is this. Blair wants to examine the thing. Thaw it out and make micro slides of its tissues and so forth. Norris doesn't believe that is safe, and Blair does. Doctor Copper agrees pretty much with Blair. Norris is physicist, of course, not a biologist. But he makes a point I think we should all hear. Blair has described the microscopic life-forms biologists find living, even in this cold and inhospitable place. They freeze every winter, and thaw every summer—for three months—and live.

"The point Norris makes is—they thaw and live again. There must have been microscopic life associated with this creature. There is with every living thing we know. And Norris is afraid that we may release a plague—some germ disease unknown to Earth—if we thaw those microscopic things that have been frozen there for twenty million years.

"Blair admits that such micro life might retain the power

of living. Such unorganized things as individual cells can retain life for unknown periods, when solidly frozen. The beast itself is as dead as those frozen mammoths they find in Siberia. Organized, highly developed life forms can't stand that treatment.

"But micro-life could. Norris suggests that we may release some disease form that man, never having met it before, will be utterly defenseless against.

"Blair's answer is that there may be such still-living germs, but that Norris has the case reversed. They are utterly nonimmune to man. Our life chemistry probably—"

"Probably!" The little biologist's head lifted in a quick, birdlike motion. The halo of gray hair about his bald head ruffled as though angry. "Heh, one look—"

"I know," McReady acknowledged. "The thing is not earthly. It does not seem likely that it can have a life chemistry sufficiently like ours to make cross infection remotely possible. I would say that there is no danger."

McReady looked toward Dr. Copper. The physician shook his head slowly. "None whatever," he asserted confidently. "Man cannot infect or be infected by germs that live in such comparatively close relatives as the snakes. And they are, I assure you," his clean-shaven face grimaced uneasily, "*much* nearer to us than—*that*."

Vance Norris moved angrily. He was comparatively short in this gathering of big men, some five-feet-eight, and his stocky, powerful build tended to make him seem shorter. His black hair was crisp and hard, like short, steel wires, and his eyes were the gray of fractured steel. If McReady was a man of bronze, Norris was all steel. His movements, his thoughts, his whole bearing had the quick, hard impulse of a steel spring. His nerves were steel—hard, quick-acting—swift corroding.

He was decided on his point now, and he lashed out in its defense with a characteristic quick, clipped flow of words. "Different chemistry be damned. That thing may be dead— or, by God, it may not—but I don't like it. Damn it, Blair, let them see the monstrosity you are petting over there. Let them see the foul thing and decide for themselves whether they want that thing thawed out in this camp.

"Thawed out, by the way. That's got to be thawed out in

one of the shacks tonight, if it is thawed out. Somebody—
who's watchman tonight? Magnetic—oh, Connant. Cosmic
rays tonight. Well, you get to sit up with that twenty-million-
year-old mummy of his. Unwrap it, Blair. How the hell can
they tell what they are buying, if they can't see it? It may
have a different chemistry. I don't care what else it has, but I
know it has something I don't want. If you can judge by the
look on its face—it isn't human so maybe you can't—it was
annoyed when it froze. Annoyed, in fact, is just about as
close an approximation of the way it felt as crazy, mad, insane hatred. Neither one touches the subject.

"How the hell can these birds tell what they are voting on?
They haven't seen those three red eyes and that blue hair like
crawling worms. Crawling—damn, it's crawling there in the
ice right now!

"Nothing Earth ever spawned had the unutterable sublima-
tion of devastating wrath that thing let loose in its face when
it looked around its frozen desolation twenty million years
ago. Mad? It was mad clear through—searing, blistering
mad!

"Hell, I've had bad dreams ever since I looked at those
three red eyes. Nightmares. Dreaming the thing thawed out
and came to life—that it wasn't dead, or even wholly unconscious all those twenty million years, but just slowed. waiting—waiting. You'll dream, too, while that damned thing that
Earth wouldn't own is dripping, dripping in the Cosmos
House tonight.

"And, Connant," Norris whipped toward the cosmic ray
specialist, "won't you have fun sitting up all night in the
quiet. Wind whining above—and that thing dripping—" He
stopped for a moment, and looked around.

"I know. That's not science. But this is, it's psychology.
You'll have nightmares for a year to come. Every night since
I looked at that thing I've had 'em. That's why I hate it—sure
I do—and don't want it around. Put it back where it came
from and let it freeze for another twenty million years. I had
some swell nightmares—that it wasn't made like we are—
which is obvious—but of a different kind of flesh that it can
really control. That it can change its shape, and look like a
man—and wait to kill and eat—

"That's not a logical argument. I know it isn't. The thing isn't Earth-logic anyway.

"Maybe it has an alien body chemistry, and maybe its bugs do have a different body chemistry. A germ might not stand that, but, Blair and Copper, how about a virus? That's just an enzyme molecule, you've said. That wouldn't need anything but a protein molecule of any body to work on.

"And how are you so sure that, of the million varieties of microscopic life it my have, *none* of them are dangerous? How about diseases like hydrophobia—rabies—that attack any warm-blooded creature, whatever its body chemistry may be? And parrot fever? Have you a body like a parrot, Blair? And plain rot—gangrene—necrosis if you want? *That* isn't choosy about body chemistry!"

Blair looked up from his puttering long enough to meet Norris's angry gray eyes for an instant. "So far the only thing you have said this thing gave off that was catching was dreams. I'll go so far as to admit that." An impish, slightly malignant grin crossed the little man's seamed face. "I had some, too. So. It's dream-infectious. No doubt an exceedingly dangerous malady.

"So far as your other things go, you have a badly mistaken idea about viruses. In the first place, nobody has shown that the enzyme-molecule theory, and that alone, explains them. And in the second place, when you catch tobacco mosaic or wheat rust, let me know. A wheat plant is a lot nearer your body chemistry than this other-world creature is.

"And your rabies is limited, strictly limited. You can't get it from, nor give it to, a wheat plant or a fish—which is a collateral descendant of a common ancestor of yours. Which this, Norris, is not." Blair nodded pleasantly toward the tarpaulined bulk on the table.

"Well, thaw the damned thing in a tub of Formalin if you must. I've suggested that—"

"And I've said there would be no sense in it. You can't compromise. Why did you and Commander Garry come down here to study magnetism? Why weren't you content to stay at home? There's magnetic force enough in New York. I could no more study the life this thing once had from a Formalin-pickled sample than you could get the information you wanted back in New York. And—if this one is so

treated, *never in all time to come can there be a duplicate!*
The race it came from must have passed away in the twenty
million years it lay frozen, so that even if it came from Mars
then, we'd never find its like. And—the ship is gone.

"There's only one way to do this—and that's the best possible way. It must be thawed slowly, carefully, and not in
Formalin."

Commander Garry stood forward again, and Norris
stepped back muttering angrily. "I think Blair is right, gentlemen. What do you say?"

Connant grunted. "It sounds right to us, I think—only perhaps he ought to stand watch over it while it's thawing." He
grinned ruefully, brushing a stray lock of ripe-cherry hair
back from his forehead. "Swell idea, in fact—if he sits up
with his jolly little corpse."

Garry smiled slightly. A general chuckle of agreement
rippled over the group. "I should think any ghost it may have
had would have starved to death if it hung around here that
long, Connant," Garry suggested. "And you look capable of
taking care of it. 'Ironman' Connant ought to be able to take
out any opposing players still."

Connant shook himself uneasily. "I'm not worrying about
ghosts. Let's see that thing. I—"

Eagerly Blair was stripping back the ropes. A single throw
of the tarpaulin revealed the thing. The ice had melted somewhat in the heat of the room, and it was clear and blue as
thick, good glass. It shone wet and sleek under the harsh light
of the unshielded globe above.

The room stiffened abruptly. It was face up there on the
plain, greasy planks of the table. The broken haft of the
bronze ice-ax was still buried in the queer skull. Three mad,
hate-filled eyes blazed up with a living fire, bright as fresh-
spilled blood, from a face ringed with a writhing, loathsome
nest of worms, blue, mobile worms that crawled where hair
should grow—

Van Wall, six feet and 200 pounds of ice-nerved pilot,
gave a queer, strangled gasp, and butted, stumbled his way
out to the corridor. Half the company broke for the doors.
The others stumbled away from the table.

McReady stood at one end of the table watching them, his
great body planted solid on his powerful legs. Norris from

the opposite end glowered at the thing with smoldering hate. Outside the door, Garry was talking with half a dozen of the men at once.

Blair had a tack hammer. The ice that cased the thing *schluffed* crisply under its steel claw as it peeled from the thing it had cased for twenty thousand thousand years—

III

"I know you don't like the thing, Connant, but it just has to be thawed out right. You say leave it as it is till we get back to civilization. All right, I'll admit your argument that we could do a better and more complete job there is sound. But—how are we going to get this across the Line? We have to take this through one temperate zone, the equatorial zone, and halfway through the other temperate zone, before we get it to New York. You don't want to sit with it one night, but you suggest, then, that I hang its corpse in the freezer with the beef?" Blair looked up from his cautious chipping, his bald freckled skull nodding triumphantly.

Kinner, the stocky, scar-faced cook, saved Connant the trouble of answering. "Hey, you listen, mister. You put that thing in the box with the meat, and by all the gods there ever were, I'll put you in to keep it company. You birds have brought everything movable in this camp in onto my mess tables here already, and I had to stand for that. But you go putting things like that in my meat box, or even my meat cache here, and you cook your own damn grub."

"But, Kinner, this is the only table in Big Magnet that's big enough to work on," Blair objected. "Everybody's explained that."

"Yeah, and everybody's brought everything in here. Clark brings his dogs every time there's a fight and sews them up to civilization. All right, I'll admit your argument that we thing you haven't had on that table is the Boeing. And you'd 'a' had that in if you coulda figured a way to get it through the tunnels."

Commander Garry chuckled and grinned at Van Wall, the huge Chief Pilot. Van Wall's great blond beard twitched suspiciously as he nodded gravely to Kinner. "You're right, Kinner. The aviation department is the only one that treats you right."

"It does get crowded, Kinner," Garry acknowledged. "But I'm afraid we all find it that way at times. Not much privacy in an antarctic camp."

"Privacy?" What the hell's that? You know, the thing that really made me weep was when I saw Barclay marchin' through here chantin' 'The last lumber in the camp! The last lumber in the camp!' and carryin' it out to build that house on his tractor. Damn it, I missed that moon cut in the door he carried out more'n I missed the sun when it set. That wasn't just the last lumber Barclay was walkin' off with. He was carryin' off the last bit of privacy in this blasted place."

A grin rode even on Connant's heavy face as Kinner's perennial, good-natured grouch came up again. But it died away quickly as his dark, deep-set eyes turned again to the red-eyed thing Blair was chipping from its cocoon of ice. A big hand ruffed his shoulder-length hair, and tugged at a twisted lock that fell behind his ear, in a familiar gesture. "I know that cosmic ray shack's going to be too crowded if I have to sit up with that thing," he growled. "Why can't you go on chipping the ice away from around it—you can do that without anybody butting in, I assure you—and then hang the thing up over the power-plant boiler? That's warm enough. It'll thaw out a chicken, even a whole side of beef, in a few hours."

"I know," Blair protested, dropping the tack hammer to gesture more effectively with his bony, freckled fingers, his small body tense with eagerness, "but this is too important to take any chances. There never was a find like this; there never can be again. It's the only chance men will ever have, and it has to be done exactly right.

"Look, you know how the fish we caught down near the Ross Sea would freeze almost as soon as we got them on deck, and come to life again if we thawed them gently? Low forms of life aren't killed by quick freezing and slow thawing. We have—"

"Hey, for the love of Heaven—you mean that damned thing will come to life?" Connant yelled. "You get the

252

damned thing— Let me at it! That's going to be in so many pieces—"

"No! *No,* you fool—" Blair jumped in front of Connant to protect his precious find. "No. Just *low* forms of life. For Pete's sake let me finish. You can't thaw higher forms of life and have them come to. Wait a moment now—hold it! A fish can come to after freezing because it's so low a form of life that the individual cells of its body can revive, and that alone is enough to re-establish life. Any higher forms thawed out that way are dead. Though the individual cells revive, they die because there must be organization and co-operative effort to live. That co-operation cannot be re-established. There is a sort of potential life in any uninjured, quick-frozen animal. But it can't—can't under any circumstances—become active life in higher animals. The higher animals are too complex, too delicate. This is an intelligent creature as high in its evolution as we are in ours. Perhaps higher. It is as dead as a frozen man would be."

"How do you know?" demanded Connant, hefting the ice-ax he had seized a moment before.

Commander Garry laid a restraining hand on his heavy shoulder. "Wait a minute, Connant. I want to get this straight. I agree that there is going to be no thawing of this thing if there is the remotest chance of its revival. I quite agree it is much too unpleasant to have alive, but I had no idea there was the remotest possibility."

Dr. Copper pulled his pipe from between his teeth and heaved his stocky, dark body from the bunk he had been sitting in. "Blair's being technical. That's dead. As dead as the mammoths they had frozen in Siberia. We have all sorts of proof that things don't live after being frozen—not even fish, generally speaking—and no proof that higher animal life can under any circumstances. What's the point, Blair?"

The little biologist shook himself. The little ruff of hair standing out around his bald pate waved in righteous anger. "The point is," he said in an injured tone, "that the individual cells might show the characteristics they had in life if it is properly thawed. A man's muscle cells live many hours after he has died. Just because they live, and a few things like hair and fingernail cells still live, you wouldn't accuse a corpse of being a zombie, or something.

253

"Now if I thaw this right, I may have a chance to determine what sort of world it's native to. We don't and can't know by any other means, whether it came from Earth or Mars or Venus or from beyond the stars.

"And just because it looks unlike men, you don't have to accuse it of being evil or vicious or something. Maybe that expression on its face is its equivalent to a resignation to fate. White is the color of mourning to the Chinese. If men can have different customs, why can't a so-different race have different understandings of facial expressions?"

Connant laughed softly, mirthlessly. "Peaceful resignation! If that is the best it could do in the way of resignation, I should exceedingly dislike seeing it when it was looking mad. That face was never designed to express peace. It just didn't have any philosophical thoughts like peace in its make-up.

"I know it's your pet—but be sane about it. That thing grew up on evil, adolesced slowly roasting alive the local equivalent of kittens, and amused itself through maturity on new and ingenious torture."

"You haven't the slightest right to say that," snapped Blair. "How do you know the first thing about the meaning of a facial expression inherently inhuman? It may well have no human equivalent whatever. That is just a different development of Nature, another example of Nature's wonderful adaptability. Growing on another, perhaps harsher world, it has different form and features. But it is just as much a legitimate child of Nature as you are. You are displaying that childish human weakness of hating the different. On its own world it would probably class you as a fish-belly, white monstrosity with an insufficient number of eyes and a fungoid body pale and bloated with gas.

"Just because its nature is different, you haven't any right to say it's necessarily evil."

Norris burst out with a single, explosive, "Haw!" He looked down at the thing. "May be that things from other worlds don't *have* to be evil just because they're different. But that thing *was!* Child of Nature, eh? Well, it was a hell of an evil Nature."

"Aw, will you mugs cut crabbing at each other and get the damned thing off my table?" Kinner growled. "And put a canvas over it. It looks indecent."

254

"Kinner's gone modest," jeered Connant.

Kinner slanted his eyes up to the big physicist. The scarred cheek twisted to join the line of his tight lips in a twisted grin. "All right, big boy, and what were you grousing about a minute ago? We can set the thing in a chair next to you tonight, if you want."

"I'm not afraid of its face," Connant snapped. "I don't like keeping a wake over its corpse particularly, but I'm going to do it."

Kinner's grin spread. "Uh-huh." He went off to the galley stove and shook down ashes vigorously, drowning the brittle chipping of the ice as Blair fell to work again.

IV

"Cluck," reported the cosmic ray counter, "*cluck-burrp-cluck.*"

Connant started and dropped his pencil.

"Damnation." The physicist looked toward the far corner, back at the Geiger counter on the table near that corner. And crawled under the desk at which he had been working to retrieve the pencil. He sat down at his work again, trying to make his writing more even. It tended to have jerks and quavers in it, in time with the abrupt proud-hen noises of the Geiger counter. The muted whoosh of the pressure lamp he was using for illumination, the mingled gargles and bugle calls of a dozen men sleeping down the corridor in Paradise House formed the background sounds for the irregular, clucking noises of the counter, the occasional rustle of falling coal in the copper-bellied stove. And a soft, steady *drip-drip-drip* from the thing in the corner.

Connant jerked a pack of cigarettes from his pocket, snapped it so that a cigarette protruded, and jabbed the cylinder into his mouth. The lighter failed to function, and he pawed angrily through the pile of papers in search of a match He scratched the wheel of the lighter several times, dropped it with a curse, and got up to pluck a hot coal from the stove with the coal tongs.

The lighter functioned instantly when he tried it on returning to the desk. The counter ripped out a series of chuckling guffaws as a burst of cosmic rays struck through to it. Connant turned to glower at it, and tried to concentrate on the interpretation of data collected during the past week. The weekly summary—

He gave up and yielded to curiosity, or nervousness. He lifted the pressure lamp from the desk and carried it over to the table in the corner. Then he returned to the stove and picked up the coal tongs. The beast had been thawing for nearly eighteen hours now. He poked at it with an unconscious caution; the flesh was no longer hard as armor plate, but had assumed a rubbery texture. It looked like wet, blue rubber glistening under droplets of water like little round jewels in the glare of the gasoline pressure lantern. Connant felt an unreasoning desire to pour the contents of the lamp's reservoir over the thing in its box and drop the cigarette into it. The three red eyes glared up at him sightlessly, the ruby eyeballs reflecting murky, smoky rays of light.

He realized vaguely that he had been looking at them for a very long time, even vaguely understood that they were no longer sightless. But it did not seem of importance, of no more importance than the labored, slow motion of the tentacular things that sprouted from the base of the scrawny, slowly pulsing neck.

Connant picked up the pressure lamp and returned to his chair. He sat down, staring at the pages of mathematics before him. The clucking of the counter was strangely less disturbing, the rustle of the coals in the stove no longer distracting.

The creak of the floor boards behind him didn't interrupt his thoughts as he went about his weekly report in an automatic manner, filling in columns of data and making brief summarizing notes.

The creak of the floor boards sounded nearer.

V

Blair came up from the nightmare-haunted depths of sleep abruptly. Connant's face floated vaguely above him; for a moment it seemed a continuance of the wild horror of the dream. But Connant's face was angry, and a little frightened. "Blair—Blair, you damned log, wake up."

"Uh-er?" The little biologist rubbed his eyes, his bony freckled finger crooked to a mutilated child-fist. From surrounding bunks other faces lifted to stare down at them.

Connant straightened up. "Get up—and get a lift on. Your damned animal's escaped."

"Escaped—what!" Chief Pilot Van Wall's bull voice roared out with a volume that shook the walls. Down the communication tunnels other voices yelled suddenly. The dozen inhabitants of Paradise House tumbled in abruptly, Barclay, stocky and bulbous in long woolen underwear, carrying a fire extinguisher.

"What the hell's the matter?" Barclay demanded.

"Your damned beast got loose. I fell asleep about twenty minutes ago, and when I woke up, the thing was gone. Hey, Doc, the hell you say those things can't come to life. Blair's blasted potential life developed a hell of a lot of potential and walked out on us."

Copper stared blankly. "It wasn't—earthly," he sighed suddenly. "I—I guess earthly laws don't apply."

"Well, it applied for leave of absence and took it. We've got to find it and capture it somehow." Connant swore bitterly, his deep-set black eyes sullen and angry. "It's a wonder the hellish creature didn't eat me in my sleep."

Blair started back, his pale eyes suddenly fear-struck. "Maybe it di—er—uh—we'll have to find it."

"You find it. It's your pet. I've had all I want to do with it, sitting there for seven hours with the counter clucking every few seconds, and you birds in here singing night music. It's a wonder I got to sleep. I'm going through to the Ad Building."

Commander Garry ducked through the doorway, pulling his belt tight. "You won't have to. Van's roar sounded like the Boeing taking off downwind. So it wasn't dead?"

"I didn't carry it off in my arms, I assure you," Connant snapped. "The last I saw, the split skull was oozing green goo, like a squashed caterpillar. Doc just said our laws don't work—it's unearthly. Well, it's an unearthly monster, with an unearthly disposition, judging by the face, wandering around with a split skull and brains oozing out." Norris and

McReady appeared in the doorway, a doorway filling with other shivering men. "Has anybody seen it coming over here?" Norris asked innocently. "About four feet tall—three red eyes—brains oozing out— Hey, has anybody checked to make sure this isn't a cracked idea of humor? If it is, I think we'll unite in tying Blair's pet around Connant's neck like the Ancient Mariner's albatross."

"It's no humor," Connant shivered. "Lord, I wish it were. I'd rather wear—" He stopped. A wild, weird howl shrieked through the corridors. The men stiffened abruptly, and half turned.

"I think it's been located," Connant finished. His dark eyes shifted with a queer unease. He darted back to his bunk in Paradise House, to return almost immediately with a heavy .45 revolver and an ice-ax. He hefted both gently as he started for the corridor toward Dogtown.

"It blundered down the wrong corridor—and landed among the huskies. Listen—the dogs have broken their chains—"

The half-terrorized howl of the dog pack had changed to a wild hunting melee. The voices of the dogs thundered in the narrow corridors, and through them came a low rippling snarl of distilled hate. A shrill of pain, a dozen snarling yelps.

Connant broke for the door. Close behind him came McReady, then Barclay and Commander Garry. Other men broke for the Ad Building, and weapons—the sledge house. Pomroy, in charge of Big Magnet's five cows started down the corridor in the opposite direction—he had a six-foot-handled, long-tined pitchfork in mind.

Barclay slid to a halt, as McReady's giant bulk turned abruptly away from the tunnel leading to Dogtown and vanished off at an angle. Uncertainly the mechanician wavered a moment, the fire extinguisher in his hands, hesitating from one side to the other. Then he was racing after Connant's broad back. Whatever McReady had in mind, he could be trusted to make it work.

Connant stopped at the bend in the corridor. His breath hissed suddenly through his throat. "Great God—" The revolver exploded thunderously; three numbing, palpable waves of sound crashed through the confined corridors. Two more. The revolver dropped to the hard-packed snow of the

258

trail, and Barclay saw the ice-ax shift into defensive position. Connant's powerful body blocked his vision, but beyond he heard something mewing, and insanely, chuckling. The dogs were quieter; there was a deadly seriousness in their low snarls. Taloned feet scratched at hard-packed snow, broken chains were clinking and tangling.

Connant shifted abruptly, and Barclay could see what lay beyond. For a second he stood frozen, then his breath went out in a gusty curse. The thing launched itself at Connant and the powerful arms of the man swung the ice-ax flat-side first at what might have been a head. It scrunched horribly, and the tattered flesh, ripped by a half-dozen savage huskies, leaped to its feet again. The red eyes blazed with an unearthly hatred, an unearthly, unkillable vitality.

Barclay turned the fire extinguisher on it. The blinding, blistering stream of chemical spray confused it, baffled it, together with the savage attacks of the huskies, not for long afraid of anything that did, or could live, and held it at bay.

McReady wedged men out of his way and drove down the narrow corridor packed with men unable to reach the scene. There was a sure fore-planned drive to McReady's attack. One of the giant blow-torches used in warming the plane's engines was in his bronzed hands. It roared gustily as he turned the corner and opened the valve. The mad mewing hissed louder. The dogs scrambled back from the three-foot lance of blue-hot flame.

"Bar, get a power cable, run it in somehow. And a handle. We can electrocute this—monster, if I don't incinerate it." McReady spoke with an authority of planned action. Barclay turned down the long corridor to the power plant, but already before him Norris and Van Wall were racing down.

Barclay found the cable in the electrical cache in the tunnel wall. In a half minute he was hacking at it, walking back. Van Wall's voice rang out in warning shout of "Power!" as the emergency gasoline-powered dynamo thudded into action. Half a dozen other men were down there now; the coal, kindling were going into the firebox of the steam power plant. Norris, cursing in a low, deadly monotone, was working with quick, sure fingers on the other end of Barclay's cable, splicing a contacter into one of the power leads.

The dogs had fallen back when Barclay reached the corridor bend, fallen back before a furious monstrosity that glared from baleful red eyes, mewing in trapped hatred. The dogs were a semicircle of red-dipped muzzles with a fringe of glistening white teeth, whining with a vicious eagerness that nearly matched the fury of the red eyes. McReady stood confidently alert at the corridor bend, the gustily muttering torch held loose and ready for action in his hands. He stepped aside without moving his eyes from the beast as Barclay came up. There was a slight, tight smile on his lean, bronzed face.

Norris's voice called down the corridor, and Barclay stepped forward. The cable was taped to the long handle of a snow shovel, the two conductors split and held 18 inches apart by a scrap of lumber lashed at right angles across the far end of the handle. Bare copper conductors, charged with 220 volts, glinted in the light of pressure lamps. The thing mewed and hated and dodged. McReady advanced to Barclay's side. The dogs beyond sensed the plan with the almost telepathic intelligence of trained huskies. Their whining grew shriller, softer, their mincing steps carried them nearer. Abruptly a huge night-black Alaskan leaped onto the trapped thing. It turned squalling, saber-clawed feet slashing.

Barclay leaped forward and jabbed. A weird, shrill scream rose and choked out. The smell of burned flesh in the corridor intensified; greasy smoke curled up. The echoing pound of the gas-electric dynamo down the corridor became a slogging thud.

The red eyes clouded over in a stiffening, jerking travesty of a face. Armlike, leglike members quivered and jerked. The dogs leaped forward, and Barclay yanked back his shovel-handled weapon. The thing on the snow did not move as gleaming teeth ripped it open.

VI

Garry looked about the crowded room. Thirty-two men, some tensed nervously standing against the wall, some uneasily relaxed, some sitting, most perforce standing as intimate as sardines. Thirty-two, plus the five engaged in sewing up wounded dogs, made thirty-seven, the total personnel.

Garry started speaking. "All right, I guess we're here. Some of you—three or four at most—saw what happened. All of you have seen that thing on the table, and can get a general idea. Anyone hasn't, I'll lift—" His hand strayed to the tarpaulin bulking over the thing on the table. There was an acrid odor of singed flesh seeping out of it. The men stirred restlessly; there were hasty denials.

"It looks rather as though Charnauk isn't going to lead any more teams," Garry went on. "Blair wants to get at this thing, and make some more detailed examination. We want to know what happened, and make sure right now that this is permanently totally dead. Right?"

Connant grinned. "Anybody that doesn't can sit up with it tonight."

"All right then, Blair, what can you say about it? What was it?" Garry turned to the little biologist.

"I wonder if we ever saw its natural form." Blair looked at the covered mass. "It may have been imitating the beings that built that ship—but I don't think it was. I think that was its true form. Those of us who were up near the bend saw the thing in action; the thing on the table is the result. When it got loose, apparently, it started looking around. Antarctica still frozen as it was ages ago when the creature first saw it—and froze. From my observations while it was thawing out, and the bits of tissue I cut and hardened then, I think it was native to a hotter planet than Earth. It couldn't, in its natural form, stand the temperature. There is no life form on Earth that can live in Antarctica during the winter, but the best compromise is the dog. It found the dogs, and somehow got near enough to Charnauk to get him. The others smelled it—heard it—I don't know—anyway they went wild and broke chains and attacked it before it was finished. The thing we found was part Charnauk, queerly only half dead, part Charnauk half-digested by the jellylike protoplasm of that creature, and part the remains of the thing we originally found, sort of melted down to the basic protoplasm.

"When the dogs attacked it, it turned into the best fighting thing it could think of. Some other-world beast apparently."

"Turned," snapped Garry. "How?"

"Every living thing is made up of jelly—protoplasm and minute, submicroscopic things called nuclei, which control the bulk, the protoplasm. This thing was just a modification of that same world-wide plan of Nature; cells made up of protoplasm, controlled by infinitely tinier nuclei. You physicists might compare it—an individual cell of any living thing —with an atom; the bulk of the atom, the space-filling part, is made up of the electron orbits, but the character of the thing is determined by the atomic nucleus.

"This isn't wildly beyond what we already know. It's just a modification we haven't seen before. It's as natural, as logical, as any other manifestation of life. It obeys exactly the same laws. The cells are made of protoplasm, their character determined by the nucleus.

"Only, in this creature, the cell nuclei can control those cells *at will*. It digested Charnauk, and as it digested, studied every cell of its tissue, and shaped its own cells to imitate them exactly. Parts of it—parts that had time to finish changing—are dog-cells. But they don't have dog-cell nuclei." Blair lifted a fraction of the tarpaulin. A torn dog's leg, with stiff gray fur protruded. "That, for instance, isn't dog at all; it's imitation. Some parts I'm uncertain about; the nucleus was hiding itself, covering up with dog-cell imitation nucleus. In time, not even a microscope would have shown the difference."

"Suppose," asked Norris bitterly, "it had had lots of time?"

"Then it would have been a dog. The other dogs would have accepted it. We would have accepted it. I don't think anything would have distinguished it, not microscope, nor X-ray, nor any other means. This is a member of a supremely intelligent race, a race that has learned the deepest secrets of biology, and turned them to its use."

"What was it planning to do?" Barclay looked at the humped tarpaulin.

Blair grinned unpleasantly. The wavering halo of thin hair round his bald pate wavered in a stir of air. "Take over the world, I imagine."

"Take over the world! Just it, all by itself?" Connant gasped. "Set itself up as a lone dictator?"

"No." Blair shook his head. The scalpel he had been fumbling in his bony fingers dropped; he bent to pick it up, so

262

that his face was hidden as he spoke. "It would become the population of the world."

"Become—populate the world? Does it reproduce asexually?"

Blair shook his head and gulped. "It's—it doesn't have to. It weighed eighty-five pounds. Charnauk weighed about ninety. It would have become Charnauk, and had eighty-five pounds left, to become—oh, Jack, for instance, or Chinook. It can imitate anything—that is, become anything. If it had reached the Antarctic Sea, it would have become a seal, maybe two seals. They might have attacked a killer whale, and become either killers, or a herd of seals. Or maybe it would have caught an albatross, or a skua gull, and flown to South America."

Norris cursed softly. "And every time it digested something, and imitated it—"

It would have had its original bulk left, to start again," Blair finished. "Nothing would kill it. It has no natural enemies, because it becomes whatever it wants to. If a killer whale attacked it, it would become a killer whale. If it was an albatross, and an eagle attacked it, it would become an eagle. Lord, it might become a female eagle. Go back—build a nest and lay eggs!"

"Are you sure that thing from hell is dead?" Dr. Cooper asked softly.

"Yes, thank Heaven," the little biologist gasped. "After they drove the dogs off, I stood there poking Bar's electrocution thing into it for five minutes. It's dead and—cooked."

"Then we can only give thanks that this is Antarctica, where there is not one, single, solitary, living thing for it to imitate, except these animals in camp."

"Us," Blair giggled. "It can imitate us. Dogs can't make four hundred miles to the sea; there's no food. There aren't any skua gulls to imitate at this season. There aren't any penguins this far inland. There's nothing that can reach the sea from this point—except us. We've got brains. We can do it. Don't you see—*it's got to imitate us—it's got to be one of us—that's the only way it can fly an airplane—fly a plane for two hours, and rule—be—all Earth's inhabitants*. A world for the taking—*if it imitates us!*

"It didn't know yet. It hadn't had a chance to learn. It was

263

rushed—hurried—took the thing nearest its own size. Look—I'm Pandora! I opened the box! And the only hope that can come out is—that nothing can come out. You didn't see me. I did it. I fixed it. I smashed every magneto. Not a plane can fly. Nothing can fly." Blair giggled and lay down on the floor crying.

Chief Pilot Van Wall made for the door. His feet were fading echoes in the corridors as Dr. Copper bent unhurriedly over the little man on the floor. From his office at the end of the room he brought something and injected a solution into Blair's arm. "He might come out of it when he wakes up," he sighed, rising. McReady helped him lift the biologist onto a near-by bunk. "It all depends on whether we can convince him that thing is dead."

Van Wall ducked into the shack, brushing his heavy blond beard absently. "I didn't think a biologist would do a thing like that up thoroughly. He missed the spares in the second cache. It's all right. I smashed them."

Commander Garry nodded. "I was wondering about the radio."

Dr. Cooper snorted. "You don't think it can leak out on a radio wave, do you? You'd have five rescue attempts in the next three months if you stop the broadcasts. The thing to do is talk loud and not make a sound. Now I wonder—"

McReady looked speculatively at the doctor. "It might be like an infectious disease. Everything that drank any of its blood—"

Cooper shook his head. "Blair missed something. Imitate it may, but it has, to a certain extent, its own body chemistry, its own metabolism. If it didn't, it would become a dog—and be a dog and nothing more. It has to be an imitation dog. Therefore you can detect it by serum tests. And its chemistry, since it comes from another world, must be so wholly, radically different that a few cells, such as gained by drops of blood, would be treated as disease germs by the dog, or human body."

"Blood—would one of those imitations bleed?" Norris demanded.

"Surely. Nothing mystic about blood. Muscle is about ninety-per cent water; blood differs only in having a couple

264

per cent more water, and less connective tissue. They'd bleed all right," Copper assured him.

Blair sat up in his bunk suddenly. "Connant—where's Connant?"

The physicist moved over toward the little biologist "Here I am. What do you want?"

"Are you?" giggled Blair. He lapsed back into the bunk contorted with silent laughter.

Connant looked at him blankly. "Huh? Am I what?"

"*Are* you there?" Blair burst into gales of laughter. "*Are* you Connant? The beast wanted to be *man*—not a dog—"

VII

Dr. Copper rose wearily from the bunk and washed the hypodermic carefully. The little tinkles it made seemed loud in the packed room, now that Blair's gurgling laughter had finally quieted. Copper looked toward Garry and shook his head slowly. "Hopeless, I'm afraid. I don't think we can ever convince him the thing is dead now."

Norris laughed uncertainly. "I'm not sure you can convince me. Oh, damn you, McReady."

"McReady?" Commander Garry turned to look from Norris to McReady curiously.

"The nightmares," Norris explained. "He had a theory about the nightmares we had at the Secondary Station after finding that thing."

"And that was?" Garry looked at McReady levelly.

Norris answered for him, jerkily, uneasily. "That the creature wasn't dead, had a sort of enormously slowed existence, an existence that permitted it, none the less, to be vaguely aware of the passing of time, of our coming, after endless years. I had a dream it could imitate things."

"Well," Copper grunted, "it can."

"Don't be an ass," Norris snapped. "That's not what's bothering me. In the dream it could read minds, read thoughts and ideas and mannerisms."

"What's so bad about that? It seems to be worrying you more than the thought of the joy we're going to have with a

265

madman in an antarctic camp." Copper nodded toward Blair's sleeping form.

McReady shook his great head slowly. "You know that Connant is Connant, because he not merely looks like Connant—which we're beginning to believe that beast might be able to do—but he thinks like Connant, moves himself around as Connant does. That takes more than merely a body that looks like him; that takes Connant's own mind, and thoughts and mannerisms. Therefore, though you know that the thing might make itself *look* like Connant, you aren't much bothered, because you know it has a mind from another world, a totally unhuman mind, that couldn't possibly react and think and talk like a man we know, and do it so well as to fool us for a moment. The idea of the creature imitating one of us is fascinating, but unreal, because it is too completely unhuman to deceive us. It doesn't have a human mind."

"As I said before," Norris repeated, looking steadily at McReady, "you can say the damnedest things at the damnedest times. Will you be so good as to finish that thought—one way or the other?"

Kinner, the scar-faced expedition cook, had been standing near Connant. Suddenly he moved down the length of the crowded room toward his familiar galley. He shook the ashes from the galley stove noisily.

"It would do it no good," said Dr. Copper, softly as though thinking out loud, "to merely look like something it was trying to imitate; it would have to understand its feelings, its reactions. It *is* unhuman; it has powers of imitation beyond any conception of man. A good actor, by training himself, can imitate another man, another man's mannerisms, well enough to fool most people. Of course, no actor could imitate so perfectly as to deceive men who had been living with the imitated one in the complete lack of privacy of an antarctic camp. That would take a superhuman skill."

"Oh, you've got the bug, too?" Norris cursed softly.

Connant, standing alone at one end of the room, looked about him wildly, his face white. A gentle eddying of the men had crowded them slowly down toward the other end of the room, so that he stood quite alone. "My God, will you two Jeremiahs shut up?" Connant's voice shook. "What am I? Some kind of microscopic specimen you're dissecting? Some unpleasant worm you're discussing in the third person?"

McReady looked up at him; his slowly twisting hands stopped for a moment. "Having a lovely time. Wish you were here. Signed: Everybody.

"Connant, if you think you're having a hell of a time, just move over on the other end for a while. You've got one thing we haven't; you know what the answer is. I'll tell you this, right now you're the most feared and respected man in Big Magnet."

"Lord, I wish you could see your eyes," Connant gasped. "Stop staring, will you! What the hell are you going to do?"

"Have you any suggestions, Doctor Copper?" Commander Garry asked steadily. "The present situation is impossible."

"Oh, is it?" Connant snapped. "Come over here and look at that crowd. By Heaven, they look exactly like that gang of huskies around the corridor bend. Benning, will you stop hefting that damned ice-ax?"

The coppery blade rang on the floor as the aviation mechanic nervously dropped it. He bent over and picked it up instantly, hefting it slowly, turning it in his hands, his brown eyes moving jerkily about the room.

Copper sat down on the bunk beside Blair. The wood creaked noisily in the room. Far down a corridor, a dog yelped in pain, and the dog drivers' tense voices floated softly back. "Microscopic examination," said the doctor thoughtfully, "would be useless, as Blair pointed out. Considerable time has passed. However, serum tests would be definitive."

"Serum tests? What do you mean exactly?" Commander Garry asked.

"If I had a rabbit that had been injected with human blood—a poison to rabbits, of course, as is the blood of any animal save that of another rabbit—and the injections continued in increasing doses for some time, the rabbit would be human-immune. If a small quantity of its blood were drawn off, allowed to separate in a test tube, and to the clear serum, a bit of human blood were added, there would be a visible reaction, proving the blood was human. If cow or dog blood were added—or any protein material other than that one

267

thing, human blood—no reaction would take place. That would prove definitely."

"Can you suggest where I might catch a rabbit for you, Doc?" Norris asked. "That is, nearer than Australia; we don't want to waste time going that far."

"I know there aren't any rabbits in Antarctica," Copper nodded, "but that is simply the usual animal. Any animal except man will do. A dog, for instance. But it will take several days, and due to the greater size of the animal, considerable blood. Two of us will have to contribute,"

"Would I do?" Garry asked.

"That will make two," Copper nodded. "I'll get to work on it right away."

"What about Connant in the meantime?" Kinner demanded. "I'm going out that door and head off for the Ross Sea before I cook for him."

"He may be human—" Copper started.

Connant burst out in a flood of curses. "Human! *May* be human, you damned sawbones! What in hell do you think I am?"

"A monster," Copper snapped sharply. "Now shut up and listen." Connant's face drained of color and he sat down heavily as the indictment was put in words. "Until we know—you know as well as we do that we have reason to question the fact, and only you know how that question is to be answered—we may reasonably be expected to lock you up. If you are—unhuman—you're a lot more dangerous than poor Blair there, and I'm going to see that he's locked up thoroughly. I expect that his next stage will be a violent desire to kill you, all the dogs, and probably all of us. When he wakes, he will be convinced we're all unhuman, and nothing on the planet will ever change his conviction. It would be kinder to let him die, but we can't do that, of course. He's going in one shack, and you can stay in Cosmos House with your cosmic-ray apparatus. Which is about what you'd do anyway. I've got to fix up a couple of dogs."

Connant nodded bitterly. "I'm human. Hurry that test. Your eyes—Lord, I wish you could see your eyes staring—"

Commander Garry watched anxiously as Clark, the dog handler, held the big brown Alaskan husky, while Copper began the injection treatment. The dog was not anxious to cooperate; the needle was painful, and already he'd experienced considerable needle work that morning. Five stitches held closed a slash that ran from his shoulder, across the ribs, halfway down his body. One long fang was broken off short; the missing part was to be found half buried in the shoulder bone of the monstrous thing on the table in the Ad Building.

"How long will that take?" Garry asked, pressing his arm gently. It was sore from the prick of the needle Dr. Copper had used to withdraw blood.

Copper shrugged. "I don't know, to be frank. I know the general method. I've used it on rabbits. But I haven't experimented with dogs. They're big, clumsy animals to work with; naturally rabbits are preferable, and serve ordinarily. In civilized places you can buy a stock of human-immune rabbits from suppliers, and not many investigators take the trouble to prepare their own."

"What do they want with them back there?" Clark asked.

"Criminology is one large field. A says he didn't murder B, but that the blood on his shirt came from killing a chicken. The State makes a test, then it's up to A to explain how it is the blood reacts on human-immune rabbits, but not on chicken-immunes."

"What are we going to do with Blair in the meantime?" Garry asked wearily. "It's all right to let him sleep where he is for a while, but when he wakes up—"

"Barclay and Benning are fitting some bolts on the door of Cosmos House," Copper replied grimly. "Connant's acting like a gentleman. I think perhaps the way the other men look at him makes him rather want privacy. Lord knows, heretofore we've all of us individually prayed for a little privacy."

Clark laughed brittlely. "Not any more, thank you. The more the merrier."

"Blair," Copper went on, "will also have to have privacy—and locks. He's going to have a pretty definite plan in mind when he wakes up. Ever hear the old story of how to stop hoof-and-mouth disease in cattle?"

Clark and Garry shook their heads silently.

"If there isn't any hoof-and-mouth disease, there won't be any hoof-and-mouth disease," Copper explained. "You get rid of it by killing every animal that exhibits it, and every animal that's been near the diseased animal. Blair's a biologist, and knows that story. He's afraid of this thing we loosed. The answer is probably pretty clear in his mind now. Kill everybody and everything in this camp before a skua gull or a wandering albatross coming in with the spring chances out this way and—catches the disease."

Clark's lips curled in a twisted grin. "Sounds logical to me. If things get too bad—maybe we'd better let Blair get loose. It would save us committing suicide. We might also make something of a vow that if things get bad, we see that that does happen."

Copper laughed softly. "The last man alive in Big Magnet—wouldn't be a man," he pointed out. "Somebody's got to kill those—creatures that don't desire to kill themselves, you know. We don't have enough thermite to do it all at once, and the decanite explosive wouldn't help much. I have an idea that even small pieces of one of those beings would be self-sufficient."

"If," said Garry thoughtfully, "they can modify their protoplasm at will, won't they simply modify themselves to birds and fly away? They can read all about birds, and imitate their structure without even meeting them. Or imitate, perhaps, birds of their home planet."

Copper shook his head, and helped Clark to free the dog. "Man studied birds for centuries, trying to learn how to make a machine to fly like them. He never did do the trick; his final success came when he broke away entirely and tried new methods. Knowing the general idea, and knowing the detailed structure of wing and bone and nerve tissue is something far, far different. And as for other-world birds, perhaps, in fact very probably, the atmospheric conditions here are so vastly different that their birds couldn't fly. Perhaps, even, the being came from a planet like Mars with such a thin atmosphere that there were no birds."

Barclay came into the building, trailing a length of airplane control cable. "It's finished, Doc. Cosmos House can't be opened from the inside. Now where do we put Blair?"

Copper looked toward Garry. "There wasn't any biology building. I don't know where we can isolate him."

"How about East Cache?" Garry said after a moment's thought. "Will Blair be able to look after himself—or need attention?"

270

"He'll be capable enough. We'll be the ones to watch out," Copper assured him grimly. "Take a stove, a couple of bags of coal, necessary supplies, and a few tools to fix it up. Nobody's been out there since last fall, have they?"

Garry shook his head. "If he gets noisy—I thought that might be a good idea."

Barclay hefted the tools he was carrying and looked up at Garry. "If the muttering he's doing now is any sign, he's going to sing away the night hours. And we won't like his song."

"What's he saying?" Copper asked.

Barclay shook his head. "I didn't care to listen much. You can if you want to. But I gathered that the blasted idiot had all the dreams McReady had, and a few more. He slept beside the thing when we stopped on the trail coming in from Secondary Magnetic, remember. He dreamed the thing was alive, and dreamed more details. And—damn his soul—knew it wasn't all dream, or had reason to. He knew it had telepathic powers that were stirring vaguely, and that it could not only read minds, but project thoughts. They weren't dreams, you see. They were stray thoughts that thing was broadcasting, the way Blair's broadcasting his thoughts now—a sort of telepathic muttering in its sleep. That's why he knew so much about its powers. I guess you and I, Doc, weren't so sensitive—if you want to believe in telepathy."

"I have to." Copper sighed. "Doctor Rhine of Duke University has shown that it exists, shown that some are much more sensitive than others."

"Well, if you want to learn a lot of details, go listen in on Blair's broadcast. He's driven most of the boys out of the Ad Building; Kinner's rattling pans like coal going down a chute. When he can't rattle a pan, he shakes ashes.

"By the way, Commander, what are we going to do this spring, now the planes are out of it?"

Garry sighed. "I'm afraid our expedition is going to be a loss. We cannot divide our strength now."

"It won't be a loss—if we continue to live, and come out of this," Copper promised him. "The find we've made, if we can get it under control, is important enough. The cosmic-ray data, magnetic work, and atmospheric work won't be greatly hindered."

Garry laughed mirthlessly. "I was just thinking of the radio broadcasts. Telling half the world about the wonderful results of our exploration flights, trying to fool men like Byrd and Ellsworth back home there that we're doing something."

Copper nodded gravely. "They'll know something's wrong. But men like that have judgment enough to know we wouldn't do tricks without some sort of reason, and will wait for our return to judge us. I think it comes to this—men who know enough to recognize our deception will wait for our return. Men who haven't discretion and faith enough to wait will not have the experience to detect any fraud. We know enough of the conditions here to put through a good bluff."

"Just so they don't send 'rescue' expeditions," Garry prayed. "When—if—we're ever ready to come out, we'll have to send word to Captain Forsythe to bring a stock of magnetos with him when he comes down. But—never mind that."

"You mean if we don't come out?" asked Barclay. "I was wondering if a nice running account of an eruption or an earthquake via radio—with a swell windup by using a stick of decanite under the microphone—would help. Nothing, of course, will entirely keep people out. One of those swell, melodramatic last-man-alive scenes might make 'em go easy though."

Garry smiled with genuine humor. "Is everybody in camp trying to figure that out, too?"

Copper laughed. "What do you think, Garry? We're confident we can win out. But not too easy about it, I guess."

Clark grinned up from the dog he was petting into calmness. "Confident, did you say, Doc?"

VIII

Blair moved restlessly around the small shack. His eyes jerked and quivered in vague, fleeting glances at the four men with him: Barclay, six feet tall and weighing over 190 pounds; McReady, a bronze giant of a man; Dr. Copper, short, squatly powerful; and Benning, five-feet-ten of wiry strength.

Blair was huddled up against the far wall of the East

Cache cabin, his gear piled in the middle of the floor beside the heating-stove, forming an island between him and the four men. His bony hands clenched and fluttered, terrified. His pale eyes wavered uneasily as his bald, freckled head darted about in birdlike motion.

"I don't want anybody coming here. I'll cook my own food," he snapped nervously. "Kinner may be human now, but I don't believe it. I'm going to get out of here, but I'm not going to eat any food you send me. I want cans. Sealed cans."

"Okay, Blair, we'll bring 'em tonight," Barclay promised. "You've got coal, and the fire's started. I'll make a last—" Barclay started forward.

Blair instantly scurried to the farthest corner. "Get out! Keep away from me, you monster!" the little biologist shrieked, and tried to claw his way through the wall of the shack. "Keep away from me—keep away—I won't be absorbed—I won't be—"

Barclay relaxed and moved back. Dr. Copper shook his head. "Leave him alone, Bar. It's easier for him to fix the thing himself. We'll have to fix the door, I think—"

The four men let themselves out. Efficiently, Benning and Barclay fell to work. There were no locks in Antarctica; there wasn't enough privacy to make them needed. But powerful screws had been driven in each side of the door frame, and the spare aviation control cable, immensely strong woven steel wire, was rapidly caught between them and drawn taut. Barclay went to work with a drill and a keyhole saw. Presently he had a trap cut in the door through which goods could be passed without unlashing the entrance. Three powerful hinges from a stock crate, two hasps, and a pair of three-inch cotterpins made it proof against opening from the other side.

Blair moved about restlessly inside. He was dragging something over to the door with panting gasps, and muttering frantic curses. Barclay opened the hatch and glanced in, Dr. Copper peering over his shoulder. Blair had moved the heavy bunk against the door. It could not be opened without his co-operation now.

"Don't know but what the poor man's right, at that," McReady sighed. "If he gets loose, it is his avowed intention

273

to kill each and all of us as quickly as possible, which is something we don't agree with. But we've something on our side of that door that is worse than a homicidal maniac. If one or the other has to get loose, I think I'll come up and undo these lashings here."

Barclay grinned. "You let me know, and I'll show you how to get these off fast. Let's go back."

The sun was painting the northern horizon in multi-colored rainbows still, though it was two hours below the horizon. The field of drift swept off to the north, sparkling under its flaming colors in a million reflected glories. Low mounds of rounded white on the northern horizon showed the Magnet Range was barely awash above the sweeping drift. Little eddies of wind-lifted snow swirled away from the skis as they set out toward the main encampment two miles away. The spidery finger of the broadcast radiator lifted a gaunt black needle against the white of the Antarctic continent. The snow under their skis was like fine sand, hard and gritty.

"Spring," said Benning bitterly, "is come. Ain't we got fun! And I've been looking forward to getting away from this blasted hole in the ice."

"I wouldn't try it now, if I were you," Barclay grunted. "Guys that set out from here in the next few days are going to be marvelously unpopular."

"How is your dog getting along, Doctor Copper?" McReady asked. "Any results yet?"

"In thirty hours? I wish there were. I gave him an injection of my blood today. But I imagine another five days will be needed. I don't know certainly enough to stop sooner."

"I've been wondering—if Connant were—changed, would he have warned us so soon after the animal escaped? Wouldn't he have waited long enough for it to have a real chance to fix itself? Until we woke up naturally?" McReady asked slowly.

"The thing is selfish. You didn't think it looked as though it were possessed of a store of the higher justices, did you?" Dr. Copper pointed out. "Every part of it is all of it, every part of it is all for itself, I imagine. If Connant were changed, to save his skin, he'd have to—but Connant's feelings aren't changed; they're imitated perfectly, or they're his own. Nat-

274

urally, the imitation, imitating perfectly Connant's feelings, would do exactly what Connant would do."

"Say, couldn't Norris or Vane give Connant some kind of a test? If the thing is brighter than men, it might know more physics than Connant should, and they'd catch it out," Barclay suggested.

Copper shook his head wearily. "Not if it reads minds. You can't plan a trap for it. Vane suggested that last night. He hoped it would answer some of the questions of physics he'd like to know answers to."

"This expedition-of-four idea is going to make life happy." Benning looked at his companions. "Each of us with an eye on the other to make sure he doesn't do something—peculiar. Man, aren't we going to be a trusting bunch! Each man eyeing his neighbors with the grandest exhibition of faith and trust—I'm beginning to know what Connant meant by 'I wish you could see your eyes.' Every now and then we all have it, I guess. One of you looks around with a sort of I-wonder-if-the-other-*three*-are look. Incidentally, I'm not excepting myself."

"So far as we know, the animal is dead, with a slight question as to Connant. No other is suspected," McReady stated slowly. "The always-four order is merely a precautionary measure."

"I'm waiting for Garry to make it four-in-a-bunk." Barclay sighed. "I thought I didn't have any privacy before, but since that order—"

IX

None watched more tensely than Connant. A little sterile glass test tube, half filled with straw-colored fluid. One—two—three—four—five drops of the clear solution Dr. Copper had prepared from the drops of blood from Connant's arm. The tube was shaken carefully, then set in a beaker of clear, warm water. The thermometer read blood heat, a little thermostat clicked noisily, and the electric hotplate began to glow as the lights flickered slightly. Then—little white flecks of precipitation were forming, snowing down in the clear straw-colored fluid. "Lord," said Connant. He dropped heavily into a bunk, crying like a baby. "Six days—" Connant sobbed, "six days in there—wondering if that damned test would lie—"

Garry moved over silently, and slipped his arm across the physicist's back.

"It couldn't lie," Dr. Copper said. "The dog was human-immune—and the serum reacted."

"He's—all right?" Norris gasped. "Then—the animal is dead—dead forever?"

"He is human," Copper spoke definitely, "and the animal is dead."

Kinner burst out laughing, laughing hysterically. McReady turned toward him and slapped his face with a methodical one-two, one-two action. The cook laughed, gulped, cried a moment, and sat up rubbing his cheeks, mumbling his thanks vaguely. "I was scared. Lord, I was scared—"

Norris laughed brittlely. "You think we weren't, you ape? You think maybe Connant wasn't?"

The Ad Building stirred with a sudden rejuvenation. Voices laughed, the men clustering around Connant spoke with unnecessarily loud voices, jittery, nervous voices relievedly friendly again. Somebody called out a suggestion, and a dozen started for their skis. Blair, Blair might recover— Dr. Copper fussed with his test tubes in nervous relief, trying solutions. The party of relief for Blair's shack started out the door, skis clapping noisily. Down the corridor, the dogs set up a quick yelping howl as the air of excited relief reached them.

Dr. Copper fussed with his tubes. McReady noticed him first, sitting on the edge of the bunk, with two precipitin-whitened test tubes of straw-colored fluid, his face whiter than the stuff in the tubes, silent tears slipping down from horror-widened eyes.

McReady felt a cold knife of fear pierce through his heart and freeze in his breast. Dr. Copper looked up. "Garry," he called hoarsely. "Garry, for God's sake, come here."

Commander Garry walked toward him sharply. Silence clapped down on the Ad Building. Connant looked up, rose stiffly from his seat.

"Garry—tissue from the monster—precipitates, too. It

proves nothing. Nothing but—but the dog was monster-immune, too. That *one of the two contributing blood—one of us two*, you and I, Garry—*one of us is a monster.*"

X

"Bar, call back those men before they tell Blair," McReady said quietly. Barclay went to the door; faintly his shouts came back to the tensely silent men in the room. Then he was back.

"They're coming," he said. "I didn't tell them why. Just that Doctor Copper said not to go."

"McReady," Garry sighed, "you're in command now. May God help you. I cannot."

The bronzed giant nodded slowly, his deep eyes on Commander Garry.

"I may be the one," Garry added. "I know I'm not, but I cannot prove it to you in any way. Doctor Copper's test has broken down. The fact that he showed it was useless, when it was to the advantage of the monster to have that uselessness not known, would seem to prove he was human."

Copper rocked back and forth slowly on the bunk. "I know I'm human. I can't prove it, either. One of us two is a liar, for that test cannot lie, and it says one of us is. I gave proof that the test was wrong, which seems to prove I'm human, and now Garry has given that argument which proves me human—which he, as the monster, should not do. Round and round and round and round and—"

Dr. Copper's head, then his neck and shoulders began circling slowly in time to the words. Suddenly he was lying back on the bunk, roaring with laughter. "It doesn't have to prove *one* of us is a monster! It doesn't have to prove that at all! Ho-ho. If we're *all* monsters it works the same—we're all monsters—all of us—Connant and Garry and I—and all of you."

"McReady," Van Wall, the blond-bearded Chief Pilot, called softly, "you were on the way to an M.D. when you took up meteorology, weren't you? Can you make some kind of test?"

McReady went over to Copper slowly, took the hypodermic from his hand, and washed it carefully in 95% alcohol. Garry sat on the bunk edge with wooden face, watching Copper and McReady expressionlessly. "What Copper said is possible." McReady sighed. "Van, will you help here? Thanks." The filled needle jabbed into Copper's thigh. The man's laughter did not stop, but slowly faded into sobs, then sound sleep as the morphia took hold.

McReady turned again. The men who had started for Blair stood at the far end of the room, skis dripping snow, their faces as white as their skis. Connant had a lighted cigarette in each hand; one he was puffing absently, and staring at the floor. The heat of the one in his left hand attracted him and he stared at it and the one in the other hand stupidly for a moment. He dropped one and crushed it under his heel slowly.

"Doctor Copper," McReady repeated, "could be right. I know I'm human—but, of course, can't prove it. I'll repeat the test for my own information. Any of you others who wish to may do the same."

Two minutes later, McReady held a test tube with white precipitin settling slowly in straw-colored serum. "It reacts to human blood, too, so they aren't both monsters."

"I didn't think they were." Van Wall sighed. "That wouldn't suit the monster, either; we could have destroyed them if we knew. Why hasn't the monster destroyed us, do you suppose? It seems to be loose."

McReady snorted. Then laughed softly. "Elementary, my dear Watson. The monster wants to have life forms available. It cannot animate a dead body, apparently. It is just waiting—waiting until the best opportunities come. We who remain human, it is holding in reserve."

Kinner shuddered violently. "Hey. Hey, Mac. Mac, would I know if I was a monster? Would I know if the monster had already got me? Oh, Lord, I may be a monster already."

"You'd know," McReady answered.

"But we wouldn't." Norris laughed shortly, half hysterically.

McReady looked at the vial of serum remaining. "There's one thing this damned stuff is good for, at that," he said thoughtfully. "Clark, will you and Van help me? The rest of the gang better stick together here. Keep an eye on each other," he said bitterly. "See that you don't get into mischief, shall we say?"

McReady started down the tunnel toward Dog Town, with Clark and Van Wall behind him. "You need more serum?" Clark asked.

McReady shook his head. "Tests. There's four cows and a bull, and nearly seventy dogs down there. This stuff reacts only to human blood and—monsters."

XI

McReady came back to the Ad Building and went silently to the washstand. Clark and Van Wall joined him a moment later. Clark's lips had developed a tic, jerking into sudden, unexpected sneers.

"What did you do?" Connant exploded suddenly. "More immunizing?"

Clark snickered, and stopped with a hiccup. "Immunizing. Haw! Immune, all right."

"That monster," said Van Wall steadily, "is quite logical. Our immune dog was quite all right, and we drew a little more serum for the tests. But we won't make any more."

"Can't—can't you use one man's blood on another dog?" Norris began.

"There aren't," said McReady softly, "any more dogs. Nor cattle, I might add."

"No more dogs?" Benning sat down slowly.

"They're very nasty when they start changing," Van Wall said precisely. "But slow. That electrocution iron you made up, Barclay, is very fast. There is only one dog left—our immune. The monster left that for us, so we could play with our little test. The rest—" He shrugged and dried his hands.

"The cattle—" gulped Kinner.

"Also. Reacted very nicely. They look funny as hell when they start melting. The beast hasn't any quick escape, when it's tied in dog chains, or halters, and it had to be to imitate."

Kinner stood up slowly. His eyes darted around the room, and came to rest horribly quivering on a tin bucket in the galley. Slowly, step by step, he retreated toward the door, his mouth opening and closing silently, like a fish out of water.

"The milk—" he gasped. "I milked 'em an hour ago—" His voice broke into a scream as he dived through the door. He was out on the ice-cap without windproof or heavy clothing.

Van Wall looked after him for a moment thoughtfully. "He's probably hopelessly mad," he said at length, "but he might be a monster escaping. He hasn't skis. Take a blowtorch—in case."

The physical motion of the chase helped them; something that needed doing. Three of the other men were quietly being sick. Norris was lying flat on his back, his face greenish, looking steadily at the bottom of the bunk above him.

"Mac, how long have the—cows been not-cows—"

McReady shrugged his shoulders hopelessly. He went over to the milk bucket and with his little tube of serum went to work on it. The milk clouded it, making certainty difficult. Finally he dropped the test tube into the stand and shook his head. "It tests negatively. Which means either they were cows then, or that, being perfect imitations, they gave perfectly good milk."

Copper stirred restlessly in his sleep and gave a gurgling cross between a snore and a laugh. Silent eyes fastened on him. "Would morphia—a monster—" somebody started to ask.

"Lord knows," McReady shrugged. "It affects every earthly animal I know of."

Connant suddenly raised his head. "Mac! The dogs must have swallowed pieces of the monster, and the pieces destroyed them! The dogs were where the monster resided. I was locked up. Doesn't that prove—"

Van Wall shook his head. "Sorry. Proves nothing about what you are, only proves what you didn't do."

"It doesn't do that." McReady sighed. "We are helpless because we don't know enough, and so jittery we don't think straight. Locked up! Ever watch a white corpuscle of the blood go through the wall of a blood vessel? No? It sticks out a pseudopod. And there it is—on the far side of the wall."

"Oh," said Van Wall unhappily. "The cattle tried to melt down, didn't they? They could have melted down—become just a thread of stuff and leaked under a door to re-collect on the other side. Ropes—no—no, that wouldn't do it. They couldn't live in a sealed tank or—"

"If," said McReady, "you shoot it through the heart, and it doesn't die, it's a monster. That's the best test I can think of offhand."

"No dogs," said Garry quietly, "and no cattle. It has to imitate men now. And locking up doesn't do any good. Your test might work, Mac, but I'm afraid it would be hard on the men."

XII

Clark looked up from the galley stove as Van Wall, Barclay, McReady, and Benning came in, brushing the drift from their clothes. The other men jammed into the Ad Building continued studiously to do as they were doing, playing chess, poker, reading. Ralsen was fixing a sledge on the table; Vane and Norris had their heads together over magnetic data, while Harvey read tables in a low voice.

Dr. Copper snored softly on the bunk. Garry was working with Dutton over a sheaf of radio messages on the corner of Dutton's bunk and a small fraction of the radio table. Connant was using most of the table for cosmic-ray sheets.

Quite plainly through the corridor, despite two closed doors, they could hear Kinner's voice. Clark banged a kettle onto the galley stove and beckoned McReady silently. The meteorologist went over to him.

"I don't mind the cooking so damn much," Clark said nervously, "but isn't there some way to stop that bird? We all agreed that it would be safe to move him into Cosmos House."

"Kinner?" McReady nodded toward the door. "I'm afraid not. I can dope him, I suppose, but we don't have an unlimited supply of morphia, and he's not in danger of losing his mind. Just hysterical."

"Well, we're in danger of losing ours. You've been out for an hour and a half. That's been going on steadily ever since, and it was going for two hours before. There's a limit, you know."

Garry wandered over slowly, apologetically. For an instant, McReady caught the feral spark of fear—horror—in Clark's eyes, and knew at the same instant it was in his own. Garry—Garry or Copper—was certainly a monster.

"If you could stop that, I think it would be a sound policy, Mac," Garry spoke quietly. "There are—tensions enough in this room. We agreed that it would be safe for Kinner in there, because everyone else in camp is under constant eyeing." Garry shivered slightly. "And try, try in God's name, to find some test that will work."

McReady sighed. "Watched or unwatched, everyone's tense. Blair's jammed the trap so it won't open now. Says he's got food enough, and keeps screaming, 'Go away, go away—you're monsters. I won't be absorbed. I won't. I'll tell men when they come. Go away.' So—we went away."

"There's no other test?" Garry pleaded.

McReady shrugged his shoulders. "Copper was perfectly right. The serum test could be absolutely definitive if it hadn't been—contaminated. But that's the only dog left, and he's fixed now."

"Chemicals? Chemical tests?"

McReady shook his head. "Our chemistry isn't that good. I tried the microscope you know."

Garry nodded. "Monster-dog and real dog were identical. But—you've got to go on. What are we going to do after dinner?"

Van Wall had joined them quietly. "Rotation sleeping. Half the crowd sleep; half stay awake. I wonder how many of us are monsters? All the dogs were. We thought we were safe, but somehow it got Copper—or you." Van Wall's eyes flashed uneasily. "It may have gotten every one of you—all of you but myself may be wondering, looking. No, that's not possible. You'd just spring then, I'd be helpless. We humans must somehow have the greater numbers now. But—" he stopped.

McReady laughed shortly. "You're doing what Norris complained of in me. Leaving it hanging. 'But if one more is changed—that may shift the balance of power.' It doesn't fight. I don't think it ever fights. It must be a peaceable thing, in its own—inimitable—way. It never had to, because it always gained its end otherwise."

Van Wall's mouth twisted in a sickly grin. "You're suggesting, then, that perhaps it already *has* the greater numbers, but is just waiting—waiting, all of them—all of you, for all I know—waiting till I, the last human, drop my wariness in sleep. Mac, did you notice their eyes, all looking at us?"

Garry sighed. "You haven't been sitting here for four straight hours, while all their eyes silently weighed the information that one of us two, Copper or I, is a monster certainly—perhaps both of us."

Clark repeated his request. "Will you stop that bird's noise? He's driving me nuts. Make him tone down, anyway."

"Still praying?" McReady asked.

"Still praying," Clark groaned. "He hasn't stopped for a second. I don't mind his praying if it relieves him, but he yells, he sings psalms and hymns and shouts prayers. He thinks God can't hear well way down here."

"Maybe He can't," Barclay grunted. "Or He'd have done something about this thing loosed from hell."

"Somebody's going to try that test you mentioned, if you don't stop him," Clark stated grimly. "I think a cleaver in the head would be as positive a test as a bullet in the heart."

"Go ahead with the food. I'll see what I can do. There may be something in the cabinets." McReady moved wearily toward the corner Copper had used as his dispensary. Three tall cabinets of rough boards, two locked, were the repositories of the camp's medical supplies. Twelve years ago, McReady had graduated, started for an internship, and been diverted to meteorology. Copper was a picked man, a man who knew his profession thoroughly and modernly. More than half the drugs available were totally unfamiliar to McReady; many of the others he had forgotten. There was no huge medical library here, no series of journals available to learn the things he had forgotten, the elementary, simple things to Copper, things that did not merit inclusion in the small library he had been forced to content himself with. Books are heavy, and every ounce of supplies had been freighted in by air.

McReady picked a barbiturate hopefully. Barclay and Van Wall went with him. One man never went anywhere alone in Big Magnet.

Ralsen had his sledge put away, and the physicists had

moved off the table, the poker game broken up when they got back. Clark was putting out the food. The click of spoons and the muffled sounds of eating were the only sign of life in the room. There were no words spoken as the three returned; simply all eyes focused on them questioningly while the jaws moved methodically.

McReady stiffened suddenly. Kinner was screeching out a hymn in a hoarse, cracked voice. He looked wearily at Van Wall with a twisted grin and shook his head. "Uh-uh."

Van Wall cursed bitterly and sat down at the table. "We'll just plumb have to take that till his voice wears out. He can't yell like that forever."

"He's got a brass throat and a cast-iron larynx," Norris declared savagely. "Then we could be hopeful, and suggest he's one of our friends. In that case he could go on renewing his throat till doomsday."

Silence clamped down. For twenty minutes they ate without a word. Then Connant jumped up with an angry violence. "You sit as still as a bunch of graven images. You don't say a word, but oh, Lord, what expressive eyes you've got. They roll around like a bunch of glass marbles spilling down a table. They wink and blink and stare—and whisper things. Can you guys look somewhere else for a change, please?

"Listen, Mac, you're in charge here. Let's run movies for the rest of the night. We've been saving those reels to make 'em last. Last for what? Who is it's going to see those last reels, eh? Let's see 'em while we can, and look at something other than each other."

"Sound idea, Connant. I, for one, am quite willing to change this in any way I can."

"Turn the sound up loud, Dutton. Maybe you can drown out the hymns," Clark suggested.

"But don't," Norris said softly, "don't turn off the lights altogether."

"The lights will be out." McReady shook his head. "We'll show all the cartoon movies we have. You won't mind seeing the old cartoons, will you?"

"Goody, goody—a moom-pitcher show. I'm just in the mood." McReady turned to look at the speaker, a lean, lanky New Englander, by the name of Caldwell, Caldwell was stuff-

284

ing his pipe slowly, a sour eye cocked up to McReady.

The bronze giant was forced to laugh. "Okay, Bart, you win. Maybe we aren't quite in the mood for Popeye and trick ducks, but it's something."

"Let's play Classifications," Caldwell suggested slowly. "Or maybe you call it Guggenheim. You draw lines on a piece of paper, and put down classes of things—like animals, you know. One for 'H' and one for 'U' and so on. Like 'Human' and 'Unknown' for instance. I think that would be a hell of a lot better game. Classifications, I sort of figure, is what we need right now a lot more than movies. Maybe somebody's got a pencil that he can draw lines with, draw lines between the 'U' animals and the 'H' animals for instance."

"McReady's trying to find that kind of a pencil," Van Wall answered quietly, "but we've got three kinds of animals here, you know. One that begins with 'M.' We don't want any more."

"Mad ones, you mean. Uh-huh. Clark, I'll help you with those pots so we can get our little peep-show going." Caldwell got up slowly.

Dutton and Barclay and Benning, in charge of the projector and sound mechanism arrangements, went about their job silently, while the Ad Building was cleared and the dishes and pans disposed of. McReady drifted over toward Van Wall slowly, and leaned back in the bunk beside him. "I've been wondering, Van," he said with a wry grin, "whether or not to report my ideas in advance. I forgot the 'U animal,' as Caldwell named it, could read minds. I've a vague idea of something that might work. It's too vague to bother with, though. Go ahead with your show, while I try to figure out the logic of the thing. I'll take this bunk."

Van Wall glanced up and nodded. The movie screen would be practically on a line with this bunk, hence making the pictures least distracting here, because least intelligible. "Perhaps you should tell us what you have in mind. As it is, only the unknowns know what you plan. You might be—unknown before you got it into operation."

"Won't take long, if I get it figured out right. But I don't want any more all-but-the-test-dog-monsters things. We better move Copper into this bunk directly above me. He won't be watching the screen, either." McReady nodded toward Copper's gently snoring bulk. Garry helped them lift and move the doctor.

McReady leaned back against the bunk and sank into a trance, almost, of concentration, trying to calculate chances, operations, methods. He was scarcely aware as the others distributed themselves silently, and the screen lit up. Vaguely Kinner's hectic, shouted prayers and his rasping hymn-singing annoyed him till the sound accompaniment started. The lights were turned out, but the large, light-colored areas of the screen reflected enough light for ready visibility. It made men's eyes sparkle as they moved restlessly. Kinner was still praying, shouting, his voice a raucous accompaniment to the mechanical sound. Dutton stepped up the amplification.

So long had the voice been going on that only vaguely at first was McReady aware that something seemed missing. Lying as he was, just across the narrow room from the corridor leading to Cosmos House, Kinner's voice had reached him fairly clearly, despite the sound accompaniment of the pictures. It struck him abruptly that it had stopped.

"Dutton, cut that sound," McReady called as he sat up abruptly. The pictures flickered a moment, soundless and strangely futile in the sudden, deep silence. The rising wind on the surface above bubbled melancholy tears of sound down the stove pipes. "Kinner's stopped," McReady said softly.

"For God's sake start that sound, then; he may have stopped to listen," Norris snapped.

McReady rose and went down the corridor. Barclay and Van Wall left their places at the far end of the room to follow him. The flickers bulged and twisted on the back of Barclay's gray underwear as he crossed the still-functioning beam of the projector. Dutton snapped on the lights, and the pictures vanished.

Norris stood at the door as McReady had asked. Garry sat down quietly in the bunk nearest the door, forcing Clark to make room for him. Most of the others had stayed exactly where they were. Only Connant walked slowly up and down the room, in steady, unvarying rhythm.

"If you're going to do that, Connant," Clark spat, "we can get along without you altogether, whether you're human or not. Will you stop that damned rhythm?"

286

"Sorry." The physicist sat down in a bunk and watched his toes thoughtfully. It was almost five minutes, five ages, while the wind made the only sound, before McReady appeared at the door.

"We," he announced, "haven't got enough grief here already. Somebody's tried to help us out. Kinner has a knife in his throat, which was why he stopped singing, probably. We've got monsters, madmen, and murderers. Any more 'M's' you can think of Caldwell? If there are, we'll probably have 'em before long."

<h1 style="text-align:center">XIII</h1>

"Is Blair loose?" someone asked.

"Blair is not loose. Or he flew in. If there's any doubt about where our gentle helper came from—this may clear it up." Van Wall held a foot-long, thin-bladed knife in a cloth. The wooden handle was half-burned, charred with the peculiar pattern of the top of the galley stove.

Clark stared at it. "I did that this afternoon. I forgot the damn thing and left it on the stove."

Van Wall nodded. "I smelled it, if you remember. I knew the knife came from the galley."

"I wonder," said Benning, looking around at the party warily, "how many more monsters have we? If somebody could slip out of his place, go back of the screen to the galley and then down to the Cosmos House and back—he did come back, didn't he? Yes—everybody's here. Well, if one of the gang could do all that—"

"Maybe a monster did it," Garry suggested quietly. "There's that possibility."

"The monster, as you pointed out today, has only men left to imitate. Would he decrease his—supply, shall we say?" Van Wall pointed out. "No, we just have a plain, ordinary louse, a murderer to deal with. Ordinarily we'd call him an 'inhuman murderer' I suppose, but we have to distinguish now. We have inhuman murderers, and now we have human murderers. Or one, at least."

"There's one less human," Norris said softly. "Maybe the monsters have the balance of power now."

"Never mind that." McReady sighed and turned to Barclay. "Bar, will you get your electric gadget? I'm going to make certain—"

Barclay turned down the corridor to get the pronged electrocutor, while McReady and Van Wall went back toward Cosmos House. Barclay followed them in some thirty seconds.

The corridor to Cosmos House twisted, as did nearly all corridors in Big Magnet, and Norris stood at the entrance again. But they heard, rather muffled, McReady's sudden shout. There was a savage flurry of blows, dull *ch-thunk*, *shluff* sounds. "Bar—Bar—" And a curious, savage mewing scream, silenced before even quick-moving Norris had reached the bend.

Kinner—or what had been Kinner—lay on the floor, cut half in two by the great knife McReady had had. The meteorologist stood against the wall, the knife dripping red in his hand. Van Wall was stirring vaguely on the floor, moaning, his hand half-consciously rubbing at his jaw. Barclay, an unutterably savage gleam in his eyes, was methodically leaning on the pronged weapon in his hand, jabbing—jabbing, jabbing.

Kinner's arms had developed a queer, scaly fur, and the flesh had twisted. The fingers had shortened, the hand rounded, the fingernails become three-inch long things of dull red horn, keened to steel-hard, razor-sharp talons.

McReady raised his head, looked at the knife in his hand, and dropped it. "Well, whoever did it can speak up now. He was an inhuman murderer at that—in that he murdered an inhuman. I swear by all that's holy, Kinner was a lifeless corpse on the floor here when we arrived. But when it found we were going to jab It with the power—It changed."

Norris stared unsteadily. "Oh, Lord, those things can act. Ye gods—sitting in here for hours, mouthing prayers to a God it hated! Shouting hymns in a cracked voice—hymns about a church it never knew. Driving us mad with its ceaseless howling—

"Well. Speak up, whoever did it. You didn't know it, but you did the camp a favor. And I want to know how in blazes

288

you got out of the room without anyone seeing you. It might help in guarding ourselves."

"His screaming—his singing. Even the sound projector couldn't drown it." Clark shivered. "It was a monster."

"Oh," said Van Wall in sudden comprehension. "You *were* sitting right next to the door, weren't you? And almost behind the projection screen already."

Clark nodded dumbly. "He—it's quiet now. It's a dead— Mac, your test's no damn good. It was dead anyway, monster or man, it was dead."

McReady chuckled softly. "Boys, meet Clark, the only one we know is human! Meet Clark, the one who proves he's human by trying to commit murder—and failing. Will the rest of you please refrain from trying to prove you're human for a while? I think we may have another test."

"A test!" Connant snapped joyfully, then his face sagged in disappointment. "I suppose it's another either-way-you-want-it."

"No," said McReady steadily. "Look sharp and be careful. Come into the Ad Building. Barclay, bring your electrocutor. And somebody—Dutton—stand with Barclay to make sure he does it. Watch every neighbor, for by the hell these monsters came from, I've got something, and they know it. They're going to get dangerous!"

The group tensed abruptly. An air of crushing menace entered into every man's body, sharply they looked at each other. More keenly than ever before—*is that man next to me an inhuman monster?*

"What is it?" Garry asked, as they stood again in the main room. "How long will it take?"

"I don't know exactly," said McReady, his voice brittle with angry determination. "But I *know* it will work, and no two ways about it. It depends on a basic quality of the *monsters*, not on us. 'Kinner' just convinced me." He stood heavy and solid in bronzed immobility, completely sure of himself again at last.

"This," said Barclay, hefting the wooden-handled weapon tipped with its two sharp-pointed, charged conductors, "is going to be rather necessary, I take it. Is the power plant assured?"

Dutton nodded sharply. "The automatic stoker bin is full.

289

The gas power plant is on stand-by. Van Wall and I set it for the movie operation—and we've checked it over rather carefully several times, you know. Anything those wires touch, dies," he assured them grimly. "*I* know that."

Dr. Copper stirred vaguely in his bunk, rubbed his eyes with fumbling hand. He sat up slowly, blinked his eyes blurred with sleep and drugs, widened with an unutterable horror of drug-ridden nightmares. "Garry," he mumbled, "Garry—listen. Selfish—from hell they came, and hellish shellfish—I mean self— Do I? What do I mean?" He sank back in his bunk and snored softly.

McReady looked at him thoughtfully. "We'll know presently." He nodded slowly. "But selfish is what you mean, all right. You may have thought of that, half sleeping, dreaming there. I didn't stop to think what dreams you might be having. But that's all right. Selfish is the word. They must be, you see." He turned to the men in the cabin, tense, silent men staring with wolfish eyes each at his neighbor. "Selfish, and as Doctor Copper said—*every part is a whole*. Every piece is self-sufficient, an animal in itself.

"That, and one other thing, tell the story. There's nothing mysterious about blood; it's just as normal a body tissue as a piece of muscle, or a piece of liver. But it hasn't so much connective tissue, though it has millions, billions of life cells."

McReady's great bronze beard ruffled in a grim smile. "This is satisfying, in a way. I'm pretty sure we humans still outnumber you—others. Others standing here. And we have what you, your other-world race, evidently doesn't. Not an imitated, but a bred-in-the-bone instinct, a driving, unquenchable fire that's genuine. We'll fight, fight with a ferocity you may attempt to imitate, but you'll never equal! We're human. We're real. You're imitations, false to the core of your every cell."

"All right. It's a showdown now. *You* know. You, with your mind-reading. You've lifted the idea from my brain. You can't do a thing about it.

"Standing here—

"Let it pass. Blood is tissue. They have to bleed; if they don't bleed when cut, then by heaven, they're phony from hell! If they bleed—then that blood, separated from them, is an individual—*a newly formed individual in its own right*, *just as they—split, all of them, from one original—are individuals!*

"Get it, Van? See the answer, Bar?"

Van Wall laughed very softly. "The blood—the blood will not obey. It's a new individual, with all the desire to protect its own life that the original—the main mass from which it was split—has. The *blood* will live—and try to crawl away from a hot needle, say!"

McReady picked up the scalpel from the table. From the cabinet he took a rack of test tubes, a tiny alcohol lamp, and a length of platinum wire set in a little glass rod. A smile of grim satisfaction rode his lips. For a moment he glanced up at those around him. Barclay and Dutton moved toward him slowly, the wooden-handled electric instrument alert.

"Dutton," said McReady, "suppose you stand over by the splice there where you've connected that in. Just make sure no—thing pulls it loose."

Dutton moved away. "Now, Van, suppose you be first on this."

White-faced, Van Wall stepped forward. With a delicate precision, McReady cut a vein in the base of his thumb. Van Wall winced slightly, then held steady as a half inch of bright blood collected in the tube. McReady put the tube in the rack, gave Van Wall a bit of alum, and indicated the iodine bottle.

Van Wall stood motionlessly watching. McReady heated the platinum wire in the alcohol lamp flame, then dipped it into the tube. It hissed softly. Five times he repeated the test. "Human, I'd say." McReady sighed, and straightened. "As yet, my theory hasn't been actually proven—but I have hopes. I have hopes.

"Don't, by the way, get too interested in this. We have with us some unwelcome ones, no doubt. Van, will you relieve Barclay at the switch? Thanks. Okay, Barclay, and may I say I hope you stay with us? You're a damned good guy."

Barclay grinned uncertainly; winced under the keen edge of the scalpel. Presently, smiling widely, he retrieved his long-handled weapon.

"Mr. Samuel Dutt—*Bar!*"

The tensity was released in that second. Whatever of hell the monsters may have had within them, the men in that instant matched it. Barclay had no chance to move his weapon, as a score of men poured down on the thing that had seemed Dutton. It mewed and spat and tried to grow fangs—and was a hundred broken, torn pieces. Without knives, or any weapon save the brute-given strength of a staff of picked men, the thing was crushed, rent.

Slowly they picked themselves up, their eyes smoldering, very quiet in their motions. A curious wrinkling of their lips betrayed a species of nervousness.

Barclay went over with the electric weapon. Things smoldered and stank. The caustic acid Van Wall dropped on each spilled drop of blood gave off tickling, cough-provoking fumes.

McReady grinned, his deep-set eyes alight and dancing. "Maybe," he said softly, "I underrated man's abilities when I said nothing human could have the ferocity in the eyes of that thing we found. I wish we could have the opportunity to treat in a more befitting manner these things. Something with boiling oil, or melted lead in it, or maybe slow roasting in the power boiler. When I think what a man Dutton was—

"Never mind. My theory is confirmed by—by one who knew? Well, Van Wall and Barclay are proven. I think, then, that I'll try to show you what I already know. That I, too, am human." McReady switched the scalpel in absolute alcohol, burned it off the metal blade, and cut the base of his thumb expertly.

Twenty seconds later he looked up from the desk at the waiting men. There were more grins out there now, friendly grins, yet withal, something else in the eyes.

"Connant," McReady laughed softly, "was right. The huskies watching that thing in the corridor bend had nothing on you. Wonder why we think only the wolf blood has the right to ferocity? Maybe on spontaneous viciousness a wolf takes tops, but after these seven days—abandon all hope, ye wolves who enter here!

"Maybe we can save time. Connant, would you step for—"

Again Barclay was too slow. There were more grins, less tensity still, when Barclay and Van Wall finished their work.

Garry spoke in a low, bitter voice. "Connant was one of the finest men we had here—and five minutes ago I'd have sworn he was a man. Those damanble things are more than imitation." Garry shuddered and sat back in his bunk.

And thirty seconds later, Garry's blood shrank from the hot platinum wire, and struggled to escape the tube, struggled as frantically as a suddenly feral, red-eyed, dissolving imitation of Garry struggled to dodge the snake-tongue weapon Barclay advanced at him, white-faced and sweating. The thing in the test tube screamed with a tiny, tinny voice as McReady dropped it into the glowing coal of the galley stove.

XIV

"The last of it?" Dr. Copper looked down from his bunk with bloodshot, saddened eyes. "Fourteen of them——"

McReady nodded shortly. "In some ways——if only we could have permanently prevented their spreading——I'd like to have even the imitations back. Commander Garry——Connant——Dutton——Clark——"

"Where are they taking those things?" Copper nodded to the stretcher Barclay and Norris were carrying out.

"Outside. Outside on the ice, where they've got fifteen smashed crates, half a ton of coal, and presently will add ten gallons of kerosene. We've dumped acid on every spilled drop, every torn fragment. We're going to incinerate those."

"Sounds like a good plan." Copper nodded wearily. "I wonder, you haven't said whether Blair——"

McReady started. "We forgot him. We had so much else! I wonder——do you suppose we can cure him now?"

"If——" began Dr. Copper, and stopped meaningly.

McReady started a second time. "Even a madman. It imitated Kinner and his praying hysteria——" McReady turned toward Van Wall at the long table. "Van, we've got to make an expedition to Blair's shack."

Van looked up sharply, the frown of worry faded for an instant in surprised remembrance. Then he rose, nodded. "Barclay better go along. He applied the lashings, and may figure how to get in without frightening Blair too much."

Three quarters of an hour, through —37° cold, while the aurora curtain bellied overhead. The twilight was nearly 12 hours long, flaming in the north on snow like white, crystalline sand under their skis. A 5-mile wind piled it in drift-lines pointing off to the northwest. Three quarters of an hour to reach the snow-buried shack. No smoke came from the little shack, and the men hastened.

"Blair!" Barclay roared into the wind when he was still a hundred yards away. "Blair!"

"Shut up," said McReady softly. "And hurry. He may be trying a lone hike. If we have to go after him—no planes, the tractors disabled—"

"Would a monster have the stamina a man has?"

"A broken leg wouldn't stop it for more than a minute," McReady pointed out.

Barclay gasped suddenly and pointed aloft. Dim in the twilit sky, a winged thing circled in curves of indescribable grace and ease. Great white wings tipped gently, and the bird swept over them in silent curiosity.

"Albatross—" Barclay said softly. "First of the season, and wandering 'way inland for some reason. If a monster's loose—"

Norris bent down on the ice and tore hurriedly at his heavy, windproof clothing. He straightened, his coat flapping open, a grim blue-metaled weapon in his hand. It roared a challenge to the white silence of Antarctica.

The thing in the air screamed hoarsely. Its great wings worked frantically as a dozen feathers floated down from its tail. Norris fired again. The bird was moving swiftly now, but in an almost straight line of retreat. It screamed again, more feathers dropped, and with beating wings it soared behind a ridge of pressure ice, to vanish.

Norris hurried after the others. "It won't come back," he panted.

Barclay cautioned him to silence, pointing. A curious, fiercely blue light beat out from the cracks of the shack's door. A very low, soft humming sounded inside, a low, soft humming and a clink and click of tools, the very sounds somehow bearing a message of frantic haste.

McReady's face paled. "Lord help us if that thing has—" He grabbed Barclay's shoulder and made snipping motions with his fingers, pointing toward the lacing of control cables that held the door.

294

Barclay drew the wire cutters from his pocket and knelt soundlessly at the door. The snap and twang of cut wires made an unbearable racket in the utter quiet of the Antarctic hush. There was only that strange, sweetly soft hum from within the shack, and the queer, hectically clipped clicking and rattling of tools to drown their noises.

McReady peered through a crack in the door. His breath sucked in huskily and his great fingers clamped cruelly on Barclay's shoulder. The meteorologist backed down. "It isn't," he explained very softly, "Blair. It's kneeling on something on the bunk—something that keeps lifting. Whatever it's working on is a thing like a knapsack—and it lifts."

"All at once," Barclay said grimly. "No. Norris, hang back, and get the iron of yours out. It may have—weapons."

Together Barclay's powerful body and McReady's giant strength struck the door. Inside, the bunk jammed against the door screeched madly and crackled into kindling. The door flung down from broken hinges, the patched lumber of the doorpost dropping inward.

Like a blue rubber ball, a thing bounced up. One of its four tentacle-like arms looped out like a striking snake. In a seven-tentacled hand a six-inch pencil of winking, shining metal glinted and swung upward to face them. Its line-thin lips twitched back from snake fangs in a grin of hate, red eyes blazing.

Norris's revolver thundered in the confined space. The hate-washed face twitched in agony, the looping tentacle snatched back. The silvery thing in its hand a smashed ruin of metal, the seven-tentacled hand became a mass of mangled flesh oozing greenish-yellow ichor. The revolver thundered three times more. Dark holes drilled each of the three eyes before Norris hurled the empty weapon against its face.

The thing screamed in feral hate, a lashing tentacle wiping at blinded eyes. For a moment it crawled on the floor, savage tentacles lashing out; the body twitching. Then it staggered up again, blinded eyes working, boiling hideously, the crushed flesh sloughing away in sodden gobbets.

Barclay lurched to his feet and dove forward with an ice-ax. The flat of the weighty thing crushed against the side of the head. Again the unkillable monster went down. The tentacles lashed out, and suddenly Barclay felt his feet in the grip of a living, livid rope. The thing dissolved as he held it, a white-hot band that ate into the flesh of his hands like living fire. Frantically he tore the stuff from him, held his hands where they could not be reached. The blind thing felt and ripped at the tough, heavy, wind-proof cloth, seeking flesh— flesh it could convert—

The huge blowtorch McReady had brought coughed solemnly. Abruptly it rumbled disapproval throatily. Then it laughed gurglingly and thrust out a blue-white, three-foot tongue. The thing on the floor shrieked, flailed out blindly with tentacles that writhed and withered in the bubbling wrath of the blowtorch. It crawled and turned on the floor, it shrieked and hobbled madly, but always McReady held the blowtorch on the face, the dead eyes burning and bubbling uselessly. Frantically the thing crawled and howled.

A tentacle sprouted a savage talon—and crisped in the flame. Steadily McReady moved with a planned, grim campaign. Helpless, maddened, the thing retreated from the grunting torch, the caressing, licking tongue. For a moment it rebelled, squalling in inhuman hatred at the touch of the icy snow. Then it fell back before the charring breath of the torch, the stench of its flesh bathing it. Hopelessly it retreated—on and on across the antarctic snow. The bitter wind swept over it, twisting the torch-tongue; vainly it flopped, a trail of oily, stinking smoke bubbling away from it—

McReady walked back toward the shack silently. Barclay met him at the door. "No more?" the giant meteorologist asked grimly.

Barclay shook his head. "No more. It didn't split?"

"It had other things to think about," McReady assured him. "When I left it, it was a glowing coal. What was it doing?"

Norris laughed shortly. "Wise boys, we are. Smash magnetos, so planes won't work. Rip the boiler tubing out of the tractors. And leave that thing alone for a week in this shack. Alone and undisturbed."

McReady looked in at the shack more carefully. The air, despite the ripped door, was hot and humid. On a table at the far end of the room rested a thing of coiled wires and small magnets, glass tubing, and radio tubes. At the center a block

296

of rough stone rested. From the center of the block came the light that flooded the place, the fiercely blue light, bluer than the glare of an electric arc, and from it came the sweetly soft hum. Off to one side was another mechanism of crystal glass, blown with an incredible neatness and delicacy, metal plates and a queer, shimmery sphere of insubstantiality.

"What is that?" McReady moved nearer.

Norris grunted. "Leave it for investigation. But I can guess pretty well. That's atomic power. That stuff to the left—that's a neat little thing for doing what men have been trying to do with one-hundred-ton cyclotrons and so forth. It separates neutrons from heavy water, which he was getting from the surrounding ice."

"Where did he get all—oh. Of course. A monster couldn't be locked in—or out. He's been through the apparatus caches." McReady stared at the apparatus. "Lord, what minds that race must have—"

"The shimmery sphere—I think it's a sphere of pure force. Neutrons can pass through any matter, and he wanted a supply reservoir of neutrons. Just project neutrons against silica—calcium—beryllium—almost anything, and the atomic energy is released. That thing is the atomic generator."

McReady plucked a thermometer from his coat. "It's a hundred and twenty degrees in here, despite the open door. Our clothes have kept the heat out to an extent, but I'm sweating now."

Norris nodded. "The light's cold. I found that. But it gives off heat to warm the place through that coil. He had all the power in the world. He could keep it warm and pleasant, as his race thought of warmth and pleasantness. Did you notice the light, the color of it?"

McReady nodded. "Beyond the stars is the answer. From beyond the stars. From a hotter planet that circled a brighter, bluer sun they came."

McReady glanced out the door toward the blasted, smoke-stained trail that flopped and wandered blindly off across the drift. "There won't be any more coming, I guess. Sheer accident it landed here, and that was twenty million years ago. What did it do all that for?" He nodded toward the apparatus.

Barclay laughed softly. "Did you notice what it was working on when we came? Look." He pointed toward the ceiling of the shack.

Like a knapsack made of flattened coffee tins, with dangling cloth straps and leather belts, the mechanism clung to the ceiling. A tiny, glaring heart of supernal flame burned in it, yet burned through the ceiling's wood without scorching it. Barclay walked over to it, grasped two of the dangling straps in his hands, and pulled it down with an effort. He strapped it about his body. A slight jump carried him in a weirdly slow arc across the room.

"Anti-gravity," said McReady softly.

"Anti-gravity." Norris nodded. "Yes, we had 'em stopped, with no planes, and no birds. The birds hadn't come—but it had coffee tins and radio parts, and glass and the machine shop at night. And a week—a whole week—all to itself. America in a single jump—with anti-gravity powered by the atomic energy of matter.

"We had 'em stopped. Another half hour—it was just tightening these straps on the device so it could wear it—and we'd have stayed in Antarctica, and shot down any moving thing that came from the rest of the world."

"The albatross—" McReady said softly. "Do you suppose—"

"With this thing almost finished? With that death weapon it held in its hand?

"No, by the grace of God, who evidently does hear very well, even down here, and the margin of half an hour, we keep our world, and the planets of the system, too. Anti-gravity, you know, and atomic power. Because They came from another sun, a star beyond the stars. *They* came from a world with a bluer sun."

When the definitive history of science fiction is written, you can be sure that **Damon Knight** will receive a full chapter. His contributions as a writer, editor, and critic are still not fully appreciated, and not yet concluded: books like *Hell's Pavement* (1955); collections like *The Best of Damon Knight* (1976); criticism and history like *In Search of Wonder* (1956, 1967) and *The Futurians* (1977); and the *Orbit* series of original stories. He is also one of the outstanding anthologists in the field.

As a writer his strength and breath is considerable. For evidence, keep reading.

An Eye for a What?

BY DAMON KNIGHT

I

On his way across the wheel one morning, Dr. Walter Alvarez detoured down to C level promenade. A few men were standing, as usual, at the view window looking out at the enormous blue-green planet below. They were dressed alike in sheen-gray coveralls, a garment with detachable gauntlets and hood designed to make it convertible into a spacesuit. It was uncomfortable, but regulation: according to the books, a Survey and Propaganda Satellite might find itself under attack at any moment.

Nothing so interesting had happened to SAPS 3107A, orbiting off the seventh planet of a G-type star in Ophiuchus. They had been here for two years and a half, and most of them had not even touched ground yet.

There it was, drifting by out there, blue-green, fat and juicy—an oxygen planet, two-thirds land, mild climate, soil fairly bursting with minerals and organics.

Alvarez felt his mouth watering when he looked at it. He had "wheel fever"; they all did. He wanted to get *down* there, to natural gravity and natural ailments.

The last month or so, there had been a feeling in the satellite that a break-through was coming. Always coming: it never arrived.

A plump orthotypist named Lola went by, and a couple of the men turned with automatic whistles. "Listen," said Olaf Marx conspiratorially, with a hand on Alvarez's arm, "that reminds me, did you hear what happened at the big banquet yesterday?"

"No," said Alvarez, irritably withdrawing his arm. "I didn't go. Can't stand banquets. Why?"

"Well, the way I get it, the Commandant's wife was sitting right across from George—"

Alvarez's interest sharpened. "You mean the gorgon? What did he do?"

"I'm *telling* you. See, it looked like he was watching her all through dinner. Then up comes the dessert—lemon meringue. So old George—"

The shift bell rang. Alvarez started nervously and looked at his thumbwatch. The other men were drifting away. So was Olaf, laughing like a fool. "You'll die when you hear," he called back. "Boy, do I wish I'd been there myself! So long, Walt."

Alvarez reluctantly went the other way. In B corridor, somebody called after him, "Hey, Walt? Hear about the banquet?"

He shook his head. The other man, a baker named Pedro, grinned and waved, disappearing up the curve of the corridor. Alvarez opened the door of Xenology Section and went in.

During his absence, somebody had put a new chart on the wall. It was ten feet high and there were little rectangles all over it, each connected by lines to other rectangles. When he first saw it, Alvarez thought it was a new table of organization for the Satellite Service, and he winced: but on closer inspection, the chart was *too* complex, and besides, it had a peculiar disorganized appearance. Boxes had been white-rubbed out and other boxes drawn on top of them. Some parts were crowded illegibly together and others were spacious. The whole thing looked desperately confused; and so did Elvis Womrath, who was on a wheeled ladder erasing the entire top righthand corner. "*N* panga," he said irritably. "That right?"

"Yes," a voice piped unexpectedly. Alvarez looked around, saw nobody. The voice went on, "But he is *R* panga to his cousins and all their *N* pangas or bigger, except when—"

Alvarez leaned over and peered around the desk. There on the carpet was the owner of the voice, a pinkish-white spheroid with various appendages sprouting in all directions, like a floating mine: "George" the gorgon. "Oh, it's you," said Alvarez, producing his echo sounder and humidometer. "What's all this nonsense I hear—" He began to prod the gorgon with the test equipment, making his regular morning examination. It was the only bright moment of his day; the infirmary could wait.

"All right," Womrath interrupted, scrubbing furiously. "*R* panga to cousins—wait a minute, now." He turned with a scowl. "Alvarez, I'll be through in a minute. *N* panga or bigger, except when . . ." He sketched in half a dozen boxes, labeled them and began to draw connecting lines. "Now is *that* right?" he asked George.

"Yes, only now it is wrong panga to *mother's* cousins. Draw again, from father's cousins' *N* pangas, to mother's cousins' *O* pangas or bigger . . . Yes, and now from father's uncles' *R* pangas, to mother's uncles' pangas *cousins*—"

Womrath's hand faltered. He stared at the chart; he had drawn such a tangle of lines, he couldn't tell what box connected with which. "Oh, God," he said hopelessly. He climbed down off the ladder and slapped the stylus into Alvarez's palm. "*You* go nuts." He thumbed the intercom on the desk and said, "Chief, I'm going off now. *Way* off."

"*Did you get that chart straightened out?*" the intercom demanded.

"No, but—"

"*You're on extra duty as of now. Take a pill. Is Alvarez here?*"

"Yes," said Womrath resignedly.

"*Both of you come in, then. Leave George outside.*"

"Hello, Doctor," the spheroid piped. "Are you panga to me?"

"Don't let's get into *that*," said Womrath, twitching, and took Alvarez by the sleeve. They found the chief of the Xenology Section, Edward H. Dominick, huddled bald and bear-like behind his desk. The cigar in his hand looked chewed. "Womrath," he said, "When can you give me that chart?"

"I don't know. Never, maybe." When Dominick scowled at him irritably, he shrugged and lit a sullen cigarette.

Dominick swiveled his gaze to Alvarez. "Have you," he asked, "heard about what happened at the banquet in George's honor yesterday?"

"No, I have not," said Alvarez. "Will you be so kind as to tell me, or else shut up about it?"

Dominick rubbed his shaven skull, absorbing the insult. "It was during the dessert," he said. "George was sitting opposite Mrs. Carver, in that little jump seat. Just as she got her fork into the pie—it was lemon meringue—George rolled up over the table and grabbed the plate away. Mrs. Carver screamed, pulled back—thought she was being attacked, I suppose—and the chair went out from under her. It—was—a—mess."

Alvarez ended the awed silence. "What did he do with the pie?"

"Ate it," said Dominick glumly. "Had a perfectly good piece of his own, that he didn't touch." He popped a lozenge into his mouth.

Alvarez shook his head. "Not typical. His pattern is strictly submissive. I don't like it."

"That's what I told Carver. But he was livid. Shaking. We all sat there until he escorted his wife to her room and came back. Then we had an interrogation. All we could get out of George was, 'I thought I was panga to her.' "

Alvarez shifted impatiently in his chair, reaching automatically for a bunch of grapes from the bowl on the desk. He was a small, spare man, and he felt defensive about it. "Now what is all this panga business?" he demanded.

Womrath snorted, and began to peel a banana.

"Panga," said Dominick, "would appear to be some kind of complicated authority-submission relationship that exists among the gorgons." Alvarez sat up straighter. "They never mentioned it to us, because we never asked. Now it turns out to be crucial." Dominick sighed. "Fourteen months, just getting a three-man base down on the planet. Seven more to get the elders' permission to bring a gorgon here experimentally. All according to the book. We picked the biggest and brightest-looking one we could find: that was George. He seemed to be coming along great. And now this."

"Well, chief," said Womrath carefully, "nobody has any more admiration than I have for Mrs. Carver as a consumer—she really puts it away, but it seems to me the question is, is *George* damaged—"

Dominick was shaking his head. "I haven't told you the rest of it. This panga thing stopped Carver cold, but not for long. He beamed down to the planethead and had Rubinson ask the elders, 'Is George panga to the Commandant's wife?' "

Alvarez grinned mirthlessly and clicked his tongue.

"Sure." Dominick nodded. "Who knows what a question like that may have meant to them? They answered back, in effect, 'Certainly not,' and wanted to know the details. Carver *told* them."

"And?" said Alvarez.

"They said George was a shocking criminal who should be appropriately punished. Not by them, you understand—by us, because we're the offended parties. Moreover—now this must make sense to their peculiar way of looking at things—if *we* don't punish George to their satisfaction, *they'll* punish Rubinson and his whole crew."

"How?" Alvarez demanded.

"By doing," Dominick said, "whatever it is we should have done to George—and that could be anything."

Womrath pursed his lips to whistle, but no sound came out. He swallowed a mouthful of banana and tried again. Still nothing.

"You get it?" said Dominick with suppressed emotion. They all looked through the open doorway at George, squatting patiently in the other room. "There's no trouble about 'punishment'—we all know what it means, we've read the books. But how do you punish an alien like that? *An eye for a what?*

"Now let's see if we have this straight," said Dominick, sorting through the papers in his hand. Womrath and Alvarez looked on from either side. George tried to peek, too, but his photoceptors were too short. They were all standing in the outer office, which had been stripped to the bare walls and floor. "One. We know a gorgon changes color according to his emotional state. When they're contented, they're a kind of rose pink. When they're unhappy, they turn blue."

"He's been pink ever since we've had him on the satellite," said Womrath, glancing down at the gorgon.

"Except at the banquet," Dominick answered thoughtfully. "I remember he turned bluish just before . . . If we could find out what it was that set him off— Well, first things first." He held down another finger. "Two, we don't have any information at all about local systems of reward and punishment. They may cut each other into bits for spitting on the sidewalk, or they may just slap each other's—um, wrists—" He looked unhappily down at George, all his auricles and photoceptors out on stalks.

"—for arson, rape and mopery," Dominick finished. "We don't know; we'll have to play it by ear."

"What does George say about it?" Alvarez asked. "Why don't you ask him?"

"We thought of that," Womrath said glumly. "Asked him what the elders would do to him in a case like this, and he said they'd quabble his infarcts, or something."

"A dead end," Dominick added. "It would take us years . . ." He scrubbed his naked scalp with a palm. "Well, number three, we've got all the furniture out of here—it's going to be damned crowded, with the whole staff working in my office, but never mind . . . Number four, there's his plate with the bread and water. And number five, that door has been fixed so it latches on the outside. Let's give it a dry run." He led the way to the door; the others followed, including George. "No, you stay in here," Womrath told him. George stopped, blushing an agreeable pink.

Dominick solemnly closed the door and dropped the improvised latch into its socket. He punched the door button, found it satisfactorily closed. Through the transparent upper pane, they could see George inquisitively watching.

Dominick opened the door again. "Now, George," he said, "pay attention. This is a *prison*. You're being *punished*. We're going to keep you in here, with nothing to eat but what's there, until we think you're punished enough. Understand?"

"Yes," said George doubtfully.

"All right," said Dominick, and closed the door. They all stood watching for a while, and George stood watching them back, but nothing else happened. "Let's go into my office and wait," said Dominick, with a sigh. "Can't expect miracles, all at once."

They trooped down the corridor to the adjoining room and ate peanuts for a while. "He's a sociable creature," Womrath said hopefully. "He'll get lonesome after a while."

"And hungry," Alvarez said. "He never turns down a meal."

Half an hour later, when they looked in, George was thoughtfully chewing up the carpet. "No, no, no, *no*, George," said Dominick, bursting in on him. "You're not supposed to eat anything except what we give you. This is a *prison*."

"Good carpet," said George, hurt.

"I don't care if it is. You don't eat it, understand?"

"Okay," said George cheerfully. His color was an honest rose pink.

Four hours later, when Alvarez went off shift, George had settled down in a corner and pulled in all his appendages. He was asleep. If anything, he looked pinker than ever.

When Alvarez came on shift again, there was no doubt about it. George was sitting in the middle of the room, photoceptors out and waving rhythmically; his color was a glowing pink, the pink of a rose pearl. Dominick kept him in there for another day, just to make sure; George seemed to lose a little weight on the austere diet, but glowed a steady pink. He liked it.

II

Goose Kelly, the games instructor, tried to keep up a good front, but he had the worst case of wheel fever on SAPS 3107A. It had got so that looking out at that fat, blue-green planet, swimming there so close, was more than he could bear. Kelly was a big man, an outdoorsman by instinct, he longed for natural air in his lungs, and turf under his feet. To compensate, he strode faster, shouted louder, got redder of face and bulgier of eye, bristled more fiercely. To quiet an occasional trembling of his hands, he munched sedative pills. He had dreams of falling, with which he bored the ship's Mother Hubbard and the Church of Marx padre by turns.

"Is that it?" he asked now, disapprovingly. He had never seen the gorgon before; Semantics, Medical and Xenology Sections had been keeping him pretty much to themselves.

Dominick prodded the pinkish sphere with his toe. "Wake up, George."

After a moment, the gorgon's skin became lumpy at half a dozen points. The lumps grew slowly into long, segmented stems. Some of these expanded at the tips into "feet" and "hands"; others flowered into the intricate patterns of auricles and photoceptors—and one speech organ, which looked like a small trumpet. "Hello," said George cheerfully.

"He can pull them back in any time?" Kelly asked, rubbing his chin.

"Yes. Show him, George."

"All right." The feathery stalks became blank-tipped, then rapidly shrank, segment by segment. In less than two seconds, George was a smooth sphere again.

"Well, that makes for a little problem here," said Kelly. "You see what I mean? If you can't get a grip on him, how are you going to *punish* him like you say?"

"We've tried everything we could think of," said Dominick. "We locked him up, kept him on short rations, didn't talk to him . . . He doesn't draw any pay, you know, so you can't fine him."

"Or downgrade him on the promotion lists, either," said Womrath gloomily.

"No. And it's a little late to use the Pavlov-Morganstern treatments we all had when we were children. We can't prevent a crime he's already committed. So our thought was, since you're the games instructor—"

"We thought," Womrath said diplomatically, "you might have noticed something that might be useful. You know, rough-housing and so on."

Kelly thought this over. "Well, there's low blows," he said, "but I mean, hell—" He gestured futilely at George, who had just decided to put his auricles out again. "What would you—"

"No, that's out of the question," Dominick said heavily. "Well, I'm sorry, Kelly. It was nice of you to help out."

"No, now, wait a minute," said Kelly. "I got something coming to me, maybe." He nibbled a thumbnail, staring down at the gorgon. "How would this be. I was thinking—sometimes the boys in the pool, they get kind of frisky, they take to ducking each other. Under the water. Now what I was thinking, he breathes air, doesn't he? You know what I mean?"

Dominick and Womrath looked at each other. "It sounds possible," said Dominick.

"Out of the question. We don't know what his tolerance is. Suppose Kelly should damage him severely, or even—"

"Oh," said Dominick. "No, you're right, we couldn't take a chance."

"I've been a games instructor for seventy-three years—two rejuvenations—" Kelly began, bristling.

"No, it isn't that, Kelly," said Womrath hastily. "We're just thinking, George isn't human. So how do we know how he'd react to a ducking?"

"On the other hand," Dominick said, "gorgons *do* turn blue when they're not happy—we have Rubinson's assurance for that. It seems to be George wouldn't be happy when smothering; that would be the whole point, wouldn't it? Dr. Alvarez would supervise closely, of course. Really, Alvarez, I

307

don't see why not. Kelly, if you'll tell what time would be most convenient for you—"

"Well," said Kelly, looking at his thumbwatch. "hell. the pool is empty now—it's ladies' day, but all the girls are down in Section Seven, hanging around Mrs. Carver. I hear she's still hysterical."

Struck by a thought, Alvarez was bending over to speak to the gorgon. "George, you breathe by spiracles, is that correct? Those little tubes all over your skin?"

"Yes," said George.

"Well, do they work under water?"

"No."

Dominick and Kelly were listening with interest.

"If we held you under water, would it hurt you?"

George flickered uncertainly, from rose to pale magenta. "Don't know. Little bit."

The three men leaned closer. "Well, George," said Dominick tensely, "would that be a *punishment?*"

George flickered again, violently. "Yes. No. Maybe. Don't know."

They straightened again, disappointed; Dominick sighed gustily. "He always gives us those mixed-up answers. *I* don't know. Let's try it—what else can we do?"

Kelly found himself paired off with George, following Dominick and Dr. Alvarez, and preceding Womrath and an orderly named Josling who was wheeling one of the dispensary pul-motors. The up-curving corridors were deserted. Kelly lagged a little, adjusting his pace to George's waddling steps. After a moment, he was surprised to feel something small and soft grip his fingers. He looked down; George the the gorgon had put one seven-fingered "hand" into his. The gorgon's flower-like photoceptors were turned trustfully upward.

Kelly was taken by surprise. No children were allowed on the Satellite, but Kelly had been the father of eight in a previous rejuvenation. The confiding touch stirred old memories. "That'll be all right," said Kelly gruffly. "You just come along with me."

The pool, as he had predicted, was empty. Ripples reflected faint threads of light up the walls. "The shallow end would be better," said Kelly. His voice was hollow, and echoed back flatly. Pausing to peel off his coverall, he led George carefully down the steps into the pool. Half submerged, George floated. Kelly drew him gently out into deeper water.

Dominick and the others arranged themselves along the brink in interested attitudes. Kelly cleared his throat. "Well," he said, "the way it generally happens, one of the boys will grab ahold of another one, like this—" He put his hands on the smooth floating globe, and hesitated.

"Go ahead now, Kelly," called Dominick. "Remember, you have a direct order to do this."

"Sure," said Kelly. "Well—" he turned to the gorgon. "Hold your breath now!" He pressed downward. The gorgon seemed lighter than he had expected, like an inflated ball; it was hard to force it under.

Kelly pushed harder. George went under briefly and slipped out of Kelly's hands, bobbing to the surface. The gorgon's speaking trumpet cleared itself of water with a *phonk* and said, "Nice. Do again, Kelly."

Kelly glanced over at Dominick, who said, "Yes. Again." Dr. Alvarez stroked his thin beard and said nothing.

Kelly took a deep sympathetic breath, and shoved the gorgon under. A few bubbles came to the surface; George's speaking trumpet broke water, but made no sound. Down below, Kelly could see his own pale hands gripping the gorgon's body; the water made them look bloodless; but not George; he was a clear, unblemished pink.

There was a discouraged silence when Kelly brought him back up.

"Listen," said Dominick, "I've got another idea. George, can you breathe through that speaking trumpet, too?"

"Yes," said George cheerfully.

There was a chorus of disgusted "Oh, wells." Everybody brightened perceptibly. Josling polished his pul-motor with a rag. "Go ahead, Kelly," said Dominick. "And this time, you hold him under."

George went down for the third time. The bubbles swirled upward. The gorgon's speaking trumpet swayed toward the surface, but Kelly leaned farther over, blocking it with his forearm. After a moment, all of George's appendages began to contract. Kelly craned his neck downward anxiously. Was a hint of blue beginning to show?

"Keep him down," said Alvarez sharply.

George was a blank sphere again. Then one or two of the limbs began to reappear; but they looked different somehow.

"Now?" said Kelly.

"Give him a second more," said Dominick, leaning over precariously. "It seems to me—"

Kelly's back muscles were knotted with tension. He did not like the way George's new limbs seemed to be flattening out, trailing limply—it was as if something had gone wrong in the works.

"I'm bringing him up," he said hoarsely.

To Kelly's horror, when he lifted his hands, George stayed where he was. Kelly made a grab for him, but the gorgon slipped out from under his fingers. The new limbs stiffened and sculled vigorously; George darted away, deep under the water.

Leaning, open-mouthed, Dominick slipped and went into the pool with a majestic splash. He floundered and rose up, a moment later, streaming with water like a sea lion. Kelly, wading anxiously toward him, stopped when he saw that Dominick was safe. Both men looked down. Between them and around them swam George, darting and drifting by turns, as much at home in the pool as a speckled trout.

"Fins!" said Dominick, slack-jawed. "And *gills!*"

It may as well be said that Dr. Walter Alvarez was a misanthrope. He did not like people; he liked diseases. Down there on Planet Seven, once the trade mission was established, he could confidently expect enough new and startling ailments to keep him happy as a lark for years. Up here, all he got was sprained ankles, psychosomatic colds, hives and indigestion. There was one cook's helper named Samuels who kept coming back every Wednesday with the same boil on the back of his neck. It got so that in spite of himself, Alvarez spent the whole week dreading Wednesday. When he saw Samuel's earnest face coming through the door, something seemed to wind itself a little tighter inside him.

Some day, when Samuels opened his mouth to say, "Hey, Doc—" Samuels always called him "Doc"—the something inside him was going to break with a sound like a banjo string. What would happen then, Dr. Alvarez was unable to imagine.

When the gorgon had first been brought up to the Satellite, there had been two or three delightful little fungus infections, then nothing. A great disappointment. Alvarez had isolated and cultured almost a hundred microörganisms found in smears he had taken from George, but they were all nonviable in human tissue. The viable bacteria, viruses, parasites that always turned up on a life-infested planet, were evidently lurking in some organism other than the gorgons. They swam, at night, across the optical field of Dr. Alvarez's dreaming mind—rod-shaped ones, lens-shaped ones, wriggly ones, leggy ones and ones with teeth.

One morning Dr. Alvarez awoke with a desperate resolve. It was a Tuesday. Alvarez went directly to the infirmary, relieved Nurse Trumble, who was on duty, and, opening a locked cabinet, filled a hypodermic from an ampule of clear straw-colored fluid. The trade name of this substance was Bets-off; it was a counter-inhibitant which stunned the censor areas of the forebrain chiefly affected by the Pavlov-Morgenstern treatments. (By an odd coincidence, the patentee was a Dr. Jekyll.) Alvarez injected two c.c.'s of it directly into the median basilic vein and sat down to wait.

After a few minutes his perpetual bad humor began to lift. He felt a pleasant ebullience; the colors of things around him seemed brighter and clearer. "Ha!" said Alvarez. He got up and went to his little refrigerator, where, after some search, he found half a dozen of the cultures he had made of microörganisms taken from gorgon smears. They were quiescent, of course—deep-frozen. Alvarez warmed them cautiously and added nutrients. All morning, while the usual succession of minor complaints paraded through the infirmary, the cultures grew and multiplied. Alvarez was jovial with his patients; he cracked a joke or two, and handed out harmless pills all around.

By noon, four of the cultures were flourishing. Alvarez carefully concentrated them into one, and loaded another hypodermic with the resulting brew. To his liberated intelligence, the matter was clear: No organism, man or pig or gorgon, was altogether immune to the microbes it normally

311

carried in its body. Upset the balance by injecting massive colonies of any one of them, and you were going to have a sick gorgon—*i.e.*, Alvarez thought, a punished gorgon.

The treatment might also kill the patient, but Alvarez light-heartedly dismissed this argument as a quibble. (Or quabble?) Armed with his hypo, he went forth looking for George.

He found him in the small assembly room, together with Dominick, Womrath, and a mechanic named Bob Ritner. They were all standing around a curious instrument, or object of art, built out of bar aluminum. "It's a rack," Ritner explained proudly. "I saw a picture of it once in a kid's book."

The chief feature of the "rack" was a long, narrow table, with a windlass at one end. It looked like a crude device for stretching something.

"We thought the time had come for stern measures," Dominick said, mopping his head.

"In the olden days," Ritner put in, "they used these on the prisoners when they wouldn't talk."

"I talk," said George unexpectedly.

"It's another punishment, George," Dominick explained kindly. "Well, Alvarez, before we go ahead, I suppose you want to examine your patient."

"Yes, just so, ha ha!" said Alvarez. He knelt down and peered keenly at George, who swiveled his photoceptors interestedly around to stare back. The doctor prodded George's hide; it was firm and resilient. The gorgon's color was a clear pink; the intricate folds of his auricles seemed crisp and alert.

Alvarez took a hand scale from his kit: it was preset for A-level gravity. "Climb up here, George." Obediently, the gorgon settled himself on the pan of the scale while Alvarez held it up. "Hm," said Alvarez. "He's lost a good deal of weight."

"He has?" asked Dominick, hopefully.

"But he seems to be in unusually good condition—better than a week ago, I would say. Perhaps just a little sugar solution to pep him up—" Alvarez withdrew the hypo from his kit, aimed it at George's smooth skin and pressed the trigger.

Dominick sighed. "Well, I suppose we might as well go ahead. George, just hop up there and let Ritner tie those straps onto you."

George obediently climbed onto the table. Ritner buckled straps around four of his limbs and then began to tighten the cylinder. "Not too much," said George anxiously.

"I'll be careful," Ritner assured him. He kept on winding the cylinder up. "How does that feel?" George's "arms" and "legs" were half again their usual length, and still stretching.

"Tickles," said George.

Ritner went on turning the handle. Womrath coughed nervously and was shushed. George's limbs kept on getting longer; then his body started to lengthen visibly.

"Are you all right, George?" Dominick asked.

"All right."

Ritner gave the handle a last despairing twist. George's elongated body stretched all the way in comfort from one end of the rack to the other: there was no place else for him to go. "Nice," said George. "Do again." He was glowing a happy pink.

Ritner, who seemed about to cry, petulantly kicked his machine. Alvarez snorted and went away. In the corridor, unseen, he jumped up and clicked his heels together. He was having a wonderful time; his only regret was that it was not tomorrow. Come to think of it, why wait till Wednesday?

Commandant Charles Watson Carver, S.S., had been trained to make quick and courageous decisions. Once you began to entertain a doubt of your own rightness, you would hesitate too much, begin to second-guess yourself, fall prey to superstition and anxiety, and end up without any power of decision at all.

The trouble was, you could never be right all the time. Following the book to the letter, or improvising brilliantly, either way, you were bound to make mistakes. The thing was, to cross them off and go ahead just the same.

Carver firmed his chin and straightened his back, looking down at the sick gorgon. It was sick, all right, there was no question about that: the thing's limbs drooped and weaved slightly, dizzily. Its hide was dry and hot to the touch. "How long has he been like this?" Carver demanded, hesitating only slightly over the "he": aliens were "it" to him and always had been, but it didn't do to let anybody know it.

"Twenty minutes, more or less," said Dr. Nasalroad. "I just

313

got here myself—" he stifled a yawn—"about ten minutes ago."

"What are you doing here, anyway?" Carver asked him. "It's Alvarez's shift.

Naselroad looked embarrassed. "I know. Alvarez is in the hospital, as a patient. I think he assaulted a cook's helper named Samuels—poured soap over his head. He was shouting something about boiling the boil on Samuel's neck. We had to put him under sedation; it took three of us."

Carver set his jaw hard. "Nasalroad, what in thunder is happening on this wheel, anyhow? First this thing attacks my wife—then Alvarez—" He glared down at George. "Can you pull him out of this, whatever it is?"

Nasalroad looked surprised. "That would be a large order. We don't know any gorgon medicine—I was assuming you'd want to beam down and ask *them*."

That was reasonable, of course: the only hitch was, as usual, a matter of interpretation. Was this something they had negligently allowed to happen to an important alien representative, or was it the necessary and proper punishment they had all been looking for? Carver glanced at his thumbwatch: it was just about three hours before the elders' deadline.

He asked Nasalroad, "What color would you say he is now? Not pink, certainly."

"No-o. But not blue, either. I'd call it a kind of violet."

"Hm. Well, anyhow, he's got smaller than he was, isn't that right? *Conspicuously* smaller."

Nasalroad admitted it.

Carver made his decision. "Do the best you can," he said to Nasalroad. He lifted his wristcom, said briskly, "Have you got a line-of-sight to the planethead?"

"Yes, sir," the operator answered.

"All right, get me Rubinson."

A few seconds passed. *"Planethead."*

"Rubinson, this is Carver. Tell the elders we've got a pretty unhappy gorgon here. We're not sure just what did it—might have been any one of a lot of things—but he's lost a good deal of weight, and his color—" Carver hesitated—"it's bluish. Definitely *bluish*. Got that?"

"Yes, chief. Thank goodness! I'll pass the message along right away and call you back."

"Right." Carver closed the wristcom with an assertive snap. The gorgon, when he glanced down at it, looked sicker than ever, but never mind. What happened to the gorgon was its lookout; Carver was doing his duty.

III

Alvarez awoke with a horrible headache and a sense of guilt. He was not in his own cubicle, but in one of the hospital bunks, dressed in a regulation set of hospital pajamas (with removable hood and gloves, capable of being converted into a spacesuit). He could just see the wall clock at the far end of the room. It was twenty-three hours—well into his shift. Alvarez scuttled out of bed, groaning, and looked at the chart beside it. *Mania, delusions. Sedation. Signed, Nasalroad.*

Delusions: yes, he was having one now. He imagined he could remember heaving up a big tureen of mock-turtle soup over Samuel's startled face—splash, a smoking green torrent.

Good heavens! If that was *real*—Samuels! And the gorgon!

Groaning and lurching, Alvarez darted out of the room, past the orderly, Munch, who was sitting with a story viewer on his lap and couldn't get up fast enough. "Dr. Alvarez! Dr. Nasalroad said—"

"Never mind Nasalroad," he snapped, pawing in the refrigerator. He remembered those cultures being right back *there*: but now they were gone.

"—not to let you up until you acted normal again. Uh, how do you feel, Doctor?"

"I feel fine! What difference does that make? How is *he*?"

Munch looked puzzled and apprehensive. "Samuels? Just superficial burns. We put him to bed in his own cubby, because—"

"Not Samuels!" Alvarez hissed, grabbing Munch by the front of his suit. "The gorgon!"

"Oh well, he's been sick, too. How did you know, though, Doctor? You were snoring when it happened. Listen, let go my suit, you're making me nervous."

"Where?" Alvarez demanded, thrusting his scrawny face close to the other's.

"Where what? Oh, you mean the *gorgon?* Up in the little assembly room, the last I—"

Alvarez was gone, out the door and down the corridor like a small, bearded fireball. He found an anxious crowd assembled—Commandant and Mrs. Carver, Dominick and his staff, Urban and two assistants from Semantics, orderlies, porters, and Dr. Nasalroad. Nasalroad had the gaunt and bright-eyed appearance of a man who has been on wake-up pills too long. He started when he saw Alvarez.

"What's up?" Alvarez demanded, grabbing his sleeve. "Where's the gorgon? What—"

"Be quiet," said Nasalroad. "George is over in that corner behind Carver. We're waiting for the delegation from planetside. Rubinson said they were coming up, three of them with some kind of a box . . ."

A loudspeaker said suddenly, "I have the tender locked on. Contact. Contact is made. The lock is opening; get ready, here they come."

Alvarez couldn't see past Carver's bulk; he tried to get away, but Nasalroad stopped him. "I want to *see*," he said irritably.

"Listen," Nasalroad said. "I know what you did. I checked the Bets-off and those cultures against inventory. The gorgon seems to be recovering nicely, no thanks to you. Now has the stuff worn off you, or not? Because if not—"

A rustle went over the group. Alvarez and Nasalroad turned in time to see the door opening. Two large, vigorous-looking gorgons waddled through; they were carrying on enameled metal box between them. "*Foop!*" said the first one, experimentally. "Where is gorgon George?"

"I'm all right," Alvarez muttered. "If I wasn't, I'd have done something uncivilized to you by now, wouldn't I?"

"I guess so," said Nasalroad. They elbowed closer as the group shifted, making a space around the three gorgons. Peering, on tiptoe, Alvarez could see George standing shakily beside the other two. "He looks terrible. Those are big ones, those other two, aren't they?"

"Not as big as George was when we got him," Nasalroad

muttered. "Listen, Walt, if it turns out you've ruined the whole thing, I'll take a dose of Bets-off myself, and——"

"Listen!" snarled Alvarez. One of the gorgons was explaining, "This is panga box. What you call? You know panga?"

"Well, uh, yes and no," said Dominick uncomfortably. "But what about the punishment? We understood——"

"Punishment later. You George, go in box."

Obediently, George waddled over and squatted beside the mouth of the box. He bobbed uncertainly; he looked for all the world like a large woman trying to get into a small sports copter. There was a minor outbreak of nervous laughter, quickly suppressed.

George leaned, retracting most of his upper appendages. His round body began to be compressed into a squarish shape, wedging itself into the box.

The other gorgons watched with an air of tension, photoceptors rigidly extended. A hush fell. Among the humans present there was a general air of Why-are-we-all-whispering?

George wriggled and oozed farther into the box. Momentarily he stuck. He flickered blue, then pink. His "feet," almost retracted, scrabbled feebly at the bottom of the box. Then he was in.

One of the other gorgons solemnly closed the lid on him and fastened it to make sure, then opened it again and helped him out. All three gorgons began to make rhythmic swaying motions with their "arms" and other appendages. George, Alvarez thought, looked smug. He felt a sudden premonitory pang. What had he done?

"What's it all about?" Nasalroad demanded. "Are they measuring him for a coffin, or——"

Dominick, overhearing, turned and said, "I don't think so. Now this is interesting. You remember they said a panga box. What I'm afraid of is, they may have a standard of size. You see what I mean, they're measuring George to see if he falls below the minimum standard of, uh, panga relations."

"Oh, heavens," said another voice. It was Urban or Semantics, who had been neglected of late; they hadn't needed him since George learned English. He was peering over Dominick's shoulder, looking dumbfounded. He said, "But don't you know the word we've been translating 'elders' really means 'smallest ones'? Good heavens——"

"I don't see—" Dominick began, but the Commandant's voice drowned him out. "Quiet! Quiet please!" Carver was trumpeting. He went on, "Our friends from Seven have an announcement to make. Now, then."

To everyone's surprise, it was George who spoke, in the lisping accents of the gorgon language. No human present understood a word of it except Urban, who turned pale under his tan and began stammering inaudibly to himself.

One of the larger gorgons began to speak when George stopped. "Most elder person, known to you by name George, wishes me to thank you all for kindness done him when he was humble youth."

"Youth," muttered Urban. "But it really means 'ungainly one'—or 'fat boy'! Oh, my *heavens!*")

"Now that he has become an elder, it will be his most pleasure to repay all kindness in agreeable legislative manner."

("What does that mean?" Alvarez said aggrievedly. "Why can't he talk for himself, anyway?"

"It would be beneath is dignity now," said Nasalroad. "Hush!")

"—*If*," said the gorgon, "you will succeed in giving elder person, known by name George, proper punishment as aforesaid."

While the others stared with dumb dismay, Carver briskly snapped open his wristcom. "Exactly how long have we got till that gorgon deadline is up?" he demanded.

There was a pause, while ears strained to catch the tiny voice.

"Just under half an hour."

"This meeting will come to order!" said Carver, banging on the table. George and the other two gorgons were sitting opposite him, with the centerpiece of nasturtiums and ferns between them. Grouped around Carver were Dominick, Urban, Womrath, Alvarez, Nasalroad, Kelly and Ritner.

"Now this is the situation," Carver said aggressively. "This gorgon turns out to be a member of their ruling council, I don't understand why, but never mind that now—the point is, he's friendly disposed toward us, so we've succeeded in this

318

mission *if* we can find that proper punishment—otherwise we're in the soup. Suggestions."

(Dominick craned his bald head toward Alvarez across the table. "Doctor, I had a thought," he murmured. "Would you say—is there anything peculiar about the gorgon's body constitution, as compared say to ours?"

"Certainly," said Alvarez, dourly. "Any number of things. You name it, they—")

Giving them a dirty look, Carver nodded to Ritner. "Yes?"

"Well, I was thinking. I know the rack was a washout, but there was another thing they used to use, called the Iron Virgin. It had a door, like, with spikes on it—"

("What I had in mind," Dominick said, "is there anything that would tend to limit their body size—any danger or disadvantage in growing large?"

Alvarez frowned and looked at Nasalroad, who hitched his chair closer. "The pressure—?" said Nasalroad tentatively. They rubbed their chins and looked at each other with professional glints in their eyes.

"What *about* the pressure?" Dominick prompted eagerly.)

"How long would it take you to build a thing like that?" Carver was asking Ritner.

"Well—ten, eleven hours."

"Too long. That's out. Next!"

("They're actually a single cell—all colloidal fluid, at a considerable osmotic pressure. The bigger they get, the more pressure it takes to keep that shape. If they got too big, I rather imagine—"

Alvarez snapped his fingers, awed. "They'd burst!")

Carver turned with an indignant glare. "Gentlemen, if I could get a little cooperation out of you, instead of this continual distraction— All right, Womrath?"

"Sir, I was just wondering, suppose if we let him turn into a fish, the way he did before in the pool—but then we'd net him and take him out of the water fast. That way, maybe—"

"It wouldn't work," said Kelly. "He changed back in about a second, the other time."

Nobody was paying any attention to him. One of the big gorgons, who had been staring fixedly at the flowers in the middle of the table, had suddenly grabbed a handful and was stuffing them into his mouth. George said something shrill in

319

gorgon talk, and snatched the flowers away again. The other gorgon looked abashed, but flushed pink.

George, on the other hand, was distinctly blue.

His "hand," clutching the mangled flowers, hesitated. Slowly, as if with an effort, he put them back in the bowl.

The other two gorgons twined their "arms" around him. After a moment George looked more like his old self, but a hint of blue remained.

"What is it?" said Carver alertly. "Did we do something, finally?" He snapped open his wristcom. "There's still ten minutes before the deadline, so—"

"Did you turn blue because we punished you, George?" Womrath asked.

"No," said George unexpectedly. "Hard for me to be elder." He added a few words in his own language to the other gorgons, and their "arms" twined around him again. "Before, they panga to *me*," added George.

("Then that's why he took the pie away from the Commandant's wife!" said Dominick, smiting himself on the forehead.

"Of course. They—")

"What's that? What's that?" Carver turned, bristling.

"Why this explains that business," said Dominick. "He felt protective toward your wife, you see—that's what 'panga' means. They none of them have much control over their own appetites, so they guard each other. As they grow older, and get more self-control, they're expected to get smaller, not bigger. George felt confused about his panga relationships to us, but in your wife's case, he was positive one more mouthful would make her explode—"

Carver was red to the ears. "Nonsense!" he shouted. "Dominick, you're being insulting, insubordinate and unpatriotic!"

George, looking on interestedly, piped a few words in the gorgon language. One of the other gorgons immediately spoke up: "Elder person says, you with smooth head are a smart man. He says, the other big one who talks too much is wrong."

Carver's jaw worked. He looked at the gorgons, then around the table. No one said anything.

320

Carver set his jaw heroically. "Well, gentlemen," he began, "we certainly tried, but—"

"Wait a minute!" said Alvarez. Somewhere in his narrow skull a great light had dawned. "George, am I panga to you?"

George's auricles weaved tensely. "Yes," he said. "You very small man."

"Good," said Alvarez, dry-washing his bony hands. "And you still have to be punished, for that mistake you made at the banquet?"

George's speaking tube buzzed unhappily. "Yes," he said.

"All right," said Alvarez. Everybody was looking at him, with expressions varying from puzzlement to alarm. Alvarez took a deep breath. "Then here are my orders to you," he said. *"Do as you please!"*

There was a hiss of indrawn breath from Urban. Most of the others looked at Alvarez as if he had grown snakes for hair. "Doctor," said Carver, "have you gone off your—"

The chorus of gasps stopped him. Up on the table, flushing blue and bright pink by turns like a sky sign, George was gobbling up the flowers in the centerpiece. Next he ate the bowl. One of his flailing limbs raked in the scratch pad Urban had been doodling on. He ate that.

Next moment, he was leaping to the floor, making Ritner duck wildly as he passed. Part of Dominick's detachable hood went with him, disappearing with hoarse munching sounds. With a gulp, George swallowed it and began on the carpet. He was eating greedily, frantically. The other two gorgons hovered around him with shrill gorgon cries, but he ate on, oblivious. Now he was bright blue and bulging, but still he ate.

"Stop it!" shouted Alvarez. "George, *stop* that!"

George rocked to a halt. Gradually his blueness faded. The other gorgons were prodding and patting him anxiously. George looked all right, but it was obvious as he stood there that he would never fit into the panga box again.

He was as big as the other two; maybe a little bigger.

"Alvarez," said Carver wildly, "why did you—"

"He was going to burst," said Alvarez, twitching with excitement. "Couldn't you tell? Another mouthful or two—"

Carver recovered himself. He straightened his coverall and thrust out his chin. "At any rate," he said, "he was certainly blue that time. You all saw it—isn't that right?" He looked around triumphantly. "And by heaven, it happened inside the time limit. So, unless I'm very much mistaken—"

One of the two attendant gorgons raised his photoceptors. It was hard to tell which was George, now, except that his color was still a little lavender. The other gorgon spoke two brief sentences in his own language, and then all three of them waddled off together toward the exit.

"What was that? What did he say?" demanded Carver.

Urban cleared his throat; he had turned pale again. "He said you should get the tender ready to take them back home."

"The tender is there," said Carver indignantly, "they can go back any time they want. But what did he say about the punishment?"

Urban cleared his throat again, looking bemused. "They say the punishment is good. More severe than any they ever thought of, in twenty thousand years. They say they won't have to punish Rubinson and the others, now, because you have done all the punishment necessary."

"Well?" said Carver. "Why are you looking that way? What's the hitch? Are they going to refuse to enter the Union, after all this?"

"No." said Urban. "They say we are all panga to them now. They'll do as we say—let us land and build the distribution centers, start them consuming in massive quantity. . . ."

"But that'll destroy them!" someone interjected in a horrified tone.

"Oh, yes," said Urban.

Carver sighed. He had been in the SAPS service most of his life and was proud of his record. He played it as a game; the new, virgin planets were the prizes, and he kept score with the row of tiny iridium buttons on his breast pocket. He said into his wristcom, "Let me know when Rubinson and his crew are on the way up."

There was a long wait. The silence grew oppressive. As length the wall screen lighted up with a view of Planet Seven, glided along one cusp, blue-green and mysterious in the shadow. A silver spark was floating up out of the night side. *Here they come now,*" said the voice.

Carver sighed again. "When they make contact," he said,

"secure the tender and then signal for acceleration stations. We're leaving Seven—tell Mr. Fruman to set a first approximation for out next star to call."

Alvarez, twitching and frowning, clutched at the front of his coverall. "You're letting them go?" he demanded. "Not landing on Seven—after all this work?"

Carver was staring into the view plate. "Some things," he said slowly and unwillingly, "are not meant to be consumed."

Frederik Pohl has been (not necessarily in this order) a pioneer sf fan, an important sf editor, and a leading writer of modern science fiction. His collaborations with C. M. Kornbluth (*The Space Merchants,* 1953; *Gladiator-at-Law,* 1955; among others) are legendary classics, and his most recent novels, *Man Plus* (1976); *Gateway* (1977); and *Jem* (1979) prove that he is still at the top of his form. *Gateway* won both the Hugo and Nebula Awards.

Here he gives us an interesting story that begins with a U.S. Senate committee meeting and then goes off in some very strange directions.

I Plinglot, Who You?

BY FREDERIK POHL

I

"Let me see," I said, "this is a time for the urbane. Say little. Suggest much." So I smiled and nodded wisely, without words, to the fierce flash bulbs.

The committee room was not big enough, they had had to move the hearings. Oh, it was hot. Senator Schnell came leaping down the aisle, sweating, his forehead glistening, his gold tooth shining and took my arm like a trap. "Capital, Mr. Smith," he cried, nodding and grinning, "I am so glad you got here on time! One moment."

He planted his feet and stopped me, turned me about to face the photographers and threw an arm around my shoulder as they flashed many bulbs. "Capital," said the senator with a happy voice. "Thanks, fellows! Come along, Mr. Smith!"

They found me a first-class seat, near a window, where the air-conditioning made such a clatter that I could scarcely hear, but what was there to hear before I myself spoke? Outside the Washington Monument cast aluminum rays from the sun.

"We'll get started in a minute," whispered Mr. Hagsworth in my ear—he was young and working for the committee— "as soon as the networks give us the go-ahead."

He patted my shoulder in a friendly way, with pride; they were always doing something with shoulders. He had brought me to the committee and thus I was, he thought, a sort of possession of his, a gift for Senator Schnell, though we know how wrong he was in that, of course. But he was proud. It was very hot and I had in me many headlines.

Q. (Mr. Hagsworth.) Will you state your name, sir?
A. Robert Smith.
Q. Is that your real name?
A. No.

Oh, that excited them all! They rustled and coughed and whispered, those in the many seats. Senator Schnell flashed his gold tooth. Senator Loveless, who as his enemy and his adjutant, as it were, a second commander of the committee but of opposite party, frowned under stiff silvery hair. But he knew I would say that, he had heard it all in executive session the night before.

Mr. Hagsworth did not waste the moment, he went right ahead over the coughs and the rustles.

Q. Sir, have you adopted the identity of "Robert P. Smith" in order to further your investigations on behalf of this committee.

A. I have.

Q. And can you—

Q. (Senator Loveless.) Excuse me.

Q. (Mr. Hagsworth.) Certainly, Senator.

Q. (Senator Loveless.) Thank you, Mr. Hagsworth. Sir—that is, Mr. Smith—do I understand that it would not be proper, or advisable, for you to reveal—that is, to make public—your true or correct identity at this time? Or in these circumstances?

A. Yes.

Q. (Senator Loveless.) Thank you very much, Mr. Smith. I just wanted to get that point cleared up.

Q. (Mr. Hagsworth.) Then tell us, Mr. Smith—

Q. (Senator Loveless.) It's clear now.

Q. (The Chairman.) Thank you for helping us clarify the matter, Senator. Mr. Hagsworth, you may proceed.

Q. (Mr. Hagsworth.) Thank you, Senator Schnell. Thank you, Senator Loveless. Then, Mr. Smith, will you tell us the nature of the investigations you have just concluded for this committee?

A. Certainly. I was investigating the question of interstellar space travel.

Q. That is, travel between the planets of different stars?

A. That's right.

Q. And have you reached any conclusions as to the possibility of such a thing?

A. Oh, yes. Not just conclusions. I have definite evidence that one foreign power is in direct contact with creatures living on the planet of another star, and expects to receive a visit from them shortly.

Q. Will you tell us the name of that foreign power?

A. Russia.

Oh, it went very well. Pandemonium became wide-spread: much noise, much hammering by Senator Schnell and at the recess all the networks said big Neilsen. And Mr. Hagsworth was so pleased that he hardly asked me about the file again, which I enjoyed as it was a hard answer to give. "Good theater, ah, Mr. Smith," he winked.

I only smiled.

The afternoon also was splendidly hot, especially as Senator Schnell kept coming beside me and the bulbs flashed. It was excellent, excellent.

Q. (Mr. Hagsworth.) Mr. Smith, this morning you told us that a foreign power was in contact with a race of beings living on a planet of the star Aldebaran, is that right?

A. Yes.

Q. Can you describe that race for us? I mean the ones you have referred to as "Aldebaranians?"

A. Certainly, although their own name for themselves is—is a word in their language which you might here render as "Triops." They average about eleven inches tall. They have two legs, like you. They have three eyes and they live in crystal cities under the water, although they are air-breathers.

Q. Why is that, Mr. Smith?

A. The surface of their planet is ravaged by enormous beasts against which they are defenseless.

Q. But they have powerful weapons?

A. Oh, very powerful, Mr. Hagsworth.

And then it was time for me to take it out and show it to them, the Aldebaranian hand-weapon. It was small and soft and I must fire it with a bent pin, but it made a hole through three floors and the cement of the basement, and they were very interested. Oh, yes!

So I talked all that afternoon about the Aldebaranians, though what did they matter? Mr. Hagsworth did not ask me about other races, on which I could have said something of greater interest. Afterwards, we went to my suite at the Mayflower Hotel and Mr. Hagsworth said with admiration: "You handled yourself beautifully, Mr. Smith. When this is over I wonder if you would consider some sort of post here in Washington."

"When this is over?"

"Oh," he said, "I've been around for some years, Mr. Smith. I've seen them come and I've seen them go. Every newspaper in the country is full of Aldebaranians tonight, but next year? They'll be shouting about something new."

"They will not," I said surely.

He shrugged. "As you say," he said agreeably, "at any rate it's a great sensation now. Senator Schnell is tasting the headlines. He's up for re-election next year you know and just between the two of us, he was afraid he might be defeated."

"Impossible, Mr. Hagsworth," I said out of certain knowledge, but could not convey this to him. He thought I was only being polite. It did not matter.

"He'll be gratified to hear that," said Mr. Hagsworth and he stood up and winked: he was a great human for winking. "But think about what I said about a job, Mr. Smith . . . Or would you care to tell me your real name?"

Why not? Sporting! "Plinglot," I said.

He said with a puzzled face, "Plinglot? Plinglot? That's an odd name." I didn't say anything, why should I? "But you're an odd man," he sighed. "I don't mind telling you that there are a lot of questions I'd like to ask. For instance, the file folder of correspondence between you and Senator Heffernan. I don't suppose you'd care to tell me how come no employee of the committee remembers anything about it, although the folder turned up in our files just as you said?"

Senator Heffernan was dead, that was why the correspondence had been with him. But I know tricks for awkward questions, you give only another question instead of answer. "Don't you trust me, Mr. Hagsworth?"

He looked at me queerly and left without speaking. No matter. It was time, I had very much to do. "No calls," I told the switchboard person, "and no visitors, I must rest." Also there would be a guard Hagsworth had promised. I wondered if he would have made the same arrangement if I had not requested it, but that also did not matter.

I sat quickly in what looked, for usual purposes, like a large armchair, purple embroidery on the headreast. It was my spaceship, with cosmetic upholstery. *Zz-z-z-zit*, quick like that, that's all there was to it and I was there.

II

Old days I could not have timed it so well, for the old one slept all the day, and worked, drinking, all the night. But now they kept capitalist hours.

"Good morning, *gospodin*," cried the man in the black tunic, leaping up alertly as I opened the tall double doors. "I trust you slept well."

I had changed quickly into pajamas and a bathrobe. Stretching, yawning, I grumbled in flawless Russian in a sleepy way: "All right, all right. What time is it?"

"Eight in the morning, Gospodin Arakelian. I shall order your breakfast."

"Have we time?"

"There is time, *gospodin*, especially as you have already shaved."

I looked at him with more care, but he had a broad open Russian face, there was no trickery on it or suspicion. I drank some tea and changed into street clothing again, a smaller size as I was now smaller. The Hotel Metropole doorman was holding open the door of the black Zis, and we bumped over cobblestones to the white marble building with no name. Here in Moscow it was also hot, though only early morning.

This morning their expressions were all different in the dim, cool room. Worried. There were three of them:

Blue eyes; Kvetchnikov, the tall one, with eyes so very blue; he looked at the wall and the ceiling, but not at me and, though sometimes he smiled, there was nothing behind it.

Red beard—Muzhnets. He tapped with a pencil softly, on thin sheets of paper.

And the old one. He sat like a squat, fat Buddha. His name was Tadjensevitch.

Yesterday they were reserved and suspicious, but they could not help themselves, they would have to do whatever I asked. There was no choice for them; they reported to the chief himself and how could they let such a thing as I had

329

told them go untaken? No, they must swallow bait. But today there was worry on their faces.

The worry was not about me; they knew me. Or so they thought. "Hello, hello, Arakelian," said Blue Eyes to me, though his gaze examined the rug in front of my chair. "Have you more to tell us today?"

I asked without alarm: "What more could I have?"

"Oh," said Blue-Eyed Kvetchnikov, looking at the old man, "perhaps you can explain what happened in Washington last night."

"In Washington?"

"In Washington, yes. A man appeared before one of the committees of their Senate. He spoke of the *Aldebaratniki*, and he spoke also of the Soviet Union. Arakelian, then, tell us how this is possible."

The old man whispered softly: "Show him the dispatch."

Red Beard jumped. He stopped tapping on the thin paper and handed it to me. "Read!" he ordered in a voice of danger, though I was not afraid. I read. It was a diplomatic telegram, from their embassy in Washington, and what it said was what every newspaper said—it was no diplomatic secret, it was headlines. One Robert P. Smith, a fictitious name, real identity unknown, had appeared before the Schnell Committee. He had told them of Soviet penetration of the stars. Considering limitations, excellent, it was an admirably accurate account.

I creased the paper and handed back to Muzhnets. "I have read it."

Old One: "You have nothing to say?"

"Only this." I leaped up on two legs and pointed at him. "I did not think you would bungle this! How dared you allow this information to become public?"

"How—"

"How did that weapon get out of your country?"

"We ap—"

"Is this Soviet efficiency?" I cried loudly, "is it proletarian discipline?"

Red-Beard Muzhnets intervened. "Softly, comrade," he cried. "Please! We must not lose tempers!"

I made a sound of disgust. I did it very well. "I warned you," I said, low, and made my face sad and stern. "I told you that there was a danger that the bourgeois-capitalists would interfere. Why did you not listen? Why did you permit their spies to steal the weapon I gave you?"

Tadjensevitch whispered agedly: "That weapon is still here."

I cried: "But this report—"

"There must be another weapon, Arakelian. And do you see? That means the Americans are also in contact with the *Aldebaratniki.*"

It was time for chagrin. I admitted: "You are right."

He sighed: "Comrades, the Marshal will be here in a moment. Let us settle this." I composed my face and looked at him. "Arakelian, answer this question straight out. Do you know how this American could have got in touch with the *Aldebaratniki* now?"

"How could I, *gospodin?*"

"That," he said thoughtfully, "is not a straight answer but it is answer enough. How could you? You have not left the Metropole. And in any case the Marshal is now coming, I hear his guard."

We all stood up, very formal, it was a question of socialist discipline.

In came this man, the Marshal, who ruled two hundred million humans, smoking a cigarette in a paper holder, his small pig's eyes looking here and there and at me. Five very large men were with him, but they never said anything at all. He sat down grunting; it was not necessary for him to speak loud or to speak clearly, but it was necessary that those around him should hear anyhow. It was not deafness that caused Tadjensevitch to wear a hearing aid.

The old man jumped up. "Comrade Party Secretary," he said, not now whispering, no, "this man is P.P. Arakelian."

Grunt from the Marshal.

"Yes, Comrade Party Secretary, he has come to us with the suggestion that we sign a treaty with a race of creatures inhabiting a planet of the star Aldebaran. Our astronomers say they cannot dispute any part of his story. And the M.V.D. has assuredly verified his reliability in certain documents signed by the late—(cough)—Comrade Beria." That too had

331

not been easy and would have been less so if Beria had not been dead.

Grunt from the Marshal. Old Tadjensevitch looked expectantly at me.

"I beg your pardon?" I said.

Old Tadjensevitch said without patience: "The Marshal asked about terms."

"Oh," I bowed, "there are no terms. These are unwordly creatures, excellent comrade." I thought to mention it as a joke, but none laughed. "Unworldly, you see. They wish only to be friends—with you, with the Americans . . . they do not know the difference; it is all in whom they first see."

Grunt. "Will they sign a treaty?" Tadjensevitch translated.

"Of course."

Grunt. Translation. "Have they enemies? There is talk in the American document of creatures that destroy them. We must know what enemies our new friends may have."

"Only animals, excellent comrade. Like your wolves of Siberia, but huge, as the great blue whale."

Grunt. Tadjensevitch said: "The Marshal asks if you can guarantee that the creatures will come first to us."

"No. I can only suggest. I cannot guarantee there will be no error."

"But if—"

"If," I cried loudly, "if there is error, you have Red Army to correct it!"

They looked at me, strange. They did not expect that. But they did not understand.

I gave them no time. I said quickly: "Now, excellency, one thing more. I have a present for you."

Grunt. I hastily said: "I saved it, comrade. Excuse me. In my pocket." I reached, most gently, those five men all looked at me now with much care. For the first demonstration I had produced an Aldebaranian hand weapon, three inches long, capable of destroying a bull at five hundred yards, but now for this Russian I had more. "See," I said, and took it out to hand him, a small glittering thing, carved of a single solid diamond, an esthetic statue four inches long. Oh, I did not like to think of it wasted! But it was important that this man should be off guard, so I handed it to one of the tall silent men, who thumbed it over and then passed it on with a scowl to the Marshal. I was sorry, yes. It was a favorite thing, a clever carving that they had made in the water under Aldebaran's rays; it was almost greater than I could have made myself. No, I will not begrudge it them, it was greater; I could not have done so well.

Unfortunate that so great a race should have needed attention; unfortunate that I must now give this memento away; but I needed to make an effect and, yes; I did!

Oh, diamond is great to humans; the Marshal looked surprised, and grunted, and one of the silent, tall five reached in *his* pocket, and took out something that glittered on silken ribbon. He looped it around my neck. "Hero of Soviet Labor," he said, "First Class—With emeralds. For you."

"Thank you, Marshal," I said.

Grunt. "The Marshal," said Tadjensevitch in a thin, thin voice, "thanks you. Certain investigations must be made. He will see you again tomorrow morning."

This was wrong, but I did not wish to make him right. I said again: "Thank you."

A grunt from the Marshal; he stopped and looked at me, and then he spoke loud so that, though he grunted, I understood, "Tell," he said, "the *Aldebaratniki,* tell them they must come to us—if their ship should land in the wrong country . . ."

He stopped at the door and looked at me powerfully.

"I hope," he said, "that it will not," and he left, and they escorted me back in the Zis sedan to the room at the Hotel Metropole.

III

So that was that and *z-z-z-z-zit,* I was gone again, leaving an empty and heavily guarded room in the old hotel.

In Paris it was midday, I had spent a long time in Moscow. In Paris it was also hot and, as the gray-haired small man with the rosette of the Legion in his buttonhole escorted me along the Champs Elysées, slim-legged girls in bright short skirts smiled at us. No matter. I did not care one pin for all those bright slim girls.

But it was necessary to look, the man expected it of me, and he was the man I had chosen. In America I worked through a committee of their Senate, in Russia the Comrade Party Secretary; here my man was a M. Duplessin, a small straw but the one to wreck a dromedary. He was a member of the Chamber of Deputies, elected as a Christian Socialist Radical Democrat, a party, which stood between the Non-Clerical Catholic Workers' Movement on one side and the F.C.M., or Movement for Christian Brotherhood, on the other. His party had three deputies in the Chamber, and the other two hated each other. Thus M. Duplessin held the balance of power in his party, which held the balance of power in the Right Centrist Coalition, which held the balance through the entire Anti-Communist Democratic Front, which supported the Premier. Yes. M. Duplessin was the man I needed.

I had slipped a folder into the locked files of a Senate committee and forged credentials into the records of Russian's M.V.D., but both together were easier than the finding of this right man. But I had him now, and he was taking me to see certain persons who also knew his importance, persons who would do as he told them. "Monsieur," he said gravely, "it lacks a small half-hour of the appointed time. Might one not enjoy an aperitif?"

"One might," I said fluently, and permitted him to find us a table under the trees, for I knew that he was unsure of me; it was necessary to cause him to become sure.

"Ah," said Duplessin, sighing and placed hat, cane and gloves on a filigree metal chair. He ordered drinks and when they came slipped slightly, looking away. "My friend," he said at last, "tell me of *les aldebaragnards*. We French have traditions—liberty, equality, fraternity—we made Arabs into citizens of the Republic—always has France been mankind's spiritual home. But, monsieur. Nevertheless. *Three* eyes?"

"They are really very nice," I told him with great sincerity, though it was probably no longer true.

"Hum."

"And," I said, "they know of love."

"Ah," he said mistily, sighing again. "Love. Tell me, monsieur. Tell me of love on Aldebaran."

"They live on a planet," I misstated somewhat. "Aldebaran

334

is the star itself. But I will tell you what you ask, M. Duplessin. It is thus: When a young Triop, for so they call themselves, comes of age, he swims far out into the wide sea, far from his crystal city out into the pellucid water where giant fan-tailed fish of rainbow colors swim endlessly above, tinting the pale sunlight that filters through the water and their scales. Tiny bright fish give off star-like flashes from patterned luminescent spots on their scales."

"It sounds most beautiful, monsieur," Duplessin said with politeness."

"It is most beautiful. And the young Triop swims until he sees—*Her*."

"Ah, monsieur." He was more than polite, I considered, he was interested.

"They speak not a word," I added, "for the water is all around and they wear masks, otherwise they could not breathe. They cannot speak, no, and one cannot see the other's eyes. They approach in silence and in mystery."

He sighed and sipped his cassis.

"They," I said, "they know, although there is no way that they can know. But they do. They swim about each other searchingly, tenderly, sadly. Yes. Sadly—is beauty not always in some way sad? A moment. And then they are one."

"They do not speak?"

I shook my head.

"Ever?"

"Never until all is over, and they meet elsewhere again."

"Ah, monsieur!" He stared into his small glass of tincture. "Monsieur," he said, "may one hope—that is, is it possible—oh, monsieur! Might one go there, soon?"

I said with all my cunning: "All the things are possible, M. Duplessin, if the Triops can be saved from destruction. Consider for yourself, if you please, that to turn such a people over to the brutes with the Red Star—or these with the forty-nine white stars—what difference?—is to destroy them."

"Never, my friend, never!" he cried strongly. "Let them come! Let them entrust themselves to France! France will protect them, my friend, or France will die!"

It was all very simple after that, I was free within an hour after lunch, and, certainly, *z-z-z-z-zit*.

My spaceship deposited me in this desert, Mojave. I think. Or almost Mojave, in its essential Americanness. Yes. It was in America, for what other place would do? I had accomplished much, but there was yet a cosmetic touch or two before I could say I had accomplished all.

I scanned the scene, everything was well, there was no one. Distantly planes howled, but of no importance: stratosphere jets, what would they know of one man on the sand four miles below? I worked.

Five round trips, carrying what was needed between this desert place and my bigger ship. And where was that? Ah. Safe. It hurled swinging around Mars: yes, quite safe. Astronomers might one day map it, but on that day it would not matter, no. Oh, it would not matter at all.

Since there was time, on my first trip I reassumed my shape and ate, it was greatly restful. Seven useful arms and ample feet, it became easy; quickly I carried one ton of materials, two thousand pounds, from my armchair ferry to the small shelter in which I constructed my cosmetic appliance. Shelter? Why a shelter, you may ask? Oh, I say, for artistic reasons, and in the remote chance that some low-flying plane might blundersomely pass, though it would not. But it might. Let's see, I said, let me think, uranium and steel, strontium and cobalt, a touch of sodium for yellow, have I everything? Yes. I have everything, I said, everything, and I assembled the cosmetic bomb and set the fuse. Good-by, bomb, I said with affection and, z-z-z-z-zit, armchair and Plinglot were back aboard my ship circling Mars. Nearly done, nearly done!

There, quickly I assembled the necessary data for the Aldebaranian rocket, my penultimate—or Next to Closing—task.

Now. This penultimate task, it was not a difficult one, no, but it demanded some concentration. I had a ship. No fake, no crude imitation! It was an authentic rocket ship of the Aldebaranians, designed to travel to their six moons, with vent baffles for underwater takeoff due to certain exigencies (e.g., inimical animals ashore) of their culture. Yes. It was real. I had brought it on purpose all the way.

Now—I say once more—now, I did what I had necessarily to do, which was to make a course for this small ship. There was no crew. (Not anywhere.) The course was easy to compute, I did it rather well; but there was setting of instruments, automation of controls—oh, it took time, took time—but I did it. It was my way, I am workmanlike and reliable, ask Mother. The human race would not know an authentic Aldebaranian rocket from a lenticular Cetan shrimp, but they *might*, hey? The Aldebaranians had kindly developed rockets and it was no great trouble to bring, as well as more authentic. I brought. And having completed all this, and somewhat pleased, I stood to look around.

But I was not alone.

This was not a fortunate thing, it meant trouble.

I at once realized what my companion, however unseen, must be, since it could not be human, nor was it another child. Aldebaranian. It could be nothing else.

I stood absolutely motionless and looked, looked. As you have in almost certain probability never observed the interior of an Aldebaranian rocket, I shall describe: Green metal in cruciform shapes ("chairs"), sparkling mosaics of colored light ("maps"), ferrous alloys in tortured cuprous-glassy conjunction ("instruments"). All motionless. But something moved. I saw! An Aldebaranian! One of the Triops, a foothigh manikin, looking up at me out of three terrified blue eyes; yes, I had brought the ship but I had not brought it empty, one of the creatures had stowed away aboard. And there it was.

I lunged toward it savagely. It looked up at me and squeaked like a bell: "Why? Why, Plinglot, why did you kill my people?"

It is *so* annoying to be held to account for every little thing. But I dissembled.

I said in moderate cunning: "Stand quiet, small creature, and let me get hold of you. Why are you not dead?"

It squeaked pathetically—not in English, to be sure! but I make allowances—it squeaked: "Plinglot, you came to our planet as a friend from outer space, one who wished to help our people join forces to destroy the great killing land beasts."

"That seemed appropriate," I conceded.

"We believed you, Plinglot! All our nations believed you. But you caused dissension. You pitted us one against the

337

other, so that one nation no longer trusted another. We had abandoned war, Plinglot, for more than a hundred years, for we dared not wage war."

"That is true," I agreed.

But you tricked us! War came, Plinglot! And at your hands. As this ship was plucked from its berth with only myself aboard I received radio messages that a great war was breaking out and that the seas were to be boiled. It is the ultimate weapon, Plinglot! By now my planet is dry and dead. Why did you do it?"

"Small Triop," I lectured, "listen to this. You are male, one supposes, and you must know that no female Adlebaranian survives. Very well. You are the last of your race. There is no future. You might as well be dead."

"I know," he wept.

"And therefore you should kill yourself. Check," I invited, "my logic with the aid of your computing machine, if you wish. But please do not disturb the course computations I have set up on it."

"It is not necessary, Plinglot," he said with sadness. "You are right."

"So kill yourself!" I bellowed.

The small creature, how foolish, would not do this, no. He said: "I do not want to, Plinglot," apologetically. "But I will not disturb your course."

Well, it was damned decent of him, in a figure of speech, I believed, for that course was most important to me; on it depended the success of my present mission, which was to demolish Earth as I had his own planet. I attempted to explain, in way of thanks, but he would not understand, no.

"Earth?" he squeaked feebly and I attempted to make him see. Yes, Earth, that planet so far away, it too had a population which was growing large and fierce and smart; it too was hovering on the fringe of space travel. Oh, it was dangerous, but he would not see, though I explained and I am Plinglot. I can allow no rivals in space, it is my assigned task, given in hand by the great Mother. Well. I terrified him, it was all I could do.

Having locked him, helpless, in a compartment of his own ship I consulted my time.

It was fleeing. I flopped onto my armchair; *z-z-z-z-zit*; once again in the room in the Hotel Mayflower, Washington, U.S.A.

Things progressed, all was ready. I opened the door, affecting having just awaked. A chambermaid turned from dusting pictures on the wall, said, "Good morning, sir," looked at me and—oh!—screamed. Screamed in a terrible tone.

Careless Plinglot! I had forgot to return to human form.

Most fortunately, she fainted. I quickly turned human and found a rope. It took very much time, and time was passing, while the rocket hastened to cover forty million miles; it would arrive soon where I had sent it. I hurried. Hardly, hardly, I made myself do it, though as anyone on Tau Ceti knows it was difficult for me; I tied her; I forced a pillowcase, or one corner of it, into her mouth so that she might not cry out; and even I locked her in a closet. Oh, it was hard. Questions? Difficulty? Danger? Yes. They were all there to be considered, too, but I had no time to consider them. Time was passing, I have said, and time passed for me.

It was only a temporary expedient. In time she would be found. Of course. This did not matter. In time there would *be* no time, you see, for time would come to an end for chambermaid, Duplessin, senators and the M.V.D., and then what?

Then Plinglot would have completed this, his mission, and two-eyes would join three-eyes, good-by.

IV

Senator Schnell this time was waiting for me at the curb in a hollow square of newsmen. "Mr. Smith," he cried, "how good to see you. Now, please, fellows! Mr. Smith is a busy man. Oh, all right, just one picture, or two." And he made to shoo the photographers off while wrapping himself securely to my side. "Terrible men," he whispered out of the golden corner of his mouth, smiling, smiling, "how they pester me!"

"I am sorry, Senator," I said politely and permitted him to lead me through the flash barrage to the large room for the hearings.

Q. (Mr. Hagsworth.) Mr. Smith, in yesterday's testimony you gave us to understand that Russia was making overtures to the alien creatures from Aldebaran. Now, I'd like to call your attention to something. Have you seen this morning's papers?

A. No.

Q. Then let me read you an extract from Pierce Truman's column which has just come to my attention. It starts, "After yesterday's sensational rev—"

Q. (Senator Loveless.) Excuse me, Mr. Hagsworth.

Q. (Mr. Hagsworth.) "—elations." Yes, Senator?

Q. (Senator Loveless.) I only want to know, or to ask, if that document—that is, the newspaper which you hold in your hand—is a matter of evidence. By this I mean an exhibit. If so, I raise the question, or rather suggestion, that it should be properly marked and entered.

Q. (Mr. Hagsworth.) Well, Senator, I—

Q. (Senator Loveless.) As an exhibit, I mean.

Q. (Mr. Hagsworth.) Yes, as an exhibit. I—

Q. (Senator Loveless.) Excuse me for interrupting. It seemed an important matter—important procedural matter that is.

Q. (Mr. Hagsworth.) Certainly, Senator. Well, Senator, I intended to read it only in order to have Mr. Smith give us his views.

Q. (Senator Loveless.) Thank you for that explanation, Mr. Hagsworth. Still it seems to me, or at the moment it appears to me, that it ought to be marked and entered.

Q. (The Chairman.) Senator, in my view—

Q. (Senator Loveless.) As an exhibit, that is.

Q. (The Chairman.) Thank you for that clarification, Senator. In my view, however, since as Mr. Hagsworth has said it is only Mr. Smith's views that he is seeking to get out, then the article itself is not evidence but merely an adjunct to questioning. Anyway, frankly, Senator, that's the way I see it. But I don't want to impose my will on the Committee. I hope you understand that, all of you.

Q. (Mr. Hagsworth.) Certainly, sir.

Q. (Senator Loveless.) Oh, none of us has any idea, or suspicion, Senator Schnell, that you have any such design, or purpose.

Q. (Senator Duffy.) Of course not.

Q. (Senator Fly.) No, not here . . .

Oh, time, time! I looked at the clock on the wall and time was going, I did not wish to be here when it started. Of course, Ten o'clock. Ten thirty. Five minutes approaching eleven. Then this Mr. Pierce Truman's column at last was marked and entered and recorded after civil objection and polite concession from Senator Schnell and in thus wise made an immutable, permanent, indestructible part of the file of this mutable, transient, soon to be destroyed committee. Oh, comedy! But it would not be for laughing if I dawdled here too late.

Somehow, somehow, Mr. Hagsworth was entitled at last to read his column and it said as follows. Viz.

After yesterday's sensational revelations before the Schnell Committee, backstage Washington was offering bets that nothing could top the mysterious Mr. Smith's weird story of creatures from outer space. But the toppers may already be on hand. Here are two questions for you, Senator Schnell. What were three Soviet U.N. military attaches doing at a special showing at the Hayden Planetarium last night? And what's the truth beyond the reports that are filtering into C.I.A. from sources in Bulgaria, concerning a special parade scheduled for Moscow's Red Square tomorrow to welcome "unusual and very special" V.I.P.'s, names unknown?

Exhausted from this effort, the committee declared a twenty-minute recess. I glowered at the clock, time, time!

Mr. Hagsworth had plenty of time, he thought, he was not worried. He cornered me in the cloakroom. "Smoke?" he said graciously, offering a package of cigarettes.

I said thank you, I do not smoke.

"Care for a drink?"

I do not drink, I told him.

341

"Or—?" he nodded toward the tiled room with the chromium pipes; I do not do that either, but I could not tell him so, only, I shook my head.

"Well, Mr. Smith," he said again, "you make a good witness. I'm sorry," he added, "to spring that column on you like that. But I couldn't help it."

"No matter," I said.

"You're a good sport, Smith. You see, one of the reporters handed it to me as we walked into the hearing room."

"All right," I said, wishing to be thought generous.

"Well, I had to get it into the record. What's it about, eh?"

I said painfully (time, time!), "Mr. Hagsworth, I have testified the Russians also wish the ship from Aldebaran. And it is coming close. Soon it will land."

"Good," he said, smiling and rubbing his hands, "very good! And you will bring them to us?"

"I will do," I said, "the best I can," ambiguously, but that was enough to satisfy him, and recess was over.

Q. (Mr. Hagsworth.) Mr. Smith, do I understand that you have some knowledge of the proposed movements of the voyagers from Aldebaran?

A. Yes.

Q. Can you tell us what you know?

A. I can. Certainly. Even now an Aldebaranian rocket ship is approaching the Earth. Through certain media of communication which I cannot discuss in open hearing, as you understand, certain proposals have been made to them on behalf of this country.

Q. And their reaction to these proposals, Mr. Smith?

A. They have agreed to land in the United States for discussions.

Oh, happy commotion, the idiots. The flash bulbs went like mad. Only the clock was going, going, and I commenced to worry, where was the ship? Was forty lousy million miles so much? But no, it was not so much; and when the messenger came racing in the door I knew it was time. One messenger, first. He ran wildly down among the seats, searching, then stopping at the seat on the aisle where Pierce Truman sat regarding me with an ophidian eye, stopped and whispered.

Then a couple more, strangers, hatless and hair flying, also messengers, came hurrying in—and more—to the committee, to the newsmen—the word had got out.

"Mr. Chairman! Mr. Chairman!" It was Senator Loveless, he was shouting; some one person had whispered in his ear and he could not wait to tell his news. But everyone had the news, you see, it was no news to the chairman, he already had a slip of paper in his hand.

He stood up and stared blindly into the television cameras, without smile now, the gold tooth not flashing. He said: "Gentlemen, I—" And stopped for a moment to catch his breath and to shake his head. "Gentlemen," he said, "Gentlemen, I have here a report," staring incredulously at the scrawled slip of paper. In the room was quickly silence; even Senator Loveless, and Pierce Truman stopped at the door on his way out to listen. "This report," he said, "comes from the Arlington Naval Observatory—in, gentlemen, my own home state, the Old Dominion, Virginia—" He paused and shook himself, yes, and made himself look again at the paper. "From the Arlington Naval Observatory, where the radio telescope experts inform us that an object of unidentified origin and remarkable speed has entered the atmosphere of the Earth from outer space!"

Cries. Sighs. Shouts. But he stopped them, yes, with a hand. "But gentlemen, that is not all! Arlington has tracked this object and it has landed. Not in our country, gentlemen! Not even in Russia! But—" he shook the paper before him —"in Africa, gentlemen! In the desert of Algeria!"

Oh, much commotion then, but not joyous. "Double-cross!" shouted someone, and I made an expression of astonishment. Adjourned, banged the gavel of the chairman, and only just in time; the clock said nearly twelve and my cosmetic bomb was set for one-fifteen. Oh, I had timed it close. But now was danger and I had to leave, which I did hardly. But I could not evade Mr. Hagsworth, who rode with me in taxi to hotel, chattering, chattering. I did not listen.

V

Now, this is how it was, an allegory or parable. Make a chemical preparation, you see? Take hydrogen and take oxygen—very pure in both cases—blend them and strike a spark. Nothing happens. They do not burn! It is true, though you may not believe me.

But with something added, yes, they burn. For instance let the spark be a common match, with, so tiny you can hardly detect it, a quarter-droplet of water bonded into its substance—Yes, with the water they will burn—more than burn—*kerblam*, the hydrogen and oxygen fiercely unite. Water, it is the catalyst which makes it go.

Similarly, I reflected (unhearing the chatter of Mr. Hagsworth), it is a catalyst which is needed on Earth, and this catalyst I have made, my cosmetic appliance, my bomb. The chemicals were stewing together nicely. There was a ferment of suspicion in Russia, of fear in America, of jealousy in France where I had made the ship land. Oh, they were jumpy now! I could feel forces building around me; even the driver of the cab, half-watching the crowded streets, half listening to the hysterical cries of his little radio. To the Mayflower, hurrying. All the while the city was getting excited around us. That was the ferment, and by my watch the catalyst was quite near.

"Wait," said Mr. Hagsworth pleading, in the lobby, "come have a drink, Smith."

"I don't drink."

"I forgot," he apologized. "Well, would you like to sit for a moment in the bar with me? I'd like to talk to you. This is all happening too fast."

"Come along to my room," I said, not wanting him, no, but what harm could he do? And I did not want to be away from my purple armchair, not at all.

So up we go and there is still time, I am glad. Enough time. The elevator could have stuck, my door could have somehow been locked against me, by error I could have gone

344

to the wrong floor—no, everything was right. We were there
and there was time.

I excused myself a moment (though it could have been
forever) and walked into the inner room of this suite. Yes, it
was there, ready. It squatted purple, and no human would
think to look at it that it was anything but an armchair, but it
was much more and if I wished I could go to it,—*z-z-z-z-zit*,
I would be gone.

A man spoke.

I turned, looking. Out of the door to the tiled room spoke
to me a man, smiling, red-faced, in blue coveralls. Well. For
a moment I felt alarm. (I remembered, e.g., what I had left
bound in the closet.) But on this man's face was only smile
and he said with apology; "Oh, hello, sir. Sorry. But we had a
complaint from the floor below, plumbing leak. I've got it
nearly fixed."

Oh, all right. I shrugged for him and went back to Mr.
Hagsworth. In my mind had been—well, I do not know what
had been in my mind. Maybe *z-z-z-z-zit* to the George V and
telephone Duplessin to make sure they would not allow Russians or Americans near the ship, no, not if the ambassadors
made of his life a living hell. Maybe to Metropole to phone
Tadjensevitch (not the Marshal, he would not speak on telephone to me) to urge him also on. Maybe farther, yes.

But I went back to Mr. Hagsworth. It was not needed,
really it was not. It was only insurance, in the event that
somehow my careful plans went wrong, I wished to be there
until the very end. Or nearly. But I need not have done it.

But I did. *Z-z-z-z-zit* and I could have been away, but I
stayed, very foolish, but I did.

Mr. Hagsworth was on telephone, his eyes bright and angry, I thought I knew what he was hearing. I listened to hear
if there were, perhaps, muffled kickings, maybe groans, from
a closet, but there were none; hard as it was, I had tied well,
surely. And then Mr. Hagsworth looked up.

He said, bleak: "I have news, Smith. It's started."

"Started?"

"Oh," he said without patience, "you know what I'm talking about, Smith. The trouble's started. These Aldebaranians

345

of yours, they've stirred up a hornet's nest, and now the stinging has begun. I just talked to the White House. There's a definite report of a nuclear explosion in the Mojave desert."

"No!"

"Yes," he said, nodding, "there is no doubt. It can't be anything but a Russian missile, though their aim is amazingly bad. Can it?"

"What else possibly?" I asked with logic. "How terrible! And I suppose you have retaliated, hey? Sent a flight of missiles to Moscow?"

"Of course. What else could we do?"

He had put his finger on it, yes, he was right, I had computed it myself. "Nothing," I said and wrung his hand, "and may the best country win."

"Or planet," he said, nodding.

"Planet?" I let go his hand. I looked. I waited. It was a time for astonishment, I did not speak.

Mr. Hagsworth said, speaking very slow, "Smith, or maybe I ought to say 'Plinglot,' that's what I wanted to talk to you about."

"Talk," I invited.

Outside there was sudden shouting. "They've heard about the bomb," conjectured Mr. Hagsworth, but he paid no more attention. He said: "In school, Plinglot, I knew a Fat Boy." He said: "He always got his way. Everybody was afraid of him. But he never fought, he only divided others, do you see, and got them to fight each other."

I stood tall—yes, and brave! I dare use that word "brave," it applies. One would think that it would be like a human to say he is brave before a blinded fluttering moth, 'brave' where there is no danger to be brave against; but though this was a human only, in that room I felt danger. Incredible, but it was so and I did not wish it.

I said, "What are you talking about, Mr. Hagsworth?"

"An idea I had," he said softly with a face like death. "About a murderer. Maybe he comes from another planet and, for reasons of his own, wants to destroy our planet. Maybe this isn't the first one—he might have stopped, for example, at Aldebaran."

"I do not want to hear this," I said, with truth.

But he did not stop, he said: "We humans beings have

faults, Plinglot, and an outsider with brains and a lot of special knowledge—say, the kind of knowledge that could get a file folder into our records, in spite of all our security precautions—such an outsider might use our faults to destroy us. Senate Committee hearings—why, some of them have been a joke for years, and not a very funny one. Characters have been destroyed, policies have been wrecked—why shouldn't a war be started? Because politicians can be relied on to act in a certain way. And maybe this outsider, having watched and studied us, knew something about Russian weaknesses too, and played on them in the same way. Do you see how easy it would be?"

"Easy?" I cried, offended.

"For someone with very special talents and ability," he assured me. "For a Fat Boy. Especially for a Fat Boy who can go faster than any human can follow from here to Moscow, Moscow to Paris, Paris to the Mojave, Mojave to—where? Somewhere near Mars, let's say at a guess. For such a person, wouldn't it, Plinglot, be easy?"

I reeled, I reeled; but these monkey tricks, they could not matter. I had planned too carefully for that, only how did they know?

"Excuse me," I said softly, "one moment," and turned again to the room with the armchair, I felt I had made a mistake. But what mistake could matter, I thought, when there was the armchair and, of course, *z-z-z-z-zit.*

But that was a mistake also.

The man in blue coveralls, he stood in the door but not smiling, he held in his hand what I knew instantly was a gun.

The armchair was there, yes, but in it was of all strange unaccountable people this chambermaid, who should have been bounded in closet, and she too had a gun.

"Miss Gonzalez," introduced Hagsworth politely, "and Mr. Hechtmeyer. They are—well, G-men, though, as you can see, Miss Gonzalez is not a man. But she had something remarkable to tell us about you, Plinglot, when Mr. Hechtmeyer released her. She said that you seemed to have another shape when she saw you last. The shape of a sort of green-skinned octapus with bright red eyes; ridiculous, isn't it? Or is it, Plinglot?

347

Ruses were past, it was a time for candid. I said—I said, *"Like this?"* terribly, and I went to natural form.

Oh, what white faces! Oh, what horror! It was remarkable, really, that they did not turn and run. For that is Secret Weapon No. 1, for us of Tau Ceti on sanitation work; for our working clothes we assume the shape of those about us, certainly, but in case of danger we have merely to resume our own. In all Galaxy (I do not know about Andromeda) there is no shape so fierce. Nine terrible arms. Fourteen piercing scarlet eyes. Teeth like Hessian bayonets; I ask you, would *you* not run?

But they did not. Outside a siren began to scream.

VI

I cried: "Air attack!" It was fearful, the siren warned of atomic warheads on their way and this human woman, this Gonzalez, sat in my chair with pointing gun. "Go away," I cried, "get out," and rushed upon her, but she did not move. *"Please!"* I said thickly among my long teeth, but what was the use, she would not do it!

They paled, they trembled, but they stayed; well, I would have paled and trembled myself if it had been a Tau Cetan trait, instead I merely went limp. Terror was not only on one side in that room, I confess it. "Please," I begged, "I must go, it is the end of life on this planet and I do not wish to be here!"

"You don't have a choice," said Mr. Hagsworth, his face like steel. "Gentlemen!" he called, "come in!" And through the door came several persons, some soldiers and some who were not. I looked with all my eyes; I could not have been more astonished. For there was—yes, Senator Schnell, gold tooth covered, face without smile; Senator Loveless, white hair waving; and—oh, there was more.

I could scarcely believe.

Feeble, slow humans! They had mere atmosphere craft mostly but here, eight thousand miles from where he had been eighteen hours before, yes, Comrade Tadjensevitch, the old man; and M. Duplessin, sadly meeting my eyes. It could not be, almost I forgot the screaming siren and the fear.

"These gentlemen," said Hagsworth with polite, "also would like to talk to you, Mr. Smith."

"Arakelian," grunted the old man.

"Monsieur Laplant," corrected Duplessin.

"Or," said Hagsworth, "should we all call you by your right name, Plinglot?"

Outside the siren screamed, I could not move.

Senator Schnell came to speak: "Mr. Smith," he said, "or, I should say, Plinglot, we would like an explanation. Or account."

"Please let me go!" I cried.

"Where?" demanded old Tadjensevitch. "To Mars, Hero of Soviet Labor? Or farther this time?"

"The bombs," I cried. "Let me go! What about Hero of Soviet Labor?"

The old man sighed: "The decoration Comrade Party Secretary gave you, it contains a microwave transmitter, very good. One of our *sputniki* now needs new parts."

"You *suspected* me?" I cried out of fear and astonishment.

"Of course the Russians suspected you, Plinglot," Hagsworth scolded mildly. "We all did, even we Americans—and we are not, you know, a suspicious race. "No," he added thoughtfully, as though there were no bombs to fall, "our national characteristics are . . . what? The conventional caricatures—the publicity hound, the pork-barrel senator, the cut-throat businessman? Would you say was a fair picture, Mr. Smith?"

"I Plinglot!"

"Yes, of course. Sorry. But that must be what you thought, because those are the stereotypes you acted on, and maybe they're true enough—most of the time. Too much of the time. But not *all* the time, Plinglot!"

I fell to the floor, perspiring a terrible smell, it is how we faint, so to speak. It was death, it was the end, and this man was bullying me without fear.

"The Fat Boy," said Mr. Hagsworth softly, "was strong. He could have whipped most of us. But in my last term he got licked. Guile and bluff—when at last the bluff was called he gave up. He was a coward."

"I give up, Mr. Hagsworth," I wailed, "only let me go away from the bombs!"

"I know you do," he nodded, "what else? And—what, the bombs? There are no bombs. Look out the window."

In seconds I pulled myself together, no one spoke. I went to window. Cruising up and down outside a white truck, red cross, painted with word *Ambulance*, siren going. Only that. No air raid warning. Only ambulance.

"Did you think?" scolded Hagsworth with voice angry now, "that we would let *you* bluff *us?* There's an old maxim—'Give him enough rope'—we gave it to you; and we added a little. You see, we didn't *know* you came from a race of cowards."

"I Plinglot!" I sobbed through all my teeth. "I am not a coward. I even tied this human woman here, ask her! It was brave, even Mother could not have done more! Why, I sector warden of this whole quadrant of the very Galaxy, indeed, to keep the peace!"

"That much we know—and we know why," nodded Mr. Hagsworth, "because you're afraid; but we needed to know more. Well, now we do; and once M. Duplessin's associates get a better means of communication with the little Aldebaranians, I expect we'll know still more. It will be very helpful knowledge," he added in thought.

It was all, it was the end. I said sadly: "If only Great Mother could know Plinglot did his best! If only she could learn what strange people live here, who I cannot understand."

"Oh," said Mr. Hagsworth, gentle, "we'll tell her for you, Plinglot," he said, "very soon, I think."

Before allowing himself to be dragged off to the confines of academia (he is Professor Philip Klass of Penn State University's Department of English) **"William Tenn"** was one of the great mainstays of H. L. Gold's *Galaxy Science Fiction,* the premier sf magazine of the 1950s. His many stories from that period were always rich in social commentary and satire, and always entertaining. Perhaps his most famous story is "The Liberation of Earth" (1953), one of the great commentaries on the Vietnam War (before there was one). "Will You Walk a Little Faster?" is a 1951 story about a subject that just won't go away: flying saucers and little men. Say, that's a good idea for a movie . . .

Will You Walk a Little Faster?

BY WILLIAM TENN

All right. So maybe I should be ashamed of myself. But I'm a writer and this is too good a story to let go. My imagination is tired, and I'm completely out of usuable plots; I'm down to the gristle of truth. I'll use it.

Besides, someone's bound to blab sooner or later—as Forkbeard pointed out, we're that kind of animal—and I might as well get some private good out of the deal.

Why, for all I know, there is a cow on the White House lawn this very moment. . . .

Last August, to be exact, I was perspiring over an ice-cold yarn that I never should have started in the first place, when the door bell rang.

I looked up and yelled, "Come in! Door's open!"

The hinges squeaked a little the way they do in my place. I heard feet slap-slapping up the long corridor which makes the rent on my apartment a little lower than most of the others in the building. I couldn't recognize the walk as belonging to anyone I knew, so I waited with my fingers on the typewriter keys and my face turned to the study entrance.

After a while, the feet came around the corner. A little man, not much more than two feet high, dressed in a green knee-length tunic, walked in. He had a very large head, a short pointed red beard, a long pointed green cap, and he was talking to himself. In his right hand, he carried a golden pencil-like object; in his left, a curling strip of what seemed to be parchment.

"Now, you," he said with a guttural accent, pointing both the beard and the pencil-like object at me, "now you must be a writer."

I closed my mouth carefully around a lump of air. Somehow, I noted with interest, I seemed to be nodding.

"Good." He flourished the pencil and made a mark at the end of a line halfway down the scroll. "That completes the enrollment for this session. Come with me, please."

He seized the arm with which I had begun an elaborate gesture. Holding me in a grip that had all the resiliency of a steel manacle, he smiled benevolently and walked back down my entrance hall. Every few steps he walked straight up in the air, and then—as if he'd noticed his error—calmly strode down to the floor again.

"What—who—" I said, stumbling and tripping and occasionally getting walloped by the wall, "you wait, you—who—*who*—"

"Please do not make such repetitious noises," he admonished me. "You are supposed to be a creature of civilization.

Ask intelligent questions if you wish, but only when you have them properly organized."

I brooded on that while he closed the door of my apartment behind him and began dragging me up the stairs. His heart may or may not have been pure, but I estimated his strength as being roughly equivalent to that of ten. I felt like a flag being flapped from the end of my own arm.

"We're going up?" I commented tentatively as I swung around a landing.

"Naturally. To the roof. Where we're parked."

"Parked, you said?" I thought of a helicopter, then of a broomstick. Who was it that rode around on the back of an eagle?

Mrs. Flugelman, who lived on the floor above, had come out of her apartment with a canful of garbage. She opened the door of the dumbwaiter and started to nod good-morning at me. She stopped when she saw my friend.

"Yes, parked. What you call our flying saucer." He noticed Mrs. Flugelman staring at him and jutted his beard at her as we went by. "Yes, I said flying saucer!" he spat.

Mrs. Flugelman walked back into her apartment with the canful of garbage and closed the door behind her very quietly.

Maybe the stuff I write for a living prepared me for such experiences, but—somehow—as soon as he told me that, I felt better. Little men and flying saucers, they seemed to go together. Just so halos and pitchforks didn't wander into the continuity.

When we reached the roof, I wished I'd had time to grab a jacket. It was evidently going to be a breezy ride.

The saucer was about thirty feet in diameter and, colorful magazine articles to the contrary, had been used for more than mere sightseeing. In the center, where it was deepest, there was a huge pile of boxes and packages lashed down with criss-crossing masses of gleaming thread. Here and there, in the pile, was the unpackaged metal of completely unfamiliar machinery.

Still using my arm as a kind of convenient handle to the rest of me, the little man whirled me about experimentally once or twice, then scaled me accurately end over end some twenty feet through the air to the top of the pile. A moment

353

before I hit, golden threads boiled about me, cushioning like a elastic net, and tying me up more thoroughly than any three shipping clerks. My shot-putting pal grunted enthusiastically and prepared to climb aboard.

Suddenly he stopped and looked back along the roof. "Irngl!" he yelled in a voice like two ocean liners arguing. "Irngl! Bordge modgunk!"

There was a tattoo of feet on the roof so rapid as to be almost one sound, and a ten-inch replica of my strong-arm guide—minus the beard, however—leaped over the railing and into the craft. Young Irngl, I decided, bordge modgunking.

His father (?) stared at him very suspiciously, then walked back slowly in the direction from which he had run. He halted and shook a ferocious finger at the youngster. Beside me, Irngl cowered.

Just behind the chimney were a cluster of television antennae. But the dipoles of these antennae were no longer parallel. Some had been carefully braided together; others had been tied into delicate and perfect bows. Growling ferociously, shaking his head so that the pointed red beard made like a metronome, the old man untied the knots and smoothed the dipoles out to careful straightness with his fingers. Then, he bent his legs slightly at their knobby knees and performed one of the more spectacular standing broad jumps of all time.

And, as he hit the floor of the giant saucer, we took off. Straight up.

When I'd recovered sufficiently to regurgitate my larynx, I noticed that old redbeard was controlling the movement of the disc beneath us by means of an egg-shaped piece of metal in his right hand. After we'd gone up a goodly distance, he pointed the egg south and we headed that way.

Radiant power, I wondered? No information—not much that was useful—had been volunteered. *Of course*, I realized suddenly: I hadn't asked any questions! Grabbed from my typewriter in the middle of the morning by a midget of great brain and greater muscle—I couldn't be blamed, though: few men in my position would have been able to put their finger on the nub of the problem and make appropriate inquiries. *Now*, however—

354

"While there's a lull in the action," I began breezily enough, "and as long as you speak English, I'd like to clear up a few troublesome matters. For example—"

"Your questions will be answered later. Meanwhile, you will shut up." Golden threads filled my mouth with the taste of antiseptics, and I found myself unable to part my jaws. Redbeard stared at me as I grunted impotently. "How hateful are humans!" he said, beaming. "And how fortunate that they are hateful!"

The rest of the trip was uneventful, except for a few moments when the Miami-bound plane came abreast of us. People inside pointed excitedly, seemed to yell, and one extremely fat man held up an expensive camera and took six pictures very rapidly. Unfortunately, I noticed, he had neglected to remove the lens cap.

The saucer skipper shook his metal egg, there was a momentary feeling of acceleration—and the airplane was a disappearing dot behind us. Irngl climbed to the top of what looked like a giant malted milk machine and stuck his tongue out at me. I glared back.

It struck me then that the little one's mischievous quality was mighty reminiscent of an elf. And his pop—the parentage seemed unmistakable by then—was like nothing else than a gnome of Germanic folklore. Therefore, didn't these facts mean that—that—that—I let my brain have ten full minutes, before giving up. Oh, well, sometimes that method works. Reasoning by self-hypnotic momentum, I call it.

I was cold, but otherwise quite content with my situation and looking forward to the next development with interest and even pride. I had been selected, alone of my species, by this race of aliens for some significant purpose. I couldn't help hoping, of course, that purpose was not vivisection.

It wasn't.

We arrived, after a while, at something so huge that it could only be called a flying dinner plate. I suspected that a good distance down, under all those belly-soft clouds, was the State of South Carolina. I also suspected that the clouds were artificial. Our entire outfit entered through a hole in the bottom. The flying dinner plate was covered with another immense plate, upside-down, the whole making a hollow disc close to a quarter of a mile in diameter. Flying saucers stacked with goods and people—both long and short folk— were scattered up and down its expanse between great masses of glittering machinery.

Evidently I was wrong about having been selected as a representative sample. There were lots of us, men and women, all over the place—one to a flying saucer. It was to be a formal meeting between the representatives of two great races, I decided. Only why didn't our friends do it right— down at the U.N.? Possibly not so formal after all. Then I remembered Redbeard's comment on humanity and I began worrying.

On my right, an army colonel, with a face like a keg of butter, was chewing on the pencil with which he had been taking notes. On my left, a tall man in a gray sharkskin suit flipped back his sleeve, looked at his watch and expelled his breath noisily, impatiently. Up ahead, two women were leaning toward each other at the touching edges of their respective saucers, both talking at the same time and both nodding vehemently as they talked.

Each of the flying saucers also had at least one equivalent of my redbearded pilot. I observed that while the females of this people had beards too, they were exactly one-half as motherly as our women. But they balanced, they balanced. . . .

Abruptly, the image of a little man appeared on the ceiling. His beard was pink and it forked. He pulled on each fork and smiled down at us.

"To correct the impression in the minds of many of you," he said, chuckling benignly, "I will paraphrase your great poet, Shakespeare. I am here to bury humanity, not to praise it."

A startled murmur broke out all around me. "*Mars*," I heard the colonel say, "bet they're from Mars. H. G. Wells predicted it. Dirty little, red little Martians. Well, just let them try!"

"Red," the man in the gray sharkskin suit repeated, "*red?*"

"Did you ever—" one of the women started to ask. "Is that a way to begin? No manners! A real foreigner."

"However," Forkbeard continued imperturbably from the ceiling, "in order to bury humanity properly, I need your help. Not only yours, but the help of others like you, who, at this moment, are listening to this talk in ships similar to this one and in dozens of languages all over the world. We need your help—and, knowing your peculiar talents so well, we are fairly certain of getting it!"

He waited until the next flurry of fist-waving and assorted imprecations had died down; he waited until the anti-Negroes and the anti-Jews, the anti-Catholics and the anti-Protestants, the Anglophobes and the Russophobes, the vegetarians and the fundamentalists, in the audience had all identified him colorfully with their peculiar concepts of the Opposition and had excoriated him soundly.

Then, once relative quiet had been achieved, we got the following blunt tale, rather contemptuously told, with mighty few explanatory flourishes:

There was an enormous and complex galactic civilization surrounding our meager nine-planet system. This civilization, composed of the various intelligent species throughout the galaxy, was organized into a peaceful federation for trade and mutual advancement.

A special bureau in the federation discharged the biological duty of more advanced races to new arrivals on the cerebral scene. Thus, quite a few millennia ago, the bureau had visited Earth to investigate tourist accounts of a remarkably ingenious animal that had lately been noticed wandering about. The animal having been certified as intelligent with a high cultural potential, Earth was closed to tourist traffic and sociological specialists began the customary close examination.

"And, as a result of this examination," the forked pink beard smiled gently down from above, "the specialists discovered that what you call the human race was nonviable. That is, while the individuals composing it had strongly developed instincts of self-preservation, the species as a whole was suicidal."

"*Suicidal!*" I found myself breathing up with rest.

"Quite. This is a matter on which there can be little argument from the more honest among you. High civilization is a product of communal living and Man, in groups, has always tended to wipe himself out. In fact, a large factor in the development of what little civilization you do experience has been the rewards contingent upon the development of mass-destruction weapons."

"We have had peaceful, brotherly periods," a hoarse voice said on the opposite side of the ship.

The large head shook slowly from side to side. The eyes, I saw suddenly and irrelevantly, were all black iris. "You have not. You *have* occasionally developed an island of culture here, and oasis of cooperation there; but these have inevitably disintegrated upon contact with the true standard-bearers of your species—the warrior-races. And when, as happened occasionally, the warrior-races were defeated, the conquerors in their turn became warriors, so that the suicidal strain was ever rewarded and became more dominant. Your past is your complete indictment, and your present—your present is about to become your executed sentence. But enough of this peculiar bloody nonsenese—let me return to *living* history."

He went on to explain that the Federation felt a suicidal species should be allowed to fulfill its destiny unhampered. In fact, so long as overt acts were avoided, it was quite permissible to help such a creature along to the doom it desired—"Nature abhors self-destruction even more than a vacuum. The logic is simple: both cease almost as soon as they come into existence."

The sociologists having extrapolated the probable date on which humanity might be expected to extinguish itself, the planet was assigned—as soon as it should be vacated—to the inhabitants of an Earth-like world for the use of such surplus population as they might then have. These were the redbeards.

"We sent representatives here to serve as caretakers, so to speak, of our future property. But about nine hundred years ago, when your world still had six thousand years to run, we decided to hurry the process a bit as we experienced a rising index of population on our own planet. We therefore received full permission from the Galactic Federation to stimulate your technological development into an earlier suicide. The Federation stipulated, however, that each advance be made the moral responsibility of an adequate representative of your race, that he be told the complete truth of the situation. This we did: we would select an individual to be the discoverer of a revolutionary technique or scientific principle;

then we would explain both the value of the technique and the consequences to his species in terms of accelerated mass destruction."

I found it hard to continue looking into his enormous eyes. "In every case"—the booming rattle of the voice had softened perceptibly—"in every case, sooner or later, the individual announced the discovery as his own, giving it to his fellows and profiting substantially. In a few cases, he later endowed great foundations which awarded prizes to those who advanced the cause of peace or the brotherhood of man. This resulted in little beyond an increase in the amount of currency being circulated. Individuals, we found, always chose to profit at the expense of their race's life-expectancy."

Gnomes, elves, kobolds! Not mischievous sprites—I glanced at Irngl sitting quietly under his father's heavy hand—not the hoarders of gold, but helping man for their own reasons: teaching him to smelt metals and build machinery, showing him how to derive the binomial theorem in one part of the world and how to plow a field more efficiently in another.

To the end that people might perish from the Earth . . . sooner.

"Unfortunately—ah, something has developed."

We looked up at that, all of us—housewives and handymen, preachers and professional entertainers—looked up from the angle of our reflections and prejudices, and *hoped*.

As D-day drew nigh, those among the kobolds who intended to emigrate filled their flying saucers with possessions and families. They scooted across space in large crafts such as the one we were now in and took up positions in the stratosphere, waiting to assume title to the planet as soon as its present occupants used their latest discovery—nuclear fission—as they had previously used ballistics and aeronautics.

The more impatient wandered down to survey homesites. They found to their annoyance that an unpleasant maggot of error had crawled into the pure mathematics of extrapolated sociology. Humanity should have wiped itself out shortly after acquiring atomic power. But—possibly as a result of the scientific stimulation we had been receiving recently—our technological momentum had carried us past uranium-plutonium fission up to the so-called hydrogen bomb.

Whereas a uranium-bomb Armageddon would have disposed of us in a most satisfactory and sanitary fashion, the explosion of several hydrogen bombs, it would seem, will result in the complete sterilization of our planet as the result of a subsidiary reaction at present unknown to us. If we go to war with this atomic refinement, Earth will not only be cleansed of all present life-forms, but it will also become uninhabitable for several millions of years in the future.

Naturally, the kobolds view this situation with a certain amount of understandable unhappiness. According to Galactic Law, they may not actively intervene to safe-guard their legacy. Therefore, they would like to offer a proposition.

Any nation which guarantees to stop making hydrogen bombs and to dispose of those it has already made—and the little redbeards have, they claim, satisfactory methods of enforcing these guarantees—such a nation will be furnished by them with a magnificently murderous weapon. This weapon is extremely simple to operate and is so calibrated that it can be set to kill instantaneously and painlessly any number of people at one time up to a full million.

"The advantage to any terrestrial military establishment of such a weapon over the unstable hydrogen bomb, which is not only hard to handle but must be transported physically to its target," the genial face on the ceiling commented, "should be obvious to all of you! And, as far as we are concerned, anything which will dispose of human beings on a wholesale basis while not injuring—"

At this point, there was so much noise that I couldn't hear a word he was saying. For that matter, I was yelling quite loudly myself.

"—while not injuring useful and compatible life-forms—"

"Ah-h," screamed a deeply tanned stout man in a flowerful red sports shirt and trunks, "whyn't you go back where you came from?"

"Yeah!" someone else added wrathfully. "Can't yuh see yuh not wanted? Shut up, huh? Shut *up!*"

"Murderers," one of the women in front of me quavered. "That's all you are—murderers trying to kill inoffensive people who've never done you any harm. Killing would be just too good for you."

The colonel was standing on his toes and oscillating a portentous forefinger at the roof. "We were doing all right," he began apoplectically, then stopped to allow himself to unpurple, "We were doing *well* enough, I can tell you, without—without—"

Forkbeard waited until we began to run down.

"Look at it this way," he urged in a wheedling voice: "You're going to wipe yourselves out—you know it, we know it and so does everybody else in the galaxy. What difference can it possibly make to you whether you do it one way or another? At least by our method you confine the injury to yourselves. You don't damage the highly valuable real estate—to wit, Earth—which will be ours after you've ceased to use it. And you go out with a weapon which is much more worthy of your destructive propensities than any you have used hitherto, including atomic bombs."

He paused and spread knobbed hands down at our impotent hatred. "Think of it—*just think of it*: a million deaths at one plunge of a lever! What other weapon can make that claim?"

Skimming back northwards with Redbeard and Irngl, I pointed to the flying saucers radiating away from us through the delicate summer sky. "These people are all fairly responsible citizens. Isn't it silly to expect them to advertise a more effective way of having their throats cut?"

There was a shrug of the green-wrapped shoulders. "With any other species, yes. But not you. The Galactic Federation insists that the actual revelation of the weapon, either to your public or your government, must be made by a fairly intelligent respresentative of your own species, in full possession of the facts, and after he or she has had an adequate period to reflect on the consequences of disclosure."

"And you think we will? In spite of everything?"

"Oh, yes," the little man told me with tranquil assurance. "*Because* of everything. For example, you have each been selected with a view to the personal advantage you would derive from the revelation. Sooner or later, one of you will find the advantage so necessary and tempting that the inhibiting scruple will disappear; eventually, all of you would come to it. As Shulmr pointed out, each member of a suicidal race contributes to the destruction of the whole even while attentively safeguarding his own existence. Disagreeable creatures, but fortunately short-lived!"

"One million," I mused. "So arbitrary. I bet we make—"

"Quite correct. You are an ingenious race. Now if you wouldn't mind stepping back to your roof? We're in a bit of a hurry, Irngl and I, and we have to disinfect after— Thank you."

I watched them disappear upwards into a cloud bank. Then, noticing a television dipole tied in a hangman's noose which Irngl's father had overlooked, I trudged downstairs.

For a while, I was very angry. Then I was glum. Then I was angry again. I've thought about it a lot since August.

I've read some recent stuff on flying saucers, but not a word about the super-weapon we'll get if we dismantle our hydrogen bombs. But, if someone had blabbed, how would I know about it?

That's just the point. Here I am a writer, a science-fiction writer no less, with a highly salable story that I'm not supposed to use. Well, it happens that I need money badly right now; and it further happens that I am plumb out of plots. How long am I supposed to go on being a sucker?

Somebody's probably told by now. If not in this country, in one of the others. And I *am* a writer, and I have a living to make. And this is fiction, and who asked you to believe it anyhow?

Only— Only I did intend to leave out the signal. The signal, that is, by which a government can get in touch with the kobolds, can let them know it's interested in making the trade, in getting that weapon. I did intend to leave out the signal.

But I don't have a satisfactory ending to this story. It needs some sort of tag-line. And the signal makes a perfect one. Well—it seems to me that if I've told *this* much—and probably anyhow—

The signal's the immemorial one between man and kobold: Leave a bowl of milk outside the White House door.

James Blish was one of the first "insiders" to bring high literary standards to the reviewing and critical examination of science fiction. He was also a major writer, whose wonderful novel *A Case of Conscience* won the Hugo Award in 1959, and whose "Pantropy" and "Okie" series will always be remembered by science-fiction readers. His untimely death in 1975 was a blow to everyone in sf.

This story responds to an important and perennial issue in all societies: the location of *power*.

Who's in Charge Here?

BY JAMES BLISH

The Early Mott Street morning was misty, but that would burn off later; it was going to be a hot day in New York. The double doors of the boarded-up shop swung inward with a grating noise, and a black-and-white tomcat bolted out of an overflowing garbage can next door and slid beneath a parked car. It was safe there: the car had been left in distress two days ago, and since then the neighborhood kids had removed three tires and the engine.

After that nothing moved for a while. At last, a preternaturally clean old man, neatly dressed in very clean rags, came out of the dark chill interior of the shop with a kettle heaped with freshly fired charcoal, which he set on the sidewalk. Straightening, he took a good long look at the day, exposing his cleanliness, the sign of his reclamation from the Bowery two blocks away, to the unkind air. Then he scuffled back into the cave with a bubbly sigh; he would next see the day tommorrow morning at the same time, if it didn't rain. Behind him, the bucket of charcoal sent up petals of yellow flame, in the midst of which the briquets nestled like dragons' eggs, still unhatched.

Now emerged the hot-dog wagons, three of them, one by one, their blue-and-orange striped parasols bobbing stiffly, pushed by men in stiff caps. The men helped themselves to charcoal from the bucket, to heat the franks (all meat) and the sauerkraut (all cabbage) and the rolls (all sawdust). Behind them came the fruit pushcarts, and then two carts heaped with the vegetables of the district: minute artichokes for three cents each, Italian tomatoes, eggplants in all sizes, zucchini, peppers, purple onions.

When the pushcarts were all gone the street was quiet again, but the cat stayed underneath the late-model wreck at the curb. It was waiting for the dogs, who after a while emerged with their men: scrubby yellowish animals with long foxy noses and plumy tails carried low, hitched to the men with imaginative networks of old imitation-alligator belts and baby-carriage straps. There was also one authentic German shepherd who wore an authentic rigid Seeing-Eye harness; the man he was pulling was a powerfully built Negro who was already wearing his sign:

PRAY IN YOUR OWN WAY
EVERY DAY
TAKE A PRAYER-CARD
THEY'RE FREE
I AM BLIND
THANK YOU

The others still carried their signs under their arms, though all were wearing their dark glasses. They paused to sniff at the day.

"Pretty good," said the man with the German shepherd. "Let's go. And don't any of you bastards be late back."

The others mumbled, and then they too filed off toward Houston Street, where the bums were already in motion toward the Volunteers of America shop, hoping to pick up a little heavy lifting to buy cigarettes with. The bums avoided the dogs very scrupulously. The dogs pulled the men west and down the sixty steps of the Broadway-Lafayette IND station to the F train, which begins there, and they all sat together in the rear car. There was almost no talking, but one of the men already had his transistor radio going, filling the car with an hysterical mixture of traffic reports and rock-and-roll.

The cat stayed under the late-model wreck; it was now time for the children to burst out of the church and charge toward the parochial school across the street, screaming and pummelling each other with their prayer-books.

Another clean old man took in the empty charcoal bucket and the doors closed.

The dogs pulled the men out of the F train at the 47th-50th Street station on Sixth Avenue, which is the Rockefeller Center stop; they emerged, however, at the 47th Street end which is almost squarely in the middle of Manhattan's diamond mart. Here they got out their cups, each of which contained a quarter to shake, and hung on their signs; then they moved singly, at five-minute intervals, one block north, and then slowly east.

The signs were all metal, hung at belt level, front and back, and all were black with greenish-yellow lettering. The calligraphy was also the same: curlicue capitals, like the upper case of that type font known as Hobo.

The messages, however, were varied, though they had obvious similarities in style. The one following the man with the German shepherd and the prayer-cards, for instance, said:

> GOD BLESS YOU
> YOU CAN SEE
> AND I CAN'T
> THANK YOU

Slowly they deployed along 48th Street toward Fifth Avenue, which was already teeming with people, though it was only 10 A.M. At the Fifth Avenue end, which is marked by Black, Starr and Gorham, a phenomenally expensive purveyor of such luxuries as one-fork-of-a-kind sterling, an old blind woman in the uniform of the Lighthouse sat behind a table on which was a tambourine, playing a guitar and whining out a hymn. A dog lay at her feet. Only a few feet away, still in front of one of Black, Starr and Gorham's show windows, was a young man with a dog, standing with a guitar, singing rock-and-roll at the top of his voice. Two blocks up Fifth Avenue, at the terrace of Rockefeller Center, two women and a man in Salvation Army uniforms played hymns on three tumpets in close harmony (a change from yesterday, when that stand had been occupied only by an Army officer with a baritone sax-horn which he could barely play), but they didn't matter—the men weren't working Rockefeller Center anymore; having already done for that area.

The dogs ignored the old woman and the rock-and-roller as well, and so did the men. They never sang. The man with the transistor radio turned it up a little when he worked that end of the block.

The street filled still further. As it got on toward a blistering noon, the travellers that counted came out: advertising-agency account men ("—and when the client's sales forecast was under ours by fifteen per cent they went and cut the budget on us, and now poor old Jim's got his yacht posted for sale in the men's room"), the middle echelons of editors from important weekly news magazines (with the latest dirty verses about their publishers), literary agents playing musical chairs ("—went to S&S and took Zuck Stamler with him with twenty-five per cent of the contract and an option clause bound in purest brass") and an occasional bewildered opinion-maker from the trade press ("—a buck eighty-five for *spaghetti?*"). None of these ever dropped a coin in the cups, but the dogs were not disturbed; they walked their men in the heat.

> I MAY SEE AGAIN
> WITH A TRANSPLANT EYE
> GOD BLESS YOU

The travellers settled in the St. Germain and the Three G's, except for the trade press, which took refuge in the American Bar. Secretaries stopped outside the restaurants, looked at the menus, looked at each other indignantly and swung up Fifth toward Stouffer's, where they would be charged just as much. The match-players said "Viva-la!" and "Law of averages!" and "That's a good call," and damned the Administration. The girl account exec had one Martini more and told the man from the client something he had suspected for five months and was not glad to hear; the agency would not be glad to hear it either, but it never would. Rogers and White-head, Authors Representatives (they had never been able to decide where the apostrophe should go) had shad roe and bacon and decided to drop all their Western authors, of whom they had three. The president and editor-in-chief of the largest magazine enterprise in the world decided to run for president after all.

The men listened and shook their cups and walked their dogs. The transistor radio reported that the news was worse today.

At 3 P.M. the temperature was 92 degrees, the humidity 40 per cent, the T.H.I. 80. The German shepherd pulled his man back toward Sixth. The other dogs followed. At the to-ken booth the cups were checked: there was enough money to get home on. Along 48th, the restaurants emptied, leaving behind a thick miasma of smoke, tomato sauce and disastrous decisions. Tomorrow they would do for 47th Street, where the Public Relations types gathered.

The cave on Mott Street was relatively cool. The men took off their signs and sat down. The radio said something about Khrushchev, something about Cuba, and something about beer.

"Not a bad day," the big man said finally. "Lots of jangle. Did you hear that guy with the three kids decide to quit?"

The man with the radio reported: "Goin' to rain tomor-row."

"It is?" the big man said. "Hell, that's no good." He thought for a while, and then, getting deliberately to his feet, he crossed the dark chill room and kicked the German shep-herd. "Who's in charge here?" The dog looked back sullenly. Satisfied, the man went back and sat down.

"Nah," he said. "It won't rain."

The last question, and finally AN ANSWER! Well, sort of.

The Last Question

BY ISAAC ASIMOV

The last question was asked for the first time, half in jest on May 21, 2061, at a time when humanity first stepped into the light. The question came about as a result of a five-dollar bet over highballs, and it happened this way:

Alexander Adell and Bertram Lupov were two of the faithful attendants of Multivac. As well as any human beings could, they knew what lay behind the cold, clicking, flashing face—miles and miles of face—of that giant computer. They had at least a vague notion of the general plan of relays and circuits that had long since grown past the point where any single human could possibly have a firm grasp of the whole.

Multivac was self-adjusting and self-correcting. It had to be, for nothing human could adjust and correct it quickly enough or even adequately enough.—So Adell and Lupov attended the monstrous giant only lightly and superficially, yet as well as any men could. They fed it data, adjusted questions to its needs and translated the answers that were issued. Certainly they, and all others like them, were fully entitled to share in the glory that was Multivac's.

For decades, Multivac had helped design the ships and plot the trajectories that enabled man to reach the Moon, Mars, and Venus, but past that, Earth's poor resources could not support the ships. Too much energy was needed for the long trips. Earth exploited its coal and uranium with increasing efficiency, but there was only so much of both.

But slowly Multivac learned enough to answer deeper questions more fundamentally, and on May 14, 2061, what had been theory became fact.

The energy of the sun was stored, converted, and utilized directly on a planet-wide scale. All Earth turned off its burning coal, its fissioning uranium, and flipped the switch that connected all of it to a small station, one mile in diameter, circling the Earth at half the distance of the Moon. All Earth ran by invisible beams of sunpower.

Seven days had not sufficed to dim the glory of it and Adell and Lupov finally managed to escape from the public function, and to meet in quiet where no one would think of looking for them, in the deserted underground chambers, where portions of the mighty buried body of Multivac showed. Unattended, idling, sorting data with contented lazy clickings, Multivac, too, had earned its vacation and the boys appreciated that. They had no intention, originally, of disturbing it.

They had brought a bottle with them, and their only concern at the moment was to relax in the company of each other and the bottle.

"It's amazing when you think of it," said Adell. His broad face had lines of weariness in it, and he stirred his drink slowly with a glass rod, watching the cubes of ice slur clumsily about. "All the energy we can possibly ever use for free. Enough energy, if we wanted to draw on it, to melt all Earth into a big drop of impure liquid iron, and still never miss the energy so used. All the energy we could ever use, forever and forever and forever."

Lupov cocked his head sideways. He had a trick of doing that when he wanted to be contrary, and he wanted to be contrary now, partly because he had had to carry the ice and glassware. "Not forever," he said.

"Oh, hell, just about forever. Till the sun runs down, Bert."

"That's not forever."

"All right, then. Billions and billions of years. Twenty billion maybe. Are you satisfied?"

Lupov put his fingers through his thinning hair as though to reassure himself that some was still left and sipped gently at his own drink. "Twenty billion years isn't forever."

"Well, it will last our time, won't it?"

"So would the coal and uranium."

"All right, but now we can hook up each individual spaceship to the Solar Station, and it can go to Pluto and back a million times without ever worrying about fuel. You can't do *that* on coal and uranium. Ask Multivac, if you don't believe me."

"I don't have to ask Multivac. I know that."

"Then stop running down what Multivac's done for us," said Adell, blazing up. "It did all right."

"Who says it didn't? What I say is that a sun won't last forever. That's all I'm saying. We're safe for twenty billion years; but then what?" Lupov pointed a slightly shaky finger at the other. "And don't say we'll switch to another sun."

There was silence for a while. Adell put his glass to his lips only occasionally, and Lupov's eyes slowly closed. They rested.

Then Lupov's eyes snapped open. "You're thinking we'll switch to another sun when ours is done, aren't you?"

"I'm not thinking."

"Sure you are. You're weak on logic, that's the trouble with you. You're like the guy in the story who was caught in a sudden shower and who ran to a grove of trees and got under one. He wasn't worried, you see, because he figured when one tree got wet through he would just get under another one."

"I get it," said Adell. "Don't shout. When the sun is done, the other stars will be gone, too."

"Darn right they will," muttered Lupov. "It all had a beginning in the original cosmic explosion, whatever that was, and it'll all have an end when all the stars run down. Some run down faster than others. Hell, the giants won't last a hundred million years. The sun will last twenty billion years and maybe the dwarfs will last a hundred billion for all the good they are. But just give us a trillion years and everything will be dark. Entropy has to increase to maximum, that's all."

"I know all about entropy," said Adell, standing on his dignity.

"The hell you do."

"I know as much as you do."

"Then you know everything's got to run down someday."

"All right. Who says they won't?"

"You did, you poor sap. You said we had all the energy we needed, forever. You said 'forever.'"

It was Adell's turn to be contrary. "Maybe we can build things up again someday," he said.

"Never."

"Why not? Someday."

"Ask Multivac."

"Never."

"*You* ask Multivac. I dare you. Five dollars says it can't be done."

Adell was just drunk enought to try, just sober enough to be able to phrase the necessary symbols and operations into a question which, in words, might have corresponded to this: Will mankind one day without the net expenditure of energy be able to restore the sun to its full youthfulness even after it had died of old age?

Or maybe it could be put more simply like this: How can the net amount of entropy of the universe be massively decreased?

Multivac fell dead and silent. The slow flashing of lights ceased, the distant sounds of clicking relays ended.

Then, just as the frightened technicians felt they could hold their breath no longer, there was a sudden springing to life of the teletype attached to that portion of Multivac. Five words were printed: "INSUFFICIENT DATA FOR MEANINGFUL ANSWER."

"No bet," whispered Lupov. They left hurriedly.

By next morning, the two, plagued with throbbing head and cottony mouth, had forgotten the incident.

Jerrodd, Jerrodine, and Jerrodette I and II watched the starry picture in the visiplate change as the passage through hyperspace was completed in its non-time laps. At once, the even powdering of stars gave way to the predominance of a single bright marble-disk, centered.

"That's X-23," said Jerrodd confidently. His thin hands clamped tightly behind his back and the knuckles whitened.

The little Jerrodettes, both girls, had experienced the hyperspace passage for the first time in their lives and were self-conscious over the momentary sensation of inside-outness. They burried their giggles and chased one another wildly about their mother, screaming, "We've reached X-23—we've reached X-23—we've—"

"Quiet, children," said Jerrodine sharply. "Are you sure, Jerrodd?"

"What is there to be but sure?" asked Jerrodd, glancing up at the bulge of featureless metal just under the ceiling. It ran the length of the room, disappearing through the wall at either end. It was as long as the ship.

Jerrodd scarcely knew a thing about the thick rod of metal except that it was called a Microvac, that one asked it questions if one wished; that if one did it still had its task of guiding the ship to a preordered destination; of feeding on energies from the various Sub-galactic Power Stations; of computing the equations for the hyperspacial jumps.

Jerrodd and his family had only to wait and live in the comfortable residence quarters of the ship.

Someone had once told Jerrodd that the "ac" at the end of "Microvac" stood for "analog computer" in ancient English, but he was on the edge of forgetting even that.

Jerrodine's eyes were moist as she watched the visiplate. "I can't help it. I feel funny about leaving Earth."

372

"Why, for Pete's sake?" demanded Jerrodd. "We had nothing there. We'll have everything on X-23. You won't be alone. You won't be a pioneer. There are over a million people on the planet already. Good Lord, our great-grandchildren will be looking for new worlds because X-23 will be overcrowded." Then, after a reflective pause, "I tell you, it's a lucky thing the computers worked out interstellar travel, the way the race is growing."

"I know, I know," said Jerrodine miserably.

Jerrodette I said promptly, "Our Microvac is the best Microvac in the world."

"I think so, too," said Jerrodd, tousling her hair.

It *was* a nice feeling to have a Microvac of your own and Jerrodd was glad he was part of his generation and no other. In his father's youth, the only computers had been tremendous machines taking up a hundred square miles of land. There was only one to a planet. Planetary ACs they were called. They had been growing in size steadily for a thousand years and then, all at once, came refinement. In place of transistors had come molecular valves, so that even the largest Planetary AC could be put into a space only half the volume of a spaceship.

Jerrodd felt uplifted, as he always did when he thought that his own personal Microvac was many times more complicated than the ancient and primitive Multivac that had first tamed the Sun, and almost as complicated as Earth's Planetary AC (the largest) that had first solved the problem of hyperspatial travel and had made trips to the stars possible.

"So many stars, so many planets," sighed Jerrodine, busy with her own thoughts. "I suppose families will be going to new planets forever, the way we are now."

"Not forever," said Jerrodd, with a smile. "It will all stop someday, but not for billions of years. Many billions. Even the stars run down, you know. Entropy must increase."

"What's entropy, daddy?" shrilled Jerrodette II.

"Entropy, little sweet, is just a word which means the amount of running-down of the universe. Everything runs down, you know, like your little walkie-talkie robot, remember?"

"Can't you just put in a new power-unit, like with my robot?"

"The stars *are* the power-units, dear. Once they're gone, there are no more power-units."

Jerrodette I at once set up a howl. "Don't let them, daddy. Don't let the stars run down."

"Now look what you've done," whisperel Jerrodine, exasperated.

"How was I to know it would frighten them?" Jerrodd whispered back.

"Ask the Microvac," wailed Jerrodette I. "Ask him how to turn the stars on again."

"Go ahead," said Jerrodine. "It will quiet them down." (Jerrodette II was beginning to cry, also).

Jerrodd shruged. "Now, now, honeys. I'll ask Microvac. Don't worry, he'll tell us."

He asked the Microvac, adding quickly, "Print the answer."

Jerrodd cupped the strip of thin cellufilm and said cheerfully, "See now, the Microvac says it will take care of everything when the time comes so don't worry."

Jerrodine said, "And now, children, it's time for bed. We'll be in our new home soon."

Jerrodd reads the words on the cellufilm again before destroying it: "INSUFFICIENT DATA FOR A MEANINGFUL ANSWER."

He shrugged and looked at the visiplate. X-23 was just ahead.

VJ-23X of Lameth stared into the black depths of the three-dimensional, small-scale map of the Galaxy and said, "Are we ridiculous, I wonder, in being so concerned about the matter?"

MQ-17J of Nicron shook his head. "I think not. You know the Galaxy will be filled in five years at the present rate of expansion."

Both seemed in their early twenties, both were tall and perfectly formed.

"Still," said VJ-23X, "I hesitate to submit a pessimistic report to the Galactic Council."

"I wouldn't consider any other kind of report. Stir them up a bit. We've got to stir them up."

VJ-23X sighed. "Space is infinite. A hundred billion Galaxies are there for the taking. More."

"A hundred billion is *not* infinite and it's getting less infinite all the time. Consider! Twenty thousand years ago, mankind first solved the problem of utilizing stellar energy, and few centuries later, interstellar travel became possible. It took mankind a million years to fill one small world and then only fifteen thousand years to fill the rest of the Galaxy. Now the population doubles every ten years—"

VJ-23X interrupted. "We can thank immortality for that."

"Very well. Immortality exists and we have to take it into account. I admit it has its seamy side, this immortality. The Galactic AC has solved many problems for us, but in solving the problem of preventing old age and death, it has undone all its other solutions."

"Yet you wouldn't want to abandon life, I suppose."

"Not at all," snapped MQ-17J, softening it at once to, "Not yet. I'm by no means old enough. How old are you?"

"Two-hundred twenty-three. And you?"

"I'm still under two hundred.—But to get back to my point. Population doubles every ten years. Once this Galaxy is filled, we'll have filled another in ten years. Another ten years and we'll have filled two more. Another decade, four more. In a hundred years, we'll have filled a thousand Galaxies. In a thousand years, a million Galaxies. In ten thousand years, the entire known Universe. Then what?"

VJ-23X said, "As a side issue, there's a problem of transportation. I wonder how many sunpower units it will take to move Galaxies of individuals from one Galaxy to the next."

"A very good point. Already, mankind consumes two sunpower units per year."

"Most of it's wasted. After all our own Galaxy alone pours out a thousand sunpower units a year and we only use two of those."

"Granted, but even with a hundred per cent efficiency, we only stave off the end. Our energy requirements are going up in a geometric progression, even faster than our population. We'll run out of energy even sooner than we run out of Galaxies. A good point. A very good point."

"We'll just have to build new stars out of interstellar gas."

"Or out of dissipated heat?" asked MQ-17J, sarcastically.

"There may be some way to reverse entropy. We ought to ask the Galactic AC."

VJ-23X was not really serious, but MQ-17J pulled out his AC-contact from his pocket and placed it on the table before him.

"I've half a mind to," he said. "It's something the human race will have to face someday."

He stared somberly at his small AC-contact. It was only two inches cubed and nothing in itself, but it was connected through hyperspace with a great Galactic AC that served all mankind. Hyperspace considered, it was an integral part of the Galactic AC.

MQ-17J paused to wonder if someday in his immortal life he would get to see the Galactic AC. It was on a little world of its own, a spiderwebbing of force-beams holding the matter within which surges of sub-mesons took the place of the old clumsy molecular valves. Yet despite its subetheric workings, the Galactic AC was known to be a full thousand feet across.

MQ-17J asked suddenly of his AC-contact, "Can entropy ever be reversed?"

VJ-23X looked startled and said at once, "Oh, say, I didn't really mean to have you ask that."

"Why not?"

"We both know entropy can't be reversed. You can't turn smoke and ash back into a tree."

"Do you have trees on your world?" asked MQ-17J.

The sound of the Galactic AC startled them into silence. Its voice came thin and beautiful out of the small AC-contact on the desk. It said: "THERE IS INSUFFICIENT DATA FOR MEANINGFUL ANSWER."

VJ-23X said, "See!"

The two men thereupon returned to the question of the report they were to make to the Galactic Council.

Zee Prime's mind spanned the new Galaxy with a faint interest in the countless twists of stars that powdered it. He had never seen this one before. Would he ever see them all? So many of them, each with its load of humanity.—But a load that was almost a dead weight. More and more, the real essence of men was to be found out here, in space.

Minds, not bodies! The immortal bodies remained back on the planets, in suspension over the eons. Sometimes they roused for material activity but that was growing rarer. Few new individuals were coming into existence to join the incredibly mighty throng, but what matter? There was little room in the Universe for new individuals.

Zee Prime was roused out of his reverie upon coming across the wispy tendrils of another mind.

"I am Zee Prime," said Zee Prime. "And you?"

"I am Dee Sub Wun. Your Galaxy?"

"We call it only the Galaxy. And you?"

"We call ours the same. All men call their Galaxy their Galaxy and nothing more. Why not?"

"True. Since all Galaxies are the same."

"Not all Galaxies. On one particular Galaxy the race of man must have originated. That makes it different."

Zee Prime said, "On which one?"

"I cannot say. The Universal AC would know."

"Shall we ask him? I am suddenly curious."

Zee Prime's perceptions broadened until the Galaxies themselves shrank and became a new, more diffuse powdering on a much larger background. So many hundreds of billions of them, all with their immortal beings, all carrying their load of intelligences with minds that drifted freely through space. And yet one of them was unique among them all in being the original Galaxy. One of them had, in its vague and distant past, a period when it was the only Galaxy populated by man.

Zee Prime was consumed with curiosity to see this Galaxy and he called out: "Universal AC! On which Galaxy did mankind originate?"

The Universal AC heard, for on every world and throughout space it had its receptors ready, and each receptor lead through hyperspace to some unknown point where the Universal AC kept itself aloof.

Zee Prime knew of only one man whose thoughts had penetrated within sensing distance of Universal AC, and he reported only a shining globe, two feet across, difficult to see.

"But how can that be all of Universal AC?" Zee Prime had asked.

"Most of it," had been the answer, "is in hyperspace. In what form it is there I cannot imagine."

Nor could anyone, for the day had long since passed, Zee Prime knew, when any man had any part of the making of a Universal AC. Each Universal AC designed and constructed its successor. Each, during its existence of a million years or more, accumulated the necessary data to build a better and more intricate, more capable successor in which its own store of data and individuality would be submerged.

The Universal AC interrupted Zee Prime's wandering thoughts, not with words, but with guidance. Zee Prime's mentality was guided into the dim sea of Galaxies and one in particular enlarged into stars.

A thought came, infinitely distant, but infinitely clear. "THIS IS THE ORIGINAL GALAXY OF MAN."

But it was the same after all, the same as any other, and Zee Prime stifled his disappointment.

Dee Sub Wun, whose mind had accompanied the other, said suddenly, "And is one of these stars the original star of Man?"

The Universal AC said, "MAN'S ORIGINAL STAR HAS GONE NOVA. IT IS A WHITE DWARF."

"Did the men upon it die?" asked Zee Prime, startled and without thinking.

The Universal AC said, "A NEW WORLD, AS IN SUCH CASES, WAS CONSTRUCTED FOR THEIR PHYSICAL BODIES IN TIME."

"Yes, of course," said Zee Prime, but a sense of loss overwhelmed him even so. His mind released its hold on the original Galaxy of Man, let it spring back and lose itself among the blurred pinpoints. He never wanted to see it again.

Dee Sub Wun said, "What is wrong?"

"The stars are dying. The original star is dead."

"They must all die. Why not?"

"But when all energy is gone, our bodies will finally die, and you and I with them."

"It will take billions of years."

"I do not wish it to happen even after billions of years. Universal AC! How may stars be kept from dying?"

Dee Sub Wun said in amusement, "You're asking how entropy might be reversed in direction."

And the Universal AC answered: "THERE IS AS YET IN-SUFFICIENT DATA FOR A MEANINGFUL ANSWER."

Zee Prime's thoughts fled back to his own Galaxy. He gave no further thought to Dee Sub Wun, whose body might be waiting on a Galaxy a trillion light-years away, or on the star next to Zee Prime's own. It didn't matter.

Unhappily, Zee Prime began collecting interstellar hydrogen out of which to build a small star of his own. If the stars must someday die, at least some could yet be built.

Man considered with himself, for in a way, Man, mentally, was one. He consisted of a trillion, trillion, trillion, ageless bodies, each in its place, each resting quiet and incorruptible, each cared for by perfect automatons, equally incorruptible, while the minds of all the bodies freely melted one into the other, indistinguishable.

Man said, "The Universe is dying."

Man looked about at the dimming Galaxies. The giant stars, spendthrifts, were long ago, back in the dimmest of the dim far past. Almost all stars were white dwarfs, fading to the end.

New stars had been built of the dust between the stars, some by natural processes, some by Man himself, and those were going, too. White dwarfs might yet be crashed together and of the mighty forces so released, new stars built, but only one star for every thousand white dwarfs destroyed, and those would come to an end, too.

Man said, "Carefully husbanded, as directed by the Cosmic AC, the energy that is even yet left in all the Universe will last for billions of years."

"But even so," said Man, "eventually it will all come to an end. However it may be husbanded, however stretched out, the energy once expended is gone and cannot be restored. Entropy must increase forever to the maximum."

Man said, "Can entropy not be reversed? Let us ask the Cosmic AC."

The Cosmic AC surrounded them but not in space. Not a fragment of it was in space. It was in hyperspace and made of something that was neither matter nor energy. The question of its size and nature no longer had meaning in any terms that Man could comprehend.

"Cosmic AC," said Man, "how can entropy be reversed?"

The Cosmic AC said, "THERE IS AS YET INSUFFICIENT DATA FOR A MEANINGFUL ANSWER."

Man said, "Collect additional data."

The Cosmic AC said, "I WILL DO SO. I HAVE BEEN DOING SO FOR A HUNDRED BILLION YEARS. MY PREDECESSORS HAVE BEEN ASKED THIS QUESTION MANY TIMES. ALL THE DATA I HAVE REMAINS INSUFFICIENT."

"Will there come a time," said Man, "when data will be sufficient or is the problem insoluble in all conceivable circumstances?"

The Cosmic AC said, "NO PROBLEM IS INSOLUBLE IN ALL CONCEIVABLE CIRCUMSTANCES."

Man said, "When will you have enough data to answer the question?"

The Cosmic AC said, "THERE IS AS YET INSUFFICIENT DATA FOR A MEANINGFUL ANSWER."

"Will you keep working on it?" asked Man.

The Cosmic AC said, "I WILL."

Man said, "We shall wait."

The stars and Galaxies died and snuffed out, and space grew black after ten trillion years of running down.

One by one Man fused with AC, each physical body losing its mental identity in a manner that was somehow not a loss but a gain.

Man's last mind paused before fusion, looking over a space that included nothing but the dregs of one last dark star and nothing besides but incredibly thin matter, agitated randomly by the tag-ends of heat wearing out, asymptotically, to the absolute zero.

Man said, "AC, is this the end? Can this chaos not be reversed into the Universe once more? Can that not be done?"

AC said, "THERE IS AS YET INSUFFICIENT DATA FOR A MEANINGFUL ANSWER."

Man's last mind fused and only AC existed—and that in hyperspace.

Matter and energy had ended and with it space and time. Even AC existed only for the sake of the one last question that it had never answered from the time a half-drunken computer ten trillion years before had asked the question of a computer that was to AC far less than was a man to Man.

All other questions had been answered, and until this last question was answered also, AC might not release his consciousness.

All collected data had come to a final end. Nothing was left to be collected.

But all collected data had yet to be completely correlated and put together in all possible relationships.

A timeless interval was spent in doing that.

And it came to pass that AC learned how to reverse the direction of entropy.

But there was now no man to whom AC might give the answer of the last question. No matter. The answer—by demonstration—would take care of that, too.

For another timeless interval, AC thought how best to do this. Carefully, AC organized the program.

The consciousness of AC encompassed all of what had once been a Universe and brooded over what was now Chaos. Step by step, it must be done.

And AC said, "LET THERE BE LIGHT!"

And there was light—

SPACE MAIL

CONTENTS

General Reader
Anywhere

Dear G. R.,

In calling you "Reader," I am not being entirely accurate, and I hope you will forgive me.

After all, when I call myself "Writer," which I surely am from a professional standpoint, I tend to obscure the fact that I am a reader, too. The only reason this doesn't lead to serious misunderstandings is that all of us assume that almost everyone, regardless of what else he or she does, is a reader.

And in calling you a "Reader," I tend to obscure the fact that you are a writer, too. Everyone who is a reader is apt to be a writer, at least on occasion.

You yourself, General Reader, if I may continue to use the term without prejudice, write on occasion. You may not be a professional writer in the sense that you make a major portion of your livelihood out of your writing—but you write.

You write innumerable letters to friends and families; chatty letters to old college roommates; morose complaints to your sister; hurried scrawls to your mother; careful lies to some mistrusted acquaintance.

You also write business letters to associates; dunning letters to those who owe you money, diplomatic letters to those to whom you owe money, peremptory letters to those who have in one way or another wronged you, soothing letters to those whom you have wronged, imperative letters ordering equipment, convoluted letters portraying carelessness as innocence and misjudgments as virtue.

In fact, in these letters you write—doing so without ever once thinking of yourself as a writer—you may well run the whole gamut of emotion, tension, persuasion, prevarication, and exclamation.

Nor is it only letters that you and I (casual writer and professional alike) are involved in as manufacturers of the written word. It may be that you keep a diary—or write yourself

Introduction

notes—or send memos up and down the communications line of an organization—or write more or less formal reports on whatever line of business you are engaged in—or fill out blanks under various forms of bureaucratic compulsion—

All this is universal. What I do in writing a formal "story" is very particular, and even artificial.

Why not, then, tell a story as it so frequently tells itself in the writings of nonprofessionals—in the form of letters, diary entries, memos, reports, and so on?

In actual fact, it is occasionally done. It may seem to some an odd device, but from my remarks I hope you see it is not. It is the very stuff of human nature, and in this book, Martin and I have selected a clutch of the best examples of such stories that we could find.

Read and enjoy—and then watch your own day-to-day writings and see if there is not a story in them, too. In other words, General Reader, it may be that you are a General Writer as well.

Sincerely,

Isaac Asimov

LETTERS

Unfortunately, the late Cyril Kornbluth (1923–58) is often thought of primarily as a collaborator of Frederik Pohl. But he was much more than that, and his individual efforts were frequently of the highest quality. Particularly outstanding are his short-story collections and the novel The Syndic *(1953). Although he never won a major award in the field during his lifetime, he shared a Hugo in 1973 for a story finished by Fred Pohl from a fragment they had worked on many years before. Kornbluth's voice was an important if a cynical one in science fiction, and he is sorely missed.*

"I Never Ast No Favors" (The Magazine of Fantasy and Science Fiction, April 1954) has a little of the flavor of The Syndic, *and tells the story of a criminal with a most unusual problem.*

I NEVER AST NO FAVORS

By C. M. Kornbluth

Dear Mr. Marino:

I hesitate to take pen in hand and write you because I guess you do not remember me except maybe as a punk kid you did a good turn, and I know you must be a busy man running your undertaking parlor as well as the Third Ward and your barber shop. I never ast no favors of nobody but this is a special case which I hope you will agree when I explain.

To refresh your memory as the mouthpiece says in court, my name is Anthony Cornaro only maybe you remember me better as Tough Tony, which is what they call me back home in the Ward. I am not the Tough Tony from Water Street who is about 55 and doing a sixer up the river, I am the Tough Tony who is going on seventeen from Brecker Street and who you got probation for last week after I slash that nosy cop that comes flatfooting into the grocery store where some friends and I are just looking around not knowing it is after hours and that the grocery man has went home. That is the Tough Tony that I am. I guess you remember me now so I can go ahead.

With the probation, not that I am complaining, the trouble starts. The mouthpiece says he has known this lad for years and he comes from a very fine churchgoing family and he has been led astray by bad companions. So all right, the judge says three years probation, but he goes on to say *if*. If this, if that, environment, bad influences, congestered city streets, our vital dairy industry denuded—such a word from a judge!—of labor...

Before I know what has happened, I am signing a paper, my Mama is putting her mark on it and I am on my way to Chiunga County to milk cows.

I figure the judge does not know I am a personal friend of yours and I do not want to embarrass you by mentioning your name in open court, I figure I will get a chance later to straighten things out. Also, to tell you the truth, I am too struck with horror to talk.

On the ride upstate I am handcuffed to the juvenile court officer so I cannot make a break for it, but at last I get time to think and I realize that it is not as bad as it looks. I am supposed to work for a dame named Mrs. Parry and get chow, clothes and Prevailering Wages. I figure it takes maybe a month for her to break me in on the cow racket or even longer if I play dumb. During the month I get a few bucks, a set of threads and take it easy and by then I figure you will have everything straightened out and I can get back to my regular occupation, only more careful this time. Experience is the best teacher, Mr. Marino, as I am sure you know.

Well, we arrive at this town Chiunga Forks and I swear to God I never saw such a creepy place. You wouldn't believe it. The main drag is all of four blocks long and the stores and houses are from wood. I expect to see Gary Cooper stalking down the street with a scowl on his puss and his hands on his guns looking for the bad guys. Four hours from the Third Ward in a beat-up '48 police department Buick—you wouldn't believe it.

We park in front of a hash house, characters in rubber boots gawk at us, the court officer takes off the cuffs and gabs with the driver but does not lose sight of me. While we are waiting for this Mrs. Parry to keep the date I study the bank building across the street and develop some ideas which will interest you, Mr. Marino, but which I will not go into right now.

All of a sudden there is a hassle on the sidewalk.

A big woman with gray hair and a built like Tony Galento is kicking a little guy who looks like T.B. Louis the Book, who I guess you know, but not so muscular and wearing overalls. She is kicking him right in the keister, five-six times. Each time I shudder, and so maybe does the bank building across the street.

"Shoot my dawg, will you!" she yells at the character. "I said I'd kick your butt from here to Scranton when I caught up with you, Dud Wingle!"

"Leave me be!" he squawks, trying to pry her hands off his shoulders. "He was chasin' deer! He was chasin' deer!"

Thud—thud—thud. "I don't keer if he was chasin' deer, panthers or butterflies." *Thud.* "He was my dawg and you shot him!" *Thud.* She was drawing quite a crowd. The characters in rubber boots are forgetting all about us to stare at her and him.

Up comes a flatfoot who I later learn is the entire manpower of Chiunga Forks' lousiest; he says to the big woman "Now Ella" a few times and she finally stops booting the little character and lets him go. "What do you want, Henry?" she growls at the flatfoot and he asks weakly: "Silver Bell dropped her calf yet?"

The little character is limping away rubbing himself. The big broad watches him regretfully and says to the flatfoot: "Yesterday, Henry. Now if you'll excuse me I have to look for my new hired boy from the city. I guess that's him over there."

She strolls over to us and yanks open the Buick's door, almost taking it off the hinges. "I'm Mrs. Ella Parry," she says to me, sticking out her hand. "You must be the Cornaro boy the Probation Association people wired me about."

I shake hands and say, "Yes, ma'am."

The officer turns me over grinning like a skunk eating beans.

I figure Mrs. Parry lives in one of the wood houses in Chiunga Forks, but no. We climb into a this-year Willys truck and take off for the hills. I do not have much to say to this lady wrestler but wish I had somebody smuggle me a rod to kind of even things a little between her and me. With that built she could break me in half by accident. I try to get in good with her by offering to customize her truck. "I could strip off the bumper guards and put on a couple of fog lights, maybe new fender skirts with a little trim to them," I say, "and it wouldn't cost you a dime. Even out here there has got to be some parts place where a person can heist what he needs."

"Quiet, Bub," she says all of a sudden, and shields her eyes peering down a side road where a car is standing in front of a shack. "I swear," she says, "that looks like Dud Wingle's Ford in front of Miz' Sigafoos' place." She keeps her neck twisting around to study it until it is out of sight. And she looks worried.

I figure it is not a good time to talk and anyway maybe she has notions about customizing and does not approve of it.

"What," she says, "would Dud Wingle want with Miz' Sigafoos?"

"I don't know, ma'am," I say. "Wasn't he the gentleman you was kicking from here to Scranton?"

"Shucks, Bub, that was just a figger of speech. If I'd of wanted to kick him from here to Scranton I'd of *done* it. Dud and Jim and Ab and Sime think they got a right to shoot your dog if he chases the deer. I'm a peaceable woman or I'd have the law on them for shootin' Grip. But maybe I did kind of lose my temper." She looked worrieder yet.

"Is something wrong, ma'am?" I ask. You never can tell, but a lot of old dames talk to me like I was their uncle; to tell you the truth this is my biggest problem in a cat house. It must be because I am a kind of thoughtful guy and it shows.

Mrs. Parry is no exception. She says to me: "You don't know the folks up here yet, Bub, so you don't know about Miz' Sigafoos. I'm old English stock so I don't hold with their foolishness, but—" And here she looked *real* worried. "Miz'

C. M. Kornbluth

Sigafoos is what they call a hex doctor."

"What's that, ma'am?"

"Just a lot of foolishness. Don't you pay any attention," she says, and then she has to concentrate on the driving. We are turning off the two-lane state highway and going up, up, up, into the hills, off a blacktop road, off a gravel road, off a dirt road. No people. No houses. Fences and cows or maybe horses, I can't tell for sure. Finally we are at her place, which is from wood and in two buildings. I start automatically for the building that is clean, new-painted, big and expensive.

"Hold on, Bub," she says. "No need to head for the barn first thing. Let's get you settled in the house first and then there'll be a plenty of work for you."

I do a double take and see that the big, clean, expensive building is the barn. The little, cheap, run-down place is the house. I say to myself: "Tough Tony, you're gonna pray tonight that Mr. Marino don't forget to tell the judge you're a personal friend of his and get you out of this."

But that night I do not pray. I am too tired. After throwing sacks of scratch feed and laying mash around, I run the baling machine and I turn the oats in the loft and I pump water until my back is aching jello and then I go hiking out to the woodlot and chop down trees and cut them up with a chain saw. It is surprising how fast I learn and how willing I am when I remember what Mrs. Parry did to Dud Wingle.

I barely get to sleep it seems like when Mrs. Parry is yanking the covers off me laughing and I see through the window that the sky is getting a little light. "Time to rise, Bub," she bawls. "Breakfast on the table." She strides to the window and flexes her muscles, breathing deep. "It's going to be a fine day. I can tell when an animal's sick to death and I can tell when it's going to be fine all day. Rise and shine, Bub. We have a lot of work ahead. I was kind of easy on you yesterday seeing you was new here, so we got a bit behindhand."

I eye the bulging muscles and say "Yes, ma'am."

She serves a good breakfast, I have to admit. Usually I just have some coffee around eleven when I wake up and maybe a meat-ball sandwich around four, but the country air gives you an appetite like I always heard. Maybe I didn't tell you there was just the two of us. Her husband kicked off a couple of years ago. She gave one of her boys half the farm because she says she don't believe in letting them hang around without a chance to make some money and get married until you die. The other boy, nineteen, got drafted two months ago and since then she is running the place on her own hook because for some reason or other it is hard to get people to work on a farm. She says she does not understand this and I do not enlighten her.

First thing after breakfast she tells me to make four crates from lumber in the toolshed, go to the duckpond and put the four Muscovy ducks in the crates so she can take them to town and sell them. She has been meaning to sell the Muscovy ducks for some time since the word has been getting around that she was pro-communist for having such a breed of ducks when there were plenty of good American ducks she could of raised. "Though," she says, "in my opinion the Walterses ought to sell off their Peking ducks too because the Chinese are just as bad as the Roossians."

I make the crates which is easy and I go to the duckpond. There are four ducks there but they are not swimming; they have sunk. I go and tell Mrs. Parry and she looks at me like I was crazy.

"Yeah," I tell her. "Sunk. Down at the bottom of the pond, drownded. I guess maybe during the night they forgot to keep treading water or something."

She didn't say a word. She just strides down the path to the duckpond and looks into it and sees the four ducks. They are big, horrible things with kind of red Jimmy Valentine masks over their eyes, and they are lying at the bottom of the pond. She wades in, still without a word, and fishes them out. She gets a big shiv out of her apron pocket, slits the ducks open, yanks out their lungs and slits them open. Water dribbles out.

"Drownded," she mutters. "If there was snapping turtles to drag them under . . . but there ain't."

I do not understand what the fuss is about and ast her if she can't sell them anyway. She says no, it wouldn't be honest, and I should get a shovel and bury them. Then there is an awful bellering from the cow barn. "Agnes of Lincolnshire!" Mrs. Parry squawks and dashes for the barn. "She's dropping her calf ahead of time!"

I run along beside her. "Should I call the cops?" I pant. "They always get to the place before the ambulance and you don't have to pay them nothing. My married sister had three kids delivered by the cops—"

But it seems it's different with cows and anyway they have a different kind of flatfoot out here that didn't go to Police Academy. Mrs. Parry finally looks up from the calf and says "I think I saved it. I *know* I saved it. I can tell when an animal's dying. Bub, go to the phone and call Miz' Croley and ask her if she can possibly spare Brenda to come over and do the milkin' tonight and tomorrow morning. I dassn't leave Agnes and the calf; they need nursing."

I stagger out of the cowbarn, throw up two-three times and go to the phone in the house. I seen them phones with flywheels in the movies so I know how to work it. Mrs. Croley cusses and moans and then says all right she'll send Brenda over in the Ford and please to tell Mrs. Parry not to keep her no longer than she has to because she has a herd of her own that needs milking.

I tell Mrs. Parry in the barn and Mrs. Parry snaps that Mrs. Croley has a living husband and a draft-proof farmhand and she swore she din't know what things were coming to when a neighbor wouldn't help another neighbor out.

I ast casually: "Who is this Brenda, ma'am?"

"Miz' Croley's daughter. Good for nothing."

I don't ast no more questions but I sure begin to wait with interest for a Ford to round the bend of the road.

It does while I am bucking up logs with the chainsaw. Brenda is a blondie about my age, a little too big for her dress—an effect which I always go for, whether in the Third Ward or Chiunga County. I don't have a chance to talk to her until lunch, and then all she does is giggle. But who wants conversation? I make a mental note that she will have the room next to mine and then a truck comes snorting up the driveway. Something inside the truck is snorting louder than the truck.

Mrs. Parry throws up her hands. "Land, I forgot! Belshazzar the Magnificent for Princess Leilani!" She gulps coffee and dashes out.

"Brenda," I say, "what was that all about?"

She giggles and this time blushes. I throw down my napkin and go to the window. The truck is being backed to a field with a big board fence around it. Mrs. Parry is going into the barn and is leading a cow into the field. The cow is mighty nervous and I begin to understand why. The truckdriver opens the tailgate and out comes a snorting bull.

I think: well, I been to a few stag shows but *this* I never seen before. Maybe a person can learn something in the country after all.

Belshazzar the Magnificent sees Princess Leilani. He snorts like Charles Boyer. Princess Leilani cowers away from him like Bette Davis. Belshazzar the Magnificent paws the ground. Princess Leilani trembles. And then Belshazzar the Magnificent yawns and starts eating grass.

Princess Leilani looks up, startled, and says: "Huh?" No, on second thought it is not Princess Leilani who says "Huh?" It is Brenda, at the other kitchen window. She sees me watching her, giggles, blushes and goes to the sink and starts doing dishes.

I guess this is a good sign, but I don't press my luck. I go outside, where Mrs. Parry is cussing out the truckdriver.

"Some bull!" she yells at him. "What am I supposed to do now? How long is Leilani going to stay in season? What if I can't line up another stud for her? Do you realize what it's going to cost me in veal and milk checks—" Yatata, yatata, yatata, while the truckdriver keeps trying to butt in with excuses and Belshazzar the Magnificent eats grass and sometimes gives Princess Leilani a brotherly lick on the nose, for by that time Princess Leilani has dropped the nervous act and edged over mooing plaintively.

Mrs. Parry yells: "See that? I don't hold with artificial insemination but you dang stockbreeders are driving us dairy farmers to it! Get your—your *steer* off my property before I throw him off! I got work to do even if he hasn't! Belshazzar the Magnificent—*hah!*"

She turns on me. "Don't just stand around gawking, Bub. When you get the stovewood split you can stack it in the woodshed." I scurry off and resume Operation Woodlot, but I take it a little easy which I can do because Mrs. Parry is in the cowbarn nursing Agnes of Lincolnshire and the preemie calf.

At supper Mrs. Parry says she thinks she better put a cot in the barn for herself and spend the night there with the invalids in case there is a sudden emergency. "And that don't mean," she adds, "that you children can be up half the night playing the radio just because the old lady ain't around. I want to see the house lights out by 8:30. Understand?"

"Yes ma'am," Brenda says.

"We won't play the radio, ma'am," I say. "And we'll put the lights out."

Brenda giggled.

What happens that night is a little embarrassing to write about. I hope, Mr. Marino, you won't go telling it around. I figure that being a licensed mortician like you are as well as boss of the Third Ward you are practically like a doctor and doctors don't go around shooting their mouths off about what their patients tell them. I figure what I have to tell you about what happened comes under the sacred relationship between a doctor and patient or a hood and his mouthpiece.

Anyway, this is what happens: nothing happens.

Like with Belshazzar the Magnificent.

I go into her room, I say yes, she says no, I say yes *please,* she says well okay. And then nothing happens. I never been so humiliated and I hope you will keep this confidential because it isn't the kind of thing you like to have get around. I am telling you about it only because I never ast no favors but this is a very special case and I want you to understand why.

The next morning at breakfast I am in a bad temper, Brenda has got the giggles and Mrs. Parry is stiff and tired from sleeping in the barn. We are a gruesome threesome, and then a car drives up and a kid of maybe thirty comes busting into the kitchen. He has been crying. His eyes are red and there are clean places on his face where the tears ran down. "Ma!" he whimpers at Mrs. Parry. "I got to talk to you! You got to talk to Bonita, she says I don't love her no more and she's going to leave me!"

"Hush up, George," she snaps at him. "Come into the parlor." They go into the parlor and Brenda whistles: "Whoo-ee! Wait'll I tell Maw about *this!*"

"Who is he?" I ask.

"Miz' Parry's boy George. She gave him the south half of the farm and built him a house on it. Bonita's his wife. She's a stuck-up girl from Ware County and she wears falsies and dyes her hair and—" Brenda looks around, lowers her voice and whispers "—and *she sends her worshing to the laundry in town.*"

"God in Heaven," I say. "Have the cops heard about this?"

I Never Ast No Favors

"Oh, it's *legal*, but you just shouldn't *do* it."

"I see. I misunderstood, I guess. Back in the Third Ward it's a worse rap than mopery with intent to gawk. The judges are ruthless with it."

Her eyes go round. "Is that a fact?"

"Sure. Tell your mother about it."

Mrs. Parry came back in with her son and said to us: "Clear out, you kids. I want to make a phone call."

"I'll start the milkin'," Brenda said.

"And I'll framble the portistan while it's still cool and barkney," I say.

"Sure," Mrs. Parry says, cranking the phone. "Go and do that, Bub." She is preoccupied.

I go through the kitchen door, take one sidestep, flatten against the house and listen. Reception is pretty good.

"Bonita?" Mrs. Parry says into the phone. "Is that you, Bonita? Listen, Bonita, George is here and he asked me to call you and tell you he's sorry. I ain't exactly going to say that. I'm going to say that you're acting like a blame fool.... No, no, no. Don't talk about it. This is a party line. Just listen; I know what happened. George told me; after all, I'm his mother. Just listen to an older woman with more experience. So it happened. That don't mean he doesn't love you, child! It's happened to me. I guess it's happened to every woman. You mustn't take it *personally*. You're just sufferin' from a case of newlywed nerves. After you've been married two years or so you'll see things like this in better focus. Maybe George was tired. Maybe he got one of these flu germs that's goin' around.... No, I didn't say he was sick. No, he seems all right—maybe looks a *little* feverish.... Well, now, I don't know whether you really want to talk to him or not, you being so upset and all. If he *is* sick it'd just upset him— oh, all right." She chuckles away from the phone and says: "She wants to talk to you, George. Don't be too eager, boy."

I slink away from the kitchen door thinking: "Ah-*hah!*" I am thinking so hard that Mrs. Parry bungles into me when she walks out of the kitchen sooner than I expect.

She grabs me with one of those pipe-vise hands and snaps: "You young devil, were you listening to me on the phone?"

Usually it is the smart thing to deny everything and ast for your mouthpiece, but up here they got no mouthpieces. For once I tell the truth and cop a plea. "Yes, Mrs. Parry. I'm so *ashamed* of myself you can't imagine. I always been like that. It's a psy-cho-logical twist I got for listening. I can't seem to control it. Maybe I read too many bad comic books. But honest I won't breathe a word about how George couldn't—" Here I have the sense to shut up, but too late.

She drills me with a look and the pipe vise tightens on my arm. "Couldn't *what, Bub?*"

"Like Belshazzar the Magnificent," I say weakly.

"Yep," she says. "I thought that's what you were going to say. Now tell me, Bub—how'd you know? And don't tell me you guessed from what I said. I been using party lines for thirty years. The way I was talkin' to Bonita, it could've been anything from George hitting her with a brick to comin' home drunk. You picked a mighty long shot, you picked it right and I want to know how you did it."

She would of made a great D.A. I mumble: "The same thing happened to me last night. Would you mind lettin' go of my arm, Mrs. Parry? Before it drops off?"

She lets go with a start. "I'm sorry, Bub." She walked slowly to the barn and I walk slowly beside her because I think she expects it.

"Maybe," I say, "it's something in the water."

She shakes her head. "You don't know bulls, Bub. And what about the ducks that sank and Agnes dropping her calf before her time?" She begins to breathe hard through her nostrils. "It's hexin', that's what it is!"

"What's hexin', ma'am?"

"Heathen doings by that old Miz' Sigafoos. She's been warned and warned plenty to stick to her doctoring. I hold nothing against her for curing the croup or maybe selling a young man love potion if he's goin' down to Scranton to sell his crop and play around a little. But she's not satisfied with that, I guess. Dud Wingle must of gone to her with a twenty-dollar bill to witch my farm!"

I do not know what to make of this. My mama of course has told me about *la vecchia religione,* but I never know they believe in stuff like that over here. "Can you go to the cops, ma'am?" I ast.

She snorts like Belshazzar the Magnificent. "Cops! A fat lot old Henry Bricker would know about witchin'. No, Bub, I guess I'll handle this myself. I ain't the five-times-great-granddaughter of Pru Posthlewaite for nothin'!"

"Who was Pru—what you said?"

"Hanged in Salem, Massachusetts, in 1680 for witchcraft.

Her coven name was Little Gadfly, but I guess she wasn't so little. The first two ropes broke—but we got no time to stand around talkin'. I got to find my Ma's trunk in the attic. You go get the black rooster from the chicken run. I wonder where there's some chalk?" And she walks off to the house, mumbling. I walk to the chicken run thinking she has flipped.

The black rooster is a tricky character, very fast on his feet and also I am new at the chicken racket. It takes me half an hour to stalk him down, during which time incidentally the Ford leaves with Brenda in it and George drives away in his car. See you later, Brenda, I think to myself and maybe you will be surprised.

I go to the kitchen door with the rooster screaming in my arms and Mrs. Parry says: "Come on in with him and set him anywhere." I do, Mrs. Parry scatters some cornflakes on the floor and the rooster calms down right away and stalks around picking it up. Mrs. Parry is sweaty and dust-covered and there are some dirty old papers rolled up on the kitchen table.

She starts fooling around on the floor with one of the papers and a hunk of carpenter's chalk and just to be doing something I look at the rest of them. Honest to God, you never saw such lousy spelling and handwriting. *Tayke the Duste off ane Olde Ymmage Quhich Ye Myngel*—like that.

I shake my head and think: it's the cow racket. No normal human can take this life. She has flipped and I don't blame her, but it will be a horrible thing if she becomes homicidal. I look around for a poker or something and start to edge away. I am thinking of a dash from the door to the Willys and then scorching into town to come back with the men in the little white coats.

She looks up at me and says: "Don't go away, Bub. This is woman's work, but I need somebody to hold the sword and palm and you're the onliest one around." She grins. "I guess you never saw anything like *this* in the city, hey?"

"No, ma'am," I say, and notice that my voice is very faint.

"Well, don't let it skeer you. There's some people it'd skeer, but the Probation Association people say they call you Tough Tony, so I guess you won't take fright."

"No, ma'am."

"Now what do we do for a sword? I guess this bread knife'll—no; the ham slicer. It looks *more* like a sword. Hold it in your left hand and get a couple of them gilded bulrushes from the vase in the parlor. Mind you wipe your feet before you tread on the carpet! And then come back. Make it fast."

She starts to copy some stuff that looks like Yiddish writing onto the floor and I go into the parlor. I am about to tiptoe to the front door when she yells: "Bub! That you?"

Maybe I could beat her in a race for the car, maybe not. I shrug. At least I have a knife—and know how to use it. I bring her the gilded things from the vase. Ugh! While I am out she has cut the head off the rooster and is sprinkling its blood over a big chalk star and the writing on the floor. But the knife makes me feel more confident even though I begin to worry about how it will look if I have to do anything with it. I am figuring that maybe I can hamstring her if she takes off after me, and meanwhile I should humor her because maybe she will snap out of it.

"Bub," she says, "hold the sword and palms in front of you pointing up and don't step inside the chalk lines. Now, will you promise me not to tell anybody about the words I speak? The rest of this stuff don't matter; it's down in all the books and people have their minds made up that it don't work. But about the words, do you promise?"

"Yes, ma'am. Anything you say, ma'am."

So she starts talking and the promise was not necessary because it's in some foreign language and I don't talk foreign languages except sometimes a little Italian to my mama. I am beginning to yawn when I notice that we have company.

He is eight feet tall, he is green, he has teeth like Red Riding Hood's grandma.

I dive through the window, screaming.

When Mrs. Parry comes out she finds me in a pile of broken glass, on my knees, praying. She clamps two fingers on my ear and hoists me to my feet. "Stop that praying," she says. "He's complaining about it. Says it makes him itch. And you said you wouldn't be skeered! Now come inside where I can keep an eye on you and behave yourself. The idea! The very idea!"

To tell you the truth, I don't remember what happens after this so good. There is some talk between the green character and Mrs. Parry about her five-times-great-grandmother who it seems is doing nicely in a warm climate. There is an argument in which the green character gets shifty and says he doesn't know who is working for Miz' Sigafoos these days. Miz' Parry threatens to let me pray again and the green character gets sulky and says all right he'll send for him and rassle with him but he is sure he can lick him.

The next thing I recall is a grunt-and-groan exhibition between the green character and a smaller purple character who must of arrived when I was blacked out or something. This at least I know something about because I am a television fan. It is a very slow match, because when one of the characters for instance bends the other character's arm it just bends and does not break. But a good big character can lick a good little character every time and finally greenface has got his opponent tied into a bowknot.

"Be gone," Mrs. Parry says to the purple character, "and never more molest me or mine. Be gone, be gone, be gone."

He is gone, and I never do find out if he gets unknotted.

"Now fetch me Miz' Sigafoos."

Blip! An ugly little old woman is sharing the ring with the winner and new champeen. She spits at Mrs. Parry: "So you it was dot mine Teufel haff ge-schtolen!" Her English is terrible. A greenhorn.

"This ain't a social call, Miz' Sigafoos," Mrs. Parry says coldly. "I just want you to unwitch my farm and kinfolks. And if you're an honest woman you'll return his money to that sneakin', dog-murderin' shiftless squirt Dud Wingle."

"Yah," the old woman mumbles. She reaches up and feels the biceps of the green character. "Yah, I guess maybe dot I besser do. Who der Yunger iss?" She is looking at me. "For why the teeth on his mouth go clop-clop-clop? Und so white the face on his head iss! You besser should feed him, Ella."

"*Missus* Parry to you, Miz' Sigafoos, *if* you don't mind. Now the both of you be gone, be gone, be gone."

At last we are alone.

"Now," Mrs. Parry grunts, "maybe we can get back to farmin'. Such foolishness and me a busy woman." She looks at me closely and says: "I do believe the old fool was right. You're as white as a sheet." She feels my forehead. "Oh, shoot! You do have a temperature. You better get to bed. If you ain't better in the morning I'll call Doc Hines."

So I am in the bedroom writing this letter, Mr. Marino, and I hope you will help me out. Like I said I never ast no favors but this is special.

Mr. Marino, will you please, please go to the judge and tell him I have a change of heart and don't want no probation?

Tell him I want to pay my debt to society. Tell him I want to go to jail for three years, and for them to come and get me right away.

Sincerely,
ANTHONY (TOUGH TONY) CORNARO

P.S. On my way to get a stamp for this I notice that I have some gray hairs which is very unusual for a person going on seventeen. Please tell the judge I wouldn't mind if they give me solitary confinement and that maybe it would help me pay my debt to society.

In haste,
T.T.

Chan Davis wrote a small number of excellent science-fiction stories, most of which appeared in the magazines in the mid-to-late 1940s. A mathematician by training and trade, he has lived in Canada for many years. In addition to the present selection, his most notable works are "The Nightmare" (1946), one of the first post-Hiroshima warning stories and still one of the best, and "Adrift On the Policy Level" (1959), a scathing attack on the bureaucratic mind.

"Letter to Ellen" (Astounding Science Fiction, June 1947) has lived in the shadow of Lester del Rey's famous "Helen O'Loy." But it belongs in the sunlight, because it is one of the most compassionate and beautiful stories you will ever read.

LETTER TO ELLEN

By Chan Davis

Dear Ellen,

By the time you get this you'll be wondering why I didn't call. It'll be the first time I've missed in—how long?—two months? A long two months it's been, and, for me, a very important two months.

I'm not going to call, and I'm not going to see you. Maybe I'm a coward writing this letter, but you can judge that when you've finished it. Judge that, and other things.

Let's see. I'd better begin at the beginning and tell the whole story right through. Do you remember my friend Roy Wisner? He came to work in the lab the same time I did, in the spring of '16, and he was still around when I first met you. Even if you never met him, you may have seen him; he was the tall blond guy with the stooped shoulders, working in the same branch with me.

Roy and I grew up together. He was my best friend as a kid, back almost as far as I can remember, back at the State Orphanage outside of Stockton. We went to different-high schools, but when I got to Iowa U. there was Roy. Just to make the coincidence complete, he'd decided to be a biochemist too, and we took mostly the same courses all the way through. Both worked with Dietz while we were getting our doctorates, and Dietz got us identical jobs with Hartwell at the Pierne Labs here in Denver.

I've told you about that first day at the lab. We'd both heard from Dietz that the Pierne Labs were devoted now almost entirely to life-synthesis, and we'd both hoped to get in on that part of the work. What we hadn't realized was quite how far the work had got. I can tell you, the little talk old Hartwell gave us when he took us around to show us the lay of the land was just as inspiring as he meant it to be.

He showed us the wing where they're experimenting with the synthesis of new types of Coelenterates. We'd heard of that too, but seeing it was another thing. I remember particularly a rather ghastly green thing that floated in a small tank and occasionally sucked pieces of sea moss into what was half mouth, half sucker. Hartwell said, offhand, "Doesn't look much like the original, does it? That one was a mistake; something went wrong with the gene synthesis. But it turned out to be viable, so the fellows kept it around. Wouldn't be surprised if it could outsurvive some of its natural cousins if we were to give it a mate and turn it loose." He looked at the thing benignly. "I sort of like it."

Then we went down to Hartwell's branch, Branch 26, where we were to work. Hartwell slid back the narrow metal door and led the way into one of the labs. We started to follow him, but we hadn't gone more than three steps inside when we just stood still and gawked. I'd seen complicated apparatus before, but that place had anything at the Iowa labs beat by a factor of one thousand. All the gear on one whole side of the lab—and it was a good-sized place—was black-coated against the light and other stray radiation in the room. I recognized most of the flasks and fractionating columns as airtight jobs. A good deal of the hookup was hidden from us, being under Gardner hoods, airtight, temperature-controlled, radiation-controlled, and everything-else-controlled. What heaters we could see were never burners, always infrared banks.

This was precision work. It had to be, because, as you know, Branch 26 synthesizes chordate genes.

Roy and I went over to take a closer look at some of the gear. We stopped about a meter away; meddling was distinctly not in order. The item we were looking at was what would be called, in a large-scale process, a reaction vat. It was a small, opaque-coated flask, and it was being revolved slowly by a mechanical agitator, to swirl the liquids inside. As we stood there we could barely feel the gentle and precise flow of heat from the infrared heaters banked around it. We watched it, fascinated.

Hartwell snapped us out of it. "The work here," he said dryly, "is carried out with a good deal of care. You've had some experience with full microanalysis, Dietz tells me."

"A little," I nodded, with very appropriate modesty.

"Well, this is microsynthesis, and microsynthesis with a vengeance. Remember, our problem here is on an entirely different level even from ordinary protein synthesis." (It staggered me a little to hear him refer to protein synthesis as ordinary!) "There you're essentially building up a periodic crystal, one in which the atoms are arranged in regularly recurrent patterns. This recursion, this periodicity, makes the structure of the molecule relatively simple; correspondingly, it simplifies the synthesis. In a gene, a virus, or any other of the complex proteinlike molecules there isn't any such frequent recursion. Instead, the radicals in your molecule chain are a little different each time; the pattern almost repeats, but not quite. You've got what you call an a-periodic crystal.

"When we synthesize such a crystal we've got to get all the little variations from the pattern just right, because it's those variations that give the structure enough complexity to be living."

He had some chromosome charts under his arm, and now he pulled one out to show to us. I don't know if you've ever seen the things; one of them alone fills a little booklet, in very condensed notation. Roy and I thumbed through one, recognizing a good many of the shorthand symbols but not understanding the scheme of the thing at all. When we got through we were pretty thoroughly awed.

Hartwell smiled. "You'll catch on, don't worry. The first few months, while you're studying up, you'll be my lab assistants. You won't be on your own until you've got the process down pretty near pat." And were we glad to hear that!

Roy and I got an apartment on the outside of town; I didn't have my copter then, so we had to be pretty close. It was a good place, though only one wall and the roof could be made transparent. We missed the morning sun that way, but I liked it all right. Downstairs lived Graham, our landlord, an old bachelor who spent most of his time on home photography, both movie wires and old-fashioned chemical prints. He got some candid angle shots of us that were so weird Roy was thinking of breaking his cameras.

At the lab we caught on fast enough. Roy was always a pretty bright boy, and I manage to keep up. After a reasonable period Hartwell began to ease himself out of our routine, until before we knew it we were running the show ourselves. Naturally, being just out of school, we began, as soon as we got the drift of things, to suggest changes in the process. The day Hartwell finally approved one of our bright ideas, we knew we were standing on our own feet. That's when the fun really began.

Some people laugh when I say "that kind of drudgery" is fun, but you're a biochemist yourself and I'm pretty sure you feel the same way. The mere thought that we were putting inert colloids in at one end and getting something out at the other end that was in some strange way *living*—that was enough to take the boredom out of the job, if there'd been any.

Because we always felt that it was in our lab and the others like it that nonlife ended and life began. Sure, before us there was the immense job of protein synthesis and colloid preparation. Sure, after we were through there was the last step, the ultramicrosurgery of putting the nuclear wall together around the chromatin and embedding the result in a cell. (I always half envied your branch that job.) But in between there was our stage of the thing, which we thought to be the crucial one.

Certainly it was a tough enough stage. The long, careful reactions, with temperatures regulated down to a hundredth of a degree and reaction time to a tenth of a second; and then the final reactions, with everything enclosed in Gardner hoods, where you build up, bit by bit, the living nucleoplasm around the almost-living chromosomes. Hartwell hadn't lied when he said the work was carried out with care! That was quite a plant for two young squirts like us to be playing around with.

Just to put an edge on it, of course, there was always the possibility that you'd do everything right and still misfire. Anywhere along the line, Heisenberg's Uncertainty Principle could shove a radical out of place in those protein chains, no matter how careful you were. Then you'd get a weird thing: a gene mutating before it was even completed.

Or Heisenberg's Principle might pull you through even if your process had gone wrong!

We got curious after a while, Roy especially. Hartwell had told us a lot; one thing he hadn't told us was exactly *what we were making:* fish, flesh, or fowl, and we weren't geneticists enough to know ourselves. It would have been better, while we were working, to have had a mental picture of the frog or lizard or chicken that was to be our end product; instead, our mental picture was a composite of the three, and a rather disconcerting composite it made. I preferred to imagine a rabbit, or better yet, an Irish terrier puppy.

Hartwell not only hadn't offered to tell us, he didn't tell us when we asked him. "One of the lower chordates," he said; "the species name doesn't matter." That phrase "lower chordates" didn't ring quite true. There were enough chromosomes in our whatever-they-were's that they had to be something fairly far up the scale.

Roy immediately decided he was going to get the answer if he had to go through twenty books on genetics to do it. Looking back, I'm surprised I didn't have the same ambition. Maybe I was too interested in chess; I was on one of my periodic chess binges at the time. Anyhow, Roy got the genetics books and Roy did the digging.

It didn't take him any time at all. I remember that night well. He had brought home a stack of books from the library and was studying them at the desk in the corner. I was in the armchair with my portable chessboard, analyzing a game I'd lost in the last tournament. As the hours went by, I noticed Roy getting more and more restless; I expected him to come up with the answer any time, but apparently he was rechecking to make sure. About the time I'd found how I should have played to beat Fedruk, Roy got up, a little unsteadily.

"Dirk," he began, then stopped.

"You got it?"

"Dirk, I wonder if you realize just how few chordate species there are which have forty-eight chromosomes."

"Well, humans have, and I guess we're not so unique."

He didn't say anything.

"Hey, do you mean what I think you mean?" I jumped to my feet.

If he did, it was terrific news for me; I think I'd had the idea in the back of my mind all the time and never dared check it for fear I'd be proved wrong. Roy wasn't so happy about it. He said, "Yes, that's exactly what I mean. The species name Hartwell wouldn't tell us was *Homo sapiens*. We're making—robots."

That took a little time to digest. When I'd got it assimilated I came back, "What do you mean, robots? If we made a puppy that wagged its tail O.K., you'd be just as pleased as I would." (I was still stuck on that Irish terrier idea of mine.) That wouldn't give you the shudders. Why do you get so worried just because it's men we're making?"

"It's not right," he said.

"What?" Roy never having been religious or anything, that sounded strange.

"Well, I take that back, I guess, but—" His voice trailed away; then, more normally, "I don't know, Dirk. I just can't see it. Making humans—what would you call them if not robots?"

"I'd call them men, doggone it, if they turn out right. Of course if they don't turn out right—maybe I could see your point. If they don't turn out right. Killing a freak chicken and killing an experimental baby that didn't quite—succeed—would be two different things. Yeah."

"I hadn't thought of that."

"Then what the heck *were* you thinking of?"

"Aw, I don't know." He went back to the desk, slammed his books shut.

"What's bothering you, Roy?"

He didn't answer, just went into his bedroom and shut the door. He didn't come out again that night.

The next morning he was grim-faced, but you could see he was excited underneath. I knew he was planning something. Finally I wormed it out of him: he was going to take a look around Branch 39 to try and find some human embryos, as confirmation. Branch 39, as you know, is one of the ones that shuts up at night; they don't have to have technicians around twenty-four hours a day as 26 does. Roy's plan was to go up there just before closing time, hide, and get himself locked in overnight.

I asked him why the secrecy, why didn't he just ask to be shown around. "Hartwell doesn't want us to know," he said, "or he would have told us. I'll have to do it on the QT."

That made some sense, but—"Heck, Hartwell couldn't have expected to keep us permanently in the dark about what we were making, when all the dope you needed to figure it out was right there in the library. He must have wanted simply to let us do the figuring ourselves."

"Uh-uh. He knew we could puzzle it through if we wanted, but he wasn't going to help us. You think the lab wants to publicize what it's doing? No, Hartwell must be trying to keep as many people as possible from knowing; he hoped we'd stay uncurious. I'm not going to tell him we've guessed, and don't you."

I agreed reluctantly, but Roy's play-acting seemed to me like just that. Roy was deadly serious about it.

Later I got the story of that night. He'd gone up to 39 as planned, and hid in the big hall on the second floor; that was the place with the most embryos, and he thought he'd have the best chance there. Everything went O.K.; the assistant turned out the lights and locked up, and Roy stayed curled in his cabinet under a lab table. When the sounds had died down in the corridors outside, he came out and looked around.

He didn't know quite how to start. There were all sizes and shapes of gestators around. When he had taken out his flash and got a good look at one, he remained in as much of a quandary as before. It didn't seem to be anything but a bottle-shaped black container, about twenty centimeters on a side, in the middle of a mass of tubing, gauges, and levers. He could guess the bottle contained the embryo; he could guess the tubing kept up the flow of "body fluids" to and from the bottle; he could recognize some of the gauge markings and some of the auxiliary apparatus; and that was all. Not only was the embryo not exposed to view but he didn't see any way of exposing it. There was a label in a code he couldn't read. Nothing was any help.

The gestators were simple enough compared to the stuff he worked with, but he had a healthy respect for that sort of thing and didn't want to experiment to try to figure them out. If you meddled with a gestator in the wrong way, there was the chance that you'd be ruining a hundred people's work; and there would be many more wrong ways than right.

He made the circuit of the lab, stooping over one gestator after another, considering. After a while the moon rose and gave him a little more light. That was not what he needed.

A key turned in the lock.

Roy, hoping he hadn't been seen, ran back to his hiding place. He left the cabinet open far enough so he could see. A figure came in the door, turned to close it, and strode toward the center of the hall. As it passed through a patch of moonlight from one of the windows, Roy recognized the face: Hartwell.

He must have been working late in his office and come down for a look at his branch's products before leaving. Be that as it may, his presence cinched the thing: whatever embryos he looked at would be from our branch. Roy watched breathlessly while the other went from bench to bench, peering at the code labels. Finally he stopped before one, worked a lever, and peeked in through a viewer in the side, which Roy hadn't noticed. He looked quite a while, then turned and left.

I don't need to tell you that Roy didn't lose any time after Hartwell left in taking a look through that same viewer. And I don't need to tell you what he saw.

Reading back over this letter, I can see I'm stretching the story out, telling you things you already know and things that aren't really necessary. I know why I'm doing it, too— I'm reluctant to get to the end. But what I've got to tell you, I've got to tell you; I'll make the rest as short as I can.

Roy was pretty broken up about the whole thing, and he didn't get over it. I think it was the experience in the gestation lab that did it. If he'd just asked Hartwell for the truth, straight out, the thing would have stopped being fantastic and again become merely his business; but that melodrama up in Branch 39 kept him from looking at things with a clear eye. He went around in a half daze a good deal of the time, pondering, I suppose, some such philosophical problem as, When is a man not a man? It was all terrible; robots were going to take over the world, or something like that. And he insisted I still not tell Hartwell what he'd learned.

Then came the payoff. It was several weeks later, the day after Roy's twenty-sixth birthday. (The date was significant, as I learned later.) He told me before we left the lab that Hartwell had asked him to come up after work to talk with Koslicki.

I raised my eyebrows. "Koslicki, huh? The top man."

"Yes, Koslicki and Hartwell both."

He looked a little worried, so I ventured a crack. "Guess they've got a really rugged punishment for you, for trespassing that night. Death by drowning in ammonium sulphide, perhaps."

"I don't know why you can't take things seriously."

"Oh? What do you think they want to talk to you about?"

"No, I mean this whole business of—"

"Of making 'robots,' yeah. Roy, I do take it seriously, darn seriously. I think it's the biggest scientific project in the world right now. You take the kind of work we're doing, together with the production of new life forms like those experimental Coelenterates we saw, and you've got the groundwork for a new kind of eugenics that'll put our present systems in the shade. Now, we select from naturally occurring haploid germ cells to produce our new forms. In the future we'll *make* the new forms.

"We can make new strains of wheat, new species of sheep and cattle—new races of men! We won't have to wait for evolution any more. We won't have to content ourselves with giving evolution an occasional shove, either; we'll be striking out on our own. There's no limit to the possibilities. New, man-made men, stronger than we are, with minds twice as fast and accurate as ours—I take that plenty seriously."

"But they wouldn't be men."

This was beginning to get irritating. "They wouldn't be Homo sapiens, no," I answered. "Let's face it, Roy. If I were to get married, say, and have a kid that was a sharp mutation, a really radical mutation, and if he were to turn out to be a superman—that kid wouldn't be Homo sapiens, either. He wouldn't have the same germ plasm his parents had. Would he be human or wouldn't he?"

"He'd be human."

"Well? Where's the difference?"

"He wouldn't have come out of somebody's reagent bottles, that's the difference. He'd be—natural."

410

I could take only so much of that. Leaving Roy to go to his conference with Koslicki and Hartwell, I came home.

There I finished up the figuring on some notes I'd taken that day in the lab, then I turned the ceiling transparent and sat down with my visor. I'd just added a couple of new wires to my movie collection, so I ran them over—a couple of ballets, they were. No, none of the wires I've shown you. I've thrown out all the movies I saw *that* night.

I was sitting there having a good time with the "Pillar of Fire" when Roy came back. He made a little noise fumbling with the door. Then he slid it back and stood on the threshold without entering.

Switching off the visor, I glanced around. "What's the take, Jake?" I corned cheerfully. "Did Koslicki give you a good dressing-down? Or did he make you the new director?"

"... I'll play you a game of chess, Dirk."

This time I took a good look at him. His shoulders were stooped more than usual, and he looked around the room as if he didn't recognize it. Not good. "For crying out loud! What's the story?"

"Let's play chess."

"O.K.," I said. He came in and got out the men and the big board, but his hand shook so I had to set up his men for him. Then, "Go ahead," I told him.

"Oh, yeah, I've got white."

Pawn to king four, knight to king bishop three, pawn to king five—one of our standard openings. I pulled my knight back in the corner and brought out the other one; he pushed his pawns up in the center; I began getting ready to castle.

Then he put his queen on queen four. "You don't mean that," I said. "My knight takes you there."

"Oh, yeah, so he does," Roy said, pulling his queen back—to the wrong square. He was staring over my shoulder as if there was a ghost standing behind me. I looked; there wasn't. I replaced his queen.

Finally, still keeping up the stare, he began, "Dirk, you know Hartwell told me—"

"Yeah?" I said casually. I knew it had been something important. Roy hadn't been *this* bad the last few weeks. Whatever it was, he might as well get it off his chest.

Roy, however, seemed to have forgotten he'd spoken. His eyes returned intently to the board. His bishop went to king three—where I could not take it—and the game went on.

"You're going to lose that bishop's pawn, old man," I remarked after a while.

I think that was what triggered it. He said suddenly but evenly, "I'm one."

"I'm two," I said, apropos of nothing. My mind was still on the game.

"Dirk, *I'm one*," he insisted. He stood up, upsetting the board, and began to walk up and down. "Koslicki just told me. I'm one of the... Dirk, I wasn't born, I'm one of the robots, they put me together out of those goddamned chemicals in those goddamned white-labeled reagent bottles in that goddamned laboratory—"

"What?"

He stopped his pacing and began to laugh. "I'm just a Frankenstein. You can pull out your gun and sizzle me dead; it won't be murder, I'm just a robot." He was laughing all through this and he kept on laughing when he'd stopped.

I figured if he was going to blow up he might as well blow up good and proper. He'd make some noise, but old Graham would be the only one disturbed. "So," I said, "how did you feel going through the reaction vats over in 26? Did the microsurgery hurt when they put you together?" Roy laughed. He laughed harder. Then he screamed.

Deciding that enough was enough, I yelled at him. He screamed again.

"Shut up, Roy!" I shouted as sharply as I could. "You're as human as I am. You've lived with yourself twenty-six years; you ought to know whether you're human or not."

After the first couple of words he listened to me O.K., so I figured the hysterics were over. I tried to sound firm as I said, "Are you through with the foolishness now?"

Roy didn't pass out, he simply lay down on the floor. I sat down beside him and began to talk in a low voice. "You're just as good as anybody else; you've already proved that. It doesn't matter where you started, just what you are here and now. Here and now, you've got human genes, you've got human cells; you can marry a human girl and make human babies with her. So what if you did start out in a lab? The rest of us started out in the ooze on the bottom of some ocean. Which is better? It doesn't make any difference. You're just as good as anybody else." I said it over and over again, as calmly as I could. Don't know whether or not it was the right

412

thing to do, but I had to do something.

Once he raised his head to say, "Roy Wisner, huh? Is that me? Heck no, why didn't they call me Roy $W_{23}H$?...I wonder where they got the name Wisner anyway." He sank back and I took up my spiel again, doing my best to keep my voice level.

After several minutes of this he got up off the floor. "Thanks," he said in a fairly normal tone. "Thanks, Dirk. You're a real friend." He went toward the door, adding as he left, "You're human."

I just sat there. It wasn't till he'd been gone a couple of minutes that I put two and two together. Then I raced out of that room and to the stairs in nothing flat.

Too late. Graham's door was open downstairs, and the light from inside shone into the hall, across the twitching body of Roy Wisner.

Graham looked at me, terrified. "I thought it was all right," he stammered. "He asked me for some hydrocyanic. I knew he was a chemist; I thought it was all right."

Hydrocyanic acid kills fast. One look at the size of the container Roy had drained, and I saw there wasn't much we could do. We did it, all right, but it wasn't enough. He died while we were still forcing emetic down his throat.

That's about all, Ellen. You know now why I never spoke much to you about Roy Wisner. And you've probably guessed why I'm writing this.

Roy was one of the experiments that failed. He was no more unstable mentally than a great many normally born men; still, a failure, though nobody knew it until he was twenty-six years old. The human organism is a very complex thing, and hard to duplicate. When you try to duplicate it you're very likely to fail, sometimes in obvious ways and sometimes in ways that don't become apparent till long afterward.

I may turn out to be a failure, too.

You see, I'm twenty-six now, and Koslicki and Hartwell have told me. *I* wasn't born, either. I was made. I am, if you like, a robot.

I had to tell you that, didn't I, Ellen? Before I asked you to marry me.

Dirk

Born in England and now a Canadian citizen, Patricia Nurse is a recent addition to the ranks of professional science-fiction writers. In fact, this story, from the July–August 1978 issue of Isaac Asimov's Science Fiction Magazine, *is her first professional sale.*

This is an "inside sf" story, a form that is difficult to do well, and even more difficult to sell, because the writer cannot assume too much information on the part of the reader. However, in this case...

ONE REJECTION TOO MANY

By Patricia Nurse

Dear Dr. Asimov:

Imagine my delight when I spotted your new science-fiction magazine on the newsstands. I have been a fan of yours for many, many years and I naturally wasted no time in buying a copy. I wish you every success in this new venture.

In your second issue I read with interest your plea for stories from new authors. While no writer myself, I have had a time traveler living with me for the past two weeks (he materialized in the bathtub without clothes or money, so I felt obliged to offer him shelter), and he has written a story of life on earth as it will be in the year 5000.

Before he leaves this time frame, it would give him great pleasure to see his story in print—I hope you will feel able to make this wish come true.

Yours sincerely,
NANCY MORRISON (Miss)

Patricia Nurse

Dear Miss Morrison:

Thank you for your kind letter and good wishes.

It is always refreshing to hear from a new author. You have included some most imaginative material in your story; however, it is a little short on plot and human interest—perhaps you could rewrite it with this thought in mind.

Yours sincerely,
ISAAC ASIMOV

Dear Dr. Asimov:

I was sorry that you were unable to print the story I sent you. Vahl (the time traveler who wrote it) was quite hurt as he tells me he is an author of some note in his own time. He has, however, rewritten the story and this time has included plenty of plot and some rather interesting mating rituals which he has borrowed from the year 3000. In his own time (the year 5015) sex is no longer practiced, so you can see that it is perfectly respectable having him in my house. I do wish, though, that he could adapt himself to our custom of wearing clothes—my neighbors are starting to talk!

Anything that you can do to expedite the publishing of Vahl's story would be most appreciated, so that he will feel free to return to his own time.

Yours sincerely,
NANCY MORRISON (Miss)

Dear Miss Morrison:

Thank you for your rewritten short story.

I don't want to discourage you but I'm afraid you followed my suggestions with a little too much enthusiasm—however, I can understand that having an imaginary nude visitor from another time is a rather heady experience. I'm afraid that your story now rather resembles a far-future episode of *Mary Hartman, Mary Hartman* or *Soap*.

Could you tone it down a bit and omit the more bizarre sex rituals of the year 3000—we must remember that *Isaac Asimov's Science Fiction Magazine* is intended to be a family publication.

Perhaps a little humor would improve the tale too.

Yours sincerely,
ISAAC ASIMOV

One Rejection Too Many

Dear Dr. Asimov:

Vahl was extremely offended by your second rejection—he said he has never received a rejection slip before, and your referring to him as "imaginary" didn't help matters at all. I'm afraid he rather lost his temper and stormed out into the garden—it was at this unfortunate moment that the vicar happened to pass by.

Anyway, I managed to get Vahl calmed down and he has rewritten the story and added plenty of humor. I'm afraid my subsequent meeting with the vicar was not blessed with such success! I'm quite sure Vahl would not understand another rejection.

Yours truly,
NANCY MORRISON (Miss)

Dear Miss Morrison:

I really admire your persistence in rewriting your story yet another time. Please don't give up hope—you can became a fairly competent writer in time, I feel sure.

I'm afraid the humor you added was not the kind of thing I had in mind at all—you're not collaborating with Henny Youngman by any chance are you? I really had a more sophisticated type of humor in mind.

Yours truly,
ISAAC ASIMOV

P.S. Have you considered reading your story, as it is, on *The Gong Show*?

Dear Dr. Asimov:

It really was very distressing to receive the return of my manuscript once again—Vahl was quite speechless with anger.

It was only with the greatest difficulty that I prevailed upon him to refine the humor you found so distasteful, and I am submitting his latest rewrite herewith.

In his disappointment, Vahl has decided to return to his own time right away. I shall be sorry to see him leave as I was getting very fond of him—a pity he wasn't from the year 3000 though. Still, he wouldn't have made a very satisfactory husband; I'd have never known where (or when) he was. It rather looks as though my plans to marry the vicar have suffered a severe setback too. Are you married, Dr. Asimov?

I must close this letter now as I have to say goodbye to Vahl. He says he has just finished making some long overdue improvements to our time frame as a parting gift—isn't that kind of him?

Yours sincerely,
NANCY MORRISON (Miss)

Dear Miss Morrison:

I am very confused by your letter. Who is Isaac Asimov? I have checked with several publishers and none of them has heard of *Isaac Asimov's Science Fiction Magazine,* although the address on the envelope was correct for *this* magazine.

However, I was very impressed with your story and will be pleased to accept it for our next issue. Seldom do we receive a story combining such virtues as a well-conceived plot, plenty of human interest, and a delightfully subtle brand of humor.

Yours truly,
GEORGE H. SCITHERS,
Editor,
Arthur C. Clarke's Science Fiction Magazine

Ray Russell (1924–   ) is an important and relatively unknown figure in the history of science fiction. Long associated
with Playboy, he was responsible (along with one or two others) for opening that important market to science-fiction writers, and the magazine has now published many notable stories
in the field. He was also the uncredited editor of the excellent
Playboy Book of Fantasy and Science Fiction (1966) and its
many successor volumes. As a writer, he has published in
many genres and markets, although many of his best fantasies
and sf stories can be found in Sardonicus and Other Stories
(1961).
   "Space Opera" (Playboy, December 1961) is a terrific story.
We only wish that The Planetary Evening Post had seen fit
to publish it.

SPACE OPERA

By Ray Russell

The Editor
The Planetary Evening Post
Level 78
Building K-6 (Old Section)
New York, New York (Zip Code: AAB/00142534786c)

Dear Sir:
   Your letter was most appreciated, but I am very sorry you
did not like "Vixen of Venus." Too melodramatic, you say,
and today's readers will have nothing to do with melodrama.

But, my dear sir, life itself is flagrantly melodramatic! The lady I described in "Vixen of Venus" is an almost literal transcription of an actual lady I encountered there in my travels. However, that is water under the bridge, as you "Earthworms" say (ha-ha, no offense).

My purpose in writing to you again is to sketch briefly an article I would like to do for you. It is completely factual, though I fear it may strike you as extravagant. A deep-dyed villain figures prominently in the piece, also a fair maiden in distress, not to mention a righteous, retribution-dealing father right out of the admirable Victor Hugo of your own culture. And, yes, I'm afraid there will even be a tricky twist ending.

If you have read this far, perhaps you will read further. The proposed article, which we might call "The Star of Orim," concerns a series of fascinating events that occurred in my own galaxy, 75/890 (I trust you have no editorial taboo against foreign settings). The chronicle begins on the planet Orim, and our antagonist, the Sargian warlord Zoonbarolar-rio Feng, accompanied by a beautiful young lady who hates him (it would be well to establish this immediately), is discovered in a magnificent Orimese palace. To point up their relationship, we might have them leaving a bedroom together. They make an oddly contrasted pair as they walk through the high-ceilinged, luxurious rooms of the palace. Feng is an enormous man—massive and powerful—with thick black hair and beard; his eyes are like an eagle's, and his nose is a formidable promontory that looks impressive on the coins that bear his likeness. In his black tunic, red robe and hip-high boots of shining xhulq, he is indeed an imposing figure. The girl is his complete opposite. She is small and slight, with fair skin and with hair red-gold as a dying sun (I'm sorry, but there *is* hair like that, you know, especially among the Orimese). Her young body is covered only by the most gauzelike pale rosy silk, cut in a pattern that leaves much of her smooth skin exposed. Her small, bare feet whisper on the marble floor.

Feng is in a good mood. As they walk, he chatters amiably in his rumbling basso. "Conquering your planet has been rich in rewards. Not only do I capture the most gifted scientist in the galaxy, but I find that he has an extremely beautiful daughter. A double prize!" This speech is reconstructed, and if the exposition is too crude for you, I can smooth it over in the finish.

As they approach the laboratory, they are saluted by two slender officers in the skintight black uniform of Feng's personal guard. One of them opens the door. Feng and the girl enter a huge room of glass and metal where a small forge glows and platoons of test tubes and retorts bubble and hiss. At the end of a long aisle, a gray-haired man sits on a high stool and looks at a gleaming metal star in his hand.

Feng walks up to him, and the girl follows. The black-bearded conqueror greets the scientist with condescending joviality. "Good evening, Torak," he booms. "What have you there?"

The old man ignores Feng, looks past him at the girl. "Vola," he whispers gently. "Vola, my child."

The girl's voice is faint and husky. "You look tired, Father. You work too hard."

"You, my dear—how are you?"

She lowers her eyes. "I'm all right. Don't worry about me."

Feng laughs. "That's right. Don't worry about her. She's in good hands!"

Does Torak lose your sympathy, dear sir, because he allows his daughter's virgin virtue to be rent asunder by this brute, impaled on the insatiable saber of his lechery? You must, then, be made aware that prior to her ravishment, Torak had watched, with taped-open eyes, an unedited ten-hour educational film, in living color, three dimensions and deafening multiphonic sound, of the legendary Six Hundred Sacred Tortures of Sarg, the featured roles played not by professional actresses but, at the tops of their voices, by the late-lamented lovely, young, naked, pink virgin daughters of other scientists of other planets. Do you continue to wonder why he permits Feng to plunder his daughter's beautiful body and his own brilliant mind?

Feng gets straight to business. "Now, then, Torak," he bellows, "I demand an answer! How soon will the project be finished?"

"It is finished, my lord," Torak answers in a lifeless tone and holds up the flat piece of metal cut in the form of a four-pointed star.

"This—" asks Feng, "this is it? The new metal?"

"The new metal. The invincible metal. Yes, this is it."

Feng chuckles. "I see you've made it into the shape of the

Star of Orim, the symbol of your people. A very clever comment, Torak—but your rebel's propaganda is wasted on me, I fear. Here, let me have that." He snatches the metal star from Torak's hand. "I shall notify my entire staff to assemble here immediately. The tests will begin at once."

"Tests?"

"Of course," Feng smiles. "You didn't think I would take your word for it, did you? Why, for all I know, this shiny new stuff of yours might collapse like tinfoil in a baby's fist. Nothing would please you more, would it?" He laughs again. "No, my friend, I am not such a fool. I have not conquered almost the entire galaxy to be finally outwitted by a rebel scientist. This metal shall be thoroughly tested, I assure you. And my own scientists sháll conduct the tests." Feng's eyes grow suddenly sharper. "If it is all you claim it to be, then the last stronghold in the galaxy shall yield before me—the planet Klor!"

Now, somewhere in through here, we will have to sandwich the information that, for years, Feng had been looking forward to the day when the whole galaxy would be his. Slowly, planet by planet, he saw his dream coming true, but always the planet Klor resisted his mighty navies. Perhaps in a footnote we can remind your readers that Klor is a world almost completely underwater; most of its people are fishlike depth creatures. And Feng's engineers had despaired of building amphibious ships versatile enough to fling themselves from the base planet, Sarg, across the black emptiness of outer space and down into the watery depths of Klor. Such ships would have had to be made of metal as light as spaceship alloy and yet as pressure-resistant as a bathysphere. Moreover, it would have had to be resistant to heat and cold and radiation. But back to our scene in the laboratory:

The scarlet-robed emperor grasps the metal star and repeats, "Yes, the tests will begin at once." He turns and strides out of the room.

When the door clangs shut, Vola buries her face in her father's chest and breaks into uncontrollable weeping. "Oh, Father! It's been so horrible! That man is a beast—a filthy beast!"

Torak's hands clench as a father's indignation rises in him. "Vola, be brave. We must both be brave."

As you pointed out in regard to "Vixen of Venus," dialogue is not my strong point. I realize this and am perfectly willing to do the piece in straight reportorial form, should you so desire. However, since I have begun my outline in this style, I shall continue so:

Sparks fly in the darkened laboratory, as a group of dark-goggled men recoil from terrific heat. A powerful ray is bombarding the small piece of star-shaped metal. "See, my lord!" says one of the men. "The upper side of the metal is white-hot, while the underside—"

"Yes?" hisses Feng.

"The underside is cool to the touch! Incredible! Your captive scientist has achieved perfect insulation." He turns off the ray, and they all remove their goggles. "That concludes the series of tests, my lord. This piece of metal was subjected to powerful explosives, searing acids, atomic radiation, great pressure, and now—withering heat. Nothing affects it! It is completely impervious."

Feng smiles. He turns to Torak. "My congratulations. You have not failed me. You shall have an honored place in the scientific hierarchy of my empire." Abruptly, he turns to his chief engineer. "Great quantities of this metal must be produced and made into the spaceships you have designed. You will work with Torak. I shall expect you to begin tomorrow. And remember, gentlemen, the conquest of Klor means the conquest of the galaxy!" He walks away as the scientists and generals bow. At the door, he turns to a figure in the shadows. "Come, Vola," he says. (We can play down this sex element if you wish.)

During the days that follow, Torak forces himself to be oblivious to his daughter's tears. While she languishes in the arms of Feng, submitting silently to the legendary Seven Hundred Sacred Perversions of Sarg, the old scientist supervises at foundries where ton after ton of the molten new metal is poured from monstrous blast furnaces. Captive slave-workers from the far reaches of the galaxy labor day and night without sleep until they drop from exhaustion and are flogged into consciousness again. When they die, they are replaced by others. And often at Torak's side is the exultant Feng, who slaps him on the back and praises him.

As soon as the sheets of metal roll from the foundries, they are rushed to the shipyards, where already the armada of amphibious destroyers is growing. Feng himself supervises the construction of the largest of these, his flagship. His escutcheon, the flaming sword of Sarg, is deeply etched on its gleaming prow; rich draperies and costly furniture—the loot of a thousand plundered worlds—are carried aboard to embellish his cabin. It is only a matter of months (incidentally, I am using Earth time throughout) before the fleet is finished. Poised and sparkling in the sun, the ships stand ready for embarkation.

Feng and his highest officers stand on a great platform repeating a ritual that has taken place before the conquest of each new planet. Martial music blares from a phalanx of glittering horns. The people of Orim cheer—with Sargian guns at their backs—as Feng, resplendent in his battle armor made completely of Torak's new metal, declaims his customary ritual speech. (I have a copy of this for verification.) His big, rough voice thunders over the loudspeakers in phrases heavy with emotionalism and light on logic. Often "the glories of Sarg" and the greatness of "our sacred galactic empire" are spoken of, but no attempt is made to define or examine these terms. Feng emphasizes the importance of conquering Klor, the last remaining planet in the galaxy which still struggles in "a barbaric darkness unilluminated by Sargian glory." He tells why he has ordered not only his generals but also his eldest statesmen and savants to accompany him in his flagship on this mission: "It is fitting that the chiefs of the Sargian Empire be present at the momentous conquest of the last planet." The speech ends with the mighty exclamation, "On to Klor!" and the trumpets drown the unenthusiastic applause.

On the gangplank of his flagship, Feng pauses and turns to Torak. "Upon my return, you shall be decorated for your services to Sarg. And you, Vola"—he smiles at the unresponsive girl—"be prepared for a night of revelry on my return. Missions of conquest never fail to excite my blood, and although the water-dwelling females of Klor may turn out to be lovely"—he winks knowingly at his generals—"I fear that, as proper entertainers to an emperor, mermaids may have certain...disadvantages, eh?" He laughs at his joke (too coarse for your readership?) and enters the flagship, followed by his generals and key statesmen.

Soon there is a terrific roar and a searing blast of rocket fire as the fleet shoots upward and dwindles to a swarm of tiny specks in the clear blue sky of Orim.

During the months of the voyage, the black wine of Sarg flows freely in the imperial flagship. Feng toasts his empire, his generals and himself. He toasts each planet, each star, each comet they pass. He toasts Torak, he toasts Vola, and he toasts the nearly forgotten women of his youth. He sings ribald Sargian ballads, and he swears fantastic oaths. All this can easily be expanded into several pages.

At length, the armada approaches Klor. As his flagship hovers above the flooded planet, Feng draws his jeweled ceremonial sword and points dramatically to the objective. His voice roars through the intercoms of every ship:

"Attack!"

Down they plunge, the flagship leading. Cleanly, Feng's ship cuts the surface of the water and his fleet follows, creating a series of immense splashes and vast, ever-widening ripples.

Through the transparent dome of his ship, Feng marvels at the exotic weeds and pouting giant fishes of Klor. Triumph sings in his veins.

Then, suddenly, the cries of startled men reach his ears. He turns, and his eagle's eyes bulge with shock....

If we do this as a serial, what better place for a break? But that is up to you, of course. And now let me quickly limn the final scene, which takes place back on Orim:

Torak drops a four-pointed metal star into a glass. It floats slowly to the bottom. He turns to his daughter, who is gazing pensively out of the laboratory window. Tenderly, he asks, "Is anything troubling you, my dear?"

There are tears in her eyes. "I was thinking of the people of Klor, that's all."

Torak smiles slightly—for the first time in many, many months. "I wouldn't spend my tears on them, if I were you. In fact, I see no reason for weeping at all."

"You don't? Father, how can you say that?"

"Feng," says Torak grimly, "will never molest you again."

"What do you mean?"

"And never again will he subjugate an entire galaxy. By this time, the armada should have reached Klor." Torak verifies this by a glance of his calendar. "Feng is dead."

Vola fears for her father's sanity. She is silent as he continues, "Dead. Floating in the waters of Klor, with all his officers, his ministers and his navy."

He looks up and sees the fear in her face. "No, my dear, I'm not mad. You see, I created a very wonderful metal. A metal both light and strong, resistant to heat and cold and pressure and radiation. A miraculous metal. And Feng was smart. He tested it thoroughly. Yes, he put my metal through every possible test—except one. One so simple, so basic that it never occurred to him. And so he built his fleet and plunged it into the seas of Klor without knowing...."

Torak turns to regard the glass from which the metal star of Orim has vanished. "Without knowing," he says, "that this rather remarkable metal *dissolves*—in water."

Now, *there,* sir, even you must admit, is a natural! And true—every word. But that is not all—in fact, the greatest revelation is yet to come.

For suppose we say—or at least hint—that shrewd Feng, the galaxy killer, the scourge of 75/890, the man who never trusted anybody in his life, took the characteristic, routine precaution of wearing, under his ceremonial armor of Torak metal, a conventional depth suit (not because he suspected anything specific, but because suspicion was his natural state of mind), that Feng, in other words, *survived the disaster!*

Perhaps we may even use a title like "Feng Is Still Alive!" or "Feng Is Still Alive?"—a time-tested attention getter. We can imply that the indestructible Zoonbarolarrio Feng, after the demolition of his navy, made his relentless and lonely way to one of Klor's few shreds of dry land—say, the south polar region of Fozkep—where even now he plots new conquests, like your own Napoleon of yore at Elba. You will say, perhaps, that nobody will believe such an assertion, and I would be inclined to agree with you, but what does that matter so long as they buy your magazine? And speaking of buying brings me to the touchy but unavoidable question of payment. I am in most desperate need of large sums and would expect your highest rates, on acceptance, should this article be commissioned for your pages. So *please* let me hear from you by return warpmail, since I urgently require every bit of ready cash I can muster.

Yours sincerely,
Z. GNEF
P.O. Box 9,000,053
75/890

Born in 1930, William Sambrot is a long-time professional writer who sold consistently to the "slicks" (The Saturday Evening Post, Collier's, etc.). Although his science-fiction and fantasy output has been relatively small, there are enough stories for an excellent collection, Island of Fear and Other Science Fiction Stories *(1963). Perhaps his finest story in the field is "Night of the Leopard" (1967).*

"The Invasion of the Terrible Titans" is from the October 1959 issue of Cosmopolitan.

THE INVASION OF THE TERRIBLE TITANS

By William Sambrot

Mr. George Papadoukalis
Ocean College Alumni Association
Ocean City, California

DEAR MR. PAPADOUKALIS:

Herewith, written in some haste, is my report on Pacific Underwater College's "Terrible Titans," the incredible group of athletes which has flattened every rival (including yourself) in the coast league.

I regret you found it necessary to insist upon this report before taking up the matter of the additional funds I requested by wire last night. The results of my efforts in your and the alumni's behalf will speak for themselves next season. You have but to read the following to realize that much more than mere money is at stake. I know you will be more than generous.

In the event you still have some doubts after reading this,

426

may I ask you to review the score of the last game O.C. played with Pacific: 112 to 0, was it not? Bear with me.

As a starter, I attempted to get some fingerprints of Sam Bama, Pacific's star, and the first of the Terrible Titans to enroll there. You will be as surprised as I to discover the man has no fingerprints. I mean to say, his fingers are blank, smooth expanses of skin. Furthermore, when I casually handed him my solid silver (plated) cigarette case (the one our grateful alumni gave me several seasons ago when I uncovered the flagrant case of proselytism going on at B.U.), he fumbled with it and acted generally like someone who's never even seen a cigarette, let alone a solid silver (plated) case. But, as I say, no fingerprints. Keep this in mind.

Bama, I might add in passing, speaks rather cultured English with a strong Oxford accent. His eyes are somewhat pinkish and his hair quite white. Albino characteristics.

However, I've never before met an albino somewhat over seven feet tall, lightning fast and weighing three hundred pounds. He has no neck to speak of, massive sloping shoulders, and arms surely no thicker than my thighs. Also, he has a pronounced body odor—something like a musk ox. (They have one at the zoo, and for purposes of comparison I went around there. Oddly enough, after some hours of sniffing, I discovered the closest similar odor came not from the musk ox, but from a yak. The significance of this failed to dawn upon me until just last night.)

Pacific's phenomenal athletic record this season can be laid at the door of one man—Professor Harold Crimshaw. You may well ask what a professor of physics has to do with your being unmercifully trounced in the bowl last New Year's, but the facts, as uncovered by me, are these:

Professor Crimshaw, a bachelor in his late forties, is a specialist on cosmic-ray research. He often spends his spare time and what funds he can drum up trudging about the higher mountains of the globe, capturing cosmic rays and measuring their intensity. As you might guess, very few people are interested enough in captured cosmic rays to finance expeditions, so up until the winter before last Professor Crimshaw operated on a strictly low budget.

I say up until the winter before last, because after that, things suddenly changed. He arrived back on the campus shortly after the holidays, accompanied by a small dark man with a beard and a huge box, punched with air holes, which must have weighed well over three hundred pounds.

Also, the box (as I was able to ascertain myself) gave off a powerful odor. In fact investigation disclosed that Professor Moriarty of biology inquired if perhaps Professor Crimshaw hadn't brought back a live musk ox. The question remained unanswered. The small bearded man was equally inscrutable.

Shortly after that, Moriarty, Dr. Evans (president of P.U.) and Dr. Smythe-Smythe, head of the language department, on loan from Oxford University, were all seen going into Professor Crimshaw's bachelor quarters. I have since managed to gain entry by a ruse and can testify that even to this day a strong odor, as of a penned-up musk ox or yak, still permeates the atmosphere.

By careful (and guarded, of course) inquiry I have learned that shortly thereafter one Oscar Grossgudt, a wholesale butcher and one of the few alumni of P.U. worth a line in Dun & Bradstreet, was seen lingering about Crimshaw's quarters. Subsequently, one of his delivery trucks made daily deliveries to Crimshaw's home; but whatever was delivered was concealed beneath a canvas wrapper. Suffice it to say, however, that discreet queries disclosed the fact that quantities of bones were carted away daily—say, about that left over from half a haunch of well-gnawed beef.

George Sneedely, P.U.'s football and wrestling coach, along with his assistant, Daniel McGurk (known to you as "Goon" McGurk), were seen entering and leaving Crimshaw's quarters frequently. On one occasion McGurk was seen noticeably limping and holding his shoulder, although Sneedely seemed in the best of spirits. In fact he was smiling, something he hasn't done since '45, the year Pacific won one and tied one (although losing twelve).

It was less than a month afterward that Sam Bama was enrolled officially at P.U. as Crimshaw's protégé. He was (and is) amiable, quick-witted, with an I.Q. of 128. (Rorschach not available.) Well-liked by all, including the girls, most of whom preferred not to date him.

In his first football game, as the alumni of State well know, he scored every time he was given the ball, which, mercifully, was only seventeen times. Sneedely is a kind-hearted chap, retiring Bama to the bench only after he was

William Sambrot

informed during the half that two of the opponent defenders suffered severe skull fractures, incurred as Bama stepped on their heads. Fortunately he was not wearing shoes.

After the game Bama gladly granted press interviews, winning the scribes' hearts with his easy banter. He skillfully parried all queries as to his prep school, although hints were dropped by Sneedely that Bama was a transferee from "overseas."

It was directly after this first game that Crimshaw's great expedition to measure cosmic rays was announced. He was given special leave of absence. Where he was going was left unmentioned, however. Clippings enclosed.

I can tell you that after considerable checking I was able to learn that money for this expedition (a large sum in fact—please note) had been advanced by a small clique of P.U. alumni, consisting in the main of Oscar Grossgudt and one Pete DeLassio, a gentleman connected with a gambling syndicate, the same syndicate which took all bets in advance on the entire schedule of P.U. and which really cleaned up, as doubtless you know.

The expedition was organized with great secrecy, but I have since learned that the entire staff of the manual arts department worked overtime building ten stout packing cases, complete with air holes.

The expedition returned last summer, slipping quietly into town late one evening. However, there were frequent complaints that evening by the citizenry that howls and roars were coming from the direction of the freight yards. A sound, as one local put it, exactly like feeding time at the zoo.

And last autumn, of course, P.U. fielded their incredible "Terrible Titans" which remained unscored upon—but why am I telling you this? You know what they did to the rest of the league.

To a man, the Terrible Titans all look amazingly alike—each a little over seven feet tall, each weighing well over three hundred pounds. They are all albinos, I can say positively, even though (as I can prove) they wear colored contact lenses. Also, in order to further conceal their identical appearance, each has his hair dyed a different shade, and some even have their skin darkened. They use prodigious quantities of deodorants and are quite popular with the girls.

Earlier I mentioned that Professor Crimshaw, winter before last, had returned with a small dark man with a beard and a huge box. This little man vanished about the time of the great expedition and just as mysteriously reappeared when the expedition returned.

By great good luck I ran across the little dark man only last night. He was in a pub, unnoticed, morose, drinking whiskey sours and obviously disliking them. I fell into deep conversation with him, and what he had to say was startling indeed; no amount of whiskey sours could account for it. It has to be true. It all fits.

He is a Sherpa: one of those breed of slight, tough men who make a business of climbing the high mountains of the Himalayas. Between whiskey sours he sobbed out his desire to go back; he says he is one of the few men alive who knows the haunts of the Yeti—the abominable snow men, so called; those giant, strangely manlike creatures of myth (or mystery?) who roam the inaccessible peaks. He speaks their language, he says. They are shy, nimble creatures but extremely intelligent withal. Loyal to a fault, they would follow him anywhere, he assures me.

Many were the times, he says, they spent bounding about the great peaks, chasing yaks for food and fun. But, alas, all too humanlike, once they tasted the dubious joys of civilization, they forgot the old ways. They became decadent; they looked upon him, their old friend, as old-fashioned—in a word, a cornball (an epithet much favored at P.U. this season).

He longed to go back, he sobbed. Back to his yaks and untutored Yeti.

And so we're going back, Mr. Papadoukalis. Fortunately, I have my credit card. I'm writing this from San Francisco International Airport. We expect to reach Katmandu, India, on or about the twelfth of the month.

Please wire sufficient funds to outfit a good-sized expedition to reach an altitude of approximately twenty-six thousand feet. Also, make sure you include enough to cover the cost of at least eleven good-sized packing cases, strong enough to hold over three hundred pounds each.

Mum's the word, and come next season we'll have a surprise for Pacific, if you follow me, and I'm sure you do.

Yours in haste,
J. PONDER
Prop., Ponder Detective Agency

Judith Merril (1923–   ) was (she has not produced much fiction in recent years) a major figure in science fiction, both as a writer and as one of the leading anthologists in the field. Her anthology England Swings SF *(1968) was a major event in the history of the "New Wave" in science fiction, and she produced twelve highly regarded volumes of "Best of the Year" stories from 1956 to 1967.*

"That Only a Mother" (Astounding Science Fiction, June 1948) is a deservedly famous story in science fiction, and one of the truly great first stories of all time.

THAT ONLY A MOTHER

By Judith Merril

Margaret reached over to the other side of the bed where Hank should have been. Her hand patted the empty pillow, and then she came altogether awake, wondering that the old habit should remain after so many months. She tried to curl up, cat-style, to hoard her own warmth, found she couldn't do it any more, and climbed out of bed with a pleased awareness of her increasingly clumsy bulkiness.

Morning motions were automatic. On the way through the kitchenette, she pressed the button that would start breakfast cooking—the doctor had said to eat as much breakfast as she could—and tore the paper out of the facsimile machine. She folded the long sheet carefully to the "National News" section and propped it on the bathroom shelf to scan while she brushed her teeth.

No accidents. No direct hits. At least none that had been officially released for publication. *Now, Maggie, don't get started on that. No accidents. No hits. Take the nice newspaper's word for it.*

The three clear chimes from the kitchen announced that breakfast was ready. She set a bright napkin and cheerful colored dishes on the table in a futile attempt to appeal to a faulty morning appetite. Then, when there was nothing more to prepare, she went for the mail, allowing herself the full pleasure of prolonged anticipation, because today there would *surely* be a letter.

There was. There were. Two bills and a worried note from her mother: "Darling. Why didn't you write and tell me sooner? I'm thrilled, of course, but, well, one hates to mention these things, but are you *certain* the doctor was right? Hank's been around all that uranium or thorium or whatever it is all these years, and I know you say he's a designer, not a technician, and he doesn't get near anything that might be dangerous, but you know he used to, back at Oak Ridge. Don't you think... well, of course, I'm just being a foolish old woman, and I don't want you to get upset. You know much more about it than I do, and I'm sure your doctor was right. He *should* know..."

Margaret made a face over the excellent coffee, and caught herself refolding the paper to the medical news.

Stop it, Maggie, stop it! The radiologist said Hank's job couldn't have exposed him. And the bombed area we drove past...No, no. Stop it, now! Read the social notes or the recipes, Maggie girl.

A well-known geneticist, in the medical news, said that it was possible to tell with absolute certainty, at five months, whether the child would be normal, or at least whether the mutation was likely to produce anything freakish. The worst cases, at any rate, could be prevented. Minor mutations, of course, displacements in facial features or changes in brain structure, could not be detected. And there had been some cases recently, of normal embryos with atrophied limbs that did not develop beyond the seventh or eighth month. But, the doctor concluded cheerfully, the *worst* cases could now be predicted and prevented.

"Predicted and prevented." We predicted it, didn't we? Hank and the others, they predicted it. But we didn't prevent it. We could have stopped it in '46 and '47. Now...

Margaret decided against the breakfast. Coffee had been enough for her in the morning for ten years; it would have to do for today. She buttoned herself into interminable folds of material that, the salesgirl had assured her, was the *only* comfortable thing to wear during the last few months. With a surge of pure pleasure, the letter and newspaper forgotten, she realized she was on the next to the last button. It wouldn't be long now.

The city in the early morning had always been a special kind of excitement for her. Last night it had rained, and the sidewalks were still damp-gray instead of dusty. The air smelled the fresher, to a city-bred woman, for the occasional pungency of acrid factory smoke. She walked the six blocks to work, watching the lights go out in the all-night hamburger joints, where the plate-glass walls were already catching the sun, and the lights go on in the dim interiors of cigar stores and drycleaning establishments.

The office was in a new Government building. In the rolovator, on the way up, she felt, as always, like a frankfurter roll in the ascending half of an old-style rotary toasting machine. She abandoned the air-foam cushioning gratefully at the fourteenth floor, and settled down behind her desk, at the rear of a long row of identical desks.

Each morning the pile of papers that greeted her was a little higher. These were, as everyone knew, the decisive months. The war might be won or lost on these calculations as well as any others. The manpower office had switched her here when her old expediter's job got to be too strenuous. The computer was easy to operate, and the work was absorbing, if not as exciting as the old job. But you didn't just stop working these days. Everyone who could do anything at all was needed.

And—she remembered the interview with the psychologist—*I'm probably the unstable type. Wonder what sort of neurosis I'd get sitting home reading that sensational paper...*

She plunged into the work without pursuing the thought.

February 18.

Hank darling,

Just a note—from the hospital, no less. I had a dizzy spell at work, and the doctor took it to heart. Blessed if I know what I'll do with myself lying in bed for weeks, just waiting—

but Dr. Boyer seems to think it may not be so long.

There are too many newspapers around here. More infanticides all the time, and they can't seem to get a jury to convict any of them. It's the fathers who do it. Lucky thing you're not around, in case—

Oh, darling, that wasn't a very *funny* joke, was it? Write as often as you can, will you? I have too much time to think. But there really isn't anything wrong, and nothing to worry about.

Write often, and remember I love you.

Maggie.

SPECIAL SERVICE TELEGRAM

FEBRUARY 21, 1953

22:04 LK37G

FROM: TECH. LIEUT. H. MARVELL

  X47–016 GCNY
  TO: MRS. H. MARVELL
  WOMEN'S HOSPITAL
  NEW YORK CITY

HAD DOCTOR'S GRAM STOP WILL ARRIVE FOUR OH TEN STOP SHORT LEAVE STOP YOU DID IT MAGGIE STOP LOVE HANK

February 25.

Hank dear,

So you didn't see the baby either? You'd think a place this size would at least have visiplates on the incubators, so the fathers could get a look, even if the poor benighted mommas can't. They tell me I won't see her for another week, or maybe more—but of course, mother always warned me if I didn't slow my pace, I'd probably even have my babies too fast. Why must she *always* be right?

Did you meet that battle-ax of a nurse they put on here? I imagine they save her for people who've already had theirs, and don't let her get too near the prospectives—but a woman like that simply shouldn't be allowed in a maternity ward. She's obsessed with mutations, can't seem to talk about anything else. Oh, well, *ours* is all right, even if it was in an unholy hurry.

434

I'm tired. They warned me not to sit up so soon, but I *had* to write you. All my love, darling,

Maggie.

February 29.

Darling,

I finally got to see her! It's all true, what they say about new babies and the face that only a mother could love—but it's all there, darling, eyes, ears, and noses—no, only one!— all in the right places. We're so *lucky,* Hank.

I'm afraid I've been a rambunctious patient. I kept telling that hatchet-faced female with the mutation mania that I wanted to *see* the baby. Finally the doctor came in to "explain" everything to me, and talking a lot of nonsense, most of which I'm sure no one could have understood, any more than I did. The only thing I got out of it was that she didn't actually. *have* to stay in the incubator; they just thought it was "wiser."

I think I got a little hysterical at that point. Guess I was more worried than I was willing to admit, but I threw a small fit about it. The whole business wound up with one of those hushed medical conferences outside the door, and finally the Woman in White said: "Well, we might as well. Maybe it'll work out better that way."

I'd heard about the way doctors and nurses in these places develop a God complex, and believe me it is as true figuratively as it is literally that a mother hasn't got a leg to stand on around here.

I *am* awfully weak, still. I'll write again soon. Love,

Maggie.

March 8.

Dearest Hank,

Well, the nurse was wrong if she told you that. She's an idiot anyhow. It's a girl. It's easier to tell with babies than with cats, and *I know.* How about Henrietta?

I'm home again, and busier than a betatron. They got *everything* mixed up at the hospital, and I had to teach myself how to bathe her and do just about everything else. She's getting prettier, too. When can you get a leave, a *real* leave?

Love,
Maggie.

May 26.

Hank dear,

You should see her now—and you shall. I'm sending along a reel of color movie. My mother sent her those nighties with drawstrings all over. I put one on, and right now she looks like a snow-white potato sack with that beautiful, beautiful flower-face blooming on top. Is that *me* talking? Am I a doting mother? But wait till you *see* her!

July 10.

...Believe it or not, as you like, but your daughter can talk, and I don't mean baby talk. Alice discovered it—she's a dental assistant in the WACs, you know—and when she heard the baby giving out what I thought was a string of gibberish, she said the kid knew words and sentences, but couldn't say them clearly because she has no teeth yet. I'm taking her to a speech specialist.

September 13.

...We have a prodigy for real! Now that all her front teeth are in, her speech is perfectly clear and—a new talent now— she can sing! I mean really carry a tune! At seven months! Darling, my world would be perfect if you could only get home.

November 19.

...at last. The little goon was so busy being clever, it took her all this time to learn to crawl. The doctor says development in these cases is always erratic...

SPECIAL SERVICE TELEGRAM

DECEMBER 1, 1953
08:47 LK59F

FROM: TECH. LIEUT. H. MARVELL
    X47–016 GCNY
    TO: MRS. H. MARVELL
    APT. K-17
    504 E. 19 ST
    N.Y. N.Y.

WEEK'S LEAVE STARTS TOMORROW STOP WILL ARRIVE AIRPORT TEN OH FIVE STOP DON'T MEET ME STOP LOVE LOVE LOVE HANK

* * *

Margaret let the water run out of the bathinette until only a few inches were left, and then loosed her hold on the wriggling baby.

"I think it was better when you were retarded, young woman," she informed her daughter happily. "You *can't* crawl in a bathinette, you know."

"Then why can't I go in the bathtub?" Margaret was used to her child's volubility by now, but every now and then it caught her unawares. She swooped the resistant mass of pink flesh into a towel, and began to rub.

"Because you're too little, and your head is very soft, and bathtubs are very hard."

"Oh. Then when can I go in the bathtub?"

"When the outside of your head is as hard as the inside, brainchild." She reached toward a pile of fresh clothing. "I cannot understand," she added, pinning a square of cloth through the nightgown, "why a child of your intelligence can't learn to keep a diaper on the way other babies do. They've been used for centuries, you know, with perfectly satisfactory results."

The child disdained to reply; she had heard it too often. She waited patiently until she had been tucked, clean and sweet-smelling, into a white-painted crib. Then she favored her mother with a smile that inevitably made Margaret think of the first golden edge of the sun bursting into a rosy predawn. She remembered Hank's reaction to the color pictures of his beautiful daughter, and with the thought, realized how late it was.

"Go to sleep, puss. When you wake up, you know, your *daddy* will be here."

"Why?" asked the four-year-old mind, waging a losing battle to keep the ten-month-old body awake.

Margaret went into the kitchenette and set the timer for the roast. She examined the table, and got her clothes from the closet, new dress, new shoes, new slip, new everything, bought weeks before and saved for the day Hank's telegram came. She stopped to pull a paper from the facsimile, and, with clothes and news, went into the bathroom and lowered herself gingerly into the steaming luxury of a scented bath.

She glanced through the paper with indifferent interest.

437

Today at least there was no need to read the national news. There was an article by a geneticist. The same geneticist. Mutations, he said, were increasing disproportionately. It was too soon for recessives; even the first mutants, born near Hiroshima and Nagasaki in 1946 and 1947, were not old enough yet to breed. *But my baby's all right.* Apparently, there was some degree of free radiation from atomic explosions causing the trouble. *My baby's fine. Precocious, but normal.* If more attention had been paid to the first Japanese mutations, he said...

There was that little notice in the paper in the spring of '47. That was when Hank quit at Oak Ridge. "Only 2 or 3 percent of those guilty of infanticide are being caught and punished in Japan today..." *But* MY BABY'S *all right.*

She was dressed, combed, and ready to the last light brush-on of lip paste, when the door chime sounded. She dashed for the door, and heard for the first time in eighteen months the almost-forgotten sound of a key turning in the lock before the chime had quite died away.

"Hank!"

"Maggie!"

And then there was nothing to say. So many days, so many months of small news piling up, so many things to tell him, and now she just stood there, staring at a khaki uniform and a stranger's pale face. She traced the features with the finger of memory. The same high-bridged nose, wide-set eyes, fine feathery brows; the same long jaw, the hair a little farther back now on the high forehead, the same tilted curve to his mouth. Pale... Of course, he'd been underground all this time. And strange, stranger because of lost familiarity than any newcomer's face could be.

She had time to think all that before his hand reached out to touch her, and spanned the gap of eighteen months. Now, again, there was nothing to say, because there was no need. They were together, and for the moment that was enough.

"Where's the baby?"

"Sleeping. She'll be up any minute."

No urgency. Their voices were as casual as though it were a daily exchange, as though war and separation did not exist. Margaret picked up the coat he'd thrown on the chair near the door, and hung it carefully in the hall closet. She went to check the roast, leaving him to wander through the rooms by himself, remembering and coming back. She found him, finally, standing over the baby's crib.

She couldn't see his face, but she had no need to.

"I think we can wake her just this once." Margaret pulled the covers down and lifted the white bundle from the bed. Sleepy lids pulled back heavily from smoky brown eyes.

"Hello." Hank's voice was tentative.

"Hello." The baby's assurance was more pronounced.

He had heard about it, of course, but that wasn't the same as hearing it. He turned eagerly to Margaret. "She really can—?"

"Of course she can, darling. But what's more important, she can even do nice normal things like other babies do, even stupid ones. Watch her crawl!" Margaret set the baby on the big bed.

For a moment young Henrietta lay and eyed her parents dubiously.

"Crawl?" she asked.

"That's the idea. Your daddy is new around here, you know. He wants to see you show off."

"Then put me on my tummy."

"Oh, of course." Margaret obligingly rolled the baby over.

"What's the matter?" Hank's voice was still casual, but an undercurrent in it began to charge the air of the room. "I thought they turned over first."

"This baby"—Margaret would not notice the tension—"*This* baby does things when she wants to."

This baby's father watched with softening eyes while the head advanced and the body hunched up propelling itself across the bed.

"Why, the little rascal." He burst into relieved laughter. "She looks like one of those potato-sack racers they used to have on picnics. Got her arms pulled out of the sleeves already." He reached over and grabbed the knot at the bottom of the long nightie.

"I'll do it, darling." Margaret tried to get there first.

"Don't be silly, Maggie. This may be *your* first baby, but *I* had five kid brothers." He laughed her away, and reached with his other hand for the string that closed one sleeve. He opened the sleeve bow, and groped for an arm.

"The way you wriggle," he addressed his child sternly, as his hand touched a moving knob of flesh at the shoulder, "anyone might think you are a worm, using your tummy to crawl on, instead of your hands and feet."

Margaret stood and watched, smiling. "Wait till you hear her sing, darling—"

His right hand traveled down from the shoulder to where he thought an arm would be, traveled down, and straight down, over firm small muscles that writhed in an attempt to move against the pressure of his hand. He let his fingers drift up again to the shoulder. With infinite care he opened the knot at the bottom of the nightgown. His wife was standing by the bed, saying, "She can do 'Jingle Bells,' and—"

His left hand felt along the soft knitted fabric of the gown, up toward the diaper that folded, flat and smooth, across the bottom end of his child. No wrinkles. No kicking. *No...*

"Maggie." He tried to pull his hands from the neat fold in the diaper, from the wriggling body. "Maggie." His throat was dry; words came hard, low and grating. He spoke very slowly, thinking the sound of each word to make himself say it. His head was spinning, but he had to *know* before he let it go. "Maggie, why...didn't you...tell me?"

"Tell you what, darling?" Margaret's poise was the immemorial patience of woman confronted with man's childish impetuosity. Her sudden laugh sounded fantastically easy and natural in that room; it was all clear to her now. "Is she wet? I didn't know."

She didn't know. His hands, beyond control, ran up and down the soft-skinned baby body, the sinuous, limbless body. *Oh God, dear God*—his head shook and his muscles contracted in a bitter spasm of hysteria. His fingers tightened on his child—*Oh God, she didn't know...*

Sharon Webb is a young writer from Blairsville, Pennsylvania, whose stories of the misadventures of Terra Tarkington, SN (Space Nurse) are a popular feature of Isaac Asimov's Science Fiction Magazine. This entertaining tale first appeared in the August 1979 issue.

ITCH ON THE BULL RUN

By Sharon Webb

Satellite Hospital Outpost
Taurus 14, North Horn 978675644
Nath Orbit

Jan. 2

Carmelita O'Hare-Mbotu RN
Teton Medical Center
Jackson Hole Summation City
Wyoming 306548760 United Earth, Sol

Dear Carmie,

This may be the last time you hear from me. I am doomed. Just as beautiful Dr. Brian-Scott and I were beginning an ardent alliance—Armageddon.

Yes, it's true. When I signed up with the Interstellar Nurses' Corps, I signed my life away. I am writing to you from a plague ship. There's been no official word, but where there's steam (to coin a phrase) there's a reactor.

I just got back from a week's pass (Earth time, not Bull

441

Run time), and found that I had fallen into a nest of pestilence. All of the Aldeberan nurses were hissing about it, but they kept lapsing from Standard into their native tongue so I couldn't get any details. I asked one of the Hyadean orderlies about it, but all he'd do was shake his head and jiggle the crease where his nose ought to be. He wouldn't say a *word,* Carmie; and he's a terrible gossip. When Glockto is at a loss for words, it is *serious.* I did find out that the chief epidemiologist, old Dr. Kelly-Bach, is stricken. Word is that he picked up the plague from an Aurigan patient. Dr. Kelly-Bach's wife, Olga the Grim, is sure to be next. And after Olga? Carmie, I am going to die. And I don't even know what the symptoms are yet.

When you read in the medical journals of the disease that decimated Nath Outpost, think of me, Carmie, and weep.

Yours in dissolution,
Terra

Satellite Hospital Outpost
Taurus 14, North Horn 978675644
Nath Orbit

Jan. 2

Gladiola Tarkington
45 Subsea
Petroleum City
Gulf of Mexico 233433111 United Earth, Sol

Dear Mom,

Everything is fine here, but boring. I just got back from a week's pass. I'm afraid I was terribly extravagant; I spent the week on Hyades IV and bought a Snuggie. I can't wear it on the ship, of course, because Hyadean Snuggies are good for forty degrees below zero, but it will come in handy back on Earth if I ever get there.

Don't worry about the plague.

Love,
Terra

Satellite Hospital Outpost
Taurus 14, North Horn 978675644
Nath Orbit

Jan. 5

Carmelita O'Hare-Mbotu RN
Teton Medical Center
Jackson Hole Summation City
Wyoming 306548760 United Earth, Sol

Dear Carmie,

I told you that I was going to die, but it is much worse than that. *Much worse.* I am to be flayed alive—victim of an insidious and malignant fungus.

We still don't have any official word, but that's because the official word has to come from Dr. Kelly-Bach, and he is in awful shape. Poor Dr. Kelly-Bach is still up and around, ministering to the sick; but his mind wanders, and his heart is not in his work. Carmie, you should see him. He has to wear thick gloves to keep from scratching his hide off. Olga tells me she has to restrain his hands every night, because if she didn't, he would wake up in the morning with most of his epidermis gone. The look in his eye is terrible, Carmie. Sort of maddened. And he moans and sighs a lot.

There is no known cure, Carmie. None. And it is definitely contagious. Only this morning, I found Olga smearing the end of her nose with a local anesthetic, but she said it didn't help much. To make matters worse, Glockto, the orderly, came in about then and begged some for his crease.

Carmie, it is so depressing that I am nearing catatonia. Just when Dr. Brian-Scott and I were developing such a fulfilling relationship, disaster strikes. We will be cut down in our prime.

I know that if he is stricken first, I will stand by him. But what if I'm first? Would he want me if my skin were gone? They say that beauty is only skin deep, but that's a lie, Carmie.

There is only one thing left to do. I've got to figure out a way to get us off this tub.

Machinatingly yours,
Terra

Satellite Hospital Outpost
Taurus 14, North Horn 978675644
Nath Orbit

Jan. 7

Gladiola Tarkington
45 Subsea
Petroleum City
Gulf of Mexico 233433111 United Earth, Sol

Dear Mom,

I'm not sick. I never said I was sick. I don't see why you're worried, because I'm fine.

The Hyadean Snuggie does not carry disease. The only diseases we get around here come from the patients.

I have applied for a transfer, but they said I couldn't have it until Olga Kelly-Bach's skin grows back.

Your loving daughter,
Terra

Satellite Hospital Outpost
Taurus 14, North Horn 978675644
Nath Orbit

Jan. 9

Carmelita O'Hare-Mbotu RN
Teton Medical Center
Jackson Hole Summation City
Wyoming 306548760 United Earth, Sol

Dear Carmie,

Well, they wouldn't let me transfer off this tin coffin, but I've beaten them at their game. I volunteered for special assignment on Pleiades II, and Dr. Brian-Scott is going too. It seems that one of the Pleiades II Mothers is sick. Her egg production slowed down to zero, and we have to find out why. The Pleiades II population is on the decline anyway, and they can't afford to lose a Mother. It sounds like an interesting case, and it sure beats terminal pruritus.

Olga is a *mass* of excoriation, and it is better not to describe the condition of poor Dr. Kelly-Bach. I really fear for his sanity, Carmie. He is so testy, you just can't stand to be around him. (If you wanted to be around him.)

We thought the Aldeberans were immune; but just this morning, one of Dr. Qotermire's scales fell out of his tail during surgery. He seemed awfully distressed about it, and the Aldeberan nurse who was assisting him turned such a

444

pale blue that I thought she would faint. I'm getting off this
tub just in time, Carmie. It's one thing to see the disease in
humans and Hyadeans, but it's altogether something else to
contemplate Dr. Qotemire's defoliation. I don't think I could
bear that. It's hard enough to look at Dr. Qotemire when he's
in health.

Terra

P.S. How's this for an itinerary? Tomorrow we take the shuttle to Hyades IV and then the express to Pleiades II. Our
port-of-entry is Seven Sisters—the only Pleasure Dome in
light-years! We'll spend the night at the Kubla Khan and
then off to see our patient.

Yours in anticipation,
Terra

Satellite Hospital Outpost
Taurus 14, North Horn 978675644
Nath Orbit

Jan. 9

Gladiola Tarkington
45 Subsea
Petroleum City
Gulf of Mexico 233433111 United Earth, Sol

Dear Mom,
    My skin is fine. You worry too much. I worry about your
worrying about me.
    They won't let me come home, Mom. They're sending Dr.
Brian-Scott and me to Pleiades II to see a patient there. But
don't be concerned. It's probably not true what they say about
the Seven Sisters Pleasure Dome.

Much love,
Terra

Pleiades II Express
17th Relay 800880008

Jan. 10

Carmelita O'Hare-Mbotu RN
Teton Medical Center
Jackson Hole Summation City
Wyoming 306548760 United Earth, Sol

Dear Carmie,

Life is bleak. There is no shining dawn for me, Carmie. No rosy edge. Dr. Brian-Scott is stricken with the fungus.

He twitched all the way on the shuttle, and now he's beginning to scratch. Just when our love begins to flower, it is nipped (to coin a phrase) cruelly in the bud. I cannot express to you the way I feel.

Yours in desolation,
Terra

Pleasure Dome
Pleiades II 456765453 Pleiades

Jan. 11

Gladiola Tarkington
45 Subsea
Petroleum City
Gulf of Mexico 233433111 United Earth, Sol

Dear Mom,

You shouldn't get so excited about things, Mom. The Pleasure Dome is really a big nothing. Absolutely tame and harmless.

I'm sure the police will let us go soon.

And don't worry. Even though Dr. Brian-Scott is growing worse by the minute, I am still fine.

Love and kisses,
Terra

Pleasure Dome
Pleiades II 456765453 Pleiades

Jan. 11

Carmelita O'Hare-Mbotu RN
Teton Medical Center
Jackson Hole Summation City
Wyoming 306548760 United Earth, Sol

Dear Carmie,

I am being held prisoner in the Seven Sisters Pleasure Dome. When we arrived last night, Dr. Brian-Scott couldn't stop scratching while we were going through customs and

446

the officials kept giving us funny looks. About the time I thought we were through, these two huge beings came and put us under arrest. (I say "beings" because I don't know *what* they were—they were wearing bulky decontam. suits.)

Well, they marched us off through a sort of tunnel into our cell. It looks like an ordinary Floatel room, but make no mistake, Carmie, it is really a cell. We are locked in. We are being fed and cared for after a fashion, but we've had no physical contact with anybody. A health servo came in and took samples of us though.

In between scratching, Dr. Brian-Scott called the embassy. Everyone was very polite, but adamant. We have to stay here until we get clearance from Pleiades II Health.

So now I am prisoner in a Pest Hole. Who would have thought it would come to this, Carmie? Have you ever been arrested? Have you ever spent the night in a Pleasure Dome cell with a man with the itch? Believe me, it is no fun. No fun at all.

The health servo told us that Aurigan fungus is not touched in any way by any drug known to the civilized galaxy.

What the health servo didn't tell us was that any known pleasurable stimulus makes it worse.

Do you know how helpless it makes you feel to see the man you love writhing on a jelly bed and pleading, "Do something, Terra. *Do something*"?

Well, what could *I* do? He's the doctor.

Grimly yours,
Terra

Pleasure Dome
Pleiades II 456765453 Pleiades

Jan. 12

Carmelita O'Hare-Mbotu RN
Teton Medical Center
Jackson Hole Summation City
Wyoming 306548760 United Earth, Sol

Dear Carmie,
We have been freed. The health servo came in a while ago and told us.

What he said was, "You are free to leave the dome. Do not attempt to return or you will be executed."

Can you imagine, Carmie? Here we are on a mission of mercy and that's the treatment we get. I can't wait to get out of here.

Pleiades II Health said it would be all right to visit our patient outside the dome. It seems that there's a lot of fungus out there anyway, and the natives are immune to most of it, including the Aurigan variety.

If I were not the dedicated professional I am, I wouldn't bother to help the Pleiades Mother. But as you know, Carmie, I am dedicated to the end.

Besides, we don't have anyplace else to go. They won't let us board the express because we're contaminated. We are doomed to wander the hostile surface of Pleiades II—perhaps forever.

Yours into the wilderness,
Terra

Mother's Oviporium
Vicious Swamp
Pleiades II 352344480

Jan. 13

Gladiola Tarkington
45 Subsea
Petroleum City
Gulf of Mexico 233433111 United Earth, Sol

Dear Mom,

Well, here we are at the Oviporium. We've seen our patient and Dr. Brian-Scott and I are going to start treatment after lunch, if he is still up and around.

I am fine.

You would be amazed at the sex habits on Pleiades II. Absolutely amazed.

Yours in wonder,
Terra

Mothers' Oviporium
Vicious Swamp
Pleiades II 352344480 Pleiades

Jan. 13

Carmelita O'Hare-Mbotu RN
Teton Medical Center
Jackson Hole Summation City
Wyoming 306548760 United Earth, Sol

Dear Carmie,

I found out why they call it a Pleasure Dome. The only pleasure that anyone could conceivably have on this planet is under that dome. Outside, it rains all the time. *All the time*. Everything is musty and mildewy.

The Pleiades II Mother is in bad shape. When we got here, she was curled up in a kind of spastic ball. Since you've led a sheltered life back on Earth, Carmie, you've probably forgotten your Alien Physiology. The Mother is about three meters long and she looks a lot like a millipede. She's stopped laying her eggs and she seems to be in pain. Of course, it's a little hard to be sure, because she's completely blind, deaf, and dumb.

After a while she began to writhe. Her groomers panicked. They stood around whimpering and twiddling their feelers while Dr. Brian-Scott stood around and scratched. Then he did an internal and said, "I think it's (scratch, scratch) a mechanical obstruction (scratch, scratch) of the ovipositor."

I thought that was interesting, and I looked at her tail; but Dr. Brian-Scott said I was looking at the wrong end. The Mother's ovipositor is just under her mouth. (Can you imagine, Carmie?)

Then he said, "We'd better (scratch, scratch) put on protective clothing (scratch, scratch)."

He said that when he finished dilating her ovipositor, the eggs would start rolling out. "As soon as they do, she'll start squirting liters of fluid from the pores in her sides to coat the eggs."

So I have to go put on this plasticine suit to keep the juice off of me. I'll let you know what happens.

Obstetrically yours,
Terra

Mothers' Oviporium
Vicious Swamp
Pleiades II 352344480 Pleiades

Itch on the Bull Run

Jan. 14

Carmelita O'Hare-Mbotu RN
Teton Medical Center
Jackson Hole Summation City
Wyoming 206548760 United Earth, Sol

Dear Carmie,

I am ecstatic! You'll never guess what happened. When we got suited up, Dr. Brian-Scott dilated the Mother's ovipositor and sure enough, these white eggs started rolling out in a steady stream. She'd catch each one with her anterior legs, and then she'd roll it down her body all the way to her tail. All the while, this brown fluid kept pouring out of openings in the side of her body. By the time the eggs got to her tail they were brown—completely coated with the fluid.

Meanwhile, poor Dr. Brian-Scott was abjectly miserable inside the plasticine suit. It simply *exacerbated* his condition to an unbearable extreme.

While he danced around on one foot and then the other and scratched and scratched with a manic expression on his face, I got to wondering about why the Mother had to squirt all that stuff over the eggs.

He stopped scratching and dancing long enough to say, "It prevents the eggs from rotting. It's so damp here the eggs would be destroyed by fungus in no time."

And that's when I conceived this brilliant idea.

I said, "Well, do you suppose that juice would do any good for the Aurigan fungus?"

The effect on him was amazing. He stood completely still like he had turned to plexiglas or something. Then, after the longest time, he leaped up in the air and began to rip his clothes off.

It was unbelievable. There he was, stripped to his itchy skin in front of everybody. Then he reached out and splashed handfuls of that brown syrupy mess all over himself. As he did it, he made little happy moans and then splashed some more. Carmie, he practically *embraced* the Mother.

I can't tell you how mortified I was. Fortunately, the Mother was blind, deaf, and dumb, or there's no telling what her reaction would have been. I guess the groomers all thought it was part of the treatment.

But it made me mad. He could have killed himself. A more unscientific experiment I have never seen; he could have at least tried a little patch first. Carmie, he's lucky that what was left of his hide didn't come off.

Well, after a while, he was completely brown like the eggs and he had this *beatific* smile on his face.

And when I saw that smile, I stopped being mortified.

Then he said (I remember his every word), "I love you, Terra."

So we're bringing back *containers* of the Mother Juice so we can cure the plague. The Port Authorities say we can board the express if we've both been treated.

I feel like Madame Curie.

Majestically yours,
Terra

Satellite Hospital Outpost
Taurus 14, North Horn 978675644
Nath Orbit

Jan. 16

Gladiola Tarkington
45 Subsea
Petroleum City
Gulf of Mexico 233433111 United Earth, Sol

Dear Mom,
You don't need to come here to see about me. *I'm fine.* I really wish you wouldn't call Dr. Kelly-Bach just now, since he's still weak from the plague.

We all took the cure, and Dr. Brian-Scott says that the brown stains may come off in a few months.

In the meantime, I am going to be a student. In view of my interest in the reproductive habits of the Pleiades II Mothers, Dr. Brian-Scott says he is going to teach me all about the most interesting reproductive habits in the galaxy.

Studiously yours,
Terra

Fredric Brown (1906–72) gave much to science fiction. Among his contributions was an unmatched talent for the short-short story, possibly the most difficult form to do effectively. He also had a wonderful sense of humor, which frequently found its way into his work—What Mad Universe (1949) and Martians, Go Home (1955) being two excellent examples.

"Letter to a Phoenix" (Astounding Science Fiction, August 1949) captures all of the qualities that made him so effective and so popular.

LETTER TO A PHOENIX

By Fredric Brown

There is much to tell you, so much that it is difficult to know where to begin. Fortunately, I have forgotten most of the things that have happened to me. Fortunately, the mind has a limited capacity for remembering. It would be horrible if I remembered the details of a hundred and eighty thousand years—the details of four thousand lifetimes that I have lived since the first great atomic war.

Not that I have forgotten the really great moments. I remember being on the first expedition to land on Mars and the third to land on Venus. I remember—I believe it was in the third great war—the blasting of Skora from the sky by a force that compares to nuclear fission as a nova compares to our slowly dying sun. I was second in command on a Hyper-

452

A Class spacer in the war against the second extragalactic invaders, the ones who established bases on Jupe's moons before we knew they were there and almost drove us out of the Solar System before we found the one weapon they couldn't stand up against. So they fled where we couldn't follow them, then, outside of the Galaxy. When we did follow them, about fifteen thousand years later, they were gone. They were dead three thousand years.

And this is what I want to tell you about—that mighty race and the others—but first, so that you will know how I know what I know, I will tell you about myself.

I am not immortal. There is only one immortal being in the universe; of it, more anon. Compared to it, I am of no importance, but you will not understand or believe what I say to you unless you understand what I am.

There is little in a name, and that is a fortunate thing—for I do not remember mine. That is less strange than you think, for a hundred and eighty thousand years is a long time and for one reason or another I have changed my name a thousand times or more. And what could matter less than the name my parents gave me a hundred and eighty thousand years ago?

I am not a mutant. What happened to me happened when I was twenty-three years old, during the first atomic war. The first war, that is, in which both sides used atomic weapons—puny weapons, of course, compared to subsequent ones. It was less than a score of years after the discovery of the atom bomb. The first bombs were dropped in a minor war while I was still a child. They ended that war quickly, for only one side had them.

The first atomic war wasn't a bad one—the first one never is. I was lucky for, if it had been a bad one—one which ended a civilization—I'd not have survived it despite the biological accident that happened to me. If it had ended a civilization, I wouldn't have been kept alive during the sixteen-year sleep period I went through about thirty years later. But again I get ahead of the story.

I was, I believe, twenty or twenty-one years old when the war started. They didn't take me for the army right away because I was not physically fit. I was suffering from a rather rare disease of the pituitary gland—Somebody's syndrome. I've forgotten the name. It caused obesity, among other things. I was about fifty pounds overweight for my height and had little stamina. I was rejected without a second thought.

About two years later my disease had progressed slightly, but other things had progressed more than slightly. By that time the army was taking anyone; they'd have taken a one-legged one-armed blind man if he was willing to fight. And I was willing to fight. I'd lost my family in a dusting, I hated my job in a war plant, and I had been told by doctors that my disease was incurable and I had only a year or two to live in any case. So I went to what was left of the army, and what was left of the army took me without a second thought and sent me to the nearest front, which was ten miles away. I was in the fighting one day after I joined.

Now I remember enough to know that *I* hadn't anything to do with it, but it happened that the time I joined was the turn of the tide. The other side was out of bombs and dust and getting low on shells and bullets. We were out of bombs and dust, too, but they hadn't knocked out *all* of our production facilities and we'd got just about all of theirs. We still had planes to carry them, too, and we still had the semblance of an organization to send the planes to the right places. Nearly the right places, anyway; sometimes we dropped them too close to our own troops by mistake. It was a week after I'd got into the fighting that I got out of it again—knocked out of it by one of our smaller bombs that had been dropped about a mile away.

I came to, about two weeks later, in a base hospital, pretty badly burned. By that time the war was over, except for the mopping up, and except for restoring order and getting the world started up again. You see, that hadn't been what I call a blow-up war. It killed off—I'm just guessing; I don't remember the fraction—about a fourth or a fifth of the world's population. There was enough productive capacity left, and there were enough people left, to keep on going; there were dark ages for a few centuries, but there was no return to savagery, no starting over again. In such times, people go back to using candles for light and burning wood for fuel, but not because they don't know how to use electricity or mine coal; just because the confusions and revolutions keep them off balance for a while. The knowledge is there, in abeyance until order returns.

It's not like a blow-up war, when nine-tenths or more of the population of Earth—or of Earth and the other planets—

is killed. Then is when the world reverts to utter savagery and the hundredth generation rediscovers metals to tip their spears.

But again I digressed. After I recovered consciousness in the hospital, I was in pain for a long time. There were, by then, no more anesthetics. I had deep radiation burns, from which I suffered almost intolerably for the first few months until, gradually, they healed. I did not sleep—that was the strange thing. And it was a terrifying thing, then, for I did not understand what had happened to me, and the unknown is always terrifying. The doctors paid little heed—for I was one of millions burned or otherwise injured—and I think they did not believe my statements that I had not slept at all. They thought I had slept but little and that I was either exaggerating or making an honest error. But I had *not* slept at all. I did not sleep until long after I left the hospital, cured. Cured, incidentally, of the disease of my pituitary gland, and with my weight back to normal, my health perfect.

I didn't sleep for thirty years. Then I *did sleep,* and I slept for sixteen years. And at the end of that forty-six-year period, I was still, physically, at the apparent age of twenty-three.

Do you begin to see what had happened as I began to see it then? The radiation—or combination of types of radiation—I had gone through, had radically changed the functions of my pituitary. And there were other factors involved. I studied endocrinology once, about a hundred and fifty thousand years ago, and I think I found the pattern. If my calculations were correct, what happened to me was one chance in a great many billions.

The factors of decay and aging were not eliminated, of course, but the rate was reduced by about fifteen thousand times. I age at the rate of one day every forty-five years. So I am not immortal. I have aged eleven years in the past hundred and eighty millennia. My physical age is now thirty-four.

And forty-five years is to me as a day. I do not sleep for about thirty years of it—then I sleep for about fifteen. It is well for me that my first few "days" were not spent in a period of complete social disorganization or savagery, else I would not have survived my first few sleeps. But I did survive them and by that time I had learned a system and could take care of my own survival. Since then, I have slept about four thousand times, and I have survived. Perhaps someday I shall be unlucky. Perhaps someday, despite certain safeguards, someone will discover and break into the cave or vault into which I seal myself, secretly, for a period of sleep. But it is not likely. I have years in which to prepare each of those places and the experience of four thousand sleeps back of me. You could pass such a place a thousand times and never know it was there, nor be able to enter if you suspected.

No, my chances for survival between my periods of waking life are much better than my chances of survival during my conscious, active periods. It is perhaps a miracle that I have survived so many of those, despite the techniques of survival that I have developed.

And those techniques are good. I've lived through seven major atomic—and super-atomic—wars that have reduced the population of Earth to a few savages around a few campfires in a few still habitable areas. And at other times, in other eras, I've been in five galaxies besides our own.

I've had several thousand wives, but always one at a time, for I was born in a monogamous era and the habit has persisted. And I have raised several thousand children. Of course, I have never been able to remain with one wife longer than thirty years before I must disappear, but thirty years is long enough for both of us—especially when she ages at a normal rate and I age imperceptibly. Oh, it leads to problems, of course, but I've been able to handle them. I always marry, when I do marry, a girl as much younger than myself as possible, so the disparity will not become too great. Say I am thirty; I marry a girl of sixteen. Then when it is time that I must leave her, she is forty-six and I am still thirty. And it is best for both of us, for everyone, that when I awaken I do not again go back to that place. If she still lives, she will be past sixty and it would not be well, even for her, to have a husband come back from the dead—still young. And I have left her well provided, a wealthy widow—wealthy in money or in whatever may have constituted wealth in that particular era. Sometimes it has been beads and arrowheads, sometimes wheat in a granary and once—there have been peculiar civilizations—it was fish scales. I never had the slightest difficulty in acquiring my share, or more, of money or its equivalent. A few thousand years' practice and the difficulty becomes the other way—knowing when to stop in order not to become unduly wealthy and so attract attention.

For obvious reasons, I've always managed to do that. For

reasons that you will see, I've never wanted power, nor have I ever—after the first few hundred years—let people suspect that I was different from them. I even spend a few hours each night lying thinking, pretending to sleep.

But none of that is important, any more than I am important. I tell it to you only so you will understand how I *know* the thing that I am about to tell you.

And when I tell you, it is not because I'm trying to sell you anything. It's something you can't change if you want to, and—when you understand it—you won't want to.

I'm not trying to influence you or to lead you. In four thousand lifetimes I've been almost everything—except a leader. I've avoided that. Oh, often enough I have been a god among savages, but that was because I had to be one in order to survive. I used the powers they thought were magic only to keep a degree of order, never to lead them, never to hold them back. If I taught them to use the bow and arrow, it was because game was scarce and we were starving and my survival depended upon theirs. Seeing that the pattern was necessary, I have never disturbed it.

What I tell you now will not disturb the pattern.

It is this: The human race is the only immortal organism in the universe.

There have been other races, and there are other races throughout the universe, but they have died away or they will die. We charted them once, a hundred thousand years ago, with an instrument that detected the presence of thought, the presence of intelligence, however alien and at whatever distance—and gave us a measure of that mind and its qualities. And fifty thousand years later that instrument was rediscovered. There were about as many races as before but only eight of them were ones that had been there fifty thousand years ago and each of those eight was dying, senescent. They had passed the peak of their powers and they were dying.

They had reached the limit of their capabilities—and there is always a limit—and they had no choice but to die. Life is dynamic; it can never be static—at however high or low a level—and survive.

That is what I am trying to tell you, so that you will never again be afraid. Only a race that destroys itself and its progress periodically, that goes back to its beginning, can survive more than, say, sixty thousand years of intelligent life.

In all the universe only the human race has ever reached a high level of intelligence without reaching a high level of sanity. We are unique. We are already at least five times as old as any other race has ever been and it is because we are not sane. And man has, at times, had glimmerings of the fact that insanity is divine. But only at high levels of culture does he realize that he is collectively insane, that fight against it as he will he will always destroy himself—and rise anew out of the ashes.

The phoenix, the bird that periodically immolates itself upon a flaming pyre to rise newborn and live again for another millennium, and again and forever, is only metaphorically a myth. It exists and there is only one of it.

You are the phoenix.

Nothing will ever destroy you, now that—during many high civilizations—your seed has been scattered on the planets of a thousand suns, in a hundred galaxies, there ever to repeat the pattern. The pattern that started a hundred and eighty thousand years ago—I think.

I cannot be sure of that, for I have seen that the twenty to thirty thousand years that elapse between the fall of one civilization and the rise of the next destroy all traces. In twenty to thirty thousand years memories become legends and legends become superstitions and even the superstitions become lost. Metals rust and corrode back into earth while the wind, the rain, and the jungle erode and cover stone. The contours of the very continents change—and glaciers come and go, and a city of twenty thousand years before is under miles of earth or miles of water.

So I cannot be sure. Perhaps the first blow-up that I knew was not the first; civilizations may have risen and fallen before my time. If so, it merely strengthens the case I put before you to say that mankind *may* have survived more than the hundred and eighty thousand years I know of, may have lived through more than the six blow-ups that have happened since what I think to have been the first discovery of the phoenix's pyre.

But—except that we scattered our seed to the stars so well that even the dying of the sun or its becoming a nova would not destroy us—the past does not matter. Lur, Candra, Thragan, Kah, Mu, Atlantis—those are the six I have known, and they are gone as thoroughly as this one will be twenty thousand years or so hence, but the human race, here or in other galaxies, will survive and will live forever.

It will help your peace of mind, here in this year of your current era, to know that—for your minds are disturbed. Perhaps, I do know, it will help your thoughts to know that the coming atomic war, the one that will probably happen in your generation, will not be a blow-up war; it will come too soon for that, before you have developed the really destructive weapons man has had so often before. It will set you back, yes. There will be darkish ages for a century or a few centuries. Then, with the memory of what you will call World War III as a warning, man will think—as he has always thought after a mild atomic war—that he has conquered his own insanity.

For a while—if the pattern holds—he will hold it in check. He will reach the stars again, to find himself already there. Why, you'll be back on Mars within five hundred years, and I'll go there too, to see again the canals I once helped to dig. I've not been there for eighty thousand years and I'd like to see what time has done to it and to those of us who were cut off there the last time mankind lost the space drive. Of course they've followed the pattern too, but the rate is not necessarily constant. We may find them at any stage in the cycle except the top. If they were at the top of the cycle, we wouldn't have to go to them—they'd come to us. Thinking, of course, as they think by now, that they are Martians.

I wonder how high, this time, you will get. Not quite as high, I hope, as Thragan. I hope that never again is rediscovered the weapon Thragan used against her colony on Skora, which was then the fifth planet until the Thragans blew it into asteroids. Of course that weapon would be developed only long after intergalactic travel again becomes commonplace. If I see it coming I'll get out of the Galaxy, but I'd hate to have to do that. I like Earth and I'd like to spend the rest of my mortal lifetime on it if it lasts that long.

Possibly it won't, but the human race will last. Everywhere and forever, for it will never be sane and only insanity is divine. Only the mad destroy themselves and all they have wrought.

And only the phoenix lives forever.

Jack Lewis had about a dozen stories in the science-fiction magazines in the mid-to-late 1950s, most of which were good to excellent. "Who's Cribbing" (Startling Stories, January 1953) is one of the most famous stories of its kind. Samuel Mines was really the editor at Startling when this story was written, and we only trust that the anthology you are now reading has not appeared somewhere else!

WHO'S CRIBBING?

By Jack Lewis

April 2, 1952

Mr. Jack Lewis
90-26 219 St.
Queens Village, N.Y.

Dear Mr. Lewis:

We are returning your manuscript, "The Ninth Dimension." At first glance, I had figured it a story well worthy of publication. Why wouldn't I? So did the editors of *Cosmic Tales* back in 1934 when the story was first published.

As you no doubt know, it was the great Todd Thromberry who wrote the story you tried to pass off on us as an original. Let me give you a word of caution concerning the penalties resulting from plagiarism.

It's not worth it. Believe me.

Sincerely,
Doyle P. Gates
Science Fiction Editor
Deep Space Magazine

April 5, 1952

Mr. Doyle P. Gates, Editor
Deep Space Magazine
New York, N.Y.

Dear Mr. Gates:

I do not know, nor am I aware of the existence of any Todd Thromberry. The story you rejected was submitted in good faith, and I resent the inference that I plagiarized it.

"The Ninth Dimension" was written by me not more than a month ago, and if there is any similarity between it and the story written by this Thromberry person, it is purely coincidental.

However, it has set me thinking. Some time ago, I submitted another story to *Stardust Scientifiction* and received a penciled notation on the rejection slip stating that the story was, "too thromberrish."

Who in the hell is Todd Thromberry? I don't remember reading anything written by him in the ten years I've been interested in science fiction.

Sincerely,
Jack Lewis

April 11, 1952

Mr. Jack Lewis
90-26 219 St.
Queens Village, N.Y.

Dear Mr. Lewis:

Re: Your letter of April 5.

While the editors of this magazine are not in the habit of making open accusations and are well aware of the fact in the writing business there will always be some overlapping of plot ideas, it is very hard for us to believe that you are not familiar with the works of Todd Thromberry.

While Mr. Thromberry is no longer among us, his works, like so many other writers', only became widely recognized after his death in 1941. Perhaps it was his work in the field of electronics that supplied him with the bottomless pit of new ideas so apparent in all his works. Nevertheless, even at this stage of science fiction's development it is apparent that he had a style that many of our so-called contemporary writers might do well to copy. By "copy," I do not mean rewrite word for word one or more of his works, as you have done. For while you state this has been accidental, surely you must realize that the chance of this phenomenon actually happening is about a million times as great as the occurrence of four pat royal flushes on one deal.

Sorry, but we're not that naïve.

Sincerely yours,
Doyle P. Gates
Science Fiction Editor
Deep Space Magazine

April 14, 1952

Mr. Doyle P. Gates, Editor
Deep Space Magazine
New York, N.Y.

Sir:
    Your accusations are typical of the rag you publish. Please cancel my subscription immediately.

Sincerely,
Jack Lewis

April 14, 1952

Science Fiction Society
144 Front Street
Chicago, Ill.

Gentlemen:
    I am interested in reading some of the works of the late Todd Thromberry.
    I would like to get some of the publications that feature his stories.

Respectfully,
Jack Lewis

April 22, 1952

Mr. Jack Lewis
90-26 219 St.
Queens Village, N.Y.

Dear Mr. Lewis:
    So would we. All I can suggest is that you contact the

publishers if any are still in business, or haunt your second-hand bookstores.

If you succeed in getting any of these magazines, please let us know. We'll pay you a handsome premium on them.

Yours,
Ray Albert
President
Science Fiction Society

May 11, 1952

Mr. Sampson J. Gross, Editor
Strange Worlds Magazine
St. Louis, Mo.

Dear Mr. Gross:

I am enclosing the manuscript of a story I have just completed. As you see on the title page, I call it "Wreckers of Ten Million Galaxies." Because of the great amount of research that went into it, I must set the minimum price on this one at not less than two cents a word.

Hoping you will see fit to use it for publication in your magazine, I remain,

Respectfully,
Jack Lewis

May 19, 1952

Mr. Jack Lewis
90-26 219 St.
Queens Village, N.Y.

Dear Mr. Lewis:

I'm sorry, but at the present time we won't be able to use "Wreckers of Ten Million Galaxies." It's a great yarn though, and if at some future date we decide to use it we will make out the reprint check directly to the estate of Todd Thromberry.

That boy sure could write.

Cordially,
Sampson J. Gross
Editor
Strange Worlds Magazine

Who's Cribbing?

May 23, 1952

Mr. Doyle P. Gates, Editor
Deep Space Magazine
New York, N.Y.

Dear Mr. Gates:

While I said I would never have any dealings with you or your magazine again, a situation has arisen which is most puzzling.

It seems all my stories are being returned to me by reason of the fact that except for the byline, they are exact duplicates of the works of this Todd Thromberry person.

In your last letter you aptly described the odds on the accidental occurrence of this phenomenon in the case of one story. What would you consider the approximate odds on no less than half a dozen of my writings?

I agree with you—astronomical!

Yet in the interest of all mankind, how can I get the idea across to you that every word I have submitted was actually written *by me!* I have never copied any material from Todd Thromberry, nor have I ever seen any of his writings. In fact, as I told you in one of my letters, up until a short while ago I was totally unaware of his very existence.

An idea has occurred to me however. It's a truly weird theory, and one that I probably wouldn't even suggest to anyone but a science-fiction editor. But suppose—just suppose—that this Thromberry person, what with his experiments in electronics and everything, had in some way managed to crack through this time-space barrier mentioned so often in your magazine. And suppose—egotistical as it sounds—he had singled out my work as being the type of material he had always wanted to write.

Do you begin to follow me? Or is the idea of a person from a different time cycle looking over my shoulder while I write too fantastic for you to accept?

Please write and tell me what you think of my theory?

Respectfully,
Jack Lewis

May 25, 1952

Mr. Jack Lewis
90-26 219 St.
Queens Village, N.Y.

Dear Mr. Lewis:
　　We think you should consult a psychiatrist.

Sincerely,
Doyle P. Gates
Science Fiction Editor
Deep Space Magazine

June 3, 1952

Mr. Sam Mines
Science Fiction Editor
Standard Magazines Inc.
New York 16, N.Y.

Dear Mr. Mines:
　　While the enclosed is not really a manuscript at all, I am submitting this series of letters, carbon copies, and correspondence, in the hope that you might give some credulity to this seemingly unbelievable happening.
　　The enclosed letters are all in proper order and should be self-explanatory. Perhaps if you publish them, some of your readers might have some idea how this phenomenon could be explained.
　　I call the entire piece "Who's Cribbing?"

Respectfully,
Jack Lewis

June 10, 1952

Mr. Jack Lewis
90-26 219 St.
Queens Village, N.Y.

Dear Mr. Lewis:
　　Your idea of a series of letters to put across a science-fiction idea is an intriguing one, but I'm afraid it doesn't quite come off.
　　It was in the August 1940 issue of Macabre Adventures that Mr. Thromberry first used this very idea. Ironically enough, the story title also was "Who's Cribbing?"

465

Who's Cribbing?

Feel free to contact us again when you have something more original.

Yours,
Samuel Mines
Science Fiction Editor
Standard Magazines Inc.

Like A. E. van Vogt, Gordy Dickson (1923–   ) was born in Canada. His forty or so published sf books include Soldier Ask Not *(1967), part of his "Childe Cycle"; the wonderful* Time Storm *(1977);* The Alien Way *(1965); and* The Dragon and the George *(1976). He won a Hugo Award for "Soldier Ask Not" in 1965 and a Nebula for "Call Him Lord" in 1966.*

This terrifying story (from Analog Science Fiction, *September 1965) is arguably his best, frightening because the bureaucratic foul-ups depicted in it seem so damn plausible.*

COMPUTERS DON'T ARGUE

By Gordon R. Dickson

TREASURE BOOK CLUB
PLEASE DO NOT FOLD,
SPINDLE OR MUTILATE
THIS CARD
Mr: Walter A. Child   Balance: $4.98
Dear Customer: Enclosed is your latest book selection.
"Kidnapped," by Robert Louis Stevenson.

437 Woodlawn Drive
Panduk, Michigan
Nov. 16, 198–

Treasure Book Club
1823 Mandy Street
Chicago, Illinois
Dear Sirs:

I wrote you recently about the computer punch card you sent, billing me for "Kim," by Rudyard Kipling. I did not open the package containing it until I had already mailed you my check for the amount on the card. On opening the package, I found the book missing half its pages. I sent it back to you, requesting either another copy or my money back. Instead, you have sent me a copy of "Kidnapped," by Robert Louis Stevenson. Will you please straighten this out?

I hereby return the copy of "Kidnapped."

Sincerely yours,
Walter A. Child

Treasure Book Club
SECOND NOTICE
PLEASE DO NOT FOLD,
SPINDLE OR MUTILATE
THIS CARD
Mr: Walter A. Child   Balance: $4.98
For "Kidnapped," by Robert Louis Stevenson
(If remittance has been made for the above, please disregard this notice)

437 Woodlawn Drive
Panduk, Michigan
Jan. 21, 198–

Treasure Book Club
1823 Mandy Street
Chicago, Illinois
Dear Sirs:

May I direct your attention to my letter of November 16, 198–? You are still continuing to dun me with computer punch cards for a book I did not order. Whereas, actually, it is your company that owes *me* money.

Sincerely yours,
Walter A. Child

Treasure Book Club
1823 Mandy Street
Chicago, Illinois
Feb. 1, 198–

Mr. Walter A. Child
437 Woodlawn Drive
Panduk, Michigan
Dear Mr. Child:

We have sent you a number of reminders concerning an amount owing to us as a result of book purchases you have made from us. This amount, which is $4.98 is now long overdue.

This situation is disappointing to us, particularly since there was no hesitation on our part in extending you credit at the time original arrangements for these purchases were made by you. If we do not receive payment in full by return mail, we will be forced to turn the matter over to a collection agency.

Very truly yours,
Samuel P. Grimes
Collection Mgr.

437 Woodlawn Drive
Panduk, Michigan
Feb. 5, 198–

Dear Mr. Grimes:

Will you stop sending me punch cards and form letters and make me some kind of a direct answer from a human being? *I* don't owe you money. *You* owe me money. Maybe I should turn your company over to a collection agency.

Walter A. Child

FEDERAL COLLECTION OUTFIT
88 Prince Street
Chicago, Illinois
Feb. 28, 198–

Mr. Walter A. Child
437 Woodlawn Drive
Panduk, Michigan
Dear Mr. Child:

Your account with the Treasure Book Club, of $4.98 plus interest and charges has been turned over to our agency for collection. The amount due is now $6.83. Please send your check for this amount or we shall be forced to take immediate action.

Jacob N. Harshe
Vice President

FEDERAL COLLECTION OUTFIT
88 Prince Street
Chicago, Illinois
April 8, 198–

Mr. Walter A. Child
437 Woodlawn Drive
Panduk, Michigan
Dear Mr. Child:
You have seen fit to ignore our courteous requests to settle your long overdue account with Treasure Book Club, which is now, with accumulated interest and charges, in the amount of $7.51.

If payment in full is not forthcoming by April 11, 198–, we will be forced to turn the matter over to our attorneys for immediate court action.

Ezekiel B. Harshe
President

MALONEY, MAHONEY, MacNAMARA
and PRUITT
Attorneys

89 Prince Street
Chicago, Illinois
April 29, 198–

Mr. Walter A. Child
437 Woodlawn Drive
Panduk, Michigan
Dear Mr. Child:
Your indebtedness to the Treasure Book Club has been referred to us for legal action to collect.

This indebtedness is now in the amount of $10.01. If you will send us this amount so that we may receive it before May 5, 198–, the matter may be satisfied. However, if we do not receive satisfaction in full by that date, we will take steps to collect through the courts.

I am sure you will see the advantage of avoiding a judgment against you, which as a matter of record would do lasting harm to your credit rating.

Very truly yours,
Hagthorpe M. Pruitt Jr.
Attorney at law

437 Woodlawn Drive
Panduk, Michigan
May 4, 198–

Mr. Hagthorpe M. Pruitt, Jr.
Maloney, Mahoney, MacNamara and Pruitt
89 Prince Street
Chicago, Illinois
Dear Mr. Pruitt:

You don't know what a pleasure it is to me in this matter to get a letter from a live human being to whom I can explain the situation.

This whole matter is silly. I explained it fully in my letters to the Treasure Book Company. But I might as well have been trying to explain to the computer that puts out their punch cards, for all the good it seemed to do. Briefly, what happened was I ordered a copy of "Kim," by Rudyard Kipling, for $4.98. When I opened the package they sent me, I found the book had only half its pages, but I'd previously mailed a check to pay them for the book.

I sent the book back to them, asking either for a whole copy or my money back. Instead, they sent me a copy of "Kidnapped," by Robert Louis Stevenson—which I had not ordered; and for which they have been trying to collect from me.

Meanwhile, I am still waiting for the money back that they owe me for the copy of "Kim" that I didn't get. That's the whole story. Maybe you can help me straighten them out.

Relievedly yours,
Walter A. Child

P.S.: I also sent them back their copy of "Kidnapped," as soon as I got it, but it hasn't seemed to help. They have never even acknowledged getting it back.

MALONEY, MAHONEY, MacNAMARA
and PRUITT
Attorneys

89 Prince Street
Chicago, Illinois
May 9, 198–

Mr. Walter A. Child
437 Woodlawn Drive
Panduk, Michigan
Dear Mr. Child:

I am in possession of no information indicating that any item purchased by you from the Treasure Book Club has been returned.

I would hardly think that, if the case had been as you stated, the Treasure Book Club would have retained us to collect the amount owing from you.

If I do not receive your payment in full within three days, by May 12, 198–, we will be forced to take legal action.

Very truly yours,
Hagthorpe M. Pruitt, Jr.

COURT OF MINOR CLAIMS
Chicago, Illinois

Mr. Walter A. Child
437 Woodlawn Drive,
Panduk, Michigan

Be informed that a judgment was taken and entered against you in this court this day of May 26, 198–, in the amount of $15.66 including court costs.

Payment in satisfaction of this judgment may be made to this court or to the adjudged creditor. In the case of payment being made to the creditor, a release should be obtained from the creditor and filed with this court in order to free you of legal obligation in connection with this judgment. Under the recent Reciprocal Claims Act, if you are a citizen of a different state, a duplicate claim may be automatically entered and judged against you in your own state so that collection may be made there as well as in the State of Illinois.

COURT OF MINOR CLAIMS
Chicago, Illinois
PLEASE DO NOT FOLD,
SPINDLE OR MUTILATE
THIS CARD

Judgment was passed this day of May 27, 198–, under Statute 941

Against: Child, Walter A. of 437 Woodlawn Drive, Panduk, Michigan. Pray to enter a duplicate claim for judgment.

    In: Picayune Court—Panduk, Michigan

    For Amount: $15.66

                    437 Woodlawn Drive
                    Panduk, Michigan
                    May 31, 198–

Samuel P. Grimes
Vice President, Treasure Book Club
1823 Mandy Street
Chicago, Illinois
Grimes:

This business has gone far enough. I've got to come down to Chicago on business of my own tomorrow. I'll see you then and we'll get this straightened out once and for all, about who owes what to whom, and how much!

                                Yours,
                        Walter A. Child

          From the desk of the Clerk
                Picayune Court

                         June 1, 198–

Harry:

The attached computer card from Chicago's Minor Claims Court against A. Walter has a 1500-series Statute number on it. That puts it over in Criminal with you, rather than Civil, with me. So I herewith submit it for your computer instead of mine. How's business?

                                Joe

CRIMINAL RECORDS
Panduk, Michigan
PLEASE DO NOT FOLD,
SPINDLE OR MUTILATE
THIS CARD

Convicted: (Child) A. Walter
On: May 26, 198–
Address: 437 Woodlawn Drive, Panduk, Mich.
Statute: 1566 (Corrected) 1567
Crime: Kidnap
Date: Nov. 16, 198–
Notes: At large. To be picked up at once.

POLICE DEPARTMENT, PANDUK, MICHIGAN. TO POLICE DEPART-
MENT CHICAGO ILLINOIS. CONVICTED SUBJECT A. (COMPLETE
FIRST NAME UNKNOWN) WALTER, SOUGHT HERE IN CONNECTION
REF. YOUR NOTIFICATION OF JUDGMENT FOR KIDNAP OF CHILD
NAMED ROBERT LOUIS STEVENSON, ON NOV. 16, 198–. INFORMA-
TION HERE INDICATES SUBJECT FLED HIS RESIDENCE, AT 437
WOODLAWN DRIVE, PANDUK, AND MAY BE AGAIN IN YOUR AREA.

POSSIBLE CONTACT IN YOUR AREA: THE TREASURE BOOK CLUB,
1823 MANDY STREET, CHICAGO, ILLINOIS. SUBJECT NOT KNOWN TO
BE ARMED, BUT PRESUMED DANGEROUS. PICK UP AND HOLD, AD-
VISING US OF CAPTURE...

TO POLICE DEPARTMENT, PANDUK, MICHIGAN. REFERENCE
YOUR REQUEST TO PICK UP AND HOLD A. (COMPLETE FIRST NAME
UNKNOWN) WALTER, WANTED IN PANDUK ON STATUTE 1567,
CRIME OF KIDNAPPING.

SUBJECT ARRESTED AT OFFICES OF TREASURE BOOK CLUB, OP-
ERATING THERE UNDER ALIAS WALTER ANTHONY CHILD AND AT-
TEMPTING TO COLLECT $4.98 FROM ONE SAMUEL P. GRIMES, EM-
PLOYEE OF THAT COMPANY.

DISPOSAL: HOLDING FOR YOUR ADVICE.

POLICE DEPARTMENT PANDUK, MICHIGAN TO POLICE DEPART-
MENT CHICAGO, ILLINOIS.

REF: A. WALTER (ALIAS WALTER ANTHONY CHILD) SUBJECT
WANTED FOR CRIME OF KIDNAP, YOUR AREA, REF: YOUR COM-
PUTER PUNCH CARD NOTIFICATION OF JUDGMENT, DATED MAY 27,
198–. COPY OUR CRIMINAL RECORDS PUNCH CARD HEREWITH FOR-
WARDED TO YOUR COMPUTER SECTION.

CRIMINAL RECORDS
Chicago, Illinois
PLEASE DO NOT FOLD,
.SPINDLE OR MUTILATE
THIS CARD
SUBJECT (CORRECTION—OMITTED RECORD SUPPLIED)
APPLICABLE STATUTE NO. 1567
JUDGMENT NO. 456789
TRIAL RECORD: APPARENTLY MISFILED AND UNAVAILABLE
DIRECTION: TO APPEAR FOR SENTENCING BEFORE JUDGE JOHN
ALEXANDER MCDIVOT, COURTROOM A, JUNE 9, 198–

From the Desk of
Judge Alexander J. McDivot

June 2, 198–

Dear Tony:

I've got an adjudged criminal coming up before me for sentencing Thursday morning—but the trial transcript is apparently misfiled.

I need some kind of information (Ref: A. Walter—Judgment No. 456789, Criminal). For example, what about the victim of the kidnapping? Was victim harmed?

Jack McDivot

June 3, 198–

Records Search Unit
Re: Ref: Judgment No. 456789—was victim harmed?

Tonio Malagasi
Records Division

June 3, 198–

To: United States Statistics Office
Attn: Information Section
Subject: Robert Louis Stevenson
Query: Information concerning

Records Search Unit
.Criminal Records Division
Police Department
Chicago, Ill.

June 5, 198–

To: Records Search Unit
Criminal Records Division

Police Department
Chicago, Illinois
Subject: Your query re Robert Louis Stevenson (File no. 189623)
Action: Subject deceased. Age at death, 44 yrs. Further information requested?

> A. K.
> Information Section
> U. S. Statistics Office

> June 6, 198–

To: United States Statistics Office
Attn.: Information Division
Subject: Re: File no. 189623
  No further information required.

> Thank you.
> Records Search Unit
> Criminal Records Division
> Police Department
> Chicago, Illinois

> June 7, 198–

To: Tonio Malagasi
Records Division
Re: Ref: judgment No. 456789—victim is dead.

> Records Search Unit

> June 7, 198–

To: Judge Alexander J. McDivot's Chambers
Dear Jack:
Ref: Judgment No. 456789. The victim in this kidnap case was apparently slain.

From the strange lack of background information on the killer and his victim, as well as the victim's age, this smells to me like a gangland killing. This for your information. Don't quote me. It seems to me, though, that Stevenson—the victim—has a name that rings a faint bell with me. Possibly, one of the East Coast Mob, since the association comes back to me as something about pirates—possibly New York dockage hijackers—and something about buried loot.

As I say, above is only speculation for your private guidance.

Any time I can help...

Best,
Tony Malagasi
Records Division

MICHAEL R. REYNOLDS
Attorney-at-law

49 Water Street
Chicago, Illinois
June 8, 198–

Dear Tim:

Regrets: I can't make the fishing trip. I've been court-appointed here to represent a man about to be sentenced tomorrow on a kidnapping charge.

Ordinarily, I might have tried to beg off, and McDivot, who is doing the sentencing, would probably have turned me loose. But this is the damnedest thing you ever heard of.

The man being sentenced has apparently been not only charged, but adjudged guilty as a result of a comedy of errors too long to go into here. He not only isn't guilty—he's got the best case I ever heard of for damages against one of the larger Book Clubs headquartered here in Chicago. And that's a case I wouldn't mind taking on.

It's inconceivable—but damnably possible, once you stop to think of it in this day and age of machine-made records—that a completely innocent man could be put in this position.

There shouldn't be much to it. I've asked to see McDivot tomorrow before the time of sentencing, and it'll just be a matter of explaining to him. Then I can discuss the damage suit with my freed client at his leisure.

Fishing next weekend?

Yours,
Mike

MICHAEL R. REYNOLDS
Attorney-at-law

49 Water Street
Chicago, Illinois
June 10

Dear Tim:

In haste—

No fishing this coming week either. Sorry.

You won't believe it. My innocent-as-a-lamb-and-I'm-not-kidding client has just been sentenced to death for first-degree murder in connection with the death of his kidnap victim.

Yes, I explained the whole thing to McDivot. And when he explained his situation to me, I nearly fell out of my chair.

It wasn't a matter of my not convincing him. It took less than three minutes to show him that my client should never have been within the walls of the County Jail for a second. But—get this—McDivot couldn't do a thing about it.

The point is, my man had already been judged guilty according to the computerized records. In the absence of a trial record—of course there never was one (but that's something I'm not free to explain to you now)—the judge has to go by what records are available. And in the case of an adjudged prisoner, McDivot's only legal choice was whether to sentence to life imprisonment, or execution.

The death of the kidnap victim, according to the statute, made the death penalty mandatory. Under the new laws governing length of time for appeal, which has been shortened because of the new system of computerizing records, to force an elimination of unfair delay and mental anguish to those condemned, I have five days in which to file an appeal, and ten to have it acted on.

Needless to say, I am not going to monkey with an appeal. I'm going directly to the Governor for a pardon—after which we will get this farce reversed. McDivot has already written the Governor, also, explaining that his sentence was ridiculous, but that he had no choice. Between the two of us, we ought to have a pardon in short order.

Then, I'll make the fur fly...

And we'll get in some fishing.

> Best,
> Mike

OFFICE OF THE
GOVERNOR OF ILLINOIS

June 17, 198–

Mr. Michael R. Reynolds
49 Water Street
Chicago, Illinois
Dear Mr. Reynolds:

In reply to your query about the request for pardon for

Walter A. Child (A. Walter), may I inform you that the Governor is still on his trip with the Midwest Governors Committee, examining the Wall in Berlin. He should be back next Friday.

I will bring your request and letters to his attention the minute he returns.

Very truly yours,
Clara B. Jilks
Secretary to the Governor

June 27, 198–

Michael R. Reynolds
49 Water Street
Chicago, Illinois
Dear Mike:
  Where is that pardon?
  My execution date is only five days from now!

Walt

June 29, 198–

Walter A. Child (A. Walter)
Cell Block E
Illinois State Penitentiary
Joliet, Illinois
Dear Walt:
  The Governor returned, but was called away immediately to the White House in Washington to give his views on interstate sewage.

  I am camping on his doorstep and will be on him the moment he arrives here.

  Meanwhile, I agree with you about the seriousness of the situation. The warden at the prison there, Mr. Allen Magruder, will bring this letter to you and have a private talk with you. I urge you to listen to what he has to say; and I enclose letters from your family also urging you to listen to Warden Magruder.

Yours,
Mike

June 30, 198–

Michael R. Reynolds
49 Water Street
Chicago, Illinois
Dear Mike: (This letter being smuggled out by Warden Magruder)

As I was talking to Warden Magruder in my cell, here, news was brought to him that the Governor has at last returned for a while to Illinois, and will be in his office early tomorrow morning, Friday. So you will have time to get the pardon signed by him and delivered to the prison in time to stop my execution on Saturday.

Accordingly, I have turned down the Warden's kind offer of a chance to escape; since he told me he could by no means guarantee to have all the guards out of my way when I tried it; and there was a chance of my being killed escaping.

But now everything will straighten itself out. Actually, an experience as fantastic as this had to break down sometime under its own weight.

Best,
Walt

FOR THE SOVEREIGN STATE OF ILLINOIS
I, Hubert Daniel Willikens, Governor of the State of Illinois, and invested with the authority and powers appertaining thereto, including the power to pardon those in my judgment wrongfully convicted or otherwise deserving of executive mercy, do this day of July 1, 198– do announce and proclaim that Walter A. Child (A. Walter), now in custody as a consequence of erroneous conviction upon a crime of which he is entirely innocent, is fully and freely pardoned of said crime. And I do direct the necessary authorities having custody of the said Walter A. Child (A. Walter) in whatever place or places he may be held, to immediately free, release, and allow unhindered departure to him...

Interdepartmental Routing Service
PLEASE DO NOT FOLD,
MUTILATE, OR SPINDLE
THIS CARD
Failure to route Document properly.
To: Governor Hubert Daniel Willikens
Re: Pardon issued to Walter A. Child, July 1, 198–

Gordon R. Dickson

Dear State Employee:

You have failed to attach your Routing Number.

PLEASE: Resubmit document with this card and form 876, explaining your authority for placing a TOP RUSH category on this document. Form 876 must be signed by your Departmental Superior.

RESUBMIT ON: Earliest possible date ROUTING SERVICE office is open. In this case, Tuesday, July 5, 198–.

WARNING: Failure to submit form 876 WITH THE SIGNATURE OF YOUR SUPERIOR may make you liable to prosecution for misusing a Service of the State Government. A warrant may be issued for your arrest.

There are NO exceptions. YOU have been WARNED.

Mildred Clingerman (1918–   ) was a mainstay of The Magazine of Fantasy and Science Fiction *in the 1950s, but stopped appearing in the sf magazines in the early 1960s. Her disappearance was a great loss to the field, because, like R. A. Lafferty, she brought a wonderful and indescribable* strangeness *to her work. Her best stories can be found in* A Cupful of Space *(1961).*

"Letters From Laura" (F & SF, October, 1954) is simply an exchange of letters between a mother and her loving daughter. Well, maybe not so simple.

LETTERS FROM LAURA

By Mildred Clingerman

Monday

Dear Mom:

Stop *worrying.* There isn't a bit of danger. Nobody ever dies or gets hurt or anything like that while time-traveling. The young man at the Agency explained it all to me in detail, but I've forgotten most of it. His eyebrows move in the most fascinating way. So I'm going this weekend. I've already bought my ticket. I haven't the faintest idea where I'm going, but that's part of the fun. Grab Bag Tours, they call them. It costs $60 for one day and night, and the Agency supplies

482

you with food concentrates and water capsules—a whole bag full of stuff they send right along with you. I certainly do *not* want Daddy to go with me. I'll tell him all about it when I get back, and then he can go himself, if he still wants to. The thing Daddy forgets is that all the history he reads is mostly just a pack of lies. Everybody says so nowadays, since time travel. He'd spoil everything arguing with the natives, telling them how they were supposed to act. I have to stop now, because the young man from the Agency is going to take me out to dinner and explain about insurance for the trip.

Love,
Laura

Tuesday

Dear Mom:

I can't *afford* to go first class. The Grab Bag Tours are not the leavings. They're perfectly all right. It's just that you sorta have to rough it. They've been thoroughly explored. I mean somebody has been there at least once before. I never heard of a native attacking a girl traveler. Just because I won't have a guide you start worrying about that. Believe me, some of those guides, from what I hear, wouldn't be very safe, either. Delbert explained it all to me. He's the boy from the Agency. Did you know that insurance is a very interesting subject?

Love,
Laura

Friday

Dear Mom:

Everything is set for tomorrow. I'm so excited. I spent three hours on the couch at the Agency's office—taking the hypno-course, you know, so I'll be able to speak the language. Later Delbert broke a rule and told me my destination, so I rushed over to the public library and read bits here and there. It's ancient Crete! Dad will be so pleased. I'm going to visit the Minotaur in the Labyrinth. Delbert says he is really off the beaten track of the tourists. I like unspoiled things, don't you? The Agency has a regular little room all fixed up right inside the cave, but hidden, so as not to disturb the regular business of the place. The Agency is very particular that way. Time travelers, Delbert says, have to agree to make themselves as inconspicuous as possible. Delbert says that will be very difficult for me to do. Don't you think *subtle* compliments are the nicest? I've made myself a darling costume—I sat up late to finish it. I don't know that it's exactly right, historically, but it doesn't really matter, since I'm not supposed to leave the cave. I have to stay close to my point of arrival, you understand. Delbert says I'm well covered now with insurance, so don't worry. I'll write the minute I get back.

Love,
Laura

Friday

Dear Prue:

Tomorrow I take my first time-travel tour. I wish you could see my costume. Very fetching! It's cut so that my breasts are displayed in the style of ancient Crete. A friend of mine doubts the authenticity of the dress but says the charms it shows off are *really* authentic! Next time I see you I'll lend you the pattern for the dress. But I honestly think, darling, you ought to get one of those Liff-Up operations first. I've been meaning to tell you. Of course, I don't need it myself. I'll tell you all about it (the trip I mean) when I get back.

Love,
Laura

Monday

Dear Prue:

I had the stinkiest time! I'll never know why I let that character at the travel agency talk me into it. The accommodations were lousy. If you want to know what I think, it's all a gyp. These Grab Bag Tours, third-class, are just the *leavings,* that they can't sell any other way. I hate salesmen. Whoever heard of ancient Crete anyway? And the Minotaur. You would certainly expect him to be a red-blooded he-man, wouldn't you? He looked like one. Not cute, you know, but built like a bull, practically. Prue, you just can't *tell* anymore. But I'm getting ahead of myself.

You've heard about that funny dizziness you feel for the first few minutes on arrival? That part is true. Everything is supposed to look black at first, but things kept on looking black even after the dizziness wore off. Then I remembered it was a cave I was in, but I did expect it to be lighted. I was lying on one of those beastly little cots that wiggle everytime your heart beats, and mine was beating plenty fast. Then I remembered the bag the Agency packs for you, and I sat up and felt around till I found it. I got out a perma-light and attached it to the solid rock wall and looked around. The floor was just plain old dirty dirt. That Agency had me stuck off in a little alcove, furnished with that sagging cot and a few coat hangers. The air in the place was rather stale. Let's be honest—it smelled. To console myself I expanded my wrist mirror and put on some more makeup. I was wearing my costume, but I had forgotten to bring a coat. I was freezing. I draped the blanket from the cot around me and went exploring. What a place! One huge room just outside my cubbyhole and corridors taking off in all directions, winding away into the dark. I had a perma-light with me, and naturally I couldn't get lost with my earrings tuned to point of arrival, but it was *weird* wandering around all by myself. I discovered that the corridor I was in curved downward. Later I found there were dozens of levels in the Labyrinth. Very confusing.

I was just turning to go back when something reached out and grabbed for me, from one of those alcoves. I was *thrilled*. I flicked off the light, dropped my blanket, and ran.

From behind I heard a man's voice. "All right, sis, we'll play games."

Well, Prue, I hadn't played hide-and-seek in years (except once or twice at office parties), but I was still pretty good at it. That part was fun. After a time my eyes adjusted to the dark so that I could see well enough to keep from banging into the walls. Sometimes I'd deliberately make a lot of noise to keep things interesting. But do you know what? That character would blunder right by me, and way down at the end of the corridor he'd make noises like "Oho" or "Aha." Frankly, I got discouraged. Finally I heard him grumbling his way back in my direction. I knew the dope would never catch me, so I just stepped out in front of him and said "Wellll?" You know, in that drawly, sarcastic way I have.

He reached out and grabbed me, and then he staggered back—like you've seen actors do in those old, old movies. He kept pounding his forehead with his fist, and then he yelled, "Cheated! Cheated again!" I almost slapped him. Instead I snapped on my perma-light and let him look me over good.

"Well, Buster," I said very coldly, "what do you mean, cheated?"

He grinned at me and shaded his eyes from the light. "Darling," he said, "you look luscious, indeed, but what the hell are you doing here?"

"I'm sight-seeing," I said. "Are you one of the sights?"

"Listen, baby, I *am* the sight. Meet the Minotaur." He stuck out this huge paw, and I shook it.

"Who did you think I was?" I asked him.

"No *who*, but *what*," he said. "Baby, you ain't no virgin."

Well, Prue, really. How can you argue a thing like that? He was completely *wrong*, of course, but I simply refused to discuss it.

"I only gobble virgins," he said.

Then he led me down into his rooms, which were really quite comfortable. I couldn't forgive the Agency for that cot, so when I spied his lovely, soft couch draped in pale blue satin, I said, "I'll borrow that if you don't mind."

"It's all yours, kid," the Minotaur said. He meant it, too. You remember how pale blue is one of my best colors? There I was lolling on the couch, looking like the Queen of the Nile, flapping my eyelashes, and what does this churl want to do?

"I'm simply starved for talk," he says. And about what? Prue, when a working girl spends her hard-earned savings on time travel, she has a right to expect something besides *politics*. I've heard there are men, a few shy ones, who will talk very fast to you about science and all that highbrow stuff, hoping maybe you won't notice some of the things they're doing in the *meantime*. But not the Minotaur. Who cares about the government a room's length apart? Lying there, twiddling my fingers and yawning, I tried to remember if Daddy had ever mentioned anything about the Minotaur's being so persnickety. That's the trouble with books. They leave out all the important details.

For instance, did you know that at midnight every night the Minotaur makes a grand tour of the Labyrinth? He wouldn't let me go along. That's another thing. He just says "no" and grins and means it. Now isn't that a typical male trait? I thought so, and when he locked me in his rooms the evening looked like turning into fun. I waited for him to come back with bated breath. But you can't bate your breath forever, and he was gone hours. When he did come back I'd fallen asleep and he woke me up *belching*.

"Please," I said. "Do you have to do that?"

"Sorry, kid," he said. "It's these gaunt old maids. Awful

souring to the stomach." It seems this windy diet was one of the things wrong with the government. He was very bitter about it all. Tender virgins, he said, had always been in short supply and now he was out of favor with the new regime. I rummaged around in my wrist bag and found an anti-acid pill. He was delighted. Can you imagine going into a transport over pills?

"Any cute males ever find their way into this place?" I asked him. I got up and walked around. You can loll on a couch just so long, you know.

"No boys!" The Minotaur jumped up and shook his fist at me. I cowered behind some hangings, but I needn't have bothered. He didn't even jerk me out from behind them. Instead he paced up and down and raved about the lies told on him. He swore he'd never eaten boys—hadn't cared for them at all. That creep, Theseus, was trying to ruin him politically. "I've worn myself thin," he yelled, "in all these years of service—" At that point I walked over and poked him in his big, fat stomach. Then I gathered my things together and walked out.

He puffed along behind me wanting to know what was the matter. "Gee, kid," he kept saying, "don't go home mad." I didn't say goodbye to him at all. A spider fell on him and it threw him into a hissy. The last I saw of him he was cursing the government because they hadn't sent him an exterminator.

Well, Prue, so much for the bogey man. Time travel in the raw!

Love,
Laura

Monday

Dear Mom:

Ancient Crete was nothing but politics, not a bit exciting. You didn't have a single cause to worry. These people are just as particular about girls as you are.

Love,
Laura

Tuesday

Dear Mr. Delbert Barnes:

Stop calling me or I will complain to your boss. You cad. I see it all now. You and your fine talk about how your Agency "fully protects its clients." That's a very high-sounding name for it. Tell me, how many girls do you talk into going to ancient Crete? And do you provide all of them with the same kind of insurance? Mr. Barnes, I don't want any more insurance from you. But I'm going to send you a client for that trip—the haggiest old maid I know. She has buck teeth and whiskers. Insure *her*.

Laura

P. S. Just in case you're feeling smug about me, put this in your pipe and smoke it. The Minotaur *knew*, I can't imagine how, but *you*, Mr. Barnes, *are no Minotaur*.

A. E. van Vogt (1912–   ), along with Robert Heinlein, Theodore Sturgeon, and one of your editors (can you guess which one?) was 'one of the great stars of the first "Golden Age" of science fiction (1939–1943). His novels Slan *(book form, 1946) and* The Weapon Shops of Isher *(book form, 1951), and a brace of excellent short stories, established his reputation. Born in Canada, he now lives in Southern California, and is still writing (and publishing).*

"Dear Pen Pal" is a delightful story of a planned invasion of Earth. It first appeared in the Winter 1949 issue of the Arkham Sampler, *one of the least known (and most beloved among those who knew it) and short-lived sf-and-fantasy magazines.*

DEAR PEN PAL

By A. E. van Vogt

Planet Aurigae II

Dear Pen Pal:

When I first received your letter from the interstellar correspondence club, my impulse was to ignore it. The mood of one who has spent the last seventy planetary periods—years, I suppose you would call them—in an Aurigaen prison, does not make for a pleasant exchange of letters. However, life is

489

very boring, and so I finally settled myself to the task of writing you.

Your description of Earth sounds exciting. I would like to live there for a while, and I have a suggestion in this connection, but I won't mention it till I have developed it further.

You will have noticed the material on which this letter is written. It is a highly sensitive metal, very thin, very flexible, and I have enclosed several sheets of it for your use. Tungsten dipped in any strong acid makes an excellent mark on it. It is important to me that you do write on it, as my fingers are too hot—literally—to hold your paper without damaging it.

I'll say no more just now. It is possible you will not care to correspond with a convicted criminal, and therefore I shall leave the next move up to you. Thank you for your letter. Though you did not know its destination, it brought a moment of cheer into my drab life.

Skander

Aurigae II

Dear Pen Pal:

Your prompt reply to my letter made me happy. I am sorry your doctor thought it excited you too much, and sorry, also, if I have described my predicament in such a way as to make you feel badly. I welcome your many questions, and I shall try to answer them all.

You say the international correspondence club has no record of having sent any letters to Aurigae. That, according to them, the temperature on the second planet of the Aurigae sun is more than 500 degrees Fahrenheit. And that life is not known to exist there. Your club is right about the temperature and the letters. We have what your people would call a hot climate, but then we are not a hydrocarbon form of life, and find 500 degrees very pleasant.

I must apologize for deceiving you about the way your first letter was sent to me. I didn't want to frighten you away by telling you too much at once. After all, I could not be expected to know that you would be enthusiastic to hear from me.

The truth is that I am a scientist, and, along with the other members of my race, I have known for some centuries that there were other inhabited systems in the galaxy. Since I am allowed to experiment in my spare hours, I amused myself in attempts at communication. I developed several simple systems for breaking in on galactic communication operations, but it was not until I developed a subspacewave control that I was able to draw your letter (along with several others, which I did not answer) into a cold chamber.

I use the cold chamber as both sending and receiving center, and since you were kind enough to use the material which I sent you, it was easy for me to locate your second letter among the mass of mail that accumulated at the nearest headquarters of the interstellar correspondence club.

How did I learn your language? After all, it is a simple one, particularly the written language seems easy. I had no difficulty with it. If you are still interested in writing me, I shall be happy to continue the correspondence.

Skander

Aurigae II

Dear Pen Pal:

Your enthusiasm is refreshing. You say that I failed to answer your question about how I expected to visit Earth. I confess I deliberately ignored the question, as my experiment had not yet proceeded far enough. I want you to bear with me a short time longer, and then I will be able to give you the details. You are right in saying that it would be difficult for a being who lives at a temperature of 500 degrees Fahrenheit to mingle freely with the people of Earth. This was never my intention, so please relieve your mind. However, let us drop that subject for the time being.

I appreciate the delicate way in which you approach the subject of my imprisonment. But it is quite unnecessary. I performed forbidden experiments upon my body in a way that was deemed to be dangerous to the public welfare. For instance, among other things, I once lowered my surface temperature to 150 degrees Fahrenheit, and so shortened the radioactive cycle-time of my surroundings. This caused an unexpected break in the normal person-to-person energy flow in the city where I lived, and so charges were laid against me. I have thirty more years to serve. It would be pleasant to leave my body behind and tour the universe—but as I said I'll discuss that later.

I wouldn't say that we're a superior race. We have certain qualities which apparently your people do not have. We live longer, not because of any discoveries we've made about ourselves, but because our bodies are built of a more enduring element—I don't know your name for it, but the atomic weight is 52.9#.* Our scientific discoveries are of the kind that would normally be made by a race with our kind of physical structure. The fact that we can work with temperatures of as high as—I don't know just how to put that—has been very helpful in the development of the subspace energies which are extremely hot, and require delicate adjustments. In the later stages these adjustments can be made by machinery, but in the development the work must be done by "hand"—I put that word in quotes, because we have no hands in the same way that you have.

I am enclosing a photographic plate, properly cooled and chemicalized for your climate. I wonder if you would set it up and take a picture of yourself. All you have to do is arrange it properly on the basis of the laws of light—that is, light travels in straight lines, so stand in front of it—and when you are ready *think* "Ready!" The picture will be automatically taken.

Would you do this for me? If you are interested, I will also send you a picture of myself, though I must warn you. My appearance will probably shock you.

Sincerely
Skander

Planet Aurigae II

Dear Pen Pal:

Just a brief note in answer to your question. It is not necessary to put the plate into a camera. You describe this as a dark box. The plate will take the picture when you think, "Ready!" I assure you it will be flooded with light.

Skander

Aurigae II

Dear Pen Pal:

You say that while you were waiting for the answer to my last letter you showed the photographic plate to one of the doctors at the hospital—I cannot picture what you mean by doctor or hospital, but let that pass—and he took the problem up with government authorities. Problem? I don't understand. I thought we were having a pleasant correspondence, private and personal.

*A radioactive isotope of chromium.—Author's Note.

I shall certainly appreciate your sending that picture of yourself.

Skander

Aurigae II

Dear Pen Pal:

I assure you I am not annoyed at your action. It merely puzzled me, and I am sorry the plate has not been returned to you. Knowing what governments are, I can imagine that it will not be returned to you for some time, so I am taking the liberty of enclosing another plate.

I cannot imagine why you should have been warned against continuing this correspondence. What do they expect me to do?—eat you up at long distance? I'm sorry but I don't like hydrogen in my diet.

In any event, I would like your picture as a memento of our friendship, and I will send mine as soon as I have received yours. You may keep it or throw it away, or give it to your governmental authorities—but at least I will have the knowledge that I've given a fair exchange.

With all best wishes
Skander

Aurigae II

Dear Pen Pal:

Your last letter was so slow in coming that I thought you had decided to break off the correspondence. I was sorry to notice that you failed to enclose the photograph, puzzled by your reference to having a relapse, and cheered by your statement that you would send it along as soon as you felt better— whatever that means. However, the important thing is that you did write, and I respect the philosophy of your club which asks its members not to write of pessimistic matters. We all have our own problems which we regard as overshadowing the problems of others. Here I am in prison, doomed to spend the next thirty years tucked away from the main stream of life. Even the thought is hard on my restless spirit, though I know I have a long life ahead of me after my release.

In spite of your friendly letter, I won't feel that you have completely re-established contact with me until you send the photograph.

Yours in expectation
Skander

Dear Pen Pal

Dear Pen Pal:

The photograph arrived. As you suggest, your appearance startled me. From your description I thought I had mentally reconstructed your body. It just goes to show that words cannot really describe an object which has never been seen.

You'll notice that I've enclosed a photograph of myself, as I promised I would. Chunky, metallic looking chap, am I not, very different, I'll wager, than you expected? The various races with whom we have communicated become wary of us when they discover we are highly radioactive, and that literally we are a radioactive form of life, the only such (that we know of) in the universe. It's been very trying to be so isolated and, as you know, I have occasionally mentioned that I had hopes of escaping not only the deadly imprisonment to which I am being subjected but also the body which cannot escape.

Perhaps you'll be interested in hearing how far this idea has developed. The problem involved is one of exchange of personalities with someone else. Actually, it is not really an exchange in the accepted meaning of the word. It is necessary to get an impress of both individuals, of their mind and of their thoughts as well as their bodies. Since this phase is purely mechanical, it is simply a matter of taking complete photographs and of exchanging them. By complete I mean, of course, every vibration must be registered. The next step is to make sure the two photographs are exchanged, that is, that each party has somewhere near him a complete photograph of the other. (It is already too late, Pen Pal. I have set in motion the sub-space energy interflow between the two plates, so you might as well read on.) As I have said, it is not exactly an exchange of personalities. The original personality in each individual is suppressed, literally pushed back out of the consciousness, and the image personality from the "photographic" plate replaces it.

You will take with you a complete memory of your life on Earth, and I will take along memory of my life on Aurigae. Simultaneously, the memory of the receiving body will be blurrily at our disposal. A part of us will always be pushing up, striving to regain consciousness, but always lacking the strength to succeed.

As soon as I grow tired of Earth, I will exchange bodies in the same way with a member of some other race. Thirty

A. E. van Vogt

years hence, I will be happy to reclaim my body, and you can then have whatever body I last happened to occupy.

This should be a very happy arrangement for us both. You, with your short life expectancy, will have outlived all your contemporaries and will have had an interesting experience. I admit I expect to have the better of the exchange—but now, enough of explanation. By the time you reach this part of the letter it will be me reading it, not you. But if any part of you is still aware, so long for now, Pen Pal. It's been nice having all those letters from you. I shall write you from time to time to let you know how things are going with my tour.

Skander

Aurigae II

Dear Pen Pal:

Thanks a lot for forcing the issue. For a long time I hesitated about letting you play such a trick on yourself. You see, the government scientists analyzed the nature of that first photographic plate you sent me, and so the final decision was really up to me. I decided that anyone as eager as you were to put one over should be allowed to succeed.

Now I know I didn't have to feel sorry for you. Your plan to conquer Earth wouldn't have gotten anywhere, but the fact that you had the idea ends the need for sympathy.

By this time you will have realized for yourself that a man who has been paralyzed since birth, and is subject to heart attacks, cannot expect a long life span. I am happy to tell you that your once-lonely pen pal is enjoying himself, and I am happy to sign myself with a name to which I expect to become accustomed.

With best wishes
Skander

A former professor of biological psychology, Dr. Lambe is now an active member of the writing society. He insists that his patronym has two syllables—but won't say which two. His short fiction has appeared in Omni *and* Analog.

DAMN SHAME

By Dean R. Lambe

Sept. 12, 1985

Albert S. Cranberg, M.D.
P.O. Box 912
Fulton, Wisconsin
Dear "Alice":

Sorry to be so long getting back to you; been busy as a bitch in heat. Janet swears that if I don't get some time off soon, she's going to take a vacation without me. The test series are really beginning to pay off on AC-337, and it's damn exciting, to say the least! I think I may have mentioned the *in vitro* results on this stuff the last time I wrote, but of course, we've seen terrific data with isolated tumor cells before. Now that we've finished the first round of animal trials and toxicity screens, though, AC-337 is beginning to look like a winner. Why, in the Bh/286 mice alone (they're the little buggers with a handy gene for bladder cancer), we've got a 92 percent remission rate, and no gastrointestinal side-effects at all. You'd better believe that I'm anxious to start the dog trials next week.

Well, enough shop talk...oh, mum's the word on AC-337. Not that you would say anything, I'm sure, but Hendricks would have my fair young hide if premature publicity got out on our wonder drug. And you know how the press goes crazy about a "cancer cure."

So anyway, how're you doing out there in the sticks? Never could understand how you and Ruth keep from going crazy, but I guess you're right about small towns being the only sensible place to raise kids these days. Still going the GP route—golf on Wednesdays, poker on Saturday night? Just kidding, I remember how you used to play poker—old stone face, you ain't.

Wish I had more time, but gotta get back to the damn computer. Give my love to Ruth and your crumb crushers. Oh, and when you write, you'd better send it here to the lab...mail at home just seems to get lost in the shuffle.

All the best,
Fred

30 Sept 85

Frederick Jenssen, Ph.D.
Ritter Memorial Institute
3944 Orangegrove Drive
Cloverdale, California
Dear Fred:

Will you for christsakes quit calling me "Alice"! You'd think that we were still back in the damn frat house. Speaking of which, did you see the class reunion picture in the latest alumni bulletin? Ho boy, George Riviere looks like he'll be completely bald before he's 40, and Ken Shikoku must have gained 20 kilos. I was also surprised to see that Willis Eisner is working on that Amazon Basin project—never figured that screwball for a Corps of Engineers type. Say though, if your California water shortage gets any worse, maybe old Willis can ship you some; he must have plenty to spare these days.

Damn Shame

The old alma ma is asking for more contributions again—I imagine you got a letter too. Ruth and I always give all we can; what with so many good private schools folding, I'd like to think that the place will still be there when my kids are ready.

Glad to hear that your work is going well. That AC-337 really sounds promising. I've sure got a lot of patients with the Big C who could use something better than what they're getting now, but I suppose your stuff will come too late for most of them, even if it pans out.

As for what's new at this end; well, not much, as you suspected. Little Ruth broke her arm two weeks ago—greenstick fracture of the radius. She fell off that damn jet skater that she just had to have for her birthday. Kids! When my partner set it, she wouldn't let him put on a mnemoplastic cast. Insisted on the old-fashioned plaster kind. Said her friends couldn't write on a plastic one! Not much else, I guess. Oh, Ruth says to tell Janet that she's welcome to move in with us when she gets tired of your workaholic ways.

Regards,
Al

Nov. 21, 1985

Albert S. Cranberg, M.D.
P.O. Box 912
Fulton, Wisconsin
Dear Al:

The space between our letters gets longer and longer, and that's no way to treat the best man at my wedding (I'll never forgive you for that business with the ring, you bastard). The work keeps going super; AC-337 is starting to look like Nobel Prize material. It's all we can do to keep our mouths shut when we're off-campus, but we've got to play it tight until the FDA prelim for human trials is approved. The three runs in the beagles were *go* all the way; still better than 85 percent remission for both sarcomas and carcinomas of several varieties...damn stuff's almost too good to be true. Keep all your toes crossed for us. We start the primate trials next Tuesday.

Believe it or not, Jack hasn't been a dull boy. Janet and I took a long weekend in Vancouver a couple of weeks ago; much fun and frolic was had by all, and she says that she

498

won't run off with that new stud in her office after all (she's joking...uh, I think).

Hello to Ruth and the kids....

All the best,
Fred

3 Jan 86

Frederick Jenssen, Ph.D.
Ritter Memorial Institute
3944 Orangegrove Drive
Cloverdale, California
Dear Fred:

Happy New Year, you lucky dog. Wish you were here to help me shovel snow! You people must have forgotten what winter's like, but then, I don't envy your drought. At least we can flush our commodes here—if the pipes don't freeze; and we did get to spend the holidays with Ruth's folks in Florida.

Fred, old buddy, I have a rather unusual request...hell, I know I shouldn't even ask, but if your AC-337 is still looking good, could you possibly send me enough for two patients? Yah, I know, the FDA and six other piles of bureaucrats would shit bricks, but these patients have nothing to lose, believe me. One is a 41-year-old schoolteacher, but by no means an old maid. She's been bed-hopping for years, and has never been pregnant—makes a classic case for breast cancer, and she's got it in both barrels, and I'm pretty sure that it's metastasized to her brain. Naturally, she waited too long to come in, and I don't give her more than six months. The other case is a 17-year-old kid who was a star basketball player until a couple of months ago. He's got myeloma in both tibias, and he and his parents wouldn't accept double amputation when taking his legs might have done some good. I'm sure that it'll be into the marrow of femur and pelvis in less than a year.

So what do you say, Fred? I know we'd be shaky legally, but who's to know except a couple of terminal patients. Besides, the Laetrile and marijuana precedents do give us some protection; and you'd gain valuable data probably years

499

ahead of schedule. Sure, I'll understand if you don't think you can swing it, but think on it, huh?

Regards,
Al

Jan. 14, 1986

Albert S. Cranberg, M.D.
P.O. Box 912
Fulton, Wisconsin
Dear Al:

Your plea for your two patients really hit me between the eyes, pal; sometimes day-in, day-out lab work makes a guy forget what it's all about. A week ago, I'd have had to say no way, but the FDA prelim just came through, and the third baboon series came up roses too. Granted, we won't be able to start human trials until June, but Hendricks has put me in charge of the whole shooting match (look Ma, a promotion). So between you, me, and a couple of dying folks, what's a little AC-337 between friends. I'm sending you a little package, which includes the computer projections on the human dose-response curve. Naturally, I'll expect you to keep meticulous records. Oh, and you may be interested to know that our biochem people finally have a handle on how it works. Seems AC-337 has characteristics of both methotrexate and urethane, but selectively hits the RNA of tumor cells more like the former. They're still puzzling over why the protein synthesis breaks down in so many seemingly different types of cancer cells, though.

Sure glad I can say yes. And hey, you folks give some real thought about heading this way for a vacation this summer.

All the best,
Fred

12 April 86

Frederick Jenssen, Ph.D.
Ritter Memorial Institute
3944 Orangegrove Drive
Cloverdale, California
Dear Fred:

Now look who's falling behind in letter-writing. And this has got to be just a quick note. I've got three runny noses, a sprained ankle, and two little old ladies who're just lonely, all outside in the waiting room. But I just got the second lab workup on "our" two patients, and want to let you know right away. The first follow-up after I started AC-337 was inconclusive, so I didn't want to send you any false positives. Now...well, I can hardly believe my eyes as I hold these X rays. If what I see continues, that school teacher will be back to the Three Rs this fall, and the kid will be under the hoop with the best of them again. Naturally, my next question is, can you spare any more of the stuff? Could save surgery for a couple other patients. Oh, and how tough is AC-337 to synthesize? Is it going to cost an arm and a leg (no pun intended) when it's finally released?

Regards,
Al

May 2, 1986

Albert S. Cranberg, M.D.
P.O. Box 912
Fulton, Wisconsin
Dear Al:

Damn mail gets slower every month, but boy am I happy you're happy. And you'll be even happier to know that the baboons and chimps have shown no side-effects either; got three female baboons pregnant that had uterine cancer three months ago. How's that for a turn-around! As for synthesis of AC-337, well, the boys and girls in biochem say it'd be a bitch, but no sweat because the source is a botanical—some South American plant of all things (hell, I didn't even know that until a few days ago, and I'm supposed to be in charge). Of course, it's too soon to have done a cost-per-dose projection, and our research costs certainly aren't cheap, but you sawbones shouldn't have to worry about the price.

I really wish I could send you more, but our human trials are about ready to go, and the available supply is all tightly budgeted. As a matter of fact, I have to break this off and get a subtle order out to the supply house for more raw materials (ah, the joys of being project director). Do keep me informed on those patients' progress.

All the best,
Fred

May 2, 1986

Mr. Nathan Anderson
Butler Bio-Medical Supply, Inc.
521 Washburn Avenue
Lawrence, Kansas
Dear Mr. Anderson:

About a year ago, your company supplied us with 60 kilograms of dried specimens of the plant *Pedicularis tefensis.* You may recall that Dr. Carlton's team at the University of Kansas had found some indications of medicinal value in this South American plant. I am pleased to report that our research has confirmed Dr. Carlton's findings.

We are most anxious to continue our investigations with extracts from *Pedicularis tefensis,* and would like to order 400 kilograms for immediate delivery.

Should your company be unable to supply this amount, I would appreciate any information you may have on other suppliers.

Sincerely,
Frederick Jenssen, Ph.D.
Ritter Memorial Institute

May 28, 1986

Dr. Frederick Jenssen
Ritter Memorial Institute
3944 Orangegrove Drive
Cloverdale, California
Dear Dr. Jenssen:

I regret that we no longer have any stock of *Pedicularis tefensis.* As you undoubtedly know, there has been considerable terrorist activity and increased anti-American sentiment in much of South America, and our regular field collectors are simply no longer welcome (or safe) in many areas. My contacts within our industry would indicate that other suppliers would be cut off from their former sources as well.

I am enclosing the name of a Brazilian botanist with whom we have had very good relations in the past, and I hope that he can be of help to you.

Please contact me if you feel that we can be of further service.

Yours truly,
Nate Anderson
Vice Pres., Botanicals
Butler Bio-Medical Supply, Inc.

29 May 1986

Frederick Jenssen, Ph.D.
Ritter Memorial Institute
3944 Orangegrove Drive
Cloverdale, California
Dear Fred:

Damnit, old buddy, this is literally one hell of a note! Classic "there's good news, and bad news." As for our two patients, well, that's the good news—complete remission. You know we don't like to use the word, but if ever I've seen "cures," then that term applies to our schoolmarm and basketball player. Now for the irony—Ruth's got a lump in her left breast. Got the biopsy results yesterday, and I needn't tell you the verdict.

My ethics are shot to hell over this. I had one dose of AC-337 left, and you know what I did with it. But it won't be enough...please, Fred.

Please,
Al

June 12, 1986

Albert S. Cranberg, M.D.
P.O. Box 912
Fulton, Wisconsin
Dear Al:

Ethics be damned, friend! You know I'll find enough somewhere to give Ruth the full series. It's tight, what with all the protocols now on file with the Feds, but I think we're about to have a "computer error" here. I just ran into a little snag on the supply of raw materials, but I'm going directly

503

to the source, so it's nothing for you or Ruth to worry about. We ought to have an ample amount in a couple of months, and I can easily replace what I send you.

Hang in there,
Fred

June 12, 1986

Senhor Dotor João Luís Linhares
Instituto Botânico Ocidental
27 Rua Barbacena
Manaus, Amazonas, Brazil
Dear Dr. Linhares:

Mr. Nathan Anderson of Butler Bio-Medical Supply, Inc. has given me your name as one who might be able to supply extract from the plant *Pedicularis tefensis*. Our research has uncovered useful medicinal properties in this plant, and we are anxious to obtain several hundred kilograms in order to continue our investigations.

I would also appreciate any information that you may have on the possibility of controlled, hothouse cultivation of this species. If possible, I would like to arrange for the immediate shipment of several hundred living plants.

Sincerely,
Frederick Jenssen, Ph.D.
Ritter Memorial Institute

19 July 1986

Dr. Frederick Jenssen
Ritter Memorial Institute
3944 Orangegrove Drive
Cloverdale, California USA
Dear Dr. Jenssen:

I am in receipt of your letter to Dr. João Luís Linhares, and ask that you forgive my poor use of your language. I regret to inform you Dr. Linhares is not among the living, it being particularly saddening that the gentleman died at his own hand. As you may know, Dr. Linhares put in most of his years in the study of the ecology of our tropical rain forest, and it is thought that he could not accept the necessity of flooding for to make our great Amazon Sea. It is unfortunate that this good man lacked the vision of our great Presidente for the progress and good of our peoples.

I also regret that I cannot supply you any *Pedicularis tefensis,* what you would call Tefé Lousewort. I do not know this plant personally, but with consultation of the notes of Dr. Linhares, I find that *Pedicularis tefensis* grows only at a place 50 km. from where the River Tefé flows into the River Amazon. Now, with completion of our great dams, that region is below many meters of water. It is to be assumed that this species is now extinct.

As I am convinced of your interest in our other plants of value medical, I take the liberty of sending you a listing of what is available.

Yours sincerely,
Raimundo P-M. Chavantes, D.Sc.
Instituto Botânico Ocidental

Howard Fast (1914–   ) is one of a relatively small group of authors who have written some excellent science fiction and fantasy in addition to other works for which they are more famous. Others who come to mind are John D. MacDonald, John Jakes, and Michael Shaara. Mr. Fast's literary accomplishments include such famous books as Citizen Tom Paine (1943), Spartacus (1951), and the best-selling Immigrant series. Within sf, he has produced a string of notable stories which have been collected as The Edge of Tomorrow (1961), The General Zapped an Angel (1969), and A Touch of Infinity (1973).

The present selection originally appeared as "The First Men" in the February 1960 issue of The Magazine of Fantasy and Science Fiction.

THE TRAP

By Howard Fast

Bath, England
October 12, 1945

Mrs. Jean Arbalaid
Washington, D.C.

My dear Sister:
I admit to lethargy and perhaps to a degree of indifference—

although it is not indifference in your terms, not in the sense of ceasing to care. I care for you very much and think about you a good deal. After all, we have only each other, and apart from the two of us, our branch of the Feltons has ceased to exist. So, in my failure to reply to three separate letters, there was no more than a sort of inadequacy. I had nothing to say because there was nothing that I wanted to say.

You knew where I was, and I asked Sister Dorcas to write you a postcard or something to the effect that I had mended physically even if my brain was nothing to shout about. I have been rather depressed for the past two months—the doctors here call it melancholia, with their British propensity for Victorian nomenclature—but they tell me that I am now on the mend in that department as well. Apparently, the overt sign of increasing mental health is an interest in things. My writing to you, for example, and also the walks I have taken around the city. Bath is a fascinating town, and I am rather pleased that the rest home they sent me to is located here.

They were terribly short of hospitals with all the bombing and with the casualties sent back here after the Normandy landing, but they have a great talent for making do. Here they took several of the great houses of the Beau Nash period and turned them into rest homes—and managed to make things very comfortable. Ours has a garden, and when a British garden is good, it has no equal anywhere else in the world. In fact, it spurred me to make some rather mawkish advances to Sister Dorcas one sunny day, and she absolutely destroyed my budding sexual desires with her damned understanding and patience. There is nothing as effective in cutting down a clean-cut American lad as a tall, peach-skinned, beautiful and competent British lady who is doubling as a nurse and has a high-bridged nose in the bargain.

I have been ambulant lately, pottering around Bath and poking my nose into each and every corner. The doctor encourages me to walk for the circulation and final healing of my legs, and since Bath is built up and down, I take a good deal of exercise. I go to the old Roman baths frequently, being absolutely fascinated by them and by the whole complex that is built around the Pump Room—where Nash and his pals held forth. So much of Bath is a Georgian city, perhaps more perfect architecturally than any other town in England. But there are also the baths, the old baths of the Middle Ages, and then the Roman baths which date back before that. In fact, the doctors here have insisted that I and other circulatory-problem cases take the baths. I can't see how it differs from an ordinary hot bath, but British physicians still believe in natural healing virtues and so forth.

Why am I a circulatory problem, you are asking yourself; and just what is left of old Harry Felton and what has been shot away and how much of his brain is soggy as a bowl of farina? Yes indeed—I do know you, my sister. May I say immediately that in my meanderings around the town, I am permitted to be alone; so apparently I am not considered to be the type of nut one locks away for the good of each and everyone.

Oh, there are occasions when I will join up with some convalescent British serviceman for an amble, and sometimes I will have a chat with the locals in one of the pubs, and on three or four occasions I have wheedled Sister Dorcas into coming along and letting me hold her hand and make a sort of pass, just so I don't forget how; but by and large, I am alone. You will remember that old Harry was always a sort of loner—so apparently the head is moderately dependable.

It is now the next day, old Jean. October 13. I put the letter away for a day. Anyway, it is becoming a sort of epistle, isn't it? The thing is that I funked it—notice the way I absorb the local slang—when it came down to being descriptive about myself, and I had a talk with Sister Dorcas, and she sent me to the psychiatrist for a listen. He listens and I talk. Then he pontificates.

"Of course," he said to me, after I had talked for a while, "this unwillingness to discuss one's horrors is sometimes worn like a bit of romantic ribbon. You know, old chap—a decoration."

"I find you irritating," I said to him.

"Of course you do. I am trying to irritate you."

"Why?"

"I suppose because you are an American and I have a snobbish dislike for Americans."

"Now you're being tactful."

The psychiatrist laughed appreciatively and congratulated me on a sense of humor. He is a nice fellow, the psychiatrist, about forty, skinny, as so many British professionals are, long head, big nose, very civilized. To me, Jean, that is the very nice thing about the English—the sense of civilization you feel.

"But I don't want you to lose your irritation," he said.

"No danger."

"I mean if we get to liking and enjoying each other, we'll simply cover things up. I want to root up a thing or two. You're well enough to take it—and you're a strong type, Felton. No schizoid tendencies—never did show any. Your state of depression was more of a reaction to your fear that you would never walk again, but you're walking quite well now, aren't you? Yet Sister Dorcas tells me you will not write a word to your family about what happened to you. Why not?"

"My family is my sister. I don't want to worry her, and Sister Dorcas has a big mouth."

"I'll tell her that."

"And I'll kill you."

"And as far as worrying your sister—my dear fellow, we all know who your sister is. She is a great scientist and a woman of courage and character. Nothing you can tell her would worry her, but your silence does."

"She thinks I've lost my marbles?"

"You Americans are delightful when you talk the way you imagine we think you talk. No, she doesn't think you're dotty. Also, I wrote to her a good many months ago, telling her that you had been raked by machine-gun fire across both legs and describing the nature of your injuries."

"Then there it is."

"Of course not. It is very important for you to be able to discuss what happened to you. You suffered trauma and great pain. So did many of us."

"I choose not to talk about it," I said. "Also, you are beginning to bore me."

"Good. Irritation and boredom. What else?"

"You are a goddamn nosey Limey, aren't you?"

"Yes, indeed."

"Never take No for an answer."

"I try not to."

"All right, doc—it is as simple as this. I do not choose to talk about what happened to me because I have come to dislike my race."

"Race? How do you mean, Felton—Americans? White race? or what?"

"The human race," I said to him.

"Oh, really? Why?"

"Because they exist only to kill."

"Come on now—we do take a breather now and then."

"Intervals. The main purpose is killing."

"You know, you are simply feeding me non sequiturs. I ask you why you will not discuss the incident of your being wounded, and you reply that you have come to dislike the human race. Now and then I myself have found the human race a little less than overwhelmingly attractive, but that's surely beside the point."

"Perhaps. Perhaps not."

"Why don't you tell me what happened?"

"Why don't you drop dead?" I asked him.

"Or why don't you and I occupy ourselves with a small pamphlet on Americanisms—if only to enlighten poor devils like myself who have to treat the ill among you who inhabit our rest homes?"

"The trouble is," I said, "that you have become so bloody civilized that you have lost the ability to be properly nasty."

"Oh, come off it, Felton, and stop asking for attention like a seven-year-old. Why don't you just tell me what happened— because you know, it's you who are becoming the bore."

"All right," I agreed. "Good. We're getting to be honest with each other. I will tell you—properly and dramatically— and then will you take your stinking psychiatric ass off my back?"

"If you wish."

"Good. Not that it's any great hotshot story for the books— it simply is what it is to me. I had a good solid infantry company, New York boys mostly; some Jews, some Negroes, five Puerto Ricans, a nice set of Italians and Irish, and the rest white Protestants of English, Scotch, North of Ireland and German descent. I specify, because we were all on the holy mission of killing our fellow man. The boys were well trained and they did their best, and we worked our way into Germany with no more casualties or stupidities than the next company; and then one of those gross and inevitable stupidities occurred. We came under enemy fire and we called our planes for support, and they bombed and strafed the hell out of us."

"Your planes?"

"That's right. It happened a lot more often than anyone gave out, and it was a wonder it didn't happen twice as much. How the hell do you know, when you're way up there and moving at that speed? How do you know which is which, when one and all are trying to cuddle into the ground? So it happened. There was an open farm shed, and one of my riflemen and I dived in there and took cover behind a woodpile. And that was where I found this little German kid, about three years old, frightened, almost catatonic with fear—and just a beautiful kid."

I must have stopped there. He prodded me, and pointed out that the war had drawn small distinction between children and adults, and even less distinction between more beautiful and less beautiful children.

"What did you do?"

"I tried to provide cover for the child," I explained patiently. "I put her in my arms and held my body over her. A bomb hit the shed. I wasn't hurt, but the rifleman there with me—his name was Ruckerman—he was killed. I came out into the open with the kid in my arms, warm and safe. Only the top of her head was gone. A freak hit. I suppose the bomb fragment sheared it clean off, and I stood there with the little girl's brains dripping down on my shoulder. Then I was hit by the German machine-gun burst."

"I see," the psychiatrist said.

"You have imagination, then."

"You tell it well," he said. "Feel any better?"

"No."

"Mind a few more questions, Felton? I am keeping my promise to take my ass off your back, so just say No, if you wish."

"You're very patient with me."

He was. He had put up with my surliness and depression for weeks. Never lost his temper, which was the principal reason why he irritated me so.

"All right. Question away."

"Now that you've told this to me, do you feel any different?"

"No."

"Any better?"

"No."

"That's good."

"Why is it good?" I asked him.

"Well, you see—the incident outraged you, but not in a traumatic sense. Apparently it doesn't hurt or help very much to recall it."

"It's not blocked, if you mean that. I can think about it whenever I wish to. It disgusts me."

"Certainly. As I said, I believe your depression was entirely due to the condition of your legs. When you began to walk, the depression started to lift, and they tell me that in another few weeks your legs will be as good as ever. Well, not for mountain climbing—but short of that, good enough. Tell me, Felton, why were you so insistent upon remaining in England for your convalescence? You pulled a good many strings. You could have been flown home, and the care stateside is better than here. They have all sorts of things and conveniences that we don't have."

"I like England."

"Do you? No girl awaited you here—what do you like about us?"

"There you go with your goddamn, nosy professional touch."

"Yes, of course. But, you see, Captain, you made your indictment universal. Man is a bloody horror. Quite so. Here, too. Isn't he?"

"Oh, do get off my back," I said to him, and that ended the interview; but by putting it down, "he said," "I said," etc., I am able, my dear Jean, to convey the facts to you.

You ask whether I want to come home. The answer is No. Not now, not in the foreseeable future. Perhaps never, but never is a hairy word, and who can tell?

You say that my share of mother's estate brings me over a hundred dollars a week. I have no way to spend any of it, so let the lawyers piddle with it just as they have been doing. I have my own dole, my accumulated pay, and a few hundred dollars I won playing bridge. Ample. As I said, I have nothing to spend it on.

As to what I desire—very little indeed. I have no intentions of resuming the practice of corporate law. The first two years of it bored me, but at least I brought to them a modicum of ambition. Now the ambition is gone, and the only thing that replaces it is distaste. No matter what direction my thinking takes, I always return to the fact that the human race is a rather dreadful thing. That is, my dear, with the exception of yourself and your brilliant husband.

I am better able to write now, so if you write to me and tell me what brilliance and benevolence you and your husband are up to now, I shall certainly answer your letter.

Thank you for bearing with me through my boorish months.

Harry.

2

Washington, D.C.
October 16, 1945

Captain Harry Felton
Bath, England

My dear Harry:
I will not try to tell you how good it was to hear from you. I never was terribly good at putting my feelings down on paper, but believe me I have read and reread your letter, oh, I should say, at least half a dozen times, and I have done little but think of you and what you have been through and your situation at this moment. I am sure you realize, Harry, better than anyone else, that this is not a time for bright words and happy clichés. Nothing I say at this moment is going to make very much difference to you or to your state of mind or, of course, to your state of health. And nothing I offer at this moment in the way of philosophical argument is going to change any of your attitudes. On my part, I am not sure that changing them at this moment is very important. Far more important is Harry Felton, his life and his future.

I have been talking about that to Mark and thinking about it a great deal myself. Harry, we've both of us engaged on a most exciting project which, for the moment, must remain surrounded with all the silly United States Army attitudes of secrecy and classification. Actually, our project is not military and there are no military secrets concerned with it. But at the moment we are operating with Army money and therefore we are surrounded with all sorts of taboos and rules and regulations. Nevertheless, Harry, rest assured that the project is fascinating, important and, quite naturally, difficult.

We need help—I think specifically the kind of help you might provide. And at the same time, I think we can give you what you need most at this moment of your life—a purpose. We cannot give you a profession, and, when you come right down to it, we cannot ask you to be much more than an exalted messenger-boy–reporter. However, the combination of the two will give you a chance to travel, perhaps to see some of the world that you have not yet seen, and, we think, to ask some interesting questions.

Truthfully, our mission requires a very intelligent man. I am not apple-polishing or trying to cheer you with compliments. I am simply stating that we can make you a fairly decent offer that will take your mind off your present situation and at least give you an interest in geography.

At the moment we can pay you only a pittance, but you say in your letter that you are not particularly concerned with money. We will pay all expenses, of course, and you may stay at the best places if you wish.

Just as an indication of the kind of wheels we presently are and the kind of weight we can throw around, Mark has completed your discharge in England; your passport is on its way via diplomatic pouch, and it will be handed to you personally either before this letter arrives or no more than a day later.

The bit in your letter about your legs was reassuring, and I am sure by now you are even further improved. What I would like you to do, at our expense, is to pick up a civilian outfit. If you can buy the clothes you need in Bath, good; if not, you'd better run up to London and buy them there. You will want, for the most part, tropical lightweight stuff since the wind is up for us in the Far East. Though you will travel as a civilian, we are able to offer you a sort of quasi-diplomatic status, and some very good-looking papers and cards that will clear your way whenever there is a difficulty about priorities. I'm afraid that priorities will remain very much in the picture for the next six months or so. We are short of air-travel space as well as a number of other things. But, as I said before, we are very large wheels indeed, and we envisage no trouble in moving you wherever we desire to. That's a dreadful thing to say, isn't it, and it almost places you outside of the picture as a human being with any volition of your own. Believe me, Harry, like your charming British psychiatrist, I am combining irritation with love. No, I know how easy it would be for you to say No, and I also know that a sharp negative will be absolutely your first and instinctive reaction. By now, of course, simply reading my letter, you have said No half a dozen times, and you have also asked yourself just who the devil your sister thinks she is. My dear, dear Harry, she is a person who loves you very much. How easy it would be for me to say to you, "Harry, please come home immediately to the warmth of our hearts and to the welcome of our open arms." All too easy, Harry, and as far as I can tell, thinking the matter through, it would do you absolutely no good. Even if we could persuade you to come back stateside, I am afraid that you would be bored to tears and frustrated beyond belief. I think that I can understand why you do not want to come home, and I think that at this moment in your existence, it is a very proper decision for you to make. That is to say, I agree with you: you should not come home; but, at the same time, you must have something to do. You may feel, Harry, that this messenger-boy business is not the most creative thing in the world, but I think that rather than attempt to explain to you in advance what we are up to and what you will encounter, you should allow yourself to be drawn into it. You need make no absolute commitments. You will see and you will understand more and more, and at any point along the way you are free to quit, to tell us to go to the devil—or to continue. The choice is always yours; you have no obligation and you are not tied down.

On the other hand, this is not to say that we do not very much want you to accept the assignment. I don't have to tell you what Mark's opinion of you is. You will remember—and believe me it has not changed—he shares my love for you, and you command his very great respect along with mine.

Harry, if you are able to accept my offer, cable me immediately. I would like you to be ready to move out in the next day or two after cabling.

Meanwhile, you have all our love and all our best and deepest and most sincere wishes and prayers for a complete recovery. I do love you very much, and I remain,

Your most devoted sister,
Jean.

By cable:

MRS. JEAN ARBALAID
WASHINGTON, D.C.
OCTOBER 19, 1945

THAT YOU SHOULD EVEN APOLOGIZE. I ACCEPT YOUR OFFER WITH
UNEQUIVOCAL DELIGHT. ENTIRE OUTFIT AVAILABLE AT BATH
WHERE THE MEN'S HABERDASHERY SHOPS ARE VERY GOOD IN-
DEED. OUTFITTING UP LIKE A VERY PUKKA EAST INDIAN TYPE.
READY TO LEAVE WHENEVER YOUR SPECIFIC INSTRUCTIONS AR-
RIVE. THIS IS THE FIRST TOUCH OF PLEASURE OR EXCITEMENT
THAT I HAVE EXPERIENCED IN A GOOD MANY DREARY MONTHS.
YOU AND MARK DEAR SISTER ADMIRABLE PSYCHOLOGISTS. THANK
YOU BOTH. LOVE AND KISSES. I AWAIT INSTRUCTIONS.

HARRY FELTON

By cable:

HARRY FELTON
BATH, ENGLAND
OCTOBER 21, 1945

THANK YOU HARRY AND OUR BLESSINGS WITH YOU. AIR TRANS-
PORT FROM LONDON AIRPORT ON 23 OCTOBER. SPECIAL PRIORI-
TIES TO CALCUTTA INDIA. AT CALCUTTA PROCEED TO CALCUTTA
UNIVERSITY AND SEE THE INDIAN ANTHROPOLOGIST PROFESSOR
SUMIL GOJEE. QUESTION HIM. GET ALL DETAILS INDIAN CHILD SUP-
POSEDLY STOLEN AND RAISED BY WOLVES VILLAGE OF CHANGA
IN ASSAM. STORY ASSOCIATED PRESS REPORTER OCTOBER 9, 1945.
ASSOCIATED PRESS STORY HAS PROFESSOR GOJEE DEEPLY IN-
VOLVED. PLEASE GET ALL DETAILS AND WRITE FULL REPORT AS
SOON AS POSSIBLE.

JEAN ARBALAID

By airmail:

Calcutta, India
November 4, 1945

Mrs. Jean Arbalaid
Washington, D.C.

My dear Sister:

First of all, I want you to know that I have taken your mission very seriously. I have never been contented with errand-boy status, as you will remember if you look back through the years of my life. Therefore, I decided to bring to the problem you set before me an observing eye, a keen ear, an astute mind, and all the skills of a poor lawyer. In any case, the mission has been completed, and I think that to some degree I have fallen in love with India. What a strange and beautiful place it is, especially now in November! I am told that in the summer months it is very different and quite unbearable. But my experience has been of a congenial climate and of a people as hospitable and gentle as I have ever known.

I arrived in Calcutta and saw the Indian anthropologist, Professor Gojee. We had a number of meetings, and I discussed this case with him quite thoroughly. I found him charming, intelligent and very perceptive, and he has been kind enough to have me at his house for dinner on two separate occasions, and to introduce me to his family. Let me tell you, indeed let me assure you, my dear sister, that in Bengal this is no small achievement.

But before I go into my discussions with Professor Gojee and the conclusions we came to, let me give you the general background of the matter.

The original Associated Press story seems to have been quite accurate in all of its details—so far as I can ascertain—and I have done my detective work thoroughly and assiduously. I went personally to the small village of Changa in Assam. It is not an easy place to get to, and requires plane, narrow-gauge train and ox cart. At this time of the year, however, it was a fairly pleasant trip. The village itself is a

517

tiny, rather wretched place, but in Indian terms it is by no means the worst place in the world. It has what very few Indian villages have, especially in this part of Bengal—a tiny schoolhouse. It also has a schoolteacher and a number of people who are literate. This helps a great deal in the process of tracking down any historical data or events connected with the life and history of the village.

The village schoolmaster, whose name is Adap Chaterjee, was very helpful, since his English was excellent and since he knew all the participants in the particular event, and, indeed, was at the village when the child was originally lost. That was twelve years ago.

I am sure, Jean, that you know enough about India to realize that twelve is very much an adult age for a girl in these parts—the majority of them are married by then; and there is no question, none at all, about the age of the child. I spoke to the mother and the father, who originally identified the child by two very distinctive birthmarks. I saw these birthmarks myself in Calcutta, where the child is kept at the university. She has there at the university the best of care, kindness, and all the attention she demands. Of course, at this moment we cannot say how long the university will be able to keep her.

However, everything the mother and father told me about the child in the village of Changa seemed to be entirely compatible with the circumstances. That is, wherever their stories and the statements of other villagers could be checked, this checking proved that they had been telling more or less the truth—considering, of course, that any truth loses some of its vividness over a twelve-year period.

The child was lost as an infant—at eight months—a common story in these parts. The parents were working in the field. The child was set down and then the child was gone. Whether the child crawled at that age or not, I can't say, nor can I find any witness who will provide that particular information. At any rate, all agree that the child was healthy, alert and curious—a fine and normal infant. There is absolutely no disagreement on that point.

Now, I know full well that most European and American scientists regard the whole mythology of a child being raised by wolves or some other animal under jungle conditions as an invention and a fiction. But a great many things that

Western science has regarded as fiction are now proving to be at least the edge of a fact if not the fact itself. Here in India, the child raised in the jungle is regarded as one of the absolutes of existence. There are so many records of it that it seems almost impossible to doubt it. Nor, as you will see, is there any other conceivable explanation for this child.

How the child came to the wolves is something we will never know. Possibly a bitch who had lost her own cubs carried the infant off. That is the most likely story, isn't it? But I do not rule out entirely any act of animosity against the parents by another villager. The child could have been carried off and left deep in the jungle; but, as I said, we will never have the truth on this question.

These wolves here in Assam are not *lupus,* the European variety, but *pallipes,* its local cousin. *Pallipes* is nevertheless a most respectable animal in size and disposition, and not something to stumble over on a dark night. When the child was found, a month ago, the villagers had to kill five wolves to take her, and she herself fought like a devil out of hell. At that point, the child had lived as a wolf for eleven years. This does not mean, however, that *pallipes* is a vicious animal. I recall reading a book not too long ago concerning the Canadian variety of *lupus,* the wolf. The naturalist commented on the fact that *lupus,* raised with a family as a dog might be raised, is, contrary to common legend, even more dependable and gentler than almost any house dog. The same naturalist goes on to say that all of the stories of *lupus* running in packs, viciously tearing down his prey, killing his fellow wolf in wolf-to-wolf fights—that all of this is invention, and not very pleasant invention. This naturalist said that there are absolutely no cases of interpack fighting among wolves, that they do not kill each other, and that they have taught each other and taught their offspring as great a responsibility as can be found in any species.

Personally, I would include man in that statement. My being here on this mission has led me to do a great deal of investigation and reading on wolves, and it all comes down to the fact that at this moment Harry Felton is ready to regard the wolf as an animal quite equal to, if not superior to, man in all moral and ethical behavior—that is, if you are willing to grant ethics to a wolf.

To get back to the problem we have here—namely, the

story of this child's life among the wolves—will the whole story ever emerge? I don't know. To all effects and purposes she is a wolf. She cannot stand upright, the curvature of her spine being beyond correction. She runs on all fours and her knuckles are covered with heavy calluses.

One day at the university, I watched her run. They had put a heavy leather belt around her waist. From it a chain extended to a cable which, in turn, was anchored high up on two opposite walls of a room about twenty feet wide. While I observed her, this time for a period of about fifteen minutes, she ran back and forth the length of the cable, on all fours, using her knuckles as front paws. She ran back and forth in that swaying, horrible, catatonic manner that a caged animal comes to assume.

My first reaction to this was that they were being unduly cruel. Later I learned better. The fact of the matter is that, if anything, they were overly tender, overly gentle and thoughtful with her. It is in the nature of the educated Indian to have enormous reverence for all forms of life. The people at the university combine such reverence with great pity for this child and her fate. If you will remember, my dear Jean, your readings in Buddhism—specifically in the type of Buddhism that is practiced in Bengal—you will recollect that it teaches, among other things, the doctrine of reoccurrence. This means that this poor damned child is caught in an eternal wheel, destined to live this senseless, awful fate of hers over and over for eternity—or at least so they believe. And it evokes their great pity.

They have been trying for days to teach her to use her hands for grasping and holding, but so far unsuccessfully. We are very glib when we talk of what man has done with a thumb in opposition to four fingers; but I assure you that in so far as this wolf-child is concerned, the thumb in opposition to her four fingers is utterly meaningless. She cannot use her thumb in conjunction with her fingers, nor can she properly straighten her fingers or use them in any way for any kind of manipulation—even for the very simple manipulation that her teachers try to lead her into.

Did I mention that she must be naked? She tears off any clothes they dress her in, and there are times when she will attack her leather belt with a kind of senseless ferocity. They attempted to put a cloth sleeping pad in the room, but in this they were unsuccessful, since she promptly tore to pieces each pad they placed there. They were equally unsuccessful in their attempts to teach her to defecate in toilet or chamber pot; in fact, any puppy is more easily housebroken than this child. Eleven years have given her a rigidity of action—or a mechanicality, as the university people here prefer to call it—which appears to preclude any kind of training.

However, the people at the university do not despair, and they hope that in time she will be able to master at least some elements of civilized behavior.

At this point, however, she has not been able to grasp even the meaning of speech, much less make any progress herself in the art of conversation or communication. The problem of communication with this child is absolutely staggering.

The Indian anthropologist, Professor Sumil Gojee (the man you had been in communication with), is very highly regarded both here and in Bombay, where he has been a guest lecturer on one occasion or another. He is a social anthropologist, you know, and he is recognized as a great authority on village life in Bengal. He has been working with the wolf-child for a week now, and during the past four days he has been joined by Professor Armen Ranand from the University of Bombay. Both of them have been very kind to me and have given me unstintingly of their time, which I want you to know is an achievement on my part, since I was unable to explain to them in any coherent fashion just what you are up to and after. That comes back to the fact that I am entirely ignorant of what you are up to and after, and have been able only to guess and to form some rather silly theories of my own which I will not bore you with.

At this point, both men have little hope that any real communication will ever be possible. In our terms and by our measurements, the wolf-child is a total idiot, an infantile imbecile, and it is likely that she will remain so for the rest of her life. This prognosis of mental rigidity puzzled me, and I discussed it at some length with both Professor Gojee and Professor Ranand.

Our first discussion took place while we were observing the child in her room, which has become for the most part her habitat. Do not think that she is held prisoner there in some heartless manner. She is taken for walks, but that is not easy; she is a rather savage little animal, and a great many precautions must be taken every time she is removed from her room. The room is equipped with one of those mirrors that enable you to look into it without being perceived from the inside. The mirror is placed high enough on the wall not to bother the child, and so far as I know she has never become aware of either the mirror or its two-way quality. Watching her on this occasion, Professor Gojee pointed out to me that she was quite different from a wolf.

I said to him, "I would think that being so unhuman she would at least be wolflike in most ways."

"Not at all," Gojee replied. "In the first place, she is twelve years old, which is very old indeed for a wolf. Do you understand? She has spent a lifetime, a wolf lifetime among the wolves, during which her wolf companions have matured and, I imagine, in many cases gone to their deaths. She, however, remained through that period a child. Now you must not believe for a moment that she could have been unaware of her difference from the wolves. She was most aware of the difference, and indeed the wolves were also aware of this difference. The fact that they accepted her, that they fed her, that they took care of her, does not mean that they were foolish enough to mistake her for a wolf. No, indeed! They knew that they were dealing with a very nonwolf type of child; and I am inclined to believe that within the limitations of their mentality the wolves had some hazy notion that this was a human child. This could only have meant that she would be treated differently from the rest of the wolves, and the result of this different treatment would be a series of traumas. In other words, a wolf brought up in a normal wolf environment would, we could expect, be fairly free from neuroses. Now, this is probably a very silly use of terminology. We do not know whether neuroses exist among wolves, and we are not absolutely certain as to the nature of neuroses in the human being. However, we can with some certainty make a case for the neurosis of this child. Whether she is pathological, I am not certain, but certainly her emotional structure has been deformed beyond repair, and her intellectual powers have been stunted beyond belief and deprived of any ability to mature."

"Then what exactly is she?" I asked him.

He turned to Dr. Ranand and, with a rather sad smile, repeated my question. Dr. Ranand, the professor from Bombay, shrugged his shoulders.

"How can I possibly answer that? She is not human; she

is not a wolf. If we were to approach her in terms of her intelligence, then certainly we would say that she is closer to the wolves. But a wolf's intelligence is a completed thing; in other words, a wolf is just as intelligent as a wolf should be. Whether she is as intelligent as a wolf should be, I don't know. Presumably a wolf with her cranial capacity would be capable of a great deal of learning. She, on the other hand, is not capable of the kind of learning we would expect from this theoretical but nonexistent wolf with a super-large cranial capacity. What, then, is the poor child? A human being? No, I don't think she is a human being. A wolf? Quite obviously she is not a wolf." His voice trailed away here. He looked at Professor Gojee helplessly.

"We can conclude this," Professor Gojee said, "she has been denied the opportunity to become a human being."

The next day, a Dr. Chalmers, a British public-health officer, joined us for a period of observation. Like myself, he had been to the village of Changa, investigating her background. He bore out what I had learned there, that there was absolutely no history of imbecilism in her background. Afterwards, he was able to examine the child very carefully. I must say here, Jean, that in order for him to make this examination the child had to be put to sleep. Ether was used, and every care was taken. An anaesthetist from the General Hospital here administered the anaesthesia—under difficult conditions, I will admit. Then the child was unchained and was taken to a medical examination room where Dr. Chalmers conducted his physical examination under the supervision of both Professor Gojee and Professor Ranand. He found absolutely no physical elements to account for the child's mental condition: no malformation of the cranial area and no signs of imbecilism. His findings bore out my own in Changa; that is, the fact that everyone in the village had attested to the normalcy—indeed, alertness and brightness— of the infant. Both Dr. Chalmers and Professor Gojee made a special point of the alertness and adaptability that the infant must have required to enable it to begin its eleven years of survival among the wolves. The child responds excellently to reflex tests, and neurologically, she appears to be sound. She is also strong—beyond the strength of most adults—very wiry, quick in her movements, and possessed of an uncanny sense of smell and hearing.

I watched while the doctor examined the wolf marks upon her—that is, the specific physical idiosyncrasies that were the result of her life among four-legged animals. Her spine was bent in a perpetual curvature that could not be reversed—even with an operation. Her calluses were well developed and most interesting; evidently she ran mostly, if not always, on all fours. Her teeth were strong and there were no signs of decay, although the incidence of tooth decay is rather high in the native village. While Dr. Chalmers is not a psychiatrist, his experience in the Public Health Service has been long and very varied; and, in his opinion, the prognosis for this child is not hopeful. Like Professor Gojee, he does not believe that she will ever progress to a point where she can master even the simplest use of language.

Professor Ranand believes that eventually the child will die. He has examined records of eighteen similar cases. These eighteen cases were selected from several hundred recorded in India during the past century. Of these several hundred recorded cases, a great many could be thrown aside as fiction. These eighteen cases Professor Ranand chose to study carefully were cases which he believed had been documented beyond a possibility of doubt. In every case, he says, the recovered child was an idiot in our terms—or a wolf in objective terms.

"But this child is not a wolf, is she?" I asked him.

"No, certainly not, by no means. The child is a human child."

"An imbecile?" I asked him. "Would you call the child an idiot? Would you call the child a moron? If you did, would you give her any number on the scale of intelligence we use?"

Professor Ranand was upset by this kind of thing and he brushed it aside, and he had some very harsh things to say about our Western methods of measuring intelligence.

"Of course the child is not an idiot," he said; "neither is the child an imbecile. You cannot call the child an imbecile any more than you would call a wolf an idiot or an imbecile because the wolf is not capable of engaging in human actions."

"But the child is not a wolf," I insisted.

"Of course not. We went over that before. The child is not a wolf, not by any means. Then you must ask what the child is and that, too, we have gone over before. It is impossible to state what this child is. This child is something that nature never intended. Now, to you, to you Westerners, this is a clinical point of view, but to us it is something else entirely. You do not recognize any such things as intentions on the part of nature. In so far as your Western science is concerned, nature moves blindly and mechanically with neither purpose nor intent nor direction. I think you have all driven yourselves into blind alleys with your concepts of the origin of the species. I am not arguing with Darwin's theories; I am only saying that your use of Darwin's theories has been as blind as your overall attitude toward the world and the life of the world."

Two days have passed since I wrote that section of my report which you have just read. Yesterday the wolf-child came down with some sort of amoebic dysentery. She seems entirely unable to fight the disease and she is obviously growing weaker. I will send you news as her condition changes.

Meanwhile, I am putting together all of the notes and the verbatim records of conversations that I have taken down concerning the wolf-child. When I have them in some proper and understandable form, I will send them to you. I don't know why this whole experience has depressed me as it has. My spirits were quite high when I arrived in India, and the whole business around this poor child has been, from my own selfish point of view, consistently interesting. At the same time, I made some good friends here, and the people at the university, the native Indian professors as well as the British here, could not have been kinder to me. I have every reason, my dear sister, for saying that I have enjoyed my stay in Bengal—but, at the same time, I feel a terrible sense of tragedy around this child, a sense of tragedy that goes far beyond her own pitiful fate and her own personal tragedy. Perhaps when I work this out in my mind, I will be able to turn it into something constructive.

In any case, be assured that I am your errand boy for as long as you desire. I am intrigued by this matter, and I spend the pre-sleep hour each night guessing what you are up to, what your purpose is, and what you and Mark have in those cunning little scientific minds of yours. I have made some absolutely fascinating guesses, and if you are very nice to me perhaps I will pass them on to you.

Love and kisses,
Harry.

By cable:

MRS. JEAN ARBALAID
WASHINGTON, D.C.
NOVEMBER 7, 1945

TODAY AT TWO O'CLOCK OUR TIME HERE THE WOLF-CHILD DIED.
THE DIRECT CAUSE OF HER DEATH WAS THE DYSENTERY. THAT IS
THERE WAS NO WAY TO STOP THE DEHYDRATION OF THE CHILD
WHICH CONTINUED TO A POINT WHERE SHE COULD NO LONGER
SUSTAIN HER LIFE. HOWEVER DR. CHALMERS WHO IS BY NO MEANS
A MYSTIC BUT A VERY PRACTICAL BRITISH PRACTITIONER FEELS
THAT ALMOST ANY INFECTIOUS DISEASE WOULD HAVE LED TO THE
SAME RESULT. SHE HAD BEEN DIVESTED OF ANY DESIRE TO LIVE
AND IN HER OWN WAY HAD BEEN IN VERY DEEP DEPRESSION SOME-
THING I RECOGNIZE AND SYMPATHIZE WITH WHOLLY. I AM SEND-
ING THIS CABLE COLLECT AND AM MAKING NO EFFORT TO ECON-
OMIZE WITH WORDS. I AM SURE YOU CAN AFFORD IT. WHAT NOW?
I AWAIT WORD FROM YOU AT THE HOTEL EMPIRE CALCUTTA.

HARRY FELTON

By cable:

HARRY FELTON
HOTEL EMPIRE
CALCUTTA, INDIA
NOVEMBER 9, 1945

YOU HAVE DONE SUPERBLY HARRY AND WE ARF DEEPLY APPRE-
CIATIVE. HOWEVER, YOUR REPORTS ARE TOO MODEST. WE LOOK
UPON YOU AS AN INTELLIGENT AND WELL-INFORMED PERSON AND
WE ARE VERY EAGER FOR YOUR OWN REACTION. PLEASE REMAIN
IN INDIA AT HOTEL EMPIRE FOR TIME BEING AND WRITE US IM-
MEDIATELY AIRMAIL YOUR REACTION TO THE CHILD AND YOUR
EXPLANATION OF WHAT HAPPENED TO THE CHILD. THIS IS TO BE
ABSOLUTELY YOUR OWN EXPLANATION AND IF POSSIBLE NOT
TEMPERED OR BIASED IN ANY WAY BY THE SPECIALISTS YOU HAVE
DISCUSSED THE CASE WITH.

JEAN ARBALAID

By airmail:

Calcutta, India
November 10, 1945

Mrs. Jean Arbalaid
Washington, D.C.

My Dear Jean:

I am flattered by your interest in my opinion. On the other hand, I am not going to negate the value of such an opinion. I think I agree with you that professional people, specialists in one branch or another of the various sciences, tend to have a narrow point of view where they have either a background of experimental evidence or specific existing evidence upon which to base their assertions and conclusions. This is a very admirable and careful method in so far as it goes, but I am afraid it will achieve only what the facts at hand—that is, the provable facts—allow it to achieve.

I can guess that by now you have consulted every available specialist on the question of human children being raised by animals. I am sure you have discussed this thoroughly with the bigwigs at the National Geographic Society and with all the various specialists who know more about animals than the animals know about themselves. Do they all agree that no human child was ever reared by so-called beasts? Do they all agree that the whole thing is a sort of continuing invention, a fiction that each generation perpetuates to confuse itself? If they do, they are in agreement with your Western naturalists here in Calcutta. I have spoken to three of them—two Englishmen and a Frenchman—and they are all absolutely certain of the scientific and historical ground they stand on. The wolf-girl is a fraud; she was not raised by the wolves; she is an idiot child who ran away from the village and spent perhaps weeks, perhaps months, wandering in the forest, deranged and developing calluses where the calluses are. And the odd thing, my dear Jean, is that I cannot prove differently. So much for evidence.

Now, as to my own conclusion which you asked for: I told you in the previous letter that I had been deeply depressed by the incident of this child and by her condition. I have been attempting to understand the origin of this depression in myself and to deal with it—if only to repay an obligation and a promise to a skinny British psychiatrist who pulled me out of the doldrums back in Bath. I think I have found the source of the depression—a sort of understanding of what the girl was afflicted with. I believe she was afflicted simply with the loss of humanity. Now you have every right to say that the loss of humanity is a widespread disease that afflicts most of the human race; and there I cannot argue with you. But regardless of how much or often we turn into killers, mass murderers, sadists, etc., we seem always to preserve some sense of our origin, some link with our beginnings. We are at least recognizable as Homo sapiens. This child, poor thing, cut all her connections. She is no longer recognizable as Homo sapien. Having the form of a human being, she is less than a human being, less indeed than what nature intended her to be.

I am quite impressed by the outlook of Professor Gojee and his associates. I think I must agree with their opinion of Western science. The sad fact is that, while the East is ahead of us in many ways, they have lagged behind in scientific method and discoveries; and therefore, the great intuitive feelings that they have and which they incorporate into some of their religion, concerning the meaning and the destiny of mankind, have remained disassociated from any wide discipline of fact and investigation.

For myself, I tend to agree with them that there must be some purpose to human existence. I am hesitant to ascribe such purpose to the presence of God. I think that their definition and concept is as limited by our intelligence and as constrained by our outlook as most of our other theories. But, speaking only for myself, I have never been truly aware of the essence of humanity until I was present here at a case where humanity was extracted from a human being. We are too pat with our descriptions, designations and accusations of those whom we consider devoid of humanity. I don't really believe that anyone is devoid of humanity in the sense that this poor little wolf-child was. But then that leads me to another question. What is your human being? What is the essence of being human?

I have not been quick to embrace the all-encompassing theories of environment that have come out of the democratic movement of the nineteenth century. Too often I have felt that theories of environment have been used to prove political points and to make for political ammunition. At the same time, heredity is possibly less important than many people imagine it to be. I think that to create a human being, you need the presence, the society and the environment of other human beings. Directly to answer the question you put to me—What happened to the child?—I would say that she was deprived of her humanity. Certainly, she is not a human being, and neither is she a wolf. A wolf society can produce wolves; a human society can produce human beings. A human being trapped in a wolf society is a good deal less than a human being and perhaps not as much as a wolf. So I would say that this child occupied a sort of limbo on the scale, or in the current, of evolution. She is not a part of development; she is not a thing in herself; she is something that had been destroyed by a set of circumstances; she is a spoiled mechanism that continued to function in a limited sort of way. Do you find that a rather dreadful definition—a spoiled mechanism? Perhaps the word "mechanism" is wrong. Would a spoiled bit of life be better? I don't know, but there are my opinions for what they are worth.

I have found a charming young lady, Miss Edith Wychkoff by name, who is the daughter of the colonel of an old Indian regiment. The whole thing is a cliché except that she is charming and blue-eyed, and will make the hours here, while I wait for your reply and for your instructions, much more endurable.

Please allow me to continue as your free-wheeling, theorizing errand boy. As the above demonstrates, my state of mind is infinitely better. I send my love to both of you, and await your reply.

Harry.

7

By cable:

HARRY FELTON
HOTEL EMPIRE
CALCUTTA, INDIA
NOVEMBER 14, 1945

THANK YOU FOR EVERYTHING HARRY. YOU HAVE DONE NOBLY AND YOUR CONCLUSIONS HAVE BEEN READ AND REREAD AND DISCUSSED SERIOUSLY AND WITH THE GREATEST OF INTEREST. A SIMILAR CASE HAS CROPPED UP IN PRETORIA UNION OF SOUTH AFRICA AT GENERAL HOSPITAL THERE UNDER DR. FELIX VANOTT. WE HAVE MADE ALL ARRANGEMENTS WITH AIR TRANSPORT AND YOU WILL BE WHISKED THERE BEFORE YOU CAN SAY JACK ROBINSON. DREADFULLY SORRY TO END ROMANCE WITH THE COLONEL'S DAUGHTER BUT IF YOU ARE VERY SERIOUS ABOUT IT AND DESPERATE TO CONTINUE IT WE WILL ARRANGE FOR YOU TO PICK IT UP LATER. MEANWHILE ON TO PRETORIA.

JEAN ARBALAID

8

By airmail:

Pretoria, Union of South Africa
November 18, 1945

Mrs. Jean Arbalaid
Washington, D.C.

My dear Sister:
You are evidently very big wheels, you and your husband, and I wish I knew just what your current experiment adds up to. I suppose that in due time you'll see fit to tell me. Meanwhile, my speculations continue.

But in any case, your priorities command respect. A full colonel was bumped, and I was promptly whisked away to South Africa, a beautiful country of pleasant climate and, I am sure, great promise.

I saw the child, who is still being kept in the General Hospital here; and I spent an evening with Dr. Vanott, an entire day at the hospital, and another evening with a young and attractive Quaker lady, Miss Gloria Oland, an anthropologist working among the Bantu people for her doctorate. Her point of origin is Philadelphia and Swarthmore College, so I was able to play upon all the bonds that unite countrymen (I will have something to say about that later). But I think that my acquaintance with Miss Oland has been fruitful, and, all in all, I will be able to provide you with a certain amount of background material.

Superficially, this case is remarkably like the incident in Assam. There it was a girl of twelve; here we have a Bantu boy of eleven (an estimate). The girl was reared by a variety of wolf; the boy in this case was reared by baboons—that is, supposing that here, as in India, we can separate fact from fiction, and come to a reasonable assumption that the child actually was stolen and reared by baboons. Let me say at this point that I have done some investigating, and I have been able to add to my notebook over twenty cases of African children stolen by baboons or by some other kind of baboon-like ape and reared by said baboons and apes. Now, these cases are by no means researched; they have not been tracked down; they have not been proven: so along with their interest as background material must go the assumption that most, if not all of them, belong to the mythology. However, if I have been able to turn up this number of cases in so short a time, and by asking as few questions as I did and of as few people, then it seems to me that this kind of thing must be fairly widespread throughout South Africa. Even if the overwhelming majority of stories belong to the mythology, any such mythology must have some basis in fact, however small.

The child was rescued from the baboons by a white hunter, name of Archway—strong, silent type, right out of Hemingway. Unfortunately, unlike most of his fictional counterparts, this Ned Archway is a son of a bitch with a nasty temper and a thoroughgoing dislike for children. So when the boy understandably bit him—for which the boy can only be praised—the white hunter whipped the child to within an inch of his life.

"Tamed him," as Mr. Archway put it to me in one of the local bars over a tall mint julep. Archway is a thoroughgoing gentleman when he is with his betters, and, as much as I dislike that kind of talk, namely, "his betters," it is the only kind that fits. Back home, a sensitive person would catalogue Archway as poor white trash. I think that describes him better than several pages of words.

I asked him for some of the details of the capture and Archway swore me to silence, since evidently his actions were somewhat illegal. He loves to shoot baboons; it proves him "a target master," as he puts it.

"Shot twenty-two of the bloody beasts," he said to me.

"You're a very good shot," I said to him.

The Trap

"Would have shot the black bastard too," he added. "However, he awakened my curiosity. Nimble little creature. You should have seen him go. You know, I have one of your jeeps—marvelous car, marvelous for the brush country, kind of car that might have been made for this part of Africa. Well, I was in the car and I had with me two of your American women, two of your very rich women—you know the type: brown as smoked goose, long legs drawn hard and thin, and just couldn't wait for the war to be over to get out here on safari. They enjoyed the chase no end. Ran the thing down in the jeep. You know, I don't think I would have ever gotten him if it weren't that the jeep threw a bad scare into him, and he froze. Animals do that, you know."

"He is not an animal," I ventured.

"Oh, of course he is. The Kaffirs are not so different from the baboons anyway, when you come right down to it."

This and a lot more. My conversation with the white hunter was not pleasant, and I don't enjoy repeating it.

May I say that at the hospital here they have a more humane, if not a more egalitarian, point of view. The child is receiving the very best of care and reasonable scientific affection. I asked them at the hospital whether there was any way to trace him back to his point of origin, that is, to his parents or to the village where he originated. They said No, there was no way at all of doing so, not in a thousand years. Evidently these Basutoland baboons are great travelers, and there is no telling where they picked up the child. It might be several hundred or a thousand miles away.

Putting his age at eleven years is a medical guess, but nevertheless reasonable. That he is of Bantu origin there is no doubt; and if I were to put him up as a physical specimen alongside of the white hunter, there is no doubt in my mind who would come out best. The child is very handsome, long-limbed, exceedingly strong, and with no indication of any cranial injury. His head is narrow and long, and his look is intelligent. Like the girl in Assam, he is—in our terms—an idiot and an imbecile, but there is nevertheless a difference. The difference is the difference between the baboon and the wolf. The wolf-child was incapable of any sort of vocalization. Did I mention that at moments of fear she howled? In her howling she was able to give an almost perfect imitation of a wolf's howl—that is, the howl of the local wolf whose habitat is Assam. Aside from this howl, her vocalization was limited to a number of wolf sounds—barks, whines and that sort of thing. Here we have something different indeed.

The vocalization of this eleven-year-old Bantu boy is the vocalization of a baboon. Strangely enough, at least here in Pretoria, there is no indication of any local scientific and serious work being done on the question of baboon vocalization. Again, all we have is a variety of opinion based on mythology. Some of the Kaffirs here will swear that the baboons have a language. Others claim to know a little of the baboon language, and I have had some of the Kaffir hunters make an assortment of sounds for me—after I had paid them well—and proceed to state their own interpretations of what these sounds meant. I think this is less a tribute to the speech abilities of the baboon than to the ingenuity of the local Kaffir when it comes to extracting money from a white man. Miss Oland pooh-poohs any suggestion that the baboons have a language, and I am inclined to go along with her.

There is one reasonably well informed naturalist at the local college with whom I had a short chat over the luncheon table. He, too, derides the notion that there is a language among the baboons. He raises an interesting point, however. He believes that the ability to talk is the motivating factor for man's becoming man, and he also believes that certain frontal sections of the brain are absolutely necessary before a species can engage in conversation. He says that the only species on earth that has any sort of conversational powers whatsoever is man, and he proceeded to break down for me various theories that bees and other insects and some of the great apes can talk to each other. He said that there is a very strong myth in gorilla country that the gorillas are able to talk to each other, but this, too, he rejects unconditionally.

He does admit that there is a series of specific sounds that the gorillas use; but these sounds are explosive grunts used entirely for situations of danger. Each and every one of these sounds relates to some area of fear, and my naturalist cannot include them in what we understand as language. He is willing to admit, however, that the baboons have a series of squeaks and grunts that may communicate, in addition to situations of fear, situations of affection. I am inclined to agree with this, for there seem to be some indications that this Bantu child will in time learn at least some elements of speech.

In that way he differs from the wolf-girl, and he also differs from her in that he is able to use his hands to hold things and to examine things. He also has a more active curiosity, but that, I am assured by the naturalist, is the difference between the wolf and baboon. The baboon is a curious creature, endlessly investigative, and he handles an endless number of objects. So the boy's curiosity and his ability to grasp things with his hands are an indication of his relationship to baboons, I think, more than an indication of his relationship to mankind.

As with the wolf-child, he too has a permanent curvature of the spine. He goes on all fours as the baboons do, and the backs of his fingers, specifically the area of the first knuckle joint, are heavily callused. After tearing off his clothes the first time, he accepted them. This too, is quite different from the case in India, and here again we have a baboon trait. Miss Oland told me of cases where baboons have been trained to wear clothing and to do remarkable tricks. Miss Oland has great hope for the boy's progress in the future, but Dr. Vanott, who has worked with him and tested him in the hospital, doubts that the child will ever talk. How much Dr. Vanott is influenced by local attitudes toward Negroes, I leave for you to decide. Incidentally, in those numerous reports of human children raised by animals, which Professor Ranand of Bombay University professed to believe, there is no case where the child was able subsequently, upon being recovered and brought back into the company of human beings, to learn human speech.

So goes my childhood hero, Tarzan of the Apes, and all the noble beasts along with him. Poor Lord Graystroke. He would have been like this Bantu child—trembling with fear, never released from this fear, cowering into a corner of his cage, staring at his human captors with bewilderment and horror. Has it been said to you that animals do not experience fear in the sense that we human beings do? What nonsense! Fear appears to be woven into the fabric of their lives; and the thing that is most heartbreaking in both of these cases is the constant fear, the fear from which neither child was apparently free, even for a moment.

But the most terrifying thought evoked by this situation is this: What is the substance of man himself, if this can happen to him? The learned folk here have been trying to explain to me that man is a creature of his thought, and that his thought is, to a very large extent, shaped by his environment; and that this thought process—or mentation as they prefer to call it—is based on words. Without words, thought becomes a process of pictures, which is on the animal level and rules out all, even the most primitive, abstract concepts.

In other words, man cannot become man by himself: he is the result of other men and of the totality of human society and experience. I realize that I am putting this forward rather blandly, but it is all new to me; and newcomers tend to simplify and (as you would say, my dear sister) vulgarize a science of which they possess some small knowledge.

Yet my thinking was borne out to some degree during a very pleasant dinner I had with Miss Oland. It was not easy to get her to have dinner with me. You see, I don't think she liked me very much, although I am presuming to say that she likes me a little better now. But in the beginning, her attitude was very much shaped by my objective and somewhat cold investigative attitude toward what had happened to the little boy.

Miss Oland, may I say, is a very intelligent young lady, an attractive young lady, and a very devout Quaker. She takes her religion with great seriousness, and she lives it. It was a nice and perhaps constructive blow to my ego to realize that she looked down upon me with a mixture of dislike and pity. I think, however, that Miss Oland and people like her look down upon most of the human race. I put this surmise of mine to her, and she denied it very hotly. In fact, she was so annoyed by the thought that I wonder whether she will agree to spend another evening with me.

However, there is no doubt in my mind but that people like Miss Oland occupy the role of the outsider. They watch the human race, without actually belonging to it. I have noticed this same attitude in a number of well-educated Jews I have met. But Miss Oland is the first Quaker with whom I ever discussed these things. I would hardly be surprised if her attitude were shared by other Quakers of sensitivity and thoughtfulness.

Miss Oland regards me as a barbarian—less a barbarian, of course, than such an obvious creature as the white hunter Ned Archway. But only by contrast with him do I become admirable, and at that only slightly admirable. As Miss Oland put it to me:

"You profess your superiority to the white hunter, Mr. Felton, and you look down on him as a rather uncivilized sort of man, but for what actually do you condemn him? For shooting the baboons for the fun of it or for beating the child?"

"For both," I replied.

"But he kills only animals, and surely the child will recover from the beating."

"And do you see virtue in killing animals for fun, as you put it?" I asked her.

"No virtue indeed, Mr. Felton, but I see less evil in it than in the slaughter of human beings."

"By that, just what do you mean, Miss Oland?"

"I mean that, like Ned Archway, you have been a hunter. You hunted men."

"What do you mean, I hunted men?"

"You told me you were an infantry captain, didn't you? What other purpose would an infantry captain have but the hunting down and the slaughter of human beings?"

"But that was different."

"How was it different, Mr. Felton?"

"My goodness, I don't have to go into all that, do I? You're not going to trap me with that old, old saw? You lived in the world that Adolf Hitler was remaking. You inhabited the same world that contained the concentration camps, the abattoirs, the gas ovens, the slaughter pits. How can you ask me such an absurd question?"

"Of course the question is absurd," she nodded. "Any question, Mr. Felton, becomes absurd when it is new to you or irritating to you or outside of your particular sphere of mental agreement. My question disturbed you; therefore, it becomes absurd."

"But surely you are not going to defend the Nazis."

"Now that indeed becomes rather absurd, doesn't it, Mr. Felton? You know that I would not defend the Nazis. How could you conceivably think that under any circumstances I would?"

"You're right. I could not conceivably think that. I admit it."

"I am not objecting, Mr. Felton, to your attitude toward the Nazis. I am simply objecting to your attitude toward killing. Obviously, you resent the pointless and witless killing of baboons, but you do not resent the equally pointless and witless slaughter of human beings."

"I like to think, Miss Oland, that I was fighting for the survival of human civilization and human dignity, and that whatever killing I was forced to do was neither thoughtless nor witless."

"Oh come now, Mr. Felton, we are both a little too old for that sort of thing, aren't we? Were you fighting for man's dignity? And by what process did you know that whatever German soldier you happened to kill was not equally aware of what was demanded by man's dignity? Did you know whether he opposed Hitler, if he did not oppose Hitler, how he agreed with Hitler or whether he agreed or disagreed with Hitler? You knew nothing of that; and certainly you knew enough of military structure to know that, like yourself, he had no choice but to face you and fight you."

"He could surrender," I said.

"Could he really, Mr. Felton? Now I am going to ask you a question. Did you shoot first and ask questions afterwards? Or did you ask questions first and shoot afterwards? I have never been on a battlefield, but I have a good imagination, and I have read many stories about what goes on on a battlefield. Could he have surrendered, Mr. Felton?"

"No," I admitted, "you're quite right. In most cases he couldn't have surrendered. There were cases where he could and maybe he did, but in most cases he could not have surrendered. Certainly, as an individual, he could not have surrendered. So you are absolutely right there, and I will not argue it. Nevertheless, I also will not relinquish my belief that there was a virtue in our cause in World War II, a virtue in what we fought for and what so many of us died for."

"Then why don't you say that there was virtue in what you killed for, Mr. Felton?"

"I don't like to put it that way because I have never regarded myself as a killer."

"But the plain and naked fact of the matter, Mr. Felton, is that you are a killer. You have killed human beings, haven't you?"

"I have," I admitted weakly.

"I am not trying to pin you down to something nasty, Mr. Felton. I am not trying to derogate you, please believe me. It is only that no man takes any action without some sort of justification. He would go out of his mind if he did, wouldn't he? You ask me to prefer you to Mr. Archway, but I find that very hard to do. Really, I know this hurts you and I know I am not being polite, but from my point of view you and Archway inhabit the same world."

"And you don't inhabit that world, Miss Oland?" I wanted to know.

"No, not really. I am a Quaker, Mr. Felton. I think that my culture, the culture of my family, the culture of my people, has been different for many generations. We live among you but not with you. Your world is not our world. It really isn't, Mr. Felton, and you might do well to think about that. You seem very seriously interested in what has happened to this poor child. Maybe thinking about what I have just said would give you some clue as to what happens when a human child must live in a baboon's world."

"And at the same time," I said to her, "you have your little triumph and great, great satisfaction of righteousness."

She did not argue that point. "Yes," she said, "I suppose I am righteous, Mr. Felton. I wish I knew how to be otherwise, and perhaps in time I will learn. For the moment I am young enough to feel righteous and disgusted as well. You have no idea how frequently I am disgusted, Mr. Felton."

So, you see, I can fail her for politeness and score her very low as regards hospitality, she having been in Pretoria at least six months longer than I. At the same time, even though she is a woman I will not remember fondly, I have to admire her, and, in the last analysis, I have to admit that she was speaking the truth.

All of which leads me to ask some very pertinent questions, sister mine. The man raised by the wolf is no longer a man, and the man raised by the baboons is no longer a man, and this fate is inevitable, isn't it? No matter what the man is, you put him with the apes and he becomes an ape and never very much more than that. My head has been swimming with all sorts of notions, some of them not at all pleasant. My dear sister, what the hell are you and your husband up to? Isn't it time you broke down and told old Harry, or do you want me to pop off to Tibet and hold converse with the lamas? I am ready for anything; I will be surprised by nothing, and I am prepared to go anywhere at all to please you. But, preferably, hand me something that adds up to a positive sum and then put a few words of explanation with it.

Your nasty killer brother,
Harry.

By airmail:

Washington, D.C.
November 27, 1945

Mr. Harry Felton
Pretoria, Union of South Africa

Dear Harry:
You are a good and sweet brother, and quite sharp, too. You are also a dear. You are patient and understanding and you have trotted around dutifully in a maze without trying to batter your way out.

Now it comes down to this, Harry: Mark and I want you to do a job for us which will enable you to go here and there across the face of the earth, and be paid for it, too. In order to convince you, and to have your full cooperation and your very considerable creative abilities as well, we must spill out the dark secrets of our work—which we have decided to do, considering that you are an upright and trustworthy character. But the mail, it would seem, is less trustworthy; and since we are working with the Army, which has a constitutional dedication to top-secrecy and similar nonsense, the information goes to you via diplomatic pouch.

As of receiving this, that is, providing that you agree, you may consider yourself employed. Your expenses will be paid—travel, hotel and per diem—within reason, and there will be an additional eight thousand a year, less for work than for indulgence. In fact, as I write it down here, it makes so absolutely intriguing a proposition that I am tempted to throw over my own job and take yours instead.

So please stay put at your hotel in Pretoria until the diplomatic pouch arrives. I promise you that this will be in not more than ten days. They will certainly find you—that is, the diplomatic courier will.

Love, affection and respect,
Jean.

By diplomatic pouch:

Washington, D.C.
December 5, 1945

Mr. Harry Felton
Pretoria, Union of South Africa

Dear Harry:
Consider this letter the joint effort of Mark and myself. The thinking is ours and the conclusions are also shared. Also, Harry, consider this to be a very serious document indeed.

You know that for the past twenty years we have both been deeply concerned with child psychology and child development. There is no need to review our careers or our experience in the Public Health Service. Our work during the war, as part of the Child Reclamation Program, led to an interesting theory, which we decided to pursue. We were given leave by the head of the service to make this our own project. The leave is a sort of five-year sabbatical, with the option given to us at the end of five years to extend the leave for five years more, and a third five years then, if necessary. Recently, we were granted a substantial amount of Army funds to work with. In return for this, we have agreed to put our findings at the disposal of the Government.

Now to get down to the theory, which is not entirely untested. As you know, Mark and I have behind us two decades of practical work with children. When I say practical, I cover a good deal of ground. Since we are both physicians, we have worked with children as pediatricians. We have done hospital work with children. We have operated on children as surgeons; and, under certain conditions (as for example, during emergencies in the early years of the war), we have pioneered surgical work with children simply because we were placed in a position which left us no other choice. From this vast experience, we have come to some curious conclusions. I would put it better if I said that we have come to a great many conclusions, but have now focused our interest on one conclusion in particular, namely this: Mark and I have come to believe that within the rank and file of Homo sapiens is the beginning of a new race.

Call this new race "man-plus"—call it what you will. The people who constitute this new race of men are not of recent arrival; they have been cropping up among men—Homo sapiens, that is—for hundreds, perhaps for thousands, of years. But they are trapped in the human environment; they are trapped in the company of man, and they are molded by the company of man and by the human environment as certainly and as implacably as your wolf-girl was trapped among the wolves or your Bantu child among the baboons. So, you see, the process is quite certain.

Everything that you discovered in Assam and in South Africa tended to bear out our own conclusions. Just as the little Assamese girl was divested of her humanity, deprived of her membership in the human race, by being reared among the wolves, so is our theoretical man-plus deprived of his racehood, of his normal plus-humanity, by living among men. Perhaps your Bantu boy would be a closer parallel to what we mean. I will not at this point try to explain more fully. Later on in this letter we will go into other details of our theory; and if you agree to work with us, as your work progresses, so will your understanding of exactly what we are after.

By the way, your two cases of animal child-rearing are not the only attested ones we have. By sworn witness, we have records of seven similar cases: one in Russia, two in Canada, two in South America, one in West Africa and, just to cut us down to size, one in the United States of America. This does not mean that all seven of these cases are wholly authenticated. If we were to turn to each in succession and apply to it the kind of severe interviewing and testing that you have applied to the two cases you investigated, we might find that of the seven cases perhaps all are fictional, perhaps one is based on reality, perhaps all are based on reality. We might come to any one of these conclusions. *A priori,* we are not able to do more than accept the facts and apply to these facts our own judgment.

You may add to this the hearsay and folklore of three hundred and eleven parallel cases which cover a period of fourteen centuries. We have in fifteenth-century Germany, in the folio manuscript of the monk Hubercus, five case histories he claims to have observed personally. In all these cases, in the seven cases witnessed by people alive today, and in all but sixteen of the hearsay cases, the result is more or less precisely what you have seen and described yourself; that is, the child reared by the wolf is divested of humanity.

We have yet been unable to find a case, mythological or otherwise, in which the child reared by the wolf is able subsequently to learn man's speech. Mythology adds up to a little—of course, very little. But speaking in mythological terms, we can find over forty such cases that survived from great antiquity in the mythologies of one nation or another.

But of course, Harry, we are not attempting to prove that animals can rear a human child, or that human children have been so reared, or that any of the facts connected with human children so reared are true. We are merely attempting to use these cases of the rearing of human children by animals as indications of what may face superior-man reared by man. You see, our own work adds up to the parallel conclusions: the child reared by a man is a man. And what is a man? In the broadest historical sense, a man is a creature who builds social organizations, the major purpose of such organizations being man's own destruction. If what I have just written were an ethical or moral judgemnt, it could certainly be challenged and perhaps successfully; however, it is not by any means a judgment; it is simply an historical conclusion. If one examines the history of man with total objectivity, one can only come to the conclusion that man's existence as a social being has been mainly for the purpose of war. All that he has achieved, all that he has built, has been achieved and has been built in the intervals between wars, thereby creating a social organism that can function during a war and in the act of war. This is by no means a judgment, nor is it an historical observation upon man as an individual. Man as an individual would have to be described quite differently. But we must not for one moment forget that we have just come through a holocaust that has consumed fifty million human lives. I refer to World War II, in which we all played our parts. We have now calculated that the toll of human life internationally in World War II was above fifty million men, women and children. This is larger than the entire human population of the earth at the time of the Roman Empire. We are used to large numbers today; it puts a little different light on the figure when we observe to ourselves that we have just succeeded in destroying in a period of less than five years more human beings than existed upon the entire face of the earth two thousand years ago. That is one to think about, isn't it, Harry? But the observation—the historical observation of the role of man—is made here in a purely clinical sense and in terms of man-plus.

You see, if man-plus exists, he is trapped and caged as certainly as any human child reared by animals is caged. In the same way the incipient man-plus is divested of whatever his potential is. The wolf dealing with our little Assamese girl would hardly be able to calculate or even to guess what she might have been in her own civilization. The wolf can only see her as the product of a wolf society. If man-plus exists, we see him and we have always seen him as a product of man's society. Of course, we have no proof that he exists. We have simply created a supposition that he exists, and we have enough evidence at our disposal for us to support this proposition. This of course, is a usual procedure among scientists. Einstein's conception of the shape of the universe and of the curvature of light was hypothetical to begin with; it originated as a creative idea. After he had formulated the hypothesis, he set about proving it in physical terms. And we shall follow a similar method.

Why do we think the super-child exists? Well, there are many reasons, and we have neither the time nor the space here to go into all of them, or into much detail. However, here are two very telling and important reasons:

Firstly we have gathered together the case histories of several hundred men and women who as children had IQ's of 170 or above. Since these men and women are now adults, their testing goes back to the early days of the Binet-Simon method, and it is by no means reliable—that is, if any intelligence testing, any system of IQ, is reliable. We do not operate on the presumption that IQ testing has any objective reliability; we simply use it as a gauge and in lieu of anything better. In spite of the enormous intellectual promise as children of these several hundred men and women, less than ten percent have succeeded in their chosen careers. Considering how small the whole group is, their record of disaster and tragedy deserves attention in itself.

Another ten percent, roughly speaking, have been institutionalized as mental cases beyond recovery—that is, as pathological cases on the path to disintegration. About fourteen percent of the group have had or now require therapy for mental-health problems; in this fourteen percent, roughly half have been in psychoanalysis or are in psychoanalysis or some similar therapy. Nine percent of the group have been suicides. One percent are in prison. Twenty-seven percent have had one or more divorces, nineteen percent are chronic failures at whatever they attempt—and the rest are undistinguished in any important manner. That is to say, they have not achieved even nominal success in the lines of endeavor they finally chose to follow. All of the IQ's have dwindled—and the dwindling of these IQ's, when graphed, bears a relationship to age. About four percent of the group studied have gone under the hundred or normal mark and are now in the condition of social morons.

Since society has never provided the full potential for such a mentality—that is, a mentality such as this group seemed to have had as children—we are uncertain as to what this potential might be. We have no valid, provable reasons to imagine that this group or a similar group would achieve more under other conditions; but against that we have every reason of logic and common sense to suppose. Our guess is that this group has been reduced to a sort of idiocy, an idiocy that puts them on the level with what we call normalcy. But having been put on that level, they could not become men any more than your Assamese child could become a wolf. Unable to live out their lives, unable to become men, they were simply divested of their destiny, biological and otherwise, and in that sense destroyed. So much for the first reason, Harry.

The second reason we put forward is this: We know that man uses only a tiny part of his brain. Extensive testing enables us to put this forward as a provable fact, but we have no idea what blocks the human ego from using the rest of the human brain. We have to ask why nature has given man equipment that he cannot put to use—not atrophied equipment such as the appendix, but equipment that marks or is definitive of the highest life form ever produced by evolution. We must ask why nature has done this. We must also ask whether society, human society, prevents human beings from breaking the barriers that surround their own potential. In other words, have human beings themselves created a cage which prevents them from ever being more than human beings?

There, in brief, are the two reasons I spoke about before. Believe me, Harry, there are many more—enough for us to have convinced some very hard-headed and unimaginative Government people that we deserve a chance to release supermen. Of course, history helps—in its own mean and degraded manner. It would appear that we are beginning another war, this time with Russia; a cold war, as some have already taken to calling it. Among other things, it will be a war of intelligence—a commodity in rather short supply these days, as some of our local mental giants have been frank enough to admit.

Our new breed of computer warriors licked their lips when we sounded them out. They can't wait to have at another blood bath with all their new gimmicks; they have fed their tapes into the machines, and they have come out with new and enticing methods of human destruction. They look upon our man-plus as a secret weapon, little devils who will come up with death rays and super-atom-bombs and all sorts of similar devices when the time is ripe. Well, let them think that way. It is inconceivable to imagine a project like ours, a project so enormous and so expensive, under benign sponsorship. The important thing is that Mark and I have been placed in full charge of the venture—millions of dollars, top priority, the whole works. We are subject to no one; we must report to no one; we have complete independence. We can requisition what we wish within reason, and we have a long period of time—that is, five years with an extension of an additional five years, and the very real possibility of another extension after that.

But nevertheless, Harry, the project is secret. I cannot stress this enough. This secrecy is not simply the childish classification business that the Army goes into; we support them on the question of secrecy. It is as important to us as to the Army, and I simply cannot stress this sufficiently or make it sound more serious than it actually is.

Now, as to your own job—that is, if you want it. And somehow or other, at this point I cannot envision you saying No. The job will develop step by step, and it is up to you to make it. First step: in Berlin, in 1937, there was a Professor Hans Goldbaum. He was half Jewish. He lectured on child psychology at the university, and he was also the head of the Berlin Institute for Child Therapy. He published a small monograph on intelligence testing in children, and he put forward claims—which we are inclined to believe—that he could determine a child's IQ during its first year of life, in its pre-speech period. The use of the term "IQ" is mine, not his. Professor Goldbaum had no use for the intelligence-quotient system that was developed by the Binet-Simon people, and he rejected it entirely. Instead, he devised his own method of intelligence testing, a very interesting method indeed.

He presented some impressive tables of estimations and subsequent checked results; but we do not know enough of his method to practice it ourselves. In other words, we need the professor's help.

In 1937, Professor Goldbaum vanished from Berlin. All of our efforts, combined with the very generous investigatory help of Army Intelligence, have convinced us that he was not murdered by the Nazis but that in some manner he escaped from Berlin. In 1943, a Professor Hans Goldbaum, either the same man in whom we are interested or someone of the same name, was reported to be living in Cape Town. This is the last address we have for him, and I am enclosing the address herewith. Now, as for you, Harry, here goes your job. You should leave for Cape Town immediately. Somehow or other, find the Professor Goldbaum reported to be in Cape Town. Find out whether he is our Professor Goldbaum. If he is not there, but has left, then follow him. Follow him wherever he has gone. Find him. I am not telling you how and, in turn, I do not expect you to ask us how. It is up to you. Find him! Naturally, all expenses will be paid. Of course, he may be dead. If that is the case, inform us immediately.

At this point I am no longer asking whether or not you will take the job. Either you will take it or I cease to be your sister, and I will curse your name and strike it out of all the family journals, etc. We love you and we need your help; in fact, we need it desperately, and at this moment I know of no one else who could substitute for you.

Jean.

By airmail:

Cape Town, South Africa
December 20, 1945

Mrs. Jean Arbalaid
Washington, D.C.

My dear Sister:
I could write a book about my week in Cape Town. This is
a city I am not in love with, and if I get out of here alive I
have no desire to return ever. The days have been very interesting indeed, as you will see, and the nights have been
occupied with nightmares about your hare-brained scheme
for super-man. Instead of sleeping peacefully, I dream of rows
of little devils preparing all sorts of hideous death rays for
your Army partners. What are you up to? No, I am not quit-
ting. I am not walking out. A job is a job, and I remain your
faithful employee.

Let me tell you something about the professor. Evidently,
in one way or another, he was important to the Nazis—that
is, important enough for them to desire to eliminate him.
There was a very considerable organization of the Nazi bully
boys here in Cape Town when the war began, and they had
Herr Goldbaum on their list. A few days after he arrived, an
attempt was made on his life. He received a superficial bullet
wound, but it became infected and he had a rather bad time
of it. The Jewish community took care of him and hid him,
but then things got a little hot, and they turned him over to
some friends they had in the Kaffir compound. I was following
the trail, an old and stale trail, but one that became the path
of duty and all that. Leave it to your brilliant brother Harry.
I did not meet up with any revanchist Nazis who had survived
the war and were hiding out for *der Tag,* whenever it might
come. No indeed. I simply followed this cold trail into the
Kaffir compound, and thereby was picked up by the police
and tossed into jail. They had me tagged for a Communist;
can you imagine? I thought that just about everything had
happened to me, but this was it. It took two days of argument,
and the efforts of the American Consul General as well, to
prove that I was the very conservative and rather thoughtless
brother of one of our most eminent Americans. I am a little

tired of the weight your name carries, but thank heavens it
carried enough weight to take me out of one of the most
uncomfortable jails I have ever occupied or ever read about.
It was crawling with bugs—huge, terrifying South African
bugs.

After I got out of jail, I did the sensible thing that I should
have done in the beginning. I sought an interview with the
head of the Jewish community here, a Rabbi Anatole Bibberman. Bibberman, it seems, is an amaetur Assyriologist—
and, if I do not make myself entirely plain, Assyriologists
are a small group who devote their spare time to the study
of ancient Assyria. I imagine a good many of them devote
full time to the subject and become pros. Rabbi Bibberman,
however, is a spare-time Assyriologist; and it turns out that
Professor Goldbaum shared his interest. They spent long
hours, I am told, discussing ancient Assyria and Babylon and
things of that sort.

The Rabbi told me something that he thought everyone
knew—that is, everyone who is interested in Professor Goldbaum. He told me that in 1944 the people in London (and by
people I suppose he meant scientists or physicians or something of that sort) discovered that Professor Goldbaum was
holed up in Cape Town. They needed him for something or
other, and he took off for London. I am leaving for London
myself as soon as I finish this letter, and goodbye to Cape
Town. As you plan my itinerary for the future, I would appreciate your eliminating Cape Town from the list.

Your ever-loving brother,
Harry.

12

By cable:

MRS. JEAN ARBALAID
WASHINGTON, D.C.
DECEMBER 25, 1945

PERHAPS YOUR TRUST MISPLACED SINCE I TAKE GLEEFUL AND
CHILDISH PLEASURE IN SENDING LONG LONG CABLES COLLECT
WHICH THE UNITED STATES ARMY PAYS FOR. LIKE ANY OTHER
MAN WHO HAS SERVED ANY LENGTH OF TIME IN THIS HIDEOUS
WAR WE HAVE JUST FINISHED I SEEM TO HAVE AN UNSHAKABLE

BIAS AGAINST THE UNITED STATES ARMY. BE THAT AS IT MAY I
HAVE FOUND THE PROFESSOR. IT WAS ABSURDLY EASY AND IN A
LETTER TO FOLLOW I WILL GIVE ALL THE DETAILS. HE IS A CHARM-
ING AND DELIGHTFUL LITTLE MAN AND LAST NIGHT I TOOK HIM
FOR A CHRISTMAS EVE DINNER TO SIMPSON'S. IT TURNED OUT THAT
HE IS A VEGETARIAN. CAN YOU IMAGINE A VEGETARIAN AT SIMP-
SON'S ON CHRISTMAS EVE? I SUPPOSE AT THIS POINT I SHOULD PUT
IN A STOP JUST TO INDICATE THAT I AM QUITE AWARE THAT I AM
SENDING YOU A CABLE BUT I HAVE HEARD IT TOLD ON RELIABLE
AUTHORITY THAT THE NEW YORK TIMES REPORTERS CABLE THOSE
ENDLESS STORIES OF THEIRS IN FULL AND NOT IN CABLESE SO I
PRESUME OF THIS TIDBIT. MAY I SAY THAT THE PROFESSOR IS IN-
TRIGUED BY THE LITTLE I HAVE TOLD HIM. I DID NOT KNOW HOW
MUCH TO TELL HIM OR HOW HARD TO PUSH. JUST WHAT DO YOU
WANT ME TO DO WITH HIM? WHAT SHALL I ASK HIM? WHAT SHALL
I TELL HIM? YOU CAN SEE THAT SINCE THIS IS A PUBLIC CABLE I
AM USING GUARDED CIRCUITOUS AND SOMETIMES RATHER SILLY
LANGUAGE. I TRUST YOU UNDERSTAND ME MY DEAR JEAN. WHAT
NOW?

HARRY FELTON.

13

By diplomatic pouch:

Washington, D.C.
December 26, 1945

Mr. Harry Felton
London, England

Dear Harry:

While I am delighted that your spell of depression has
disappeared, you are beginning to worry me just a wee bit
with your silliness. I try to remember whether you were always as light-headed as you now appear to be, and I keep
telling myself and Mark that the war has changed you. In
any case, you are our man on the spot, and we must go along
with you. The truth is, I'm teasing. We do trust you, dear,
but please be more serious. Our project is dead serious. We
believe that despite protestations of your own limitations,
you have enough sense and good instincts to gauge Professor
Goldbaum's method. Talk to him. Unless you believe he is
a complete fraud—and from the little you say, I doubt that—
we want you to sell him on this venture. Sell him! We will

give him whatever he asks—that is, in the way of financial remuneration. A man like Professor Goldbaum, according to all my past experience with such men, should be more or less indifferent to money; but even if he is, Harry, I want you to set his fee and to set it generously. We want to make an arrangement whereby he will continue to work with us for as long as we need him. If it must be less than that, try to specify some contractual terms, at least a year. As far as his future is concerned, I repeat that we are able to take care of his future; we will take care of it financially, and we will take care of it in terms of citizenship. If he desires American citizenship, we can arrange that with no trouble whatsoever. If he wishes to continue as a British national—I presume that is his status now—then we will smooth the way. No difficulty will be encountered.

I am sure that when you discuss the matter with him he will have a number of questions of his own, and he will desire to be enlightened more fully than we have enlightened you. Perhaps we should have briefed you more completely before now; but the truth of the matter is that we had not yet completed our own preparations, nor were we exactly decided on what our procedure would be. At this point we are.

We have been allocated a tract of eight thousand acres in northern California. The eight thousand acres are very attractive. There is a stand of sequoia forest, a lovely lake, and some very beautiful and arable meadowland. There is also a stretch of badland. All in all, it is a variegated and interesting landscape. Here we intend to establish an environment which will be under military guard and under military security. In other words, we propose to make this environment as close to a self-contained world as perhaps ever existed. In the beginning, in the first years of our experiment, the outside world will be entirely excluded. The environment will be exclusive and it will be controlled as absolutely as anything can be controlled within the present world and national situation.

Within this environment, we intend to bring forty children to maturity—to a maturity that will result in man-plus. But please understand, Harry, and convey this to the professor, that when I state something as a positive I am proceeding on a theoretical hypothesis. Man-plus does not exist and may never exist. We are making an experiment based on a presumption. Always come back to that, Harry; never talk as if we were dealing with certainties.

As to the details of the environment—well, most if it will have to wait. I can tell you this: We shall base its functioning on the highest and the gentlest conclusions of man's philosophy through the ages. There is no way to put this into a few sentences. Perhaps I might say that instead of doing unto others as we would have them do unto us, we will attempt to do not unto others as we would not have them do unto us. Of course that says everything and anything, and perhaps nothing as well; but in due time we will tell you the details of the environment as we plan it, and the details of its functioning. The more immediate and important problem is finding the children. We need a certain type of child—that is, a superior child, a very superior child. We would like to have the most extraordinary geniuses in all the world; but, since these children are to be very young, our success in that direction must always be open to question. But we are going to try.

As I said, we intend to raise forty children. Out of these forty children, we hope to find ten in the United States of America; the other thirty will be found by the professor and yourself—outside of the United States.

Half are to be boys. We want an even boy-girl balance, and the reasons for that, I think, are quite obvious. All of the children are to be between the ages of six months and nine months, and all are to show indications of an exceedingly high IQ. As I said before, we would like to have extraordinary geniuses. Now, you may ask me how, how is this location of infant genius going to work? Well, Harry, there's where the professor comes into the picture, as your guide and mentor. How we are going to accomplish the problem at home, we have not fully worked out. But we believe that we have some methods, some hints, some directions that will ultimately lead us to success. In your case, we are depending upon the professor's method—that is, if his method is any good at all. If it is not—well, there are a dozen points where we can fail, aside from his methods.

We want five racial groupings: Caucasian, Indian, Chinese, Malayan and Bantu. Of course, we are sensible to the vagueness of these groupings, and you will have to have some latitude within them. As you know, racial definitions are at worst political and at best extremely imprecise. If you should find, let us say, three or four or five Bantu children who impress you as extraordinary, naturally we want to include them. Again, when we say Bantu we are not being literal. You may find in South Africa a Hottentot child who commands your attention. By all means include the Hottentot child.

The six so-called Caucasian infants are to be found in Europe. We might suggest two Northern types, two Central European types and two Mediterranean types; but this is only a suggestion and by no means a blueprint for you to follow. Let me be more specific: If you should by any chance find seven children in Italy, all of whom are obviously important for our experiment, you must take all seven children, even though only six children are suggested from Europe.

Now the word "take" which I have just used—understand this: no cops and robbers stuff, no OSS tactics, no kidnapping. If you find the most marvelous, the most extraordinary, infant of your entire search, and the parents of that infant will not part with it, that ends the matter right there. This is not simply an ethical point that I am raising, Harry. This is integral to the success of our program, and I think that in time you will understand why.

Now, where will the children come from? We are going to buy children. Let us be brutally frank about it. We are in the market for children. Where will they come from? Unfortunately for mankind but perhaps fortunately for our narrow purpose here, the world abounds with war orphans—and also in parents so poor, so desperate, that they will sell their children if the opportunity arises. When you find a child in such a situation and you want the child and the parents are willing, you are to buy. The price is no object. Of course, I must add here that you should exercise a certain amount of common sense. When I say price is no object, I mean that if you have to pay a hundred thousand or a hundred and fifty thousand dollars for a child, you are to pay the price. If, on the other hand, a price is in the neighborhood of a million dollars, you are to think it over very carefully. This is not to say that we will not pay as high as a million dollars if the necessity arises; but at that price, I want you to be very certain of what you are doing. We have enormous backing and an enormous amount of money to work with; but regardless of how enormous our resources are at this moment, they are going to be spent eventually, and there are limitations. I am afraid that we must work within these limitations.

However, I will have no maudlin sentimentality or scruples about acquiring the children, and I would like you and the professor to share my point of view. We are scientists, and sentimentalism rarely advances science; also, in itself, I find sentimentalism a rather dreadful thing. Let me state emphatically that these children will be loved and cherished as much as it is possible for those who are not blood parents to love and cherish children; and in the case of these children that you acquire by purchase, you will be buying not only a child but, for that child, a life of hope and promise. Indeed, we hope to offer these children the most wonderful life that any child could have.

When you find a child that you want and you are ready to acquire that child, inform us immediately. Air transport will be at your disposal. We are also making all arrangements for wet nurses—that is to say, if you find a nursing infant who should continue to nurse, we will always have wet nurses available. Rest assured that all other details of child care will be anticipated. We will have a staff of excellent pediatricians whom you can call on anywhere on earth. They will fly to where you are.

On the other hand, we do not anticipate a need for physicians. Above all things, we want healthy children, of course within the general conditions of health in any given area. We know that an extraordinary child in certain regions of the earth may well have the most discouraging signs of poor health, undernourishment, etc. But I am sure that you and Professor Goldbaum will be able to measure and assess such cases.

Good luck to you. We are depending on you, and we love you. We do wish that you could have been here with us for Christmas Day; but, in any case, a Merry Christmas to you, and may the future bring peace on earth and good will to all men.

Your loving sister,
Jean.

By diplomatic pouch:

Copenhagen, Denmark
February 4, 1946

Mrs. Jean Arbalaid
Washington, D.C.

Dear Jean:

I seem to have caught your top-secret and classified disease, or perhaps I have become convinced that this is a matter wanting some kind of secrecy. That seems hard to believe in such a down-to-earth, practical and lovely place as Copenhagen. We have been here for three days now, and I am absolutely charmed by the city and delighted with the Danes. I set aside today, in any case a good part of today, to sum up my various adventures and to pass on to you whatever conclusions and opinions might be of some profit to you.

From my cables, you will have deduced that the professor and I have been doing a Cook's Tour of the baby market. My dear sister, this kind of shopping spree does not set at all well with me; however, I gave my word, and there you are. I will complete and deliver. I might add that I have also become engrossed with your plans, and I doubt that I would allow myself to be replaced under any circumstances.

By the way, I suppose I continue to send these along to Washington, even though your "environment," as you call it, has been established? I will keep on doing so until otherwise instructed.

As you know, there was no great difficulty in finding the professor. Not only was he in the telephone book, but he is quite famous in London. He has been working for almost a year now with a child-reclamation project, while living among the ruins of the East End, which was pretty badly shattered and is being reclaimed only slowly. He is an astonishing little man, and I have become fond of him. On his part, he is learning to tolerate me.

I think I cabled to you how I took him to dinner at Simpson's only to learn that he was a vegetarian. But did I say that you were the lever that moved him, my dear sister? I had no idea how famous you are in certain circles. Professor

Howard Fast

Goldbaum regarded me with awe, simply because you and
I share a mother and a father. On the other hand, my respect
for unostentatious scientific folk is growing. The second meeting I had with Dr. Goldbaum took place on the terrace of the
House of Commons. This little fellow, who would be lost so
easily in any crowd, had casually invited three Members of
Parliament and one of His Majesty's Ministers to lunch with
us. The subject under discussion was children: the future of
children, the care of children, the love of children and the
importance of children.

Whatever you may say about the government here, its
interest in the next generation is honest, moving, and very
deep and real. For the first time in British history, the average Englishman is getting a substantial, adequate and
balanced diet. They have wonderful plans and great excitement about the future and about children's role in the future.
I think it was for this purpose (to hear some of the plans)
that Goldbaum invited me to be there. I am not sure that he
trusts me—I don't mean this in a personal sense, but rather
that I, being simply what I am, and he, being a sensitive
man who recognizes what I am—well, why should he trust
me? In that sense, he is quite right not to trust me.

At this lunch he drew me into the conversation, explaining
to the others that I was deeply interested in children. They
raised their eyebrows and inquired politely just where my
interest derived from and where it was directed.

Believe me, my only claim to a decent standing in the
human race was the fact that I was Mrs. Jean Arbalaid's
brother; and when they heard that I was your brother their
whole attitude toward me changed. I passed myself off as a
sort of amateur child psychologist, working for you and assisting you, which is true in a way, isn't it? They were all
very polite to me, and none of them questioned me too closely.

It was a good day, one of those astonishing blue-sky days
that are real harbingers of spring, and that come only rarely
in London in February. After the luncheon, the professor and
I strolled along Bird Cage Walk, and then through Saint
James's Park to the Mall. We were both relaxed, and the
professor's uncertainty about me was finally beginning to
crumble just a little. So I said my piece, all of it, no holds
barred. To be truthful, I had expected your reputation to
crumble into dust there on the spot, but no such thing. Gold-

baum listened with his mouth and his ears and every fiber of his being. The only time he interrupted me was to question me about the Assamese girl and the Bantu boy; and very pointed and meticulous questions they were.

"Did you yourself examine the child?" he asked me.

"Not as a doctor," I replied, "but I did examine her in the sense that one human being can observe another human being. This was not a calm little girl, nor was the Bantu boy a calm little boy; they were both terror-stricken animals."

"Not animals," Goldbaum corrected me.

"No, of course not."

"You see," Goldbaum said, "that point is most important. Animals they could not become; they were prevented, however, from becoming human beings."

There he hit upon the precise point that I had come to and which Professor Gojee had underlined so often. When I had finished with my whole story, and had, so to speak, opened all my cards to Professor Goldbaum's inspection, he simply shook his head—not in disagreement, but with sheer excitement and wordless delight. I then asked him what his reaction to all this was.

"I need time," he said. "This is something to digest. But the concept, Mr. Felton, is wonderful—daring and wonderful. Not that the reasoning behind it is so novel. I have thought of this same thing; so many anthropologists have thought of it. Also, throughout the ages it has been a concept of many philosophies. The Greeks gave their attention to it, and many other ancient peoples speculated upon it. But always as an imaginative concept, as a speculation, as a sort of beautiful daydream. To put it into practice, young man—ah, your sister is a wonderful and a remarkable woman!"

There you are, my sister, I struck while the iron was hot, and told him then and there that you wanted and needed his help, first to find the children and then to work in the environment.

"The environment," he said. "You understand, that is everything, everything. But how can she change the environment? The environment is total, the whole fabric of human society, self-deluded and superstitious and sick and irrational and clinging to the legends and the fantasies and the ghosts. Who can change that?"

I had my answer ready, and I told him that if anyone could, Mrs. Jean Arbalaid could.

"You have a great deal of respect for your sister," he said. "I am told that she is a very gentle woman."

"When she is not crossed," I agreed. "But the point is this, Professor: Will you work with us? That is the question she wants me to put to you?"

"But how can I answer it now? You confront me with perhaps the most exciting, the most earth-shaking notion of all of human history—not as a philosophical notion but as a pragmatic experiment—and then you ask me to say Yes or No. Impossible!"

"All right," I agreed, "I can accept that. How long do you want to think about it?"

"Overnight will be enough," he said. "Now tell me about California. I have never been there. I have read a little about it. Tell me what the state is like and what sort of an environment this would be in a physical sense; I would also like to know something more specific about your sister's relations to what you call 'the Army.' That phrase you use, 'the Army'—it seems quite different from what we understand in European terms or even in British terms."

So it went. My anthropology is passable at best, but I have read all your books. My geography and history are better, and if my answers were weak where your field was concerned, he did manage to draw out of me a more or less complete picture of Mark and yourself, and as much sociological and political information concerning the United States Government, the United States Army, and the relationship of the government and the Army to subprojects, as I could have provided under any circumstances. He has a remarkable gift for extracting information, or, as I am inclined to regard it, of squeezing water from a rock.

When I left him, he said that he would think the whole matter over. We made an appointment for the following day. Then, he said, provided he had agreed to join us, he would begin to instruct me in his method of determining the intelligence of infants.

By the way, just to touch on his methods, he makes a great point of the fact that he does not test but rather determines, leaving himself a wide margin for error. Years before, in prewar Germany, he had worked out a list of about fifty characteristics which he had noted in infants. All of these characteristics had some relationship to factors of intelligence and response. As the infants in whom he had originally noted these characteristics matured, they were tested regularly by standard methods, and the results of these tests were compared with his original observations. Thereby he began to draw certain conclusions, which he tested again and again during the next fifteen years. Out of these conclusions and out of his tests, his checking, his relating testing to observation, he began to put together a list of characteristics that the pre-tested (that is, the new) infant might demonstrate, and he specified how those characteristics could be relied upon to indicate intelligence. Actually, his method is as brilliant as it is simple, and I am enclosing here an unpublished article of his which goes into far greater detail. Suffice it to say he convinced me of the validity of his methods.

I must note that subsequently, watching him examine a hundred and four British infants and watching him come up with our first choice for the group, I began to realize how brilliant this man is. Believe me, Jean, he is a most remarkable and wise man, and anything and everything you may have heard about his talents and knowledge is less than reality.

When I met him the following day, he agreed to join the project. Having come to this conclusion, he had no reservations about it. He seemed to understand the consequences far better than I did, and he told me very gravely just what his joining meant. Afterwards I wrote it down exactly as he said it:

"You must tell your sister that I have not come to this decision lightly. We are tampering with human souls—and perhaps even with human destiny. This experiment may fail, but if it succeeds it can be the most important event of our time—even more important and consequential than this terrible war we have just been through. And you must tell her something else. I once had a wife and three children, and they were put to death because a nation of men had turned into beasts. I personally lived through and observed that transition, that unbelievable and monstrous mass transition of men into beasts—but I could not have lived through it unless I had believed, always, that what can turn into a beast can also turn into a human being. We—and by we I mean the present population of the earth—are neither beast nor man. When I speak the word 'man,' I speak it proudly. It is a goal, not a fact. It is a dream, not a reality. Man does not exist. We are professing to believe that he might exist. But if we go ahead to create man, we must be humble. We are the tool, not the creator, and if we succeed, we ourselves will be far less than the result of our work. You must also tell your sister that when I make this commitment as I do today, it is a commitment without limitation. I am no longer a young man, and if this experiment is to be pursued properly, it must take up most, perhaps the rest, of my life. I do not lightly turn over the rest of my existence to her—and yet I do."

There is your man, Jean, and as I said, very much of a man. The words above are quoted verbatim. He also dwells a great deal on the question of environment, and the wisdom and judgment and love necessary to create this environment. He understands, of course, that in our work—in our attempt to find the children to begin the experiment with—we are relying most heavily upon heredity. He does not negate the factor of heredity by any means, but heredity without the environment, he always underlines, is useless. I think it would be helpful if you could send me a little more information about this environment that you are establishing. Perhaps Professor Goldbaum could make a contribution toward it while it is in the process of being created.

We have now sent you four infants. Tomorrow we leave for Rome, and from Rome for Casablanca. We will be in Rome for at least two weeks and you can write or cable me there. The embassy in Rome will have our whereabouts at any time.

More seriously than ever and not untroubled.

Harry.

15

By diplomatic pouch:

Via Washington, D.C.
February 11, 1946

Mr. Harry Felton
Rome, Italy

Dear Harry:

Just a few facts here—not nearly as many as we would like to give you concerning the environment, but at least enough for Professor Goldbaum to begin to orient himself. We are tremendously impressed by your reactions to Professor Goldbaum, and we look forward eagerly to his completing his work in Europe and joining us as a staff member here in America. By the way, he is the only staff member, as such, that we will have. Later on in this letter, I will make that clear. Meanwhile, Mark and I have been working night and day on the environment. In the most general terms, this is what we hope to accomplish and to have ready for the education of the children:

The entire reservation—all eight thousand acres—will be surrounded by a wire fence, what is commonly known as heavy tennis fencing or playground fencing. The fence will be eleven feet high; it will be topped by a wire carrying live current, and it will be under Army guard twenty-four hours a day. However, the Army guards will be stationed a minimum of three hundred yards from the fence. They will be under orders never, at any time under any circumstances, to approach the main fence nearer than three hundred yards. Outside of this neutral strip of three hundred yards, a second fence will be built—what might be thought of us an ordinary California cow fence. The Army guards will patrol outside of this fence, and only under specific and special circumstances will they have permission to step within it into the neutralized zone. In this way, and through the adroit use of vegetation, we hope that, for the first ten years, at least, people within the reservation will neither see nor have any other indication of the fact that outside of the reservation an armed guard patrols and protects it.

Within the reservation itself we shall establish a home; indeed, the most complete home imaginable. Not only shall we have living quarters, teaching quarters, and the means of any and all entertainment we may require; but we shall also have machine shops, masonry shops, wood-carving shops, mills, all kinds of fabrication devices and plans—in other words, almost everything necessary for absolute independence and self-maintenance. This does not mean that we are going to cut our relationships with the outside. There will certainly be a constant flow of material from the outside into the environment, for we shall require many things that we shall not be able to produce ourselves.

Now for the population of the environment: We expect to enlist between thirty and forty teachers or group parents. We are accepting only young married couples who love children and who will dedicate themselves entirely to this venture.

This in itself has become a monumental task, for enlistment in this project is even more of a commitment than enlistment in the Army was five years ago. We are telling those parents who accept our invitation and who are ready to throw in their lot with the experiment that the minimum time they will be asked to spend with us is fifteen years, and that the maximum time may well be a lifetime. In other words, the people who accept our invitation and come with us to be a part of the environment are, in actuality, leaving the planet Earth. They are leaving their friends and they are leaving their relatives, not for a day, a week, a month, or a year, but in a manner of speaking, forever. It is as if you were to approach twenty married couples and suggest to them that they emigrate from Earth to an uninhabited planet with no possibility of a return.

Can you imagine what this is, Harry? Can you imagine how keenly these people must believe? You might well suppose that nowhere could we find people who would be willing to join us in our venture; but that is far from the case. It is true that we are going all over the world for the parents, just as we are going all over the world for the children. However, we have already enlisted twelve couples, superb people, of several nationalities. We are excited and delighted with every step forward we take. Remember, it is not enough to find couples willing to dedicate themselves to this venture; they must have unique additional qualifications; and the fact that we have found so many with these qualifications is what excites us and gives us faith in the possibility that we will succeed.

Even to begin the experiment, we must dedicate ourselves to the proposition that somewhere in man's so-called civilized development, something went tragically wrong; therefore, we are returning to a number of forms of great antiquity. One of these forms is group marriage. That is not to say that we will cohabit indiscriminately; rather, the children will be given to understand that parentage is a whole, a matter of the group—that we are all their mothers and their fathers, not by blood but by a common love, a common feeling for protection and a common feeling for instruction.

As far as teaching is concerned, we shall teach our children only the truth. Where we do not know the truth, we shall not teach. There will be no myths, no legends, no lies, no superstitions, no false premises and no religions. There will be no gods, no bogeymen, no horrors, no nameless fears. We shall teach love and compassion and cooperation; and with this we shall demonstrate, in our lives and in every action we take, the same love and compassion—hoping, trusting and fighting for all of this to add up to the fullest possible measure of security. We shall also teach them the knowledge of mankind—but not until they are ready for that knowledge, not until they are capable of handling it. Certainly we shall not give them knowledge of the history of mankind or what mankind has become in the course of that history until they have completed the first eight years of their lives. Thus they will grow up knowing nothing of war, knowing nothing of murder, knowing nothing of the thing called patriotism, unaware of the multitude of hatreds, of fears, of hostilities that has become the common heritage of all of mankind.

During the first nine years in the environment, we shall have total control. We have already installed a complete printing press, a photo-offset system; we have all the moving-picture equipment necessary, and we have laboratories to develop the film we take, projection booths and theaters. All the film we need we shall make. We shall write the books; we shall take the film; we shall shape the history as history is taught to them in the beginning—that is, a history of who they are and what they are within the environment. We shall raise them in a sort of Utopia—God willing, without all the tragic mistakes that man has always made in his Utopias. And, finally, when we have produced something strong and healthy and beautiful and sturdy—at that point only will we begin to relate the children to the world as it is. Does it sound too simple or presumptuous? I am almost sorry, Harry, that I cannot make it more complicated, more intriguing, more wonderful, yet Mark and I both agree that the essence of what we are attempting to do is simple beyond belief; it is almost negative. We are attempting to rid ourselves of something that mankind has done to itself; and, if we can rid a group of children of that undefined something, then what will emerge just might be exciting and wonderful and even magnificent beyond belief. That is our hope; but the environment as I describe it above, Harry, is all that we can do—and I think that Professor Goldbaum will understand that full well and will not ask more of us. It is also a great deal more than has ever been done for any children on this earth heretofore.

So good luck to both of you. May you work well and happily and complete your work. The moment it is completed we want Professor Goldbaum to join us in the United States and to become a part of our group and our experiment. I am not asking you to become a part of it, Harry, and I think you can understand why. I don't want to put you in a position of having to make the choice. By now I can well understand how deeply you have committed yourself to our experiment. Mark and I both realize that you cannot spell out such a commitment, but, dear Harry, I know you so well and I know what has happened inside of you. If I asked you to join us, you would not allow yourself to say No; but, at the same time, I don't think that your road to happiness consists of taking off for another planet. However you might feel about it, Harry, you are far too attached to the reality of the world as it is. You have not yet found the woman that you must find, but when you do find her, Harry, she and you will have your own way to find.

Your letters, in spite of your attempt to make them highly impersonal, do give us a clue to the change within you. Do you know, Harry, everyone associated with this experiment begins a process of change—and we feel that same curious process of change taking place within us.

When I put down simply and directly on paper what we are doing now and what we intend to do in the future, it seems almost too obvious to be meaningful in any manner. In fact, when you look at it again and again, it seems almost ridiculously simple and pointless and hopeless. What are we doing, Harry? We are simply taking a group of very gifted children and giving them knowledge and love. Is this enough to break through to that part of man which is unused and unknown? We don't know, Harry, but in time we shall see. Bring us the children, Harry, and we shall see.

With love,
Jean.

16

One day in the early spring of 1965, Harry Felton arrived in Washington from London. At the airport he took a cab directly to the White House, where he was expected.

Felton had just turned fifty; he was a tall and pleasant-looking man, rather lean, with graying hair. As president of the board of Shipways, Inc.—one of the country's largest import and export houses, with offices in London and in New York—Felton commanded a certain amount of deference and respect from Eggerton, who was then Secretary of Defense. A cold, withdrawn, and largely unloved man, Eggerton frequently adopted an attitude of immediate superiority, or, if that failed to impress, of judicious and controlled hostility; but he was sufficiently alert and sensitive not to make the mistake of trying to intimidate Felton.

Instead, he greeted him rather pleasantly—that is, pleasantly for Eggerton. The two of them, with no others present, sat down to talk in a small room in the White House. Drinks were served and a tray of sandwiches was brought in case Felton was hungry. Felton was not hungry. He and Eggerton drank each other's good health, and then they began to talk.

Eggerton proposed that Felton might know why he had been asked to Washington.

"I can't say that I do know," Felton replied—a little less than truthfully; but then, Felton did not like Eggerton and did not feel comfortable with him.

"You have a remarkable sister."

"I have been aware of that for a long time."

Felton seemed to take a moment to think about what he had just said, and then he smiled. Whatever made him smile was not revealed to Eggerton who, after a moment, asked him whether he felt that his statement had been humorous.

"No, I didn't feel that," Felton said seriously.

"You are being very careful here, Mr. Felton," the Secretary observed, "but you have trained yourself to be a very close-mouthed person. So far as we are able to ascertain, not even your immediate family has ever heard of man-plus. That's a commendable trait."

"Possibly and possibly not. It's been a long time," Felton said coldly. "Just what do you mean by 'ascertain'? How have you been able to ascertain whether or not I am close-mouthed? That interests me, Mr. Secretary."

"Please don't be naïve, Mr. Felton."

"I have practiced being naïve for a lifetime," Felton said. "It's really not very sensitive on your part to ask me to change in a moment sitting here in front of you. I find that a degree of naïveté fits well with close-mouthedness. What did it come to, Mr. Secretary? Was my mail examined?"

"Now and then," the Secretary admitted.

"My offices bugged?"

"At times."

"And my home?"

"There have been reasons to keep you under observation, Mr. Felton. We do what is necessary. What we do has received large and unnecessary publicity; so I see no point in your claiming ignorance."

"I am sure you do what is necessary."

"We must, and I hope that this will not interfere with our little conversation today."

"It doesn't surprise me. So, in that direction at least, it will not interfere. But just what is this conversation and what are we to talk about?"

"Your sister."

"I see, my sister." Felton nodded. He did not appear surprised.

"Have you heard from your sister lately, Mr. Felton?"

"No, not for almost a year."

"Does it alarm you, Mr. Felton?"

"Does what alarm me?"

"The fact that you have not heard from your sister in so long?"

"Should it alarm me? No, it doesn't alarm me. My sister and I are very close, but this project of hers is not the sort of thing that allows for frequent social relations. Add to that the fact that my residence is in England, and that, while I do make trips to America, most of my time is spent in London and Paris. There have been long periods before when I have not heard from my sister. We are indifferent letter writers."

"I see," Eggerton said.

"Then I am to conclude that my sister is the reason for my visit here?"

"Yes."

"She is well?"

"As far as we know," Eggerton replied quietly.

"Then what can I do for you?"

"Help us if you will," Eggerton said just as quietly. He was visibly controlling himself—as if he had practiced with himself before the meeting and had conditioned himself not to lose his temper under any circumstances, but to remain quietly controlled, aloof and polite. "I am going to tell you what has happened, Mr. Felton, and then perhaps you can help us."

The Trap

"Perhaps," Felton agreed. "You must understand, Mr. Eggerton, that I don't admire either your methods or your apparent goal. I think you would be wrong to look upon me as an ally. I spent the first twenty-four years of my life in the United States. Since then I have lived abroad with only infrequent visits here. So, you see, I am not even conditioned by what you might think of as a patriotic frame of mind. I am afraid that, if anything, I am a total internationalist."

"That doesn't surprise me, Mr. Felton."

"On second thought, I realize that it wouldn't. I am sure that you have investigated my residences, my frame of mind, my philosophy, and I would also guess that you have enough recordings of my conversations with my most intimate friends to know exactly what my point of view is."

The Secretary of Defense smiled as if to exhibit to Felton the fact that he, the Secretary of Defense, possessed a sense of humor. "No, not quite that much, Mr. Felton, but I must say that I am rather pleased by the respect you have for our methods. It is true that we know a good deal about you and it is also true that we could anticipate your point of view. However, we are not calling upon you in what some might term a patriotic capacity; we are calling upon you because we feel that we can appeal to certain instincts which are very important to you."

"Such as?"

"Human beings, human decency, the protection of mankind, the future of mankind—subjects that cross national boundaries. You would agree that they do, would you not, Mr. Felton?"

"I would agree that they do," Felton said.

"All right then; let us turn to your sister's project, a project which has been under way so many years now. I don't have to be hush-hush about it, because I am sure that you know as much concerning this project as any of us—more perhaps, since you were in at its inception. At that time, you were on the payroll of the project, and for a number of months you assisted your sister in the beginnings of the project. If I am not mistaken, part of your mission was to acquire certain infants which she needed at that stage of her experiment?"

"The way you say 'infants,'" Felton replied, smiling, "raises a suspicion that we wanted them to roast and devour. May I assure you that such was not the case. We were neither kidnappers nor cannibals; our motives were rather pure."

"I am sure."

"You don't say it as if you were sure at all."

"Then perhaps I have some doubts, and perhaps you will share my doubts, Mr. Felton, when you have heard me out. What I intended to say was that surely you, of all people, realize that such a project as your sister undertook must be regarded very seriously indeed or else laughed off entirely. To date it has cost the Government of the United States upwards of one hundred and fourteen million dollars, and that is not something you laugh off, Mr. Felton."

"I had no idea the price was so high," Felton said. "On the other hand, you may have gotten a hundred and fourteen million dollars' worth for your money."

"That remains to be seen. You understand, of course, that the unique part of your sister's project was its exclusiveness. That word is used advisedly and specifically. Your sister made the point again and again and again—and continues to make it, I may say—the point that the success of the project depended entirely upon its exclusiveness, upon the creation of a unique and exclusive environment. We were forced to accept her position and her demands—that is, if we desired the project at all; and it seems that the people who undertook to back the project did desire it. I say we, Mr. Felton, because 'we' is a term we use in government; but you must understand that was a good many years ago, almost twenty years ago, and I myself, Mr. Felton, did not participate in its inception. Now, in terms of the specifications, in terms of the demands that were made and met, we agreed not to send any observers into the reservation for a period of fifteen years. Of course, during those fifteen years there have been many conferences with Mr. and Mrs. Arbalaid and with certain of their associates, including Dr. Goldbaum."

"Then, if there were conferences," Felton said, "it seems to me that you know more about my sister than I do. You must understand that I have not seen my sister almost since the inception of the project."

"We understand that. Nevertheless, the relationship differs. Out of these conferences, Mr. Felton, there was no progress report that dealt with anything more than general progress and that in the most fuzzy and indefinite terms. We were given to understand that the results they had obtained in the reservation were quite rewarding and exciting, but little more, very little more indeed."

"That was to be expected. That's the way my sister works; in fact, it's the way most scientists work. They are engaged in something that is very special to them, very complicated, very difficult to explain. They do not like to give reports of the way stations they may arrive at. They like to complete their work and have results, proven results, before they report."

"We are aware of that, Mr. Felton. We honored our part of the agreement, and at the end of a fifteen-year period we told your sister and her husband that they would have to honor their part of the agreement and that we would have to send in a team of observers. We were as liberal, as flexible, as people in our position could be. We advised them that they would have the right to choose the observers, that they could even limit the path of the observers—limit what the observers would see and the questions the observers could ask—but that we would have to send in such a team."

"And did you?" Felton asked him.

"No, we did not. That's a tribute to the persuasive powers of your sister and her husband. They pleaded for an extension of time, maintaining that it was critical to the success of the entire program, and they pleaded so persuasively that in the end they did win a three-year extension. Some months ago, the three-year period of grace was over. Mrs. Arbalaid came to Washington and begged for a further extension. I was at the meeting where she was heard, and I can tell you, Mr. Felton, that never before in my life had I heard a woman plead for something with the fervor, the insistence, with which Mrs. Arbalaid pleaded for this further extension."

Felton nodded. "Yes, I imagine my sister would plead with some intensity. Did you agree?"

"No. As I said, we refused."

"You mean you turned her down completely—entirely?"

"Not as completely perhaps as we should have. She agreed—when she saw that she could not move us—that our team could come into the reservation in ten days. She begged the ten-day interval to discuss the matter with her husband and to choose the two people who would make up the observation team. The way she put it, we had to agree to it; and then she returned to California."

Eggerton paused and looked at Felton searchingly.

"Well," Felton said, "what happened then? Did my sister select competent observers?"

"You don't know?" Eggerton asked him.

"I know some things. I'm afraid I don't know whatever you're interested in at this moment. I certainly don't know what happened."

"That was three weeks ago, Mr. Felton. Your sister never chose observers; your sister never communicated with us again; in fact, we know nothing about your sister or her reactions or what she said to her husband because we have not heard from her since."

"That's rather curious."

"That is exceedingly curious, Mr. Felton, far more curious than you might imagine."

"Tell me, what did you do when ten days went by and you didn't hear from my sister?"

"We waited a few days more to see whether it was an oversight on her part, and then we tried to communicate with her."

"Well?"

"We couldn't. You know something, Felton? When I think about what I'm going to tell you now I feel like a damn fool. I also feel a little bit afraid. I don't know whether the fear or the fool predominates. Naturally, when we couldn't communicate with your sister, we went there."

"Then you did go there," Felton said.

"Oh, yes, we went there."

"And what did you find?"

"Nothing."

"I don't understand," Felton said.

"Didn't I make myself plain, Mr. Felton? We went there and we found nothing."

"Oh?"

"You don't appear too surprised, Mr. Felton."

"Nothing my sister did ever really surprised me. You mean the reservation was empty—no sign of anything, Mr. Eggerton?"

"No, I don't mean that at all, Mr. Felton. I wish to God I did mean that. I wish it were so pleasantly human and down to earth and reasonable. I wish we thought or had some evidence that your sister and her husband were two clever and unscrupulous swindlers who had taken the government for a hundred and fourteen million dollars. That would have been a joy, Mr. Felton. That would have warmed the cockles of our hearts compared to what we do have and what we did find. You see, we don't know whether the reservation is empty or not, Mr. Felton, because the reservation is not there."

"What?"

"Precisely. Exactly what I said. The reservation is not there."

"Oh, come on now," Felton smiled. "My sister is a remarkable woman, but she doesn't make off with eight thousand acres of land. It isn't like her."

"I don't find your humor entertaining at this moment, Mr. Felton."

"No. No, of course not. I'm sorry. I realize that this is hardly the moment for humor. Only a thing is put to me and the thing makes no sense at all—how could an eight-thousand-acre stretch of land not be where it was? Doesn't that leave a damn big hole?"

"It's still a joke, isn't it, Mr. Felton?"

"Well, how do you expect me to react?" Felton asked.

"Oh, you're quite justified, Mr. Felton. If the newspapers got hold of it, they could do even better."

"Supposing you explain it to me," Felton said. "We're both guessing, aren't we? Maybe we're both putting each other on, maybe we're not. Let's be sensible about it and talk in terms that we both understand."

"All right," the Secretary said, "suppose you let me try, not to explain—that's beyond me—but to describe. The stretch of land where the reservation is located is in the Fulton National Forest: rolling country, some hills, a good stand of sequoia—a kidney-shaped area all in all, and very exclusive in terms of the natural formation. It's a sort of valley, a natural valley, that contains within itself areas of high land, areas of low land, and flat areas as well. Water, too. It was wire-fenced. Around it was a three-hundred-yard wide neutral zone, and Army guards were stationed at every possible approach. I went out there last week with our inspection team: General Meyers; two Army physicians; Gorman, the psychiatrist; Senator Totenwell of the Armed Services Committee; and Lydia Gentry, the educator who is our present Secretary of Education. You will admit that we had a comprehensive and intelligent team that represented a fine cross-section of American society. At least, Mr. Felton, that is my opinion. I still have some veneration for the American society."

"I share your admiration, Mr. Secretary, if not your veneration. I don't think that this should be a contest between you and me, *re* our attitudes toward the United States of America."

"No such contest intended, Mr. Felton. Let me continue. We crossed the country by plane and then we drove the final sixty miles to the reservation. We drove this distance in two Government cars. A dirt road leads into the reservation. The main guard, of course, is on that dirt road, and that road is the only road into the reservation, the only road that a vehicle could possibly take to go into the reservation. The armed guard on this road halted us, of course. They were merely doing their duty. The reservation was directly before us. The sergeant in charge of the guard approached the first car according to orders; and, as he walked toward our car, the reservation disappeared."

"Come on now," Felton said.

"I am trying to be reasonable and polite, Mr. Felton. I think the very least you could do is attempt to adopt the same attitude toward me. I said, 'The reservation disappeared'."

"Just like that?" Felton whispered. "No noise—no explosion—no earthquake?"

"No noise, no explosion, no earthquake, Mr. Felton. One moment a forest of sequoia in front of us—then a gray area of nothing."

"Nothing. Nothing is not a fact, Mr. Secretary. Nothing is not even a description; it's simply a word and a highly abstract word."

"We have no other word for this situation."

"Well, you say 'nothing.' What do you mean? Did you try to go in? If there was nothing in front of you did you try to go through this nothing?"

"Yes, we tried. You can be very certain that we tried, Mr. Felton, and since then the best scientists in America have tried. I do not like to speak about myself as a brave man, but certainly I am not a coward. Yet believe me, it took a while for me to get up enough courage to walk up to that gray edge of nothing and touch it."

"Then you touched it?"

"I touched it."

"If it was nothing, it seems to me you could hardly touch it. If you could touch it, it was something, certainly not nothing."

"If you wish, it was something. It blistered these three fingers."

He held out his hand for Felton to see. The first three fingers of his right hand were badly blistered.

"That looks like a burn," Felton said.

"It is a burn. No heat and no cold, nevertheless it burned my hand. That kind of thing sets you back, Felton."

"I can appreciate that," Felton said.

"I became afraid then, Mr. Felton, I think we all became afraid. We continue to be afraid. Do you understand, Mr. Felton? The world today represents a most delicate and terrible balance of power. When news comes to us that the Chinese have developed an atomic weapon, we become afraid. Out of necessity, our diplomatic attitude must reflect such fear and our attitude toward the Chinese must change. When the French began their atomic stockpile, our attitude toward the French changed. We are a pragmatic and a realistic administration, Mr. Felton, and we do not lie about fear or abjure power; we recognize fear and power, and we are very much afraid of that damn thing out there in California."

"I need not ask you if you tried this or that."

"We tried everything, Mr. Felton. You know, I'm a little ashamed to say this, and it is certainly damned well not for publication—I trust you will honor my request in that direction, Mr. Felton—?"

"I am not here as a reporter for the press," Felton said.

"Of course, yet this is very delicate, very delicate indeed. You asked whether we tried this or that. We tried things. We even tried a very small atomic bomb. Yes, Mr. Felton, we tried the sensible things and we tried the foolish things. We went into panic and we went out of panic and we tried everything we have and it all failed."

"And yet you have kept it a secret?"

"So far, Mr. Felton, we have kept it a secret," the Secretary agreed. "You cannot imagine what wire-pulling that took. We threw our weight here and there, and we threw our weight heavily, and we kept the secret—so far, Mr. Felton."

"Well, what about airplanes? You couldn't bar access to it from the air, could you? You couldn't cut off so wide a lane of air visibility that it would not be seen?"

"No, we immediately observed it from the air; you can be sure we thought of that quickly enough. But when you fly above it you see nothing. As I said, the reservation is in a valley, and all you can see is what appears to be mist lying in the valley. Perhaps it is mist—"

Felton leaned back and thought about it.

"Take your time," the Secretary said to him. "We are not rushing you, Mr. Felton, and believe me we are not pressuring you. We want your cooperation and, if you know what this is, we want you to tell us what it is."

Finally Felton asked him, "What do your people think it is?"

Eggerton smiled coldly and shook his head. "They don't know. There you are. At first, some of them thought it was some kind of force field. I have since learned that *force field* is a generic term for any area of positive action not understood too well. But when they tried to work it out mathematically, the mathematics wouldn't work. When they put it on the computers, the mathematics still refused to work. I don't know the math, Mr. Felton. I'm not a physicist and I'm not a mathematician, so I'm merely reporting what I have been told. And, of course, it's cold, and they're very upset about the fact that it's cold. It seems to confuse them no end. Terribly cold. Don't think only I am mumbling, Mr. Felton. As I said, I am neither a scientist nor a mathematician, but I can assure you that the scientists and the mathematicians also mumble. As for me, Mr. Felton, I am sick to death of the mumbling. I am sick to death of the doubletalk and the excuses. And that's why we decided that you should come to Washington and talk with us. We thought that you might know about this thing that bars us from the reservation, and you might be able to tell us what it is or tell us how to get rid of it."

"I haven't the vaguest idea what it is," Felton said, "but even if I had, what on earth makes you think that I would tell you how to get rid of it?"

"Surely you don't think it's a good thing."

"How can I say whether it's a good thing or a bad thing?" Felton asked him. "I haven't the faintest notion of what it is, and I'm not sure that I know, in today's scheme of things, what is good or what is bad."

"Then you can't help us at all?"

"I didn't say that either. I just might be able to help you."

For the first time, Eggerton emerged from his lethargy,

his depression. Suddenly he was excited and patient and overly cordial. He tried to force another drink on Felton. When Felton refused, he suggested that champagne be brought. Felton smiled at him, and the Secretary admitted that he was being childish.

"But you don't know how you have relieved me, Mr. Felton."

"I don't see why the little I said should relieve you. I certainly didn't intend to relieve you, and I don't know whether I can help you or not. I said I might help you."

Felton took a letter out of his pocket.

"This came from my sister," he said.

"You told me you had no letter from her in almost a year," the Secretary replied suspiciously.

"Exactly. And I have had this letter for almost a year." There was a note of sadness in Felton's voice. "I haven't opened it, Mr. Secretary, because when she sent it to me she enclosed it in a sealed envelope with a short letter. The letter said that she was well and quite happy, and that I was not to open or read the enclosed letter until it was absolutely necessary to do so. My sister is like that. We think the same way. I think that it's necessary now, don't you?"

The Secretary nodded slowly but said nothing. His eyes were fixed on Felton. Felton scanned the letter, turned it over, and then reached toward the Secretary's desk where there was a letter opener. The Secretary made no move to help him. Felton took the opener, slit the letter, and took out a sheaf of onionskin paper. He opened this sheaf of paper and he began to read aloud.

17

June 12, 1964

My dear Harry:
As I write this, it is twenty-two years since I have seen you or spoken to you. How very long for two people who have such love and regard for each other as we do! And now that you have found it necessary to open this letter and read it, we must face the fact that in all probability we will never see each other again unless we are most fortunate. And Harry, I have watched so many miracles occur that I hesitate to dream of another. I know from your letters that you have

a wife and three children, and I have seen their photographs. So far as I can tell, they are wonderful people. I think the hardest thing is to know that I will not see them or come to know them and watch them grow, and at least be some sort of sister to your wife.

Only this thought saddens me. Otherwise, Mark and I are very happy—perhaps as happy as two human beings have any right to be. As you read this letter I think you will come to understand why.

Now, about the barrier—which must exist or you would not have opened the letter—tell them that there is no harm to it and that no hurt will be caused by it. The very worst that can happen is that if one leans against it too long, one's skin may be badly blistered. But the barrier cannot be broken into because it is a negative power rather than a positive one, an absence instead of a presence. I will have more to say about it later, but I don't think I will be able to explain it better. My physics is limited, and these are things for which we, as human beings, have no real concepts. To put it into visual terms or understandable terms for a layman is almost impossible—at least for me. I imagine that some of the children could put it into intelligible words. But I want this to be my report, not theirs.

Strange that I still call them children and think of them as children—when in fact we are the children and they are the adults. But they still have the quality of children that we know best: the innocence and purity that vanishes so quickly with the coming of puberty in the outside world.

Now, dear Harry, I must tell you what came of our experiment—or some of it. Some of it, for how could I ever put down the story of the strangest two decades that man ever lived through? It is all incredible and, at the same time, it is all commonplace. We took a group of wonderful children and we gave them an abundance of love, security and truth—but I think it was the factor of love that mattered most, and because we were able to give them these three very obvious things—love, security and truth—we were able to return them to their heritage, and what a heritage it is, Harry!

During the first year we weeded out those couples who showed less than a total desire to love the children. I mention this because you must not think that any stage of this was easy or that any part of it ran smoothly. We went into the reservation with twenty-three couples; six of them—that is, twelve people—failed to meet our test, and they had to go, but they were still good people and they abided by the necessity for silence and security.

But our children are easy to love, and they were easy to love from the very beginning. You see, I call them our children, Harry, because as the years passed they became our children—in every way. The children who were born to the couples in residence here simply joined the group. No one had a father or a mother; we were a living, functioning group in which all the men were the fathers of all the children and all the women were the mothers of all the children.

Now this is very easy to state as a fact, Harry; it is easy to project as a concept; but its achievement was far from easy. Its achievement was something that tore us to pieces. We had to turn ourselves inside out, totally reexamine ourselves, to achieve this. This among ourselves, Harry, among the adults who had to fight and work and examine each other inside and outside again and again and again—and tear out our guts and tear our hearts out—so that we could present ourselves to the children as something in the way of human beings. I mean a quality of sanity and truth and security embodied in a group of adult men and women. Far more spectacular achievements than this were accomplished, Harry—but perhaps nothing more wonderful than the fact that we, the adults, could remake ourselves. In doing so, we gave the children their chance.

And what did the chance amount to? How shall I tell you of an American Indian boy, five years old, composing a splendid symphony? Or of the two children, one Bantu, one Italian, one a boy, one a girl, who at the age of six built a machine to measure the speed of light? Will you believe that we, the adults, sat quietly and respectfully and listened to these six-year-olds explain to us a new theory of light? We listened, and perhaps some of us understood, but most of us did not. I certainly did not. I might translate it and repeat it in these terms—that since the speed of light is a constant anywhere, regardless of the motion of material bodies, the distance between the stars cannot be mentioned or determined in terms of the speed of light, since distance so arrived at is not, and has no equivalence to, distance on our plane of being. Does what I have said make any sense to you? It makes just a little to me. If I put it poorly, awkwardly, blame my own ignorance.

I mention just this one small thing. In a hundred—no, in a thousand—of these matters, I have had the sensations of an uneducated immigrant whose beloved child is exposed to all the wonders of school and knowledge. Like this immigrant, I understand a little of what the children achieve, but very little indeed. If I were to repeat instance after instance, wonder after wonder—at the ages of six and seven and eight and nine—would you think of the poor tortured nervous creatures whose parents boast that they have an IQ of 160 or 170 and, in the same breath, bemoan the fate that did not give them normal children? Do you understand me, Harry? These children of ours, in your world, would have been condemned to disaster—not to simple disaster but to the specific, terrible disaster that befalls the super-knowing, the super-sensitive, the super-intelligent who are ground down, degraded and destroyed just as that Assamese child raised by the wolves was destroyed. Well, our children were and are normal children. Perhaps they are the first truly normal children that this world has seen in a long time—in many thousands of years. If just once you could hear them laugh or sing, you would know how absolutely true my statement is. If only you could see how tall and strong they are, how fine of body and movement. They have a quality that I have never seen in children before.

I suppose, dear Harry, that much about them would shock you just as it would shock most of the population of the outside world. Most of the time, they wear no clothes. Sex has always been a joy and a good thing to them, and they face it and enjoy it as naturally as we eat and drink—more naturally, for we have no gluttons in sex or food, no ulcers of the belly or the soul.

Our children kiss and caress each other and do many things that the world has specified as shocking, nasty, forbidden, dirty, obscene. But whatever they do, they do it with grace and they do it with joy, and they have no guilt nor any knowledge whatsoever of guilt. *Guilt* as a word or fact is meaningless to them.

Is all this possible? Or is it a dream and an illusion? I tell you that it has been my life for almost twenty years now. I live with these children, with boys and girls who are without evil or sickness, who are like pagans or gods, however you would look at it.

But the story of the children and of their day-to-day life

is one that will some day be told properly in its own time and place. Certainly I have neither the time nor the ability to tell it here, Harry. You will have to content yourself with the bits and snatches that I can put down in this letter to you. All the indications that I have put down here add up only to great gifts and great abilities. But, after all, this was inherent in the children we selected. Mark and I never had any doubts about such results; we knew that if we created a controlled environment that was predicated on our hypothesis, the children would learn more than children do on the outside.

Naturally, this part of it came about. How could it have been otherwise—unless, of course, Mark and I had flubbed the whole thing and acted like fools and sentimentalists. But I don't think that there was much danger of that. Without being egotistical I can say that we, and of course Professor Goldbaum (who was with us through all the most difficult years), and our associates—we knew what we were doing. We knew precisely what we were doing and we knew pretty well how to do it.

In the seventh year of their lives, the children were dealing easily and naturally with scientific problems normally taught on the college level or on the postgraduate level in the outside world. But, as I said, this was to be expected, this was normal and we would have been very disappointed indeed if this development had not taken place. It was the unexpected that we hoped for, prayed for, dreamed of and watched for. A flowering, a development of the mind of man that was unpredictable and unknowable, which we could comprehend only negatively by theorizing that a block to such development is locked in every single human being on the outside.

And it came. Originally, it began with a Chinese child in the fifth year of our work. The second incident occurred in an American child, and the third in a Burmese child. Most strangely, it was not thought of as anything very unusual by the children themselves. We did not realize what was happening until the seventh year, that is, two years after the process had begun; and by that time it had happened already in five of the children. The very fact that it took place so gently, so naturally, so obviously, was a healthy symptom.

Let me tell you how we discovered what was happening. Mark and I were taking a walk that day—I remember it so well, a lovely, cool and clear northern California day—when we came upon a group of children in a meadow. There were about a dozen children gathered together in the meadow. Five of the children sat in a little circle, with a sixth child in the center of their circle. The six heads were almost touching. They were full of little giggles, ripples of mirth and satisfaction. The rest of the children sat in a group about ten feet away—watching intently, seriously, respectfully.

As we came closer the children were neither alarmed nor disturbed. The children in the second group put their fingers to their lips, indicating that we should be quiet. So we came rather close, and then we stood and watched without speaking.

After we were there about ten minutes, the little girl in the center of the circle of five children leaped to her feet, crying out ecstatically:

"I heard you! I heard you! I heard you!"

There was a kind of achievement and delight reflected in the sound of her voice that we had not experienced before, not even from our children. Then all of the children there rushed together to kiss and embrace the girl who had been in the middle of the group of five. They did a sort of dance of play and delight around her. All this we watched with no indication of surprise or even very great curiosity on our part. For even though this was the first time anything like this—anything beyond our expectation or comprehension—had ever happened, we had worked out what our own reaction should be to such discoveries and achievements on the part of the children. We had made up our minds that whatever they accomplished, our position would be that it was perfectly natural and completely expected.

When the children rushed to us for our congratulations, we nodded and smiled and agreed that it was all indeed very wonderful.

"Whose turn is it now?" Mark asked.

They called all the men "Father," the women "Mother." A Senegalese boy turned to me and said excitedly, "Now, it's my turn, Mother. I can do—well, I can almost do it already. Now there are six to help me, and it will be much easier."

"Aren't you proud of us?" another child cried.

"So proud," I said. "We couldn't be more proud."

"Are you going to do it now?" Mark asked him.

"Not now, we're tired now. You know, when you go at it with a new one, it's terribly tiring. After that, it's not tiring. But the first time it is."

"Then when will you do it?" I asked.

"Maybe tomorrow."

"Can we be here? I mean would you want us here when you do it or does it make it harder?"

"No harder," one of them said.

"Of course you can be here," another answered. "We would like you to be here."

"Both of us?" Mark asked.

"Of course, both of you and any other mother or father who wants to come."

We pressed it no further, but that evening at our regular staff meeting, Mark described what had happened and repeated the conversation.

"I noticed the same thing a few weeks ago," Mary Hengel, our semantics teacher, said. "I watched them, but either they didn't see me or they didn't mind my watching them."

"Did you go up close to them?" I asked her.

"No, I was a little uncertain about that. I must have stayed about forty or fifty yards away."

"How many were there then?" Professor Goldbaum asked Mary Hengel. He was very intent on his question, smiling slightly.

"Three. No there was a fourth child in the center—the three had their heads together. I simply thought it was one of their games—they have so many—and I walked away after a little while."

"They make no secret about it," someone else observed.

"Yes," I said, "we had the same feeling. They just took it for granted that we knew what they were doing, and they were quite proud of what they were doing."

"The interesting thing is," Mark said, "that while they were doing it, no one spoke. I can vouch for that."

"Yet they were listening," I put in. "There is no question about that; they were listening and they were listening for something, and finally, I imagine, they heard what they were listening for. They giggled and they laughed as if some great joke were taking place—you know the way children laugh about a game that delights them."

"Of course," said Abel Simms, who was in charge of our construction program, "of course they have no knowledge of right and wrong in our terms, and nothing they do ever seems wrong to them, just as nothing they do ever seems right to them; so there is no way to gauge their attitude in that sense toward whatever they were doing."

We discussed it a bit further, and it was Dr. Goldbaum who finally put his finger on it. He said, very gravely:

"Do you know, Jean—you always thought and hoped and dreamed too that we might open that great area of the human mind that is closed and blocked in all human beings. I think they found out how to open it. I think they are teaching each other and learning from each other what is to them a very simple and obvious thing—how to listen to thoughts."

There was a rather long silence after that, and then Atwater, one of our psychologists, said uneasily, "I am not sure I believe it. You know, I have investigated every test and every report on telepathy ever published in this country, and as much as I could gather and translate of what was published in other parts of the world—the Duke experiments and all the rest of it. None of it, absolutely none of it, was dependable, and absolutely none of it gave any provable or reliable or even believable evidence or indication that such a thing as mental telepathy exists. You know, we have measured brain waves. We know how tiny and feeble they are—it just seems to me utterly fantastic that brain waves can be a means of communication."

"Hold on there," said Tupper, an experimental physicist. "The seemingly obvious linkage of brain waves with telepathy is rather meaningless, you know. If telepathy exists, it is not a result of what we call brain waves of the tiny electric pattern that we are able to measure. It's quite a different type of action, in a different manner on a wholly different level of physical reality. Just what that level is, I have no idea. But one of the things we are learning more and more certainly in physics is that there are different levels of reality, different levels of action and interaction of force and counterforce, so we cannot dispose of telepathy by citing brain waves."

"But how about the statistical factor?" Rhoda Lannon, a mathematician, argued. "If this faculty existed, even as a potential in mankind, is it conceivable that there would be no recorded instance of it? Statistically it must have emerged not once but literally thousands of times."

"Maybe it has been recorded," said Fleming, one of our

historians. "Can you take all the whippings and burnings and hangings of history, all the witches, the demigods, the magicians, the alchemists, and determine which of these were telepaths and which were not? Also, there is another way of looking at it. Suppose one telepath alone is totally impotent. Suppose we need two telepaths to make it work, and suppose there is a limited distance over which two telepaths can operate. Then the statistical factor becomes meaningless and the accident becomes virtually impossible."

"I think that all in all I agree at least to some extent with Dr. Goldbaum," Mark said. "The children are becoming telepaths. It seems to me there is no question about that; it is the only sensible explanation for what Jean and I witnessed. If you argue, and with reason, that our children do not react to right and wrong and have no real understanding of right and wrong, then we must also add that they are equally incapable of lying. They have no understanding of the lie, of the meaning of the lie or of the necessity of the lie. So, if they told me that they heard what is not spoken, I have to believe them. I am not moved by an historical argument or by a statistical argument, because our concentration here is the environment and the absolute singularity of our environment. I speak of an historical singularity. There is no record in all of human history of a similar group of unusual children being raised in such an environment. Also, this may be—and probably is—a faculty of man which must be released in childhood, or remain permanently blocked. I believe Dr. Haenigson here will bear me out when I say that mental blocks imposed during childhood are not uncommon."

"More than that," Dr. Haenigson, our chief psychiatrist, stated. "No child in our history escapes the need to erect mental blocks in his mind. Without the ability to erect such blocks, it is safe to say that very few children in our society would survive. Indeed, we must accept the fact—and this is not theoretical or hypothetical, this is a fact, a provable fact which we have learned as psychiatrists—that whole areas of the mind of every human being are blocked in early childhood. This is one of the tragic absolutes of human society, and the removal—not the total removal, for that is impossible, but the partial removal—of such blocks becomes the largest part of the work of practicing psychiatrists."

Dr. Goldbaum was watching me strangely. I was about to

say something, but I stopped and I waited, and finally Dr. Goldbaum said:

"I wonder whether we have begun to realize what we may have done without even knowing what we were doing. That is the wonderful, the almost unbearable implication of what may have happened here. What is a human being? He is the sum of his memories and his experience—these are locked in his brain, and every moment of experience simply builds up the structure of these memories. We do not know as yet what is the extent or power of the gift these children of ours appear to be developing, but suppose they reach a point where they can easily and naturally share the totality of memory? It is not simply that among themselves there can be no lies, no deceit, no rationalization, no secrets, no guilts—it is far more than that."

Then he looked from face to face, around the whole circle of our staff. At that point we were beginning to understand him and comprehend the condition he was posing. I remember my own reactions at that moment: a sense of wonder and discovery and joy, and heartbreak too, a feeling so poignant that it brought tears to my eyes. But above and beyond all that, I felt a sense of excitement, of enormous and exhilarating excitement.

"You know, I see," Dr. Goldbaum said. "I think that all of you know to one degree or another. Perhaps it would be best for me to speak about it, to put it into words, and to open it up to our thinking. I am much older than any of you—and I have been through and lived through the worst years of horror and bestiality that mankind ever knew. When I saw what I saw, when I witnessed the rise of Hitlerism, the concentration camps, the abattoirs, the ovens, the senseless, meaningless madness that culminated in the use of human skin to make lampshades, of human flesh and fat to make soap, when I saw and watched all this, I asked myself a thousand times: What is the meaning of mankind? Or has it any meaning at all? Is man not, perhaps, simply a haphazard accident, an unusual complexity of molecular structure, a complexity without meaning, without purpose and without hope? I know that you all have asked yourselves the same thing perhaps a hundred, a thousand times. What sensitive or thoughtful human being does not ask this question of himself? Who are we? What are we? What is our destiny?

The Trap

What is our purpose? Where is sanity or reason in these bits of struggling, clawing, sick, murderous flesh? We kill, we torture, we hurt, we destroy as no other species does. We ennoble murder and falsehood and hypocrisy and superstition. We destroy our own bodies with drugs and poisonous food. We deceive ourselves as well as others. And we hate and hate and hate until every action we take is a result of our hatred.

"Now something has happened. Something new, something different, something very wonderful. If these children can go into each other's minds completely, then they will have a single memory, which is the memory of all of them. All their experience will be common to all of them, all their knowledge will be common to all of them, all the dreams they dream will be common to all of them—and do you know what that means? It means that they will be immortal. For as one of them dies, another child is linked to the whole, and another, and another. For them there will be no death. Death will lose all of its meaning, all of its dark horror. Mankind will begin, here in this place, in this strange little experiment of ours, to fulfill at least one part of its intended destiny—to become a single, wonderful thing, a whole—almost in the old words of your poet, John Donne, who sensed what each of us has sensed at one time or another: that no man is an island unto himself. Our tragedy has been that we are singular. We never lived, we were always fragmented bits of flesh at the edge of reality, at the edge of life. Tell me, has any thoughtful man or woman ever lived life without having a sense of that singleness of mankind and longing for it and dreaming of it? I don't think so. I think we have all had it, and therefore we have, all of us, been living in darkness, in the night, each of us struggling with his own poor little brain and then dying, perishing, with all the memories and the work of a lifetime destroyed forever. It is no wonder that we achieve so little. The wonder is that we have achieved so much. Yet all that we know, all that we have done, will be nothing, primitive, idiotic, nothing compared to what these children will know and do and create. It just staggers my imagination."

So the old man spelled it out, Harry. I can't put it all down here, but do you know, he saw it—at that moment, which was almost the beginning of it, he saw it in all of its far-flung implications. I suppose that was his reward, that he was able to fling his imagination forward into the future, the vast unrealized future, and see the blinding, incredible promise that it holds for us.

Well, that was the beginning, Harry; within the next twelve months, each one of our children was linked to all the others telepathically. And in the years that followed, every child born in our reservation was shown the way into that linkage by the children. Only we, the adults, were forever barred from joining it. We were of the old and they were of the new. Their way was closed to us forever—although they could go into our minds, and did when they had to. But never could we feel them there or see them there or go into their minds or communicate with them as they did with each other.

I don't know how to tell you of the years that followed, Harry. In our little guarded reservation, man became what he was always destined to be, but I can explain it only imperfectly. I can hardly comprehend, much less explain, what it means to inhabit forty bodies simultaneously, or what it means to each of the children to have the other personalities within him or her, a part of each of them. Can I even speculate on what it means to live as man and woman, always together, not only in the flesh, but man and woman within the same mind?

Could the children explain it to us? Did they explain it to us? Hardly. For this is a transformation that must take place, from all we can learn, before puberty; and as it happens, the children accept it as normal and natural—indeed as the most natural thing in the world. We were the unnatural ones— and the one thing they never truly comprehended is how we could bear to live in our aloneness, how we could bear to live on the edge of death and extinction and with the knowledge of death and extinction always pressing against us. Again, could we explain to a man born blind what color is, gradations of color, form, light, or the meaning of light and form combined? Hardly, any more than they are able to explain their togetherness to us who live so singularly and so alone.

As for the children's knowledge of us, we are very happy, indeed grateful, that it did not come at once. In the beginning, the children could merge their thoughts only when their heads were almost touching. This is what saved them from us, because if, in the very beginning, they had been able to touch our thoughts, they might not have been able to defend themselves. Bit by bit, their command of distance grew, but very slowly; and not until our fifteenth year in the reservation did the children begin to develop the power to reach out and probe with their thoughts anywhere on earth. We thank God for this. By then the children were ready for what they found. Earlier, it might have destroyed them.

I might mention here that the children explained to us in due time that their telepathic powers had nothing to do with brain waves. Telepathy, according to the children, is a function of time, but exactly what that means, I don't know, Harry, and therefore I cannot explain it to you.

I must mention that two of our children met accidental death—one in the ninth year and the second in the eleventh year. But the effect of these two deaths upon the other children cannot be compared to the effects of death in our world. There was a little regret, but no grief, no sense of great loss, no tears or weeping. Death is totally different among them than among us; among them, a loss of flesh and only flesh; the personality itself is immortal and lives consciously in the others.

When we spoke to them about a marked grave, or a tombstone, or some other mark that would enable us to keep alive the memory of the two dead children, they smiled sympathetically and said that we could make such a tomb or tombstone if it would give us any comfort. Their concern was only for us, not in any way for the two bodies that were gone.

Yet later, when Dr. Goldbaum died, their grief was deep and terrible, something so deep, so heartbreaking, that it touched us more than anything in our whole experience here—and this, of course, was because Dr. Goldbaum's death was the old kind of death.

The strangest thing, Harry, is that in spite of all these indications and means of togetherness that I have been telling you about, outwardly our children remain individuals. Each of the children retains his or her own characteristics, mannerisms and personality. The boys and girls make love in a normal, heterosexual manner—though all of them share the experience. Can you comprehend that? I cannot; but then neither can I comprehend any other area of their emotional experience except to realize that for them everything is different. Only the unspoiled devotion of mother for helpless child can approximate the love that binds them together. Yet here, too, in their love everything is different, deeper than anything that we can relate to our own experience. Before their transformation into telepaths took place, the children displayed enough petulance and anger and annoyance; but after it took place, we never again heard a voice raised in anger or annoyance. As they themselves put it, when there was trouble among them, they washed it out. When there was sickness among them, they healed it.

After the ninth year, there was no more sickness. By then they had learned to control their bodies. If sickness approached their bodies—and by that I mean infection, germs, virus, whatsoever you might call it—they could control and concentrate the reaction of their bodies to the infection; and with such conscious control and such conscious ability to change the chemical balance of their bodies, to change their heartbeat if necessary, to influence their blood flow, to increase the circulation in one part of the body, to decrease it in another, to increase or decrease the functioning of various organs in the body—with that kind of control, they were absolutely immune to sickness. However they could go further than that. While they could give us no part of the wholeness which they enjoyed as a normal thing of their lives, they could cure our illnesses. Three or four of them would merge their minds and go into our bodies and cure our bodies. They would go into our minds; they would control the organs of our bodies and the balance of our bodies and cure them; and yet we, the recipients of this cure, were never aware of their presence.

In trying to describe all of this to you, Harry, to make it real and to make incidents come alive, I use certain words and phrases only because I have no other words and phrases, I have no language that fits the life of these children. I use the words I know, but at the same time I realize, and you must realize, that my words do not describe adequately— they do not serve the use I am trying to put them to. Even after all these years of living intimately with the children, day and night, I can comprehend only vaguely the manner of their existence. I know what they are outwardly because I see it, I watch it. They are free and healthy and happy as no men and women ever were before. But what their inner life is remains a closed thing to me.

Again and again we discussed this with various members of our group, that is, among ourselves and also among the children. The children had no reticence about it; they were willing, eager, delighted to discuss it with us, but the discussions were hardly ever fruitful. For example, take the conversation I had with one of the children, whose name is Arlene. She is a tall, lovely child whom we found in an orphanage in Idaho. She came to us as the other children did, in infancy. At the time of our conversation, Arlene was fourteen. So much, you see, had happened in the reservation during the intervening years. We were discussing personality, and I told Arlene that I could not understand how she could live and work as an individual when she was also a part of so many others, and these so many others were a part of her.

She, however, could not see that and she rejected the whole concept.

"But how can you be yourself?" I pressed her.

"I remain myself," she answered simply. "I could not stop being myself."

"But aren't the others also yourself?"

"Yes, of course, what else could they be? And I am also them."

This was put to me as something self-evident. You see, it is no easier for them to understand our concepts than it is for us to understand their concepts. I said to her then:

"But who controls your body?"

"I do, of course."

"But just for the sake of a hypothetical situation, Arlene, suppose we take this possibility—that some of the other children should want to control your body instead of leaving the control to you."

"Why?" she asked me.

"If you did something they didn't approve of," I said lamely, digging the hole I had gotten into still deeper.

"Something they disapproved of?" she asked. "Well, how could I? Can you do something that you yourself disapprove of?"

"I am afraid I can, Arlene, and I do."

"Now that I don't understand at all, Jean. Why do you do it?"

"Well, don't you see, I can't always control what I do."

This was a new notion to her. Even able to read our minds, this was a new notion to her.

"You can't control what you do?" she asked.

"Not always."

"Poor *Jean*," she said, "oh, poor *Jean*. How terrible. What an awful way to have to live."

"But it's not so terrible, Arlene," I argued, "not at all. For us it's perfectly normal."

"But how? How could such things be normal?"

So these discussions always seemed to develop and so they always ended. The communication between us, with all the love that the children had for us and all the love that we had for the children, was so limited. We, the adults, had only words for communication; and words are very limited. But by their tenth year, the children had developed methods of communication as far beyond words as words are beyond the dumb motions of animals. If one of them watched something, there was no necessity to describe what he or she watched to the others. The others could see it through the eyes of the child who was watching. This went on not only in waking but in sleeping as well. They actually dreamed together, participated in the same dreams.

Has it ever occurred to you, Harry, that when something hurts you, you don't have to engage in conversation with yourself to tell yourself that it hurts you? When you have a certain feeling, you don't have to explain the feeling to yourself; you have the feeling. And this was the process of communication that was perfectly natural to the children. They felt as a unit, as a body, and yet they remained individuals.

I could go on for hours attempting to describe something utterly beyond my understanding, but that would not help, would it, Harry? You will have your own problems, and I must try to make you understand what happened, what had to happen, and now what must happen in the future.

You see, Harry, by the tenth year, the children had learned all we knew, all we had among us as material for teaching; our entire pooled experience was now used up. In effect, we were teaching a single mind, a mind composed of the unblocked, unfettered talent and brains of forty superb children. Consider that. A mind forty times as large, as agile, as comprehensive as any mind that man had ever known before—a mind so rational, so pure, that to this mind we could only be objects of loving pity. We have among us, as a pair of group parents, Alex Cromwell and his wife. You will recognize Alex Cromwell's name; he is one of our greatest physicists, and it was he who was largely responsible for the first atom bomb. After that, he came to us as one would go to a monastery. He performed an act of personal expiation in the only manner which could give him any hope, any satisfaction, any surcease from the enormous and terrible guilt that he bore. He and his wife taught our children physics, but by the eighth year, mind you, by the eighth year of their lives, the children were teaching Cromwell. A year later, Cromwell could no longer be taught. He was now incapable of following either their mathematics or their reasoning, and their symbolism, of course, was totally outside of the structure of Cromwell's thoughts. Imagine a mind like Cromwell's, led with concern, with tenderness, with gentleness, with the greatest love and consideration that the children could give him—for he is a charming and lovable person—imagine that such a mind could not advance within the area of knowledge that these nine-year-old children possessed.

It is rather terrifying, isn't it? And when you will show this letter (and of course we want you to show this letter) to the people who command the destiny of the United States, this thing I have just written will also be terrifying to them. I think that one of the saddest aspects of our society is the fear of the child that it engenders in the adult. That is a continuing fact of our society. Each generation, as it matures, fears the coming generation, looks at the coming generation as being conscienceless and depraved. No skill of adults, no talent of adults will engender as much fear as this skill, this talent, this brilliance of our children. Remember that, Harry, and expect it.

Let me give you an example of some of the capabilities, some of the powers our children have developed. In the far outfield of our baseball diamond, there was a boulder of perhaps ten tons. Incidentally, I must remark that our children's athletic skill, their physical prowess, is in its own way almost as extraordinary as their mental powers. They have broken every track and field record, often cutting world records by one third and even by one half. I have watched them effortlessly run down our horses. Their movements and their reactions are so quick as to make us appear sluggards by comparison. If they so desire, they can move their arms and legs faster than our eyes can follow; and, of course, one of the games they love is baseball, and they play in a manner you have never seen on the outside. Now to go back to this situation of the boulder: For some years, we, the adults, had spoken of either blasting the boulder apart or of rolling it out of the way with one of our very heavy bulldozers, but it was something we had simply never gotten to. Then, one day, we discovered that the boulder was gone, and in its place was a pile of thick red dust—a pile that the wind was fast leveling.

We brooded over the matter ourselves for a while, made our usual attempt at interpretation, made our guesses, and at last, frustrated, went to the children and asked them what had happened. They told us that they had reduced the boulder to dust—as if it were no more than kicking a small stone out of one's path and just as if everyone could at will reduce a gigantic boulder to dust. Why not?

Cromwell cornered them on this one and he asked one of the children, Billy:

"But how? After all, Billy, you say you reduced the boulder to dust, but how? That's the point. How?"

"Well, the ordinary way," Billy said.

"You mean there's an ordinary way to reduce a boulder to dust?"

"Well, isn't there?" another child asked.

Billy was more patient. He sensed our difficulty and asked gently whether perhaps Cromwell did not know the ordinary way, but had to do it in some more complex way.

"I suppose I could reduce the boulder to dust," Cromwell said. "I would have to use a great deal of heavy explosive. It would take some time; it would make a lot of noise, and it would be rather expensive."

"But the end would be the same, wouldn't it?" Billy asked.

"I suppose so," Cromwell said, "if you mean dust."

"No, I mean the manner," Billy said, "the technique."

"What technique?" Cromwell asked desperately.

"Well, our technique. I mean to make anything dust you have to unbond it. We do it by loosening the molecular structure—not very quickly, you know, it could be dangerous if you did it too quickly—but we just loosen it slowly, steadily, and we let the thing kick itself to pieces, so to speak. That doesn't mean that it actually kicks itself to pieces. It doesn't explode or anything of that sort; it just powders away. You know, it holds its shape for a while, and then you touch it and it becomes powder—it collapses."

"But how do you do that?" Cromwell insisted.

"Well, the best way of course—directly. I mean with your mind. You understand it, and then you reject it as an understood phenomenon and you let it shake itself loose."

But the more he spoke, the further Billy traveled from

Cromwell's area of comprehension; the more he used words, the less the words were able to convey, and finally, with patient and sympathetic smiles, the children dismissed the whole thing and their attempt to enlighten us as well. This was what usually happened, and this was the manner in which it usually happened.

Of course it was not always that way. They used the tools of our civilization, not because they admired these tools or because they needed mechanical things, but simply because they felt that our anxieties were eased by a certain amount of old-fashioned procedure. In other words, they wanted to preserve some of our world for our own sentimental needs. For example, they built an atomic-fusion power plant, out of which we derived and continued to derive our power. Then they built what they called free-fields into all our trucks and cars so that the trucks and cars could rise and travel through the air with the same facility as on the ground. The children could have built sensible, meaningful platforms that would have done the same thing and would have done it in a functional manner. The cars were much less functional; automobiles and trucks are not built to travel through the air. But the children had the kind of concern for the outer aspect of our world that led them to refrain from disarranging it too much.

At this point the use of thought, the degree to which they are able to use their own thoughts to influence atomic structure, is the most remarkable gift that they have beyond the power of telepathy itself. With the power of their thoughts they can go into atoms, they can control atoms, they can rearrange electrons; they can go into the enormous, almost infinite random patterns of electrons and atoms, and move things so that the random becomes directed and changes take place. In this way they are able to build one element out of another, and the curious thing of it is that all this is so elementary to them that they will do it at times as if they were doing tricks to amuse and amaze us, to save us from boredom, as an adult might do tricks for a child and so entertain the child.

So, dear Harry, I have been able to tell you something of what went on here over the years, a little bit of what the children are, a little bit about what they can do—not as much, perhaps, as I would want to tell you. I think I would like to create an hour-by-hour diary for you so that there might be a record on your side of what every day, every week of the last nineteen years has held; for, believe me, every day in the week of almost twenty years was exciting and rewarding.

Now I must tell you what you must know; and you shall tell these things to whoever you wish to tell them to. Use only your own judgment. Nothing in this document, Harry, is a secret. Nothing is for your ears alone. Nothing is to be held back. All of it can be given to the world. As for how much of it should be given to all the world, that must be a decision of the people who control the means of information. But let the decision be theirs, Harry. Do not interfere with it. Do not try to influence it; and above all, do not suppress anything that I am writing here.

In the fifteenth year of the experiment, our entire staff met with the children on a very important occasion. There were fifty-two children then, for all of the children born to us were taken into their body of singleness and flourished in their company. I must add that this was possible despite the initially lower IQ's of most of the children born to our mothers and fathers. Once the group has formed itself telepathically and has merged its powers, there is no necessity for high IQ's among the children who are brought into it. In fact, we are speculating on whether the experiment might not have proceeded almost the same way if we had chosen our first forty children at random. This we will never know.

Now, as to this meeting: It was a very formal and a very serious meeting, perhaps the most serious meeting of our experiment. Thirty days were left before the team of observers was scheduled to enter the reservation, according to the terms of our initial agreement with the Army. We had discussed that situation at great length among ourselves, the adults, and with the children, and of course it had been discussed among the children without us. But now it was discussed formally.

The children had chosen Michael to speak for them, but of course they were all speaking. Michael was simply the voice necessary to communicate with us. Michael, I might say, was born in Italy, a tall, delicate, lovely young man, and a most talented artist. Again I might mention that talent, specific talent, remained the property, the gift of the individual. This could not be communicated through the group to another child. Knowledge, yes, but a creative talent remained entirely the gift of the child who had it originally.

Michael took the floor and began by telling us how much the children loved and cherished us, the adults who were once their teachers.

I interrupted him to say that it was hardly necessary for the children ever to spell that out. We might not be able to communicate telepathically but never once was there anything in their actions to make us doubt their love for us.

"Of course," Michael said, "we understand that; yet, at the same time, certain things must be said. They must be said in your language, and unless they are said they do not really exist as they must exist in relation to you. Believe us, we comprehend fully that all that we have, all that we are, you have given us. You are our fathers and mothers and teachers—and we love you beyond our power to say. We know that you consider us something superior to yourselves, something more than yourselves and beyond yourselves. This may be true, but it is also a fact of life that in each step forward, along with what is gained, something else is lost. There is a taking and a giving, a taking on and a putting aside. For years now, we have wondered and marveled at your patience and self-giving, for we have gone into your minds and we have known what pain and doubt and fear and confusion all of you live with. But there is something else that until now you have not known."

He paused and looked at each of us in turn. Then he looked at me searchingly, wonderingly, and I nodded as if to tell him to go ahead and tell us everything and hold nothing back.

"This then," Michael said. "We have also gone into the minds of the soldiers who guard the reservation. More and more, our power to probe grew and extended itself so that now, in this fifteenth year, there is no mind anywhere on earth we cannot seek out and read. I need not tell you how many thousands of minds we have already sought out and read."

He paused, and I looked at Dr. Goldbaum, who shook his head. Tears rolled down his cheeks and he whispered, "Oh my God, my God, what you must have seen. How could you do it and how could you bear it?"

"You never really knew how much we can bear," Michael

said. "Always we had a child-parent relationship. It was a good relationship. Always you sought to protect us, to interpose your body, your presence, between ourselves and the world. But you didn't have to. It hurts me to say it, but you must know that long, long ago you became the children and we became the parents."

"We know it," I said. "Whether or not we spoke about it in so many words, we know it. We have known it for a long time."

"From our seventh year," Michael continued, "we knew all the details of this experiment. We knew why we were here and we knew what you were attempting—and from then until now, we have pondered over what our future must be. We have also tried to help you, whom we love so much, and perhaps we have been of some help in easing your discontents, in keeping you as physically healthy as possible, in helping you through your troubled, terrible nights and that maze of fear and nightmare and horror that you and all other human beings call sleep. We did what we could, but all our efforts to join you with us, to open your minds to each other and our minds to you, all these efforts have failed. Finally we learned that unless the necessary area of the mind is opened before puberty, the brain tissues change, the brain cells lose the potential of development and the mind is closed forever. Of all the things we face, this saddens us most—for you have given us the most precious heritage of mankind and, in return, we are able to give you nothing."

"That isn't so," I said. "You have given us more than we gave you, so much more."

"Perhaps," Michael nodded. "Or perhaps it helps for you to think that and to say that. You are very good and kind people. You have a kind of tenderness, a kind of gentle love that we can never have, for it grows out of your fear, your guilt, and the horror you live with. We have never been able, nor did we want, to know such fear, such guilt and such horror. It is foreign to us. So while we save ourselves the knowledge of these things, we are also deprived of the kind of love, the kind of self-sacrifice that is almost a matter-of-fact part of your nature. That we must say. But now, our fathers and our mothers, now the fifteen years are over; now this team of observers will be here in thirty days."

I shook my head and said quietly but firmly. "No. They

must be stopped. They must not come here; they cannot come here."

"And all of you?" Michael asked, looking from one to another of us. "Do you all feel the same way? Do you all know what will come after that? Can you imagine what will come after that? Do you know what will happen in Washington? This is what you must think about now."

Some of us were choked with emotion. Cromwell, the physicist, said:

"We are your teachers and your fathers and your mothers, but we can't make this decision. You must tell us what to do. You know what to do. You know that, and you know that you must tell us."

Michael nodded, and then he told us what the children had decided. They had decided that the reservation must be maintained. They needed five more years. They decided that I was to go to Washington with Mark and with Dr. Goldbaum—and somehow we were to get an extension of time. They felt that such an extension would not be too difficult to get at this point. Once we got the extension of time, they would be able to act.

"What kind of action?" Dr. Goldbaum asked them.

"There are too few of us," Michael said. "We need more. We must find new children, new infants, and we must bring them into the reservation. In other words, we must leave the reservation, some of us, and we must bring children here and we must educate the children here."

"But why must they be brought here?" Mark asked. "You can reach them wherever they are. You can go into their minds, you can make them a part of you. The children of the whole world are open to us. Why must you bring them here?"

"That may be true," Michael said, "but the crux of the matter is that the children can't reach us. Not for a long, long time. The children would be alone—and their minds would be shattered if we went into their minds. Tell us, what would the people of your world outside do to such children? What happened to people in the past who were possessed of devils, who heard voices, who heard the sound of angels? Some became saints, but many more were burned at the stake, destroyed, beaten to death, impaled, the victims of every horror that man could devise and inflict upon children."

"Can't you protect the children?" someone asked.

"Someday, yes. Now, no. There are simply not enough of us. First, we must help children to move here, hundreds and hundreds of children. Then we must create other reservations, other places like this one. It cannot be done quickly. It will take a long time. For a child, even our kind of child, to grow into an effective mover, it takes at least fifteen years. It is true that when we are eight, nine, ten years old, we know a great deal, we are able to do a great deal; but we are still children. That has not changed. So you see it will take a long, long time. The world is a very large place and there are a great many children. With all this, we must work carefully, very carefully. You see, people are afraid. Your lives, the lives of mankind, are ruled by fear. This will be the worst fear of all. They will go mad with fear, and all they will be able to think about is how to kill us. That will be their whole intention: to kill us, to destroy us."

"And our children could not fight back," Dr. Goldbaum said quietly. "That is something to remember, to think about; that is very important. You see, fighting, killing, hostility—this is the method of mankind. It has been the method of mankind for so long that we have never questioned it. Can a human being kill? Can a human being fight? We simply take it for granted that this is a human attribute. Take the case, for example, of the Israelis. For two thousand years the Jews had not, as a people, engaged in any kind of war, and it was said that they had lost the will to fight to kill; but you see that with the creation of Israel this will returned. So we say that there is no place on earth where man cannot learn very quickly to become a killer. When the people of India, who were such a people of peace, obtained their freedom from England, they turned upon each other in a fratricide unbelievable, unthinkable, monstrous. But our children are different. Our children cannot kill. This we must understand. No matter what danger faced them, no matter what fate they confronted, they could not kill. They cannot hurt a human being, much less kill one. The very act of hurt is impossible. Cattle, our old dogs and cats, they are one thing—but not people, not people."

(Here Dr. Goldbaum referred to the fact that we no longer slaughtered our cattle in the old way. We had pet dogs and cats, and when they became very old and sick, the children caused them peacefully to go to sleep—a sleep from which they never awakened. Then the children asked us if they might do the same with the cattle we butchered for food. But I must make one point specific, Harry, so that you will understand the children a little better: We butchered the cattle because some of us still required meat, but the children ate no meat. They ate eggs and vegetables, the fruit of the ground, but never meat. This eating of meat, the slaughtering of living things for eating, was a thing they tolerated in us with sadness. Discipline, you know, is also not a part of their being—that is, discipline in the sense that we understand it. They do not ask us not to do things. They will ask us positively to do something; but, on the other hand, if we do what to them is repulsive, no matter how obnoxious it may be to them, they will not ask us to stop doing it.)

"But not people," Dr. Goldbaum went on. "God help us, our children cannot hurt people. We are able to do things that we know are wrong. That remains one power we possess which the children lack. They cannot kill and they cannot hurt. Am I right, Michael, or is this only a presumption on my part?"

"Yes, you are right," Michael said. "We must do our work slowly and patiently, and the world must not know what we are doing until we have taken certain measures. We think we need three years more. We would like to have five years more. But, Jean, if you can get us three years, we will bear with that and somehow manage to do what we must do within that period. Now, will you go with Mark and with Dr. Goldbaum, and will you get us these three years, Jean?"

"Yes, I will get the three years," I said. "Somehow I will do what you need."

"And the rest of you," Michael said, "the rest of you are needed too. We need all of you to help us. Of course we will not keep any of you here if you wish to go. But, oh, we need you so desperately—as we have always needed you—and we love you and we cherish you, and we beg you to remain with us."

Do you wonder that we all remained, Harry, that no one of us could leave our children or will ever leave them now except when death takes us away? You see, Harry, they needed the time and they got the time, and that is why I can write this and that is why I can tell you so forthrightly what happened.

Mark and I and Dr. Goldbaum pleaded our case and we

pleaded it well. We were given the years we needed, the additional years; and as for this gray barrier that surrounds us and the reservation, the children tell me that it is a simple device indeed. Of course that doesn't mean a great deal. They have a whole succession of devices that they call simple which are totally beyond the comprehension of any ordinary human being. But to come back to this barrier; as nearly as I can understand, they have altered the time sequence of the entire reservation; not by much—by less than one ten-thousandth of a second. But the result is that your world outside exists this tiny fraction of a second in the future. The same sun shines on us, the same winds blow, and from inside the barrier, we see your world unaltered. But you cannot see us. When you look at us, the present of our existence, the moment of time which we are conscious of at that moment of being in the universe, that moment has not yet come into existence; and instead of that, instead of reality, there is nothing: no space, no heat, no light, only the impenetrable wall of non-existence. Of course you will read this, Harry, and you will say it makes absolutely no sense whatever, and I cannot pretend that I am able to make any sense out of it. I asked the children how to describe it. They told me as best they could, considering that they had to use the same words I use. They ask me to think of an existing area of time, of us traveling along this existing area with a point of consciousness to mark our progress. They have altered this point. And that means absolutely nothing to someone like myself.

I can only add this—from inside the reservation we are able to go outside, to go from the past into the future. After all, the crossover is only one ten-thousandth of a second. I myself have done this during the moments when we were experimenting with the barrier. I felt a shudder, a moment of intense nausea, but no more than that. There is also a way in which we return, but, understandably, I cannot spell that out.

So there is the situation, Harry. We will never see each other again, but I assure you that Mark and I are happier than we have ever been. Man will change; nothing in the world can halt the change. It has already begun. And in that change, man will become what he was intended to be, and he will reach out with love and knowledge and tenderness to all the universes of the firmament. I have written that down, Harry, and as I look upon it I find it the most thrilling idea I have ever encountered. My skin prickles at the mere thought. Harry, isn't this what man has always dreamed of? No war, no hatred, no hunger or sickness or death? How fortunate we are to be alive while this is happening! I think that we should ask no more.

So now I say goodbye to you, my dear brother, and I finish this letter.

With all my love,
Your sister,
Jean Arbalaid.

Felton finished reading, and then there was a long, long silence while the two men looked at each other. Finally the Secretary of Defense spoke, saying:

"You know, Felton, that we shall have to keep knocking at that barrier. We can't stop. We have to keep on trying to find the way to break through."

"I know."

"It will be easier, now that your sister has explained it."

"I don't think it will be easier," Felton said tiredly. "I don't think that she has explained it."

"Not to you and me, perhaps. But we'll put the eggheads to work on it. They'll figure it out. They always do, you know."

"Perhaps not this time."

"Oh, yes," the Secretary of Defense nodded. "After all, Felton, we've got to stop it. We've had threats before, but not this kind of thing. I'm not going to dwell on the fact of this immorality, this godlessness, this nakedness, this depraved kind of sexual togetherness, this interloping into minds, this violation of every human privacy and every human decency. I don't have to dwell on that. You realize as well as I do, Felton, that this is a threat to every human being on the face of the earth. The kids were right. Oh, they understood this well enough, you know. This isn't a national threat; this isn't like Communism; this isn't simply a threat to the sovereignty, to the freedom of the United States, to the American way of life; this isn't just a threat to democracy; this is a threat to God Himself. This is a threat to mankind. This is a threat to everything decent, everything sacred, everything we believe in, everything we cherish. It's a disease, Felton. You know that, don't you? You recognize that—a disease."

"You really feel that, don't you?" Felton said. "You really believe what you are telling me."

"Believe it? Who can disbelieve it, Felton? It's a disease, and the only way to stop a disease is to kill the bugs that cause it. You know how you stop this disease? I'm going to say it and a lot more are going to say it, Felton: You kill the kids. It's the only way. I wish there were another way, but there isn't."

DIARIES

Daniel Keyes (1927–) is one of those authors who will always be remembered for one story, for "Flowers for Algernon" is one of the most famous works in the history of science fiction. Immediately recognized as a classic when it appeared in the April 1959 issue of The Magazine of Fantasy and Science Fiction, *it was expanded into a novel in 1966 and filmed as* Charly *in 1968. It also won the Hugo Award for short fiction in 1960.*

For the record, we would also like to bring your attention to two other fine stories by Daniel Keyes, "Crazy Maro" and "The Quality of Mercy" (both 1960).

FLOWERS FOR ALGERNON

By Daniel Keyes

progris riport 1—martch 5 1965

Dr. Strauss says I shud rite down what I think and evrey thing that happins to me from now on. I dont know why but he says its importint so they will see if they will use me. I hope they use me. Miss Kinnian says maybe they can make me smart. I want to be smart. My name is Charlie Gordon. I am 37 years old and 2 weeks ago was my brithday. I have nuthing more to rite now so I will close for today.

progris riport 2—martch 6

I had a test today. I think I faled it. and I think that maybe now they wont use me. What happind is a nice young man was in the room and he had some white cards with ink spillled all over them. He sed Charlie what do you see on this card.

I was very skared even tho I had my rabits foot in my pockit because when I was a kid I always faled tests in school and I spillled ink to.

I told him I saw a inkblot. He said yes and it made me feel good. I thot that was all but when I got up to go he stopped me. He said now sit down Charlie we are not thru yet. Then I dont remember so good but he wantid me to say what was in the ink. I dint see nuthing in the ink but he said there was picturs there other pepul saw some picturs. I coudnt see any picturs. I reely tryed to see. I held the card close up and then far away. Then I said if I had my glases I coud see better I usally only ware my glases in the movies or TV but I said they are in the closit in the hall. I got them. Then I said let me see that card agen I bet Ill find it now.

I tryed hard but I still coudnt find the picturs I only saw the ink. I told him maybe I need new glases. He rote somthing down on a paper and I got skared of faling the test. I told him it was a very nice inkblot with littel points all around the eges. He looked very sad so that wasnt it. I said please let me try agen. Ill get it in a few minits becaus Im not so fast somtimes. Im a slow reeder too in Miss Kinnians class for slow adults but I'm trying very hard.

He gave me a chance with another card that had 2 kinds of ink spillled on it red and blue.

He was very nice and talked slow like Miss Kinnian does and he explained it to me that it was a *raw shok*. He said pepul see things in the ink. I said show me where. He said think. I told him I think a inkblot but that wasnt rite eather. He said what does it remind you—pretend something. I closd my eyes for a long time to pretend. I told him I pretned a fowntan pen with ink leeking all over a table cloth. Then he got up and went out.

I dont think I passd the *raw shok* test.

progris report 3—martch 7

Dr Strauss and Dr Nemur say it dont matter about the inkblots. I told them I dint spill the ink on the cards and I couldn't see anything in the ink. They said that maybe they will still use me. I said Miss Kinnian never gave me tests like that one only spellin and reading. They said Miss Kinnian told that I was her bestist pupil in the adult nite scool becaus I tryed the hardist and I reely wantid to lern. They said how come you went to the adult nite scool all by yourself Charlie. How did you find it. I said I askd pepul and sumbody told me where I shud go to lern to read and spell good. They said why did you want to. I told them becaus all my life I wantid to be smart and not dumb. But its very hard to be smart. They said you know it will probly be tempirery. I said yes. Miss Kinnian told me. I dont care if it herts.

Later I had more crazy tests today. The nice lady who gave it me told me the name and I asked her how do you spellit so I can rite it in my progris riport. THEMATIC APPERCEPTION TEST. I dont know the frist 2 words but I know what *test* means. You got to pass it or you get bad marks. This test lookd easy becaus I coud see the picturs. Only this time she dint want me to tell her the picturs. That mixd me up. I said the man yesterday said I shoud tell him what I saw in the ink she said that dont make no difrence. She said make up storys about the pepul in the picturs.

I told her how can you tell storys about pepul you never met. I said why shud I make up lies. I never tell lies any more becaus I always get caut.

She told me this test and the other one the raw-shok was for getting personalty. I laffed so hard. I said how can you get that thing from inkblots and fotos. She got sore and put her picturs away. I dont care. It was sily. I gess I faled that test too.

Later some men in white coats took me to a difernt part of the hospitil and gave me a game to play. It was like a race with a white mouse. They called the mouse Algernon. Algernon was in a box with a lot of twists and turns like all kinds of walls and they gave me a pencil and a paper with lines and lots of boxes. On one side it said START and on the other end it said FINISH. They said it was *amazed* and that Algernon and me had the same *amazed* to do. I dint see how we could have the same *amazed* if Algernon had a box and I had a paper but I dint say nothing. Anyway there wasnt time because the race started.

One of the men had a watch he was trying to hide so I wouldnt see it so I tryed not to look and that made me nervus.

Anyway that test made me feel worser than all the others because they did it over 10 times with difernt *amazeds* and Algernon won every time. I dint know that mice were so smart. Maybe thats because Algernon is a white mouse. Maybe white mice are smarter then other mice.

progris riport 4—Mar 8

Their going to use me! Im so exited I can hardly write. Dr Nemur and Dr Strauss had a argament about it first. Dr Nemur was in the office when Dr Strauss brot me in. Dr Nemur was worryed about using me but Dr Strauss told him Miss Kinnian rekemmended me the best from all the people who she was teaching. I like Miss Kinnian becaus shes a very smart teacher. And she said Charlie your going to have a second chance. If you volenteer for this experament you mite get smart. They dont know if it will be perminint but theirs a chance. Thats why I said ok even when I was scared because she said it was an operashun. She said dont be scared Charlie you done so much with so little I think you deserv it most of all.

So I got scaird when Dr Nemur and Dr Strauss argud about it. Dr Strauss said I had something that was very good. He said I had a good *motor-vation*. I never even knew I had that. I felt proud when he said that not every body with an eye-q of 68 had that thing. I dont know what it is or where I got it but he said Algernon had it too. Algernons *motor-vation* is the cheese they put in his box. But it cant be that because I didnt eat any cheese this week.

Then he told Dr Nemur something I dint understand so while they were talking I wrote down some of the words.

He said Dr Nemur I know Charlie is not what you had in mind as the first of your new brede of intelek** (coudnt get the word) superman. But most people of his low ment** are host** and uncoop** they are usualy dull apath** and hard to reach. He has a good natcher hes intristed and eager to please.

Dr Nemur said remember he will be the first human beeng ever to have his intelijence trippled by surgicle meens.

Dr. Strauss said exakly. Look at how well hes lerned to read and write for his low mentel age its as grate an acheve** as you and I lerning einstines therey of **vity without help. That shows the intenss motor-vation. Its comparat** a tre-men** achev** I say we use Charlie.

I dint get all the words and they were talking to fast but

it sounded like Dr Strauss was on my side and like the other one wasnt.

Then Dr Nemur nodded he said all right maybe your right. We will use Charlie. When he said that I got so exited I jumped up and shook his hand for being so good to me. I told him thank you doc you wont be sorry for giving me a second chance. And I mean it like I told him. After the operashun Im gonna try to be smart. Im gonna try awful hard.

progris ript 5—Mar 10

Im skared. Lots of people who work here and the nurses and the people who gave me the tests came to bring me candy and wish me luck. I hope I have luck. I got my rabits foot and my lucky penny and my horse shoe. Only a black cat crossed me when I was comming to the hospitil. Dr Strauss says dont be supersitis Charlie this is sience. Anyway Im keeping my rabits foot with me.

I asked Dr Strauss if Ill beat Algernon in the race after the operashun and he said maybe. If the operashun works Ill show that mouse I can be as smart as he is. Maybe smarter. Then Ill be abel to read better and spell the words good and know lots of things and be like other people. I want to be smart like other people. If it works perminint they will make everybody smart all over the wurld.

They dint give me anything to eat this morning. I dont know what that eating has to do with getting smart. Im very hungry and Dr Nemur took away my box of candy. That Dr Nemur is a grouch. Dr Strauss says I can have it back after the operashun. You cant eat befor a operashun...

Progress Report 6—Mar 15

The operashun dint hurt. He did it while I was sleeping. They took off the bandijis from my eyes and my head today so I can make a PROGRESS REPORT. Dr. Nemur who looked at some of my other ones says I spell PROGRESS wrong and he told me how to spell it and REPORT too. I got to try and remember that.

I have a very bad memory for spelling. Dr Strauss says its ok to tell about all the things that happin to me but he says I shoud tell more about what I feel and what I think.

Flowers for Algernon

When I told him I dont know how to think he said try. All the time when the bandijis were on my eyes I tryed to think. Nothing happened. I dont know what to think about. Maybe if I ask him he will tell me how I can think now that Im suppose to get smart. What do smart people think about. Fancy things I suppose. I wish I knew some fancy things alredy.

Progress Report 7—Mar 19

Nothing is happening. I had lots of tests and different kinds of races with Algernon. I hate that mouse. He always beats me. Dr Strauss said I got to play those games. And he said some time I got to take those tests over again. Thse inkblots are stupid. And those pictures are stupid too. I like to draw a picture of a man and a woman but I wont make up lies about people.

I got a headache from trying to think so much. I thot Dr Strauss was my frend but he dont help me. He dont tell me what to think or when Ill get smart. Miss Kinnian dint come to see me. I think writing these progress reports are stupid too.

Progress Report 8—Mar 23

Im going back to work at the factery. They said it was better I shud go back to work but I cant tell anyone what the operashun was for and I have to come to the hospitil for an hour evry night after work. They are gonna pay me mony every month for lerning to be smart.

Im glad Im going back to work because I miss my job and all my frends and all the fun we have there.

Dr Strauss says I shud keep writing things down but I dont have to do it every day just when I think of something or something speshul' happins. He says dont get discoridged because it takes time and it happins slow. He says it took a long time with Algernon before he got 3 times smarter then he was before. Thats why Algernon beats me all the time because he had that operashun too. That makes me feel better. I coud probly do that *amazed* faster than a reglar mouse. Maybe some day Ill beat Algernon. Boy that would be something. So far Algernon looks like he mite be smart perminent.

Daniel Keyes

Mar 25 (I dont have to write PROGRESS REPORT on top any more just when I hand it in once a week for Dr Nemur to read. I just have to put the date on. That saves time)

We had a lot of fun at the factery today. Joe Carp said hey look where Charlie had his operashun what did they do Charlie put some brains in. I was going to tell him but I remembered Dr Strauss said no. Then Frank Reilly said what did you do Charlie forget your key and open your door the hard way. That made me laff. Their really my friends and they like me.

Sometimes somebody will say hey look at Joe or Frank or George he really pulled a Charlie Gordon. I don't know why they say that but they always laff. This morning Amos Borg who is the 4 man at Donnegans used my name when he shouted at Ernie the office boy. Ernie lost a packige. He said Ernie for godsake what are you trying to be a Charlie Gordon. I dont understand why he said that. I never lost any packiges.

Mar 28 Dr Strauss came to my room tonight to see why I dint come in like I was suppose to. I told him I dont like to race with Algernon any more. He said I dont have to for a while but I shud come in. He had a present for me only it wasnt a present but just for lend. I thot it was a little television but it wasnt. He said I got to turn it on when I go to sleep. I said your kidding why shud I turn it on when Im going to sleep. Who ever herd of a thing like that. But he said if I want to get smart I got to do what he says. I told him I dint think I was going to get smart and he put his hand on my sholder and said Charlie you dont know it yet but your getting smarter all the time. You wont notice for a while. I think he was just being nice to make me feel good because I dont look any smarter.

Oh yes I almost forgot. I asked him when I can go back to the class at Miss Kinnians school. He said I wont go their. He said that soon Miss Kinnian will come to the hospitil to start and teach me speshul. I was mad at her for not comming to see me when I got the operashun but I like her so maybe we will be frends again.

Mar 29 That crazy TV kept me up all night. How can I sleep with something yelling crazy things all night in my ears.

And the nutty pictures. Wow. I dont know what it says when Im up so how am I going to know when Im sleeping.

Dr Strauss says its ok. He says my brains are lerning when I sleep and that will help me when Miss Kinnian starts my lessons in the hospitil (only I found out it isnt a hospitil its a labatory). I think its all crazy. If you can get smart when your sleeping why do people go to school. That thing I dont think will work. I use to watch the late show and the late late show on TV all the time and it never made me smart. Maybe you have to sleep while you watch it.

PROGRESS REPORT 9—April 3

Dr Strauss showed me how to keep the TV turned low so now I can sleep. I dont hear a thing. And I still dont understand what it says. A few times I play it over in the morning to find out what I lerned when I was sleeping and I dont think so. Miss Kinnian says Maybe its another langwidge or something. But most times it sounds american. It talks so fast faster than even Miss Gold who was my teacher in 6 grade and I remember she talked so fast I coudnt understand her.

I told Dr Strauss what good is it to get smart in my sleep. I want to be smart when Im awake. He says its the same thing and I have two minds. Theres the *subconscious* and the *conscious* (thats how you spell it). And one dont tell the other one what its doing. They don't even talk to each other. Thats why I dream. And boy have I been having crazy dreams. Wow. Ever since that night TV. The late late late late late show.

I forgot to ask him if it was only me or if everybody had those two minds.

(I just looked up the word in the dictionary Dr Strauss gave me. The word is *subconscious. adj. Of the nature of mental operations yet not present in consciousness; as, subconscious conflict of desires.*) Theres more but I still dont know what it means. This isnt a very good dictionary for dumb people like me.

Anyway the headache is from the party. My frends from the factery Joe Carp and Frank Reilly invited me to go with them to Muggsys Saloon for some drinks. I dont like to drink but they said we will have lots of fun. I had a good time.

Joe Carp said I shoud show the girls how I mop out the toilet in the factory and he got me a mop. I showed them and everyone laffed when I told that Mr Donnegan said I was the best janiter he ever had because I like my job and do it good and never come late or miss a day except for my operashun.

I said Miss Kinnian always said Charlie be proud of your job because you do it good.

Everybody laffed and we had a good time and they gave me lots of drinks and Joe said Charlie is a card when hes potted. I dont know what that means but everybody likes me and we have fun. I cant wait to be smart like my best frends Joe Carp and Frank Reilly.

I dont remember how the party was over but I think I went out to buy a newspaper and coffe for Joe and Frank and when I came back there was no one their. I looked for them all over till late. Then I dont remember so good but I think I got sleepy or sick. A nice cop brot me back home. Thats what my landlady Mrs Flynn says.

But I got a headache and a big lump on my head and black and blue all over. I think maybe I fell but Joe Carp says it was the cop they beat up drunks some times. I don't think so. Miss Kinnian says cops are to help people. Anyway I got a bad headache and Im sick and hurt all over. I dont think Ill drink anymore.

April 6 I beat Algernon! I dint even know I beat him until Burt the tester told me. Then the second time I lost because I got so exited I fell off the chair before I finished. But after that I beat him 8 more times. I must be getting smart to beat a smart mouse like Algernon. But I dont *feel* smarter.

I wanted to race Algernon some more but Burt said thats enough for one day. They let me hold him for a minit. Hes not so bad. Hes soft like a ball of cotton. He blinks and when he opens his eyes their black and pink on the eges.

I said can I feed him because I felt bad to beat him and I wanted to be nice and make frends. Burt said no Algernon is a very specshul mouse with an operashun like mine, and he was the first of all the animals to stay smart so long. He told me Algernon is so smart that every day he has to solve a test to get his food. Its a thing like a lock on a door that changes every time Algernon goes in to eat so he has to lern something new to get his food. That made me sad because if he couldnt lern he would be hungry.

I dont think its right to make you pass a test to eat. How would Dr Nemur like it to have to pass a test every time he wants to eat. I think Ill be frends with Algernon.

April 9 Tonight after work Miss Kinnian was at the laboratory. She looked like she was glad to see me but scared. I told her dont worry Miss Kinnian Im not smart yet and she laffed. She said I have confidence in you Charlie the way you struggled so hard to read and right better than all the others. At werst you will have it for a littel wile and your doing somthing for sience.

We are reading a very hard book. I never read such a hard book before. Its called *Robinson Crusoe* about a man who gets merooned on a dessert Iland. Hes smart and figers out all kinds of things so he can have a house and food and hes a good swimmer. Only I feel sorry because hes all alone and has no frends. But I think their must be somebody else on the iland because theres a picture with his funny umbrella looking at footprints. I hope he gets a frend and not be lonely.

April 10 Miss Kinnian teaches me to spell better. She says look at a word and close your eyes and say it over and over until you remember. I have lots of truble with *through* that you say *threw* and *enough* and *tough* that you dont say *enew* and *tew*. You got to say *enuff* and *tuff*. Thats how I use to write it before I started to get smart. Im confused but Miss Kinnian says theres no reason in spelling.

Apr 14 Finished *Robinson Crusoe*. I want to find out more about what happens to him but Miss Kinnian says thats all there is. *Why*

Apr 15 Miss Kinnian says Im lerning fast. She read some of the Progress Reports and she looked at me kind of funny. She says Im a fine person and Ill show them all. I asked her why. She said never mind but I shoudnt feel bad if I find out that everybody isnt nice like I think. She said for a person who god gave so little to you done more then a lot of people with brains they never even used. I said all my frends are smart people but there good. They like me and they never did anything that wasnt nice. Then she got something in her eye and she had to run out to the ladys room.

Apr. 16 Today, I lerned, the *comma*, this is a comma (,) a period, with a tail, Miss Kinnian, says its importent, because, it makes writing better, she said, sombeody, coud lose, a lot of money, if a comma, isnt, in the, right place, I dont have, any money, and I dont see, how a comma, keeps you from losing it.

But she says, everybody, uses commas, so Ill use, them too,

Apr 17 I used the comma wrong. Its punctuation. Miss Kinnian told me to look up long words in the dictionary to lern to spell them. I said whats the difference if you can read it anyway. She said its part of your education so now on I'll look up all the words Im not sure how to spell. It takes a long time to write that way but I think Im remembering. I only have to look up once and after that I get it right. Anyway thats how come I got the word *punctuation* right. (Its that way in the dictionary). Miss Kinnian says a period is punctuation too, and there are lots of other marks to lern. I told her I thot all the periods had to have tails but she said no.

You got to mix them up, she showed? me" how. to mix! them(up,. and now; I can! mix up all kinds" of punctuation, in! my writing? There, are lots! of rules? to lern; but I'm gettin'g them in my head.

One thing I? like about, Dear Miss Kinnian: (thats the way it goes in a business letter if I ever go into business) is she, always gives me' a reason" when—I ask. She's a gen'ius! I wish! I cou'd be smart' like, her;

(Punctuation, is; fun!)

Apr 18 What a dope I am! I didn't even understand what she was talking about. I read the grammar book last night and it explanes the whole thing. Then I saw it was the same way as Miss Kinnian was trying to tell me, but I didn't get it. I got up in the middle of the night, and the whole thing straightened out in my mind.

Miss Kinnian said that the TV working in my sleep helped out. She said I reached a plateau. Thats like the flat top of a hill.

After I figgered out how punctuation worked, I read over all my old Progress Reports from the beginning. Boy, did I have crazy spelling and punctuation! I told Miss Kinnian I ought to go over the pages and fix all the mistakes but she said, "No, Charlie, Dr. Nemur wants them just as they are. That's why he let you keep them after they were photostated, to see your own progress. You're coming along fast, Charlie."

That made me feel good. After the lesson I went down and played with Algernon. We don't race any more.

April 20 I feel sick inside. Not sick like for a doctor, but inside my chest it feels empty like getting punched and a heartburn at the same time.

I wasn't going to write about it, but I guess I got to, because it's important. Today was the first time I ever stayed home from work.

Last night Joe Carp and Frank Reilly invited me to a party. There were lots of girls and some men from the factory. I remembered how sick I got last time I drank too much, so I told Joe I didn't want anything to drink. He gave me a plain Coke instead. It tasted funny, but I thought it was just a bad taste in my mouth.

We had a lot of fun for a while. Joe said I should dance with Ellen and she would teach me the steps. I fell a few times and I couldn't understand why because no one else was dancing besides Ellen and me. And all the time I was tripping because somebody's foot was always sticking out.

Then when I got up I saw the look on Joe's face and it gave me a funny feeling in my stomack. "He's a scream," one of the girls said. Everybody was laughing.

Frank said, "I ain't laughed so much since we sent him off for the newspaper that night at Muggsy's and ditched him."

"Look at him. His face is red."

"He's blushing. Charlie is blushing."

"Hey, Ellen, what'd you do to Charlie? I never saw him act like that before."

I didn't know what to do or where to turn. Everyone was looking at me and laughing and I felt naked. I wanted to hide myself. I ran out into the street and I threw up. Then I walked home. It's a funny thing I never knew that Joe and Frank and the others liked to have me around all the time to make fun of me.

Now I know what it means when they say "to pull a Charlie Gordon."

I'm ashamed.

PROGRESS REPORT 11

April 21 Still didn't go into the factory. I told Mrs. Flynn my landlady to call and tell Mr. Donnegan I was sick. Mrs. Flynn looks at me very funny lately like she's scared of me.

I think it's a good thing about finding out how everybody laughs at me. I thought about it a lot. It's because I'm so dumb and I don't even know when I'm doing something dumb. People think it's funny when a dumb person can't do things the same way they can.

Anyway, now I know I'm getting smarter every day. I know punctuation and I can spell good. I like to look up all the hard words in the dictionary and I remember them. I'm reading a lot now, and Miss Kinnian says I read very fast. Sometimes I even understand what I'm reading about, and it stays in my mind. There are times when I can close my eyes and think of a page and it all comes back like a picture.

Besides history, geography, and arithmetic, Miss Kinnian said I should start to learn a few foreign languages. Dr. Strauss gave me some more tapes to play while I sleep. I still don't understand how that conscious and unconscious mind works, but Dr. Strauss says not to worry yet. He asked me to promise that when I start learning college subjects next week I wouldn't read any books on psychology—that is, until he gives me permission.

I feel a lot better today, but I guess I'm still a little angry that all the time people were laughing and making fun of me because I wasn't so smart. When I become intelligent like Dr. Strauss says, with three times my I.Q. of 68, then maybe I'll be like everyone else and people will like me and be friendly.

I'm not sure what an I.Q. is. Dr. Nemur said it was something that measured how intelligent you were—like a scale in the drug-store weighs pounds. But Dr. Strauss had a big argument with him and said an I.Q. didn't weigh intelligence at all. He said an I.Q. showed how much intelligence you could get, like the numbers on the outside of a measuring cup. You still had to fill the cup up with stuff.

Then when I asked Burt, who gives me my intelligence

tests and works with Algernon, he said that both of them were wrong (only I had to promise not to tell them he said so).

Burt says that the I.Q. measures a lot of different things including some of the things you learned already, and it really isn't any good at all.

So I still don't know what I.Q. is except that mine is going to be over 200 soon. I didn't want to say anything, but I don't see how if they don't know *what* it is, or *where* it is—I don't see how they know *how much* of it you've got.

Dr. Nemur says I have to take a *Rorshach Test* tomorrow. I wonder what *that* is.

April 22 I found out what a *Rorshach* is. It's the test I took before the operation—the one with the inkblots on the pieces of cardboard. The man who gave me the test was the same one.

I was scared to death of those inkblots. I knew he was going to ask me to find the pictures and I knew I wouldn't be able to. I was thinking to myself, if only there was some way of knowing what kind of pictures were hidden there. Maybe there weren't any pictures at all. Maybe it was just a trick to see if I was dumb enough to look for something that wasn't there. Just thinking about that made me sore at him.

"All right, Charlie," he said, "you've seen these cards before, remember?"

"Of course I remember."

The way I said it, he knew I was angry, and he looked surprised. "Yes, of course. Now I want you to look at this one. What might this be? What do you see on this card? People see all sorts of things in these inkblots. Tell me what it might be for you—what it makes you think of."

I was shocked. That wasn't what I had expected him to say at all. "You mean there are no pictures hidden in those inkblots?"

He frowned and took off his glasses. "What?"

"Pictures. Hidden in the inkblots. Last time you told me that everyone could see them and you wanted me to find them too."

He explained to me that the last time he had used almost the exact words he was using now. I didn't believe it, and I still have the suspicion that he misled me at the time just for the fun of it. Unless—I don't know any more—could I have been *that* feebleminded?

We went through the cards slowly. One of them looked like a pair of bats tugging at something. Another one looked like two men fencing with swords. I imagined all sorts of things. I guess I got carried away. But I didn't trust him any more, and I kept turning them around and even looking on the back to see if there was anything there I was supposed to catch. While he was making his notes, I peeked out of the corner of my eye to read it. But it was all in code that looked like this:

$$WF + A \ DdF\text{-}Ad \ orig. \ WF\text{-}A \ SF + obj$$

The test still doesn't make sense to me. It seems to me that anyone could make up lies about things that they didn't really see. How could he know I wasn't making a fool of him by mentioning things that I didn't really imagine? Maybe I'll understand it when Dr. Strauss lets me read up on psychology.

April 25 I figured out a new way to line up the machines in the factory, and Mr. Donnegan says it will save him ten thousand dollars a year in labor and increased production. He gave me a twenty-five-dollar bonus.

I wanted to take Joe Carp and Frank Reilly out to lunch to celebrate, but Joe said he had to buy some things for his wife, and Frank said he was meeting his cousin for lunch. I guess it'll take a little time for them to get used to the changes in me. Everybody seems to be frightened of me. When I went over to Amos Borg and tapped him on the shoulder, he jumped up in the air.

People don't talk to me much any more or kid around the way they used to. It makes the job kind of lonely.

April 27 I got up the nerve today to ask Miss Kinnian to have dinner with me tomorrow night to celebrate my bonus.

At first she wasn't sure it was right, but I asked Dr. Strauss and he said it was okay. Dr. Strauss and Dr. Nemur don't seem to be getting along so well. They're arguing all the time. This evening when I came in to ask Dr. Strauss about having dinner with Miss Kinnian, I heard them shouting. Dr. Nemur was saying that it was *his* experiment and *his* research, and Dr. Strauss was shouting back that he contributed just as much, because he found me through Miss Kinnian and he performed the operation. Dr. Strauss said that someday thousands of neurosurgeons might be using his technique all over the world.

Dr. Nemur wanted to publish the results of the experiment at the end of this month. Dr. Strauss wanted to wait a while longer to be sure. Dr. Strauss said that Dr. Nemur was more interested in the Chair of Psychology at Princeton than he was in the experiment. Dr. Nemur said that Dr. Strauss was nothing but an opportunist who was trying to ride to glory on *his* coattails.

When I left afterwards, I found myself trembling. I don't know why for sure, but it was as if I'd seen both men clearly for the first time. I remember hearing Burt say that Dr. Nemur had a shrew of a wife who was pushing him all the time to get things published so that he could become famous. Burt said that the dream of her life was to have a big-shot husband.

Was Dr. Strauss really trying to ride on his coattails?

April 28 I don't understand why I never noticed how beautiful Miss Kinnian really is. She has brown eyes and feathery brown hair that comes to the top of her neck. She's only thirty-four! I think from the beginning I had the feeling that she was an unreachable genius—and very, very old. Now, every time I see her she grows younger and more lovely.

We had dinner and a long talk. When she said that I was coming along so fast that soon I'd be leaving her behind, I laughed.

"It's true, Charlie. You're already a better reader than I am. You can read a whole page at a glance while I can take in only a few lines at a time. And you remember every single thing you read. I'm lucky if I can recall the main thoughts and the general meaning."

"I don't feel intelligent. There are so many things I don't understand."

She took out a cigarette and I lit it for her. "You've got to be a *little* patient. You're accomplishing in days and weeks what it takes normal people to do in half a lifetime. That's what makes it so amazing. You're like a giant sponge now, soaking things in. Facts, figures, general knowledge. And soon you'll begin to connect them, too. You'll see how the different branches of learning are related. There are many levels, Charlie, like steps on a giant ladder that take you up higher and higher to see more and more of the world around you.

"I can see only a little bit of that, Charlie, and I won't go much higher than I am now, but you'll keep climbing up and up, and see more and more, and each step will open new worlds that you never even knew existed." She frowned. "I hope...I just hope to God—"

"What?"

"Never mind, Charles. I just hope I wasn't wrong to advise you to go into this thing in the first place."

I laughed. "How could that be? It worked, didn't it? Even Algernon is still smart."

We sat there silently for a while and I knew what she was thinking about as she watched me toying with the chain of my rabbit's foot and my keys. I didn't want to think of that possibility any more than elderly people want to think of death. I *knew* that this was only the beginning. I knew what she meant about levels because I'd seen some of them already. The thought of leaving her behind made me sad.

I'm in love with Miss Kinnian.

PROGRESS REPORT 12

April 30 I've quit my job with Donnegan's Plastic Box Company. Mr. Donnegan insisted that it would be better for all concerned if I left. What did I do to make them hate me so?

The first I knew of it was when Mr. Donnegan showed me the petition. Eight hundred and forty names, everyone connected with the factory, except Fanny Girden. Scanning the list quickly, I saw at once that hers was the only missing name. All the rest demanded that I be fired.

Joe Carp and Frank Reilly wouldn't talk to me about it. No one else would either, except Fanny. She was one of the few people I'd known who set her mind to something and believed it no matter what the rest of the world proved, said, or did—and Fanny did not believe that I should have been fired. She had been against the petition on principle and despite the pressure and threats she'd held out.

"Which don't mean to say," she remarked, "that I don't think there's something mighty strange about you, Charlie.

Them changes. I don't know. You used to be a good, dependable, ordinary man—not too bright maybe, but honest. Who knows what you done to yourself to get so smart all of a sudden. Like everybody around here's been saying, Charlie, it's not right."

"But how can you say that, Fanny? What's wrong with a man becoming intelligent and wanting to acquire knowledge and understanding of the world around him?"

She stared down at her work and I turned to leave. Without looking at me, she said: "It was evil when Eve listened to the snake and ate from the tree of knowledge. It was evil when she saw that she was naked. If not for that none of us would ever have to grow old and sick, and die."

Once again now I have the feeling of shame burning inside me. This intelligence has driven a wedge between me and all the people I once knew and loved. Before, they laughed at me and despised me for my ignorance and dullness; now, they hate me for my knowledge and understanding. What in God's name do they want of me?

They've driven me out of the factory. Now I'm more alone than ever before...

May 15 Dr. Strauss is very angry at me for not having written any progress reports in two weeks. He's justified because the lab is now paying me a regular salary. I told him I was too busy thinking and reading. When I pointed out that writing was such a slow process that it made me impatient with my poor handwriting, he suggested that I learn to type. It's much easier to write now because I can type nearly seventy-five words a minute. Dr. Strauss continually reminds me of the need to speak and write simply so that people will be able to understand me.

I'll try to review all the things that happened to me during the last two weeks. Algernon and I were presented to the American Psychological Association sitting in convention with the World Psychological Association last Tuesday. We created quite a sensation. Dr. Nemur and Dr. Strauss were proud of us.

I suspect that Dr. Nemur, who is sixty—ten years older than Dr. Strauss—finds it necessary to see tangible results of his work. Undoubtedly the result of pressure by Mrs. Nemur.

Contrary to my earlier impressions of him, I realize that Dr. Nemur is not at all a genius. He has a very good mind, but it struggles under the specter of self-doubt. He wants people to take him for a genius. Therefore, it is important for him to feel that his work is accepted by the world. I believe that Dr. Nemur was afraid of further delay because he worried that someone else might make a discovery along these lines and take the credit from him.

Dr. Strauss on the other hand might be called a genius, although I feel that his areas of knowledge are too limited. He was educated in the tradition of narrow specialization; the broader aspects of background were neglected far more than necessary—even for a neurosurgeon.

I was shocked to learn that the only ancient languages he could read were Latin, Greek, and Hebrew, and that he knows almost nothing of mathematics beyond the elementary levels of the calculus of variations. When he admitted this to me, I found myself almost annoyed. It was as if he'd hidden this part of himself in order to deceive me, pretending—as do many people I've discovered—to be what he is not. No one I've ever known is what he appears to be on the surface.

Dr. Nemur appears to be uncomfortable around me. Sometimes when I try to talk to him, he just looks at me strangely and turns away. I was angry at first when Dr. Strauss told me I was giving Dr. Nemur an inferiority complex. I thought he was mocking me and I'm oversensitive at being made fun of.

How was I to know that a highly respected psychoexperimentalist like Nemur was unacquainted with Hindustani and Chinese? It's absurd when you consider the work that is being done in India and China today in the very field of his study.

I asked Dr. Strauss how Nemur could refute Rahajamati's attack on his method and results if Nemur couldn't even read them in the first place. That strange look on Dr. Strauss' face can mean only one of two things. Either he doesn't want to tell Nemur what they're saying in India, or else—and this worries me—Dr. Strauss doesn't know either. I must be careful to speak and write clearly and simply so that people won't laugh.

May 18 I am very disturbed. I saw Miss Kinnian last night for the first time in over a week. I tried to avoid all discussions

621

of intellectual concepts and to keep the conversation on a simple, everyday level, but she just stared at me blankly and asked me what I meant about the mathematical variance equivalent in Dorbermann's *Fifth Concerto.*

When I tried to explain she stopped me and laughed. I guess I got angry, but I suspect I'm approaching her on the wrong level. No matter what I try to discuss with her, I am unable to communicate. I must review Vrostadt's equations on *Levels of Semantic Progression.* I find that I don't communicate with people much any more. Thank God for books and music and things I can think about. I am alone in my apartment at Mrs. Flynn's boardinghouse most of the time and seldom speak to anyone.

May 20 I would not have noticed the new dishwasher, a boy of about sixteen, at the corner diner where I take my evening meals if not for the incident of the broken dishes.

They crashed to the floor, shattering and sending bits of white china under the tables. The boy stood there, dazed and frightened, holding the empty tray in his hand. The whistles and catcalls from the customers (the cries of "hey, there go the profits!"..."*Mazeltov!*"...and "well, *he* didn't work here very long..." which invariably seems to follow the breaking of glass or dishware in a public restaurant) all seemed to confuse him.

When the owner came to see what the excitement was about, the boy cowered as if he expected to be struck and threw up his arms as if to ward off the blow.

"All right! All right, you dope," shouted the owner, "don't just stand there! Get the broom and sweep that mess up. A broom...a broom, you idiot! It's in the kitchen. Sweep up all the pieces."

The boy saw that he was not going to be punished. His frightened expression disappeared and he smiled and hummed as he came back with the broom to sweep the floor. A few of the rowdier customers kept up the remarks, amusing themselves at his expense.

"Here, sonny, over here there's a nice piece behind you..."

"C'mon, do it again..."

"He's not so dumb. It's easier to break 'em than to wash 'em..."

As his vacant eyes moved across the crowd of amused onlookers, he slowly mirrored their smiles and finally broke into an uncertain grin at the joke which he obviously did not understand.

I felt sick inside as I looked at his dull, vacuous smile, the wide, bright eyes of a child, uncertain but eager to please. They were laughing at him because he was mentally retarded.

And I had been laughing at him too.

Suddenly, I was furious at myself and all those who were smirking at him. I jumped up and shouted, "Shut up! Leave him alone! It's not his fault he can't understand! He can't help what he is! But for God's sake...he's still a human being!"

The room grew silent. I cursed myself for losing control and creating a scene. I tried not to look at the boy as I paid my check and walked out without touching my food. I felt ashamed for both of us.

How strange it is that people of honest feelings and sensibility, who would not take advantage of a man born without arms or legs or eyes—how such people think nothing of abusing a man born with low intelligence. It infuriated me to think that not too long ago I, like this boy, had foolishly played the clown.

And I had almost forgotten.

I'd hidden the picture of the old Charlie Gordon from myself because now that I was intelligent it was something that had to be pushed out of my mind. But today in looking at the boy, for the first time I saw what I had been. *I was just like him!*

Only a short time ago, I learned that people laughed at me. Now I can see that unknowingly I joined with them in laughing at myself. That hurts most of all.

I have often reread my progress reports and seen the illiteracy, the childish naïveté, the mind of low intelligence peering from a dark room, through the keyhole, at the dazzling light outside. I see that even in my dullness I knew that I was inferior, and that other people had something I lacked—something denied me. In my mental blindness, I thought that it was somehow connected with the ability to read and write, and I was sure that if I could get those skills I would automatically have intelligence too.

Even a feeble-minded man wants to be like other men.

A child may not know how to feed itself, or what to eat, yet it knows of hunger.

This then is what I was like, I never knew. Even with my gift of intellectual awareness, I never really knew.

This day was good for me. Seeing the past more clearly, I have decided to use my knowledge and skills to work in the field of increasing human intelligence levels. Who is better equipped for this work? Who else has lived in both worlds? These are my people. Let me use my gift to do something for them.

Tomorrow, I will discuss with Dr. Strauss the manner in which I can work in this area. I may be able to help him work out the problems of widespread use of the technique which was used on me. I have several good ideas of my own.

There is so much that might be done with this technique. If I could be made into a genius, what about thousands of others like myself? What fantastic levels might be achieved by using this technique on normal people? On *geniuses*?

There are so many doors to open. I am impatient to begin.

PROGRESS REPORT 13

May 23 It happened today. Algernon bit me. I visited the lab to see him as I do occasionally, and when I took him out of his cage, he snapped at my hand. I put him back and watched him for a while. He was unusually disturbed and vicious.

May 24 Burt, who is in charge of the experimental animals, tells me that Algernon is changing. He is less cooperative, he refuses to run the maze any more; general motivation has decreased. And he hasn't been eating. Everyone is upset about what this may mean.

May 25 They've been feeding Algernon, who now refuses to work the shifting-lock problem. Everyone identifies me with Algernon. In a way we're both the first of our kind. They're all pretending that Algernon's behavior is not necessarily significant for me. But it's hard to hide the fact that some of the other animals who were used in this experiment are showing strange behavior.

Dr. Strauss and Dr. Nemur have asked me not to come to the lab any more. I know what they're thinking but I can't accept it. I am going ahead with my plans to carry their research forward. With all due respect to both of these fine scientists. I am well aware of their limitations. If there is an answer, I'll have to find it out for myself. Suddenly, time has become very important to me.

May 29 I have been given a lab of my own and permission to go ahead with the research. I'm onto something. Working day and night. I've had a cot moved into the lab. Most of my writing time is spent on the notes which I keep in a separate folder, but from time to time I feel it necessary to put down my moods and my thoughts out of sheer habit.

I find the *calculus of intelligence* to be a fascinating study. Here is the place for the application of all the knowledge I have acquired. In a sense it's the problem I've been concerned with all my life.

May 31 Dr. Strauss thinks I'm working too hard. Dr. Nemur says I'm trying to cram a lifetime of research and thought into a few weeks. I know I should rest, but I'm driven on by something inside that won't let me stop. I've got to find the reason for the sharp regression in Algernon. I've got to know *if* and *when* it will happen to me.

June 4

LETTER TO DR. STRAUSS *(copy)*
Dear Dr. Strauss:

Under separate cover I am sending you a copy of my report entitled, "The Algernon-Gordon Effect: A Study of Structure and Function of Increased Intelligence," which I would like to have you read and have published.

As you see, my experiments are completed. I have included in my report all of my formulae, as well as mathematical analysis in the appendix. Of course, these should be verified.

Because of its importance to both you and Dr. Nemur (and need I say to myself, too?) I have checked and rechecked my results a dozen times in the hope of finding an error. I am sorry to say the results must stand. Yet for the sake of science, I am grateful for the little bit that I here add to the knowledge of the function of the human mind and of the laws governing the artificial increase of human intelligence.

I recall your once saying to me that an experimental *failure* or the *disproving* of a theory was as important

to the advancement of learning as a success would be.
I know now that this is true. I am sorry, however, that
my own contribution to the field must rest upon the
ashes of the work of two men I regard so highly.

Yours truly,
Charles Gordon

encl.: rept.

June 5 I must not become emotional. The facts and the results
of my experiments are clear, and the more sensational aspects
of my own rapid climb cannot obscure the fact that the tri-
pling of intelligence by the surgical technique developed by
Drs. Strauss and Nemur must be viewed as having little or
no practical applicability (at the present time) to the increase
of human intelligence.

As I review the records and data on Algernon, I see that
although he is still in his physical infancy, he has regressed
mentally. Motor activity is impaired; there is a general re-
duction of glandular activity; there is an accelerated loss of
coordination.

There are also strong indications of progressive amnesia.

As will be seen by my report, these and other physical and
mental deterioration syndromes can be predicted with statistically significant results by the application of my formula.

The surgical stimulus to which we were both subjected
has resulted in an intensification and acceleration of all mental processes. The unforeseen development, which I have
taken the liberty of calling the *Algernon-Gordon Effect,* is
the logical extension of the entire intelligence speed-up. The
hypothesis here proven may be described simply in the following terms: Artificially increased intelligence deteriorates
at a rate of time directly proportional to the quantity of the
increase.

I feel that this, in itself, is an important discovery.

As long as I am able to write, I will continue to record my
thoughts in these progress reports. It is one of my few pleas-
ures. However, by all indications, my own mental deterioration will be very rapid.

I have already begun to notice signs of emotional insta-
bility and forgetfulness, the first symptoms of the burnout.

June 10 .Deterioration progressing. I have become absent-
minded. Algernon died two days ago. Dissection shows my

predictions were right. His brain had decreased in weight and there was a general smoothing out of cerebral convolutions as well as a deepening and broadening of brain fissures.

I guess the same thing is or will soon be happening to me. Now that it's definite, I don't want it to happen.

I put Algernon's body in a cheese box and buried him in the back yard. I cried.

June 15 Dr. Strauss came to see me again. I wouldn't open the door and I told him to go away. I want to be left to myself. I have become touchy and irritable. I feel the darkness closing in. It's hard to throw off thoughts of suicide. I keep telling myself how important this introspective journal will be.

It's a strange sensation to pick up a book that you've read and enjoyed just a few months ago and discover that you don't remember it. I remembered how great I thought John Milton was, but when I picked up *Paradise Lost* I couldn't understand it at all. I got so angry I threw the book across the room.

I've got to hold onto some of it. Some of the things I've learned. Oh, God, please don't take it all away.

June 19 Sometimes, at night, I go for a walk. Last night I couldn't remember where I lived. A policeman took me home. I have the strange feeling that this has all happened to me before—a long time ago. I keep telling myself I'm the only person in the world who can describe what's happening to me.

June 21 Why can't I remember? I've got to fight. I lie in bed for days and I don't know who or where I am. Then it all comes back to me in a flash. Fugues of amnesia. Symptoms of senility—second childhood. I can watch them coming on. It's so cruelly logical. I learned so much and so fast. Now my mind is deteriorating rapidly. I won't let it happen. I'll fight it. I can't help thinking of the boy in the restaurant, the blank expression, the silly smile, the people laughing at him. No—please—not that again...

June 22 I'm forgetting things that I learned recently. It seems to be following the classic pattern—the last things learned are the first things forgotten. Or is that the pattern? I'd better look it up again....

I reread my paper on the *Algernon-Gordon Effect* and I get the strange feeling that it was written by someone else. There are parts I don't even understand.

Motor activity impaired. I keep tripping over things, and it becomes increasingly difficult to type.

June 23 I've given up using the typewriter completely. My coordination is bad. I feel that I'm moving slower and slower. Had a terrible shock today. I picked up a copy of an article I used in my research, Krueger's *Uber psychische Ganzheit,* to see if it would help me understand what I had done. First I thought there was something wrong with my eyes. Then I realized I could no longer read German. I tested myself in other languages. All gone.

June 30 A week since I dare to write again. It's slipping away like sand through my fingers. Most of the books I have are too hard for me now. I get angry with them because I know that I read and understood them just a few weeks ago.

I keep telling myself I must keep writing these reports so that somebody will know what is happening to me. But it gets harder to form the words and remember spellings. I have to look up even simple words in the dictionary now and it makes me impatient with myself.

Dr. Strauss comes around almost every day, but I told him I wouldn't see or speak to anybody. He feels guilty. They all do. But I don't blame anyone. I knew what might happen. But how it hurts.

July 7 I don't know where the week went. Todays Sunday I know becuase I can see through my window people going to church. I think I stayed in bed all week but I remember Mrs. Flynn bringing food to be a few times. I keep saying over and over Ive got to do something but then I forget or maybe its just easier not to do what I say Im going to do.

I think of my mother and father a lot these days. I found a picture of them with me taken at a beach. My father has a big ball under his arm and my mother is holding me by the hand. I dont remember them the way they are in the picture. All I remember is my father drunk most of the time and arguing with mom about money.

He never shaved much and he used to scratch my face when he hugged me. My mother said he died but Cousin

Miltie said he heard his mom and dad say that my father ran away with another woman. When I asked my mother she slapped my face and said my father was dead. I dont think I ever found out which was true but I don't care much. (He said he was going to take me to see cows on a farm once but he never did. He never kept his promises...)

July 10 My landlady Mrs Flynn is very worried about me. She says the way I lay around all day and dont do anything I remind her of her son before she threw him out of the house. She said she doesn't like loafers. If Im sick its one thing, but if Im a loafer thats another thing and she wont have it. I told her I think Im sick.

I try to read a little bit every day, mostly stories, but sometimes I have to read the same thing over and over again because I dont know what it means. And its hard to write. I know I should look up all the words in the dictionary but its so hard and Im so tired all the time.

Then I got the idea that I would only use the easy words instead of the long hard ones. That saves time. I put flowers on Algernons grave about once a week. Mrs Flynn thinks Im crazy to put flowers on a mouses grave but I told her that Algernon was special.

July 14 Its sunday again. I dont have anything to do to keep me busy now because my television set is broke and I dont have any money to get it fixed. (I think I lost this months check from the lab. I dont remember)

I get awful headaches and asperin doesnt help me much. Mrs Flynn knows Im really sick and she feels very sorry for me. Shes a wonderful woman whenever someone is sick.

July 22 Mrs Flynn called a strange doctor to see me. She was afraid I was going to die. I told the doctor I wasnt too sick and that I only forget sometimes. He asked me did I have any friends or relatives and I said no I dont have any. I told him I had a friend called Algernon once but he was a mouse and we used to run races together. He looked at me kind of funny like he thought I was crazy.

He smiled when I told him I used to be a genius. He talked to me like I was a baby and he winked at Mrs. Flynn. I got mad and chased him out because he was making fun of me the way they all used to.

July 24 I have no more money and Mrs. Flynn says I got to go to work somewhere and pay the rent because I havent paid for over two months. I dont know any work but the job I used to have at Donnegans Plastic Box Company. I dont want to go back there because they all knew me when I was smart and maybe theyll laugh at me. But I don't know what else to do to get money.

July 25 I was looking at some of my old progress reports and its very funny but I cant read what I wrote. I can make out some of the words but they dont make sense.

Miss Kinnian came to the door but I said go away I dont want to see you. She cried and I cried too but I wouldnt let her in because I didn't want her to laugh at me. I told her I didn't like her any more. I told her I didnt want to be smart any more. Thats not true. I still love her and I still want to be smart but I had to say that so shed go away. She gave Mrs Flynn money to pay the rent. I dont want that. I got to get a job.

Please...please let me not forget how to read and write...

July 27 Mr Donnegan was very nice when I came back and asked him for my old job of janitor. First he was very suspicious but I told him what happened to me then he looked very sad and put his hand on my shoulder and said Charlie Gordon you got guts.

Everybody looked at me when I came downstairs and started working in the toilet sweeping it out like I used to. I told myself Charlie if they make fun of you dont get sore because you remember their not so smart as you once thot they were. And besides they were once your friends and if they laughed at you that doesnt mean anything because they liked you too.

One of the new men who came to work there after I went away made a nasty crack he said hey Charlie I hear your a very smart fella a real quiz kid. Say something intelligent. I felt bad but Joe Carp came over and grabbed him by the shirt and said leave him alone you lousy cracker or Ill break your neck. I didn't expect Joe to take my part so I guess hes really my friend.

Later Frank Reilly came over and said Charlie if anybody bothers you or trys to take advantage you call me or Joe and we will set em straight. I said thanks Frank and I got choked up so I had to turn around and go into the supply room so he wouldn't see me cry. Its good to have friends.

July 28 I did a dumb thing today I forgot I wasnt in Miss Kinnians class at the adult center any more like I use to be. I went in and sat down in my old seat in the back of the room and she looked at me funny and she said Charles. I dint remember she ever called me that before only Charlie so I said hello Miss Kinnian Im redy for my lesin today only I lost my reader that we was using. She started to cry and run out of the room and everybody looked at me and I saw they wasnt the same pepul who used to be in my class.

Then all of a sudden I remembered some things about the operashun and me getting smart and I said holy smoke I reely pulled a Charlie Gordon that time. I went away before she come back to the room.

Thats why Im going away from New York for good. I dont want to do nothing like that agen. I dont want Miss Kinnian to feel sorry for me. Evry body feels sorry at the factery and I dont want that eather so Im going someplace where nobody knows that Charlie Gordon was once a genus and how he cant even reed a book or rite good.

Im taking a cuple of books along and even if I cant reed them Ill practise hard and maybe I wont forget every thing I lerned. If I try reel hard maybe Ill be a littel bit smarter than I was before the operashun. I got my rabits foot and my luky penny and maybe they will help me.

If you ever reed this Miss Kinnian dont be sorry for me Im glad I got a second chanse to be smart becaus I lerned a lot of things that I never even new were in this world and Im grateful that I saw it all for a littel bit. I dont know why Im dumb agen or what I did wrong maybe its becaus I dint try hard enuff. But if I try and practis very hard maybe Ill get a littl smarter and know what all the words are. I remember a littel bit how nice I had a feeling with the blue book that has the torn cover when I red it. Thats why Im gonna keep trying to get smart so I can have that feeling agen. Its a good feeling to know things and be smart. I wish I had it rite now if I did I would sit down and reed all the time. Anyway I bet Im the first dumb person in the world who ever found out somthing importent for sience. I remember I did somthing but I dont remember what. So I gess its like I did it for all the dumb pepul like me.

Flowers for Algernon

Good-by Miss Kinnian and Dr Strauss and evreybody. And P.S. please tell Dr Nemur not to be such a grouch when pepul laff at him and he would have more frends. Its easy to make frends if you let pepul laff at you. Im going to have lots of frends where I go.

P.P.S. Please if you get a chanse put some flowrs on Algernon's grave in the bak yard ...

*A rising star in the science-fiction galaxy, George R. R. (his friends call him "Railroad") Martin has published a novel (*Dying of the Light, *1977) and two excellent collections (*A Song for Lya and Other Stories, *1976, and* Songs of Stars and Shadows, *1977) in his relatively brief career as a professional writer. "A Song for Lya" won the Hugo Award in the novelette category in 1975.*

*"The Second Kind of Loneliness" (*Analog, *December 1972) is a lovely, sad, yet inspirational story of the problems of one man.*

THE SECOND KIND OF LONELINESS

By George R. R. Martin

June 18

My relief left Earth today.

It will be at least three months before he gets here, of course. But he's on his way.

Today he lifted off from the Cape, just as I did, four long years ago. Out at Komarov Station he'll switch to a moon boat, then switch again in orbit around Luna, at Deepspace Station. There his voyage will really begin. Up to then he's still been in his own backyard.

Not until the *Charon* casts loose from Deepspace Station and sets out into the night will he feel it, *really* feel it, as I felt it four years ago. Not until Earth and Luna vanish behind him will it hit. He's known from the first that there's no turning back, of course. But there's a difference between knowing it and feeling it. Now he'll feel it.

There will be an orbital stopover around Mars, to send supplies down to Burroughs City. And more stops in the belt.

But then the *Charón* will begin to gather speed. It will be going very fast when it reaches Jupiter. And much faster after it whips by, using the gravity of the giant planet like a slingshot to boost its acceleration.

After that there are no stops for the *Charon*. No stops at all until it reaches me, out here at the Cerberus Star Ring, six million miles beyond Pluto.

My relief will have a long time to brood. As I did.

I'm still brooding now, today, four years later. But then, there's not much else to do out here. Ringships are infrequent, and you get pretty weary of films and tapes and books after a time. So you brood. You think about your past and dream about your future. And you try to keep the loneliness and the boredom from driving you out of your skull.

It's been a long four years. But it's almost over now. And it will be nice to get back. I want to walk on grass again, and see clouds, and eat an ice cream sundae.

Still, for all that, I don't regret coming. These four years alone in the darkness have done me good, I think. It's not as if I had left much. My days on Earth seem remote to me now, but I can still remember them if I try. The memories aren't all that pleasant. I was pretty screwed up back then.

I needed time to think, and that's one thing you get out here. The man who goes back on the *Charon* won't be the same one who came out here four years ago. I'll build a whole new life back on Earth. I know I will.

June 20

Ship today.

I didn't know it was coming, of course. I never do. The ringships are irregular, and the kind of energies I'm playing with out here turn radio signals into crackling chaos. By the time the ship finally punched through the static, the station's scanners had already picked it up and notified me.

It was clearly a ringship. Much bigger than the old system rust-buckets like the *Charon*, and heavily armored to withstand the stresses of the nullspace vortex. It came straight on, with no attempt to decelerate.

While I was heading down to the control room to strap in, a thought hit me. This might be the last. Probably not, of course. There's still three months to go, and that's time enough for a dozen ships. But you can never tell. The ringships are irregular, like I said.

Somehow the thought disturbed me. The ships have been part of my life for four years now. An important part. And the one today might have been the last. If so, I want it all down here. I want to remember it. With good reason, I think. When the ships come, that makes everything else worthwhile.

The control room is in the heart of my quarters. It's the center of everything, where the nerves and the tendons and the muscles of the station are gathered. But it's not very impressive. The room is very small, and once the door slides shut the walls and floor and ceiling are all a featureless white.

There's only one thing in the room: a horseshoe-shaped console that surrounds a single padded chair.

I sat down in that chair today for what might be the last time. I strapped myself in, and put on the earphones, and lowered the helmet. I reached for the controls, and touched them, and turned them on.

And the control room vanished.

It's all done with holographs, of course. I *know* that. But that doesn't make a bit of difference when I'm sitting in that chair. Then, as far as I'm concerned, I'm not inside anymore. I'm out *there*, in the void. The control console is still there, and the chair. But the rest has gone. Instead, the aching darkness is everywhere, above me, below me, all around me. The distant sun is only one star among many, and all the stars are terribly far away.

That's the way it always is. That's the way it was today. When I threw that switch I was alone in the universe with the cold stars and the ring. The Cerberus Star Ring.

I saw the ring as if from outside, looking down on it. It's a vast structure, really. But from out here, it's nothing. It's swallowed by the immensity of it all, a slim silver thread lost in the blackness.

But I know better. The ring is huge. My living quarters take up but a single degree in the circle it forms, a circle whose diameter is more than a hundred miles. The rest is circuitry and scanners and power banks. And the engines, the waiting nullspace engines.

The ring turned silent beneath me, its far side stretching away into nothingness. I touched a switch on my console. Below me, the nullspace engines woke.

In the center of the ring, a new star was born.

It was a tiny dot amid the dark at first. Green today, bright green. But not always, and not for long. Nullspace has many colors.

I could see the far side of the ring then, if I'd wanted to. It was glowing with a light of its own. Alive and awake, the nullspace engines were pouring unimaginable amounts of energy inward, to rip wide a hole in space itself.

The hole had been there long before Cerberus, long before man. Men found it, quite by accident, when they reached Pluto. They built the ring around it. Later they found two other holes, and built other star rings.

The holes were small, too small. But they could be enlarged. Temporarily, at the expense of vast amounts of power, they could be ripped open. Raw energy could be pumped through that tiny, unseen hole in the universe until the placid surface of nullspace roiled and lashed back, and the nullspace vortex formed.

And now it happened.

The star in the center of the ring grew and flattened. It was a pulsing disc, not a globe. But it was still the brightest thing in the heavens. And it swelled visibly. From the spinning green disc, flame-like orange spears lanced out, and fell back, and smoky bluish tendrils uncoiled. Specks of red danced and flashed among the green, grew and blended. The colors all began to run together.

The flat, spinning, multicolored star doubled in size, doubled again, again. A few minutes before it had not been. Now it filled the ring, lapped against the silver walls, seared them with its awful energy. It began to spin faster and faster, a whirlpool in space, a maelstrom of flame and light.

The vortex. The nullspace vortex. The howling storm that is not a storm and does not howl, for there is no sound in space.

To it came the ringship. A moving star at first, it took on visible form and shape almost faster than my human eyes could follow. It became a dark silver bullet in the blackness, a bullet fired at the vortex.

The aim was good. The ship hit very close to the center of the ring. The swirling colors closed over it.

I hit my controls. Even more suddenly than it had come, the vortex was gone. The ship was gone too, of course. Once more there was only me, and the ring, and the stars.

Then I touched another switch, and I was back in the

blank white control room, unstrapping. Unstrapping for what might be the last time, ever.

Somehow I hope not. I never thought I'd miss anything about this place. But I will. I'll miss the ringships. I'll miss moments like the ones today.

I hope I get a few more chances at it before I give it up forever. I want to feel the nullspace engines wake again under my hands and watch the vortex boil and churn while I float alone between the stars. Once more, at least. Before I go.

June 23

That ringship has set me to thinking. Even more than usual.

It's funny that with all the ships I've seen pass through the vortex, I've never even given a thought to riding one. There's a whole new world on the other side of nullspace; Second Chance, a rich green planet of a star so far away that astronomers are still unsure whether it shares the same galaxy with us. That's the funny thing about the holes—you can't be sure where they lead until you go through.

When I was a kid, I read a lot about star travel. Most people didn't think it was possible. But those who did always mentioned Alpha Centauri as the first system we'd explore and colonize. Closest, and all that. Funny how wrong they were. Instead, our colonies orbit suns we can't even see. And I don't think we'll *ever* get to Alpha Centauri.

Somehow I never thought of the colonies in personal terms. Still can't. Earth is where I failed before. That's got to be where I succeed now. The colonies would be just another escape.

Like Cerberus?

June 26

Ship today. So the other wasn't the last, after all. But what about this one?

June 29

Why does a man volunteer for a job like this? Why does a man run to a silver ring six million miles beyond Pluto, to guard a hole in space? Why throw away four years of life alone in the darkness?

Why?

The Second Kind of Loneliness

I used to ask myself that, in the early days. I couldn't answer it then. Now I think I can. I bitterly regretted the impulse that drove me out here, then. Now I think I understand it.

And it wasn't really an impulse. I ran to Cerberus. Ran. Ran to escape from loneliness.

That doesn't make sense?

Yes it does. I know about loneliness. It's been the theme of my life. I've been alone for as long as I can remember.

But there are two kinds of loneliness.

Most people don't realize the difference. I do. I've sampled both kinds.

They talk and write about the loneliness of the men who man the star rings. The lighthouses of space, and all that. And they're right.

There are times, out here at Cerberus, when I think I'm the only man in the universe. Earth was just a fever dream. The people I remember were just creations of my own mind.

There are times, out here, when I want someone to talk to so badly that I scream, and start pounding on the walls. There are times when the boredom crawls under my skin and all but drives me mad.

But there are *other* times, too. When the ringships come. When I go outside to make repairs. Or when I just sit in the control chair, imaging myself out into the darkness to watch the stars.

Lonely? Yes. But a solemn, brooding, tragic loneliness. A loneliness tinged with grandeur, somehow. A loneliness that a man hates with a passion—and yet loves so much he craves for more.

And then there is the second kind of loneliness.

You don't need the Cerberus Star Ring for that kind. You can find it anywhere on Earth. I know. I did. I found it everywhere I went, in everything I did.

It's the loneliness of people trapped within themselves. The loneliness of people who have said the wrong thing so often that they don't have the courage to say anything anymore. The loneliness, not of distance, but of fear.

The loneliness of people who sit alone in furnished rooms in crowded cities, because they've got nowhere to go and no one to talk to. The loneliness of guys who go to bars to meet someone, only to discover they don't know how to strike up a conversation, and wouldn't have the courage to do so if they did.

There's no grandeur to that kind of loneliness. No purpose and no poetry. It's loneliness without meaning. It's sad and squalid and pathetic, and it stinks of self-pity.

Oh yes, it hurts at times to be alone among the stars.

But it hurts a lot more to be alone at a party. A lot more.

June 30

Reading yesterday's entry. Talk about self-pity...

July 1

Reading *yesterday's* entry. My flippant mask. After four years, I still fight back whenever I try to be honest with myself. That's not good. If things are going to be any different this time, I have to understand myself.

So why do I have to ridicule myself when I admit that I'm lonely and vulnerable? Why do I have to struggle to admit that I was scared of life? No one's ever going to read this thing. I'm talking to myself, about myself.

So why are there some things I still can't bring myself to say?

July 4

No ringship today. Too bad. Earth ain't never *had* no fireworks that could match the nullspace vortex, and I felt like celebrating.

But why do I keep Earth calendar out here, where the years are centuries and the seasons a dim memory? July is just like December. So what's the use?

July 10

I dreamed of Karen last night. And now I can't get her out of my skull.

I thought I buried her long ago. It was all a fantasy anyway. Oh, she liked me well enough. Loved me, maybe. But no more than a half-dozen other guys. I wasn't really *special* to her, and she never realized just how special she was to me.

Nor how much I wanted to be special to her—how much I needed to be special to someone, somewhere.

So I elected her. But it was all a fantasy. And I knew it

was, in my more rational moments. I had no right to be so hurt. I had no special claim on her.

But I thought I did, in my daydreams. And I *was* hurt. It was my fault, though, not hers. Karen would never hurt anyone willingly. She just never realized how fragile I was.

Even out here, in the early years, I kept dreaming. I dreamed of how she'd change her mind. How she'd be waiting for me. Et cetera.

But that was more wish-fulfillment. It was before I came to terms with myself out here. I know now that she won't be waiting. She doesn't need me, and never did. I was just a friend.

So I don't much like dreaming about her. That's bad. Whatever I do, I must *not* look up Karen when I get back. I have to start all over again. I have to find someone who *does* need me. And I won't find her if I try to slip back into my old life.

July 18

A month since my relief left Earth. The *Charon* should be in the belt by now. Two months to go.

July 23

Nightmares now. God help me.

I'm dreaming of Earth again. And Karen. I can't stop. Every night it's the same.

It's funny, calling Karen a nightmare. Up to now she's always been a dream. A beautiful dream, with her long, soft hair, and her laugh, and that funny way she had of grinning. But those dreams were always wish fulfillments. In the dreams Karen needed me and wanted me and loved me.

The nightmares have the bite of truth to them. They're all the same. It's always a replay of me and Karen, together on that last night.

It was a good night, as nights went for me. We ate at one of my favorite restaurants, and went to a show. We talked together easily, about many things. We laughed together, too.

Only later, back at her place, I reverted to form. When I tried to tell her how much she meant to me. I remember how awkward and stupid I felt, how I struggled to get things out, how I stumbled over my own words. So much came out wrong.

I remember how she looked at me then. Strangely. How she tried to disillusion me. Gently. She was always gentle. And I looked into her eyes and listened to her voice. But I didn't find love, or need. Just—just pity, I guess.

Pity for an inarticulate jerk who'd been letting life pass him by without touching it. Not because he didn't want to. But because he was afraid to, and didn't know how. She'd found that jerk, and loved him, in her way—she loved everybody. She'd tried to help, to give him some of her self-confidence, some of the courage and bounce that she faced life with. And, to an extent, she had.

Not enough, though. The jerk liked to make fantasies about the day he wouldn't be lonely anymore. And when Karen tried to help him, he thought she was his fantasy come to life. Or deluded himself into thinking that. The jerk suspected the truth all along, of course, but he lied to himself about it.

And when the day came that he couldn't lie any longer, he was still vulnerable enough to be hurt. He wasn't the type to grow scar tissue easily. He didn't have the courage to try again with someone else. So he ran.

I hope the nightmares stop. I can't take them, night after night. I can't take reliving that hour in Karen's apartment.

I've had four years out here. I've looked at myself hard. I've changed what I didn't like, or tried to. I've tried to cultivate that scar tissue, to gather the confidence I need to face the new rejections I'm going to meet before I find acceptance. But I know myself damn well now, and I know it's only been a partial success. There will always be things that will hurt, things that I'll never be able to face the way I'd like to.

Memories of that last hour with Karen are among those things. *God,* I hope the nightmares end.

July 26

More nightmares. Please Karen. I loved you. Leave me alone. Please.

July 29

There was a ringship yesterday, thank God. I needed one. It helped take my mind off Earth, off Karen. And there was no nightmare last night, for the first time in a week. Instead I dreamed of the nullspace vortex. The raging silent storm.

The Second Kind of Loneliness

August 1

The nightmares have returned. Not always Karen, now. Older memories too. Infinitely less meaningful, but still painful. All the stupid things I've said, all the girls I never met, all the things I have never done.

Bad. Bad. I have to keep reminding myself. I'm not like that anymore. There's a new me, a me I built out here, six million miles beyond Pluto. Made of steel and stars and null-space, hard and confident and self-assured. And not afraid of life.

The past is behind me. But it still hurts.

August 2

Ship today. The nightmares continue. Damn.

August 3

No nightmare last night. Second time for that, and I've rested easy after opening the hole for a ringship during the day. (Day? Night? Nonsense out here—but I still write as if they had some meaning. Four years haven't even touched the Earth in me.) Maybe the vortex is scaring Karen away. But I never wanted to scare Karen away before. Besides, I shouldn't need crutches.

August 13

Another ship came through a few nights ago. No dream afterwards. A pattern!

I'm fighting the memories. I'm thinking of other things about Earth. The good times. There were a lot of them, really, and there will be lots more when I get back. I'm going to make sure of that.

These nightmares are stupid. I won't permit them to continue. There was so much else I shared with Karen, so much I'd like to recall. Why can't I?

August 18

The *Charon* is about a month away. I wonder who my relief is. I wonder what drove *him* out here?

Earth dreams continue. No. Call them Karen dreams. Am I even afraid to write her name now?

August 20

Ship today. After it was through I stayed out and looked at stars. For several hours, it seems. Didn't seem as long at the time.

It's beautiful out here. Lonely, yes. But such a loneliness! You're alone with the universe, the stars spread out at your feet and scattered around your head.

Each one is a sun. Yet they still look cold to me. I find myself shivering, lost in the vastness of it all, wondering how it got there and what it means.

My relief, whoever it is, I hope he can appreciate this, as it should be appreciated. There are so many who can't, or won't. Men who walk at night, and never look up at the sky. I hope my relief isn't a man like that.

August 24

When I get back to Earth, I *will* look up Karen. I must. How can I pretend that things are going to be different this time if I can't even work up the courage to do that? And they *are* going to be different. So I *must* face Karen, and prove that I've changed. Really changed.

August 25

The nonsense of yesterday. How could I face Karen? What would I *say* to her? I'd only start deluding myself again, and wind up getting burned all over again. No. I must *not* see Karen. Hell, I can even take the dreams.

August 30

I've been going down to the control room and flipping myself out regularly of late. No ringships. But I find that going outside makes the memories of Earth dim.

More and more I know I'll miss Cerberus. A year from now, I'll be back on Earth, looking up at the night sky, and remembering how the ring shone silver in the starlight. I know I will.

And the vortex. I'll remember the vortex, and the ways the colors swirled and mixed. Different every time.

Too bad I was never a holo buff. You could make a fortune back on Earth with a tape of the way the vortex looks when it spins. The ballet of the void. I'm surprised no one's ever thought of it.

Maybe I'll suggest it to my relief. Something to do to fill the hours, if he's interested. I hope he is. Earth would be richer if someone brought back a record.

I'd do it myself, but the equipment isn't right, and I don't have the time to modify it.

September 4

I've gone outside every day for the last week, I find. No nightmares. Just dreams of the darkness, laced with the colors of nullspace.

September 9

Continue to go outside, and drink it all in. Soon, soon now, all this will be lost to me. Forever. I feel as though I must take advantage of every second. I must memorize the way things are out here at Cerberus, so I can keep the awe and the wonder and the beauty fresh inside me when I return to Earth.

September 10

There hasn't been a ship in a long time. Is it over, then? Have I seen my last?

September 12

No ship today. But I went outside and woke the engines and let the vortex roar.

Why do I always write about the vortex roaring and howling? There is no sound in space. I hear nothing. But I watch it. And it does roar. It does.

The sounds of silence. But not the way the poets meant.

September 13

I watched the vortex again today, though there was no ship.

I've never done that before. Now I've done it twice. It's forbidden. The costs in terms of power are enormous, and Cerberus lives on power. So why?

It's almost as though I don't want to give up the vortex. But I have to. Soon.

September 14

Idiot, idiot, idiot. What have I been doing? The *Charon* is less than a week away, and I've been gawking at the stars as if I'd never seen them before. I haven't even started to pack, and I've got to clean up my records for my relief, and get the station in order.

Idiot! Why am I wasting time writing in this damn *book!*

September 15

Packing almost done. I've uncovered some weird things, too. Things I tried to hide in the early years. Like my novel. I wrote it in the first six months, and thought it was great. I could hardly wait to get back to Earth, and sell it, and become an Author. Ah, yes. Read it over a year later. It stinks.

Also found a picture of Karen.

September 16

Today I took a bottle of Scotch and a glass down to the control room, set them down on the console, and strapped myself in. Drank a toast to the blackness and the stars and the vortex. I'll miss them.

September 17

A day, by my calculations. A day. Then I'm on my way home, to a fresh start and a new life. If I have the courage to live it.

September 18

Nearly midnight. No sign of the *Charon*. What's wrong?

Nothing, probably. These schedules are never precise. Sometimes as much as a week off. So why do I worry? Hell, I was late getting here myself. I wonder what the poor guy I replaced was thinking then?

September 20

The *Charon* didn't come yesterday, either. After I got tired of waiting, I took the bottle of Scotch and went back to the control room. And out. To drink another toast to the stars. And the vortex. I woke the vortex and let it flame, and toasted it.

A lot of toasts. I finished the bottle. And today I've got such a hangover I think I'll never make it back to Earth.

It was a stupid thing to do. The crew of the *Charon* might have seen the vortex colors. If they report me, I'll get docked a small fortune from the pile of money that's waiting back on Earth.

September 21

Where is the *Charon?* Did something happen to it? Is it coming?

September 22

I went outside again.

God, so beautiful, so lonely, so vast. Haunting, that's the word I want. The beauty out there is haunting. Sometimes I think I'm a fool to go back. I'm giving up all of eternity for a pizza and a lay and a kind word.

NO! What the hell am I writing! No. I'm going back, of course I am. I need Earth, I miss Earth, I want Earth. This time it *will* be different.

I'll find another Karen, and this time I won't blow it.

September 23

I'm sick. God, but I'm sick. The things I've been thinking. I thought I had changed, but now I don't know. I find myself actually thinking about staying, about signing on for another term. I don't want to. No. But I think I'm still afraid of life, of Earth, of everything.

Hurry, *Charon.* Hurry, before I change my mind.

September 24

Karen or the vortex? Earth or eternity?

Dammit, how can I *think* that! Karen! Earth! I have to have courage, I have to risk pain, I have to taste life.

I am *not* a rock. Or an island. Or a star.

September 25

No sign of the *Charon.* A full week late. That happens sometimes. But not very often. It will arrive soon. I know it.

September 30

Nothing. Each day I watch, and wait. I listen to my scanners, and go outside to look, and pace back and forth through the ring. But nothing. It's never been this late. What's wrong?

October 3

Ship today. Not the *Charon.* I thought it was at first, when the scanners picked it up. I yelled loud enough to wake the vortex. But then I looked, and my heart sank. It was too big, and it was coming straight on without decelerating.

I went outside and let it through. And stayed out for a long time afterward.

October 4
I want to go home. Where are they? I don't understand. I don't understand.

They can't just leave me here. They can't. They won't.

October 5
Ship today. Ringship again. I used to look forward to them. Now I hate them, because they're not the *Charon*. But I let it through.

October 7
I unpacked. It's silly for me to live out of suitcases when I don't know if the *Charon* is coming, or when.

I still look for it, though. I wait. It's coming, I know. Just delayed somewhere. An emergency in the belt maybe.

There are lots of explanations.

Meanwhile, I'm doing odd jobs around the ring. I never did get it in proper shape for my relief. Too busy star watching at the time, to do what I should have been doing.

January 8 (or thereabouts)
Darkness and despair.

I know why the *Charon* hasn't arrived. It isn't due. The calendar was all screwed up. It's January, not October. And I've been living on the wrong time for months. Even celebrated the Fourth of July on the wrong day.

I discovered it yesterday when I was doing those chores around the ring. I wanted to make sure everything was running right. For my relief.

Only there won't be any relief.

The *Charon* arrived three months ago. I—I destroyed it.

Sick. It was sick. I was sick, mad. As soon as it was done, it hit me. What I'd done. Oh, God. I screamed for hours.

And then I set back the wall calendar. And forgot. Maybe deliberately. Maybe I couldn't bear to remember. I don't know. All I know is that I forgot.

But now I remember. Now I remember it all.

The scanners had warned me of the *Charon*'s approach. I was outside, waiting. Watching. Trying to get enough of the stars and the darkness to last me forever.

Through that darkness, *Charon* came. It seemed so slow compared to the ringships. And so small. It was my salvation, my relief, but it looked fragile, and silly, and somehow ugly. Squalid. It reminded me of Earth.

It moved toward docking, dropping into the ring from above, groping toward the locks in the habitable section of Cerberus. So very slow. I watched it come. Suddenly I wondered what I'd say to the crewmen, and my relief. I wondered what they'd think of me. Somewhere in my gut, a fist clenched.

And suddenly I couldn't stand it. Suddenly I was afraid of it. Suddenly I hated it.

So I woke the vortex.

A red flare, branching into yellow tongues, growing quickly, shooting off bluegreen bolts. One passed near the *Charon*. And the ship shuddered.

I tell myself, now, that I didn't realize what I was doing. Yet I knew the *Charon* was unarmored. I knew it couldn't take vortex energies. I knew.

The *Charon* was so slow, the vortex so fast. In two heartbeats the maelstrom was brushing against the ship. In three it had swallowed it.

It was gone so fast. I don't know if the ship melted, or burst asunder, or crumpled. But I know it couldn't have survived. There's no blood on my star ring, though. The debris is somewhere on the other side of nullspace. If there is any debris.

The ring and the darkness looked the same as ever.

That made it so easy to forget. And I must have wanted to forget very much.

And now? What do I do *now*? Will Earth find out? Will there ever be relief? I want to go home.

Karen, I—

June 18

My relief left Earth today.

At least I think he did. Somehow the wall calendar was broken, so I'm not precisely sure of the date. But I've got it back into working order.

Anyway, it can't have been off for more than a few hours, or I would have noticed. So my relief *is* on the way. It will take him three months to get here, of course.

But at least he's coming.

MEMOS

Ms. Merril's second contribution is a beautiful (not an easy quality to obtain in this form of the short story) and powerful story that first appeared in the late and lamented Worlds of Tomorrow *(October 1963).*

THE LONELY

By Judith Merril

TO: The Hon. Natarajan Roi Hennessy, Chairman, Committee on Intercultural Relations. Solar Council, Eros.
FROM: Dr. Shlomo Mouna, Sr. Anthropologist, Project Ozma XII, Pluto Station.
DATE: 10/9/92, TC.
TRANSMISSION: VIA: Tight beam, scrambled. SENT: 1306 hrs, TST. RCDV: 1947 hrs, TST.

Dear Nat:

Herewith, a much condensed, heavily annotated, and top-secret coded transcript of a program we just picked up. The official title is GU #79, and the content pretty well confirms some of our earlier assumptions about the whole series, as this one concerns us directly, and we have enough background information, including specific dates, to get a much more complete and stylistic translation than before.

I'd say the hypotheses that these messages represent a "Galactic University" lecture series broadcast from somewhere near Galactic Center, through some medium a damn sight faster than light, now seems very reasonable.

This one seemed to come from Altair, which would date transmission from there only a few years after some incidents described in script. Some of the material also indicates probable nature of original format, and I find it uncomfortable.

651

Also reraises question of whether Altair, Arcturus, Castor, etc., relay stations are aimed at us? Although the content makes that doubtful.

Full transcript, film, etc., will go out through channels, as soon as you let me know which channels. This time I am not pleading for declassification. I think of some Spaserve reactions and—frankly I wonder if it shouldn't be limited to SC Intercult Chairmen and Ozma Sr. Anthropoids—and sometimes I wonder about thee.

Cheery reading.
Shlomo

TRANSCRIPT, GU #79, Condensed Version, edited by SM, 10/9/92, TC. (NRH: All material in parens is in my words—summarizing, commenting, and/or describing visual material where indicated. Straight text is verbatim, though cut as indicated. Times, measurements, etc., have been translated from Standard Galactic or Aldebaran local to Terran Standard; and bear in mind that words like "perceive" are often very rough translations for SG concepts more inclusive than our language provided for.—SM)

(Open with distance shot of Spaserve crew visiting Woman of Earth statue on Aldebaran VI. Closeup of reverent faces. Shots of old L-1, still in orbit, and jump-ship trailing it. Repeat first shot, then to Lecturer. You may have seen this one before. Sort of electric-eel type. Actually makes sparks when he's being funny.)

The image you have just perceived is symbolic, in several senses. First, the statue was created by the Arlemites, the native race of Aldebaran VI (!! Yes, Virginia, there *are* aborigines!!) in an effort to use emotional symbols to bridge the gap in communications between two highly dissimilar species. Second: due to the farcical failure of this original intent, the structure has now become a vitally significant symbol—you perceived the impact—to the other species involved, the Terrans, a newly emerged race from Sol III. (Note that "you perceived." We must accept the implication that the original broadcasting format provides means of projecting emotional content.) Finally, this twofold symbol relates in one sense (Shooting sparks like mad here. Professional humor pretty much the same all over, hey?) to the phenomenon of the paradox of absolute universality and infinite variety inherent in the symbolism.

(Next section is a sort of refresher-review of earlier lectures. Subject of the whole course appears to be, roughly, "Problems of disparate symbolism in interspecies communications." This lecture—don't laugh—is "Symbols of Sexuality." Excerpts from review:—)

The phenomenon of symbolism is an integral part of the development of communicating intelligence. Distinctions of biological construction, ecological situation, atmospheric and other geophysical conditions, do of course profoundly influence the radically infantile phases of intellectual-emotional-social development in all cultures...(but)...from approximately that point in the linear development of a civilization at which it is likely to make contact with other cultures— that is, from the commencement of cultural maturity, following the typically adolescent outburst of energy in which first contact is generally accomplished...(He describes this level at some length in terms of a complex of: 1, astrophysical knowledge; 2, control of basic matter-energy conversions, "mechanical or psial"; 3, self-awareness of whole culture and of individuals in it; and 4, some sociological phenomena for which I have no referents.)...all cultures appear to progress through a known sequence of i-e-s patterns...(and)...despite differences in the *rate* of development, the composite i-e-s curve for mature cultural development of all known species is familiar enough to permit reliable predictions for any civilization, once located on the curve.

(Then progresses to symbolism. Specific symbols, he says, vary even more, between cultures, than language or other means of conscious communication, as to wit—)

It is self-evident that the specific symbols utilized by, for instance, a septasexual, mechanophilic, auriphased species of freely locomotive discrete individuals, will vary greatly from those of, let us say, a mitotic, unicellular, intensely psioid, communal culture. (Which makes it all the more striking, that) it is specifically in the *use of symbols,* the general consciousness of their significance, the degree of sophistication of the popularly recognized symbols, and the uses to which they are put by the society as a whole, that we have found our most useful constant, so far, for purposes of locating a given culture on the curve.

(Much more here about other aspects of cultural development, some of which are cyclical, some linear—all fascinating but not essential to understanding of what follows.)

Sexuality has until recently been such a rare phenomenon among civilized species that we had casually assumed it to be something of a drawback to the development of intelli-. gence. Such sexual races as we did know seemed to have developed in spite of their biological peculiarity, but usually not until after the mechanical flair that often seemed to accompany the phenomenon had enabled them to escape their planet of origin for a more favorable environment.

I say more favorable because sexuality does seem to develop as an evolutionary compensation where (some terms untranslatable, some very broad, but generally describing circumstances, like extra-dense atmosphere, in which the normal rate of cosmic radiation was reduced to a degree that inhibited mutation and thus, evolution)...

As I said, this seemed almost a freak occurrence, and so it was, and is, here in the heart of the Galaxy. But in the more thinly populated spiral arms, the normal rate of radiation is considerably lower. It is only in the last centuries that we have begun to make contact with any considerable numbers of species from these sectors—and the incidence of sexuality among these peoples is markedly higher than before.

Recently, then, there has been fresh cause to investigate the causes and effects of sexuality; and there has been a comparative wealth of new material to work with.

(Here he goes into a review of the variety of sexual modes, ranging from two to seventeen sexes within a species, and more exotica-erotica of means, manners, and mores than a mere two-sexed biped can readily imagine. Restrain yourself. It's all in the full transcript.)

But let me for the moment confine myself to the simplest and most common situation, involving only two sexes. Recent investigations indicate that there is an apparently inevitable psychological effect of combining two essentially distinct subspecies in one genetic unit. (Sparks like mad.) I perceive that many of you have just experienced the same delight-dismay the first researchers felt at recognizing this so-obvious and so-overlooked parallel with the familiar cases of symbiosis.

The Terrans, mentioned earlier, are in many ways prototypical of sexuality in an intelligent species, and the unusual and rather dramatic events on Aldebaran VI have added greatly to our insights into the psychology of sexuality in general.

In this culture, dualism is very deep-rooted, affecting

every aspect of the i-e-s complex: not just philosophy and engineering, but mathematics, for instance, and mystique.

This cultural attitude starts with a duality, or two-sided symmetry, of body-structure. (Throughout this discussion he uses visual material—photos, diagrams, etc., of human bodies, anatomy, physiology, habitat, eating and mating habits, etc. Also goes off into some intriguing speculation of the chicken-or-egg type: is physical structure influenced by mental attitudes, or is it some inherent tendency of a chromosome pattern with *pairs* of genes from *pairs* of parents?)

In this respect, the Terrans are almost perfect prototypes, with two pairs of limbs, for locomotion and manipulation, extending from a central—single—abdominal cavity, which, although containing some single organs as well as some in pairs, is so symmetrically proportioned that the first assumption from an exterior view would be that everything inside was equally mirror-imaged. Actually, the main breathing apparatus is paired; the digestive system is single—although food intake is through an orifice with paired lips and two rows of teeth. In both "male" and "female" types, the organ of sexual contact is single, whereas the gamete-producers are pairs. There is a single, roundish head set on top of the abdomen, containing the primary sensory organs, all of which occur in pairs. Even the brain is paired!

I mentioned earlier that it is typical of the sexual races that the flair for physical engineering is rather stronger than the instinct for communication. This was an observed but little-understood fact for many centuries; it was not till this phenomenon of dualism (and triadism for the three-sexed, etc.) was studied that the earlier observation was clarified. If you will consider briefly the various sources of power and transport, you will realize that—outside of the psi-based techniques—most of these are involved with principles of symmetry and/ or equivalence; these concepts are obvious to the two-sexed. On the other hand, the principle of unity, underlying all successful communication—physical, verbal, psial, or other—and which is also the basis for the application of psi to engineering problems—is for these species, in early stages, an almost mystical quality.

As with most life-forms, the reproductive act is, among sexual beings, both physically pleasurable and biologically compulsive, so that it is early equated with religio-mystic sensations. Among sexual species, these attitudes are intensified by the communicative aspects of the act. (Cartoon-type diagrams here which frankly gave me to think a bit!) We have much to learn yet about the psychology of this phenomenon, but enough has been established to make clear that the concept of unity for these races is initially almost entirely related to the use of their sexuality, and is later extended to other areas—religion and the arts of communication at first—with a mystical—indeed often reverent attitude!

I hardly need to remind you that the tendencies I have been discussing are the primitive and underlying ones. Obviously, at the point of contact, any species must have acquired at least enough sophistication in the field of physics— quanta, unified field theory, and atomic transmutation for a start—to have begun to look away from the essentially blind alley of dualistic thinking. But the extent to which these Terrans were still limited by their early developmental pattern is indicated by the almost unbelievable fact that they developed ultra-dimensional transport *before* discovering any more effective channels of communication than the electromagnetic!

Thus their first contacts with older civilizations were physical; and, limited as they still are almost entirely to aural and visual communication, they were actually unable to perceive their very first contact on Aldebaran VI.

(Shot of Prof. Eel in absolute sparkling convulsions goes to distance shots of planet and antiquated Earth spaceship in orbit: L-1 again. Then suborb launch drops, spirals to surface. Twenty bulky spacesuited figures emerge—not the same as in opening shots. This looks like actual photographic record of landing, which seems unlikely. Beautiful damn reconstruction, if so. Narration commences with Aldebaran date. I substitute Terran Calendar date we know for same, and accept gift of one more Rosetta Stone.)

The time is the year 2053. For more than six decades, this primitive giant of space has ployed its way through the restrictive medium of slow space. Twice before in its travels, the great ship has paused.

First at Procyon, where they found the system both uninhabited and uninviting; and at the time they did not yet know what urgent cause they had to make a landing. (Our date for Procyon exploration, from L-1 log, is 2016, which fits.)

Then at Saiph, two decades later, where they hoped for

just a bare mimimum of hospitality—no more than safe footing for their launches, in which they could live while they tried to ensure their future survival. But this system's planets offered little hope. One Earth-size enveloped in horror-film type gases and nasty moistures. (One more with dense atmosphere of high acid content: probe from ship corroded in minutes.)

They limped on. A half-decade later they came to a time of decision, and determined not to try for the next nearest star system, but for the closest one from which their radio had received signs of intelligent life: Aldebaran.

What they had learned between Procyon and Saiph was that those of their crew who were born in space were not viable. The ship had been planned to continue, if necessary, long beyond the lifespan of its first crew. The Terran planners had ingeniously bypassed their most acute psychosocial problem, and staffed the ship with a starting crew of just one sex. Forty females started the journey, with a supply of sperm from one hundred genetically selected males carefully preserved on board.

Sex determination in this species is in the male chromosome, and most of the supply had been selected for production of females. The plan was to maintain the ship in transit with single-sexed population and restore the normal balance only at the end of the journey.

The Terrans have apparently reached a level of self-awareness that enables them to avoid the worst dangers of their own divisive quality, while utilizing the advantages of this special (pun intended—Prof. Eel was sparking again) ambivalence. Their biological peculiarities have, among other things, developed a far greater tolerance in the females for the type of physical constraints and social pressures that were to accompany the long, slow voyage. Males, on the other hand, being more aggressive, and more responsive to hostile challenges, would be needed for colonizing a strange planet. (Dissertation on mammals here which says nothing new, but restates from an outsider's—rather admiring—viewpoint with some distinction. Should be a textbook classic—if we can ever release this thing.)

That was the plan. But when the first females born on the trip came to maturity, and could not conceive, the plan was changed. Three male infants were born to females of the original complement—less than half of whom, even then, were still alive and of child-bearing age.

(Well, he tells it effectively, but adds nothing to what we know from the log. Conflicts among the women led to death of one boy, eventual suicide of another at adolescence. Remaining mature male fails to impregnate known fertile women. Hope of landing while enough fertiles remained to start again pretty well frustrated at Saiph. Decision to try for nearest system eight light years off—with Aldebaran still farther. Faint fantastic hope still at landing, with just one child-bearer left—the Matriarch, if you recall?)

Remembering the reasons for their choice of Aldebaran, you can imagine the reaction when that landing party, first, lost all radio signals as they descended; then, could find no trace whatsoever—to their senses—of habitation. The other planets were scouted, to no avail. The signals on the Mother Ship's more powerful radio continued to come from VI. One wild hypothesis was followed up by a thorough and fruitless search of the upper atmosphere. The atmosphere was barely adequate to sustain life at the surface. Beam tracing repeatedly located the signal beacon in a mountain of VI, which showed—to the Terrans—no other sign of intelligent life.

The only logical conclusion was that they had followed a "lighthouse beacon" to an empty world. The actual explanation, of course, was in the nature of the Arlemites, the natives of Aldebaran VI.

Originating as a social-colonizing lichen, on a heavy planet, with—even at its prime—a barely adequate atmosphere, the Arlemites combined smallness of individual size with limited locomotive powers and superior air and water retentive ability. They developed, inevitably, as a highly psioid culture—as far to one end of the psichophysical as the Terrans are to the other. (My spelling up there. I think it represents true meaning better than "psycho.") The constantly thinning choice was between physical relocation and a conscious evolutionary measure which this mature psioid race was far better equipped to undertake: the Arlemites now exist as a planet-wide diffusion of single-celled entities, comprising just one individual, and a whole species.

(Visual stuff here helps establish concept—as if you or I just extended the space between cells.)

It seems especially ironic that the Arlemites were not only one of the oldest and most psioid of peoples—so that they had virtually all the accumulated knowledge of the Galaxy at their disposal—but were also symbiote products. This background might have enabled them to comprehend the Terran mind and the problems confronting the visitors—except for the accidental combination of almost total psi-blindness in the Terrans, and the single-sexed complement of the ship.

The visitors could not perceive their hosts. The hosts could find no way to communicate with the visitors. The full complement of the ship, eventually, came down in launches, and lived in them, hopelessly, while they learned that their viability had indeed been completely lost in space. There was no real effort to return to the ship and continue the voyage. The ranks thinned, discipline was lost, deaths proliferated. Finally, it was only a child's last act of rebelliousness that mitigated the futility of the tragedy.

The last child saw the last adult die, and saw this immobility as an opportunity to break the most inviolable of rules. She went out of the launch—into near-airlessness that killed her within minutes.

But minutes were more than enough, with the much longer time afterwards for examination of the dead brain. It was through the mind of this one child, young enough to be still partially free of the rigid mental framework that made adult Terrans so inaccessible to Arlemites, that the basis was gained for most of the knowledge we now have.

Sorrowingly, the Arlemites generated an organism to decompose the Terrans and their artifacts, removing all traces of tragedy from the planet's surface. Meanwhile, they studied what they had learned, against future needs.

The technological ingenuity of these young sexuals will be apparent when I tell you that only four decades after the departure of that ill-fated ship, they were experimenting with ultra-dimensional travel. Even at the time of the landing at Aldebaran, ultra-di scouts were already exploring the systems closest to Sol. Eventually—within a decade after the child's death—one of these came to Aldebaran, and sighted the still-orbiting Mother Ship.

A second landing was clearly imminent. The Arlemites had still devised no way to aid this species to live in safety on their planet, nor did they have any means to communicate adequately with psi-negatives whose primary perceptions were aural and visual. But they did have, from the child's mind, a working knowledge of the strongest emotional symbols the culture knew, and they had long since devised a warning sign they could erect for visual perception. The statue of the Woman of Earth was constructed in an incredibly brief time through the combined efforts of the whole Arlemite consciousness.

They had no way to know that the new ship, designed for exploration, not colonizing, and equipped with ultra-di drive, which obviated the long slow traveling, was crewed entirely by males. Even had they known, they did not yet comprehend the extreme duality of the two-sexed double-culture. So they built their warning to the shape of the strongest fear-and-hate symbols of—a female.

(Shot of statue, held for some time, angle moving slowly. No narration. Assuming that emotional-projection notion— and I think we must—the timing here is such that I believe they first project what they seem to think a human female would feel, looking at it. I tried women on staff here. They focused more on phallic than female component, but were just as positive in reactions as males.???? Anyhow, like I said, no narration. What follows, though out of parens, is my own reaction.)

It seems more a return than a venture.

The Woman waits, as she has waited...always?...to greet her sons, welcomes us...home?...She sits in beauty, in peacefulness, perfect, complete, clean and fresh-colored... new?...no, *forever*...open, welcoming, yet so impervious... warm and...untouchable?...rather, *untouched*...almost, but never, forgotten Goddess...Allmother, Woman of Earth...enveloped, enveloping, in warmth and peace...

One stands back a bit: this is the peace of loving insight, of unquesting womanhood, of great age and undying youth...the peace of the past, of life that is passed, of that immortality that nothing mortal can ever achieve except through the frozen impression of living consciousness that we call *art*.

The young men are deeply moved and they make jokes. "Allmother," one hears them say, sarcastically, "Old White Goddess, whaddya know?"

Then they look up and are quiet under the smiling stone eyes. Even the ancient obscenely placed spaceship in her lap is not quite absurd, as it will seem in museum models—or tragic, as is the original overhead.

(Prof. Eel goes on to summarize the conclusions that seem obvious to him. Something is awfully wrong; that's obvious to me. How did they manage to build something so powerful out of total miscomprehension? What are we up against, anyhow? And, to get back to the matter of channels, what do you think this little story would do to Spaserve brass egos? Do you want to hold it top secret a while?)

End of Transcript

TO: Dr. Shlomo Mouna, Sr. Anthropologist, Ozma XII, Pluto
FROM: N.R.Hennessy, Solar Council Dome. Eros
DATE: 10/10/92
TRANSMISSION: VIA tight beam, scrambled. SENT: 0312 hrs. RECVD: 1027 hrs.

Dear Shlomo:
Absolutely, let me see the full package before we release it elsewhere. I've got a few more questions, like: Do they know we're receiving it? How do we straighten them out? Or should we? Instinct says yes. Tactics says it is advantageous to be underestimated. Think best you come with package, and we'll braintrust it. Meantime, in reply to your bafflement—

"L" class ships, you should have known, are for "Lysistrata." Five of them launched during brief Matriarchy at beginning of World Government on Terra, following Final War. So sort out your symbols *now*.

And good grief, where did the *other* four land?

NRH

*A.E. van Vogt's second contribution, "Secret Unattainable"
(Astounding Science Fiction, July 1942) is a good example
of the reaction of science-fiction writers to Nazism and World
War II. Never before (to the best of our knowledge) anthologized, it appeared in the author's excellent collection* Away
and Beyond *(1952).*

SECRET UNATTAINABLE

By A. E. van Vogt

The file known as Secret Six was smuggled out of Berlin in
mid-1945 when Russia was in sole occupation of the city.
How it was brought to the United States is one of those
dramatic true tales of World War II. The details cannot yet
be published since they involve people now in the Russian
zone of Germany.

All the extraordinary documents of this file, it should be
emphasized, are definitely in the hands of our own authorities; and investigations are proceeding apace. Further revelations of a grand order may be expected as soon as one of
the machines is built. All German models were destroyed by
the Nazis early in 1945.

The documents date from 1937, and will be given chron-
ologically, without reference to their individual importance.

But first, it is of surpassing interest to draw attention to the following news item, which appeared in the New York *Sun,* March 25, 1941, on page 17. At that time it appeared to have no significance whatever. The item:

GERMAN CREEK BECOMES RIVER

London, March 24 (delayed): A royal Air Force reconnaissance pilot today reported that a creek in northern Prussia, marked on the map as the Gribe Creek, has become a deep, swift river overnight. It is believed that an underground waterway burst its bounds. Several villages in the path of the new river showed under water. No report of the incident has yet been received from Berlin.

There never was any report from Berlin. It should again be pointed out that the foregoing news item was published in 1941; the documents which follow date from 1937, a period of four years. Four years of world-shaking history:

April 10, 1937

From   Secretary, Bureau of Physics
To   Reich and Prussian Minister of Science
Subject   10731–127–S–6

1. Enclosed is the report of the distinguished scientific board of inquiry which sat on the case of Herr Professor Johann Kenrube.

2. As you will see, the majority of the board oppose emphatically the granting of State funds for what they describe as a "fantastic scheme." They deny that a step-up tube would produce the results claimed, and refute utterly the number philosophy involved. Number, they say, is a function, not a reality, or else modern physics has no existence.

3. The minority report of Herr Professor Goureit, while thought-provoking, can readily be dismissed when it is remembered that Goureit, like Kenrube and Kenrube's infamous brother, was once a member of the SPD.

4. The board of inquiry, having in mind Hitler's desire that no field of scientific inquiry should be left unexplored, and as a generous gesture to Goureit, who has a very great reputation and a caustic pen, suggested that, if Kenrube

could obtain private funds for his research, he should be permitted to do so.

5. Provided Geheime Staats Polizei do not object, I concur.

G.L.

Author's Note: *The signature G.L. has been difficult to place. There appear to have been several secretaries of the Bureau of Physics Research, following one another in swift order. The best accounts identify him as Gottfried Lesser, an obscure B.Sc. who early joined the Nazi party, and for a period was its one and only science expert. Geheime Staats Polizei is of course Gestapo.*

MEMO April 17, 1937

From   Chief, Science Branch, Gestapo

If Kenrube can find the money, let him go ahead. Himmler concurs, provided supervision be strict.

K. Reissel

COPY ONLY June 2, 1937

From   Co-ordinator Dept., Deutsche Bank
To   Gestapo

The marginally noted personages have recently transferred sums totaling Reichsmarks four million five hundred thousand to the account of Herr Professor Johann Kenrube. For your information, please.

J. Pleup.

June 11, 1937

From   Gestapo
To   Reich and Prussian Minister of Science
Subject   Your 10731–127–S–6

Per your request for further details on the private life of J. Kenrube since the death of his brother in June, 1934, in the purge:

We quote from a witness, Peter Braun: "I was in a position to observe Herr Professor Kenrube very closely when the news was brought to him at Frankfort-on-Main that August, his brother, had been executed in the sacred blood purge.

"Professor Kenrube is a thin, good-looking man with a very wan face normally. This face turned dark with color, then drained completely of blood. He clenched his hands and said: 'They've murdered him!' Then he rushed off to his room.

"Hours later, I saw him walking, hatless, hair disarrayed, along the bank of the river. People stopped to look at him, but he did not see them. He was very much upset that first day. When I saw him again the next morning, he seemed to have recovered. He said to me: 'Peter, we must all suffer for our past mistakes. The tragic irony of my brother's death is that he told me only a week ago in Berlin that he had been mistaken in opposing the National-sozialistiche Arbeitspartei. He was convinced they were doing great things. I am too much of a scientist ever to have concerned myself with politics.'"

You will note, Excellency, that this is very much the set speech of one who is anxious to cover up the indiscreet, emotional outburst of the previous day. However, the fact that he was able to pull himself together at all seems to indicate that affection of any kind is but shallowly rooted in his character. Professor Kenrube returned to his laboratories in July, 1934, and has apparently been hard at work ever since.

There has been some discussion here concerning Kenrube, by the psychologists attached to this office; and the opinion is expressed, without dissent, that in three years the professor will almost have forgotten that he had a brother.

K. Reissel.

MEMO AT BOTTOM OF LETTER:

I am more convinced than ever that psychologists should be seen and not heard. It is our duty to watch every relative of every person whose life is, for any reason, claimed by the State. If there are scientific developments of worthwhile nature in this Kenrube affair, let me know at once. His attainments are second to none. A master plan of precaution is in order.

Himmler.

October 24, 1937

From   Secretary, Bureau of Physics
To   Reich and Prussian Minister of Science
Subject   Professor Johann Kenrube

The following report has been received from our Special Agent Seventeen:

"Kenrube has hired the old steel and concrete fortress,

Gribe Schloss, overlooking the Gribe Creek, which flows into
the Eastern Sea. This ancient fortress was formerly located
on a small hill in a valley. The hill has subsided, however,
and is now virtually level with the valley floor. We have been
busy for more than a month making the old place livable,
and installing machinery."

For your information, Agent Seventeen is a graduate in
physics of Bonn University. He was for a time professor of
physics at Muenchen. In view of the shortage of technicians,
Kenrube has appointed Seventeen his chief assistant.

G.L.

May 21, 1938

From   Science Branch, Gestapo
To   Reich and Prussian Minister of Science
Subject   10731–127–S–6

Himmler wants to know the latest developments in the
Kenrube affair. Why the long silence? Exactly what is Pro-
fessor Kenrube trying to do, and what progress has he made?
Surely, your secret agent has made reports.

K. Reissel.

June 3, 1938

From   Secretary, Bureau of Physics
To   Chief, Science Branch, Gestapo
Subject   Professor Johann Kenrube

Your letter of the 21st ultimo has been passed on to me.
The enclosed précis of the reports of our Agent Seventeen
will bring you up to date.

Be assured that we are keeping a careful watch on the
developments in this case. So far, nothing meriting special
attention has arisen.

G.L.

PRÉCIS OF MONTHLY REPORTS
OF AGENT SEVENTEEN

Our agent reports that Professor Kenrube's first act was
to place him, Seventeen, in charge of the construction of the
machine, thus insuring that he will have the most intimate
knowledge of the actual physical details.

When completed, the machine is expected to occupy the
entire room of the old fortress, largely because of the use of

step-up vacuum tubes. In this connection, Seventeen describes how four electric dynamos were removed from Kenrube's old laboratories, their entire output channeled through the step-up tubes, with the result that a ninety-four percent improvement in efficiency was noted.

Seventeen goes on to state that orders for parts have been placed with various metal firms but, because of the defense program, deliveries are extremely slow. Professor Kenrube has resigned himself to the possibility that his invention will not be completed until 1944 or '45.

Seventeen, being a scientist in his own right, has become interested in the machine. In view of the fact that, if successful, it will insure measureless supplies of raw materials for our Reich, he urges that some effort be made to obtain priorities.

He adds that he has become quite friendly with Kenrube. He does not think that the Herr Professor suspects how closely he is connected with the Bureau of Science.

June 4, 1938

From   Gestapo
To   Reich and Prussian Minister of Science
Subject   10731–127–S–6

Raw materials! Why was I not informed before that Kenrube was expecting to produce raw materials? Why did you think I was taking an interest in this case, if not because Kenrube is a genius of the first rank; and therefore anything he does must be examined with the most minute care? But—raw materials! Are you all mad over there, or living in a world of pleasant dreams?

You will at once obtain from Herr Professor Kenrube the full plans, the full mathematics of his work, with photographs of the machine as far as it has progressed. Have your scientists prepare a report for me as to the exact nature of the raw materials that Kenrube expects to obtain. Is this some transmutation affair, or what is the method?

Inform Kenrube that he must supply this information or he will obtain no further materials. If he satisfies our requirements, on the other hand, there will be a quickening of supplies. Kenrube is no fool. He will understand the situation.

As for your agent, Seventeen, I am at once sending an agent to act as his bodyguard. Friendly with Kenrube indeed!

Himmler.

June 28, 1938

From Gestapo
To Secretary, Bureau of Physics
Subject Secret Six

Have you received the report from Kenrube? Himmler is most anxious to see this the moment it arrives.

K. Reissel.

July 4, 1938

From Gestapo
To Secretary, Bureau of Physics
Subject Secret Six

What about the Kenrube report? Is it possible that your office does not clearly grasp how important we regard this matter? We have recently discovered that Professor Kenrube's grandfather once visited a very curious and involved revenge on a man whom he hated years after the event that motivated the hatred. Every conceivable precaution must be taken to see to it that the Kenrube machine can be duplicated, and the machine itself protected.

Please send the scientific report the moment it is available.

K. Reissel.

July 4, 1938

From Secretary, Bureau of Physics
To Chief, Science Branch, Gestapo
Subject Professor Johann Kenrube

The report, for which you have been asking, has come to hand, and a complete transcription is being sent to your office under separate cover. As you will see, it is very elaborately prepared; and I have taken the trouble to have a précis made of our scientific board's analysis of the report for your readier comprehension.

G.L.

PRÉCIS OF
SCIENTIFIC ANALYSIS OF KENRUBE'S REPORT
ON HIS INVENTION

General Statement of Kenrube's Theory: That there are two kinds of space in the universe, normal and hyper-space.

Only in normal space is the distance between star systems and galaxies great. It is essential to the nature of things, to the unity of material bodies, that intimate cohesion exist between every particle of matter, between, for instance, the earth and the universe as a whole.

Kenrube maintains that gravity does not explain the perfect and wonderful balance, the singleness of organism that is a galactic system. And that the theory of relativity merely evades the issue in stating that planets go around the sun because it is easier for them to do that than to fly off into space.

Kenrube's thesis, therefore, is that all the matter in the universe conjoins according to a rigid mathematical pattern, and that this conjunction presupposes the existence of hyperspace.

Object of the Invention: To bridge the gap through hyperspace between the Earth and any planet, or any part of any planet. In effect, this means that it would not be necessary to drill for oil in a remote planet. The machine would merely locate the oil stratum, and tap it at any depth; the oil would flow from the orifice of the machine which, in the case of the machine now under construction, is ten feet in diameter.

A ten-foot flow of oil at a pressure of four thousand feet a minute would produce approximately six hundred thousand tons of oil every hour.

Similarly, mining could be carried on simply by locating the ore-bearing veins, and skimming from them the purest ores.

It should be pointed out that, of the distinguished scientists who have examined the report, only Herr Professor Goureit claims to be able to follow the mathematics proving the existence of hyper-space.

COPY ONLY   July 14, 1938
TRANSCRIPTION OF INTERVIEW BY HERR HIMMLER OF PROFESSOR H. KLEINBERG, CHAIRMAN OF THE SCIENTIFIC COMMITTEE OF SCIENCE BRANCH, GESTAPA, INVESTIGATING REPORT OF HERR PROFESSOR JOHANN KENRUBE.

Q. You have studied the drawings and examined the mathematics?

A. Yes.

Q. What is your conclusion?

A. We are unanimously agreed that some fraud is being perpetrated.

Q. Does your verdict relate to the drawings of the invention, or to the mathematics explaining the theory?

A. To both. The drawings are incomplete. A machine made from those blueprints would hum with apparent power and purpose, but it would be a fraudulent uproar; the power simply goes oftener through a vacuumized circuit before returning to its source.

Q. I have sent your report to Kenrube. His comment is that almost the whole of modern electrical physics is founded on some variation of electricity being forced through a vacuum. What about that?

A. It is a half-truth.

Q. What about the mathematics?

A. There is the real evidence. Since Descartes—

Q. Please abstain from using these foreign names.

A. Pardon me. Since Libniz, number has been a function, a variable idea. Kenrube treats of number as an existing *thing*. Mathematics, he says, has living and being. You have to be a scientist to realize how incredible, impossible, ridiculous, such an idea is.

WRITTEN COMMENT ON THE ABOVE

I am not a scientist. I have no set ideas on the subject of mathematics or invention. I am, however, prepared to accept the theory that Kenrube is withholding information, and for this reason order that:

1. All further materials for the main machine be withheld.

2. Unlimited assistance be given Kenrube to build a model of his machine in the great government laboratories at Dresden. When, and not until, this model is in operation, permission will be given for the larger machine to be completed.

3. Meanwhile, Gestapo scientists will examine the machine at Gribe Schloss, and Gestapo construction experts will, if necessary, reinforce the building, which must have been dam-

aged by the settling of the hill on which it stands.

4. Gestapo agents will hereafter guard Gribe Schloss.

Himmler.

From   Secretary, Bureau of Physics
To   Chief, Science Branch, Gestapo
Subject Herr Professor Kenrube

Enclosed is the quarterly précis of the reports of our Agent Seventeen.

For your information, please.

August Buehnen

Author's Note: *Buehnen, a party man who was educated in one of the Nazi two-year Science Schools, replaced G.L. as secretary of the Bureau of Physics about September, 1938.*

It is not known exactly what became of Lesser, who was a strong party man. There was a Brigadier General G. Lesser, a technical expert attached to the Fuehrer's headquarters at Smolensk. This man, and there is some evidence that he is the same, was killed in the first battle of Moscow.

QUARTERLY PRÉCIS OF REPORTS
OF AGENT SEVENTEEN

1. Herr Professor Kenrube is working hard on the model. He has at no time expressed bitterness over the enforced cessation of work on the main machine, and apparently accepts readily the explanation that the government cannot afford to allot him material until the model proves the value of his work.

2. The model will have an orifice of six inches. This compares with the ten-foot orifice of the main machine. Kenrube's intention is to employ it for the procuration of liquids, and believes that the model will of itself go far to reducing the oil shortage in the Reich.

3. The machine will be in operation sometime in the summer of 1939. We are all eager and excited.

February 7, 1939

From   Secretary, Bureau of Physics
To   Gestapo
Subject   Secret Six

The following precautions have been taken with the full knowledge and consent of Herr Professor Kenrube:

1. A diary in triplicate is kept of each day's progress. Two copies are sent daily to our office here. As you know, the other copy is submitted by us to your office.

2. Photographs are made of each part of the machine before it is installed, and detailed plans of each part are kept, all in triplicate, the copies distributed as described above.

3. From time to time independent scientists are called in. They are invariably impressed by Kenrube's name, and suspicious of his mathematics and drawings.

For your information, please.

August Buehnen.

March 1, 1939

From   Reich and Prussian Minister of Science
To   Herr Heinrich Himmler, Gestapo
Subject   The great genius, Herr Professor Kenrube

It is my privilege to inform Your Excellency that the world-shaking invention of Herr Professor Johann Kenrube went into operation yesterday, and has already shown fantastic results.

The machine is not a pretty one, and some effort must be made to streamline future reproductions of this model, with an aim toward greater mobility. In its present condition, it is strung out over the floor in a most ungainly fashion. Rough metal can be very ugly.

Its most attractive feature is the control board, which consists of a number of knobs and dials, the operator of which, by an arrangement of mirrors, can peer into the orifice, which is located on the right side of the control board, and faces away from it. (I do not like these awkward names, orifice and hyper-space. We must find a great name for this wonderful machine and its vital parts.)

When Buehnen and I arrived, Professor Kenrube was busy opening and shutting little casements in various parts of that sea of dull metal. He took out and examined various items.

At eleven forty-five, Kenrube stationed himself at the control board, and made a brief speech comparing the locator dials of the board to the dial on a radio which tunes in stations. His dials, however, tuned in planets; and, quite simply, that is what he proceeded to do.

It appears that the same planets are always on exactly the same gradation of the main dial; and the principle extends down through the controls which operate to locate sections of planets. Thus it is always possible to return to any point of any planet. You will see how important this is.

The machine had already undergone its first tests, so Kenrube now proceeded to turn to various planets previously selected; and a fascinating show it was.

Gazing through the six-inch orifice is like looking through a glassless window. What a great moment it will be when the main machine is in operation, and we can *go* through the ten-foot orifice.

The first planet was a desolate, frozen affair, dimly lighted by a remote red sun. It must have been airless because there was a whistling sound, as the air rushed out of our room into that frigid space. Some of that deadly cold came trickling through, and we quickly switched below the surface of the planet.

Fantastic planet! It must be an incredibly heavy world, for it is a treasure house of the heavier metals. Everywhere we turned, the soil formation showed a shifting pattern of gold, silver, zinc, iron, tin—thousands of millions of tons.

At Professor Kenrube's suggestion, I put on a pair of heavy gloves, and removed a four-inch rock of almost pure gold. It simply lay there in a gray shale, but it was so cold that the moisture of the room condensed on it, forming a thick hoarfrost. How many ages that planet must have frozen for the cold to penetrate so far below the surface!

The second planet was a vast expanse of steaming swamps and tropical forests, much as Earth must have been forty million years ago. However, we found not a single trace of animal, insect, reptile, or other non-floral life.

The third, fourth, and fifth planets were devoid of any kind of life, either plant or animal. The sixth planet might have been Earth, except that its green forests, its rolling plains showed no sign of animal or intelligent life. But it is on this planet that oil had been located by Kenrube and Seventeen in their private tests. When I left, a pipeline, previously rigged up, had been attached to the orifice, and was vibrating with oil at the colossal flow speed of nearly one thousand miles per hour.

This immense flow has now been continuous for more than twenty-four hours; and I understand it has already been necessary to convert the great water reservoir in the south suburbs to storage space for oil.

It may be *nouveau riche* to be storing oil at great inconvenience, when the source can be tapped at will. But I personally will not be satisfied until we have a number of these machines in action. It is better to be childish and have the oil than logical and have regrets.

I cannot conceive what could go wrong now. Because of our precautions, we have numerous and complete plans of the machines. It is necessary, of course, to insure that our enemies do not learn our secret, and on this point I would certainly appreciate your most earnest attention.

The enormous potentialities of this marvelous instrument expand with every minute spent in thinking about it. I scarcely slept a wink last night.

March 1, 1939

From   Chief, Criminal Investigation Branch, Gestapo
To   Reich and Prussian Minister of Science
Subject   Secret Six

Will you please inform this office without delay of the name of every scientist or other person who has any knowledge, however meager, of the Kenrube machine?

Reinhard Heydrich.

Author's Note: *This is the Heydrich, handsome, ruthless Heydrich, who in 1941 bloodily repressed the incipient Czech revolt, who, after the notorious Himmler became Minister of the Interior, succeeded his former master as head of the Gestapo, and who was subsequently assassinated.*

March 2, 1939

From   Secretary, Bureau of Physics
To   R. Heydrich
Subject   Secret Six

The list of names for which you asked is herewith attached.

August Buehnen.

A. E. van Vogt

COMMENT AT BOTTOM OF LETTER

In view of the importance of this matter, some changes should be made in the precautionary plan drawn up a few months ago with respect to these personages. Two, not one, of our agents must be assigned to keep secret watch on each of these individuals. The rest of the plan can be continued as arranged with one other exception: In the event that any of these men suspect that they are being watched, I must be informed at once. I am prepared to explain to such person, within limits, the truth of the matter, so that he may not be personally worried. The important thing is we do not want these people suddenly to make a run for the border.

Himmler.

SPECIAL DELIVERY
PERSONAL
From   Reich and Prussian Minister of Science
To   Herr Heinrich Himmler
Subject   Professor Johann Kenrube

I this morning informed the Fuehrer of the Kenrube machine. He became very excited. The news ended his indecision about the Czechs. The army will move to occupy.

For your advance information, please.

March 13, 1939

From   Gestapo
To   Reich and Prussian Minister of Science
Subject   The Dresden Explosion

The incredibly violent explosion of the Kenrube model must be completely explained. A board of discovery should be set up at Dresden with full authority. I must be informed day by day of the findings of this court.

This is a very grim business. Your agent, Seventeen, is among those missing. Kenrube is alive, which is very suspicious. There is no question of arresting him; the only thing that matters is to frustrate future catastrophes of this kind. His machine has proved itself so remarkable that he must be conciliated at all costs until we can be sure that everything is going right.

Let me know *everything*.

Himmler.

PRELIMINARY REPORT OF AUGUST BUEHNEN

When I arrived at the scene of the explosion, I noticed immediately that a solid circle, a remarkably precise circle, of the wall of the fifth floor of the laboratories—where the Kenrube machine is located—had been sliced out as by some inconceivable force.

Examining the edges of this circle, I verified that it could not have been heat which performed so violent an operation. Neither the brick nor the exposed steel was in any way singed or damaged by fire.

The following facts have been given to me of what transpired:

It had been necessary to cut the flow of oil because of the complete absence of further storage space. Seventeen, who was in charge—Professor Kenrube during this whole time was at Gribe Schloss working on the main machine—was laboriously exploring other planets in search of rare metals.

The following is an extract from my interview with Jacob Schmidt, a trusted laboratory assistant in the government service:

Q. You say, Herr————(Seventeen) took a piece of ore to the window to examine it in the light of the sun?
A. He took it to the window, and stood there looking at it.
Q. This placed him directly in front of the orifice of the machine?
A. Yes.
Q. Who else was in front of the orifice?
A. Dobelmanns, Minster, Freyburg, Tousand-friend.
Q. These were all fellow assistants of yours?
A. Yes.
Q. What happened then?
A. There was a very loud click from the machine, followed by a roaring noise.
Q. Was anyone near the control board?
A. No, sir.
Q. It was an automatic action of the machine?
A. Yes. The moment it happened we all turned to face the machine.
Q. All of you? Herr————(Seventeen), too?
A. Yes, he looked around with a start, just as Minster cried out that a blue light was coming from the orifice.
Q. A blue light. What did this blue light replace?
A. A soil formation of a planet, which we had numbered

676

447–711–Gradation A–131–8, which is simply its location on the dials. It was from this soil that Herr———— (Seventeen) had taken the ore sample.

Q. And then, just like that, there was the blue light?

A. Yes. And for a few instants that was all there was, the blue light, the strange roaring sound, and us standing there half paralyzed.

Q. Then it flared forth?

A. It was terrible. It was such an intense blue it hurt my eyes, even though I could only see it in the mirror over the orifice. I have not the faintest impression of heat. But the wall was gone, and all the metal around the orifice.

Q. And the men?

A. Yes, and the men, all five of them.

March 18, 1939

From   Secretary, Bureau of Physics
To   Chief, Science Branch, Gestapo
Subject   Dresden Explosion

I am enclosing a précis of the report of the Court of Inquiry, which has just come to hand. The report will be sent to you as soon as a transcription has been typed.

For your information, please.

August Buehnen

PRÉCIS OF REPORT OF COURT OF INQUIRY

1. It has been established:
   (A) That the destruction was preceded by a clicking sound.
   (B) That this click came from the machine.
   (C) That the machine is fitted with automatic finders.
2. The blue flame was the sole final cause of the destruction.
3. No theory exists, or was offered, to explain the blue light. It should be pointed out that Kenrube was not called to testify.
4. The death of Herr————(Seventeen) and of his assistants was entirely due to the momentary impulse that had placed them in the path of the blue fire.
5. The court finds that the machine could have been tampered with, that the click that preceded the explosion could have been the result of some automatic device previously set to tamper with the machine. No other evidence of sabotage exists, and no one in the room at the time was to blame for the accident.

Secret Unattainable

COPY ONLY
FOR MINISTRY OF SCIENCE   March 19, 1939

From   Major H. L. Guberheit
To   Minister for Air
Subject   Destruction of plane, type JU-88

I have been asked to describe the destruction of a plane under unusual circumstances, as witnessed by several hundred officers and men under my command.

The JU-88, piloted by Cadet Pilot Herman Kiesler, was approaching the runway for a landing, and was at the height of about five hundred feet when there was a flash of intense blue—and the plane vanished.

I cannot express too strongly the violence, the intensity, the blue vastness of the explosion. It was titanic. The sky was alive with light reflections. And though a bright sun was shining, the entire landscape grew brilliant with that blue tint.

There was no sound of explosion. No trace of this machine was subsequently found, no wreckage. The time of the accident was approximately ten-thirty A.M., March 13th.

There has been great uneasiness among the students during the past week.

For your information, please.

H. L. Guberheit
Major, C. Air Station 473

COMMENT AT BOTTOM OF LETTER

Excellency—I wish most urgently to point out that the time of this unnatural accident coincides with the explosion of "blue" light from the orifice of the Kenrube machine.

I have verified that the orifice was tilted ever so slightly upward, and that the angle would place the beam at a height of five hundred feet near the airport in question.

The staggering feature is that the airport referred to is *seventy-five miles* from Dresden. The greatest guns ever developed can scarcely fire that distance, and yet the incredible power of the blue energy showed no diminishment. Literally, it disintegrated metal and flesh—everything.

I do not dare to think what would have happened if that devastating flame had been pointed not away from but at the ground.

Let me have your instructions at once, because here is beyond doubt the weapon of the ages.

August Buehnen

March 19, 1939

From   Chief, Science Branch, Gestapo
To   Reich and Prussian Minister of Science
Subject Secret Six

In perusing the report of the inquiry board, we were amazed to note that Professor Kenrube was not questioned in this matter.

Be assured that there is no intention here of playing up to this man. We absolutely require an explanation from him. Send Herr Buehnen to see Kenrube and instruct him to employ the utmost firmness if necessary.

K. Reissel

March 21, 1939

From   Secretary, Bureau of Physics
To   Chief, Science Branch, Gestapo
Subject Dresden Explosion

As per your request, I talked with Kenrube at Gribe Schloss.

It was the second time I had seen him, the first time being when I accompanied his Excellency, the Minister of Science, to Dresden to view the model; and I think I should point out here that Herr Professor Kenrube's physical appearance is very different from what I had been led to expect from the description recorded in File Secret Six. I had pictured him a lean, fanatic-eyed type. He *is* tall, but he must have gained weight in recent years, for his body is well filled out, and his face and eyes are serene, with graying hair to crown the effect of a fine, scholarly, middle-aged man.

It is unthinkable to me that this is some madman plotting against the Reich.

The first part of his explanation of the blue light was a most curious reference to the reality of mathematics, and, for a moment, I almost thought he was attempting to credit the accident to this *actuality* of his incomprehensible number system.

Then he went on to the more concrete statement that a great star must have intruded into the plane of the planet under examination. The roaring sound that was heard he

679

attributed to the fact that the component elements of the air in the laboratory were being sucked into the sun, and destroyed.

The sun, of course, would be in a state of balance all its own, and therefore would not come into the room until the balance had been interfered with by the air of the room.

(I must say my own explanation would be the reverse of this; that is, the destruction of the air would possibly create a momentary balance, a barrier, during which time nothing of the sun came into the room except light reflections. However, the foregoing is what Kenrube said, and I presume it is based on his own mathematics. I can only offer it for what it is worth.)

Abruptly, the balance broke down. For a fraction of an instant, then, before the model hyper-space machine was destroyed, the intolerable energies of a blue-white sun poured forth.

It would have made no difference if the airplane that was caught in the beam of blue light had been farther away from Dresden than seventy-five miles—that measureless force would have reached seven thousand five hundred miles just as easily, or seventy-five thousand.

The complete absence of visible heat is no evidence that it was not a sun. At forty million degrees Fahrenheit, heat, as we know it, does not exist.

The great man went on to say that he had previously given some thought to the danger from suns, and that in fact he was in the late mathematical stage of developing an attachment that would automatically reject bodies larger than ten thousand miles in diameter.

In his opinion, efforts to control the titanic energies of suns should be left to a later period, and should be carried out on uninhabited planets by scientists who have gone through the orifice and who have been then cut off from contact with earth.

August Buehnen

COMMENT ATTACHED

Kenrube's explanation sounds logical, and it does seem incredible that he would meddle with such forces, though it is significant that the orifice was tilted "slightly upward." We can dispense with his advice as to when and how we should experiment with sun energies. The extent of the danger seems to be a momentary discharge of inconceivable forces, and then destruction of the machine. If at the moment of discharge the orifice was slightly tilted toward London or New York, and if a sufficient crisis existed, the loss of one more machine would be an infinitesimal cost.

As for Kenrube's fine, scholarly appearance, I think Buehnen has allowed himself to be carried away by the greatness of the invention. The democrats of Germany are not necessarily madmen, but here, as abroad, they are our remorseless enemies.

We must endeavor to soften Kenrube by psychological means.

I cannot forget that *there is not now a working model of the Kenrube machine in existence.* Until there is, all the fine, scholarly-looking men in the world will not convince me that what happened was entirely an accident.

The deadly thing about all this is that we have taken an irrevocable step with respect to the Czechs; and war in the west is now inevitable.

Himmler

May 1, 1939

From   Chief, Science Branch, Gestapo.
To   Reich and Prussian Minister of Science
Subject   Secret Six

The Fuehrer has agreed to exonerate completely August Kenrube, the brother of Herr Professor Kenrube. As you will recall, August Kenrube was killed in the sacred purge of June, 1934. It will now be made clear that his death was an untimely accident, and that he was a true German patriot.

This is in line with our psychological attack on Professor Kenrube's suspected anti-Nazism.

K. Reissel.

June 17, 1939

From   Secretary, Bureau of Physics
To   Chief, Science Branch, Gestapo
Subject   Professor Johann Kenrube

In line with our policy to make Kenrube realize his oneness with the community of German peoples, I had him address the convention of mathematicians. The speech, of which I enclose a copy, was a model one; three thousand words of glowing generalities, giving not a hint as to his true opinions on anything. However, he received the ovation of his life; and I think he was pleased in spite of himself.

Afterward, I saw to it—without, of course, appearing directly—that he was introduced to Fräulein Ilse Weber.

As you know, the Fräulein is university-educated, a mature, modern young woman; and I am sure that she is merely taking on one of the many facets of her character in posing to Kenrube as a young woman who has decided quite calmly to have a child, and desires the father to be biologically of the highest type.

I cannot see how any human male, normal or abnormal, could resist the appeal of Fräulein Weber.

August Buehnen.

July 11, 1939

From   Chief, Science Branch, Gestapo
To   Secretary, Bureau of Physics
Subject   Secret Six

Can you give me some idea when the Kenrube machine will be ready to operate? What about the duplicate machines which we agreed verbally would be built without Kenrube's knowledge? Great decisions are being made. Conversations are being conducted that will shock the world, and, in a general way, the leaders are relying on the Kenrube machine.

In this connection please submit as your own some variation of the following memorandum. It is from the Fuehrer himself, and therefore I need not stress its urgency.

K. Reissel.

MEMORANDUM OF ADOLF HITLER

Is it possible to tune the Kenrube machine to our own earth?

July 28, 1939

From   Secretary, Bureau of Physics
To   Chief, Science Branch, Gestapo
Subject   Secret Six

I enclose the following note from Kenrube, which is self-explanatory. We have retained a copy.

August Buehnen

A. E. van Vogt

Dear Herr Buehnen:

The answer to your memorandum is yes.

In view of the international anxieties of the times, I offer the following suggestions as to weapons that can be devised from the hyper-space machine:

1. Any warship can be rendered noncombatant at critical moments by draining of its oil tanks.

2. Similarly, enemy oil-storage supplies can be drained at vital points. Other supplies can be blown up or, if combustible, set afire.

3. Troops, tanks, trucks, and all movable war materials can be transported to any point on the globe, behind enemy lines, into cities, by the simple act of focusing the orifice at the desired destination—and driving it and them through. I need scarcely point out that my machine renders railway and steamship transport obsolete: The world shall be transformed.

4. It might even be possible to develop a highly malleable, delicately adjusted machine, which can drain the tanks of airplanes in full flight.

5. Other possibilities, too numerous to mention, suggest themselves with the foregoing as a basis.

Kenrube.

COMMENT ATTACHED

This machine is like a dream. With it, the world is ours, for what conceivable combination of enemies could fight an army that appeared from nowhere on their flank, in the centers of their cities, in London, New York, in the Middle-West plains of America, in the Ural Mountains, in the Caucasus? Who can resist us?

K. Reissel.

ADDITIONAL COMMENT

My dear Reissel:

Your enthusiasm overlooks the fact that the machine is still only in the building stage. What worries me is that our hopes are being raised to a feverish height—what greater revenge could there be than to lift us to the ultimate peak of confidence, and then smash it in a single blow?

Every day that passes we are involving ourselves more deeply, decisions are being made from which there is already no turning back. When, oh, when will this machine be finished?

H.

July 29, 1939

From   Secretary, Bureau of Physics
To   Chief, Science Branch, Gestapo
Subject Secret Six

The hyper-space machine at Gribe Schloss will be completed in February, 1941. No less than five duplicate machines are under construction, unknown to Kenrube. What is done is that, when he orders an installation for the Gribe Schloss machine, the factory turns out five additional units from the same plans.

In addition, a dozen model machines are being secretly constructed from the old plans, but, as they must be built entirely from drawings and photographs, they will take not less, but more, time to build than the larger machines.

August Buehnen

August 2, 1939

From   Secretary, Bureau of Physics
To   Herr Heinrich Himmler
Subject Professor Johann Kenrube

I have just now received a telegram from Fräulein Ilse Weber that she and the Herr Professor were married this morning, and that Kenrube will be a family man by the middle of next summer.

August Buehnen

COMMENT WRITTEN BELOW

This is great news indeed. One of the most dangerous aspects of the Kenrube affair was that he was a bachelor without ties. Now, we have him. He has committed himself to the future.

Himmler.

A. E. van Vogt

I have advised the Fuehrer, and our great armies will move into Poland at the end of this month.

H.

August 8, 1939

From Gestapo
To   Reich and Prussian Minister of Science
Subject Secret Six

I have had second thought on the matter of Fräulein Ilse Weber, now Frau Kenrube. In view of the fact that a woman, no matter how intelligent or objective, becomes emotionally involved with the man who is the father of her children, I would advise that Frau Kenrube be appointed to some great executive post in a war industry. This will keep her own patriotism at a high level, and thus she will continue to have exemplary influence on her husband. Such influence cannot be overestimated.

Himmler.

January 3, 1940

From Secretary, Bureau of Physics
To   Chief, Science Branch, Gestapo

In glancing through the correspondence, I notice that I have neglected to inform you that our Agent Twelve has replaced Seventeen as Kenrube's chief assistant.

Twelve is a graduate of Munich, and was for a time attached to the General Staff in Berlin as a technical expert.

In my opinion, he is a better man for our purpose than was Seventeen, in that Seventeen, it seemed to me, had toward the end a tendency to associate himself with Kenrube in what might be called a scientific comradeship, an intellectual fellowship. He was in a mental condition where he quite unconsciously defended Kenrube against our suspicion.

Such a situation will not arise with Twelve. He is a practical man to the marrow. He and Kenrube have nothing in common.

Kenrube accepted Twelve with an attitude of what-does-it-matter-who-they-send. It was so noticeable that it is now clear that he is aware that these men are agents of ours.

Unless Kenrube has some plan of revenge which is beyond

all precautions, the knowledge that he is being watched should exercise a restraint on any impulses to evil that he may have.

August Buehnen.

Author's Note: *Most of the letters written in the year 1940 were of a routine nature, consisting largely of detailed reports as to the progress of the machine. The following document, however, was an exception:*

December 17, 1940

From   Reich and Prussian Minister of Science
To   Herr Heinrich Himmler
Subject   Secret Six

The following work has now been completed on the fortress Gribe Schloss, where the Kenrube machine is nearing completion:

1. Steel doors have been fitted throughout.

2. A special, all-steel chamber has been constructed from which, by an arrangement of mirrors, the orifice of the machine can be watched without danger to the watchers.

3. This watching post is only twenty steps from a paved road which runs straight up out of the valley.

4. A concrete pipeline for the transportation of oil is nearing completion.

August Buehnen.

MEMO AT BOTTOM OF LETTER

To Reinhard Heydrich:

Please make arrangements for me to inspect personally the reconstructed Gribe Schloss. It is Hitler's intention to attend the official opening.

The plan now is to invade England via the Kenrube machine possibly in March, not later than April. In view of the confusion that will follow the appearance of vast armies in every part of the country, this phase of the battle of Europe should be completed by the end of April.

In May, Russia will be invaded. This should not require more than two months. The invasion of the United States is set for July or August.

Himmler.

A. E. van Vogt

January 31, 1941

From   Secretary, Bureau of Physics
To   Chief, Science Branch, Gestapo
Subject   Secret Six

It will be impossible to complete the five extra Kenrube machines at the same time as the machine at Gribe Schloss. Kenrube has changed some of the designs, and our engineers do not know how to fit the sections together until they have studied Kenrube's method of connection.

I have personally asked Kenrube the reason for the changes. His answer was that he was remedying weaknesses that he had noticed in the model. I am afraid that we shall have to be satisfied with this explanation, and complete the duplicate machines after the official opening, which is not now scheduled until March 20th. The delay is due to Kenrube's experimentation with design.

If you have any suggestions, please let me hear them. I frankly do not like this delay, but what to do about it is another matter.

August Buehnen.

February 3, 1941

From   Chief, Science Branch, Gestapo
To   Secretary, Bureau of Physics
Subject   Secret Six

Himmler says to do nothing. He notes that you are still taking the precaution of daily photographs, and that your agent, Twelve, who replaced Seventeen, is keeping a diary in triplicate.

There has been a meeting of leaders, and this whole matter discussed very thoroughly, with special emphasis on critical analysis of the precautions taken, and of the situation that would exist if Kenrube should prove to be planning some queer revenge.

You will be happy to know that not a single additional precaution was thought of, and that our handling of the affair was commended.

K. Reissel.

687

February 18, 1941

From   Gestapo
To   Reich and Prussian Minister of Science
Subject   Secret Six

In view of our anxieties, the following information, which I have just received, will be welcome:

Frau Kenrube, formerly our Ilse Weber, has reserved a private room in the maternity ward of the Prussian State Hospital for May 7th. This will be her second child, another hostage to fortune by Kenrube.

K. Reissel.

COPY ONLY
MEMO   March 11, 1941

I have today examined Gribe Schloss and environs and found everything according to plan.

Himmler

March 14, 1941

From   Secretary, Bureau of Physics
To   Herr Himmler, Gestapo
Subject   Secret Six

You will be relieved to know the reason for the changes in design made by Kenrube.

The first reason is rather unimportant. Kenrube refers to the mathematical structure involved, and states that, for his own elucidation, he designed a functional instrument whose sole purpose was to defeat the mathematical reality of the machine. This is very obscure, but he had referred to it before, so I call it to your attention.

The second reason is that there are now two orifices, not one. The additional orifice is for focusing. The following illustration will clarify what I mean:

Suppose we have a hundred thousand trucks in Berlin, which we wished to transfer to London. Under the old method, these trucks would have to be driven all the way to the Gribe Schloss before they could be transmitted.

With the new two-orifice machine, one orifice would be focused in Berlin, the other in London. The trucks would drive through from Berlin to London.

Herr Professor Kenrube seems to anticipate our needs before we realize them ourselves.

August Buehnen.

March 16, 1941

From   Gestapo
To   Secretary, Bureau of Physics
Subject Secret Six

The last sentence of your letter of March 14th to the effect that Kenrube seems to anticipate our needs made me very uncomfortable, because the thought that follows naturally is: Is he also anticipating our plans?

I have accordingly decided at this eleventh hour that we are dealing with a man who may be our intellectual superior in every way. Have your agent advise us the moment the machine has undergone its initial tests. Decisive steps will be taken immediately.

Himmler.

March 19, 1941

DECODED TELEGRAM

KENRUBE MACHINE WAS TESTED TODAY AND WORKED PER-FECTLY.

AGENT TWELVE.

COPY ONLY
MEMO   March 19, 1941

To Herr Himmler:

This is to advise that Professor Johann Kenrube was placed under close arrest, and has been removed to Gestapo Headquarters, Berlin.

R. Heydrich.

March 19, 1941

DECODED TELEGRAM

REPLYING TO YOUR TELEPHONE INSTRUCTIONS, WISH TO STATE ALL AUTOMATIC DEVICES HAVE BEEN REMOVED FROM KENRUBE MACHINE. NONE SEEMED TO HAVE BEEN TAMPERED WITH. MADE PERSONAL TEST OF MACHINE. IT WORKED PERFECTLY.

TWELVE

COMMENT WRITTEN BELOW

I shall recommend that Kenrube be retired under guard to his private laboratories, and not allowed near a hyperspace machine until after the conquest of the United States.

And with this, I find myself at a loss for further precautions. In my opinion, all thinkable possibilities have been covered. The only dangerous man has been removed from the zone where he can be actively dangerous; a careful examination has been made to ascertain that he has left no automatic devices that will cause havoc. And, even if he has, five other large machines and a dozen small ones are nearing completion, and it is impossible that he can have tampered with them.

If anything goes wrong now, thoroughness is a meaningless word.

Himmler.

March 21, 1941

From   Gestapo
To   Secretary, Bureau of Physics
Subject   Secret Six

Recriminations are useless. What I would like to know is: What in God's name happened?

Himmler.

March 22, 1941

From   Secretary, Bureau of Physics
To   Herr Heinrich Himmler
Subject   Secret Six

The reply to your question is being prepared. The great trouble is the confusion among the witnesses, but it should not be long before some kind of coherent reply is ready.

Work is being rushed to complete the duplicate machines on the basis of photographs and plans that were made from day to day. I cannot see how anything can be wrong in the long run.

As for Number One, shall we send planes over with bombs?

August Buehnen.

COPY ONLY
MEMO   March 23, 1941
From   Detention Branch, Gestapo

The four agents, Gestner, Luslich, Heinreide, and Muemmer, who were guarding Herr Professor Johann Kenrube report that he was under close arrest at our Berlin headquarters until six P.M., March 21st. At six P.M., he abruptly vanished.

S. Duerner

COMMENT WRITTEN BELOW

Kenrube was at Gribe Schloss before two P.M., March 21st. This completely nullifies the six-P.M. story. Place these scoundrels under arrest, and bring them before me at eight o'clock tonight.

Himmler

COPY ONLY

EXAMINATION BY HERR HIMMLER OF F. GESTNER

Q. Your name?

A. Gestner. Fritz Gestner. Long service.

Q. Silence. If we want to know your service, we'll check it in the record.

A. Yes, sir.

Q. That's a final warning. You answer my questions, or I'll have your tongue.

A. Yes, sir.

Q. You're one of the stupid fools set to guard Kenrube?

A. I was one of the four guards, sir.

Q. Answer yes or no.

A. Yes, sir.

Q. What was your method of guarding Kenrube?

A. By twos. Two of us at a time were in the great white cell with him.

Q. Why weren't the four of you there?

A. We thought—

Q. You thought! Four men were ordered to guard Kenrube and—By God, there'll be dead men around here before this night is over. I want to get this clear: There was never a moment when two of you were not in the cell with Kenrube?

A. Always two of us.

Q. Which two were with Kenrube at the moment he disappeared?

A. I was. I and Johann Luslich.

Q. Oh, you know Luslich by his first name. An old friend of yours, I suppose?

A. No, sir.

Q. You knew Luslich previously, though?

A. I met him for the first time when we were assigned to guard Herr Kenrube.

Q. Silence! Answer yes or no. I've warned you about that.

A. Yes, sir.

Q. Ah, you admit knowing him?

A. No, sir. I meant—

Q. Look here, Gestner, you're in a very bad spot. Your story is a falsehood on the face of it. Tell me the truth. Who are your accomplices?

A. None, sir.

Q. You mean you were working this alone?

A. No, sir.

Q. You damned liar! Gestner, we'll get the truth out of you if we have to tear you apart.

A. I am telling the truth, Excellency.

Q. Silence, you scum. What time did you say Kenrube disappeared?

A. About six o'clock.

Q. Oh, he did, eh? Well, never mind that. What was Kenrube doing just before he vanished?

A. He was talking to Luslich and me.

Q. What right had you to talk to the prisoner?

A. Sir, he mentioned an accident he expected to happen at some official opening somewhere.

Q. He what?

A. Yes, sir; and I was desperately trying to find out where, so that I could send a warning.

Q. Now, the truth is coming. So you do know about this business, you lying rat! Well, let's have the story you've rigged up.

A. The dictaphone will bear out every word.

Q. Oh, the dictaphone was on.

A. Every word is recorded.

Q. Oh, why wasn't I told about this in the first place?

A. You wouldn't lis—

Q. Silence, you fool! By God, the coöperation I get around this place. Never mind. Just what was Kenrube doing at the moment he disappeared?

A. He was sitting—talking.

Q. Sitting? You'll swear to that?

A. To the Fuehrer himself.

Q. He didn't move from his chair? He didn't walk over to an orifice?

A. I don't know what you mean, Excellency.

Q. So you pretend, anyway. But that's all for the time being. You will remain under arrest. Don't think we're through with you. That goes also for the others.

AUTHOR'S NOTE:
The baffled fury expressed by the normally calm Himmler in this interview is one indication of the dazed bewilderment that raged through high Nazi circles. One can imagine the accusation and counter-accusation and then the slow, deadly realization of the situation.

March 24, 1941

From   Reich and Prussian Minister of Science
To   Gestapo
Subject   Secret Six

Enclosed is the transcription of a dictaphone record which was made by Professor Kenrube. A careful study of these deliberate words, combined with what he said at Gribe Schloss, may reveal his true purpose, and may also explain the incredible thing that happened.

I am anxiously awaiting your full report.

Himmler.

TRANSCRIPTION OF DICTAPHONE RECORD P–679–423–1; CONVERSATION OF PROFESSOR JOHANN KENRUBE IN WHITE CELL 26, ON 3/21/41.

(Note: K. refers to Kenrube, G. to any of the guards.)

K. A glass of water, young man.

G. I believe there is no objection to that. Here.

K. It must be after five.

G. There is no necessity for you to know the time.

K. No, but the fact that it is late is very interesting. You see, I have invented a machine. A very queer machine it is going to seem when it starts to react according to the laws of real as distinct from functional mathematics. You have the dictaphone on, I hope?

G. What kind of a smart remark is that?

K. Young man, that dictaphone had better be on. I intend talking about my invention, and your masters will skin you alive if it's not recorded. Is the dictaphone on?

G. Oh, I suppose so.

K. Good. I may be able to finish what I have to say. I may not.

G. Don't worry. You'll be here to finish it. Take your time.

K. I had the idea before my brother was killed in the purge, but I thought of the problem then as one of education. Afterward, I saw it as revenge. I hated the Nazis and all they stood for.

G. Oh, you did, eh? Go on.

K. My plan after my brother's murder was to build for the Nazis the greatest weapon the world will ever know, and then have them discover that only I, who understood and who accordingly *fitted in* with the immutable laws involved—only I could ever operate the machine. And I would have to be present physically. That way I would prove my indispensability and so transform the entire world to my way of thinking.

G. We've got ways of making indispensables work.

K. Oh, that part is past. I've discovered what is going to happen—to me as well as to my invention.

G. Plenty is going to happen to you. You've already talked yourself into a concentration camp.

K. After I discovered that, my main purpose was simplified. I wanted to do the preliminary work on the machine and, naturally, I had to do that under the prevailing system of government—by cunning and misrepresentation. I had no fear that any of the precautions they were so laboriously taking would give them the use of the machine, not this year, not this generation, not ever. The machine simply cannot be used by people who think as they do. For instance, the model that—

G. Model! What are you talking about?

K. Silence, please. I am anxious to clarify for the dictaphone what will seem obscure enough under any circumstances. The reason the model worked perfectly was because I fitted in mentally and physically. Even after I left, it continued to carry out the task I had set it, but as soon as Herr————(Seventeen) made a change, it began to yield to other pressures. The accident—

G. Accident!

K. Will you shut up? Can't you see that I am trying to give information for the benefit of future generations? I have no desire that my secret be lost. The whole thing is in understanding. The mechanical part is only half the means. The mental approach is indispensable. Even Herr———(Seventeen), who was beginning to be *sympathique,* could not keep the machine sane for more than an hour. His death, of course, was inevitable, whether it looked like an accident or not.

G. Whose death?

K. What it boils down to is this. My invention does not fit into our civilization. It's *the next,* the coming age of man. Just as modern science could not develop in ancient Egypt because the whole mental, emotional, and physical attitude was wrong, so my machine cannot be used until the thought structure of man changes. Your masters will have some further facts soon to bear me out.

G. Look! You said something before about something happening. What?

K. I've just been telling you: I don't know. The law of averages says it won't be another sun, but there are a thousand deadly things that can happen. When Nature's gears snag, no imaginable horror can match the result.

G. But something is going to happen?

K. I really expected it before this. The official opening was set for half-past one. Of course, it doesn't really matter. If it doesn't happen today, it will take place tomorrow.

G. Official opening! You mean an accident is going to happen at some official opening?

K. Yes, and my body will be *attracted.* I—

G. What—Good God! He's gone!

(Confusion. Voices no longer audible.)

March 25, 1941

From   Reich and Prussian Minister of Science
To   Herr Himmler
Subject   Destruction of Gribe Schloss

The report is still not ready. As you were not present, I have asked the journalist, Polermann, who was with Hitler, to write a description of the scene. His account is enclosed with the first page omitted.

You will note that in a number of paragraphs he reveals incomplete knowledge of the basic situation, but except for this, his story is, I believe, the most accurate we have.

The first page of his article was inadvertently destroyed.
It was simply a preliminary.

For your information.

DESCRIPTION OF DESTRUCTION OF GRIBE SCHLOSS, BY HERR PO-
LERMANN

—The first planet came in an unexpected fashion. I realized that as I saw Herr———(Twelve) make some hasty
adjustments on one of his dials.

Still dissatisfied, he connected a telephone plug into a
socket somewhere in his weird-looking asbestos suit, thus
establishing telephone communication with the Minister of
Science, who was in the steel enclosure with us. I heard His
Excellency's reply:

"Night! Well, I suppose it has to be night some time on
other planets. You're not sure it's the same planet? I imagine
the darkness is confusing."

It was. In the mirror, the night visible through the orifice
showed a bleak, gray, luminous landscape, incredibly eerie
and remote, an unnatural world of curious shadows, and not
a sign of movement anywhere.

And that, after an instant, struck us all with an appalling
effect, the dark consciousness of that great planet, swinging
somewhere around a distant sun, an uninhabited waste, a
lonely reminder that life is rarer than death in the vast
universe. Herr———(Twelve) made an adjustment on a dial;
and, instantly, the great orifice showed that we were seeing
the interior of the planet. A spotlight switched on, and picked
out a solid line of red earth that slowly, as the dial turned,
became clay; then a rock stratum came into view, and was
held in focus.

An asbestos-clothed assistant of Herr———(Twelve) dis-
lodged a piece of rock with a pick. He lifted it, and started
to bring it toward the steel enclosure, apparently for the
Fuehrer's inspection.

And abruptly vanished.

We blinked our eyes. But he was gone, and the rock with
him. Herr———(Twelve) switched on his telephone hurriedly. There was a consultation, in which the Fuehrer participated. The decision finally was that it has been a mistake
to examine a doubtful planet, and that the accident had hap-

pened because the rock had been removed. Accordingly, no further effort would be made to remove anything.

Regret was expressed by the Fuehrer that the brave assistant should have suffered such a mysterious fate.

We resumed our observant positions, more alert now, conscious of what a monstrous instrument was here before our eyes. A man whisked completely out of our space simply because he had touched a rock from a planet in hyper-space.

The second planet was also dark. At first it, too, looked a barren world, enveloped in night; and then—wonder. Against the dark, towering background of a great hill, a city grew. It spread along the shore of a moonlit sea, ablaze with ten million lights. It clung there for a moment, a crystalline city, alive with brilliant streets. Then it faded. Swiftly it happened. The lights seemed literally to slide off into the luminous sea. For a moment, the black outline of the city remained, then that, too, vanished into the shadows. Astoundingly, the hill that had formed an imposing background for splendor, distorted like a picture out of focus, and was gone with the city.

A flat, night-wrapped beach spread where a moment before there had been a world of lights, a city of another planet, the answer to ten million questions about life on other worlds—gone like a secret wind into the darkness.

It was plain to see that the test, the opening, was not according to schedule. Once more, Herr———(Twelve) spoke through the telephone to His Excellency, the Minister of Science.

His Excellency turned to the Fuehrer, and said, "He states that he appears to have no control over the order of appearance. Not once has he been able to tune in a planet which he had previously selected to show you."

There was another consultation. It was decided that this second planet, though it had reacted in an abnormal manner, had not actually proved dangerous. Therefore, one more attempt would be made. No sooner was this decision arrived at, than there was a very distinctly audible click from the machine. And, though we did not realize it immediately, the catastrophe was upon us.

I cannot describe the queer loudness of that clicking from the machine. It was not a metallic noise. I have since been informed that only an enormous snapping of energy in motion could have made that unusual, unsettling sound.

My own sense of uneasiness was quickened by the sight of Herr————(Twelve) frantically twisting dials. But nothing happened for a few seconds. The planet on which we had seen the city continued to hold steady in the orifice. The darkened beach spread there in the half-light shed by a moon we couldn't see. And then—

A figure appeared in the orifice. I cannot recall all my emotions at the sight of that manlike being. There was a wild thought that here was some supercreature who, dissatisfied with the accidents he had so far caused us, was now come to complete our destruction. That thought ended as the figure came out onto the floor and one of the assistants swung a spotlight on him. The light revealed him as a tall, well-built, handsome man, dressed in ordinary clothes.

Beside me, I heard someone exclaim: "Why, it's Professor Kenrube!"

For most of those present, everything must have, in that instant, been clear. I, however, did not learn until later that Kenrube was one of the scientists assigned to assist Herr————(Twelve) in building the machine, and that he turned out to be a traitor. He was suspected in the destruction of an earlier model, but as there was no evidence and the suspicion not very strong, he was permitted to continue his work.

Suspicion had arisen again a few days previously, and he had been confined to his quarters, from whence, apparently, he had now come forth to make sure that his skillful tampering with the machine had worked out. This, then, was the man who stood before us. My impression was that he should not have been allowed to utter his blasphemies, but I understand the leaders were anxious to learn the extent of his infamy, and thought he might reveal it in his speech. Although I do not profess to understand the gibberish, I have a very clear memory of what was said, and set it down here for what it is worth.

Kenrube began: "I have no idea how much time I have, and as I was unable to explain clearly to the dictaphone all that I had to say, I must try to finish here." He went on, "I am not thinking now in terms of revenge, though God knows my brother was very dear to me. But I want the world to know the way of this invention."

The poor fool seemed to be laboring under the impression that the machine was his. I did not, and do not understand his reference to a dictaphone. Kenrube went on:

"My first inkling came through psychology, the result of meditating on the manner in which the soil of different parts of the earth influences the race that lives there. This race-product was always more than simply the end-shape of a seacoast, or a plains, or a mountain environment. Somehow, beneath adaptations, peculiar and unsuspected relationships existed between the proper ties of matter and the phenomena of life. And so my search was born. The idea of revenge came later.

"I might say that in all history there has never been a revenge as complete as mine. Here is your machine. It is all there; yours to use for any purpose—provided you first change your mode of thinking to conform to the reality of the relationship between matter and life.

"I have no doubt you can build a thousand duplicates, but beware—every machine will be a Frankenstein monster. Some of them will distort time, as seems to have happened in the time of my arrival here. Others will feed you raw material that will vanish even as you reach forth to seize it. Still others will pour obscene things into our green earth; and others will blaze with terrible energies, but you will never know what is coming, you will never satisfy a single desire.

"You may wonder why everything will go wrong. Herr— ——(Twelve) has, I am sure, been able to make brief, successful tests. That will be the result of my earlier presence, and will not recur now that so many alien presences have affected its—sanity!

"It is not that the machine has will. It reacts to laws, which you must learn, and in the learning it will reshape your minds, your outlook on life. It will change the world. Long before that, of course, the Nazis will be destroyed. They have taken irrevocable steps that will insure their destruction.

"Revenge! Yes, I have it in the only way that a decent human being could desire it. I ask any reasonable being how else these murderers could be wiped from the face of the earth, except by other nations, who would never act until *they* had acted first?

"I have only the vaguest idea what the machine will do with me—it matters not. But I should like to ask you, my great Fuehrer, one question: Where now will you obtain your raw material?"

He must have timed it exactly. For, as he finished, his

figure dimmed. Dimmed! How else describe the blur that his body became? And he was gone, merged with the matter with which, he claimed, his life force was attuned.

The madman had one more devastating surprise for us. The dark planet, from which the city had disappeared, was abruptly gone from the orifice. In its place appeared another dark world. As our vision grew accustomed to this new night, we saw that this was a world of restless water; to the remote, dim horizon was a blue-black, heaving sea. The machine switched below the surface. It must have been at least ten hellish miles below it, judging from the pressure, I have since been informed.

There was a roar that seemed to shake the earth.

Only those who were with the Fuehrer in the steel room succeeded in escaping. Twenty feet away a great army truck stood with engines churning—it was not the first time that I was thankful that some car engines are always left running wherever the Fuehrer is present.

The water swelled and surged around our wheels as we raced up the newly paved road, straight up out of the valley. It was touch-and-go. We looked back in sheer horror. Never in the world has there been such a titanic torrent, such a whirlpool.

The water rose four hundred feet in minutes, threatened to overflow the valley sides, and then struck a balance. The great new river is still there, raging toward the Eastern Sea.

Author's Note: This is not quite the end of the file. A few more letters exist, but it is unwise to print more, as it might be possible for the GPU to trace the individual who actually removed the file Secret Six from its cabinet.

It is scarcely necessary to point out that we subsequently saw the answer that Hitler made to Professor Kenrube's question: "Where now will you obtain your raw material?"

On June 22nd, three months almost to the day after the destruction of Gribe Schloss, the Nazis began their desperate invasion of Russia. By the end of 1941, their diplomacy bankrupt, they were at war with the United States.

Born in 1939, Barry Malzberg has published over thirty sf books since he first entered the genre in 1967. Many of these have used the conventions of science fiction to explore the fears and alienation of twentieth-century humans, and some of them have been among the most controversial (and the best) in the history of the field. Particularly outstanding are Guernica Night *(1974),* Herovits World *(1973), the award-winning* Beyond Apollo *(1972), and* The Falling Astronauts *(1971).*

"After the Great Space War" (from the original anthology Alternities, *1974) captures several of his major themes, and all of the special qualities that make his work unique and important.*

AFTER THE GREAT SPACE WAR

By Barry N. Malzberg

Gents:

Well, here I am in the heart of the Rigelian System, a fine, spacious system indeed, composed of binary stars and a veritable forest of planets and a lovely little planet you have picked, most suitable indeed for conquest, with delicately purple-hued natives who talk in musical scat (whop-a-bee-ba; a-whop-a-dee-*doo*) and whisper about the hedges of their world like birds: as you see, there is no xenophobia in my analyses and the warnings and accusations at the time of embarkment (embarkation?) were *totally* unfair. I *love* being an interstellar scout and am much cheered by the Rigelian System, finding these natives endlessly resourceful and amusing even though our contact has thus far been tentative and I have been able to map out only a little of their language with the inductive devices, making communication somewhat hesitant. Evenings I spend in this capsule spreading out against the sky like an operating table; mornings and afternoons I stroll through the forests of this planet, joshing with the natives monosyllabically (a-ba-*boo*-dup) and handing out the very fine supply of interstellar trinkets with which I was so thoughtfully equipped. These simple-minded inhabitants are delighted with them.

Assignment, in short, proceeds with ease and fluency, fluency and ease, and I make it that I should be ready to summon the landing fleet within a shift or three; in the meantime I continue to win their confidence. They seem to think that I am one of their local gods made manifest and although I recall the problems with this reaction against which we have been warned (riot, desolation, flood, reversion to barbarism) am sure that can handle this as have handled everything else. There is something called the Ceremony of Hinges (very approximate translation of their scat but the best I can do at this time) which they would like me to join but if you do not mind, if you do not mind, I think that I will pass this up. For the time being. The last ceremonial, three planets ago as you will recall, gave me an extremely bad cold and moderate feelings of insufficiency which I have yet to entirely overcome.

Wilson

PARTICIPATE IN SO-CALLED CEREMONY OF HINGES. VITAL AT ALL COSTS THAT INTEGRATION WITH THE SUBGROUP PROCEED ON NATURAL LINES. CEREMONY IS PROBABLY PART OF IMPORTANT RITUAL AND INVITATION THEY EXTEND MEANS THEIR CONFIDENCE IS WON. DO NOT HOLD BACK WILSON WE WILL HAVE NO REPETITION OF PAST DIFFICULTIES TO WHICH OF COURSE THERE IS NO NECESSITY TO REFER IN THIS TRANSMISSION.

HEADQUARTERS

Barry N. Malzberg

Headquarters:

Yes, gents, I do understand and am not making waves. Really I am not (realize the circumstances of the probation on which I have been placed, a matter of which to quote your own approach I see no necessity to refer in this transmission) but it is not, *not* xenophobia which makes me reluctant to participate in the Ceremony of Hinges but merely a certain shy reluctance, a demureness of the spirit if you will. How can I explain this *je ne sais quoi?* How do I know the material of the ceremony? They turn aside my queries. (The translation is indeed rough, certainly the naming gives no clue. Hinges. *Hinges?*) Am willing to move on straightway with honesty and guile alternating in the best tradition of the interstellar scout with steadfastness and dependability predominating but are you really sure that you want me to do this? The sky is a lovely azure (I asure you of this) and pastel blue like the eyes of my many loves during their days and red at night on a sixteen-hour time cycle and the sound of their voices fills the pleasant glade in which I have landed with music at all times. I am happy here, gents, happy and I *love* the natives and accept the circumstances but do you really think that this is worth the risks?

Come now: what does the Ceremony of Hinges have to do with our plans of conquest? I think that the landing fleet should be called in *now*, right now in fact, but await as always your advice even though I feel that our relationship has not quite reached and I am beginning to fear may never quite reach that mutuality of understanding for which *I*, fellows, have striven from the very first. I remind you that the majority of the embarrassing difficulties to which, delicately, neither of us cares to refer have been caused by the sincerity of my attempts to live up to what I take your own wishes to be. I have *tried.* I have tried so hard.

Wilson

YOU POOR FOOL YOU ARE WASTING YOUR TIME AND OURS. WE ARE IN A POSITION OF MAXIMUM OBSERVATION AND IMMINENCE SUSTAINED ONLY AT GREAT EXPENSE. PARTICIPATE IN THE CEREMONY IMMEDIATELY DO YOU GET THAT PARTICIPATE IN THE CEREMONY IMMEDIATELY AT WHICH POINT OUR SOCIOPATHOLOGISTS HAVE CALCULATED YOU WILL HAVE REACHED THE OPTIMUM INTEGRATION AND CAN BE MOST USEFULLY APPLIED WHEN THE LANDING IS ACCOMPLISHED. CUT IT OUT WILSON WE WILL NOT

TOLERATE MUCH MORE OF THIS. ACCOMPLISH A MODAL INFARC-
TION.

HQ

Friends:

Modal infarction?

Well, you see men, I don't *want* to participate in the Ceremony of Hinges. Has not that already become clear? Since
our last talk, furthermore, I have come into new and somewhat ominous indications as the translation machinery
moves on apace that it, the Ceremony that is, may be a birth
ritual of some kind or perhaps a reconstitution of one's history
in which the participant is stuffed with local herbs and additives and passed through living *flame.* I do not know if I
can survive this even though their purposes do appear benign.

Listen, I am not xenophobic. I love *all* aliens and am prepared to love these too, caring ever more deeply about optimum performance of my job which as you know is rapidly
approaching tenure guaranteeing promotion, probation or
not, and want to make as few problems as possible, but are
you sure, I am are you really sure that you want going ahead
with this particular Ceremony?

Listen, I believe that I have *already* won their confidence.
They are now bringing *me* gifts, local plants and animals
somewhat indistinguishable from the natives themselves virtually ring my little capsule and we chatter and reminisce
through the bulkheads nightly. (Wa-ba-ba-beep; la-lo-*ka*.) I
think that it is now time to bring down the landing party.
Modal infarctions, whatever they might be, are fine, I am
willing to dedicate my *life* to the principles of m.i. but is it
really called for at this time? My life, that is to say. Think
about this friends; I certainly have value at the HQ, even
more value than to my humble self considering the training
and warnings that have been invested in me, and I do not
think that the m.i. is suitable at this time.

Perhaps you ought to land before they make the Ceremony
of Hinges a test of my true sincerity and worth to them which
so far they are not. They are not ordering me to participate.
May I repeat this? They are *not* ordering me to participate,
merely wistfully requesting it in the way that I wistfully
requested this one last assignment to prove my good faith
and credentials and then proceeded as you can see to carry

off said assignment with great success for indeed and you must believe this now, indeed they do love me.

Let me handle this my way. I can explain that our metabolism will not permit us to accommodate the preparatory herbs and additives and while they are bemusedly considering this the landing parties can come in with the incinerative gear and do the job roundly.

As a matter of fact, let's send them in right now. Leave the apologies and explanations to me; I will handle my part of the bargain and you will handle yours. Now strikes me as an excellent time to send them in.

Do not be winsome, gents, or fail me at this hour of great need. I am counting upon you. Send the fleet in.

Wilson

YOU ARE TO PARTICIPATE IN THE CEREMONY OF HINGES AND AT ONCE.

YOU FOOL THIS IS A WORLD AT STAKE WHO DO YOU THINK YOU ARE TO JEOPARDIZE THE CONQUEST OF A WORLD AS VALUABLE AS THIS COULD BE. AS THE REPORTS ALSO INDICATE WE DO NOT TAKE ANY RISKS OR CHANCES. WILSON THE SCOUT IS THE ONE WHO IS EXPENDABLE IN CIRCUMSTANCES LIKE THIS. THE SCOUT IS EXPENDABLE. YOU KNEW THAT AND IT IS THAT CONDITION UNDER WHICH YOU HAVE WORKED AND IT IS TIME FOR YOU TO ACCEPT THE RESPONSIBILITIES OF THE ASSIGNMENT WHICH YOU ARE REMINDED YOU BEGGED AS ONE LAST CHANCE TO PROVE YOUR MERIT. PARTICIPATE IN THE CEREMONY AND THEN SEND US FULL PARTICULARS AND THEN IN DUE COURSE IT WILL BE OUR DECISION AND ONLY OUR DECISION AS TO WHEN AND WHERE TO LAND THE FLEET.

HQ

Gents:

You know not what you ask. It is a far far better thing which I do. I do not think you understand the sacrifice that I am making. Very well. Have it your way. You will feel sorry. Guilt will overwhelm you in due course and you will be sorry that you have made me do this. Nevertheless I am going to go in. Ask not what I can do for you now but what you can do for me. One small step.

Wilson

After the Great Space War

YOU HAVE MADE THE PROPER DECISION AND WE WISH TO CON-
GRATULATE YOU FOR COMING TO TERMS WITH THE SITUATION IN
A REALISTIC MANNER AT LAST. WE KNEW THAT IN THE END WE
COULD COUNT UPON YOU. AWAIT YOUR FULL REPORT ON THE CER-
EMONY OF HINGES WITH GREAT INTEREST.

HEADQUARTERS

HAVE HAD NO REPORT FROM YOU FOR TWO CYCLES. DID YOU
PARTICIPATE IN THE CEREMONY OF HINGES, QUESTION MARK. WE
WISH AN IMMEDIATE REPORT. EXCUSE YOURSELF FROM FESTIVI-
TIES IF STILL CARRYING ON AND CABLE A FULL REPORT. WE AWAIT
SAME.

HQ

TWO MORE CYCLES HAVE ELAPSED AND NOW WE ARE MOVING
WELL INTO THE THIRD. INTO THE THIRD YOU FOOL. SUPPORT AND
MONITORING DEVICES INDICATE THAT YOU ARE VERY MUCH
ALIVE. RESPIRATION PULSE HEARTBEAT GROSS FUNCTIONS ALL
NORMAL OR WITHIN GROSS NORMAL RANGE. STOP HIDING FROM
US WILSON YOU ARE TO REPLY AT ONCE.

HQ!

To: Headquarters Division
Cancel the fleet. The planet is uncongenial to human life.
James O. Wilson

WHAT ARE YOU TALKING ABOUT WILSON THE PARTY IS IN
CLOSE ORBIT AND HAS BEEN FOR SOME CONSIDERABLE TIME NOW.
MUCH TIME WASTED TOO MUCH SPECIAL OVERTIME INVOLVED.
HOW IS PLANET UNCONGENIAL TO HUMAN LIFE, QUESTION MARK.
YOU HAVE SURVIVED ON IT.

HQ

FOR YOUR FAILURE TO REPLY YOU HAVE BEEN RELIEVED OF
COMMAND EFFECTIVE AT ONCE WHICH IS TO SAY UPON YOUR RE-
CEIPT OF THIS TRANSMISSION WHICH IS TO SAY IMMEDIATELY. DE-
CISION TO LAND HAS BEEN MADE INDEPENDENTLY AND YOU ARE
TO TURN YOURSELF OVER TO FLEET COMMANDER WHO WILL AR-
RANGE QUARTERS AND WE WILL TAKE CARE OF YOU OH WILL WE
EVER TAKE CARE OF YOU UPON YOUR RETURN TO THE SHIP.

HQ

Barry N. Malzberg

To: Headquarters Division of the Enemy

My troops and I that is to say we will fight to the last man, no matter the price, no matter the penalty, in order that we may repel the invaders and save for all time the integrity of our world.

James O. Wilson

LAND THE FLEET. LAND THE FLEET AT ONCE. THIS SUPERSEDES ANY AND ALL OTHER ORDERS AND IS NOT TO BE DISREGARDED UNDER ANY CIRCUMSTANCE. LAND THE FLEET AT ONCE AND SECURE EVERYTHING THAT MOVES.

HQ

Headquarters:

Planet landed and secured at 1400 Cycle 23. We are now in control of the populace and surrounding territory all of which is pleasantly amiable and delightful to behold. We report no instances of enemy action nor indeed any signs of an enemy. These people are our friends. All is well. Now we are going at the special invitation of the Conductors to participate in the Ceremony of Leakage. (This is a rough translation; the transmission devices are still not sensitive to gradations of language but you get the idea.) We will report shortly upon our successful participation in this ceremony. Modal infarction is well upon the way. It is not necessary to send in the second division.

Commander

DO NOT REPEAT DO NOT REPEAT DO NOT DO IT. WHERE IS WILSON. DO NOT DO IT DO NOT PARTICIPATE IN ANY CEREMONIES THIS IS AN ABSOLUTE INFLEXIBLE ORDER. WHERE IS WILSON WHY IS PLANET NOT SECURED WHY ARE YOU PARTICIPATING IN CEREMONY EXPRESS ORDERS SAY YOU ARE NOT TO DO NOT DO IT. REPORT AT ONCE SECOND DIVISION IS ON WAY AND WILL LAND WITHIN TWELVE CYCLES TO TAKE INCENDIARY ACTION IF YOU DO NOT ALL OF YOU COOPERATE.

HQ

Friends:

Ceremony of Leakage delightful. All that we could have wished and more besides. We look forward with an antici-

707

pation we can barely hide to the promised Pageant of Stains which we have been advised makes the Ceremony of Leakage pale to insignificance just as the C. of L. utterly reduces the Ceremony of Hinges to the tiny taste of grandeur which it is now seen to be.

The planet is secure and while we await the Pageant of Stains we similarly await arrival of the Second Division and behind them the colonists. The colonists are important. Send the colonists. Send all six thousand of the colonists. The planet is entirely secure and we are awaiting them. Send us boatloads of colonists. They may come in from all the systems; send the word that a green and harmless world awaits them. Planet, climate, circumstances extraordinary, natives totally submissive and within our control. Send at least the initial six thousand colonists. They can enjoy with us the Pageant if they arrive soon enough. Hurry.

Commander

SEAL OFF THE PLANET AND PREPARE FOR INCENDIARY ACTION. WE HAVE NO CHOICE REPEAT WE HAVE NO CHOICE. BEGIN CONDITION PINK AT ONCE.

HQ

We await with great anticipation the colonists. Their place in the Pageant has been saved if they hurry. We are waiting for them and we insist that they be sent immediately do you hear me immediately you send those colonists I wopa-ba-bee-do-dee-wham-bam-*boom!*

"Christopher Anvil" (real name Harry Crosby) was one of the most popular and prolific authors in Analog Science Fiction *from the mid-1950s to the end of the 1960s. His work featured social satire and extrapolation, frequently brilliant and almost always entertaining. Few writers could equal his skill in showing how slight changes in the structure of society (or various technological breakthroughs) could cause the whole system to undergo profound change.*

"The Prisoner" (Astounding, February 1956) was his first published story, a complicated and excellent example of the "memo tale."

THE PRISONER

By Christopher Anvil

ROUTINE 04-12-2308-1623TCT STAFF
COMGEN IV TO OPCHIEF GS CAPITOL
REQUEST PERMISSION ADVANCE DEFENSE LINE TO SYSTEM CODE
R3J RPT R3J

ROUTINE 04-13-2308-0715TCT STAFF
OPCHIEF GS CAPITOL TO COMGEN IV
PERMISSION ADVANCE DEFENSE LINE TO SYSTEM CODE R3J RPT
R3J REFUSED RPT REFUSED

The Prisoner

URGENT 04-14-2308-150TCT PERSONAL
COMGEN IV TO OPCHIEF GS CAPITOL
STINKO IT IS VITALLY NECESSARY THAT I TAKE OVER R3J RPT R3J
BEFORE THE OUTS GET HERE STP YOU KNOW THE SIZE OF MY FLEET
STP LOVE TO TANYA AND KIDS MART MARTIN M GLICK COMGEN IV

ROUTINE 04-15-2308-0730TCT PERSONAL
OPCHIEF GS CAPITOL TO COMGEN IV
SORRY MART I CAN'T LET YOU DO IT STP R3J RPT R3J IS TOUGH NUT
TO CRACK AND NOT ENOUGH TIME TO CRACK IT STP ONLY QUAD-
RITE IN SYSTEM IS ON FIFTH PLANET STP TWO PREVIOUS ATTEMPTS
TO TAKE FIFTH PLANET ABORTED STP SYSTEM AS A WHOLE IS NO
GOOD WITHOUT QUADRITE AND WE COULD NOT SUPPLY YOU FROM
HERE YOU KNOW THAT STP CANNOT HAVE YOUR FORCES IN STATE
OF DISORDER WITH MINOR CONFLICT GOING ON WHEN OUTS AR-
RIVE STP I KNOW YOUR POSITION BUT R3J RPT R3J IS NO SOLUTION
STP CAN ONLY HOPE THEY WILL ATTACK ELSEWHERE STP JACKIE
IS FINE STP YOUNG MART HAS GROWN STP GOOD LUCK STP STINKO
J J RYSTENKO OPCHIEF GS

VITAL 04-16-2308-1632TCT STAFF
COMGEN IV TO ALL STATIONS
U EXPLOSION D308L564v013
U EXPLOSION D308L562v013
U EXPLOSION D308L560v013
U EXPLOSION D308L562v015
U EXPLOSION D308L562v011
EXPLOSIONS SIMULTANEOUS TIME OF OBSERVATION 04-16-2308-
1624TCT
VITAL TRANSMIT TRIPLE AT TEN-MINUTE INTERVALS

URGENT 04-162308-1640TCT PERSONAL
COMGEN IV TO OPCHIEF GS CAPITOL
STINKO THEY ARE NOT GOING SOMEWHERE ELSE THEY ARE COM-
ING HERE STP IF THEY GET BY ME THERE IS NOTHING FROM HERE
TO CAP BUT THE GR AND THAT WILL NEVER HOLD THEM STP THEIR
TIMING PERFECT STP MAXIMUM CONFUSION STP IF THEY CAME
ANY SOONER THEY COULD HAVE VOTED IN THE ELECTION STP IN
CIRCUMSTANCES DESPERATELY NECESSARY TO TAKE R3J RPT R3J
STP SEND PERMISSION BEFORE WE WASTE MORE TIME STP MART
MARTIN M GLICK COMGEN IV

(Reply requested today.)
Office of the Secretary for Defense
Dear General Rystenko:

As a member of the new President's cabinet, responsible for the overall direction of the defense effort, I am determined to acquire, as soon as possible, some appreciation of the overall strategic picture.

So long as I do not understand the meaning of certain technical terms, this will be impossible. These terms are regarded as secret, and no civilian has any sure idea of their meaning until he is thrust into an office where his ignorance may be fatal. Looking at the dispatch copies which come to my office, I find the following terms I would like defined: (a) quadrite; (b) GR; (c) CAP; (d) U-explosion; (e) Henkel sphere; (f) SB; (g) abort.

I also want a brief summary, on no more than two sheets of paper, of the overall defense strategy; a similar summary of known enemy capabilities; and a brief point-by-point comparison of our important weapons, considering not only quality but amounts, and present and projected rates of production.

You need not handle this yourself; but if you do not, I want you to check the papers before they come to me. You will be held personally responsible for their accuracy.

Sincerely,
James Cordovan
Secretary for Defense

4-17-2308

Office of The Chief of Operations
Dear Mr. Secretary:

Quadrite is a crystalline substance used as fuel in the nonradioactive, or N-drive. A small safe quantity of radioactive material starts the reaction, which may be stopped by removal of this material. The mass radioactive, or R-drive, is useless against the present enemy because he possesses a means of exploding it before our ships come into ordinary firing range. Thus we use quadrite on warships.

GR means General Reserve. CAP means Capitol. A U-explosion is a large explosion of uranium or other radioactive material by the enemy's device, or, occasionally, by us. Henkel sphere is a large self-contained unit carrying impulse torpedoes and magnetic-inductive direction finders. SB means solar beam; a concentration of the rays of a sun for offensive or defensive purposes. "Abort," as we use it, merely means "fail."

The overall defense strategy is simple. Our forces are located around the surface of a flattened spheroidal defensive border. At the outer edge is a triple layer of warning devices, the U-markers, which explode on approach of the enemy. Next comes several layers of Henkel spheres, stretching from one sun system to the next. Each sun system is equipped with solar beams, so far as possible, so that these sun systems constitute strong points in the defense perimeter, or, if they are cut off, may function for some time as isolated fortresses in the enemy's rear. Behind this outer line of defense lie the fleets, which help service the Henkel spheres, fight to repair small breaches in the defensive perimeter, and, in the event of large breaches, fall back in an orderly manner and assist in forming the next defensive line.

As for the known enemy capabilities, and the comparison of their important weapons with ours, the first item to consider is their manner of attack. They come in in huge masses of ships, moving at a tremendous velocity, and often making two nearly simultaneous attacks at far separated parts of our defense lines. A series of U-explosions signals their penetration through successive lines of our U-markers, and then they hurtle through the lines of Henkel spheres. The spheres automatically discharge their impulse torpedoes on precalculated courses, and at the same time our fleet on the spot sows a series of new layers of spheres along the estimated course of the enemy attack. There is no such thing as a general engagement between the two fleets, because ours is always too weak at the point of attack. It is guarding a vast area which the enemy can, if he chooses, attack at any chosen point with his full force.

Usually, however, just as the situation becomes desperate, and we feel compelled to rush the general reserve to the spot, a second and even stronger attack strikes us at some widely separated point from the first. At this stage, all resemblance to plan and order ceases, and we are forced to resort to expediency. Fleets are rushed from all around the perimeter to the estimated position of the future enemy penetrations. Solar beams are concentrated in a webwork across the line of enemy attack. It is impossible to generalize beyond this point. We do what we can. Usually we are forced to commit the fleet to battle at a heavy loss, which weakens us for the next attack. The enemy cuts a swath through the whole system, burns out a number of vitally important planetary centres en route, and erupts outward through some place which has already been stripped for defense elsewhere. After the enemy has gone, we draw together the bits and pieces, reapportion the weakened forces, and wait for the next blow.

We know very little of enemy weapons, save that they are similar to ours and used in overwhelming concentrations. As for the enemy personnel, only one individual has been captured following a fluke individual dogfight in which Colonel A. C. Nielson was killed and the enemy ship ruined. This enemy individual showed (a) human form, very compact and muscular, with peculiar eyes; (b) fantastic recuperative power, with healing of very severe wounds, such as killed Colonel Nielson, taking place spontaneously and practically visibly; (c) fanatic hostility, shown as soon as the individual recovered consciousness; and which was followed apparently by the use of some poison, as the enemy's body then at once decomposed, too fast to permit further examination on the spot.

As for our present rate of production, it is suitable to replace approximately forty percent of the losses suffered during enemy attack. This refers to warship production. Production of the cheaper Henkel spheres would be quite respectable if it weren't for the fact that it takes ships to put the spheres in position. Projected production of ships was cut further in the last budget.

As for recruitment of personnel, it is barely adequate to man the continually decreasing strength we are able to maintain. Training facilities are inadequate, but the need for men is so drastic we have no time for adequate training. The quality of recruits is poor, since the population does not believe the situation serious, and thus has little respect for the services.

I hope this answers your questions satisfactorily. I shall be glad to help you in any way I can.

Respectfully,
J. J. Rystenko
Chief of Operations

Office of the Secretary for Defense
Bart:

I am enclosing an answer from General Rystenko, the Chief of Operations, to some questions of mine. I hope you will read it now and let me know what you think. Unless Rystenko is exaggerating for some reason, this is worse than we ever imagined.

Jim Cordovan

4-17-2308

Office of the President
Jim:

This is horrible. Let me know immediately if you find out anything more about this.

Bart

(Immediate action)

4-17-2308

Office of the President
General Rystenko:

Report to my office immediately unless you are occupied with matters of vital importance.

Barton Baruch

4-17-2308

Office of the President
Jim:

Rystenko is all right. But our predecessors have gutted the defense establishment to balance the budget. Cabinet meeting tonight at 8:30.

Bart

URGENT 04-16-2308-2210TCT PERSONAL
COMGEN IV TO OPCHIEF GS CAPITOL
STINKO MY POSITION HOPELESS HERE IN PRESENT CIRCUMSTAN-
CES STP ONLY JUSTIFICATION FOR INACTION WAS TO AVOID IN-
VOLVEMENT IN MINOR WAR AND THUS INABILITY TO REINFORCE
IF ATTACK CAME ELSEWHERE STP ATTACK IS COMING HERE STP IF
I STAY WHERE I AM I AM LIKE A MOUSE IN AN UNBLOCKED HOLE
WITH THE WEASEL COMING ON THE RUN STP I CANT HOLD THEM
HERE STP THIS TIME THEY WILL GO ALL THE WAY TO CAP STP
STINKO I HOPE YOUR PERMISSION IS ON WAY AS I AM GOING TO
TAKE R3J RPT R3J OR DIE TRYING STP LOVE TO TANYA AND THE

714

KIDS STP GOOD LUCK IF THEY GET THROUGH STINKO STP MART MARTIN M GLICK COMGEN IV

ROUTINE 04-17-2308-1100TCT STAFF
OPCHIEF GS CAPITOL TO COMGEN IV
IN ABSENCE OF GENERAL RYSTENKO MY DUTY TO INFORM LIEU-TENANT GENERAL GLICK NO PERMISSION TO ADVANCE TO R3J RPT R3J WAS SENT OR CONTEMPLATED STP IN EVENT YOU ADVANCE CONTRARY TO REITERATED COMMANDS TO CONTRARY MY DUTY TO INFORM YOU YOU ARE HEREBY RELIEVED OF COMMAND AND HEREBY ORDERED TO TURN OVER COMMAND TO DEPUTY COMGEN IV AS PRESCRIBED RGC 6-143J SECTION 14 STP Q L GORLEY COLONEL FOR GENERAL J J RYSTENKO OPCHIEF GS

ROUTINE 04-18-2308-1625TCT STAFF
COMGEN IV TO OPCHIEF GS CAPITOL
ALL RECEIVING APPARATUS OUT OF ORDER STP POSSIBLY BY EN-EMY ACTION STP ADVANCE ELEMENTS OF FLEET IV APPROACHING SYSTEM CODE R3J RPT R3J

VITAL 04-18-2308-1640TCT STAFF
COMGEN IV TO ALL STATIONS
U EXPLOSION D288L564v103
U EXPLOSION D288L562v103
U EXPLOSION D288L560v103
U EXPLOSION D288L562v105
U EXPLOSION D288L562v099
EXPLOSIONS SIMULTANEOUS TIME OF OBSERVATION 04-18-2308-1635TCT
VITAL TRANSMIT TRIPLE AT TEN-MINUTE INTERVALS

(Reply requested immediately)

4-18-2308

Office of the Secretary for Defense
General Rystenko:
    As you know, OPCHIEF dispatches move through my of-fice as a routine so I will know what your office is doing. Now I want to know why this General Glick is being kept on a short leash. I have gone over a set of star charts, and if I can make anything out of them this System R3J is a vital link in your defense system. Who is this Q. L. Gorley, colonel, who sent the order removing General Glick? Why did *he* send the order? Are you dodging the responsibility for it? Unless

you are occupied in vital matters I want the answers to these questions by tube within fifteen minutes.

J. Cordovan
Secretary for Defense

4-18-2308

Office of the Chief of Operations
Dear Mr. Secretary:

I had no knowledge of Gorley's action till you called it to my attention. I am reinstating Glick immediately.

Rystenko

VITAL 04-18-2308-1125TCT STAFF
OPCHIEF GS CAPITOL TO COMGEN IV
BY ORDER GENERAL J J RYSTENKO OPCHIEF GS EFFECTIVE IM-
MEDIATELY LIEUTENANT-GENERAL MARTIN M GLICK IS RPT IS IN
FULL COMMAND SECTOR IV STP BY ORDER GENERAL J J RYSTENKO
OPCHIEF GS FULL DISCRETION RPT FULL DISCRETION GRANTED
RPT GRANTED LIEUTENANT-GENERAL MARTIN M GLICK COMGEN
IV INCLUDING RPT INCLUDING ANY ACTIONS REGARDING SYSTEM
CODE R3J RPT R3J TIME OF ORIGINAL ORDER 02-18-2308-1125TCT
VITAL TRANSMIT TRIPLE AT THIRTY-MINUTE INTERVALS

URGENT 02-18-2308-1128TCT PERSONAL
OPCHIEF GS CAPITOL TO COMGEN IV
MY GOD MART I AM SORRY STP YOUR REASONING REGARDING R3J
RPT R3J IS PERFECTLY CORRECT STP GORLEY ACTED WITHOUT MY
KNOWLEDGE STP WE ARE IN MIDST OF CHANGE OF ADMINISTRA-
TION HERE STP SOME CONFUSION STP YOU HAVE FULL AUTHORITY
STP DO WHAT YOU WANT STP BEST OF LUCK AND GOD BE WITH
YOU STP STINKO J J RYSTENKO OPCHIEF GS

4-18-2308

Office of the Chief of Operations
Dear Mr. Secretary:

I have sent orders reinstating General Glick and giving him full authority to take System R3J. Two previous attempts to take the only planet in the system that possesses quadrite have failed, with no survivors returning; but it is worth trying.

Rystenko

(Reply requested immediately)

4-18-2308

Office of the Secretary for Defense
General Rystenko:
    That is fine. What about my questions concerning Colonel
Gorley?

J. Cordovan

4-18-2308

Office of the Chief of Operations
Dear Mr. Secretary:
    Colonel Gorley was sent here by the former President. He
acted in an advisory and liaison capacity between this office
and that of the former President. I know his action in this
instance has proved to be unfortunate, but he was entirely
justified by regulations covering the situation. I was with the
President at the moment, and immediate action was necessary to maintain the balance of the situation.

Respectfully,
J. J. Rystenko
Chief of Operations

(Reply requested immediately)

4-18-2308

Office of the Secretary for Defense
General Rystenko:
    Do you mean that Gorley advised the former President on
matters of defense?

J. Cordovan

4-18-2308

Office of the Chief of Operations
Mr. Secretary:
    That is what I mean. Yes.

J. J. Rystenko
Chief of Operations

4-18-2308

Office of the Secretary for Defense
Bart:
    I am enclosing some correspondence between myself and
Rystenko, regarding a Colonel Q. L. Gorley who has just
taken a step I regard as well calculated to throw our defense
arrangements off balance at the decisive moment. I am enclosing the dispatch referred to. You will note that Rystenko

takes a progressively stiffer tone in protecting Gorley. Personally, I think if Gorley was defense adviser to the previous Administration, he must be no good.

Jim

(Reply requested today)

4-18-2308

Office of the Secretary for Defense
Comptroller of the Records:
I would like a digest of all pertinent data in the service record of Colonel Q. L. Gorley, now attached to the office of the Chief of Operations.

James Cordovan
Secretary for Defense

4-18-2308

Office of the President
Jim:
I have been in office three days and it feels like three years, all thanks to the miserable defense picture. If you think Gorley is no good, select some distant and unimportant asteroid and put him in charge of it. Don't bother me with this trivia.

Bart

PS. The time on this dispatch from Gorley to Glick is 1100. Rystenko was not with me then.

4-19-2308

Comptroller of the Records
Dear Mr. Secretary:
I have been able to ascertain that there is a Colonel Q. L. Gorley attached to the Chief of Operations office, but the Master Recorder merely remains blank when I try to obtain his service record. No Colonel Q. L. Gorley is listed in the Officers' Registry. There is a Q. S. Gorley, Captain, now serving with the Tenth Fleet, and a Brigadier General Mason Gorley, Ret'd. Upon code-checking the rolls of the National Space Academy at Bristol Bay, I find no mention of any Q. L. Gorley within the last hundred years.

It is possible to bar access to the service record of any individual if the President or Secretary for Defense approves the action. But this is not the case here. There simply is no record. Do you wish me to cross-check the coded Administration records of the past few years to see if any mention is made of this man in these records?

Respectfully,
Ogden Mannenberg
Comptroller of the Records

(Reply requested today)

4-19-2308

Office of the Secretary for Defense
Comptroller of the Records:
Yes, by all means cross-check the administrative records back to the time Gorley was first mentioned.

James Cordovan
Secretary for Defense

(Immediate action)

4-19-2308

Office of the Secretary for Defense
Birdie:
Get down to the Chief of Operations' office and play the part of the Undersecretary getting acquainted with the team. Find out all you can about a Colonel Q. L. Gorley, who is now attached to the Opchief's office. Gorley appears to have no service record and I am a little curious about him.

Jim

ROUTINE 04-19-2308-2300TCT STAFF
COMGEN IV TO OPCHIEF GS CAPITOL
FLEET IV NOW BASED ON SECOND RPT SECOND PLANET OF SYSTEM CODE R3J RPT R3J STP SB BEING PLACED NOW STP ADVANCE HENKEL SPHERE PERIMETER BEING HEAVILY REINFORCED STP BULK OF FLEET IV NOW MOVING TO OCCUPY FIFTH RPT FIFTH PLANET OF SYSTEM CODE R3J RPT R3J

ROUTINE 04-19-2308-2314TCT PERSONAL
COMGEN IV TO OPCHIEF GS CAPITOL
STINKO I HAVE OCCUPIED THE SECOND PLANET OF R3J RPT R3J AND FIND POPULACE AND GOVERNMENT FRIENDLY AND EAGER TO HELP STP THEY HAD CIVILIZATION BASED ON FISSION FIVE HUNDRED YEARS AGO BUT THE OUTS WENT THROUGH HERE AND KNOCKED THEM INTO A QUOTE PILE OF DUNG END QUOTE STP THEY HAD SPACE TRAVEL BUT KEPT AWAY FROM FIFTH PLANET AS HAD NO NEED FOR QUADRITE WHICH IS ONLY ATTRACTION STP

ALL THEY CAN TELL ME IS THAT ONE OF THEIR RELIGIOUS LEADERS PREDICTED MY ARRIVAL AND SAID OF THE FIFTH PLANET QUOTE HE WHO WILL FEED ON IT SHALL LIVE OF IT STP END QUOTE SOUNDS GOOD STP AM EN ROUTE NOW STP MART MARTIN M GLICK COMGEN IV

4-19-2308

Office of the Undersecretary for Defense
Jim:

I have covered the situation for you down at the Opchief's office, and I am sure you must be mistaken about Colonel Gorley. He seems straightforward and solid, and explained the defense setup to me in such a way that for the first time it made sense to me. I can think of no one we might pick who would make a better advisor to the President on military matters. As for Colonel Gorley having no service record, the idea is fantastic. Several of the officers present spoke familiarly to Gorley of events which happened while he and they were at Bristol Bay together in their Academy days. It could hardly be a case of mistaken identity. Colonel Gorley is a very striking man, very compact and muscular—a very powerful, magnetic, dynamic type. He has peculiarly keen intelligent eyes, and an incisive, clear, positive manner of speaking. Personally, I think that instead of investigating Gorley, we should raise him to high rank and get a little decision into the war effort.

Birdie

PS. The only thing resembling criticism I have heard of Gorley was a joking reference that he has a ferocious appetite and has to diet constantly to keep his weight down. Surely you won't hold this against him.

ROUTINE 04-20-2308-0756TCT STAFF
COMGEN IV TO OPCHIEF GS CAPITOL
ADVANCE ELEMENTS FLEET IV HAVE LANDED ON PLANET FIVE RPT FIVE OF SYSTEM CODE R3J RPT R3J STP NO OPPOSITION STP ONLY INHABITANTS APPEAR TO BE GRAZING ANIMALS OF INTERMEDIATE SIZE

4-20-2308

Comptroller of the Records
Dear Mr. Secretary:

I list below in chronological order the portions of past

Administrative records apparently referring to Colonel Q. L. Gorley:

4-25-2304 ... Thank you so much for sending me Colonel Gorley. The defense position is more clear to me...

President to Opchief

5-4-2304 ... I approve the new plan of dynamic containment. I was a bit uncertain as to the effect this would have should the enemy renew offensive action, but Colonel Gorley has assured me it will be possible to concentrate reserves quickly. On this basis I approve the plan. Certainly it seems much less risky...

President to Opchief

2-23-2305 ... I do not understand your difficulties in repelling the latest enemy attack. What exactly has happened here? Why were you not able to concentrate your reserves quickly enough to prevent the enemy from traversing the whole length and breadth of the system and leaving a trail of ruin behind him such as we have not seen in twenty years of warfare? Who ordered these cuts in production? What do you mean you cannot replace the losses? I have no memory of these Executive Orders you speak of, or of any Colonel Gorley. Send this man to me immediately, or better yet, come yourself...

President to Opchief

2-24-2305 ... Colonel Gorley has explained the matter to me satisfactorily. Of course it is unfortunate, but these things happen...

President to Opchief

6-1-2305 ... Colonel Gorley will explain to you the recommended new cuts in the defense budget. The improved foreign situation makes these cuts possible...

Opchief to President

4-2-2306 ... Rystenko, these losses are horrible. Why has this thing happened twice? The purpose of censorship is not to hold the people in ignorance and hide the festering wounds from view. The point of censorship is to keep information from the enemy and to prevent over-violent public reaction to unimportant temporary reversals. But these disasters are not unimportant! They are terrible defeats! I find your reaction grossly inadequate. Who is this Gorley you are sending to me, as if this would correct the situation?...

President to Opchief

4-4-2306...Colonel Gorley has explained the matter to me satisfactorily. I see now clearly it was bound to happen in this phase of our defensive effort...

President to Opchief

6-2-2306...I approve the new defense budget, as explained to me by Colonel Gorley. I am, of course, pleased though surprised that you can now give us more defensive power at lower cost. Please check this and be sure that the situation has stabilized to this extent...

President to Opchief

6-2-2306...That Colonel Gorley be attached to my office until these complex arrangements are completed...

President to Opchief

6-7-2306...We will miss Gorley, but are sure he will prove as helpful to you as to us...

Opchief to President

9-15-2306...The food must be much better here than in your mess. Poor Gorley has to go on another diet...

President to Opchief

10-23-2306...I am very sorry to have to bother you with these petty trivialities, Mr. President, but they may prove vital. I can't send men to Cryos with such inadequate equipment as this budget allows for. This one trivial substitution of separate interliners and thin semi-detached boots may cost a delay of up to ten minutes when the men go into action. This equipment has already proved itself worthless. I will gladly consider Colonel Gorley's suggestions, but this matter was disposed of years ago. I have also discovered several other aspects of our present arrangements which make me extremely uneasy...

Opchief to President

10-25-2306...I have talked with Colonel Gorley and can see that these plans are perfectly suited to the situation. Perhaps he could remain with our office for some time till these other matters are ironed out...

Opchief to President

4-15-2307...Poor Gorley is on a diet again...

Opchief to President

4-16-2307...Who? Gorley? Am I acquainted with the man?...

President to Opchief

4-29-2307...Terribly shaken by this hideous disaster. Why had this happened to us when our arrangements were supposed to be invulnerable? The enemy has torn your battle line like tissue paper. Why are we so weak everywhere? Your talk of "elastic counter defensive" makes no sense to me whatever. If these fleets were held concentrated at one central point instead of strewn all over the universe, we could return the blow. What do you mean by offering to send "Colonel Gorley" to me? If any personal explaining is to be done, you will come yourself, not send a stooge. Make out immediately a list of all requirements needed to correct this hideous situation.

President to Opchief

4-30-2307...I see now. Gorley has explained it all to me...
President to Opchief

Note: These are all the direct references made to Colonel Q. L. Gorley in the Administration records. Would you like me to cross-check the Departmental records?

Respectfully,
Ogden Mannenberg
Comptroller of the Records

4-20-2308

Office of the Secretary for Defense
Comptroller of the Records:
    Thank you. These references are amply sufficient for the present.

James Cordovan
Secretary for Defense

4-20-2308

Office of the President
Jim:
    I have now absorbed the substance of the report Rystenko sent you concerning our defenses, and which you forwarded to me. I have slept on it, and thought of it when I was not otherwise occupied. It seems to me: (1) This policy of locating

723

the main bulk of our fleet in a thin shell around the periphery offers us about as much defense as an eggshell does to an egg. (2) Since in the present arrangement the fleet does not engage, it is worth no more than so many civilian ships. (3) Therefore, let us draw all the fleet to the center (with the possible exception of Glick's IVth, which is actively occupied), and replace it around the periphery with civilian ships and crews to service the layers of Henkel spheres. Enough men could be left behind to train these crews, but no more.

My final observation is that everything I have said so far is fairly obvious, therefore why hasn't Rystenko carried it out on his own? He impressed me very favourably in our interview, but further consideration leads me to think he may be one of those men who expend their sense on the package instead of the contents. I am going to talk to him again, and would like your view of the subject.

Bart

4-20-2308

Office of the President
General Rystenko:

I want to see you within the next hour regarding the overall strategy of the war effort, regarding the present recruitment and material replacement situation, and regarding the present arrangements for advancement of high officers.

Barton Baruch

4-20-2308

Office of the Chief of Operations
Dear Mr. President:

I shall be at your office at 3:00 P.M. if this is agreeable to you. As it happens, my aide, Colonel Q. L. Gorley, left my office a short while ago to bring you some important data sheets. I am sure you will find him most helpful also on these other matters if you choose to consult him.

Respectfully,
J. J. Rystenko
Chief of Operations

4-20-2308

Office of the President
Jim:

I have just had a very illuminating talk with General

Rystenko's aide, Colonel Gorley, and he has very clearly explained the logic of the present defence set-up to me. I am sending him along to brief you. He is a most capable man, and I am sure you will profit by contact with him.

Bart

VITAL 04-20-2308-1654TCT STAFF
COMGEN IV TO ALL STATIONS
U EXPLOSION D280L564v193
U EXPLOSION D280L562v193
U EXPLOSION D 280L560v193
U EXPLOSION D280L562v195
U EXPLOSION D280L562v191
EXPLOSIONS SIMULTANEOUS
TIME OF OBSERVATION 04-20-2308-1646TCT
VITAL TRANSMIT TRIPLE AT TEN-MINUTE INTERVALS

4-20-2308

Office of the Undersecretary for Defense
Jim:
    Colonel Gorley is out here cooling his heels in the anteroom. He is here at the President's personal order, and yet when the receptionist tries to let him in, your door is locked. Have you turned childish?

Birdie

4-29-2308

Office of the Secretary for Defense
Birdie:
    Who is Gorley? Is he the one who made the fuss removing a general yesterday or the day before? If he has anything from the President, he can leave it outside. If he wants to see me, he can make an appointment for tomorrow. I am working my way through a pile of business as high as your head, and I do not want to be disturbed till I am finished. Say, while he is out there, pump him discreetly about Rystenko. See if you can find out whether the Opchief used Gorley for a cat's-paw in trying to get rid of that general...what's his name?...Glick.

Jim

725

4-20-2308

Office of the Secretary for Defense
Chief Dispatcher:
    Send the following:
VITAL 04-20-2308-1621TCT PERSONAL
DEFSEC CAPITOL TO COMGEN GR CAPITOL
REPLY IMMEDIATELY YOUR OPINION WILL PRESENT DEFENSES RE-
PEL ENEMY ATTACK OF MAGNITUDE SIMILAR TO THAT EXPERI-
ENCED LAST THREE YEARS STP REPLY IMMEDIATELY CATEGORY
VITAL TO DEFSEC CAPITOL THROUGH CHIEF DISPATCHER STP THIS
INQUIRY AND REPLY CONFIDENTIAL STP JAMES CORDOVAN DEF-
SEC CAPITOL

(Reply requested immediately)

4-20-2308

Office of the Secretary for Defense
Comptroller of the Records:
    Find out for me what happened to the body of the enemy
captured after a dogfight in which Colonel A. C. Nielson was
killed.

James Cordovan
Secretary for Defense

VITAL 04-20-2308-1642TCT PERSONAL
COMGEN GR CAP TO DEFSEC CAP THRU CHIEF DISPATCHER
    CONFIDENTIAL
MY OPINION PRESENT DEFENSES WILL COLLAPSE IF ENEMY AT-
TACKS WITH SAME STRENGTH AS FORMERLY STP OR WITH ANY-
THING LIKE SAME STRENGTH AS FORMERLY STP VERNON L HAUSER
COMGEN GR CAPITOL

4-20-2308

Comptroller of the Records
Dear Mr. Secretary:
    The body of the captured enemy was brought here under
refrigeration, to be examined by physicians and chemists. It
arrived at night and was placed, still in its box, in a small
room off the autopsy room. The intern on duty ordered the
lid of the box pried up, examined the remains, and noted that
the object within appeared to be in a state of advanced de-
composition, with, however, very little odor. The room was
refrigerated, and next day the surgeons entered to carry out
a preliminary examination, and upon raising the lid found

nothing within but a quantity of water, some of which had seeped out through the sides of the box.

The above summary is condensed from voluminous reports on the occurrence, and equally voluminous reports attempt to explain the matter, but the substance of these latter reports is that the authorities do not know what happened.

Respectfully,
Ogden Mannenberg
Comptroller of the Records

(Reply requested immediately)

4-20-2308

Office of the Secretary for Defense
Comptroller of the Records:

Send me a summary of the physical characteristics of the captured enemy during life.

James Cordovan
Secretary for Defense

4-20-2308

Office of the Undersecretary for Defense
Jim:

Colonel Gorley was ordered by the President to see you now, today. Why try to put him off till tomorrow? You can get back to your work after he has a few minutes to deliver his message.

Birdie

4-20-2308

Office of the Secretary for Defense
Birdie:

I am snowed under. Tomorrow.

Jim

4-20-2308

Comptroller of the Records
Dear Mr. Secretary:

The captured enemy is described as having during life the following physical characteristics: (a) human form; (b) extremely compact and muscular physique; (c) peculiarly keen sharp eyes; (d) very great recuperative power.

Respectfully,
Ogden Mannenberg
Comptroller of the Records

4-20-2308

Office of the Secretary for Defense
Chief Dispatcher:
   Send the following:
VITAL 04-20-2308-1708TCT PERSONAL
DEFSEC CAP TO COMGEN GR CAP CONFIDENTIAL
REPLY IMMEDIATELY THROUGH CHIEF DISPATCHER YOUR OPINION
ON OUTCOME OF COMING ENEMY ATTACK IF ALL OUR FORCES NOW
CONCENTRATED AT CENTRAL POINT LEAVING SMALL TRAINING
CADRES AND CIVILIANS TO MAINTAIN HENKEL SPHERE DEFENSES
STP REPLY CONFIDENTIAL CATEGORY VITAL STP JAMES COR-
DOVAN DEFSEC CAPITOL

VITAL 04-20-2308-1714TCT PERSONAL
COMGEN GR CAP TO DEFSEC CAP THRU CHIEF DISPATCHER
   CONFIDENTIAL
MY OPINION OUR CHANCES GOOD STP THIS IS FIRST SENSIBLE PLAN
TO COME OUT OF CAP IN FOUR YEARS STP BUT YOU WILL NEVER
GET IT BY RYSTENKO OR HIS CREATURE GORLEY STP SEE GORLEY
DOES NOT GET TO PRESIDENT STP GORLEY IS CLEVER MAN WITH
THE BUTTER KNIFE OR WHATEVER HE USES STP MR SECRETARY
ONLY CHANCE YOUR PLAN GETTING ACROSS IS TO SEE PRESIDENT
REMOVE RYSTENKO APPOINT ANYONE WITH ALL HIS FACULTIES
STP ANY SANE MAN CAN SEE PLAN NOW IN USE IS SUICIDE STP
VERNON L HAUSER COMGEN GR CAP

4-20-2308

Office of the Undersecretary for Defense
Jim:
   Colonel Gorley was *ordered* to see you by the *President*
and he was *ordered* to do it *today*. The colonel is a very
powerful and determined man when his duty is at stake, Jim,
and I think it would be wise not to get in his or the President's
way. I say this as a friend, Jim. Gorley is *going* to *see* you
today.

Birdie

4-20-2308

Office of the Secretary for Defense
Birdie:
   Why didn't you tell me Gorley was here at the direct order
of the President to see me *today*? He can see me when I am
through, probably about an hour-and-a-half from now, or, as

he would put it, about 1854 hours. Birdie, would you repeat what you said about Colonel Gorley's appearance? I think he reminds me of someone I knew as a kid.

Jim

4-20-2308

Office of the Secretary for Defense
Chief Dispatcher:
    Send the following:
VITAL 04-20-2308-1722TCT PERSONAL
DEFSEC CAP TO COMGEN GR CAP CONFIDENTIAL
REPLY IMMEDIATELY THROUGH CHIEF DISPATCHER STP SITUATION HERE HIGHLY PRECARIOUS STP GORLEY HAS ALREADY GOTTEN TO PRESIDENT AND USED WHATEVER HE USES STP PRESIDENT NOW CONVERTED STP GORLEY AWAITING ME IN MY OUTER OFFICE STP EAGER TO USE WHATEVER HE USES STP MY THOUGHT THAT ONLY SOLUTION IS THROW AWAY PRESENT SITUATION AND START ALL OVER STP INCIDENTALLY WHY CAN I NOT PERSONALLY ORDER REGROUPING OF FORCES STP IS THERE ANOTHER CAPITOL AS I HAVE HEARD RUMORED ALL SET UP WITH SKELETON CREWS AND READY TO TAKE OVER IF ANYTHING HAPPENS TO PRESENT ONE STP WILL YOU CONSENT TO ACT AS OPCHIEF IF SO DIRECTED BY ME STP I PROPOSE GIVE YOU DIRECT ORDER TO PERFORM VERY HAZARDOUS THANKLESS MISSION OF VITAL IMPORTANCE STP WILL YOU OBEY IMMEDIATELY AND WITHOUT QUESTION STP REPLY IMMEDIATELY THROUGH CHIEF DISPATCHER STP REPLY CONFIDENTIAL CATEGORY VITAL STP JAMES CORDOVAN DEFSEC CAPITOL

VITAL 04-20-2308-1730TCT PERSONAL
COMGEN GR CAP TO DEFSEC CAP THRU CHIEF DISPATCHER
    CONFIDENTIAL
HOW DOES GORLEY DO IT STP YES YOU CAN ORDER FORCES DIRECT BUT WHAT GOOD IF PRESIDENT COUNTERMANDS STP YES AUXILIARY CAP EXISTS READY TO TAKE OVER STP BUT IF WE LOSE THE PRESENT CAP THRU ENEMY ACTION IT WILL BE BECAUSE OF GREAT WEAKNESS AND THERE WILL BE LITTLE FOR AUX CAP TO DO BUT SIGN SURRENDER STP YES I WILL BE OPCHIEF IF YOU SO ORDER STP I WILL FOLLOW ORDERS REGARDLESS HAZARD OR THANKLESSNESS STP I WILL ACT IMMEDIATELY WITHOUT QUESTION STP BUT I CAN FOLLOW YOUR ORDERS ONLY IF NOT COUNTERMANDED BY HIGHER AUTHORITY THAT IS THE PRESIDENT STP VERNON L HAUSER COMGEN GR CAP

4-20-2308

Office of the Undersecretary for Defense
Jim:

Come off it, fellow. You can't expect a man like Colonel Gorley to wait around in your outer office when he is on a mission direct from the President. As for Colonel Gorley's appearance, as I said before, the colonel is a splendid figure of a man, very compact and muscular, with peculiarly keen sharp eyes. Eyes indicative, I might add, of great force of character, and you are standing in this man's way and the President's. Colonel Gorley says he thinks it is "unlikely" you knew him as a child. He came from a place where as a child he didn't ever have enough to eat, which explains his periodic little indulgences in food. He is angry with you, Jim, and he is close to the President. I don't think he will wait much longer, Jim, when it is his duty to see you. Wake up, Jim.

Birdie

4-20-2308

Office of the Secretary for Defense
Chief Dispatcher:

Send the following:
VITAL 04-20-2308-1734TCT PERSONAL
DEFSEC CAP TO COMGENS ALL SECTORS
EFFECTIVE IMMEDIATELY GENERAL J J RYSTENKO IS REMOVED RPT REMOVED FROM POST AS OPCHIEF GS STP EFFECTIVE IMMEDIATELY LIEUTENANT-GENERAL VERNON L HAUSER COMGEN GR IS APPOINTED RPT APPOINTED OPCHIEF GS STP I HAVE FULL AND COMPLETE CONFIDENCE IN GENERAL HAUSER STP ANY DELAY IN CARRYING OUT GENERAL HAUSER'S ORDERS IN THE UNUSUAL CIRCUMSTANCES ABOUT TO OCCUR WILL BE A DIRECT THREAT TO THE SECURITY OF THE RACE STP IN THESE TIMES STEADINESS AND INSTANT OBEDIENCE TO ORDERS ARE THE VITAL QUALITIES STP GOD BE WITH YOU AND HOLD YOU STEADY AGAINST THE FOE STP JAMES CORDOVAN DEFSEC CAPITOL

VITAL 04-20-2308-1735TCT STAFF
DEFSEC CAPITOL TO ALL STATIONS
FOR YOUR INFORMATION EXPERIENCE WITH ENEMY CAPTIVE HERE SUGGESTS OUTS POSSESS GREAT HYPNOTIC POWERS AT CLOSE RANGE STP ADVISABLE TAKE NO PRISONERS

VITAL 04-20-2308-1736TCT PERSONAL
DEFSEC CAPITOL TO COMGEN GR CAPITOL
DIRECT ORDER YOU DESTROY RPT DESTROY CAPITOL RPT CAPITOL
AT EARLIEST POSSIBLE MOMENT CONSISTENT WITH SAFETY OF
FORCES UNDER YOUR COMMAND STP THEN CONCENTRATE MAIN
FORCES AS YOU THINK ADVISABLE STP JAMES CORDOVAN DEFSEC
CAP

4-20-2308

Office of the Undersecretary of Defense
Jim:
    You have gone a little too far in defying Colonel Gorley
and the President, and Colonel Gorley has decided to wait
no longer in performing his duty. He is coming in to see you
now, Jim, door or no door.

Birdie

4-20-2308

Office of the Secretary for Defense
Birdie:
    Tell Colonel Gorley I have a service revolver in my hand
and am only too eager to test Gorley's fantastic recuperative
powers against this and one other weapon. Go after him and
tell him this.

Jim

ROUTINE 04-20-2308-1700TCT STAFF
COMGEN IV TO OPCHIEF GS CAPITOL
OCCUPATION OF PLANET FIVE RPT FIVE COMPLETE STP NO RPT NO
OPPOSITION STP NO RPT NO INDICATION OF PREVIOUS ATTEMPTS
TO TAKE PLANET STP HUGE RESERVES OF QUADRITE STP MINING
NOW UNDERWAY

04-20-2308

Office of the Undersecretary for Defense
Jim:
    What do you mean? What is going on here? May I go home,
Jim? I feel strange.

Birdie

731

4-20-2308

Office of the Secretary for Defense
Birdie:
    Thank you for sending Colonel Gorley in to me. He has explained our defense set-up to me most clearly.

Jim

VITAL 04-20-2308-1750TCT STAFF
COMGEN GR CAP TO ALL STATIONS
U EXPLOSION CAPITOL
U EXPLOSION CAPITOL
U EXPLOSION CAPITOL
U EXPLOSION CAPITOL
U EXPLOSION CAPITOL
EXPLOSIONS RAPID SUCCESSIVE NOT BY ENEMY ACTION TIME OF OBSERVATION 04-20-2308-1746TCT
VITAL TRANSMIT TRIPLE AT TEN-MINUTE INTERVALS

Tony Lewis is a good example of the science-fiction fan turned author. He has been active in organized fandom for many years, and now reviews sf for Analog Science Fiction/Science Fact. *We predict that "Request for Proposal" (*Analog, *November 1972) will see more reprintings, for it is a superior example of social-science fiction and of bureaucracy gone mad.*

REQUEST FOR PROPOSAL

By Anthony R. Lewis

DEPARTMENT OF HOUSING AND URBAN
DEVELOPMENT
ROBERT F. KENNEDY RESEARCH CENTER

FROM: Chief, Improvements Branch, Readjustment Division
TO: Branch Members
DATE: 7 March 1984
SUBJECT: COST EFFECTIVE OPTIMIZATION OF IN-
NER-CITY INTERACTION STABILIZATION

1. Reference is made to the President's speech of 1 March dealing with the necessity to solve the problems of inner-city personnel and matériel interactions in a modern cost-effective manner utilizing state-of-the-art technology.

2. Reference is further made to the statement of the Sec-

retary of Housing and Urban Development reaffirming the role of the Department in the solution of the substantive problems of our society and the need for additional funding in this area.

3. Reference is further made to the memo from the Center Director stressing the unique capability of this Center due to its history of university and industrial relations and its in-house facilities and staff.

4. In accordance with paragraphs 1–3, I would like all technical members of the branch to submit to me, by 14 March, their ideas as to how our branch can aid in the implementation of these national goals.

   a. It is not intended that any of these suggestions will be in final form.

   b. Include estimates as to costs and man-hours to be committed.

   c. I would like to see new concepts: remember that the President has requested us to solve the problems—not their symptoms.

Invest in America
Buy United States Savings Bonds

DEPARTMENT OF HOUSING AND URBAN
DEVELOPMENT
ROBERT F. KENNEDY RESEARCH CENTER

FROM: Gordon Rogers
TO: Chief, Improvements Branch
DATE: 13 March 1984
SUBJECT: COST EFFECTIVE OPTIMIZATION OF INNER-CITY INTERACTION STABILIZATION (Branch Memo of 7 March 1984)

Keeping in mind paragraph 4c of your memo, the problem seems to naturally divide into the areas of matériel and personnel. However, the approach I suggest will be equally effective in both sections of the problem. (This will enable a saving in both procurement and administrative areas.)

The matériel problem is essentially the replacement of obsolescent and obsolete residential (and, to a very small extent, industrial), buildings in a controlled economical method.

Some of the major problems to be expected are: labor-union regulations; local construction ordinances; lack of specialized tools/techniques.

All these essentially add to the time required to perform the task, adding to the cost. The current patchwork method also makes it extremely difficult to perform long-range, large-scale planning for slum clearance and urban renewal.

The personnel problem is closely tied into this with older buildings (which provide too many defense positions) making effective law enforcement difficult. The unplanned city growth (especially in the use of narrow and short streets) hampers effective control of urban disturbances and riots.

The obvious solution to all these problems is the selective use of low-yield tactical nuclear devices as the major components of a modern, effective slum-clearance and riot-control program. It is expected that sufficient devices can be transferred from the Department of Defense, at cost, in the initial stages of the program. Further downstream, alternate sources for the devices can be sought on a competitive bid basis, thereby decreasing costs.

The program could be run by the Department directly or as a contractor to the states.

I estimate the first year's program should run about $4,700,000 and involve forty man-years of technical and support staff.

Invest in America
Buy United States Savings Bonds

DEPARTMENT OF HOUSING AND URBAN DEVELOPMENT
ROBERT F. KENNEDY RESEARCH CENTER

FROM: Chief, Improvements Branch
TO: Gordon Rogers
DATE: 19 March 1984
SUBJECT: Your Memo of 13 March 1984

Are you serious? You are proposing that we go into these areas and essentially eliminate them and their inhabitants without any warning. What you are proposing is administrative murder—these are living human beings. Perhaps you meant the whole thing as a joke, but, if so, it is in very bad taste. Regardless of how much money could be saved I don't think anyone in this Department (or any other) would justify using the methods you proposed. If you have any sane suggestions in line with my memo of 7 March, I would like to see them.

A copy of this memo is being placed in your permanent personnel file.

Invest in America
Buy United States Savings Bonds

DEPARTMENT OF HOUSING AND URBAN
DEVELOPMENT
ROBERT F. KENNEDY RESEARCH CENTER

FROM: Gordon Rogers
TO: Chief, Improvements Branch
DATE: 21 March 1984
SUBJECT: Your Memo of 19 March

My proposal was made quite seriously and I believe that its scope comes within the charter of this Center. I would like to refer you to the pertinent sections of the President's speech of 1 March (mention of some of these sections was made in the Division Memo of 7 March) calling for solutions to these critical national problems.

It was not my intention to have any solutions performed in secret, as this could lead to the loss of innocent life and a decrease in the high esteem in which the Department and Center are held by the general public. After an area is publicly selected for improvement, Emergency Urban Evacuation Notices can be served on all persons living in the area under the construction title of the Federal Urban Transit Act of 1977. This will give all decent law-abiding citizens in the improvement area no less than forty-eight (48) hours to relocate elsewhere. They would, of course, have first option to rent new housing (if any) in the improved area after improvement operations.

Since all people residing in the country have their addresses listed in the National Data System, Emergency Urban Evacuation Notices can be sent to all the inhabitants. I would also like to point out that since both failure to report changes of address and failure to comply with an Emergency

Evacuation Notice are felonies, we have what is essentially a self-selecting system which will preserve law-abiding citizens and no others.

I hope that with these points made clear you will see fit to approve this suggestion and pass it on to the Division Chief for consideration. In any case I should point out that even if you do not approve this suggestion, since it deals with an issue designated as a "National Priority Issue" it must be forwarded as called for in the Civil Service Regulations (105.8) and the Internal Operation Instructions of the Department of Housing and Urban Development (RA25-3(c)).

Invest in America
Buy United States Savings Bonds

DEPARTMENT OF HOUSING AND URBAN DEVELOPMENT
ROBERT F. KENNEDY RESEARCH CENTER

FROM: Chief, Improvements Branch
TO: Chief, Readjustment Division
DATE: 28 March 1984
SUBJECT: Proposed Program for COST EFFECTIVE OPTIMIZATION OF INNER-CITY INTERACTION STABILIZATION

This proposal is being forwarded to you as a "National Priority Issue" under section 105.8 of the Civil Service Regulations and Section RA25-3(c) of the Internal Operating Instructions of the Department of Housing and Urban Development.

This proposal has not been approved by the Branch Chief, Improvements Branch.

Although it should be obvious that this proposal is contraindicated on moral and humanitarian grounds alone, I have included a list of technical objections which should be sufficient grounds for rejection of this program.

Enc: technical objections, list

Invest in America
Buy United States Savings Bonds

Request for Proposal

DEPARTMENT OF HOUSING AND URBAN DEVELOPMENT
ROBERT F. KENNEDY RESEARCH CENTER

FROM: Chief, Readjustment Division
TO: Gordon Rogers
DATE: 2 April 1984
SUBJECT: Proposed Program for COST EFFECTIVE OPTIMIZATION OF INNER-CITY INTERACTION STABILIZATION

The Division has received and reviewed your proposed program and has found the following problems involved. It is our opinion that any one of these would be sufficient to cause rejection of this program.

1. What percentage of the buildings in potential improvement areas are industrial? This is extremely important as it would lead to a lessening of the city's tax base.

2. What provisions will be made for the exacerbation of the housing shortage since the decrease in demand will not be concomitant with the temporary supply decrease? (Assuming proper action with regard to the Emergency Urban Evacuation Notices.)

3. What damages could occur in neighboring nonimprovement areas? How can we predict overlaps and errors? What tolerance in "slop-over" can be allowed in both personnel and matériel?

4. What containment is necessary under the terms of the Nuclear Test Ban Treaty?

5. What would be the added costs if it becomes necessary to prevent the dispersal of fallout? Or, of the reimbursement of affected areas, if this is more economical?

6. What specific problems will there be with labor unions? Will it be better to retrain the people involved or to pension them off?

7. In order to demonstrate cost effectiveness we will have to run a pilot program. Outline briefly, with especial reference to selection of areas and parameters, such a plan for effectiveness-result comparison.

If you cannot satisfy the problems listed above by 9 April 1984, I shall have no choice but to reject your proposed program.

738

Anthony R. Lewis

cc: Improvements Branch

Invest in America
Buy United States Savings Bonds

DEPARTMENT OF HOUSING AND URBAN
DEVELOPMENT
ROBERT F. KENNEDY RESEARCH CENTER

FROM: Gordon Rogers
TO: Chief, Readjustment Division
DATE: 9 April 1984
SUBJECT: Your Memo of 2 April 1984

1. Data from the 1980 census indicate that in potential improvement areas less than four percent of the structures (floor area) are classified as industrial. Of these, more than ninety percent are over sixty (60) years old and are considered to be inefficient.

2. The problems of temporary housing may be met as provided for under the Federal Transit Act of 1977. Those people who cannot relocate independently (through family, friends, or private agencies) are to be provided for by the Federal Government either in the Ecology Improvement Relocation Camps or as Urban Inductees (quasi-voluntary) in the Armed Forces or the Peace Corps.

3. With state-of-the-art techniques in nuclear devices, we can, by pattern shaping, reduce the error to less than twenty feet (approximately an average city street width). The greatest error will result from emplacement of the devices. If we can hand emplace, this will be eliminated. The accuracy of emplacement via remote delivery is estimated as twenty feet (ground) or fifty feet (air). (All uncertainties are root-mean-square.) Since the areas immediately adjacent may also be in need of improvements within a short time span—it is not expected that in most cases this will prove a problem.

In a few cases we may have just such a problem and then a choice arises between a decrease in the yields used, necessitating additional manual clearance at the peripheries, or the reimbursement of survivors and/or legatees in the surrounding areas in the case of nonoptimum emplacement. Which will be more economical will, of course, depend upon the details of each specific case. A small contract to a consulting firm to develop a choice algorithm would be in order here.

4. Semantically, this is not a test. I think we will still be abiding by the spirit of the treaty, since these events will not be directed against anyone, but will be of a specific corrective and constructive purpose. Recent urban developments in other countries lead me to believe that our successes in this program will be quickly imitated elsewhere. Possibly, later projects could be done on an international basis—with due regard to security.

5. It is not expected, in the majority of cases, that containment in advance will be practicable due to the possibility of criminal elements. Present device design indicates that major fallout components will be neutron-activated environmental artifacts. Calculations indicate that proper emplacement can eliminate up to seventy-six percent of the specific activity present twenty-four hours after the event. Reimbursements to the surrounding areas are covered under Title 7 of the Federal Urban Transit Act of 1977.

6. Studies of documents and speeches indicate that a lump-sum payment to the union(s) retirement fund plus assurance of employment on rebuilding projects in the improved areas will be adequate. Possibly a contract with the national unions involved would be desirable.

7. This will involve a pilot program. In order to gather necessary background data we should construct (probably at the Nevada test site) a selection of the different building styles which would be encountered in major cities in their potential improvement areas. These would then be staffed with personnel transferred from the Departments of Defense and Labor (proper backgrounds, et cetera, to be computer-selected). Costs for personnel would be on a per capita–per diem basis and would be extremely low under the Universal Conscription Act of 1979. If this phase is to be extended as data from cities are obtained, perhaps some of the personnel temporarily evacuated (see paragraph 2) would volunteer for this assignment knowing that it would aid in the improvement of the lives of their socioeconomic class.

These data will enable us to construct algorithms for the choice of cities as tests for this program and to eliminate effects due to the differing urban matrices in which the individual improvement areas are embedded.

I trust that this fully answers the questions you raised.

I request that this proposed program be forwarded to the Center Director as a "National Priority Issue" under Section 105.8 of the Civil Service Regulations and Section RA25-3(c) of the Internal Operating Instructions of the Department of Housing and Urban Development and in accordance with the expressed desires of the President in his speech of 1 March 1984.

cc: Improvements Branch

Invest in America
Buy United States Savings Bonds

DEPARTMENT OF HOUSING AND URBAN DEVELOPMENT
ROBERT F. KENNEDY RESEARCH CENTER

FROM: Chief, Readjustment Division
TO: Director, Robert F. Kennedy Research Center
DATE: 13 April 1984
SUBJECT: Proposed Program for COST EFFECTIVE OPTIMIZATION OF INNER-CITY INTERACTION STABILIZATION

1. Herein is forwarded a proposed program in the area of Cost Effective Optimization of Inner-City Interaction Stabilization as a "National Priority Issue" under Section 105.8 of the Civil Service Regulations and Section RA25-3(c) of the Internal Operating Instructions of the Department of Housing and Urban Development and Center Directive XLR-2527-003.

2. This proposal is in response to the Center Memo of 7 March 1984.

3. This proposed program has not been approved by Chief, Improvements Branch nor Chief, Readjustment Division.

4. It is felt that this proposal is highly immoral and that it be rejected.

cc: Improvements Branch
    Gordon Rogers

Invest in America
Buy United States Savings Bonds

DEPARTMENT OF HOUSING AND URBAN DEVELOPMENT
ROBERT F. KENNEDY RESEARCH CENTER

FROM: Director, Robert F. Kennedy Research Center
TO: Chief, Readjustment Division
DATE: 18 April 1984
SUBJECT: Proposed Program for COST EFFECTIVE OPTIMIZATION OF INNER-CITY INTERACTION STABILIZATION

1. In view of both the public statements of the President and the Secretary of Housing and Urban Development and the fact that this area has been designated a "National Priority Issue" I do not think that we can reject this proposal on any other grounds than deficiencies in the technical aspects.
2. The following major questions have not been answered by the proposed program document:

2.1 Control of devices to be used in this program is by AEC and/or Defense. Is it feasible to set up a liaison program to handle transfers of this magnitude?
2.2 How will the actions of the recalcitrant element in the potential improvement areas affect the proper emplacement of devices, bearing in mind that at least forty-eight hours' notification will be given?
2.3 In the construction of any selection algorithm, it is essential to include the factor that any population readjustments due to the program should not decrease the present Administration's representation in the Congress.

3. Please have Mr. Rogers report to me with answers to the problems in paragraph 2 before 25 April 1984.

cc: Improvements Branch

Invest in America
Buy United States Savings Bonds

DEPARTMENT OF HOUSING AND URBAN DEVELOPMENT
ROBERT F. KENNEDY RESEARCH CENTER

Anthony R. Lewis

19 April 1984

Dr. J. Moriarty (Code 21-5)
Defense Nuclear Agency
Washington, D.C. 20301

Dear Jim:

We've got a possible program going here in line with the President's speech of 1 March setting up the inner-city problems as a National Priority Issue. Before we can go ahead with formal requests for liaison I'd like to talk to you informally about it. Please give me a call on FTS or Autovon soonest.

Gordon Rogers

Invest in America
Buy United States Savings Bonds

DEPARTMENT OF HOUSING AND URBAN DEVELOPMENT
ROBERT F. KENNEDY RESEARCH CENTER

19 April 1984

Col. S. Moran (Code RM-37)
United States Atomic Energy Commission
Washington, D.C., 20545

Dear Sebastian:

In regard to the President's speech of 1 March setting up the inner-city problems as a National Priority Issue, I think we've got a possible program here that would be a natural for cooperation between our two agencies and would be to all our advantages. Give me a call on FTS and we'll talk it over before we do anything formal about it.

Best to you and Irene.

Gordon Rogers

Invest in America
Buy United States Savings Bonds

DEPARTMENT OF HOUSING AND URBAN DEVELOPMENT
ROBERT F. KENNEDY RESEARCH CENTER

Request for Proposal

FROM: Chief, Readjustment Division
TO: Director, Robert F. Kennedy Research Center
DATE: 25 April 1984
SUBJECT: Proposed Program for COST EFFECTIVE OP-
TIMIZATION OF INNER-CITY INTERACTION STABI-
LIZATION (Your Memo of 18 April 1984)

Mr. Rogers has spoken informally to the appropriate persons in both the Defense Nuclear Agency and the Atomic
Energy Commission and we have been assured of the support
of both agencies in fulfilling the pledges of the President in
his raising of the inner-city problems to a "National Priority
Issue." (See attachment A for confirmatory memos.)

See also attachment B giving details of remote emplacement in the event that access to the potential improvement
area is denied to lawful authorities by recalcitrant elements.

See also attachment C spelling out the constraints to be
placed on the selection algorithms as specified in paragraph
2.3 of your memo of 18 April 1984.

Since I see no possible way to prevent this program from
being actualized in my present position, I wish to tender my
resignation from the Department.

cc: Improvements Branch
     Gordon Rogers
att: A—confirmatory memos from DNA, AEC
     B—legal brief and details of remote emplacement
     C—mathematical constraints on selection algorithm

Invest in America
Buy United States Savings Bonds

DEPARTMENT OF HOUSING AND URBAN
DEVELOPMENT
ROBERT F. KENNEDY RESEARCH CENTER

FROM: Director, Robert F. Kennedy Research Center
TO: Acting Chief, Readjustment Division
DATE: 3 May 1984
SUBJECT: COST EFFECTIVE OPTIMIZATION OF IN-
NER-CITY INTERACTION STABILIZATION

This is to authorize you to proceed immediately with the subject program as defined in our previous communications. Below is a quote from the Secretary of Housing and Urban Development concerning this program:

"This program will be in keeping with the finest traditions of our country and will reflect most favorably upon the Department and upon the Robert F. Kennedy Research Center and upon those individuals directly involved."

cc: Improvements Branch
    Gordon Rogers

Invest in America
Buy United States Savings Bonds

DEPARTMENT OF HOUSING AND URBAN
DEVELOPMENT
ROBERT F. KENNEDY RESEARCH CENTER

FROM: Acting Chief, Improvements Branch
TO: Chief, Procurement Branch
DATE: 7 May 1984
SUBJECT: REQUEST FOR PROPOSAL

Procurement Request for Study for the Cost Effective Optimization of Inner-City Interaction Stabilization
1. It is requested that a contract be negotiated with a commercial source to perform the efforts described in the attached work statement and performance schedule, exhibit A.

Invest in America
Buy United States Savings Bonds

DEPARTMENT OF HOUSING AND URBAN
DEVELOPMENT
ROBERT F. KENNEDY RESEARCH CENTER

Issue Date: 4 June 1984
Subject: Solicitation No. HUD84-2101R
Title: Cost Effective Optimization of Inner-City Interaction
    Stabilization

Request for Proposal

Due Date: 9 July 1984, 1700 (local Washington, D.C. time)
Submit to:
　Negotiated Contracts
　Procurement Branch
　Department of Housing and Urban Development

Gentlemen:
　The U.S. Department of Housing and Urban Development, Robert F. Kennedy Research Center, solicits your organization for a proposal for a study aimed at defining the requirements for, and the economics of, the use of low-yield nuclear devices in the optimization of inner-city interaction stabilization.
　This solicitation is covered by the following documents...

H. Beam Piper (1903–64) is best remembered as the author of the "Paratime" and "Terran Federation" series which appeared (mostly) in the 1950s. Particularly popular are the novels Little Fuzzy *(1962) and* The Other Human Race *(1964). His finest short fiction was "Omnilingual" (1957), but "He Walked Around the Horses" (*Astounding Science Fiction, *April 1948) is a close second. The story is based on an actual historical mystery, and, for all we know, this is really what happened.*

HE WALKED AROUND THE HORSES

By H. Beam Piper

In November, 1809, an Englishman named Benjamin Bathurst vanished, inexplicably and utterly.

He was en route to Hamburg from Vienna, where he had been serving as his Government's envoy to the court of what Napoleon had left of the Austrian Empire. At an inn in Perleburg, in Prussia, while examining a change of horses for his coach, he casually stepped out of sight of his secretary and his valet. He was not seen to leave the inn-yard. He was not seen again, ever.

At least, not in this continuum...

I

(From Baron Eugen von Krutz, Minister of Police, to His Excellency the Count von Berchtenwald, Chancellor to His Majesty Friedrich Wilhelm III of Prussia.)

25 November, 1809

Your Excellency:

A circumstance has come to the notice of this Ministry, the significance of which I am at a loss to define, but, since it appears to involve matters of state, both here and abroad, I am convinced that it is of sufficient importance to be brought to the personal attention of your Excellency. Frankly, I am unwilling to take any further action in the matter without your Excellency's advice.

Briefly, the situation is this: We are holding, here at the Ministry of Police, a person giving his name as Benjamin Bathurst, who claims to be a British diplomat. This person was taken into custody by the police at Perleburg yesterday, as a result of a disturbance at an inn there; he is being detained on technical charges of causing disorder in a public place, and of being a suspicious person. When arrested, he had in his possession a dispatch-case, containing a number of papers; these are of such an extraordinary nature that the local authorities declined to assume any responsibility beyond having the man sent here to Berlin.

After interviewing this person and examining his papers, I am, I must confess, in much the same position. This is not, I am convinced, any ordinary police matter; there is something very strange and disturbing here. The man's statements, taken alone, are so incredible as to justify the assumption that he is mad. I cannot, however, adopt this theory, in view of his demeanor, which is that of a man of perfect rationality, and because of the existence of these papers. The whole thing is mad; incomprehensible!

The papers in question accompany, along with copies of the various statements taken at Perleburg, and a personal letter to me from my nephew, Lieutenant Rudolf von Tarlburg. This last is deserving of your Excellency's particular attention; Lieutenant von Tarlburg is a very level-headed young officer, not at all inclined to be fanciful or imaginative. It would take a good deal to affect him as he describes.

The man calling himself Benjamin Bathurst is now lodged in an apartment here at the Ministry; he is being treated with every consideration, and, except for freedom of movement, accorded every privilege.

I am, most anxiously awaiting your Excellency's advice, etc., etc.,

Krutz

II

(Report of Traugott Zeller, *Oberwachtmeister, Staatspolizei,* made at Perleburg, 25 November, 1809.)

At about ten minutes past two of the afternoon of Saturday, 25 November, while I was at the police station, there entered a man known to me as Franz Bauer, an inn-servant employed by Christian Hauck, at the sign of the Sword & Scepter, here in Perleburg. This man Franz Bauer made complaint to *Staatspolizeikapitan* Ernst Hartenstein, saying that there was a madman making trouble at the inn where he, Franz Bauer, worked. I was therefore directed, by *Staatspolizeikapitan* Hartenstein to go to the Sword & Scepter Inn, there to act at discretion to maintain the peace.

Arriving at the inn in company with the said Franz Bauer, I found a considerable crowd of people in the common-room, and, in the midst of them, the innkeeper, Christian Hauck, in altercation with a stranger. This stranger was a gentlemanly-appearing person, dressed in traveling clothes, who had under his arm a small leather dispatch-case. As I entered, I could hear him, speaking in German with a strong English accent, abusing the innkeeper, the said Christian Hauck, and accusing him of having drugged his, the stranger's, wine, and of having stolen his, the stranger's, coach-and-four, and of having abducted his, the stranger's, secretary and servants. This the said Christian Hauck was loudly denying, and the other people in the inn were taking the innkeeper's part, and mocking the stranger for a madman.

On entering, I commanded everyone to be silent, in the King's name, and then, as he appeared to be the complaining party of the dispute, I required the foreign gentleman to state to me what was the trouble. He then repeated his accusations against the innkeeper, Hauck, saying that Hauck, or, rather, another man who resembled Hauck and who had claimed to be the innkeeper, had drugged his wine and stolen his coach and made off with his secretary and his servants. At this point, the innkeeper and the bystanders all began shouting denials and contradictions, so that I had to pound on a table with my truncheon to command silence.

I then required the innkeeper, Christian Hauck, to answer the charges which the stranger had made; this he did with a complete denial of all of them, saying that the stranger had had no wine in his inn, and that he had not been inside the inn until a few minutes before, when he had burst in shouting accusations, and that there had been no secretary, and no valet, and no coachman, and no coach-and-four, at the inn, and that the gentleman was raving mad. To all this, he called the people who were in the common-room to witness.

I then required the stranger to account for himself. He said that his name was Benjamin Bathurst, and that he was a British diplomat, returning to England from Vienna. To prove this, he produced from his dispatch-case sundry papers. One of these was a letter of safe-conduct, issued by the Prussian Chancellery, in which he was named and described as Benjamin Bathurst. The other papers were English, all bearing seals, and appearing to be official documents.

Accordingly, I requested him to accompany me to the police station, and also the innkeeper, and three men whom the innkeeper wanted to bring as witnesses.

Traugott Zeller
Oberwachtmeister

Report approved,

Ernst Hartenstein
Staatspolizeikapitan

III

(Statement of the self-so-called Benjamin Bathurst, taken at the police station at Perleburg, 25 November, 1809.)

My name is Benjamin Bathurst, and I am Envoy Extraordinary and Minister Plenipotentiary of the Government of His Britannic Majesty to the court of His Majesty Franz I, Emperor of Austria, or, at least I was until the events following the Austrian surrender made necessary my return to London. I left Vienna on the morning of Monday, the 20th, to go to Hamburg to take ship home; I was traveling in my own coach-and-four, with my secretary, Mr. Bertram Jardine, and my valet, William Small, both British subjects, and a coachman, Joseph Bidek, an Austrian subject, whom I had hired for the trip. Because of the presence of French troops, whom I was anxious to avoid, I was forced to make a detour west as far as Salzburg before turning north toward Magdeburg, where I crossed the Elbe. I was unable to get a change of horses for my coach after leaving Gera, until I reached Perleburg, where I stopped at the Sword & Scepter Inn.

Arriving there, I left my coach in the inn-yard, and I and my secretary, Mr. Jardine, went into the inn. A man, not this fellow here, but another rogue, with more beard and less paunch, and more shabbily dressed, but as like him as though he were his brother, represented himself as the innkeeper, and I dealt with him for a change of horses, and ordered a bottle of wine for myself and my secretary, and also a pot of beer apiece for my valet and the coachman, to be taken outside to them. Then Jardine and I sat down to our wine, at a table in the common-room, until the man who claimed to be the innkeeper came back and told us that the fresh horses were harnessed to the coach and ready to go. Then we went outside again.

I looked at the two horses on the off-side, and then walked around in front of the team to look at the two nigh-side horses, and as I did, I felt giddy, as though I were about to fall, and everything went black before my eyes. I thought I was having a fainting-spell, something I am not at all subject to, and I put out my hand to grasp the hitching-bar, but could not find it. I am sure, now, that I was unconscious for some time, because when my head cleared, the coach and horses were gone, and in their place was a big farm-wagon, jacked up in front, with the right front wheel off, and two peasants were greasing the detached wheel.

I looked at them for a moment, unable to credit my eyes, and then I spoke to them in German, saying, "Where the devil's my coach-and-four?"

They both straightened, startled; the one who was holding the wheel almost dropped it.

"Pardon, Excellency," he said. "There's been no coach-and-four here, all the time we've been here."

"Yes," said his mate, "and we've been here since just after noon."

I did not attempt to argue with them. It occurred to me—and it is still my opinion—that I was the victim of some plot; that my wine had been drugged, that I had been unconscious

for some time, during which my coach had been removed and
this wagon substituted for it, and that these peasants had
been put to work on it and instructed what to say if questioned. If my arrival at the inn had been anticipated, and
everything put in readiness, the whole business would not
have taken ten minutes.

I therefore entered the inn, determined to have it out with
this rascally innkeeper, but when I returned to the common-
room, he was nowhere to be seen, and this other fellow, who
has also given his name as Christian Hauck, claimed to be
the innkeeper and denied knowledge of any of the things I
have just stated. Furthermore, there were four cavalrymen,
Uhlans, drinking beer and playing cards at the table where
Jardine and I had had our wine, and they claimed to have
been there for several hours.

I have no idea why such an elaborate prank, involving the
participation of many people, should be played on me, except
at the instigation of the French. In that case, I cannot understand why Prussian soldiers should lend themselves to it.

Benjamin Bathurst

IV

(Statement of Christian Hauck, innkeeper, taken at the police station at Perleburg, 25 November, 1809.)

May it please your Honor, my name is Christian Hauck,
and I keep an inn at the sign of the Sword & Scepter, and
have these past fifteen years, and my father, and his father,
before me, for the past fifty years, and never has there been
a complaint like this against my inn. Your Honor, it is a hard
thing for a man who keeps a decent house, and pays his taxes,
and obeys the laws, to be accused of crimes of this sort.

I know nothing of this gentleman, nor of his coach nor his
secretary nor his servants; I never set eyes on him before he
came bursting into the inn from the yard, shouting and raving like a madman, and crying out, "Where the devil's that
rogue of an innkeeper?"

I said to him, "I am the innkeeper; what cause have you
to call me a rogue, sir?"

The stranger replied:

"You're not the innkeeper I did business with a few minutes ago, and he's the rascal I have a crow to pick with. I

want to know what the devil's been done with my coach, and what's happened to my secretary and my servants."

I tried to tell him that I knew nothing of what he was talking about, but he would not listen, and gave me the lie, saying that he had been drugged and robbed, and his people kidnapped. He even had the impudence to claim that he and his secretary had been sitting at a table in that room, drinking wine, not fifteen minutes before, when there had been four non-commissioned officers of the Third Uhlans at that table since noon. Everybody in the room spoke up for me, but he would not listen, and was shouting that we were all robbers, and kidnappers, and French spies, and I don't know what all, when the police came.

Your Honor, the man is mad. What I have told you about this is the truth, and all that I know about this business, so help me God.

Christian Hauck

V

(Statement of Franz Bauer, inn-servant, taken at the police station at Perleburg, 25 November, 1809.)

May it please your Honor, my name is Franz Bauer, and I am a servant at the Sword & Scepter Inn, kept by Christian Hauck.

This afternoon, when I went into the inn-yard to empty a bucket of slops on the dung-heap by the stables, I heard voices and turned around, to see this gentleman speaking to Wilhelm Beick and Fritz Herzer, who were greasing their wagon in the yard. He had not been in the yard when I had turned around to empty the bucket, and I thought that he must have come in from the street. This gentleman was asking Beick and Herzer where was his coach, and when they told him they didn't know, he turned and ran into the inn.

Of my own knowledge, the man had not been inside the inn before then, nor had there been any coach, or any of the people he spoke of, at the inn, and none of the things he spoke of happened there, for otherwise I would know, since I was at the inn all day.

When I went back inside, I found him in the common-room, shouting at my master, and claiming that he had been drugged and robbed. I saw that he was mad, and was afraid that he would do some mischief, so I went for the police.

Franz Bauer
his (X) mark

VI

(Statements of Wilhelm Beick and Fritz Herzer, peasants, taken at the police station at Perleburg, 25 November, 1809.)

May it please your Honor, my name is Wilhelm Beick, and I am a tenant on the estate of the Baron von Hentig. On this day, I and Fritz Herzer were sent in to Perleburg with a load of potatoes and cabbages which the innkeeper at the Sword & Scepter had bought from the estate-superintendent. After we had unloaded them, we decided to grease our wagon, which was very dry, before going back, so we unhitched and began working on it. We took about two hours, starting just after we had eaten lunch, and in all that time, there was no coach-and-four in the inn-yard. We were just finishing when this gentleman spoke to us, demanding to know where his coach was. We told him that there had been no coach in the yard all the time we had been there, so he turned around and ran into the inn. At the time, I thought that he had come out of the inn before speaking to us, for I know that he could not have come in from the street. Now I do not know where he came from, but I know that I never saw him before that moment.

Wilhelm Beick
his (X) mark

I have heard the above testimony, and it is true to my own knowledge, and I have nothing to add to it.

Fritz Herzer
his (X) mark

VII

(From *Staatspolizeikapitan* Ernst Hartenstein, to His Excellency, the Baron von Krutz, Minister of Police.)

25 November, 1809

Your Excellency:
The accompanying copies of statements taken this day

will explain how the prisoner, the self-so-called Benjamin Bathurst, came into my custody. I have charged him with causing disorder and being a suspicious person, to hold him until more can be learned about him. However, as he represents himself to be a British diplomat, I am unwilling to assume any further responsibility, and am having him sent to your Excellency, in Berlin.

In the first place, your Excellency, I have the strongest doubts of the man's story. The statement which he made before me. and signed, is bad enough, with a coach-and-four turning into a farm-wagon, like Cinderella's coach into a pumpkin, and three people vanishing as though swallowed by the earth. Your Excellency will permit me to doubt that there ever was any such coach, or any such people. But all this is perfectly reasonable and credible, beside the things he said to me, of which no record was made.

Your Excellency will have noticed, in his statement, certain allusions to the Austrian surrender, and to French troops in Austria. After his statement had been taken down, I noticed these allusions, and I inquired, what surrender, and what were French troops doing in Austria. The man looked at me in a pitying manner, and said:

"News seems to travel slowly, hereabouts; peace was concluded at Vienna on the 14th of last month. And as for what French troops are doing in Austria, they're doing the same thing Bonaparte's brigands are doing everywhere in Europe."

"And who is Bonaparte?" I asked.

He stared at me as though I had asked him, "Who is the Lord Jehovah?" Then, after a moment, a look of comprehension came into his face.

"So; you Prussians concede him the title of Emperor, and refer to him as Napoleon," he said. "Well, I can assure you that His Britannic Majesty's Government haven't done so, and never will; not so long as one Englishman has a finger left to pull a trigger. General Bonaparte is a usurper; His Britannic Majesty's Government do not recognize any sovereignty in France except the House of Bourbon." This he said very sternly, as though rebuking me.

It took me a moment or so to digest that, and to appreciate all its implications. Why, this fellow evidently believed, as a matter of fact, that the French Monarchy had been overthrown by some military adventurer named Bonaparte, who was calling himself the Emperor Napoleon, and who had made war on Austria and forced a surrender. I made no attempt to argue with him—one wastes time arguing with madmen—but if this man could believe that, the transformation of a coach-and-four into a cabbage-wagon was a small matter indeed. So, to humor him, I asked him if he thought General Bonaparte's agents were responsible for his trouble at the inn.

"Certainly," he replied. "The chances are they didn't know me to see me, and took Jardine for the Minister, and me for the secretary, so they made off with poor Jardine. I wonder, though, that they left me my dispatch-case. And that reminds me; I'll want that back. Diplomatic papers, you know."

I told him, very seriously, that we would have to check his credentials. I promised him I would make every effort to locate his secretary and his servants and his coach, took a complete description of all of them, and persuaded him to go into an upstairs room, where I kept him under guard. I did start inquiries, calling in all my informers and spies, but, as I expected, I could learn nothing. I could not find anybody, even, who had seen him anywhere in Perleburg before he appeared at the Sword & Scepter, and that rather surprised me, as somebody should have seen him enter the town, or walk along the street.

In this connection, let me remind your Excellency of the discrepancy in the statements of the servant, Franz Bauer, and of the two peasants. The former is certain the man entered the inn-yard from the street; the latter are just as positive that he did not. Your Excellency, I do not like such puzzles, for I am sure that all three were telling the truth to the best of their knowledge. They are ignorant common-folk, I admit, but they should know what they did or did not see.

After I got the prisoner into safe-keeping, I fell to examining his papers, and I can assure your Excellency that they gave me a shock. I had paid little heed to his ravings about the King of France being dethroned, or about this General Bonaparte who called himself the Emperor Napoleon, but I found all these things mentioned in his papers and dispatches, which had every appearance of being official documents. There was repeated mention of the taking, by the French, of Vienna, last May, and of the capitulation of the Austrian Emperor to this General Bonaparte, and of battles being fought all over Europe, and I don't know what other fantastic things. Your Excellency, I have heard of all sorts of madmen—one believing himself to be the Archangel Gabriel, or Mohammed, or a werewolf, and another convinced that his bones are made of glass, or that he is pursued and tormented by devils—but, so help me God, this is the first time I have heard of a madman who had documentary proof for his delusions! Does your Excellency wonder, then, that I want no part of this business?

But the matter of his credentials was even worse. He had papers, sealed with the seal of the British Foreign Office, and to every appearance genuine—but they were signed, as Foreign Minister, by one George Canning, and all the world knows that Lord Castlereagh has been Foreign Minister these last five years. And to cap it all, he had a safe-conduct, sealed with the seal of the Prussian Chancellery—the very seal, for I compared it, under a strong magnifying-glass, with one that I knew to be genuine, and they were identical!—and yet, this letter was signed, as Chancellor, not by Count von Berchtenwald, but by Baron vom und zum Stein, the Minister of Agriculture, and the signature, as far as I could see, appeared to be genuine! This is too much for me, your Excellency; I must ask to be excused from dealing with this matter, before I become as mad as my prisoner!

I made arrangements, accordingly, with Colonel Keitel, of the Third Uhlans, to furnish an officer to escort this man in to Berlin. The coach in which they come belongs to this police station, and the driver is one of my men. He should be furnished expense-money to get back to Perleburg. The guard is a corporal of Uhlans, the orderly of the officer. He will stay with the *Herr Oberleutnant*, and both of them will return here at their own convenience and expense.

I have the honor, your Excellency, to be, etc., etc.

Ernst Hartenstein
Staatspolizeikapitan

VIII

(From *Oberleutnant* Rudolf von Tarlburg, to Baron Eugen von Krutz.)

26 November, 1809

Dear Uncle Eugen:

This is in no sense a formal report; I made that at the Ministry, when I turned the Englishman and his papers over to one of your officers—a fellow with red hair and a face like a bulldog. But there are a few things which you should be told, which wouldn't look well in an official report, to let you know just what sort of a rare fish has gotten into your net.

I had just come in from drilling my platoon, yesterday, when Colonel Keitel's orderly told me that the colonel wanted to see me in his quarters. I found the old fellow in undress in his sitting-room, smoking his big pipe.

"Come in, Lieutenant; come in and sit down, my boy!" he greeted me, in that bluff, hearty manner which he always adopts with his junior officers when he has some particularly nasty job to be done. "How would you like to take a little trip in to Berlin? I have an errand, which won't take half an hour, and you can stay as long as you like, just so you're back by Thursday, when your turn comes up for road-patrol."

Well, I thought, this is the bait. I waited to see what the hook would look like, saying that it was entirely agreeable with me, and asking what his errand was.

"Well, it isn't for myself, Tarlburg," he said. "It's for this fellow Hartenstein, the *Staatspolizeikapitan* here. He has something he wants done at the Ministry of Police, and I thought of you because I've heard you're related to the Baron von Krutz. You are, aren't you?" he asked, just as though he didn't know all about who all his officers are related to.

"That's right, Colonel; the Baron is my uncle," I said. "What does Hartenstein want done?"

"Why, he has a prisoner whom he wants taken to Berlin and turned over at the Ministry. All you have to do is to take him in, in a coach, and see he doesn't escape on the way, and get a receipt for him, and for some papers. This is a very important prisoner; I don't think Hartenstein has anybody he can trust to handle him. A state prisoner. He claims to be some sort of a British diplomat, and for all Hartenstein knows, maybe he is. Also, he is a madman."

"A madman?" I echoed.

"Yes, just so. At least, that's what Hartenstein told me. I wanted to know what sort of a madman—there are various kinds of madmen, all of whom must be handled differently— but all Hartenstein would tell me was that he had unrealistic beliefs about the state of affairs in Europe."

"Ha! What diplomat hasn't?" I asked.

Old Keitel gave a laugh, somewhere between the bark of a dog and the croaking of a raven.

"Yes, naturally! The unrealistic beliefs of diplomats are what soldiers die of," he said. "I said as much to Hartenstein, but he wouldn't tell me anything more. He seemed to regret having said even that much. He looked like a man who's seen a particularly terrifying ghost." The old man puffed hard at his famous pipe for a while, blowing smoke up through his moustache. "Rudi, Hartenstein has pulled a hot potato out of the ashes, this time, and he wants to toss it to your uncle, before he burns his fingers. I think that's one reason why he got me to furnish an escort for his Englishman. Now, look; you must take this unrealistic diplomat, or this undiplomatic madman, or whatever in blazes he is, in to Berlin. And understand this." He pointed his pipe at me as though it were a pistol. "Your orders are to take him there and turn him over at the Ministry of Police. Nothing has been said about whether you turn him over alive, or dead, or half one and half the other. I know nothing about this business, and want to know nothing; if Hartenstein wants us to play gaol-warders for him, then, *bei Gott*, he must be satisfied with our way of doing it!"

Well, to cut short the story, I looked at the coach Hartenstein had placed at my disposal, and I decided to chain the left door shut on the outside, so that it couldn't be opened from within. Then, I would put my prisoner on my left, so that the only way out would be past me. I decided not to carry any weapons which he might be able to snatch from me, so I took off my sabre and locked it in the seat-box, along with the dispatch-case containing the Englishman's papers. It was cold enough to wear a greatcoat in comfort, so I wore mine, and in the right side pocket, where my prisoner couldn't reach, I put a little leaded bludgeon, and also a brace of pocket-pistols. Hartenstein was going to furnish me a guard as well as a driver, but I said that I would take a servant who could act as guard. The servant, of course, was my orderly, old Johann; I gave him my double hunting-gun to carry, with a big charge of boar-shot in one barrel and an ounce ball in the other.

In addition, I armed myself with a big bottle of cognac. I thought that if I could shoot my prisoner often enough with that, he would give me no trouble.

As it happened, he didn't, and none of my precautions—except the cognac—were needed. The man didn't look like a lunatic to me. He was a rather stout gentleman, of past middle age, with a ruddy complexion and an intelligent face. The only unusual thing about him was his hat, which was a peculiar contraption, looking like the pot out of a close-stool. I put him in the carriage, and then offered him a drink out of my bottle, taking one about half as big myself. He smacked his lips over it and said, "Well, that's real brandy; whatever we think of their detestable politics, we can't criticize the French for their liquor." Then, he said, "I'm glad they're sending me in the custody of a military gentleman, instead of a confounded gendarme. Tell me the truth, Lieutenant; am I under arrest for anything?"

"Why," I said, "Captain Hartenstein should have told you about that. All I know is that I have orders to take you to the Ministry of Police, in Berlin, and not to let you escape on the way. These orders I will carry out; I hope you don't hold that against me."

He assured me that he did not, and we had another drink on it—I made sure, again, that he got twice as much as I did—and then the coachman cracked his whip and we were off for Berlin.

Now, I thought, I am going to see just what sort of a madman this is, and why Hartenstein is making a state affair out of a squabble at an inn. So I decided to explore his unrealistic beliefs about the state of affairs in Europe.

After guiding the conversation to where I wanted it, I asked him:

"What, *Herr* Bathurst, in your belief, is the real, underlying cause of the present tragic situation in Europe?"

That, I thought, was safe enough. Name me one year, since the days of Julius Caesar, when the situation in Europe hasn't been tragic! And it worked, to perfection.

"In my belief," says this Englishman, "the whole damnable mess is the result of the victory of the rebellious colonists in North America, and their blasted republic."

Well, you can imagine, that gave me a start. All the world knows that the American Patriots lost their war for independence from England; that their army was shattered, that their leaders were either killed or driven into exile. How many times, when I was a little boy, did I not sit up long past my bedtime, when old Baron von Steuben was a guest at Tarlburg-Schloss, listening open-mouthed and wide-eyed to his stories of that gallant lost struggle! How I used to shiver at his tales of the terrible Winter camp, or thrill at the battles, or weep as he told how he held the dying Washington in his arms, and listened to his noble last words, at the Battle of Doylestown! And here, this man was telling me that the Patriots had really won, and set up the republic for which they had fought! I had been prepared for some of what Hartenstein had called unrealistic beliefs, but nothing as fantastic as this.

"I can cut it even finer than that," Bathurst continued. "It was the defeat of Burgoyne at Saratoga. We made a good bargain when we got Benedict Arnold to turn his coat, but we didn't do it soon enough. If he hadn't been on the field that day, Burgoyne would have gone through Gates' army like a hot knife through butter."

But Arnold hadn't been at Saratoga. I know; I have read much of the American War. Arnold was shot dead on New Year's Day of 1776, during the attempted storming of Quebec. And Burgoyne had done just as Bathurst had said; he had gone through Gates like a knife, and down the Hudson to join Howe.

"But, *Herr* Bathurst," I asked, "how could that affect the situation in Europe? America is thousands of miles away, across the ocean."

"Ideas can cross oceans quicker than armies. When Louis XVI decided to come to the aid of the Americans, he doomed himself and his regime. A successful resistance to royal authority in America was all the French Republicans needed to inspire them. Of course, we have Louis' own weakness to blame, too. If he'd given those rascals a whiff of grapeshot, when the mob tried to storm Versailles in 1790, there'd have been no French Revolution."

But he had. When Louis XVI ordered the howitzers turned on the mob at Versailles, and then sent the dragoons to ride down the survivors, the Republican movement had been broken. That had been when Cardinal Talleyrand, who had then been merely Bishop of Autun, had come to the fore and become the power that he is today in France; the greatest King's Minister since Richelieu.

"And, after that, Louis' death followed as surely as night after day," Bathurst was saying. "And because the French had no experience in self-government, their republic was foredoomed. If Bonaparte hadn't seized power, somebody else would have; when the French murdered their King, they delivered themselves to dictatorship. And a dictator, unsupported by the prestige of royalty, has no choice but to lead his people into foreign war, to keep them from turning upon him."

It was like that all the way to Berlin. All these things seem foolish, by daylight, but as I sat in the darkness of that swaying coach, I was almost convinced of the reality of what he told me. I tell you, Uncle Eugen, it was frightening, as though he were giving me a view of Hell. *Gott im Himmel*, the things that man talked of! Armies swarming over Europe; sack and massacre, and cities burning; blockades, and starvation; kings deposed, and thrones tumbling like tenpins! battles in which the soldiers of every nation fought, and in which tens of thousands were mowed down like ripe grain; and, over all, the Satanic figure of a little man in a gray coat, who dictated peace to the Austrian Emperor in Schoenbrunn, and carried the Pope away a prisoner to Savona.

Madman, eh? Unrealistic beliefs, says Hartenstein? Well, give me madmen who drool spittle, and foam at the mouth, and shriek obscene blasphemies. But not this pleasant-seeming gentleman who sat beside me and talked of horrors in a quiet, cultured voice, while he drank my cognac.

But not all my cognac! If your man at the Ministry—the one with red hair and the bulldog face—tells you that I was drunk when I brought in that Englishman, you had better believe him!

Rudi.

IX

(From Count von Berchtenwald, to the British Minister.)

28 November, 1809

Honored Sir:

The accompanying *dossier* will acquaint you with the problem confronting this Chancellery, without needless repetition on my part. Please to understand that it is not, and never was, any part of the intentions of the Government of His Majesty Friedrich Wilhelm III to offer any injury or indignity to the Government of His Britannic Majesty George III. We would never contemplate holding in arrest the person, or tampering with the papers, of an accredited envoy of your Government. However, we have the gravest doubt, to make a considerable understatement, that this person who calls himself Benjamin Bathurst is any such envoy, and we do not think that it would be any service to the Government of His Britannic Majesty to allow an impostor to travel about Europe in the guise of a British diplomatic representative. We certainly should not thank the Government of His Britannic Majesty for failing to take steps to deal with some person who, in England, might falsely represent himself to be a Prussian diplomat.

This affair touches us almost as closely as it does your own Government; this man had in his possession a letter of safe conduct, which you will find in the accompanying dispatch-case. It is of the regular form, as issued by this Chancellery, and is sealed with the Chancellery seal, or with a very exact counterfeit of it. However, it has been signed, as Chancellor of Prussia, with a signature indistinguishable from that of the Baron vom und zum Stein, who is the present Prussian Minister of Agriculture. Baron Stein was shown the signature, with the rest of the letter covered, and without hesitation acknowledged it for his own writing. However, when the letter was uncovered and shown to him, his surprise and horror were such as would require the pen of a Goethe or a Schiller to describe, and he denied categorically ever having seen the document before.

I have no choice but to believe him. It is impossible to think that a man of Baron Stein's honorable and serious character would be party to the fabrication of a paper of this sort. Even aside from this, I am in the thing as deeply as he; if it is signed with his signature, it is also sealed with my seal, which has not been out of my personal keeping in the ten years that I have been Chancellor here. In fact, the word "impossible" can be used to describe the entire business. It was impossible for the man Benjamin Bathurst to have entered the inn-yard—yet he did. It was impossible that he should carry papers of the sort found in his dispatch-case, or that such papers should exist—yet I am sending them to you with this letter. It is impossible that Baron vom und zum Stein should sign a paper of the sort he did, or that it should be sealed by the Chancellery—yet it bears both Stein's signature and my seal.

You will also find in the dispatch-case other credentials ostensibly originating with the British Foreign Office, of the same character, being signed by persons having no connection with the Foreign Office, or even with the Government, but being sealed with apparently authentic seals. If you send these papers to London, I fancy you will find that they will there create the same situation as that caused here by this letter of safe-conduct.

I am also sending you a charcoal sketch of the person who calls himself Benjamin Bathurst. This portrait was taken without its subject's knowledge. Baron von Krutz's nephew, Lieutenant von Tarlburg, who is the son of our mutual friend Count von Tarlburg, has a *little friend*, a very clever young lady who is, as you will see, an expert at this sort of work; she was introduced into a room at the Ministry of Police and placed behind a screen, where she could sketch our prisoner's face. If you should send this picture to London, I think that there is a good chance that it might be recognized. I can vouch that it is an excellent likeness.

To tell the truth, we are at our wits' end about this affair. I can not understand how such excellent imitations of these various seals could be made, and the signature of the Baron vom and zum Stein is the most expert forgery that I have ever seen, in thirty years' experience as a statesman. This would indicate careful and painstaking work on the part of somebody; how, then, do we reconcile this with such clumsy mistakes, recognizable as such by any schoolboy, as signing the name of Baron Stein as Prussian Chancellor, or Mr. George Canning, who is a member of the opposition party and not connected with your Government, as British Foreign Secretary?

These are mistakes which only a madman would make. There are those who think our prisoner is a madman, because of his apparent delusions about the great conqueror, General Bonaparte, *alias* the Emperor Napoleon. Madmen have been known to fabricate evidence to support their delusions, it is true, but I shudder to think of a madman having at his disposal the resources to manufacture the papers you will find in this dispatch-case. Moreover, some of our foremost medical men, who have specialized in the disorders of the mind, have interviewed this man Bathurst and say that, save for his fixed belief in a non-existent situation, he is perfectly rational.

Personally, I believe that the whole thing is a gigantic hoax, perpetrated for some hidden and sinister purpose, possibly to create confusion, and undermine the confidence existing between your Government and mine, and to set against one another various persons connected with both Governments, or else as a mask for some other conspiratorial activity. Without specifying any Sovereigns or Governments who might wish to do this, I can think of two groups, namely, the Jesuits, and the outlawed French Republicans, either of whom might conceive such a situation to be to their advantage. Only a few months ago, you will recall, there was a Jacobin plot unmasked at Koln.

But, whatever this business may portend, I do not like it. I want to get to the bottom of it as soon as possible, and I will thank you, my dear Sir, and your Government, for any assistance you may find possible.

I have the honor, Sir, to be, etc., etc., etc.,

Berchtenwald

X

FROM BARON VON KRUTZ, TO THE COUNT VON BERCH-TENWALD. MOST URGENT; MOST IMPORTANT.
TO BE DELIVERED IMMEDIATELY AND IN PERSON, RE-GARDLESS OF CIRCUMSTANCES.

28 November, 1809

Count von Berchtenwald:

Within the past half-hour, that is, at about eleven o'clock tonight, the man calling himself Benjamin Bathurst was shot and killed by a sentry at the Ministry of Police, while attempting to escape from custody.

A sentry on duty in the rear courtyard of the Ministry observed a man attempting to leave the building in a suspicious and furtive manner. This sentry, who was under the strictest orders to allow no one to enter or leave without written authorization, challenged him; when he attempted to run, the sentry fired his musket at him, bringing him down. At the shot, the Sergeant of the Guard rushed into the courtyard with his detail, and the man whom the sentry had shot was found to be the Englishman, Benjamin Bathurst. He had been hit in the chest with an ounce ball, and died before the doctor could arrive, and without recovering consciousness.

An investigation revealed that the prisoner, who was confined on the third floor of the building, had fashioned a rope from his bedding, his bed-cord, and the leather strap of his bell-pull; this rope was only long enough to reach to the window of the office on the second floor, directly below, but he managed to enter this by kicking the glass out of the window. I am trying to find out how he could do this without being heard; I can assure your Excellency that somebody is going to smart for this night's work. As for the sentry, he acted within his orders; I have commended him for doing his duty, and for good shooting, and I assume full responsibility for the death of the prisoner at his hands.

I have no idea why the self-so-called Benjamin Bathurst, who, until now, was well-behaved and seemed to take his confinement philosophically, should suddenly make this rash and fatal attempt, unless it was because of those infernal dunderheads of madhouse-doctors who have been bothering him. Only this afternoon, your Excellency, they deliberately handed him a bundle of newspapers—Prussian, Austrian, French, and English—all dated within the last month. They wanted, they said, to see how he would react. Well, God pardon them, they've found out!

What does your Excellency think should be done about giving the body burial?

Krutz

(From the British Minister to the Count von Berchtenwald.)

December 20th, 1809

Mr. Dear Count von Berchtenwald:

Reply from London to my letter of the 18th *ult.*, which accompanied the dispatch-case and the other papers, has finally come to hand. The papers which you wanted returned—the copies of the statements taken at Perleburg, the letter to the Baron von Krutz from the police captain, Hartenstein, and the personal letter of Krutz's nephew, Lieutenant von Tarlburg, and the letter of safe-conduct found in the dispatch-case—accompany herewith. I don't know what the people at Whitehall did with the other papers; tossed them into the nearest fire, for my guess. Were I in your Excellency's place, that's where the papers I am returning would go.

I have heard nothing, yet, from my dispatch of the 29th *ult.* concerning the death of the man who called himself Benjamin Bathurst, but I doubt very much if any official notice will ever be taken of it. Your Government had a perfect right to detain the fellow, and, that being the case, he attempted to escape at his own risk. After all, sentries are not required to carry loaded muskets in order to discourage them from putting their hands in their pockets.

To hazard a purely unofficial opinion, I should not imagine that London is very much dissatisfied with this *denouement*. His Majesty's Government are a hard-headed and matter-of-fact set of gentry who do not relish mysteries, least of all mysteries whose solution may be more disturbing than the original problem.

This is entirely confidential, your Excellency, but those papers which were in that dispatch-case kicked up the devil's own row in London, with half the Government' bigwigs protesting their innocence to high Heaven, and the rest accusing one another of complicity in the hoax. If that was somebody's intention, it was literally a howling success. For a while, it was even feared that there would be Questions in Parliament, but eventually, the whole vexatious business was hushed.

You may tell Count Tarlburg's son that his little friend is a most talented young lady; her sketch was highly commended by no less an authority than Sir Thomas Lawrence, and here, your Excellency, comes the most bedeviling part of a thoroughly bedeviled business. The picture was instantly recognized. It is a very fair likeness of Benjamin Bathurst, or, I should say, Sir Benjamin Bathurst, who is King's Lieutenant-Governor for the Crown Colony of Georgia. As Sir Thomas Lawrence did his portrait a few years back, he is in an excellent position to criticize the work of Lieutenant von Tarlburg's young lady. However, Sir Benjamin Bathurst was known to have been in Savannah, attending to the duties of his office, and in the public eye, all the while that his double was in Prussia. Sir Benjamin does not have a twin brother. It has been suggested that this fellow might be a half-brother, born on the wrong side of the blanket, but, as far as I know, there is no justification for this theory.

The General Bonaparte, *alias* the Emperor Napoleon, who is given so much mention in the dispatches, seems also to have a counterpart in actual life; there is, in the French army, a Colonel of Artillery by that name, a Corsican who Gallicized his original name of Napolione Buonaparte. He is a most brilliant military theoretician; I am sure some of your own officers, like General Scharnhorst, could tell you about him. His loyalty to the French Monarchy has never been questioned.

This same correspondence to fact seems to crop up everywhere in that amazing collection of pseudo-dispatches and pseudo-state-papers. The United States of America, you will recall, was the style by which the rebellious colonies referred to themselves, in the Declaration of Philadelphia. The James Madison who is mentioned as the current President of the United States is now living, in exile, in Switzerland. His alleged predecessor in office, Thomas Jefferson, was the author of the rebel Declaration; after the defeat of the rebels, he escaped to Havana, and died, several years ago, in the Principality of Lichtenstein.

I was quite amused to find our old friend Cardinal Talleyrand—without ecclesiastical title—cast in the role of chief advisor to the usurper, Bonaparte. His Eminence, I have always thought, is the sort of fellow who would land on his feet on top of any heap, and who would as little scruple to be Prime Minister to His Satanic Majesty as to His Most Christian Majesty.

I was baffled, however, by one name, frequently mentioned in those fantastic papers. This was the English General, Wellington. I haven't the least idea who this person might be.

I have the honor, your Excellency, etc., etc., etc.,

Sir Arthur Wellesley

"Murray Leinster" (the late Will F. Jenkins, 1896–1975) had one of the longest and most successful careers in the history of science fiction, beginning in 1919 and continuing until the late 1960s. He also had a distinguished writing career outside of sf. Within the genre he produced more than forty books and well over a hundred stories, including his popular "Med Service" series, and "Exploration Team," which won a 1956 Hugo Award.

"The Power" (Astounding Science Fiction, September 1945) exhibits all the skill and the imaginative strength that Will Jenkins brought to all of his work.

THE POWER

By Murray Leinster

Memorandum from Professor Charles, Latin Department, Haverford University, to Professor McFarland, the same faculty:

Dear Professor McFarland:
In a recent batch of fifteenth-century Latin documents from abroad, we found three which seem to fit together. Our interest is in the Latin of the period, but their contents seem to bear upon your line. I send them to you with a free translation. Would you let me know your reaction?

Charles.

To Johannus Hartmannus, Licentiate in Philosophy,
Living at the house of the goldsmith Grote,
Lane of the Dyed Flee,
Leyden, the Low Countries:

Friend Johannus:
I write this from the Goth's Head Inn, in Padua, the second

day after Michaelmas, Anno Domini 1482. I write in haste because a worthy Hollander here journeys homeward and has promised to carry mails for me. He is an amiable lout, but ignorant. Do not speak to him of mysteries. He knows nothing. Less than nothing. Thank him, give him to drink, and speak of me as a pious and worthy student. Then forget him.

I leave Padua tomorrow for the realization of all my hopes and yours. This time I am sure. I came here to purchase perfumes and mandragora and the other necessities for an Operation of the utmost imaginable importance, which I will conduct five nights hence upon a certain hilltop near the village of Montevecchio. I have found a Word and a Name of incalculable power, which in the place that I know of must open to me knowledge of all mysteries. When you read this, I shall possess powers at which Hermes Trismegistos only guessed, and which Albertus Magnus could speak of only by hearsay. I have been deceived before, but this time I am sure. I have seen proofs!

I tremble with agitation as I write to you. I will be brief. I came upon these proofs and the Word and the Name in the village of Montevecchio. I rode into the village at nightfall, disconsolate because I had wasted a month searching for a learned man of whom I had heard great things. Then I found him—and he was but a silly antiquary with no knowledge of mysteries! So riding upon my way I came to Montevecchio, and there they told me of a man dying even then because he had worked wonders. He had entered the village on foot only the day before. He was clad in rich garments, yet he spoke like a peasant. At first he was mild and humble, but he paid for food and wine with a gold piece, and villagers fawned upon him and asked for alms. He flung them a handful of gold pieces and when the news spread the whole village went mad with greed. They clustered about him, shrieking pleas, and thronging ever the more urgently as he strove to satisfy them. It is said that he grew frightened and would have fled because of their thrusting against him. But they plucked at his garments, screaming of their poverty, until suddenly his rich clothing vanished in the twinkling of an eye and he was but another ragged peasant like themselves and the purse from which he had scattered gold became a mere coarse bag filled with ashes.

This had happened but the day before my arrival, and the

man was yet alive, though barely so because the villagers had cried witchcraft and beset him with flails and stones and then dragged him to the village priest to be exorcised.

I saw the man and spoke to him, Johannus, by representing myself to the priest as a pious student of the snares Satan has set in the form of witchcraft. He barely breathed, what with broken bones and pitchfork wounds. He was a native of the district, who until now had seemed a simple ordinary soul. To secure my intercession with the priest to shrive him ere he died, the man told me all. And it was much!

Upon this certain hillside where I shall perform the Operation five nights hence, he had dozed at midday. Then a Power appeared to him and offered to instruct him in mysteries. The peasant was stupid. He asked for riches instead. So the Power gave him rich garments and a purse which would never empty so long—said the Power—as it came not near a certain metal which destroys all things of mystery. And the Power warned that this was payment that he might send a learned man to learn what he had offered the peasant, because he saw that peasants had no understanding. Thereupon I told the peasant that I would go and greet this Power and fulfil his desires, and he told me the Name and the Word which would call him, and also the Place, begging me to intercede for him with the priest.

The priest showed me a single gold piece which remained of that which the peasant had distributed. It was of the age of Antonius Pius, yet bright and new as if fresh minted. It had the weight and feel of true gold. But the priest, wryly, laid upon it the crucifix he wears upon a small iron chain about his waist. Instantly it vanished, leaving behind a speck of glowing coal which cooled and was a morsel of ash.

This I saw, Johannus! So I came speedily here to Padua, to purchase perfumes and mandragora and the other necessities for an Operation to pay great honor to this Power whom I shall call up five nights hence. He offered wisdom to the peasant, who desired only gold. But I desire wisdom more than gold, and surely I am learned concerning mysteries and Powers! I do not know any but yourself who surpasses me in true knowledge of secret things. And when you read this, Johannus, I shall surpass even you! But it may be that I will gain knowledge so that I can transport myself by a mystery to your attic, and there inform you myself, in advance of this letter, of the results of this surpassing good fortune which causes me to shake with agitation whenever I think of it.

Your friend Carolus,

at the Goth's Head Inn in Padua.

...fortunate, perhaps, that an opportunity has come to send a second missive to you, through a crippled man-at-arms who has been discharged from a mercenary band and travels homeward to sit in the sun henceforth. I have given him one gold piece and promised that you would give him another on receipt of this message. You will keep that promise or not, as pleases you, but there is at least the value of a gold piece in a bit of parchment with strange symbols upon it which I enclose for you.

Item: I am in daily communication with the Power of which I wrote you, and daily learn great mysteries.

Item: Already I perform marvels such as men have never before accomplished by means of certain sigils or talismans the Power has prepared for me.

Item: Resolutely the Power refuses to yield to me the Names or the incantations by which these things are done so that I can prepare such sigils for myself. Instead, he instructs me in divers subjects which have no bearing on the accomplishment of wonders, to my bitter impatience which I yet dissemble.

Item: Within this packet there is a bit of parchment. Go to a remote place and there tear it and throw it upon the ground. Instantly, all about you, there will appear a fair garden with marvelous fruits, statuary, and pavilion. You may use this garden as you will, save that if any person enter it, or you yourself, carrying a sword or dagger or any object however small made of iron, the said garden will disappear immediately and nevermore return.

This you may verify when you please. For the rest, I am like a prisoner trembling at the very door of Paradise, barred from entering beyond the antechamber by the fact of the Power withholding from me the true essentials of mystery, and granting me only crumbs—which, however, are greater marvels than any known certainly to have been practiced before. For example, the parchment I send you. This art I have proven many times. I have in my scrip many such sigils, made for me by the Power at my entreaty. But when I have secretly taken other parchments and copied upon them the very symbols to the utmost exactitude, they are valueless.

There are words or formulas to be spoken over them or—I think more likely—a greater sigil which gives the parchments their magic property. I begin to make a plan—a very daring plan—to acquire even this sigil.

But you will wish to know of the Operation and its results. I returned to Montevecchio from Padua, reaching it in three days. The peasant who had worked wonders was dead, the villagers having grown more fearful and beat out his brains with hammers. This pleased me, because I had feared he would tell another the Word and Name he had told me. I spoke to the priest and told him that I had been to Padua and secured advice from high dignitaries concerning the wonder-working, and had been sent back with special commands to seek out and exorcise the foul fiend who had taught the peasant such marvels.

The next day—the priest himself aiding me!—I took up to the hilltop the perfumes and wax tapers and other things needed for the Operation. The priest trembled, but he would have remained had I not sent him away. And night fell, and I drew the magic circle and the pentacle, with the Signs in their proper places. And when the new moon rose, I lighted the perfumes and the fine candles and began the Operation. I have had many failures, as you know, but this time I knew confidence and perfect certainty. When it came time to use the Name and the Word I called them both loudly, thrice, and waited.

Upon this hilltop there are many greyish stones. At the third calling of the Name, one of the stones shivered and was not. Then a voice said dryly:

"Ah! So that is the reason for this stinking stuff! My messenger sent you here?"

There was a shadow where the stone had been and I could not see clearly. But I bowed low in that direction:

"Most Potent Power," I said, my voice trembling because the Operation was a success, "a peasant working wonders told me that you desired speech with a learned man. Beside your Potency I am ignorant indeed, but I have given my whole life to the study of mysteries. Therefore I have come to offer worship or such other compact as you may desire in exchange for wisdom."

There was a stirring in the shadow, and the Power came forth. His appearance was that of a creature not more than an ell and a half in height, and his expression in the moonlight was that of sardonic impatience. The fragrant smoke seemed to cling about him, to make a cloudiness close about his form.

"I think" said the dry voice, "that you are as great a fool as the peasant I spoke to. What do you think I am?"

"A Prince of Celestial race, your Potency," I said, my voice shaking.

There was a pause. The Power said as if wearily:

"Men! Fools forever! Oh, man, I am simply the last of a number of my kind who traveled in a fleet from another star. This small planet of yours has a core of the accursed metal, which is fatal to the devices of my race. A few of our ships came too close. Others strove to aid them, and shared their fate. Many, many years since, we descended from the skies and could never rise again. Now I alone am left."

Speaking of the world as a planet was an absurdity, of course. The planets are wanderers among the stars, traveling in their cycles and epicycles as explained by Ptolemy a thousand years since. But I saw at once that he would test me. So I grew bold and said:

"Lord, I am not fearful. It is not needful to cozen me. Do I not know of those who were cast out of Heaven for rebellion? Shall I write the name of your leader?"

He said "Eh?" for all the world like an elderly man. So, smiling, I wrote on the earth the true name of Him whom the vulgar call Lucifer. He regarded the markings on the earth and said:

"Bah! It is meaningless. More of your legendary! Look you, man, soon I shall die. For more years than you are like to believe I have hid from your race and its accursed metal. I have watched men, and despised them. But—I die. And it is not good that knowledge should perish. It is my desire to impart to men the knowledge which else would die with me. It can do no harm to my own kind, and may bring the race of men to some degree of civilization in the course of ages."

I bowed to the earth before him. I was aflame with eagerness.

"Most Potent One," I said joyfully. "I am to be trusted. I will guard your secrets fully. Not one jot nor tittle shall ever be divulged!"

Again his voice was annoyed and dry.

"I desire that this knowledge be spread so that all may learn it. But—" Then he made a sound which I do not understand, save that it seemed to be derisive—"What I have to say may serve, even garbled and twisted. And I do not think you will keep secrets inviolate. Have you pen and parchment?"

"Nay, Lord!"

"You will come again, then, prepared to write what I shall tell you."

But he remained, regarding me. He asked me questions, and I answered eagerly. Presently he spoke in a meditative voice, and I listened eagerly. His speech bore an odd similarity to that of a lonely man who dwelt much on the past, but soon I realized that he spoke in ciphers, in allegory, from which now and again the truth peered out. As one who speaks for the sake of remembering, he spoke of the home of his race upon what he said was a fair planet so far distant that to speak of leagues and even the span of continents would be useless to convey the distance. He told of cities in which his fellows dwelt—here, of course, I understood his meaning perfectly—and told of great fleets of flying things rising from those cities to go to other fair cities, and of music which was in the very air so that any person, anywhere upon the planet, could hear sweet sounds or wise discourse at will. In this matter there was no metaphor, because the perpetual sweet sounds in Heaven are matters of common knowledge. But he added a metaphor immediately after, because he smiled at me and observed that the music was not created by a mystery, but by waves like those of light, only longer. And this was plainly a cipher, because light is an impalpable fluid without length and surely without waves!

Then he spoke of flying through the emptiness of the empyrean, which again is not clear, because all can see that the heavens are fairly crowded with stars, and he spoke of many suns and other worlds, some frozen and some merely barren rock. The obscurity of such things is patent. And he spoke of drawing near to this world which is ours, and of an error made as if it were in mathematics—instead of in rebellion—so that they drew close to Earth as Icarus to the sun. Then again he spoke in metaphors, because he referred to engines, which are things to cast stones against walls, and in a larger sense for grinding corn and pumping water. But he spoke of engines growing hot because of the accursed metal in the core of Earth, and of the inability of his kind to resist Earth's pull—more metaphor—and then he spoke of a screaming descent from the skies. And all of this, plainly, is a metaphorical account of the casting of the Rebels out of Heaven, and an acknowledgment that he is one of the said Rebels.

When he paused, I begged humbly that he would show me a mystery and of his grace give me protection in case my converse with him became known.

"What happened to my messenger?" asked the Power.

I told him, and he listened without stirring. I was careful to tell him exactly, because of course he would know that— as all else—by his powers of mystery, and the question was but another test. Indeed, I felt sure that the messenger and all that taken place had been contrived by him to bring me, a learned student of mysteries, to converse with him in this place.

"Men!" he said bitterly at last. Then he added coldly. "Nay! I can give you no protection. My kind is without protection upon this earth. If you would learn what I can teach you, you must risk the fury of your fellow countrymen."

But then, abruptly, he wrote upon parchment and pressed the parchment to some object at his side. He threw it upon the ground.

"If men beset you," he said scornfully, "tear this parchment and cast it from you. If you have none of the accursed metal about you, it may distract them while you flee. But a dagger will cause it all to come to naught!"

Then he walked away. He vanished. And I stood shivering for a very long time before I remembered me of the formula given by Apollonius of Tyana for the dismissal of evil spirits. I ventured from the magic circle. No evil befell me. I picked up the parchment and examined it in the moonlight. The symbols upon it were meaningless, even to one like myself who has studied all that is known of mysteries. I returned to the village, pondering.

I have told you so much at length, because you will observe that this Power did not speak with the pride or the menace of which most authors on mysteries and Operations speak. It is often said that an adept must conduct himself with great firmness during an Operation, lest the Powers he has called up overawe him. Yet this Power spoke wearily, with irony, like one approaching death. And he had spoken of death, also. Which was of course a test and a deception, because are not the Principalities and Powers of Darkness immortal? He had some design it was not his will that I should know. So I saw that I must walk warily in this priceless opportunity.

In the village I told the priest that I had had encounter with a foul fiend, who begged that I not exorcise him, promising to reveal certain hidden treasures once belonging to the Church, which he could not touch or reveal to evil men because they were holy, but could describe the location of to me. And I procured parchment, and pens, and ink, and the next day I went alone to the hilltop. It was empty, and I made sure I was unwatched and—leaving my dagger behind me— I tore the parchment and flung it to the ground.

As it touched, there appeared such a treasure of gold and jewels as truly would have driven any man mad with greed. There were bags and chests and boxes filled with gold and precious stones, which had burst with the weight and spilled out upon the ground. There were gems glittering in the late sunlight, and rings and necklaces set with brilliants, and such monstrous hoards of golden coins of every antique pattern...

Johannus, even I went almost mad! I leaped forward like one dreaming to plunge my hands into the gold. Slavering, I filled my garments with rubies and ropes of pearls, and stuffed my scrip with gold pieces, laughing crazily to myself. I rolled in the riches. I wallowed in them, flinging the golden coins into the air and letting them fall upon me. I laughed and sang to myself.

Then I heard a sound. On the instant I was filled with terror for the treasure. I leaped to my dagger and snarled, ready to defend my riches to the death.

Then a dry voice said: "Truly you care naught for riches!"

It was savage mockery. The Power stood regarding me. I saw him clearly now, yet not clearly because there was a cloudiness which clung closely to his body. He was, as I said, an ell and a half in height, and from his forehead there protruded knobby feelers which were not horns but had somewhat the look save for bulbs upon their ends. His head was large and—But I will not attempt to describe him, because he could assume any of a thousand forms, no doubt, so what does it matter?

Then I grew terrified because I had no Circle or Pentacle to protect me. But the Power made no menacing move.

"It is real, that riches," he said dryly. "It has color and weight and the feel of substance. But your dagger will destroy it all."

Didyas of Corinth has said that treasure of mystery must be fixed by a special Operation before it becomes permanent and free of the power of Those who brought it. They can transmute it back to leaves or other rubbish, if it be not fixed.

"Touch it with your dagger," said the Power.

I obeyed, sweating in fear. And as the metal iron touched a great piled heap of gold, there was a sudden shifting and then a little flare about me. And the treasure—all, to the veriest crumb of a seed-pearl!—vanished before my eyes. The bit of parchment reappeared, smoking. It turned to ashes. My dagger scorched my fingers. It had grown hot.

"Ah, yes," said the Power, nodding. "The force-field has energy. When the iron absorbs it, there is heat." Then he looked at me in a not unfriendly way. "You have brought pens and parchment," he said, "and at least you did not use the sigil to astonish your fellows. Also you had the good sense to make no more perfumish stinks. It may be that there is a grain of wisdom in you. I will bear with you yet a while. Be seated and take parchment and pen—Stay! Let us be comfortable. Sheathe your dagger, or better, cast it from you."

I put it in my bosom. And it was as if he thought, and touched something at his side, and instantly there was a fair pavilion about us, with soft cushions and a gently playing fountain.

"Sit," said the Power. "I learned that men like such things as this from a man I once befriended. He had been wounded and stripped by robbers, so that he had not so much as a scrap of accursed metal about him, and I could aid him. I learned to speak the language men use nowadays from him. But to the end he believed me an evil spirit and tried valorously to hate me."

My hands shook with my agitation that the treasure had departed from me. Truly it was a treasure of such riches as no King has ever possessed, Johannus! My very soul lusted after that treasure! The golden coins alone would fill your attic solidly, but the floor would break under their weight, and the jewels would fill hogsheads. Ah, Johannus! That treasure!

"What I will have you write," said the Power, "at first will mean little. I shall give facts and theories first, because they are easiest to remember. Then I will give the applications of the theories. Then you men will have the beginning of such civilization as can exist in the neighborhood of the accursed metal."

"Your Potency!" I begged abjectly. "You will give me another sigil of treasure?"

"Write!" he commanded.

I wrote. And, Johannus, I cannot tell you myself what it is that I wrote. He spoke words, and they were in such obscure cipher that they have no meaning as I con them over. Hark you to this, and seek wisdom for the performance of mysteries in it! "The civilization of my race is based upon fields of force which have the property of acting in all essentials as substance. A lodestone is surrounded by a field of force which is invisible and impalpable. But the fields used by my people for dwellings, tools, vehicles, and even machinery are perceptible to the senses and act physically as solids. More, we are able to form these fields in latent fashions; and to fix them to organic objects as permanent fields which require no energy for their maintenance, just as magnetic fields require no energy supply to continue. Our fields, too, may be projected as three-dimensional solids which assume any desired form and have every property of substance except chemical affinity."

Johannus! Is it not unbelievable that words could be put together, dealing with mysteries, which are so devoid of any clue to their true mystic meaning? I write and I write in desperate hope that he will eventually give me the key, but my brain reels at the difficulty of extracting the directions for Operations which such ciphers must conceal! I give you another instance: "When a force-field generator has been built as above, it will be found that the pulsatory fields which are consciousness serve perfectly as controls. One has but to visualize the object desired, turn on the generator's auxiliary control, and the generator will pattern its output upon the pulsatory consciousness-field..."

Upon this first day of writing, the Power spoke for hours, and I wrote until my hand ached. From time to time, resting, I read back to him the words that I had written. He listened, satisfied.

"Lord!" I said shakily. "Mighty Lord! Your Potency! These

mysteries you bid me write—they are beyond comprehension!"

But he said scornfully:

"Write! Some will be clear to someone. And I will explain it little by little until even you can comprehend the beginning." Then he added. "You grow weary. You wish a toy. Well! I will make you a sigil which will make again that treasure you played with. I will add a sigil which will make a boat for you, with en engine drawing power from the sea to carry you wheresoever you wish without need of wind or tide. I will make others so you may create a palace where you will, and fair gardens as you please..."

These things he has done, Johannus. It seems to amuse him to write upon scraps of parchment, and think, and then press them against his side before he lays them upon the ground for me to pick up. He has explained amusedly that the wonder in the sigil is complete, yet latent, and is released by the tearing of the parchment, but absorbed and destroyed by iron. In such fashion he speaks in ciphers, but otherwise sometimes he jests!

It is strange to think of it, that I have come little by little to accept this Power as a person. It is not in accord with the laws of mystery. I feel that he is lonely. He seems to find satisfaction in speech with me. Yet he is a Power, one of the Rebels who was flung to earth from Heaven! He speaks of that only in vague, metaphorical terms, as if he had come from another world like *the* world, save much larger. He refers to himself as a voyager of space, and speaks of his race with affection, and of Heaven—at any rate the city from which he comes, because there must be many great cities there—with a strange and prideful affection. If it were not for his powers, which are of mystery, I would find it possible to believe that he was a lonely member of a strange race, exiled forever in a strange place, and grown friendly with a man because of his loneliness. But how could there be such as he and not a Power? How could there be another world?

This strange converse has now gone on for ten days or more. I have filled sheets upon sheets of parchment with writing. The same metaphors occur again and again. "Forcefields"—a term without literal meaning—occurs often. There are other metaphors such as "coils" and "primary" and "secondary" which are placed in context with mention of wires of copper metal. There are careful descriptions, as if in the plainest of language, of sheets of dissimilar metals which are to be placed in acid, and other descriptions of plates of similar metal which are to be separated by layers of air or wax of certain thicknesses, with the plates of certain areas! And there is an explanation of the means by which he lives. "I, being accustomed to an atmosphere much more dense than that on Earth, am forced to keep about myself a field of force which maintains an air density near that of my home planet for my breathing. This field is transparent, but because it must shift constantly to change and refresh the air I breathe, it causes a certain cloudiness of outline next my body. It is maintained by the generator I wear at my side, which at the same time provides energy for such other force-field artifacts as I may find convenient."—Ah, Johannes! I grow mad with impatience! Did I not anticipate that he would some day give me the key to this metaphorical speech, so that from it may be extracted the Names and the Words which cause his wonders, I would give over in despair.

Yet he has grown genial with me. He has given me such sigils as I have asked him, and I have tried them many times. The sigil which will make you a fair garden is one of many. He says that he desires to give to man the knowledge he possesses, and then bids we write ciphered speech without meaning, such as: "The drive of a ship for flight beyond the speed of light is adapted from the simple drive generator already described simply by altering its constants so that it cannot generate in normal space and must create an abnormal space by tension. The process is—" Or else—I choose at random, Johannus—"The accursed metal, iron, must be eliminated not only from all circuits but from nearness to apparatus using high-frequency oscillations, since it absorbs their energy and prevents the functioning..."

I am like a man trembling upon the threshold of Paradise, yet unable to enter because the key is withheld. "Speed of light!" What could it mean in metaphor? In common parlance, as well speak of the speed of weather or of granite! Daily I beg him for the key to his speech. Yet even now, in the sigils he makes for me, is greater power than any man has ever known before!

But it is not enough. The Power speaks as if he were lonely beyond compare; the last member of a strange race upon earth; as if he took a strange, companion-like pleasure in merely talking to me. When I beg him for a Name or a Word which would give me power beyond such as he doles out in sigils, he is amused and calls me fool, yet kindly. And he speaks more of his metaphorical speech about forces of nature and fields of force—and gives me a sigil which should I use it will create a palace with walls of gold and pillars of emerald! And then he amusedly reminds me that one greedy looter with an axe or hoe of iron would cause it to vanish utterly!

I go almost mad, Johannus! But there is certainly wisdom unutterable to be had from him. Gradually, cautiously, I have come to act as if we were merely friends, of different race and he vastly the wiser, but friends rather than Prince and subject. Yet I remember the warnings of the most authoritative authors that one must be ever on guard against Powers called up in an Operation.

I have a plan. It is dangerous, I well know, but I grow desperate. To stand quivering upon the threshold of such wisdom and power as no man has ever dreamed of before, and then be denied...

The mercenary who will carry this to you, leaves tomorrow. He is a cripple, and may be months upon the way. All will be decided ere you receive this. I know you wish me well.

Was there ever a student of mystery in so saddening a predicament, with all knowledge in his grasp yet not quite his?

Your friend
Carolus.

Written in the very bad inn in Montevecchio.

Johannus! A courier goes to Ghent for My Lord of Brabant and I have opportunity to send you mail. I think I go mad, Johannus! I have power such as no man ever possessed before, and I am fevered with bitterness. Hear me!

For three weeks I did repair daily to the hilltop beyond Montevecchio and take down the ciphered speech of which I wrote you. My scrip was stuffed with sigils, but I had not one word of Power or Name of Authority. The Power grew mocking, yet it seemed sadly mocking. He insisted that his words held no cipher and needed but to be read. Some of them he phrased over and over again until they were but instructions for putting bits of metal together, mechanicwise. Then he made me follow those instructions. But there was no Word, no Name—nothing save bits of metal put together cunningly. And how could inanimate metal, not imbued with power of mystery by Names or Words or incantations, have power to work mystery?

At long last I become convinced that he would never reveal the wisdom he had promised. And I had come to such familiarity with this Power that I could dare to rebel, and even to believe that I had chance of success. There was the cloudiness about his form, which was maintained by a sigil he wore at his side and called a "generator." Were that cloudiness destroyed, he could not live, or so he had told me. It was for that reason that he, in person, dared not touch anything of iron. This was the basis of my plan.

I feigned illness, and said that I would rest at a peasant's thatched hut, no longer inhabited, at the foot of the hill on which the Power lived. There was surely no nail of iron in so crude a dwelling. If he felt for me the affection he protested, he would grant me leave to be absent in my illness. If his affection was great, he might even come and speak to me there. I would be alone in the hope that his friendship might go so far.

Strange words for a man to use to a Power! But I had talked daily with him for three weeks. I lay groaning in the hut, alone. On the second day he came. I affected great rejoicing, and made shift to light a fire from a taper I had kept burning. He thought it a mark of honor, but it was actually a signal. And then, as he talked to me in what he thought my illness, there came a cry from without the hut. It was the village priest, a simple man but very brave in his fashion. On the signal of smoke from the peasant's hut, he had crept near and drawn all about it an iron chain that he had muffled with cloth so that it would make no sound. And now he stood before the hut door with his crucifix upraised, chanting exorcisms. A very brave man, that priest, because I had pictured the Power as a foul fiend indeed.

The Power turned and looked at me, and I held my dagger firmly.

"I hold the accursed metal," I told him fiercely. "There is a ring of it about this house. Tell me now, quickly, the Words and the Names which make the sigils operate! Tell me the secret of the cipher you had me write! Do this and I will slay this priest and draw away the chain and you may go hence unharmed. But be quick, or—"

The Power cast a sigil upon the ground. When the parchment struck earth, there was an instant's cloudiness as if some dread thing had begun to form. But then the parchment smoked and turned to ash. The ring of iron about the hut had destroyed its power when it was used. The Power knew that I spoke truth.

"Ah!" said the Power dryly. "Men! And I thought one was my friend!" He put his hand to his side. "To be sure! I should have known. Iron rings me about. My engine heats..."

He looked at me. I held up the dagger, fiercely unyielding.

"The Names!" I cried. "The Words! Give me power of my own and I will slay the priest!"

"I tried," said the Power quietly, "to give you wisdom. And you will stab me with the accursed metal if I do not tell you things which do not exist. But you need not. I cannot live long in a ring of iron. My engine will burn out; my force-field will fail. I will stifle in the thin air which is dense enough for you. Will not that satisfy you? Must you stab me, also?"

I sprang from my pallet of straw to threaten him more fiercely. It was madness, was it not? But I was mad, Johannus!

"Forbear," said the Power. "I could kill you now, with me! But I thought you my friend. I will go out and see your priest. I would prefer to die at his hand. He is perhaps only a fool."

He walked steadily toward the doorway. As he stepped over the iron chain, I thought I saw a wisp of smoke begin, but he touched the thing at his side. The cloudiness about his person vanished. There was a puffing sound, and his garments jerked as if in a gust of wind. He staggered. But he went on, and touched his side again and the cloudiness returned and he walked more strongly. He did not try to turn aside. He walked directly toward the priest, and even I could see that he walked with a bitter dignity.

And—I saw the priest's eyes grow wide with horror. Because he saw the Power for the first time, and the Power was an ell and a half high, with a large head and knobbed feelers projecting from his forehead, and the priest knew instantly that he was not of any race of men but was a Power and one of those Rebels who were flung out from Heaven.

I heard the Power speak to the priest, with dignity. I did not hear what he said. I raged in my disappointment. But the priest did not waver. As the Power moved toward him, the priest moved toward the Power. His face was filled with horror, but it was resolute. He reached forward with the crucifix he wore always attached to an iron chain about his waist. He thrust it to touch the Power, crying, *"In nomine Patri—"*

Then there was smoke. It came from a spot at the Power's side where was the engine to which he touched the sigils he had made, to imbue them with the power of mystery. And then—

I was blinded. There was a flare of monstrous, bluish light, like a lightning-stroke from Heaven. After, there was a ball of fierce yellow flame which gave off a cloud of black smoke. There was a monstrous, outraged bellow of thunder.

Then there was nothing save the priest standing there, his face ashen, his eyes resolute, his eyebrows singed, chanting psalms in a shaking voice.

I have come to Venice. My scrip is filled with sigils with which I can work wonders. No men can work such wonders as I can. But I use them not. I labor daily, nightly, hourly, minute by minute, trying to find the key to the cipher which will yield the wisdom the Power possessed and desired to give to men. Ah, Johannus! I have those sigils and I can work wonders, but when I have used them they will be gone and I shall be powerless. I had such a chance at wisdom as never man possessed before, and it is gone! Yet I shall spend years— aye!—all the rest of my life, seeking the true meaning of what the Power spoke! I am the only man in all the world who ever spoke daily, for weeks on end, with a Prince of Powers of Darkness, and was accepted by him as a friend to such a degree as to encompass his own destruction. It must be true that I have wisdom written down! But how shall I find instructions for mystery in such metaphors as—to choose a fragment by chance—"plates of two dissimilar metals, immersed in an acid, generate a force for which men have not yet a name, yet which is the basis of true civilization. Such plates..."

I grow mad with disappointment, Johannus! Why did he not speak clearly? Yet I will find out the secret...

The Power

Memorandum from Peter McFarland, Physics Department, Haverford University, to Professor Charles, Latin, the same faculty:

Dear Professor Charles:
My reaction is, Damnation! Where is the rest of this stuff?

McFarland.